A TWIST

AND

AS THE CROW FLIES

Jeffrey Archer's writing career has spanned almost thirty years. His bestselling novels, which range from *Not a Penny More, Not a Penny Less* to *Kane and Abel* and *The Eleventh Commandment*, have sold over 120 million copies throughout the world.

In August 2001, he was sentenced to four years in prison for perjury. During that time he wrote three highly praised and bestselling works of non-fiction entitled *Prison Diaries*. He was released in July 2003.

He is married with two children and lives in London and Granchester.

ALSO BY JEFFREY ARCHER

NOVELS

Not a Penny More, Not a Penny Less
Shall We Tell the President?
Kane & Abel
The Prodigal Daughter
First Among Equals
A Matter of Honour
Honour Among Thieves
The Fourth Estate
The Eleventh Commandment
Sons of Fortune
False Impression

The Gospel According to Judas by Benjamin Iscariot
(with Frank Moloney)

SHORT STORIES

A Quiver Full of Arrows
Twelve Red Herrings
The Collected Short Stories
To Cut a Long Story Short
Cat O'Nine Tales

PLAYS

Beyond Reasonable Doubt
Exclusive
The Accused

PRISON DIARIES

Volume One – Belmarsh: Hell
Volume Two – Wayland: Purgatory
Volume Three – North Sea Camp: Heaven

SCREENPLAYS

Mallory: Walking off the Map
False Impression

JEFFREY ARCHER

A TWIST IN THE TALE

AND

AS THE CROW FLIES

PAN BOOKS

A Twist in the Tale first published 1988 by Hodder and Stoughton Ltd.
First published in paperback 1989 by Coronet.
First published by Pan Books 2003.
As the Crow Flies first published 1991 by Hodder and Stoughton Ltd.
First published in paperback 1992 by Coronet.
First published by Pan Books 2003.

This omnibus first published 2008 by Pan Books
an imprint of Pan Macmillan Ltd
Pan Macmillan, 20 New Wharf Road, London N1 9RR
Basingstoke and Oxford
Associated companies throughout the world
www.panmacmillan.com

ISBN 978-0-330-45775-0

1 3 5 7 9 8 6 4 2

A CIP catalogue record for this book is available from
the British Library.

Printed and bound in Great Britain by
Mackays of Chatham plc, Chatham, Kent

A TWIST IN THE TALE

To Henry and Suzanne

AUTHOR'S NOTE

Of these twelve short stories, gathered in my travels from Tokyo to Trumpington, ten are based on known incidents – some embellished with considerable licence. Only two are totally the result of my own imagination.

I would like to thank all those people who allowed me to learn some of their innermost secrets.

J.A.
September 1988

Contents

The Perfect Murder

IF I hadn't changed my mind that night I would never have found out the truth.

I couldn't believe that Carla had slept with another man, that she had lied about her love for me – and that I might be second or even third in her affections.

Carla had phoned me at the office during the day, something I had told her not to do, but since I also warned her never to call me at home she hadn't been left with a lot of choice. As it turned out, all she had wanted to let me know was that she wouldn't be able to make it for what the French so decorously call a "*cinq à sept*". She had to visit her sister in Fulham who had been taken ill, she explained.

I was disappointed. It had been another depressing day, and now I was being asked to forgo the one thing that would have made it bearable.

"I thought you didn't get on well with your sister," I said tartly.

There was no immediate reply from the other end. Eventually Carla asked, "Shall we make it next Tuesday, the usual time?"

"I don't know if that's convenient," I said. "I'll call you on Monday when I know what my plans are." I put down the receiver.

Wearily, I phoned my wife to let her know I was on the way home – something I usually did from the phone box outside Carla's flat. It was a trick I often used to make Elizabeth feel she knew where I was every moment of the day.

Most of the office staff had already left for the night so I gathered together some papers I could work on at home. Since the new company had taken us over six months ago, the management had not only sacked my Number Two in the accounts department but expected me to cover his work as well as my own. I was hardly in a position to complain, since my new boss made it abundantly clear that if I didn't like the arrangement I should feel free to seek employment elsewhere. I might have, too, but I couldn't think of many firms that would readily take on a man who had reached that magic age somewhere between the sought-after and the available.

As I drove out of the office car park and joined the evening rush hour I began to regret having been so sharp with Carla. After all, the role of the other woman was hardly one she delighted in. The feeling of guilt persisted, so that when I reached the corner of Sloane Square, I jumped out of my car and ran across the road.

"A dozen roses," I said, fumbling with my wallet.

A man who must have made his profit from lovers selected twelve unopened buds without comment. My choice didn't show a great deal of imagination but at least Carla would know I'd tried.

I drove on towards her flat, hoping she had not yet left for her sister's, that perhaps we might even find time for a quick drink. Then I remembered that I had already told my wife I was on the way home. A few minutes' delay could be explained by a traffic jam, but that lame excuse could hardly cover my staying on for a drink.

When I arrived at Carla's home I had the usual trouble finding a parking space, until I spotted a gap that would just take a Rover opposite the paper shop. I stopped and would have backed into the space had I not noticed a man coming out of the entrance to her block of flats. I wouldn't have given it a second thought if Carla hadn't followed him a moment later. She stood there in the doorway, wearing a loose blue housecoat. She leaned forward to give her departing visitor a kiss that could hardly have been described as sisterly. As she closed the door I drove my car round the corner and double-parked.

I watched the man in my rear-view mirror as he crossed the road, went into the newsagent and a few moments later reappeared with an evening paper and what looked like a packet of cigarettes. He walked to his car, a blue BMW, stopped to remove a parking ticket from his windscreen and appeared to curse. How long had the BMW been there? I even began to wonder if he had been with Carla when she phoned to tell me not to come round.

The man climbed into the BMW, fastened his seat belt and lit a cigarette before driving off. I took his parking meter space in part-payment for my woman. I didn't consider it a fair exchange. I checked up and down the street, as I always did, before getting out and walking over to the block of flats. It was already dark and no one gave me a second glance. I pressed the bell marked 'Moorland'.

When Carla opened the front door I was greeted with a huge smile which quickly turned into a frown, then just as quickly back to a smile. The first smile must have been meant for the BMW man. I often wondered why she wouldn't give me a front-door key. I stared into those blue eyes that had first captivated me so many months ago. Despite her smile, those eyes now revealed a coldness I had never seen before.

She turned to re-open the door and let me into her ground-floor flat. I noticed that under her housecoat she was wearing the wine-red negligee I had given her for Christmas. Once inside the flat I found myself checking round the room I knew so well. On the glass table in the centre of the room stood the 'Snoopy' coffee mug I usually drank from, empty. By its side was Carla's mug, also empty, and a dozen roses arranged in a vase. The buds were just beginning to open.

I have always been quick to chide and the sight of the flowers made it impossible for me to hide my anger.

"And who was the man who just left?" I asked.

"An insurance broker," she replied, removing the mugs from the table.

"And what was he insuring?" I asked. "Your love-life?"

"Why do you automatically assume he's my lover?" Her voice had begun to rise.

"Do you usually have coffee with an insurance broker in your negligee? Come to think of it, *my* negligee."

"I'll have coffee with whom I damn well please," she said, "and wearing what I damn well please, especially when you are on your way home to your wife."

"But I had wanted to come to you –"

"And then return to your wife. In any case, you're always telling me I should lead my own life and not rely on you," she added, an argument Carla often fell back on when she had something to hide.

"You know it's not that easy."

"I know it's easy enough for you to jump into bed with me whenever it suits you. That's all I'm good for, isn't it?"

"That's not fair."

"Not fair? Weren't you hoping for your usual at six so you could still be home at seven in time for supper with Elizabeth?"

"I haven't made love to my wife in years!" I shouted.

"We only have your word for that," she spat out with scorn.

"I have been utterly faithful to you."

"Which means I always have to be to you, I suppose?"

"Stop behaving like a whore."

Carla's eyes flashed as she leaped forward and slapped me across the face with all the strength she could muster.

I was still slightly off-balance when she raised her arm a second time, but as her hand came swinging towards me I blocked it and was even able to push her back against the mantelpiece. She recovered quickly and came flying at me again.

In a moment of uncontrolled fury, just as she was about to launch herself on me, I clenched my fist and took a swing at her. I caught her on the side of the chin, and she wheeled back from the impact. I watched her put an arm out to break her fall. But before she had the chance to leap back up and retaliate, I turned and strode out, slamming the flat door behind me.

I ran down the hall, out on to the street, jumped into my car and drove off quickly. I couldn't have been with her for more than ten minutes. Although I felt like murdering her at the time I regretted having hit her long before I reached home. Twice I nearly turned back. Everything she had complained about was fair and I wondered if I dared phone her from home. Although Carla and I had only been lovers for a few months, she must have known how much I cared.

If Elizabeth had intended to comment on my being late, she changed her mind the moment I handed her the roses. She began to arrange them in a vase while I poured myself a large whisky. I waited for her to say something as I rarely drank before dinner but she seemed preoccupied with the flowers. Although I had already made up my mind to phone Carla and try to make amends, I decided I couldn't do it from home. In any case, if I waited until the morning when I was back in the office, she might by then have calmed down a little.

I woke early the next day and lay in bed, considering what form my apology should take. I decided to invite her to lunch at the little French bistro she liked so much, half way between my office and hers. Carla always appreciated seeing me in the middle of the day, when she knew it couldn't be for sex. After I had shaved and dressed I joined Elizabeth for breakfast, and seeing there was nothing interesting on the front page, I turned to the financial section. The company's shares had fallen again, following City forecasts of poor interim profits. Millions would undoubtedly be wiped off our share value following such a bad piece of publicity. I already knew that when it came to publishing the annual accounts it would be a miracle if the company didn't declare a loss.

After gulping down a second cup of coffee I kissed my wife on the cheek and made for the car. It was then that I decided to drop a note through Carla's letterbox rather than cope with the embarrassment of a phone call.

"Forgive me," I wrote. "Marcel's, one o'clock. *Sole Véronique* on a Friday. Love, Casaneva." I rarely wrote to Carla, and when I did I only ever signed it with her chosen nickname.

I took a short detour so that I could pass her home but was held up by a traffic jam. As I approached the flat I could see that the hold-up was being caused by some sort of accident. It had to be quite a serious one because there was an ambulance blocking the other side of the road and delaying the flow of oncoming vehicles. A traffic warden was trying to help but she was only slowing things down even more. It was obvious that it was going to be impossible to park anywhere near Carla's flat, so I resigned myself to phoning her from the office. I did not relish the prospect.

I felt a sinking feeling moments later when I saw that the ambulance was parked only a few yards from the front door to her block of flats. I knew I was being irrational but I began to fear the worst. I tried to convince myself it was probably a road accident and had nothing to do with Carla.

It was then that I spotted the police car tucked in behind the ambulance.

As I drew level with the two vehicles I saw that Carla's front door was wide open. A man in a long white coat came scurrying out and opened the back of the ambulance. I stopped my car to observe more carefully what was going on, hoping the man behind me would not become impatient. Drivers coming from the other direction raised a hand to thank me for allowing them to pass. I thought I could let a dozen or so through before anyone would start to complain. The traffic warden helped by urging them on.

Then a stretcher appeared at the end of the hall. Two uniformed orderlies carried a shrouded body out on to the road and placed it in the back of the ambulance. I was unable to see the face because it was covered by the sheet, but a third man, who could only have been a detective, walked immediately behind the stretcher. He was carrying a plastic bag, inside which I could make out a red garment that I feared was the negligee I had given Carla.

I vomited my breakfast all over the passenger seat, my head finally resting on the steering wheel.

A moment later they closed the ambulance door, a siren started up and the traffic warden began waving me on. The ambulance moved quickly off and the man behind me started to press his horn. He was, after all, only an innocent bysitter. I lurched forward and later couldn't recall any part of my journey to the office.

Once I had reached the office car park I cleared up the mess on the passenger seat as best I could and left a window open before taking a lift to the washroom on the seventh floor. I tore my lunch invitation to Carla into little pieces and flushed them down the lavatory. I walked into my room on the twelfth floor a little after eight thirty, to find the managing director pacing up and down in front of my desk, obviously waiting for me. I had quite forgotten that it was Friday and he always expected the latest completed figures to be ready for his consideration.

This Friday it turned out he also wanted the projected accounts for the months of May, June and July. I promised they would be on his desk by midday. The one thing I needed was a clear morning and I was not going to be allowed it.

Every time the phone rang, the door opened or anyone even spoke to me, my heart missed a beat – I assumed it could only be the police. By midday I had finished some sort of report for the managing director, but I knew he would find it neither adequate nor accurate. As soon as I had deposited the papers with his secretary, I left for an early lunch. I realised I wouldn't be able to eat anything, but at least I could get hold of the first edition of the

Standard and search for any news they might have picked up about Carla's death.

I sat in the corner of my local pub where I knew I couldn't be seen from behind the bar. A tomato juice by my side, I began slowly to turn the pages of the paper.

She hadn't made page one. She hadn't made the second, third or fourth page. And on page five she rated only a tiny paragraph. "Miss Carla Moorland, aged 31, was found dead at her home in Pimlico earlier this morning." I remember thinking at the time they hadn't even got her age right. "Detective Inspector Simmons, who has been put in charge of the case, said that an investigation was being carried out and they were awaiting the pathologist's report but to date they had no reason to suspect foul play."

After that piece of news I even managed a little soup and a roll. Once I had read the report a second time I made my way back to the office car park and sat in my car. I wound down the other front window to allow more fresh air in before turning on the *World At One* on the radio. Carla didn't even get a mention. In the age of pump shotguns, drugs, Aids and gold bullion robberies the death of a thirty-two-year-old industrial personal assistant had passed unnoticed by the BBC.

I returned to my office to find on my desk a memo containing a series of questions that had been fired back from the managing director, leaving me in no doubt as to how he felt about my report. I was able to deal with nearly all his queries and return the answers to his secretary before I left the office that night, despite spending most of the afternoon trying to convince myself that whatever had caused Carla's death must have happened after I left and could not possibly have been connected with my hitting her. But that red negligee kept returning to my thoughts. Was there any way they could trace it back to me? I had bought it at Harrods – an extravagance, but I felt certain it couldn't be unique and it was still the only serious present I'd ever given her. But the note that was attached – had Carla destroyed it? Would they discover who Casaneva was?

I drove directly home that evening, aware that I would never again be able to travel down the road Carla had lived in. I listened to the end of the *PM* programme on my car radio and as soon as I reached home switched on the six o'clock news. I turned to Channel Four at seven and back to the BBC at nine. I returned to ITV at ten and even ended up watching *Newsnight*.

Carla's death, in their combined editorial opinion, must have been less important than a Third-Division football result between Reading and Walsall. Elizabeth continued reading her latest library book, oblivious to my possible peril.

I slept fitfully that night, and as soon as I heard the papers pushed through the letterbox the next morning I ran downstairs to check the headlines.

"DUKAKIS NOMINATED AS CANDIDATE" stared up at me from the front page of *The Times*.

I found myself wondering, irrelevantly, if he would ever be President. "President Dukakis" didn't sound quite right to me.

I picked up my wife's *Daily Express* and the

three-word headline filled the top of the page: “LOVERS’ TIFF MURDER”.

My legs gave way and I fell to my knees. I must have made a strange sight, crumpled up on the floor trying to read that opening paragraph. I couldn’t make out the words of the second paragraph without my spectacles. I stumbled back upstairs with the papers and grabbed the glasses from the table on my side of the bed. Elizabeth was still sleeping soundly. Even so, I locked myself in the bathroom where I could read the story slowly and without fear of interruption.

Police are now treating as murder the death of a beautiful Pimlico secretary, Carla Moorland, 32, who was found dead in her flat early yesterday morning. Detective Inspector Simmons of Scotland Yard, who is in charge of the case, initially considered Carla Moorland’s death to be due to natural causes, but an X-ray has revealed a broken jaw which could have been caused in a fight.

An inquest will be held on April 19th.

Miss Moorland’s daily, Maria Lucia (48), said – exclusively to the *Express* – that her employer had been with a man friend when she had left the flat at five o’clock on the night in question. Another witness, Mrs Rita Johnson, who lives in the adjoining block of flats, stated she had seen a man leaving Miss Moorland’s flat at around six, before entering the newsagents opposite and later driving away. Mrs Johnson added that she couldn’t be sure of the make of the car but it might have been a Rover . . .

"Oh, my God," I exclaimed in such a loud voice that I was afraid it might have woken Elizabeth. I shaved and showered quickly, trying to think as I went along. I was dressed and ready to leave for work even before my wife had woken. I kissed her on the cheek but she only turned over, so I scribbled a note and left it on her side of the bed, explaining that I had to spend the morning in the office as I had an important report to complete.

On my journey to work I rehearsed exactly what I was going to say. I went over it again and again. I arrived on the twelfth floor a little before eight and left my door wide open so I would be aware of the slightest intrusion. I felt confident that I had a clear fifteen, even twenty minutes before anyone else could be expected to arrive.

Once again I went over exactly what I needed to say. I found the number in the L–R directory and scribbled it down on a pad in front of me before writing five headings in block capitals, something I always did before a board meeting.

BUS STOP
COAT
NO. 19
BMW
TICKET

Then I dialled the number.

I took off my watch and placed it in front of me. I had read somewhere that the location of a telephone call can be traced in about three minutes.

A woman's voice said, "Scotland Yard."

"Inspector Simmons, please," was all I volunteered.

"Can I tell him who's calling?"

"No, I would prefer not to give my name."

"Yes, of course, sir," she said, evidently used to such callers.

Another ringing tone. My mouth went dry as a man's voice announced "Simmons" and I heard the detective speak for the first time. I was taken aback to find that a man with so English a name could have such a strong Glaswegian accent.

"Can I help you?" he asked.

"No, but I think I can help you," I said in a quiet tone which I pitched considerably lower than my natural speaking voice.

"How can you help me, sir?"

"Are you the officer in charge of the Carla-whatever-her-name-is case?"

"Yes, I am. But how can you help?" he repeated.

The second hand showed one minute had already passed.

"I saw a man leaving her flat that night."

"Where were you at the time?"

"At the bus stop on the same side of the road."

"Can you give me a description of the man?" Simmons's tone was every bit as casual as my own.

"Tall. I'd say five eleven, six foot. Well built. Wore one of those posh City coats – you know, the black ones with a velvet collar."

"How can you be so sure about the coat?" the detective asked.

"It was so cold standing out there waiting for the No. 19 that I wished it had been me who was wearing it."

"Do you remember anything in particular that happened after he left the flat?"

"Only that he went into the paper shop opposite before getting into his car and driving away."

"Yes, we know that much," said the Detective Inspector. "I don't suppose you recall what make of car it was?"

Two minutes had now passed and I began to watch the second hand more closely.

"I think it was a BMW," I said.

"Do you remember the colour by any chance?"

"No, it was too dark for that." I paused. "But I saw him tear a parking ticket off the windscreen, so it shouldn't be too hard for you to trace him."

"And at what time did all this take place?"

"Around six fifteen to six thirty, Inspector," I said.

"And can you tell me . . . ?"

Two minutes fifty-eight seconds. I put the phone back on the hook. My whole body broke out in a sweat.

"Good to see you in the office on a Saturday morning," said the managing director grimly as he passed my door. "Soon as you're finished whatever you're doing I'd like a word with you."

I left my desk and followed him along the corridor into his office. For the next hour he went over my projected figures, but however hard I tried I couldn't concentrate. It wasn't long before he stopped trying to disguise his impatience.

"Have you got something else on your mind?" he asked as he closed his file. "You seem preoccupied."

"No," I insisted, "just been doing a lot of overtime lately," and stood up to leave.

Once I had returned to my office, I burnt the piece of paper with the five headings and left to go home. In the first edition of the afternoon paper, the "Lovers' Tiff" story had been moved back to page seven. They had nothing new to report.

The rest of Saturday seemed interminable but my wife's *Sunday Express* finally brought me some relief.

"Following up information received in the Carla Moorland 'Lovers' Tiff' murder, a man is helping the police with their inquiries." The commonplace expressions I had read so often in the past suddenly took on a real meaning.

I scoured the other Sunday papers, listened to every news bulletin and watched each news item on television. When my wife became curious I explained that there was a rumour in the office that the company might be taken over again, which meant I could lose my job.

By Monday morning the *Daily Express* had named the man in "The Lovers' Tiff murder" as Paul Menzies (51), an insurance broker from Sutton. His wife was at a hospital in Epsom under sedation while he was being held in the cells of Brixton Prison under arrest. I began to wonder if Mr Menzies had told Carla the truth about *his* wife and what *his* nickname might be. I poured myself a strong black coffee and left for the office.

Later that morning, Menzies appeared before the magistrates at the Horseferry Road court, charged with the murder of Carla Moorland. The police had been successful in opposing bail, the *Standard* reassured me.

* * *

It takes six months, I was to discover, for a case of this gravity to reach the Old Bailey. Paul Menzies passed those months on remand in Brixton Prison. I spent the same period fearful of every telephone call, every knock on the door, every unexpected visitor. Each one created its own nightmare. Innocent people have no idea how many such incidents occur every day. I went about my job as best I could, often wondering if Menzies knew of my relationship with Carla, if he knew my name or if he even knew of my existence.

It must have been a couple of months before the trial was due to begin that the company held its annual general meeting. It had taken some considerable creative accountancy on my part to produce a set of figures that showed us managing any profit at all. We certainly didn't pay our shareholders a dividend that year.

I came away from the meeting relieved, almost elated. Six months had passed since Carla's death and not one incident had occurred during that period to suggest that anyone suspected I had even known her, let alone been the cause of her death. I still felt guilty about Carla, even missed her, but after six months I was now able to go for a whole day without fear entering my mind. Strangely, I felt no guilt about Menzies's plight. After all, it was he who had become the instrument that was going to keep me from a lifetime spent in prison. So when the blow came it had double the impact.

It was on August 26th – I shall never forget it – that I received a letter which made me realise it might be necessary to follow every word of the trial.

However much I tried to convince myself I should explain why I couldn't do it, I knew I wouldn't be able to resist it.

That same morning, a Friday – I suppose these things always happen on a Friday – I was called in for what I assumed was to be a routine weekly meeting with the managing director, only to be informed that the company no longer needed me.

"Frankly, in the last few months your work has gone from bad to worse," I was told.

I didn't feel able to disagree with him.

"And you have left me with no choice but to replace you."

A polite way of saying, "You're sacked."

"Your desk will be cleared by five this evening," the managing director continued, "when you will receive a cheque from the accounts department for £17,500."

I raised an eyebrow.

"Six months' compensation, as stipulated in your contract when we took over the company," he explained.

When the managing director stretched out his hand it was not to wish me luck, but to ask for the keys of my Rover.

I remember my first thought when he informed me of his decision: at least I would be able to attend every day of the trial without any hassle.

Elizabeth took the news of my sacking badly but only asked what plans I had for finding a new job. During the next month I pretended to look for a position in another company but realised I couldn't hope to settle down to anything until the case was over.

On the morning of the trial all the popular papers had colourful background pieces. The *Daily Express* even displayed on its front page a flattering picture of Carla in a swimsuit on the beach at Marbella: I wondered how much her sister in Fulham had been paid for that particular item. Alongside it was a profile photo of Paul Menzies which made him look as if he were already a convict.

I was amongst the first to be told in which court at the Old Bailey the case of the Crown v. Menzies would be tried. A uniformed policeman gave me detailed directions and along with several others I made my way to Court No. 4.

Once I had reached the courtroom I filed in and made sure that I sat on the end of my row. I looked round thinking everyone would stare at me, but to my relief no one showed the slightest interest.

I had a good view of the defendant as he stood in the dock. Menzies was a frail man who looked as if he had recently lost a lot of weight; fifty-one, the newspapers had said, but he looked nearer seventy. I began to wonder how much I must have aged over the past few months.

Menzies wore a smart, dark blue suit that hung loosely on him, a clean shirt and what I thought must be a regimental tie. His grey thinning hair was swept straight back; a small silver moustache gave him a military air. He certainly didn't look like a murderer or much of a catch as a lover, but anyone glancing towards me would probably have come to the same conclusion. I searched around the sea of faces for Mrs Menzies but no one in the court fitted the newspaper description of her.

We all rose when Mr Justice Buchanan came in.

"The Crown v. Menzies," the clerk of the court read out.

The judge leaned forward to tell Menzies that he could be seated and then turned slowly towards the jury box.

He explained that, although there had been considerable press interest in the case, their opinion was all that mattered because they alone would be asked to decide if the prisoner were guilty or not guilty of murder. He also advised the jury against reading any newspaper articles concerning the trial or listening to anyone else's views, especially those who had not been present in court: such people, he said, were always the first to have an immutable opinion on what the verdict should be. He went on to remind the jury how important it was to concentrate on the evidence because a man's life was at stake. I found myself nodding in agreement.

I glanced round the court hoping there was nobody there who would recognise me. Menzies's eyes remained fixed firmly on the judge, who was turning back to face the prosecuting counsel.

Even as Sir Humphrey Mountcliff rose from his place on the bench I was thankful he was against Menzies and not me. A man of dominating height with a high forehead and silver grey hair, he commanded the court not only with his physical presence but with a voice that was never less than authoritative.

To a silent assembly he spent the rest of the morning setting out the case for the prosecution. His eyes rarely left the jury box except occasionally to peer down at his notes.

He reconstructed the events as he imagined

they had happened that evening in April.

The opening address lasted two and a half hours, shorter than I'd expected. The judge then suggested a break for lunch and asked us all to be back in our places by ten past two.

After lunch Sir Humphrey called his first witness, Detective Inspector Simmons. I was unable to look directly at the policeman while he presented his evidence. Each reply he gave was as if he were addressing me personally. I wondered if he suspected all along that there was another man. Simmons gave a highly professional account of himself as he described in detail how they had found the body and later traced Menzies through two witnesses and the damning parking ticket. By the time Sir Humphrey sat down few people in that court could have felt that Simmons had arrested the wrong man.

Menzies's defence counsel, who rose to cross-examine the Detective Inspector, could not have been in greater contrast to Sir Humphrey. Mr Robert Scott, QC, was short and stocky, with thick bushy eyebrows. He spoke slowly and without inflection. I was happy to observe that one member of the jury was having difficulty in staying awake.

For the next twenty minutes Scott took the Detective Inspector painstakingly back over his evidence but was unable to make Simmons retract anything substantial. As the Inspector stepped out of the witness box I felt confident enough to look him straight in the eye.

The next witness was a Home Office pathologist, Dr Anthony Mallins, who, after answering a few preliminary questions to establish his professional status, moved on to answer an inquiry from Sir Humphrey that took everyone by surprise. The pathologist informed the court that there was clear evidence to suggest that Miss Moorland had had sexual intercourse shortly before her death.

"How can you be so certain, Dr Mallins?"

"Because I found traces of blood group B on the deceased's upper thigh, while Miss Moorland was later found to be blood group O. There were also traces of seminal fluid on the negligee she was wearing at the time of her death."

"Are these common blood groups?" Sir Humphrey asked.

"Blood group O is common," Dr Mallins admitted. "Group B, however, is fairly unusual."

"And what would you say was the cause of her death?" Sir Humphrey asked.

"A blow or blows to the head, which caused a broken jaw, and lacerations at the base of the skull which may have been delivered by a blunt instrument."

I wanted to stand up and say, "I can tell you which!" when Sir Humphrey said, "Thank you, Dr Mallins. No more questions. Please wait there."

Mr Scott treated the doctor with far more respect than he had Inspector Simmons, despite Mallins being the defendant's witness.

"Could the blow on the back of Miss Moorland's head have been caused by a fall?" he asked.

The doctor hesitated. "Possibly," he agreed. "But that wouldn't explain the broken jaw."

Mr Scott ignored the comment and pressed on.

"What percentage of people in Britain are blood group B?"

"About five, six per cent," volunteered the doctor.

"Two and a half million people," said Mr Scott, and waited for the figure to sink in before he suddenly changed tack.

But as hard as he tried he could not shift the pathologist on the time of death or on the fact that sexual intercourse must have taken place around the hours his client had been with Carla.

When Mr Scott sat down the judge asked Sir Humphrey if he wished to re-examine.

"I do, my Lord. Dr Mallins, you told the court that Miss Moorland suffered from a broken jaw and lacerations on the back of her head. Could the lacerations have been caused by falling on to a blunt object after the jaw had been broken?"

"I must object, my Lord," said Mr Scott, rising with unusual speed. "This is a leading question."

Mr Justice Buchanan leaned forward and peered down at the doctor. "I agree, Mr Scott, but I would like to know if Dr Mallins found blood group O, Miss Moorland's blood group, on any other object in the room?"

"Yes, my Lord," replied the doctor. "On the edge of the glass table in the centre of the room."

"Thank you, Dr Mallins," said Sir Humphrey. "No more questions."

Sir Humphrey's next witness was Mrs Rita Johnson, the lady who claimed she had seen everything.

"Mrs Johnson, on the evening of April 7th, did you see a man leave the block of flats where Miss Moorland lived?" Sir Humphrey asked.

"Yes, I did."

"At about what time was that?"

"A few minutes after six."

"Please tell the court what happened next."

"He walked across the road, removed a parking ticket, got into his car and drove away."

"Do you see that man in the court today?"

"Yes," she said firmly, pointing to Menzies, who at this suggestion shook his head vigorously.

"No more questions."

Mr Scott rose slowly again.

"What did you say was the make of the car the man got into?"

"I can't be sure," Mrs Johnson said, "but I think it was a BMW."

"Not a Rover as you first told the police the following morning?"

The witness did not reply.

"And did you actually see the man in question remove a parking ticket from the car windscreen?" Mr Scott asked.

"I think so, sir, but it all happened so quickly."

"I'm sure it did," said Mr Scott. "In fact, I suggest to you that it happened so quickly that you've got the wrong man and the wrong car."

"No, sir," she replied, but without the same conviction with which she had delivered her earlier replies.

Sir Humphrey did not re-examine Mrs Johnson. I realised that he wanted her evidence to be forgotten by the jury as quickly as possible. As it was, when she left the witness box she also left everyone in court in considerable doubt.

Carla's daily, Maria Lucia, was far more convincing. She stated unequivocally that she had seen

Menzies in the living room of the flat that afternoon when she arrived a little before five. However, she had, she admitted, never seen him before that day.

"But isn't it true," asked Sir Humphrey, "that you usually only work in the mornings?"

"Yes," she replied. "Although Miss Moorland was in the habit of bringing work home on a Thursday afternoon so it was convenient for me to come in and collect my wages."

"And how was Miss Moorland dressed that afternoon?" asked Sir Humphrey.

"In her blue morning coat," replied the daily.

"Is this how she usually dressed on a Thursday afternoon?"

"No, sir, but I assumed she was going to have a bath before going out that evening."

"But when you left the flat was she still with Mr Menzies?"

"Yes, sir."

"Do you remember anything else she was wearing that day?"

"Yes, sir. Underneath the morning coat she wore a red negligee."

My negligee was duly produced and Maria Lucia identified it. At this point I stared directly at the witness but she showed not a flicker of recognition. I thanked all the gods in the Pantheon that I had never once been to visit Carla in the morning.

"Please wait there," were Sir Humphrey's final words to Miss Lucia.

Mr Scott rose to cross-examine.

"Miss Lucia, you have told the court that the purpose of the visit was to collect your wages. How long were you at the flat on this occasion?"

"I did a little clearing up in the kitchen and ironed a blouse, perhaps twenty minutes."

"Did you see Miss Moorland during this time?"

"Yes, I went into the drawing room to ask if she would like some more coffee but she said no."

"Was Mr Menzies with her at the time?"

"Yes, he was."

"Were you at any time aware of a quarrel between the two of them or even raised voices?"

"No, sir."

"When you saw them together did Miss Moorland show any signs of distress or need of help?"

"No, sir."

"Then what happened?"

"Miss Moorland joined me in the kitchen a few minutes later, gave me my wages and I let myself out."

"When you were alone in the kitchen with Miss Moorland, did she give any sign of being afraid of her guest?"

"No, sir."

"No more questions, my Lord."

Sir Humphrey did not re-examine Maria Lucia and informed the judge that he had completed the case for the prosecution. Mr Justice Buchanan nodded and said he felt that was enough for the day; but I wasn't convinced it was enough to convict Menzies.

When I got home that night Elizabeth did not ask me where I had been, and I did not volunteer any information. I spent the evening pretending to go over job applications.

* * *

The following morning I had a late breakfast and read the papers before returning to my place at the end of a row in Court No. 4, only a few moments before the judge made his entrance.

Mr Justice Buchanan, having sat down, adjusted his wig before calling on Mr Scott to open the case for the defence. Mr Scott, QC, was once again slow to rise – a man paid by the hour, I thought uncharitably. He started by promising the court that his opening address would be brief, and he then remained on his feet for the next two and a half hours.

He began the case for the defence by going over in detail the relevant parts, as he saw them, of Menzies's past. He assured us all that those who wished to dissect it later would only find an unblemished record. Paul Menzies was a happily married man who lived in Sutton with his wife and three children, Polly, aged twenty-one, Michael, nineteen, and Sally, sixteen. Two of the children were now at university and the youngest had just completed her GCSE. Doctors had advised Mrs Menzies not to attend the trial, following her recent release from hospital. I noticed two of the women on the jury smile sympathetically.

Mr Menzies, Mr Scott continued, had been with the same firm of insurance brokers in the City of London for the past six years and, although he had not been promoted, he was a much respected member of the staff. He was a pillar of his local community, having served with the Territorial Army and on the committee of the local camera club. He had once even stood for the Sutton council. He could hardly be described as a serious candidate as a murderer.

Mr Scott then went on to the actual day of the killing and confirmed that Mr Menzies had an appointment with Miss Moorland on the afternoon in question, but in a strictly professional capacity with the sole purpose of helping her with a personal insurance plan. There could have been no other reason to visit Miss Moorland during office hours. He did not have sexual intercourse with her and he certainly did not murder her.

The defendant had left his client a few minutes after six. He understood she had intended to change before going out to dinner with her sister in Fulham. He had arranged to see her the following Wednesday at his office for the purpose of drawing up the completed policy. The defence, Mr Scott went on, would later produce a diary entry that would establish the truth of this statement.

The charge against the accused was, he submitted, based almost completely on circumstantial evidence. He felt confident that, when the trial reached its conclusion, the jury would be left with no choice but to release his client back into the bosom of his loving family. "You must end this nightmare," Mr Scott concluded. "It has gone on far too long for an innocent man."

At this point the judge suggested a break for lunch. During the meal I was unable to concentrate or even take in what was being said around me. The majority of those who had an opinion to give now seemed convinced that Menzies was innocent.

As soon as we returned, at ten past two, Mr Scott called his first witness: the defendant himself.

Paul Menzies left the dock and walked slowly over to the witness box. He took a copy of the New

Testament in his right hand and haltingly read the words of the oath, from a card which he held in his left.

Every eye was fixed on him while Mr Scott began to guide his client carefully through the minefield of evidence.

Menzies became progressively more confident in his delivery as the day wore on, and when at four thirty the judge told the court, "That's enough for today," I was convinced that he would get off, even if only by a majority verdict.

I spent a fitful night before returning to my place on the third day fearing the worst. Would Menzies be released and would they then start looking for me?

Mr Scott opened the third morning as gently as he had begun the second, but he repeated so many questions from the previous day that it became obvious he was only steadying his client in preparation for prosecuting counsel. Before he finally sat down he asked Menzies for a third time, "Did you ever have sexual intercourse with Miss Moorland?"

"No, sir. I had only met her for the first time that day," Menzies replied firmly.

"And did you murder Miss Moorland?"

"Certainly not, sir," said Menzies, his voice now strong and confident.

Mr Scott resumed his place, a look of quiet satisfaction on his face.

In fairness to Menzies, very little which takes place in normal life could have prepared anyone for cross-examination by Sir Humphrey Mountcliff. I could not have asked for a better advocate.

"I'd like to start, if I may, Mr Menzies," he began, "with what your counsel seems to set great store by as proof of your innocence."

Menzies's thin lips remained in a firm straight line.

"The pertinent entry in your diary which suggests that you made a second appointment to see Miss Moorland, the murdered woman" – three words Sir Humphrey was to repeat again and again during his cross-examination – "for the Wednesday after she had been killed."

"Yes, sir," said Menzies.

"This entry was made – correct me if I'm wrong – following your Thursday meeting at Miss Moorland's flat."

"Yes, sir," said Menzies, obviously tutored not to add anything that might later help prosecuting counsel.

"So when did you make that entry?" Sir Humphrey asked.

"On the Friday morning."

"After Miss Moorland had been killed?"

"Yes, but I didn't know."

"Do you carry a diary on you, Mr Menzies?"

"Yes, but only a small pocket diary, not my large desk one."

"Do you have it with you today?"

"I do."

"May I be allowed to see it?"

Reluctantly Menzies took a small green diary out of his jacket pocket and handed it over to the clerk of the court, who in turn passed it on to Sir Humphrey. Sir Humphrey began to leaf through the pages.

"I see that there is no entry for your appointment with Miss Moorland for the afternoon on which she was murdered?"

"No, sir," said Menzies. "I put office appointments only in my desk diary, personal appointments are restricted to my pocket diary."

"I understand," said Sir Humphrey. He paused and looked up. "But isn't it strange, Mr Menzies, that you agreed to an appointment with a client to discuss further business and you then trusted it to memory, when you so easily could have put it in the diary you carry around with you all the time before transferring it?"

"I might have written it down on a slip of paper at the time, but as I explained that's a personal diary."

"Is it?" said Sir Humphrey as he flicked back a few more pages. "Who is David Paterson?" he asked.

Menzies looked as if he were trying to place him.

"Mr David Paterson, 112 City Road, 11.30, January 9th this year," Sir Humphrey read out to the court. Menzies looked anxious. "We could subpoena Mr Paterson if you can't recall the meeting," said Sir Humphrey helpfully.

"He's a client of my firm," said Menzies in a quiet voice.

"A client of your firm," Sir Humphrey repeated slowly. "I wonder how many of those I could find if I went through your diary at a more leisurely pace?" Menzies bowed his head as Sir Humphrey passed the diary back to the clerk, having made his point.

"Now I should like to turn to some more important questions . . ."

"Not until after lunch, Sir Humphrey," the

judge intervened. "It's nearly one and I think we'll take a break now."

"As you wish, my Lord," came back the courteous reply.

I left the court in a more optimistic mood, even though I couldn't wait to discover what could be more important than that diary. Sir Humphrey's emphasis on little lies, although they did not prove Menzies was a murderer, did show he was hiding something. I became anxious that during the break Mr Scott might advise Menzies to admit to his affair with Carla, and thus make the rest of his story appear more credible. To my relief, over the meal I learned that under English law Menzies could not consult his counsel while he was still in the witness box. I noticed when we returned to court that Mr Scott's smile had disappeared.

Sir Humphrey rose to continue his cross-examination.

"You have stated under oath, Mr Menzies, that you are a happily married man."

"I am, sir," said the defendant with feeling.

"Was your first marriage as happy, Mr Menzies?" asked Sir Humphrey casually. The defendant's cheeks drained of their colour. I quickly looked over towards Mr Scott who could not mask that this was information with which he had not been entrusted.

"Take your time before you answer," said Sir Humphrey.

All eyes turned to the man in the witness box.

"No," said Menzies and quickly added, "but I was very young at the time. It was many years ago and all a ghastly mistake."

"All a ghastly mistake?" repeated Sir Humphrey, looking straight at the jury. "And how did that marriage end?"

"In divorce," Menzies said quite simply.

"And what were the grounds for that divorce?"

"Cruelty," said Menzies, "but . . ."

"But . . . would you like me to read out to the jury what your first wife swore under oath in court that day?"

Menzies stood there shaking. He knew that "No" would damn him and "Yes" would hang him.

"Well, as you seem unable to advise us I will, with your permission, my Lord, read the statement made before Mr Justice Rodger on June 9th, 1961, at the Swindon County Court by the first Mrs Menzies." Sir Humphrey cleared his throat. "'He used to hit me again and again, and it became so bad that I had to run away for fear he might one day kill me.'" Sir Humphrey emphasised the last five words.

"She was exaggerating," shouted Menzies from the witness box.

"How unfortunate that poor Miss Carla Moorland cannot be with us today to let us know if your story about her is also an exaggeration."

"I object, my Lord," said Mr Scott. "Sir Humphrey is harassing the witness."

"I agree," said the judge. "Tread more carefully in future, Sir Humphrey."

"I apologise, my Lord," said Sir Humphrey, sounding singularly unapologetic. He closed the file to which he had been referring and replaced it on the desk in front of him before taking up a new one. He opened it slowly, making sure all in the court were following every movement before he extracted a single sheet of paper.

"How many mistresses have you had since you were married to the second Mrs Menzies?"

"Objection, my Lord. How can this be relevant?"

"My Lord, it is relevant, I respectfully suggest. I intend to show that this was not a business relationship that Mr Menzies was conducting with Miss Moorland but a highly personal one."

"The question can be put to the defendant," ruled the judge.

Menzies said nothing as Sir Humphrey held up the sheet of paper in front of him and studied it.

"Take your time because I want the exact number," Sir Humphrey said, looking over the top of his glasses.

The seconds ticked on as we all waited.

"Hm – three, I think," Menzies said eventually in a voice that just carried. The gentlemen of the press began scribbling furiously.

"Three," said Sir Humphrey, staring at his piece of paper in disbelief.

"Well, perhaps four."

"And was the fourth Miss Carla Moorland?" Sir Humphrey asked. "Because you had sexual intercourse with her that evening, didn't you?"

"No, I did not," said Menzies, but by this time few in that courtroom could have believed him.

"Very well then," continued Sir Humphrey, as he placed the piece of paper on the bench in front of him. "But before I return to your relationship with

Miss Moorland, let us discover the truth about the other four."

I stared at the piece of paper from which Sir Humphrey had been reading. From where I was seated I could see that there was nothing written on it at all. A blank white sheet lay before him.

I was finding it hard to keep a grin off my face. Menzies's adulterous background was an unexpected bonus for me and the press – and I couldn't help wondering how Carla would have reacted if she had known about it.

Sir Humphrey spent the rest of the day making Menzies relate the details of his previous relationships with the four mistresses. The court was agog and the journalists continued to scribble away, knowing they were about to have a field day. When the court rose Mr Scott's eyes were closed.

I drove home that night feeling not a little pleased with myself; like a man who had just completed a good day's work.

On entering the courtroom the following morning I noticed people were beginning to acknowledge other regulars and nod. I found myself falling into the same pattern and greeted people silently as I took my regular position on the end of the bench.

Sir Humphrey spent the morning going over some of Menzies's other misdemeanours. We discovered that he had served in the Territorial Army for only five months and left after a misunderstanding with his commanding officer over how many hours he should have been spending on exercises during weekends and how much he had claimed in expenses for those hours. We also learned that his attempts to get on the local council sprung more from anger at being refused planning permission to build on a piece of land adjoining his house than from an altruistic desire to serve his fellow men. To be fair, Sir Humphrey could have made the Archangel Gabriel look like a soccer hooligan; but his trump card was still to come.

"Mr Menzies, I should now like to return to your version of what happened on the night Miss Moorland was killed."

"Yes," sighed Menzies in a tired voice.

"When you visit a client to discuss one of your policies, how long would you say such a consultation usually lasts?"

"Usually half an hour, an hour at the most," said Menzies.

"And how long did the consultation with Miss Moorland take?"

"A good hour," said Menzies.

"And you left her, if I remember your evidence correctly, a little after six o'clock."

"That is correct."

"And what time was your appointment?"

"At five o'clock, as was shown clearly in my desk diary," said Menzies.

"Well, Mr Menzies, if you arrived at about five to keep your appointment with Miss Moorland and left a little after six, how did you manage to get a parking fine?"

"I didn't have any small change for the meter at the time," said Menzies confidently. "As I was already a couple of minutes late, I just risked it."

"You just risked it," repeated Sir Humphrey slowly. "You are obviously a man who takes risks, Mr Menzies. I wonder if you would be good enough to look at the parking ticket in question."

The clerk handed it up to Menzies.

"Would you read out to the court the hour and minute that the traffic warden has written in the little boxes to show when the offence occurred."

Once again Menzies took a long time to reply.

"Four sixteen to four thirty," he said eventually.

"I didn't hear that," said the judge.

"Would you be kind enough to repeat what you said for the judge?" Sir Humphrey asked.

Menzies repeated the damning figures.

"So now we have established that you were in fact with Miss Moorland some time before four sixteen, and not, as I suggest you later wrote in your diary, five o'clock. That was just another lie, wasn't it?"

"No," said Menzies. "I must have arrived a little earlier than I realised."

"At least an hour earlier, it seems. And I also suggest to you that you arrived at that early hour because your interest in Carla Moorland was not simply professional?"

"That's not true."

"Then it wasn't your intention that she should become your mistress?"

Menzies hesitated long enough for Sir Humphrey to answer his own question. "Because the business part of your meeting finished in the usual half hour, did it not, Mr Menzies?" He waited for a response but still none was forthcoming.

"What is your blood group, Mr Menzies?"

"I have no idea."

Sir Humphrey without warning changed tack: "Have you heard of DNA, by any chance?"

"No," came back the puzzled reply.

"Deoxyribonucleic acid is a proven technique that shows genetic information can be unique to every individual. Blood or semen samples can be matched. Semen, Mr Menzies, is as unique as any fingerprint. With such a sample we would know immediately if you raped Miss Moorland."

"I didn't rape her," Menzies said indignantly.

"Nevertheless sexual intercourse did take place, didn't it?" said Sir Humphrey quietly.

Menzies remained silent.

"Shall I recall the Home Office pathologist and ask him to carry out a DNA test?"

Menzies still made no reply.

"And check your blood group?" Sir Humphrey paused. "I will ask you once again, Mr Menzies. Did sexual intercourse between you and the murdered woman take place that Thursday afternoon?"

"Yes, sir," said Menzies in a whisper.

"Yes, sir," repeated Sir Humphrey so that the whole court could hear it.

"But it wasn't rape," Menzies shouted back at Sir Humphrey.

"Wasn't it?" said Sir Humphrey.

"And I swear I didn't kill her."

I must have been the only person in that courtroom who knew he was telling the truth. All Sir Humphrey said was, "No more questions, my Lord."

Mr Scott tried manfully to resurrect his client's credibility during re-examination but the fact that Menzies had been caught lying about his relationship with Carla made everything he had said previously appear doubtful.

If only Menzies had told the truth about being

Carla's lover, his story might well have been accepted. I wondered why he had gone through the charade – in order to protect his wife? Whatever the motive, it had only ended by making him appear guilty of a crime he hadn't committed.

I went home that night and ate the largest meal I had had for several days.

The following morning Mr Scott called two more witnesses. The first turned out to be the vicar of St Peter's, Sutton, who was there as a character witness to prove what a pillar of the community Menzies was. After Sir Humphrey had finished his cross-examination the vicar ended up looking like a rather kind, unworldly old man, whose knowledge of Menzies was based on the latter's occasional attendance at Sunday matins.

The second was Menzies's superior at the company they both worked for in the City. He was a far more impressive figure but he was unable to confirm that Miss Moorland had ever been a client of the company.

Mr Scott put up no more witnesses and informed Mr Justice Buchanan that he had completed the case for the defence. The judge nodded and, turning to Sir Humphrey, told him he would not be required to begin his final address until the following morning.

That heralded the signal for the court to rise.

Another long evening and an even longer night had to be endured by Menzies and myself. As on every other day during the trial, I made sure I was in my place the next morning before the judge entered.

Sir Humphrey's closing speech was masterful.

Every little untruth was logged so that one began to accept that very little of Menzies's testimony could be relied on.

"We will never know for certain," said Sir Humphrey, "for what reason poor young Carla Moorland was murdered. Refusal to succumb to Menzies's advances? A fit of temper which ended with a blow that caused her to fall and later die alone? But there are, however, some things, members of the jury, of which we can be quite certain.

"We can be certain that Menzies was with the murdered woman that day before the hour of four sixteen because of the evidence of the damning parking ticket.

"We can be certain that he left a little after six because we have a witness who saw him drive away, and he does not himself deny this evidence.

"And we can be certain that he wrote a false entry in his diary to make you believe he had a business appointment with the murdered woman at five, rather than a personal assignation some time before.

"And we can now be certain that he lied about having sexual intercourse with Miss Moorland a short time before she was killed, though we cannot be certain if intercourse took place before or after her jaw had been broken." Sir Humphrey's eyes rested on the jury before he continued.

"We can, finally, establish, beyond reasonable doubt, from the pathologist's report, the time of death and that, therefore, Menzies was the last person who could possibly have seen Carla Moorland alive.

"Therefore no one else could have killed Carla

Moorland – for do not forget Inspector Simmons's evidence – and if you accept that, you can be in no doubt that only Menzies could have been responsible for her death. And how damning you must have found it that he tried to hide the existence of a first wife who had left him on the grounds of his cruelty, and the four mistresses who left him we know not why or how. Only one less than Bluebeard," Sir Humphrey added with feeling.

"For the sake of every young girl who lives on her own in our capital, you must carry out your duty, however painful that duty might be. And find Menzies guilty of murder."

When Sir Humphrey sat down I wanted to applaud.

The judge sent us away for another break. Voices all around me were now damning Menzies. I listened contentedly without offering an opinion. I knew that if the jury convicted Menzies the file would be closed and no eyes would ever be turned in my direction. I was seated in my place before the judge appeared at ten past two. He called on Mr Scott.

Menzies's counsel put up a spirited defence of his client, pointing out that almost all the evidence that Sir Humphrey had come up with had been circumstantial, and that it was even possible someone else could have visited Carla Moorland after his client had left that night. Mr Scott's bushy eyebrows seemed almost to have a life of their own as he energetically emphasised that it was the prosecution's responsibility to prove their case beyond reasonable doubt and not his to disprove it, and that, in his opinion, his learned friend, Sir Humphrey, had failed to do so.

During his summing-up Scott avoided any mention of diary entries, parking tickets, past mistresses, sexual intercourse or questions of his client's role in the community. A latecomer listening only to the closing speeches might have been forgiven for thinking the two learned gentlemen were summarising different cases.

Mr Scott's expression became grim as he turned to face the jury for his summation. "The twelve of you," he said, "hold the fate of my client in your hands. You must, therefore, be certain, I repeat, certain beyond reasonable doubt that Paul Menzies could have committed such an evil crime as murder.

"This is not a trial about Mr Menzies's lifestyle, his position in the community or even his sexual habits. If adultery were a crime I feel confident Mr Menzies would not be the only person in this courtroom to be in the dock today." He paused as his eyes swept up and down the jury.

"For this reason I feel confident that you will find it in your hearts to release my client from the torment he has been put through during the last seven months. He has surely been shown to be an innocent man deserving of your compassion."

Mr Scott sank down on the bench having, I felt, given his client a glimmer of hope.

The judge told us that he would not begin his own summing-up until Monday morning.

The weekend seemed interminable to me. By Monday I had convinced myself that enough members of the jury would feel there just had not been sufficient evidence to convict.

As soon as the trial was under way the judge

began by explaining once again that it was the jury alone who must make the ultimate decision. It was not his job to let them know how he felt, but only to advise them on the law.

He went back over all the evidence, trying to put it in perspective, but he never gave as much as a hint as to his own opinions. When he had completed his summing-up late that afternoon he sent the jury away to consider their verdict.

I waited with nearly as much anxiety as Menzies must have done while I listened to others giving their opinion as the minutes ticked by in that little room. Then, four hours later, a note was sent up to the judge.

He immediately asked the jury to return to their places while the press flooded back into the courtroom, making it look like the House of Commons on Budget Day. The clerk dutifully handed up the note to Mr Justice Buchanan. He opened it and read what only twelve other people in the courtroom could have known.

He handed it back to the clerk who then read the note to a silent court.

Mr Justice Buchanan frowned before asking if there were any chance of a unanimous verdict being reached if he allowed more time. Once he had learned that it was proving impossible he reluctantly nodded his agreement to a majority verdict.

The jury disappeared downstairs again to continue their deliberations, and did not return to their places for another three hours. I could sense the tension in the court as neighbours sought to give opinions to each other in noisy whispers. The clerk called for silence as the judge waited for everyone to settle before he instructed the clerk to proceed.

When the clerk rose, I could hear the person next to me breathing.

"Would the Foreman please stand?"

I rose from my place.

"Have you reached a verdict on which at least ten of you are agreed?"

"We have, sir."

"Do you find the defendant, Paul Menzies, guilty or not guilty?"

"Guilty," I replied.

Clean Sweep Ignatius

FEW showed much interest when Ignatius Agarbi was appointed Nigeria's Minister of Finance. After all, the cynics pointed out, he was the seventeenth person to hold the office in seventeen years.

In Ignatius's first major policy statement to Parliament he promised to end graft and corruption in public life and warned the electorate that no one holding an official position could feel safe unless he led a blameless life. He ended his maiden speech with the words, "I intend to clear out Nigeria's Augean stables."

Such was the impact of the minister's speech that it failed to get a mention in the Lagos *Daily Times*. Perhaps the editor considered that, since the paper had covered the speeches of the previous sixteen ministers *in extenso*, his readers might feel they had heard it all before.

Ignatius, however, was not to be disheartened by the lack of confidence shown in him, and set about his new task with vigour and determination. Within days of his appointment he had caused a minor official at the Ministry of Trade to be jailed for falsifying documents relating to the import of grain. The next to feel the bristles of Ignatius's new broom was a leading Lebanese financier, who was deported without trial for breach of the exchange control regulations. A month later came an event which even Ignatius considered a personal coup: the arrest of the Inspector General of Police for accepting bribes – a perk the citizens of Lagos had in the past considered went with the job. When four months later the Police Chief was sentenced to eighteen months in jail, the new Finance Minister finally made the front page of the Lagos *Daily Times*. A leader on the centre page dubbed him "Clean Sweep Ignatius", the new broom every guilty man feared. Ignatius's reputation as Mr Clean continued to grow as arrest followed arrest and unfounded rumours began circulating in the capital that even General Otobi, the Head of State, was under investigation by his own Finance Minister.

Ignatius alone now checked, vetted and authorised all foreign contracts worth over one hundred million dollars. And although every decision he made was meticulously scrutinised by his enemies, not a breath of scandal ever became associated with his name.

When Ignatius began his second year of office as Minister of Finance even the cynics began to acknowledge his achievements. It was about this time that General Otobi felt confident enough to call Ignatius in for an unscheduled consultation.

The Head of State welcomed the Minister to Dodan Barracks and ushered him to a comfortable chair in his study overlooking the parade ground.

"Ignatius, I have just finished going over the latest budget report and I am alarmed by your conclusion that the Exchequer is still losing millions of dollars each year in bribes paid to go-betweens by foreign companies. Have you any idea into whose pockets this money is falling? That's what I want to know."

Ignatius sat bolt upright, his eyes never leaving the Head of State.

"I suspect a great percentage of the money is ending up in private Swiss bank accounts but I am at present unable to prove it."

"Then I will give you whatever added authority you require to do so," said General Otobi. "You can use any means you consider necessary to ferret out these villains. Start by investigating every member of my Cabinet, past and present. And show no fear or favour in your endeavours, no matter what their rank or connections."

"For such a task to have any chance of success I would need a special letter of authority signed by you, General . . ."

"Then it will be on your desk by six o'clock this evening," said the Head of State.

"And the rank of Ambassador Plenipotentiary whenever I travel abroad."

"Granted."

"Thank you," said Ignatius, rising from his chair on the assumption that the audience was over.

"You may also need this," said the General as they walked towards the door. The Head of State handed Ignatius a small automatic pistol. "Because I suspect by now that you have almost as many enemies as I."

Ignatius took the pistol from the soldier awkwardly, put it in his pocket and mumbled his thanks.

Without another word passing between the two men, Ignatius left his leader and was driven back to his Ministry.

Without the knowledge of the Governor of the Central Bank of Nigeria, and unhindered by any senior civil servants, Ignatius enthusiastically set about his new task. He researched alone at night, and by day discussed his findings with no one. Three months later he was ready to pounce.

The Minister selected the month of August to make an unscheduled visit abroad, as it was the time when most Nigerians went on holiday, and his absence would therefore not be worthy of comment.

He asked his Permanent Secretary to book him, his wife and their two children on a flight to Orlando, and to be certain that the tickets were charged to his personal account.

On their arrival in Florida, the family checked into the local Marriott Hotel. Ignatius then informed his wife, without warning or explanation, that he would be spending a few days in New York on business before rejoining them for the rest of the holiday. The following morning he left his family to the mysteries of Disney World while he took a flight to New York. It was a short taxi ride from LaGuardia to Kennedy, where, after a change of clothes and the purchase of a return tourist ticket for cash, he boarded a Swissair flight for Geneva unobserved.

Once he had arrived, Ignatius booked into an inconspicuous hotel, retired to bed and slept soundly for eight hours. Over breakfast the following morning he studied the list of banks he had so carefully drawn up after completing his research in Nigeria: each name was written out boldly in his own hand. Ignatius decided to start with Gerber et Cie whose building, he observed from the hotel bedroom, took up half the Avenue de Parchine. He checked the telephone number with the concierge before placing a call. The chairman agreed to see him at twelve o'clock.

Carrying only a battered briefcase, Ignatius arrived at the bank a few minutes before the appointed hour – an unusual occurrence for a Nigerian, thought the young man dressed in a smart grey suit, white shirt and grey silk tie, who was waiting in the marble hall to greet him. He bowed to the Minister, introducing himself as the chairman's personal assistant, and explained that he would accompany Ignatius to the chairman's office. The young executive led the Minister to a waiting lift and neither man uttered another word until they had reached the eleventh floor. A gentle tap on the chairman's door elicited "*Entrez*," which the young man obeyed.

"The Nigerian Minister of Finance, sir."

The chairman rose from behind his desk and stepped forward to greet his guest. Ignatius could not help noticing that he too wore a grey suit, white shirt and grey silk tie.

"Good morning, Minister," the chairman said. "Won't you have a seat?" He ushered Ignatius towards a low glass table surrounded by comfortable chairs on the far side of the room. "I have ordered coffee for both of us if that is acceptable."

Ignatius nodded, placed the battered briefcase on the floor by the side of his chair and stared out of the large plate-glass window. He made some small-talk about the splendid view of the magnificent fountain while a girl served all three men with coffee.

Once the young woman had left the room Ignatius got down to business.

"My Head of State has requested that I visit your bank with a rather unusual request," he began. Not a flicker of surprise appeared on the face of the chairman or his young assistant. "He has honoured me with the task of discovering which Nigerian citizens hold numbered accounts with your bank."

On learning this piece of information only the chairman's lips moved. "I am not at liberty to disclose –"

"Allow me to put my case," said the Minister, raising a white palm. "First, let me assure you that I come with the absolute authority of my government." Without another word, Ignatius extracted an envelope from his inside pocket with a flourish. He handed it to the chairman who removed the letter inside and read it slowly.

Once he had finished reading, the banker cleared his throat. "This document, I fear, sir, carries no validity in my country." He replaced it in the envelope and handed it back to Ignatius. "I am, of course," continued the chairman, "not for one moment doubting that you have the full backing of your Head of State, both as a Minister and an Ambassador, but that does not change the bank's rule of confidentiality in such matters. There are no circumstances in which we would release the names of any of our account holders without their authority. I'm sorry to be of so little help, but those are, and will always remain, the bank rules." The chairman rose to his feet, as he considered the meeting was now at an end; but he had not bargained for Clean Sweep Ignatius.

"My Head of State," said Ignatius, softening his tone perceptibly, "has authorised me to approach your bank to act as the intermediary for all future transactions between my country and Switzerland."

"We are flattered by your confidence in us, Minister," replied the chairman, who remained standing. "However, I feel sure that you will understand that it cannot alter our attitude to our customers' confidentiality."

Ignatius remained unperturbed.

"Then I am sorry to inform you, Mr Gerber, that our Ambassador in Geneva will be instructed to make an official communiqué to the Swiss Foreign Office about the lack of co-operation your bank has shown concerning requests for information about our nationals." He waited for his words to sink in. "You could avoid such embarrassment, of course, by simply letting me know the names of my countrymen who hold accounts with Gerber et Cie and the amounts involved. I can assure you we would not reveal the source of our information."

"You are most welcome to lodge such a communiqué, sir, and I feel sure that our Minister will explain to your Ambassador in the most courteous of diplomatic language that the Foreign Ministry does not have the authority under Swiss law to demand such disclosures."

"If that is the case, I shall instruct my own

Ministry of Trade to halt all future dealings in Nigeria with any Swiss nationals until these names are revealed."

"That is your privilege, Minister," replied the chairman, unmoved.

"And we may also have to reconsider every contract currently being negotiated by your countrymen in Nigeria. And in addition I shall personally see to it that no penalty clauses are honoured."

"Would you not consider such action a little precipitate?"

"Let me assure you, Mr Gerber, that I would not lose one moment of sleep over such a decision," said Ignatius. "Even if my efforts to discover those names were to bring your country to its knees I would not be moved."

"So be it, Minister," replied the chairman. "However, it still does not alter the policy or the attitude of this bank to confidentiality."

"If that remains the case, sir, this very day I shall give instructions to our Ambassador to close our Embassy in Geneva and I shall declare your Ambassador in Lagos *persona non grata.*"

For the first time the chairman raised his eyebrows.

"Furthermore," continued Ignatius, "I will hold a conference in London which will leave the world's press in no doubt of my Head of State's displeasure with the conduct of this bank. After such publicity I feel confident you will find that many of your customers would prefer to close their accounts, while others who have in the past considered you a safe haven may find it necessary to look elsewhere."

The Minister waited but still the chairman did not respond.

"Then you leave me no choice," said Ignatius, rising from his seat.

The chairman stretched out his arm, assuming that at last the Minister was leaving, only to watch with horror as Ignatius placed a hand in his jacket pocket and removed a small pistol. The two Swiss bankers froze as the Nigerian Minister of Finance stepped forward and pressed the muzzle against the chairman's temple.

"I need those names, Mr Gerber, and by now you must realise I will stop at nothing. If you don't supply them immediately I'm going to blow your brains out. Do you understand?"

The chairman gave a slight nod, beads of sweat appearing on his forehead. "And he will be next," said Ignatius, gesturing towards the young assistant, who stood speechless and paralysed a few paces away.

"Get me the names of every Nigerian who holds an account in this bank," Ignatius said quietly, looking towards the young man, "or I'll blow your chairman's brains all over his soft pile carpet. Immediately, do you hear me?" he added sharply.

The young man looked towards the chairman, who was now trembling but said quite clearly, "*Non, Pierre, jamais.*"

"*D'accord,*" replied the assistant in a whisper.

"You can't say I didn't give you every chance." Ignatius pulled back the hammer. The sweat was now pouring down the chairman's face and the young man had to turn his eyes away as he waited in terror for the pistol shot.

"Excellent," said Ignatius, as he removed the gun from the chairman's head and returned to his seat. Both the bankers were still trembling and quite unable to speak.

The Minister picked up the battered briefcase by the side of his chair and placed it on the glass table in front of him. He pressed back the clasps and the lid flicked up.

The two bankers stared down at the neatly packed rows of hundred-dollar bills. Every inch of the briefcase had been taken up. The chairman quickly estimated that it probably amounted to around five million dollars.

"I wonder, sir," said Ignatius, "how I go about opening an account with your bank?"

A la Carte

ARTHUR Hapgood was demobbed on November 3rd, 1946. Within a month he was back at his old workplace on the shop-floor of the Triumph factory on the outskirts of Coventry.

The five years spent in the Sherwood Foresters, four of them as a quartermaster seconded to a tank regiment, only underlined Arthur's likely post-war fate, despite having hoped to find more rewarding work once the war was over. However, on returning to England he quickly discovered that in a "land fit for heroes" jobs were not that easy to come by, and although he did not want to go back to the work he had done for five years before war had been declared, that of fitting wheels on cars, he reluctantly, after four weeks on the dole, went to see his former works' manager at Triumph.

"The job's yours if you want it, Arthur," the works' manager assured him.

"And the future?"

"The car's no longer a toy for the eccentric rich or even just a necessity for the businessman," the works' manager replied. "In fact," he continued, "management are preparing for the 'two-car family'."

"So they'll need even more wheels to be put on cars," said Arthur forlornly.

"That's the ticket."

Arthur signed on within the hour and it was only a matter of days before he was back into his old routine. After all, he often reminded his wife, it didn't take a degree in engineering to screw four knobs on to a wheel a hundred times a shift.

Arthur soon accepted the fact that he would have to settle for second best. However, second best was not what he planned for his son.

Mark had celebrated his fifth birthday before his father had even set eyes on him, but from the moment Arthur returned home he lavished everything he could on the boy.

Arthur was determined that Mark was not going to end up working on the shop-floor of a car factory for the rest of his life. He put in hours of overtime to earn enough money to ensure that the boy could have extra tuition in maths, general science and English. He felt well rewarded when the boy passed his eleven-plus and won a place at King Henry VIII Grammar School, and that pride did not falter when Mark went on to pass five O-levels and two years later added two A-levels.

Arthur tried not to show his disappointment when, on Mark's eighteenth birthday, the boy informed him that he did not want to go to university.

"What kind of career *are* you hoping to take up then, lad?" Arthur enquired.

"I've filled in an application form to join you on the shop-floor just as soon as I leave school."

"But why would you –"

"Why not? Most of my friends who're leaving this term have already been accepted by Triumph, and they can't wait to get started."

"You must be out of your mind."

"Come off it, Dad. The pay's good and you've shown that there's always plenty of extra money to be picked up with overtime. And I don't mind hard work."

"Do you think I spent all those years making sure you got a first-class education just to let you end up like me, putting wheels on cars for the rest of your life?" Arthur shouted.

"That's not the whole job and you know it, Dad."

"You go there over my dead body," said his father. "I don't care what your friends end up doing, I only care about you. You could be a solicitor, an accountant, an army officer, even a schoolmaster. Why should you want to end up at a car factory?"

"It's better paid than schoolmastering for a start," said Mark. "My French master once told me that he wasn't as well off as you."

"That's not the point, lad –"

"The point is, Dad, I can't be expected to spend the rest of my life doing a job I don't enjoy just to satisfy one of your fantasies."

"Well, I'm not going to allow you to waste the rest of your life," said Arthur, getting up from the breakfast table. "The first thing I'm going to do when I get in to work this morning is see that your application is turned down."

"That isn't fair, Dad. I have the right to –"

But his father had already left the room, and did not utter another word to the boy before leaving for the factory.

For over a week father and son didn't speak to each other. It was Mark's mother who was left to come up with the compromise. Mark could apply for any job that met with his father's approval and as long as he completed a year at that job he could, if he still wanted to, reapply to work at the factory. His father for his part would not then put any obstacle in his son's way.

Arthur nodded. Mark also reluctantly agreed to the solution.

"But only if you complete the full year," Arthur warned solemnly.

During those last days of the summer holiday Arthur came up with several suggestions for Mark to consider, but the boy showed no enthusiasm for any of them. Mark's mother became quite anxious that her son would end up with no job at all until, while helping her slice potatoes for dinner one night, Mark confided that he thought hotel management seemed the least unattractive proposition he had considered so far.

"At least you'd have a roof over your head and be regularly fed," his mother said.

"Bet they don't cook as well as you, Mum," said Mark as he placed the sliced potatoes on the top of the Lancashire hot-pot. "Still, it's only a year."

During the next month Mark attended several

interviews at hotels around the country without success. It was then that his father discovered that his old company sergeant was head porter at the Savoy: immediately Arthur started to pull a few strings.

"If the boy's any good," Arthur's old comrade-in-arms assured him over a pint, "he could end up as a head porter, even a hotel manager." Arthur seemed well satisfied, even though Mark was still assuring his friends that he would be joining them a year to the day.

On September 1st, 1959, Arthur and Mark Hapgood travelled together by bus to Coventry station. Arthur shook hands with the boy and promised him, "Your mother and I will make sure it's a special Christmas this year when they give you your first leave. And don't worry – you'll be in good hands with 'Sarge'. He'll teach you a thing or two. Just remember to keep your nose clean."

Mark said nothing and returned a thin smile as he boarded the train. "You'll never regret it . . ." were the last words Mark heard his father say as the train pulled out of the station.

Mark regretted it from the moment he set foot in the hotel.

As a junior porter he started his day at six in the morning and ended at six in the evening. He was entitled to a fifteen-minute mid-morning break, a forty-five-minute lunch break and another fifteen-minute break around mid-afternoon. After the first month had passed he could not recall when he had been granted all three breaks on the same day, and he quickly learned that there was no one to whom he could protest. His duties consisted of carrying guests' cases up to their rooms, then lugging them back down again the moment they wanted to leave. With an average of three hundred people staying in the hotel each night the process was endless. The pay turned out to be half what his friends were getting back home and as he had to hand over all his tips to the head porter, however much overtime Mark put in, he never saw an extra penny. On the only occasion he dared to mention it to the head porter he was met with the words, "Your time will come, lad."

It did not worry Mark that his uniform didn't fit or that his room was six foot by six foot and overlooked Charing Cross Station, or even that he didn't get a share of the tips; but it did worry him that there was nothing he could do to please the head porter – however clean he kept his nose.

Sergeant Crann, who considered the Savoy nothing more than an extension of his old platoon, didn't have a lot of time for young men under his command who hadn't done their national service.

"But I wasn't *eligible* to do national service," insisted Mark. "No one born after 1939 was called up."

"Don't make excuses, lad."

"It's not an excuse, Sarge. It's the truth."

"And don't call me 'Sarge'. I'm 'Sergeant Crann' to you, and don't you forget it."

"Yes, Sergeant Crann."

At the end of each day Mark would return to his little box-room with its small bed, small chair and tiny chest of drawers, and collapse exhausted. The only picture in the room – of the Laughing Cavalier

– was on the calendar that hung above Mark's bed. The date of September 1st, 1960, was circled in red to remind him when he would be allowed to re-join his friends at the factory back home. Each night before falling asleep he would cross out the offending day like a prisoner making scratch marks on a wall.

At Christmas Mark returned home for a four-day break, and when his mother saw the general state of the boy she tried to talk his father into allowing Mark to give up the job early, but Arthur remained implacable.

"We made an agreement. I can't be expected to get him a job at the factory if he isn't responsible enough to keep to his part of a bargain."

During the holiday Mark waited for his friends outside the factory gate until their shift had ended and listened to their stories of weekends spent watching football, drinking at the pub and dancing to the Everly Brothers. They all sympathised with his problem and looked forward to him joining them in September. "It's only a few more months," one of them reminded him cheerfully.

Far too quickly, Mark was on the journey back to London, where he continued unwillingly to hump cases up and down the hotel corridors for month after month.

Once the English rain had subsided the usual influx of American tourists began. Mark liked the Americans, who treated him as an equal and often tipped him a shilling when others would have given him only sixpence. But whatever the amount Mark received Sergeant Crann would still pocket it with the inevitable, "Your time will come, lad."

One such American for whom Mark ran around diligently every day during his fortnight's stay ended up presenting the boy with a ten-bob note as he left the front entrance of the hotel.

Mark said, "Thank you, sir," and turned round to see Sergeant Crann standing in his path.

"Hand it over," said Crann as soon as the American visitor was well out of earshot.

"I was going to the moment I saw you," said Mark, passing the note to his superior.

"Not thinking of pocketing what's rightfully mine, was you?"

"No, I wasn't," said Mark. "Though God knows I earned it."

"Your time will come, lad," said Sergeant Crann without much thought.

"Not while someone as mean as you is in charge," replied Mark sharply.

"What was that you said?" asked the head porter, veering round.

"You heard me the first time, Sarge."

The clip across the ear took Mark by surprise.

"You, lad, have just lost your job. Nobody, but nobody, talks to me like that." Sergeant Crann turned and set off smartly in the direction of the manager's office.

The hotel manager, Gerald Drummond, listened to the head porter's version of events before asking Mark to report to his office immediately. "You realise I have been left with no choice but to sack you," were his first words once the door was closed.

Mark looked up at the tall, elegant man in his long, black coat, white collar and black tie. "Am I allowed to tell you what actually happened, sir?" he asked.

Mr Drummond nodded, then listened without interruption as Mark gave his version of what had taken place that morning, and also disclosed the agreement he had entered into with his father. "Please let me complete my final ten weeks," Mark ended, "or my father will only say I haven't kept my end of our bargain."

"I haven't got another job vacant at the moment," protested the manager. "Unless you're willing to peel potatoes for ten weeks."

"Anything," said Mark.

"Then report to the kitchen at six tomorrow morning. I'll tell the third chef to expect you. Only if you think the head porter is a martinet just wait until you meet Jacques, our *maître chef de cuisine*. He won't clip your ear, he'll cut it off."

Mark didn't care. He felt confident that for just ten weeks he could face anything, and at five thirty the following morning he exchanged his dark blue uniform for a white top and blue and white check trousers before reporting for his new duties. To his surprise the kitchen took up almost the entire basement of the hotel, and was even more of a bustle than the lobby had been.

The third chef put him in the corner of the kitchen, next to a mountain of potatoes, a bowl of cold water and a sharp knife. Mark peeled through breakfast, lunch and dinner, and fell asleep on his bed that night without even enough energy left to cross a day off his calendar.

For the first week he never actually saw the fabled Jacques. With seventy people working in the kitchens Mark felt confident he could pass his whole period there without anyone being aware of him.

Each morning at six he would start peeling, then hand over the potatoes to a gangling youth called Terry who in turn would dice or cut them according to the third chef's instructions for the dish of the day. Monday sauté, Tuesday mashed, Wednesday French-fried, Thursday sliced, Friday roast, Saturday croquette . . . Mark quickly worked out a routine which kept him well ahead of Terry and therefore out of any trouble.

Having watched Terry do his job for over a week Mark felt sure he could have shown the young apprentice how to lighten his workload quite simply, but he decided to keep his mouth closed: opening it might only get him into more trouble, and he was certain the manager wouldn't give him a second chance.

Mark soon discovered that Terry always fell badly behind on Tuesday's shepherd's pie and Thursday's Lancashire hot-pot. From time to time the third chef would come across to complain and he would glance over at Mark to be sure that it wasn't him who was holding the process up. Mark made certain that he always had a spare tub of peeled potatoes by his side so that he escaped censure.

It was on the first Thursday morning in August (Lancashire hot-pot) that Terry sliced off the top of his forefinger. Blood spurted all over the sliced potatoes and on to the wooden table as the lad began yelling hysterically.

"Get him out of here!" Mark heard the *maître chef*

de cuisine bellow above the noise of the kitchen as he stormed towards them.

"And you," he said, pointing at Mark, "clean up mess and start slicing rest of potatoes. I 'ave eight hundred hungry customers still expecting to feed."

"Me?" said Mark in disbelief. "But –"

"Yes, you. You couldn't do worse job than idiot who calls himself trainee chef and cuts off finger." The chef marched away, leaving Mark to move reluctantly across to the table where Terry had been working. He felt disinclined to argue while the calendar was there to remind him that he was down to his last twenty-five days.

Mark set about a task he had carried out for his mother many times. The clean, neat cuts were delivered with a skill Terry would never learn to master. By the end of the day, although exhausted, Mark did not feel quite as tired as he had in the past.

At eleven that night the *maître chef de cuisine* threw off his hat and barged out of the swing doors, a sign to everyone else they could also leave the kitchen once everything that was their responsibility had been cleared up. A few seconds later the door swung back open and the chef burst in. He stared round the kitchen as everyone waited to see what he would do next. Having found what he was looking for, he headed straight for Mark.

"Oh, my God," thought Mark. "He's going to kill me."

"How is your name?" the chef demanded.

"Mark Hapgood, sir," he managed to splutter out.

"You waste on 'tatoes, Mark Hapgood," said the

chef. "You start on vegetables in morning. Report at seven. If that *crétin* with half finger ever returns, put him to peeling 'tatoes."

The chef turned on his heel even before Mark had the chance to reply. He dreaded the thought of having to spend three weeks in the middle of the kitchens, never once out of the *maître chef de cuisine*'s sight, but he accepted there was no alternative.

The next morning Mark arrived at six for fear of being late and spent an hour watching the fresh vegetables being unloaded from Covent Garden market. The hotel's supply manager checked every case carefully, rejecting several before he signed a chit to show the hotel had received over three thousand pounds' worth of vegetables. An average day, he assured Mark.

The *maître chef de cuisine* appeared a few minutes before seven thirty, checked the menus and told Mark to score the Brussels sprouts, trim the French beans and remove the coarse outer leaves of the cabbages.

"But I don't know how," Mark replied honestly. He could feel the other trainees in the kitchen edging away from him.

"Then I teach you," roared the chef. "Perhaps only thing you learn is if hope to be good chef, you able to do everyone's job in kitchen, even 'tato peeler's."

"But I'm hoping to be a . . ." Mark began and then thought better of it. The chef seemed not to have heard Mark as he took his place beside the new recruit. Everyone in the kitchen stared as the chef began to show Mark the basic skills of cutting, dicing and slicing.

"And remember other idiot's finger," the chef said on completing the lesson and passing the razor-sharp knife back to Mark. "Yours can be next."

Mark started gingerly dicing the carrots, then the Brussels sprouts, removing the outer layer before cutting a firm cross in the stalk. Next he moved on to trimming and slicing the beans. Once again he found it fairly easy to keep ahead of the chef's requirements.

At the end of each day, after the head chef had left, Mark stayed on to sharpen all his knives in preparation for the following morning, and would not leave his work area until it was spotless.

On the sixth day, after a curt nod from the chef, Mark realised he must be doing something half-right. By the following Saturday he felt he had mastered the simple skills of vegetable preparation and found himself becoming fascinated by what the chef himself was up to. Although Jacques rarely addressed anyone as he marched round the acre of kitchen except to grunt his approval or disapproval – the latter more commonly – Mark quickly learned to anticipate his needs. Within a short space of time he began to feel that he was part of a team – even though he was only too aware of being the novice recruit.

On the deputy chef's day off the following week Mark was allowed to arrange the cooked vegetables in their bowls and spent some time making each dish look attractive as well as edible. The chef not only noticed but actually muttered his greatest accolade – "*Bon.*"

During his last three weeks at the Savoy Mark

did not even look at the calendar above his bed.

One Thursday morning a message came down from the under-manager that Mark was to report to his office as soon as was convenient. Mark had quite forgotten that it was August 31st – his last day. He cut ten lemons into quarters, then finished preparing the forty plates of thinly sliced smoked salmon that would complete the first course for a wedding lunch. He looked with pride at his efforts before folding up his apron and leaving to collect his papers and final wage packet.

"Where you think you're going?" asked the chef, looking up.

"I'm off," said Mark. "Back to Coventry."

"See you Monday then. You deserve day off."

"No, I'm going home for good," said Mark.

The chef stopped checking the cuts of rare beef that would make up the second course of the wedding feast.

"Going?" he repeated as if he didn't understand the word.

"Yes. I've finished my year and now I'm off home to work."

"I hope you found first-class hotel," said the chef with genuine interest.

"I'm not going to work in a hotel."

"A restaurant, perhaps?"

"No, I'm going to get a job at Triumph."

The chef looked puzzled for a moment, unsure if it was his English or whether the boy was mocking him.

"What is – Triumph?"

"A place where they manufacture cars."

"You will manufacture cars?"

"Not a whole car, but I will put the wheels on."

"You put cars on wheels?" the chef said in disbelief.

"No," laughed Mark. "Wheels on cars."

The chef still looked uncertain.

"So you will be cooking for the car workers?"

"No. As I explained, I'm going to put the wheels on the cars," said Mark slowly, enunciating each word.

"That not possible."

"Oh yes it is," responded Mark. "And I've waited a whole year to prove it."

"If I offered you job as commis chef, you change mind?" asked the chef quietly.

"Why would you do that?"

"Because you 'ave talent in those fingers. In time I think you become chef, perhaps even good chef."

"No, thanks. I'm off to Coventry to join my mates."

The head chef shrugged. "*Tant pis*," he said, and without a second glance returned to the carcass of beef. He glanced over at the plates of smoked salmon. "A wasted talent," he added after the swing door had closed behind his potential protégé.

Mark locked his room, threw the calendar in the wastepaper basket and returned to the hotel to hand in his kitchen clothes to the housekeeper. The final action he took was to return his room key to the under-manager.

"Your wage packet, your cards and your PAYE. Oh, and the chef has phoned up to say he would be happy to give you a reference," said the under-manager. "Can't pretend that happens every day."

"Won't need that where I'm going," said Mark. "But thanks all the same."

He started off for the station at a brisk pace, his small battered suitcase swinging by his side, only to find that each step took a little longer. When he arrived at Euston he made his way to Platform 7 and began walking up and down, occasionally staring at the great clock above the booking hall. He watched first one train and then another pull out of the station bound for Coventry. He was aware of the station becoming dark as shadows filtered through the glass awning on to the public concourse. Suddenly he turned and walked off at an even brisker pace. If he hurried he could still be back in time to help chef prepare dinner that night.

Mark trained under Jacques le Renneu for five years. Vegetables were followed by sauces, fish by poultry, meats by pâtisserie. After eight years at the Savoy he was appointed second chef, and had learned so much from his mentor that regular patrons could no longer be sure when it was the *maître chef de cuisine*'s day off. Two years later Mark became a master chef, and when in 1971 Jacques was offered the opportunity to return to Paris and take over the kitchens of the George Cinq – an establishment that is to Paris what Harrods is to London – Jacques agreed, but only on condition that Mark accompanied him.

"It is wrong direction from Coventry," Jacques warned him, "and in any case they sure to offer you my job at the Savoy."

"I'd better come along otherwise those Frogs will never get a decent meal."

"Those Frogs," said Jacques, "will always know when it's my day off."

"Yes, and book in even greater numbers," suggested Mark, laughing.

It was not to be long before Parisians were flocking to the George Cinq, not to rest their weary heads but to relish the cooking of the two-chef team.

When Jacques celebrated his sixty-fifth birthday the great hotel did not have to look far to appoint his successor.

"The first Englishman ever to be *maître chef de cuisine* at the George Cinq," said Jacques, raising a glass of champagne at his farewell banquet. "Who would believe it? Of course, you will have to change your name to Marc to hold down such a position."

"Neither will ever happen," said Mark.

"Oh yes it will, because I 'ave recommended you."

"Then I shall turn it down."

"Going to put cars on wheels, *peut-être*?" asked Jacques mockingly.

"No, but I have found a little restaurant on the Left Bank. With my savings alone I can't quite afford the lease, but with your help . . ."

Chez Jacques opened on the rue du Plaisir on the Left Bank on May 1st, 1982, and it was not long before those customers who had taken the George Cinq for granted transferred their allegiance.

Mark's reputation spread as the two chefs pioneered "nouvelle cuisine", and soon the only way anyone could be guaranteed a table at the restaurant in under three weeks was to be a film star or a Cabinet Minister.

The day Michelin gave Chez Jacques their third

star Mark, with Jacques's blessing, decided to open a second restaurant. The press and customers then quarrelled amongst themselves as to which was the finer establishment. The booking sheets showed clearly the public felt there was no difference.

When in October 1986 Jacques died, at the age of seventy-one, the restaurant critics wrote confidently that standards were bound to fall. A year later the same journalists had to admit that one of the five great chefs of France had come from a town in the British Midlands they could not even pronounce.

Jacques's death only made Mark yearn more for his homeland, and when he read in the *Daily Telegraph* of a new development to be built in Covent Garden he called the site agent to ask for more details.

Mark's third restaurant was opened in the heart of London on February 11th, 1987.

Over the years Mark Hapgood often travelled back to Coventry to see his parents. His father had retired long since but Mark was still unable to persuade either parent to take the trip to Paris and sample his culinary efforts. But now he had opened in the country's capital he hoped to tempt them.

"We don't need to go up to London," said his mother, laying the table. "You always cook for us whenever you come home, and we read of your successes in the papers. In any case, your father isn't so good on his legs nowadays."

"What do you call this, son?" his father asked a few minutes later as noisette of lamb surrounded by baby carrots was placed in front of him.

"Nouvelle cuisine."

"And people pay good money for it?"

Mark laughed and the following day prepared his father's favourite Lancashire hot-pot.

"Now that's a real meal," said Arthur after his third helping. "And I'll tell you something for nothing, lad. You cook it almost as well as your mother."

A year later Michelin announced the restaurants throughout the world that had been awarded their coveted third star. *The Times* let its readers know on its front page that Chez Jacques was the first English restaurant ever to be so honoured.

To celebrate the award Mark's parents finally agreed to make the journey down to London, though not until Mark had sent a telegram saying he was reconsidering that job at British Leyland. He sent a car to fetch his parents and had them installed in a suite at the Savoy. That evening he reserved the most popular table at Chez Jacques in their name.

Vegetable soup followed by steak and kidney pie with a plate of bread and butter pudding to end on were not the table d'hôte that night, but they were served for the special guests on Table 17.

Under the influence of the finest wine, Arthur was soon chatting happily to anyone who would listen and couldn't resist reminding the head waiter that it was his son who owned the restaurant.

"Don't be silly, Arthur," said his wife. "He already knows that."

"Nice couple, your parents," the head waiter confided to his boss after he had served them with their coffee and supplied Arthur with a cigar.

"What did your old man do before he retired? Banker, lawyer, schoolmaster?"

"Oh no, nothing like that," said Mark quietly. "He spent the whole of his working life putting wheels on cars."

"But why would he waste his time doing that?" asked the waiter incredulously.

"Because he wasn't lucky enough to have a father like mine," Mark replied.

Not The Real Thing

GERALD Haskins and Walter Ramsbottom had been eating cornflakes for over a year.

"I'll swap you my MC and DSO for your VC," said Walter, on the way to school one morning.

"Never," said Gerald. "In any case, it takes ten packet tops to get a VC and you only need two for an MC or a DSO."

Gerald went on collecting packet tops until he had every medal displayed on the back of the packet.

Walter never got the VC.

Angela Bradbury thought they were both silly.

"They're only replicas," she continually reminded them, "not the real thing, and *I* am only interested in the real thing," she told them haughtily.

Neither Gerald nor Walter cared for Angela's opinion at the time, both boys still being more interested in medals than the views of the opposite sex.

Kellogg's offer of free medals ended on January

1st, 1950, just at the time when Gerald had managed to complete the set.

Walter gave up eating cornflakes.

Children of the Fifties were then given the opportunity to discover the world of Meccano. Meccano demanded eating even more cornflakes and within a year Gerald had collected a large enough set to build bridges, pontoons, cranes and even an office block.

Gerald's family nobly went on munching cornflakes, but when he told them he wanted to build a whole town – Kellogg's positively final offer – it took nearly all his friends in the fifth form at Hull Grammar School to assist him in consuming enough breakfast cereal to complete his ambition.

Walter Ramsbottom refused to be of assistance.

Angela Bradbury's help was never sought.

All three continued on their separate ways.

Two years later, when Gerald Haskins won a place at Durham University, no one was surprised that he chose to read engineering and listed as his main hobby collecting medals.

Walter Ramsbottom joined his father in the family jewellery business and started courting Angela Bradbury.

It was during the spring holiday in Gerald's second year at Durham that he came across Walter and Angela again. They were sitting in the same row at a Bach quintet concert in Hull Town Hall. Walter told him in the interval that they had just become engaged but had not yet settled on a date for the wedding.

Gerald hadn't seen Angela for over a year but

this time he did listen to her opinions, because like Walter he fell in love with her.

He replaced eating cornflakes with continually inviting Angela out to dinner in an effort to win her away from his old rival.

Gerald notched up another victory when Angela returned her engagement ring to Walter a few days before Christmas.

Walter spread it around that Gerald only wanted to marry Angela because her father was chairman of the Hull City Amenities Committee and he was hoping to get a job with the council after he'd taken his degree at Durham. When the invitations for the wedding were sent out, Walter was not on the guest list.

Mr and Mrs Haskins travelled to Multavia for their honeymoon, partly because they couldn't afford Nice and didn't want to go to Cleethorpes. In any case, the local travel agent was making a special offer for those considering a visit to the tiny kingdom that was sandwiched between Austria and Czechoslovakia.

When the newly married couple arrived at their hotel in Teske, the capital, they discovered why the terms had been so reasonable.

Multavia was, in 1959, going through an identity crisis as it attempted to adjust to yet another treaty drawn up by a Dutch lawyer in Geneva, written in French, but with the Russians and Americans in mind. However, thanks to King Alfons III, their shrewd and popular monarch, the kingdom continued to enjoy uninterrupted grants from the West and non-disruptive visits from the East.

The capital of Multavia, the Haskins were quickly to discover, had an average temperature of 92°F in June, no rainfall and the remains of a sewerage system that had been indiscriminately bombed by both sides between 1939 and 1944. Angela actually found herself holding her nose as she walked through the cobbled streets. The People's Hotel claimed to have forty-five rooms, but what the brochure did not point out was that only three of them had bathrooms and none of those had bath plugs. Then there was the food, or lack of it; for the first time in his life Gerald lost weight.

The honeymoon couple were also to discover that Multavia boasted no monuments, art galleries, theatres or opera houses worthy of the name and the outlying country was flatter and less interesting than the fens of Cambridgeshire. The kingdom had no coastline and the only river, the Plotz, flowed from Germany and on into Russia, thus ensuring that none of the locals trusted it.

By the end of their honeymoon the Haskins were only too pleased to find that Multavia did not boast a national airline. BOAC got them home safely, and that would have been the end of Gerald's experience of Multavia had it not been for those sewers – or the lack of them.

Once the Haskins had returned to Hull, Gerald took up his appointment as an assistant in the engineering department of the city council. His first job was as a third engineer with special responsibility for the city's sewerage. Most ambitious young men would have treated such an appointment as nothing more than a step on life's ladder. Gerald however did not. He quickly made contact with all the leading sewerage companies, their advisers as well as his opposite numbers throughout the county.

Two years later he was able to put in front of his father-in-law's committee a paper showing how the council could save a considerable amount of the ratepayers' money by redeveloping its sewerage system.

The committee were impressed and decided to carry out Mr Haskins's recommendation, and at the same time appointed him second engineer.

That was the first occasion Walter Ramsbottom stood for the council; he wasn't elected.

When, three years later, the network of little tunnels and waterways had been completed, Gerald's diligence was rewarded by his appointment as deputy borough engineer. In the same year his father-in-law became Mayor and Walter Ramsbottom became a councillor.

Councils up and down the country were now acknowledging Gerald as a man whose opinion should be sought if they had any anxieties about their sewerage system. This provoked an irreverent round of jokes at every Rotary Club dinner Gerald attended, but they nevertheless still hailed him as the leading authority in his field, or drain.

When in 1966 the Borough of Halifax considered putting out to tender the building of a new sewerage system they first consulted Gerald Haskins – Yorkshire being the one place on earth where a prophet is with honour in his own country.

After spending a day in Halifax with the town council's senior engineer and realising how much had to be spent on the new system, Gerald remarked to his wife, not for the first time, "Where there's muck there's brass." But it was Angela who was shrewd enough to work out just how much of that brass her husband could get hold of with the minimum of risk. During the next few days Gerald considered his wife's proposition and when he returned to Halifax the following week it was not to visit the council chambers but the Midland Bank. Gerald did not select the Midland by chance; the manager of the bank was also chairman of the planning committee on the Halifax borough council.

A deal that suited both sides was struck between the two Yorkshiremen, and with the bank's blessing Gerald resigned his position as deputy borough engineer and formed a private company. When he presented his tender, in competition with several large organisations from London, no one was surprised that Haskins of Hull was selected unanimously by the planning committee to carry out the job.

Three years later Halifax had a fine new sewerage system and the Midland Bank was delighted to be holding Haskins of Hull's company account.

Over the next fifteen years Chester, Runcorn, Huddersfield, Darlington, Macclesfield and York were jointly and severally grateful for the services rendered to them by Gerald Haskins, of Haskins & Co plc.

Haskins & Co (International) plc then began contract work in Dubai, Lagos and Rio de Janeiro. In 1983 Gerald received the Queen's Award for Industry from a grateful government, and a year later he was made a Commander of the British Empire by a grateful monarch.

The investiture took place at Buckingham Palace in the same year as King Alfons III of Multavia died and was succeeded by his son King Alfons IV. The newly crowned King decided something had finally to be done about the drainage problems of Teske. It had been his father's dying wish that his people should not go on suffering those unseemly smells, and King Alfons IV did not intend to bequeath the problem to *his* son.

After much begging and borrowing from the West, and much visiting and talking with the East, the newly anointed monarch decided to invite tenders for a new sewerage system in the kingdom's capital.

The tender document supplying several pages of details and listing the problems facing any engineer who wished to tackle the problem arrived with a thud on most of the boardroom tables of the world's major engineering companies. Once the paperwork had been seriously scrutinised and the realistic opportunity for a profit considered, King Alfons IV received only a few replies. Nevertheless, the King was able to sit up all night considering the merits of the three interested companies that had been shortlisted. Kings are also human, and when Alfons discovered that Gerald had chosen Multavia for his honeymoon some twenty-five years before it tipped the balance. By the time Alfons IV fell asleep that morning he had decided to accept Haskins & Co (International) plc's tender.

And thus Gerald Haskins made his second visit to Multavia, this time accompanied by a site manager, three draughtsmen and eleven engineers. Gerald had a private audience with the King and assured him the job would be completed on time and for the price specified. He also told the King how much he was enjoying his second visit to his country. However, when he returned to England he assured his wife that there was still little in Multavia that could be described as entertainment before or after the hour of seven.

A few years later and after some considerable haggling over the increase in the cost of materials, Teske ended up with one of the finest sewerage systems in Central Europe. The King was delighted – although he continued to grumble about how Haskins & Co had over-run the original contract price. The words "contingency payment" had to be explained to the monarch several times, who realised that the extra two hundred and forty thousand pounds would in turn have to be explained to the East and "borrowed" from the West. After many veiled threats and "without prejudice" solicitors' letters, Haskins & Co received the final payment but not until the King had been given a further grant from the British government, a payment which involved the Midland Bank, Sloane Street, transferring a sum of money to the Midland Bank, High Street, Hull, without Multavia ever getting their hands on it. This was after all, Gerald explained to his wife, how most overseas aid was distributed.

Thus the story of Gerald Haskins and the drainage problems of Teske might have ended, had not the

British Foreign Secretary decided to pay a visit to the kingdom of Multavia.

The original purpose of the Foreign Secretary's European trip was to take in Warsaw and Prague, in order to see how *glasnost* and *perestroika* were working in those countries. But when the Foreign Office discovered how much aid had been allocated to Multavia and after they explained to their minister its role as a buffer state, the Foreign Secretary decided to accept King Alfons's long-standing invitation to visit the tiny kingdom. Such excursions to smaller countries by British Foreign Secretaries usually take place in airport lounges, a habit the British picked up from Henry Kissinger, and later Comrade Gorbachev; but not on this occasion. It was felt Multavia warranted a full day.

As the hotels had improved only slightly since the time of Gerald's honeymoon, the Foreign Secretary was invited to lodge at the palace. He was asked by the King to undertake only two official engagements during his brief stay: the opening of the capital's new sewerage system, and a formal banquet.

Once the Foreign Secretary had agreed to these requests the King invited Gerald and his wife to be present at the opening ceremony – at their own expense. When the day of the opening came the Foreign Secretary delivered the appropriate speech for the occasion. He first praised Gerald Haskins on a remarkable piece of work in the great tradition of British engineering, then commended Multavia for her shrewd common sense in awarding the contract to a British company in the first place. The Foreign Secretary omitted to mention the fact that the

British government had ended up underwriting the entire project. Gerald, however, was touched by the minister's words and said as much to the Foreign Secretary after the latter had pulled the lever that opened the first sluice gate.

That evening in the palace there was a banquet for over three hundred guests, including the ambassadorial corps and several leading British businessmen. There followed the usual interminable speeches about "historic links", Multavia's role in Anglo-Soviet affairs and the "special relationship" with Britain's own royal family.

The highlight of the evening, however, came after the speeches when the King made two investitures. The first was the award of the Order of the Peacock (Second Class) to the Foreign Secretary. "The highest award a commoner can receive," the King explained to the assembled audience, "as the Order of the Peacock (First Class) is reserved for royalty and heads of state."

The King then announced a second investiture. The Order of the Peacock (Third Class) was to be awarded to Gerald Haskins, CBE, for his work on the drainage system of Teske. Gerald was surprised and delighted as he was conducted from his place on the top table to join the King, who leaned forward to put a large gold chain encrusted with gems of various colours and sizes over his visitor's head. Gerald took two respectful paces backwards and bowed low, as the Foreign Secretary looked up from his seat and smiled encouragingly at him.

Gerald was the last foreign guest to leave the banquet that night. Angela, who had left on her own over two hours before, had already fallen asleep by the time Gerald returned to their hotel room. He placed the chain on the bed, undressed, put on his pyjamas, checked his wife was still asleep and then placed the chain back over his head to rest on his shoulders.

Gerald stood and looked at himself in the bathroom mirror for several minutes. He could not wait to return home.

The moment Gerald got back to Hull he dictated a letter to the Foreign Office. He requested permission to be allowed to wear his new award on those occasions when it stipulated on the bottom right-hand corner of invitation cards that decorations and medals should be worn. The Foreign Office duly referred the matter to the Palace where the Queen, a distant cousin of King Alfons IV, agreed to the request.

The next official occasion at which Gerald was given the opportunity to sport the Order of the Peacock was the Mayor-making ceremony held in the chamber of Hull's City Hall, which was to be preceded by dinner at the Guildhall.

Gerald returned especially from Lagos for the occasion and even before changing into his dinner jacket couldn't resist a glance at the Order of the Peacock (Third Class). He opened the box that held his prize possession and stared down in disbelief: the gold had become tarnished and one of the stones looked as if it were coming loose. Mrs Haskins stopped dressing in order to steal a glance at the order. "It's not gold," she declared with a simplicity that would have stopped the IMF in their tracks.

Gerald offered no comment and quickly fixed the

loose stone back in place with Araldite but he had to admit to himself that the craftmanship didn't bear careful scrutiny. Neither of them mentioned the subject again on their journey to Hull's City Hall.

Some of the guests during the Mayor's dinner that night at the Guildhall enquired after the history of the Order of the Peacock (Third Class), and although it gave Gerald some considerable satisfaction to explain how he had come by the distinction and indeed the Queen's permission to wear it on official occasions, he felt one or two of his colleagues had been less than awed by the tarnished peacock. Gerald also considered it was somewhat unfortunate that they had ended up on the same table as Walter Ramsbottom, now the Deputy Mayor.

"I suppose it would be hard to put a true value on it," said Walter, staring disdainfully at the chain.

"It certainly would," said Gerald firmly.

"I didn't mean a monetary value," said the jeweller with a smirk. "That would be only too easy to ascertain. I meant a sentimental value, of course."

"Of course," said Gerald. "And are you expecting to be the Mayor next year?" he asked, trying to change the subject.

"It is the tradition," said Walter, "that the Deputy succeeds the Mayor if he doesn't do a second year. And be assured, Gerald, that I shall see to it that you are placed on the top table for that occasion." Walter paused. "The Mayor's chain, you know, is fourteen-carat gold."

Gerald left the banquet early that evening determined to do something about the Order of the

Peacock before it was Walter's turn to be Mayor.

None of Gerald's friends would have described him as an extravagant man and even his wife was surprised at the whim of vanity that was to follow. At nine o'clock the next morning Gerald rang his office to say he would not be in to work that day. He then travelled by train to London to visit Bond Street in general and a famed jeweller in particular.

The door of the Bond Street shop was opened for Gerald by a sergeant from the Corps of Commissionaires. Once he had stepped inside Gerald explained his problem to the tall, thin gentleman in a black suit who had come forward to welcome him. He was then led to a circular glass counter in the middle of the shop floor.

"Our Mr Pullinger will be with you in a moment," he was assured. Moments later Asprey's fine-gems expert arrived and happily agreed to Gerald's request to value the Order of the Peacock (Third Class). Mr Pullinger placed the chain on a black velvet cushion before closely studying the stones through a small eye glass.

After a cursory glance he frowned with the disappointment of a man who has won third prize at a shooting range on Blackpool pier.

"So what's it worth?" asked Gerald bluntly after several minutes had elapsed.

"Hard to put a value on something so intricately" – Pullinger hesitated – "unusual."

"The stones are glass and the gold's brass, that's what you're trying to say, isn't it, lad?"

Mr Pullinger gave a look that indicated that he could not have put it more succinctly himself.

"You might possibly be able to get a few hundred pounds from someone who collects such objects, but . . ."

"Oh, no," said Gerald, quite offended. "I have no interest in selling it. My purpose in coming up to London was to find out if you can *copy* it."

"Copy it?" said the expert in disbelief.

"Aye," said Gerald. "First, I want every stone to be the correct gem according to its colour. Second, I expect a setting that would impress a duchess. And third, I require the finest craftsman put to work on it in nothing less than eighteen-carat gold."

The expert from Asprey's, despite years of dealing with Arab clients, was unable to conceal his surprise.

"It would not be cheap," he uttered *sotto voce*: the word "cheap" was one of which Asprey's clearly disapproved.

"I never doubted that for one moment," said Gerald. "But you must understand that this is a once-in-a-lifetime honour for me. Now when could I hope to have an estimate?"

"A month, six weeks at the most," replied the expert.

Gerald left the plush carpet of Asprey's for the sewers of Nigeria. When a little over a month later he flew back to London, he travelled in to the West End for his second meeting with Mr Pullinger.

The jeweller had not forgotten Gerald Haskins and his strange request, and he quickly produced from his order book a neatly folded piece of paper. Gerald unfolded it and read the tender slowly. Requirement for customer's request: twelve diamonds, seven amethysts, three rubies and a sapphire, all to be of the most perfect colour and of the highest quality. A peacock to be sculpted in ivory and painted by a craftsman. The entire chain then to be moulded in the finest eighteen-carat gold. The bottom line read: "Two hundred and eleven thousand pounds – exclusive of VAT."

Gerald, who would have thought nothing of haggling over an estimate of a few thousand pounds for roofing material or the hire of heavy equipment, or even a schedule of payments, simply asked, "When will I be able to collect it?"

"One could not be certain how long it might take to put together such a fine piece," said Mr Pullinger. "Finding stones of a perfect match and colour will, I fear, take a little time." He paused. "I am also hoping that our senior craftsman will be free to work on this particular commission. He has been rather taken up lately with gifts for the Queen's forthcoming visit to Saudi Arabia so I don't think it could be ready before the end of March."

Well in time for next year's Mayor's banquet, thought Gerald. Councillor Ramsbottom would not be able to mock him this time. Fourteen-carat gold, had he said?

Lagos and Rio de Janeiro both had their sewers down and running long before Gerald was able to return to Asprey's. And he only set his eyes on the unique prize a few weeks before Mayor-making day.

When Mr Pullinger first showed his client the finished work the Yorkshireman gasped with delight. The Order was so magnificent that Gerald found it necessary to purchase a string of pearls from Asprey's to ensure a silent wife.

On his return to Hull he waited until after dinner to open the green leather box from Asprey's and surprise her with the new Order. "Fit for a monarch, lass," he assured his wife but Angela seemed preoccupied with her pearls.

After Angela had left to wash up, her husband continued to stare for some time at the beautiful jewels so expertly crafted and superbly cut before he finally closed the box. The next morning he reluctantly took the piece round to the bank and explained that it must be kept safely locked in the vaults as he would only be requiring to take it out once, perhaps twice, a year. He couldn't resist showing the object of his delight to the bank manager, Mr Sedgley.

"You'll be wearing it for Mayor-making day, no doubt?" Mr Sedgley enquired.

"If I'm invited," said Gerald.

"Oh, I feel sure Ramsbottom will want all his old friends to witness the ceremony. Especially you, I suspect," he added without explanation.

Gerald read the news item in the Court Circular of *The Times* to his wife over breakfast: "It has been announced from Buckingham Palace that King Alfons IV of Multavia will make a state visit to Britain between April 7th and 11th."

"I wonder if we will have an opportunity to meet the King again," said Angela.

Gerald offered no opinion.

In fact Mr and Mrs Gerald Haskins received two

invitations connected with King Alfons's official visit, one to dine with the King at Claridge's – Multavia's London Embassy not being large enough to cater for such an occasion – and the second arriving a day later by special delivery from Buckingham Palace.

Gerald was delighted. The Peacock, it seemed, was going to get three outings in one month, as their visit to the Palace was ten days before Walter Ramsbottom would be installed as Mayor.

The state dinner at Claridge's was memorable and although there were several hundred other guests Gerald still managed to catch a moment with his host, King Alfons IV who, he found to his pleasure, could not take his eyes off the Order of the Peacock (Third Class).

The trip to Buckingham Palace a week later was Gerald and Angela's second, following Gerald's investiture in 1984 as a Commander of the British Empire. It took Gerald almost as long to dress for the state occasion as it did his wife. He took some time fiddling with his collar to be sure that his CBE could be seen to its full advantage while the Order of the Peacock still rested squarely on his shoulders. Gerald had asked his tailor to sew little loops into his tailcoat so that the Order did not have to be continually readjusted.

When the Haskins arrived at Buckingham Palace they followed a throng of bemedalled men and tiara'd ladies through to the state dining room where a footman handed out seating cards to each of the guests. Gerald unfolded his to find an arrow pointing to his name. He took his wife by the arm and guided her to their places.

He noticed that Angela's head kept turning whenever she saw a tiara.

Although they were seated some distance away from Her Majesty at an offshoot of the main table, there was still a minor royal on Gerald's left and the Minister of Agriculture on his right. He was more than satisfied. In fact the whole evening went far too quickly, and Gerald was already beginning to feel that Mayor-making day would be something of an anti-climax. Nevertheless, Gerald imagined a scene where Councillor Ramsbottom was admiring the Order of the Peacock (Third Class), while he was telling him about the dinner at the Palace.

After two loyal toasts and two national anthems the Queen rose to her feet. She spoke warmly of Multavia as she addressed her three hundred guests, and affectionately of her distant cousin the King. Her Majesty added that she hoped to visit his kingdom at some time in the near future. This was greeted with considerable applause. She then concluded her speech by saying it was her intention to make two investitures.

The Queen created King Alfons IV a Knight Commander of the Royal Victorian Order (KCVO), and then Multavia's Ambassador to the Court of St James a Commander of the same order (CVO), both being personal orders of the monarch. A box of royal blue was opened by the Court Chamberlain and the awards placed over the recipients' shoulders. As soon as the Queen had completed her formal duties, King Alfons rose to make his reply.

"Your Majesty," he continued after the usual formalities and thanks had been completed. "I also would like to make two awards. The first is to an Englishman who has given great service to my country through his expertise and diligence" – the King then glanced in Gerald's direction – "a man," he continued, "who completed a feat of sanitary engineering that any nation on earth could be proud of and indeed, Your Majesty, it was opened by your own Foreign Secretary. We in the capital of Teske will remain in his debt for generations to come. We therefore bestow on Mr Gerald Haskins, CBE, the Order of the Peacock (Second Class)."

Gerald couldn't believe his ears.

Tumultuous applause greeted a surprised Gerald as he made his way up towards their Majesties. He came to a standstill behind the throned chairs somewhere between the Queen of England and the King of Multavia. The King smiled at the new recipient of the Order of the Peacock (Second Class) as the two men shook hands. But before bestowing the new honour upon him, King Alfons leaned forward and with some difficulty removed from Gerald's shoulders his Order of the Peacock (Third Class).

"You won't be needing this any longer," the King whispered in Gerald's ear.

Gerald watched in horror as his prize possession disappeared into a red leather box held open by the King's private secretary, who stood poised behind his sovereign. Gerald continued to stare at the private secretary, who was either a diplomat of the highest order or had not been privy to the King's plan, for his face showed no sign of anything untoward. Once Gerald's magnificent prize had been safely removed, the box snapped closed like a safe of which Gerald had not been told the combination.

Gerald wanted to protest, but remained speechless.

King Alfons then removed from another box the Order of the Peacock (Second Class) and placed it over Gerald's shoulders. Gerald, staring at the indifferent coloured glass stones, hesitated for a few moments before stumbling a pace back, bowing, and then returning to his place in the great dining room. He did not hear the waves of applause that accompanied him; his only thought was how he could possibly retrieve his lost chain immediately the speeches were over. He slumped down in the chair next to his wife.

"And now," continued the King, "I wish to present a decoration that has not been bestowed on anyone since my late father's death. The Order of the Peacock (First Class), which it gives me special delight to bestow on Her Majesty Queen Elizabeth II."

The Queen rose from her place as the King's private secretary once again stepped forward. In his hands was held the same red leather case that had snapped shut so firmly on Gerald's unique possession. The case was re-opened and the King removed the magnificent Order from the box and placed it on the shoulders of the Queen. The jewels sparkled in the candlelight and the guests gasped at the sheer magnificence of the piece.

Gerald was the only person in the room who knew its true value.

"Well, you always said it was fit for a monarch," his wife remarked as she touched her string of pearls.

"Aye," said Gerald. "But what's Ramsbottom going to say when he sees this?" he added sadly, fingering the Order of the Peacock (Second Class). "He'll know it's not the real thing."

"I don't see it matters that much," said Angela.

"What do you mean, lass?" asked Gerald. "I'll be the laughing stock of Hull on Mayor-making day."

"You should start reading the evening papers, Gerald, and stop looking in mirrors and then you'd know Walter isn't going to be Mayor this year."

"Not going to be Mayor?" repeated Gerald.

"No. The present Mayor has opted to do a second term so Walter won't be Mayor until next year."

"Is that right?" said Gerald with a smile.

"And if you're thinking what I think you're thinking, Gerald Haskins, this time it's going to cost you a tiara."

Just Good Friends

I woke up before him feeling slightly randy but I knew there was nothing I could do about it.

I blinked and my eyes immediately accustomed themselves to the half light. I raised my head and gazed at the large expanse of motionless white flesh lying next to me. If only he took as much exercise as I did he wouldn't have that spare tyre, I thought unsympathetically.

Roger stirred restlessly and even turned over to face me, but I knew he would not be fully awake until the alarm on his side of the bed started ringing. I pondered for a moment whether I could go back to sleep again or should get up and find myself some breakfast before he woke. In the end I settled for just lying still on my side day-dreaming, but making sure I didn't disturb him. When he did eventually open his eyes I planned to pretend I was still asleep – that way he would end up getting breakfast for me. I began to go over the things that needed to be done after he had left for the office. As long as I was at home ready to greet him when he returned from work, he didn't seem to mind what I got up to during the day.

A gentle rumble emanated from his side of the bed. Roger's snoring never disturbed me. My affection for him was unbounded, and I only wished I could find the words to let him know. In truth, he was the first man I had really appreciated. As I gazed at his unshaven face I was reminded that it hadn't been his looks which had attracted me in the pub that night.

I had first come across Roger in the Cat and Whistle, a public house situated on the corner of Mafeking Road. You might say it was our local. He used to come in around eight, order a pint of mild and take it to a small table in the corner of the room just beyond the dartboard. Mostly he would sit alone, watching the darts being thrown towards double top but more often settling in one or five, if they managed to land on the board at all. He never played the game himself, and I often wondered, from my vantage point behind the bar, if he were fearful of relinquishing his favourite seat or just had no interest in the sport.

Then things suddenly changed for Roger – for the better, was no doubt how he saw it – when one evening in early spring a blonde named Madeleine, wearing an imitation fur coat and drinking double gin and its, perched on the stool beside him. I had never seen her in the pub before but she was obviously known locally, and loose bar talk led me to believe it couldn't last. You see, word was about that she was looking for someone whose horizons stretched beyond the Cat and Whistle.

In fact the affair – if that's what it ever came to –

lasted for only twenty days. I know because I counted every one of them. Then one night voices were raised and heads turned as she left the small stool just as suddenly as she had come. His tired eyes watched her walk to a vacant place at the corner of the bar, but he didn't show any surprise at her departure and made no attempt to pursue her.

Her exit was my cue to enter. I almost leapt from behind the bar and, moving as quickly as dignity allowed, was seconds later sitting on the vacant stool beside him. He didn't comment and certainly made no attempt to offer me a drink, but the one glance he shot in my direction did not suggest he found me an unacceptable replacement. I looked around to see if anyone else had plans to usurp my position. The men standing round the dartboard didn't seem to care. Treble seventeen, twelve and a five kept them more than occupied. I glanced towards the bar to check if the boss had noticed my absence, but he was busy taking orders. I saw Madeleine was already sipping a glass of champagne from the pub's only bottle, purchased by a stranger whose stylish double-breasted blazer and striped bow tie convinced me she wouldn't be bothering with Roger any longer. She looked well set for at least another twenty days.

I looked up at Roger – I had known his name for some time, although I had never addressed him as such and I couldn't be sure that he was aware of mine. I began to flutter my eyelashes in a rather exaggerated way. I felt a little stupid but at least it elicited a gentle smile. He leaned over and touched my cheek, his hands surprisingly gentle. Neither of us felt the need to speak. We were both lonely and it seemed unnecessary to explain why. We sat in silence, he occasionally sipping his beer, I from time to time rearranging my legs, while a few feet from us the darts pursued their undetermined course.

When the publican cried, "Last orders," Roger downed the remains of his beer while the dart players completed what had to be their final game.

No one commented when we left together and I was surprised that Roger made no protest as I accompanied him back to his little semi-detached. I already knew exactly where he lived because I had seen him on several occasions standing at the bus queue in Dobson Street in a silent line of reluctant morning passengers. Once I even positioned myself on a nearby wall in order to study his features more carefully. It was an anonymous, almost commonplace face but he had the warmest eyes and the kindest smile I had observed in any man.

My only anxiety was that he didn't seem aware of my existence, just constantly preoccupied, his eyes each evening and his thoughts each morning only for Madeleine. How I envied that girl. She had everything I wanted – except a decent fur coat, the only thing my mother had left me. In truth, I have no right to be catty about Madeleine, as her past couldn't have been more murky than mine.

All that had taken place well over a year ago and, to prove my total devotion to Roger, I have never entered the Cat and Whistle since. He seemed to have forgotten Madeleine because he never once spoke of her in front of me. An unusual man, he didn't question me about any of my past relationships either.

Perhaps he should have. I would have liked him to know the truth about my life before we'd met, though it all seems irrelevant now. You see, I had been the youngest in a family of four so I always came last in line. I had never known my father, and I arrived home one night to discover that my mother had run off with another man. Tracy, one of my sisters, warned me not to expect her back. She turned out to be right, for I have never seen my mother since that day. It's awful to have to admit, if only to oneself, that one's mother is a tramp.

Now an orphan, I began to drift, often trying to stay one step ahead of the law – not so easy when you haven't always got somewhere to put your head down. I can't even recall how I ended up with Derek – if that was his real name. Derek, whose dark sensual looks would have attracted any susceptible female, told me that he had been on a merchant steamer for the past three years. When he made love to me I was ready to believe anything. I explained to him that all I wanted was a warm home, regular food and perhaps in time a family of my own. He ensured that one of my wishes was fulfilled, because a few weeks after he left me I ended up with twins, two girls. Derek never set eyes on them: he had returned to sea even before I could tell him I was pregnant. He hadn't needed to promise me the earth; he was so good-looking he must have known I would have been his just for a night on the tiles.

I tried to bring up the girls decently, but the authorities caught up with me this time and I lost them both. I wonder where they are now? God knows. I only hope they've ended up in a good home. At least they inherited Derek's irresistible looks, which can only help them through life. It's just one more thing Roger will never know about. His unquestioning trust only makes me feel more guilty, and now I never seem able to find a way of letting him know the truth.

After Derek had gone back to sea I was on my own for almost a year before getting part-time work at the Cat and Whistle. The publican was so mean that he wouldn't have even provided food and drink for me, if I hadn't kept to my part of the bargain.

Roger used to come in about once, perhaps twice a week before he met the blonde with the shabby fur coat. After that it was every night until she upped and left him.

I knew he was perfect for me the first time I heard him order a pint of mild. A pint of mild – I can't think of a better description of Roger. In those early days the barmaids used to flirt openly with him, but he didn't show any interest. Until Madeleine latched on to him I wasn't even sure that it was women he preferred. Perhaps in the end it was my androgynous looks that appealed to him.

I think I must have been the only one in that pub who was looking for something more permanent.

And so Roger allowed me to spend the night with him. I remember that he slipped into the bathroom to undress while I rested on what I assumed would be my side of the bed. Since that night he has never once asked me to leave, let alone tried to kick me out. It's an easy-going relationship. I've never known him raise his voice or scold me unfairly. Forgive the cliché, but for once I have fallen on my feet.

Brr. Brr. Brr. That damned alarm. I wished I could have buried it. The noise would go on and on until at last Roger decided to stir himself. I once tried to stretch across him and put a stop to its infernal ringing, only ending up knocking the contraption on to the floor, which annoyed him even more than the ringing. Never again, I concluded. Eventually a long arm emerged from under the blanket and a palm dropped on to the top of the clock and the awful din subsided. I'm a light sleeper – the slightest movement stirs me. If only he had asked me I could have woken him far more gently each morning. After all, my methods are every bit as reliable as any man-made contraption.

Half awake, Roger gave me a brief cuddle before kneading my back, always guaranteed to elicit a smile. Then he yawned, stretched and declared as he did every morning, "Must hurry along or I'll be late for the office." I suppose some females would have been annoyed by the predictability of our morning routine – but not this lady. It was all part of a life that made me feel secure in the belief that at last I had found something worthwhile.

Roger managed to get his feet into the wrong slippers – always a fifty-fifty chance – before lumbering towards the bathroom. He emerged fifteen minutes later, as he always did, looking only slightly better than he had when he entered. I've learned to live with what some would have called his foibles, while he has learned to accept my mania for cleanliness and a need to feel secure.

"Get up, lazy-bones," he remonstrated but then only smiled when I re-settled myself, refusing to leave the warm hollow that had been left by his body.

"I suppose you expect me to get your breakfast before I go to work?" he added as he made his way downstairs. I didn't bother to reply. I knew that in a few moments' time he would be opening the front door, picking up the morning newspaper, any mail, and our regular pint of milk. Reliable as ever, he would put on the kettle, then head for the pantry, fill a bowl with my favourite breakfast food and add my portion of the milk, leaving himself just enough for two cups of coffee.

I could anticipate almost to the second when breakfast would be ready. First I would hear the kettle boil, a few moments later the milk would be poured, then finally there would be the sound of a chair being pulled up. That was the signal I needed to confirm it was time for me to join him.

I stretched my legs slowly, noticing my nails needed some attention. I had already decided against a proper wash until after he had left for the office. I could hear the sound of the chair being scraped along the kitchen lino. I felt so happy that I literally jumped off the bed before making my way towards the open door. A few seconds later I was downstairs. Although he had already taken his first mouthful of cornflakes he stopped eating the moment he saw me.

"Good of you to join me," he said, a grin spreading over his face.

I padded over towards him and looked up expectantly. He bent down and pushed my bowl towards me. I began to lap up the milk happily, my tail swishing from side to side.

It's a myth that we only swish our tails when we're angry.

The Steal

CHRISTOPHER and Margaret Roberts always spent their summer holiday as far away from England as they could possibly afford. However, as Christopher was the classics master at St Cuthbert's, a small preparatory school just north of Yeovil, and Margaret was the school matron, their experience of four of the five continents was largely confined to periodicals such as the *National Geographic Magazine* and *Time*.

The Roberts' annual holiday each August was nevertheless sacrosanct and they spent eleven months of the year saving, planning and preparing for their one extravagant luxury. The following eleven months were then spent passing on their discoveries to the "offspring": the Roberts, without children of their own, looked on all the pupils of St Cuthbert's as "offspring".

During the long evenings when the "offspring" were meant to be asleep in their dormitories, the Roberts would pore over maps, analyse expert opinion and then finally come up with a shortlist to consider. In recent expeditions they had been as far afield as Norway, Northern Italy and Yugoslavia, ending up the previous year exploring Achilles' island, Skyros, off the east coast of Greece.

"It has to be Turkey this year," said Christopher after much soul-searching. A week later Margaret came to the same conclusion, and so they were able to move on to Phase Two. Every book on Turkey in the local library was borrowed, consulted, re-borrowed and re-consulted. Every brochure obtainable from the Turkish Embassy or local travel agents received the same relentless scrutiny.

By the first day of the summer term, charter tickets had been paid for, a car hired, accommodation booked and everything that could be insured comprehensively covered. Their plans lacked only one final detail.

"So what will be our 'steal' this year?" asked Christopher.

"A carpet," Margaret said, without hesitation. "It has to be. For over a thousand years Turkey has produced the most sought-after carpets in the world. We'd be foolish to consider anything else."

"How much shall we spend on it?"

"Five hundred pounds," said Margaret, feeling very extravagant.

Having agreed, they once again swapped memories about the "steals" they had made over the years. In Norway, it had been a whale's tooth carved in the shape of a galleon by a local artist who soon after had been taken up by Steuben. In Tuscany, it had been a ceramic bowl found in a small village where they cast and fired them to be sold in Rome at exorbitant prices: a small blemish which only an expert would have noticed made it a "steal". Just outside Skopje the Roberts had visited a local glass factory and acquired a water jug moments after it had been blown in front of their eyes, and in Skyros they had picked up their greatest triumph to date, a fragment of an urn they discovered near an old excavation site. The Roberts reported their find immediately to the authorities, but the Greek officials had not considered the fragment important enough to prevent it being exported to St Cuthbert's.

On returning to England Christopher couldn't resist just checking with the senior classics don at his old *alma mater*. He confirmed the piece was probably twelfth century. This latest "steal" now stood, carefully mounted, on their drawing room mantelpiece.

"Yes, a carpet would be perfect," Margaret mused. "The trouble is, everyone goes to Turkey with the idea of picking up a carpet on the cheap. So to find a really good one. . . ."

She knelt and began to measure the small space in front of their drawing room fireplace.

"Seven by three should do it," she said.

Within a few days of term ending, the Roberts travelled by bus to Heathrow. The journey took a little longer than by rail but at half the cost. "Money saved is money that can be spent on the carpet," Margaret reminded her husband.

"Agreed, Matron," said Christopher, laughing.

On arrival at Heathrow they checked their baggage on to the charter flight, selected two non-smoking seats and, finding they had time to spare, decided to watch other planes taking off to even more exotic places.

It was Christopher who first spotted the two passengers dashing across the tarmac, obviously late.

"Look," he said, pointing at the running couple. His wife studied the overweight pair, still brown from a previous holiday, as they lumbered up the steps to their plane.

"Mr and Mrs Kendall-Hume," Margaret said in disbelief. After hesitating for a moment, she added, "I wouldn't want to be uncharitable about any of the offspring, but I do find young Malcolm Kendall-Hume a . . ." She paused.

"'Spoilt little brat'?" suggested her husband.

"Quite," said Margaret. "I can't begin to think what his parents must be like."

"Very successful, if the boy's stories are to be believed," said Christopher. "A string of second-hand garages from Birmingham to Bristol."

"Thank God they're not on our flight."

"Bermuda or the Bahamas would be my guess," suggested Christopher.

A voice emanating from the loudspeaker gave Margaret no chance to offer her opinion.

"Olympic Airways Flight 172 to Istanbul is now boarding at Gate No. 37."

"That's us," said Christopher happily as they began their long route-march to their departure gate.

They were the first passengers to board, and once shown to their seats they settled down to study the guidebooks of Turkey and their three files of research.

"We must be sure to see Diana's Temple when we visit Ephesus," said Christopher, as the plane taxied out on to the runway.

"Not forgetting that at that time we shall be only a few kilometres away from the purported last home of the Virgin Mary," added Margaret.

"Taken with a pinch of salt by serious historians," Christopher remarked as if addressing a member of the Lower Fourth, but his wife was too engrossed in her book to notice. They both continued to study on their own before Christopher asked what his wife was reading.

"*Carpets – Fact and Fiction* by Abdul Verizoglu – seventeenth edition," she said, confident that any errors would have been eradicated in the previous sixteen. "It's most informative. The finest examples, it seems, are from Hereke and are woven in silk and are sometimes worked on by up to twenty young women, even children, at a time."

"Why young?" pondered Christopher. "You'd have thought experience would have been essential for such a delicate task."

"Apparently not," said Margaret. "Herekes are woven by those with young eyes which can discern intricate patterns sometimes no larger than a pinpoint and with up to nine hundred knots a square inch. Such a carpet," continued Margaret, "can cost as much as fifteen, even twenty, thousand pounds."

"And at the other end of the scale? Carpets woven in old leftover wool by old leftover women?" suggested Christopher, answering his own question.

"No doubt," said Margaret. "But even for our humble purse there are some simple guidelines to follow."

Christopher leaned over so that he could be sure

to take in every word above the roar of the engines.

"The muted reds and blues with a green base are considered classic and are much admired by Turkish collectors, but one should avoid the bright yellows and oranges," read his wife aloud. "And never consider a carpet that displays animals, birds or fishes, as they are produced only to satisfy Western tastes."

"Don't they like animals?"

"I don't think that's the point," said Margaret. "The Sunni Muslims, who are the country's religious rulers, don't approve of graven images. But if we search diligently round the bazaars we should still be able to come across a bargain for a few hundred pounds."

"What a wonderful excuse to spend all day in the bazaars."

Margaret smiled, before continuing. "But listen. It's most important to bargain. The opening price the dealer offers is likely to be double what he expects to get and treble what the carpet is worth." She looked up from her book. "If there's any bargaining to be done it will have to be carried out by you, my dear. They're not used to that sort of thing at Marks & Spencer."

Christopher smiled.

"And finally," continued his wife, turning a page of her book, "if the dealer offers you coffee you should accept. It means he expects the process to go on for some time as he enjoys the bargaining as much as the sale."

"If that's the case they had better have a very large pot percolating for us," said Christopher as he closed his eyes and began to contemplate the pleasures that awaited him. Margaret only closed her books on carpets when the plane touched down at Istanbul airport, and at once opened file Number One, entitled "Pre-Turkey".

"A shuttle bus should be waiting for us at the north side of the terminal. It will take us on to the local flight," she assured her husband as she carefully wound her watch forward two hours.

The Roberts were soon following the stream of passengers heading in the direction of passport control. The first people they saw in front of them were the same middle-aged couple they had assumed were destined for more exotic shores.

"Wonder where they're heading," said Christopher.

"Istanbul Hilton, I expect," said Margaret as they climbed into a vehicle that had been declared redundant by the Glasgow Corporation Bus Company some twenty years before. It spluttered out black exhaust fumes as it revved up before heading off in the direction of the local THY flight.

The Roberts soon forgot all about Mr and Mrs Kendall-Hume once they looked out of the little aeroplane windows to admire the west coast of Turkey highlighted by the setting sun. The plane landed in the port of Izmir just as the shimmering red ball disappeared behind the highest hill. Another bus, even older than the earlier one, ensured that the Roberts reached their little guest house just in time for late supper.

Their room was tiny but clean and the owner much in the same mould. He greeted them both with exaggerated gesturing and a brilliant smile which augured well for the next twenty-one days.

Early the following morning, the Roberts checked over their detailed plans for Day One in file Number Two. They were first to collect the rented Fiat that had already been paid for in England, before driving off into the hills to the ancient Byzantine fortress at Selcuk in the morning, to be followed by the Temple of Diana in the afternoon if they still had time.

After breakfast had been cleared away and they had cleaned their teeth, the Roberts left the guest house a few minutes before nine. Armed with their hire car form and guidebook, they headed off for Beyazik's Garage where their promised car awaited them. They strolled down the cobbled streets past the little white houses, enjoying the sea breeze until they reached the bay. Christopher spotted the sign for Beyazik's Garage when it was still a hundred yards ahead of them.

As they passed the magnificent yachts moored alongside the harbour, they tested each other on the nationality of each flag, feeling not unlike the "offspring" completing a geography test.

"Italian, French, Liberian, Panamanian, German. There aren't many British boats," said Christopher, sounding unusually patriotic, the way he always did, Margaret reflected, the moment they were abroad.

She stared at the rows of gleaming hulls lined up like buses in Piccadilly during the rush hour; some of the boats were even bigger than buses. "I wonder what kind of people can possibly afford such luxury?" she asked, not expecting a reply.

"Mr and Mrs Roberts, isn't it?" shouted a voice from behind them. They both turned to see a now-familiar figure dressed in a white shirt and white shorts, wearing a hat that made him look not unlike the "Bird's Eye" captain, waving at them from the bow of one of the bigger yachts.

"Climb on board, me hearties," Mr Kendall-Hume declared enthusiastically, more in the manner of a command than an invitation.

Reluctantly the Roberts walked the gang-plank.

"Look who's here," their host shouted down a large hole in the middle of the deck. A moment later Mrs Kendall-Hume appeared from below, dressed in a diaphanous orange sarong and a matching bikini top. "It's Mr and Mrs Roberts – you remember, from Malcolm's school."

Kendall-Hume turned back to face the dismayed couple. "I don't remember your first names, but this is Melody and I'm Ray."

"Christopher and Margaret," the schoolmaster admitted as handshakes were exchanged.

"What about a drink? Gin, vodka or . . . ?"

"Oh, no," said Margaret. "Thank you very much, we'll both have an orange juice."

"Suit yourselves," said Ray Kendall-Hume. "You must stay for lunch."

"But we couldn't impose . . ."

"I insist," said Mr Kendall-Hume. "After all, we're on holiday. By the way, we'll be going over to the other side of the bay for lunch. There's one hell of a beach there, and it will give you a chance to sunbathe and swim in peace."

"How considerate of you," said Christopher.

"And where's young Malcolm?" asked Margaret.

"He's on a scouting holiday in Scotland. Doesn't like to mess about in boats the way we do."

For the first time he could recall Christopher felt some admiration for the boy. A moment later the engine started thunderously.

On the trip across the bay, Ray Kendall-Hume expounded his theories about "having to get away from it all". "Nothing like a yacht to ensure your privacy and not having to mix with the *hoi polloi.*" He only wanted the simple things in life: the sun, the sea and an infinite supply of good food and drink.

The Roberts could have asked for nothing less. By the end of the day they were both suffering from a mild bout of sunstroke and were also feeling a little seasick. Despite white pills, red pills and yellow pills, liberally supplied by Melody, when they finally got back to their room that night they were unable to sleep.

Avoiding the Kendall-Humes over the next twenty days did not prove easy. Beyazik's, the garage where their little hire car awaited them each morning and to which it had to be returned each night, could only be reached via the quayside where the Kendall-Humes' motor yacht was moored like an insuperable barrier at a gymkhana. Hardly a day passed that the Roberts did not have to spend some part of their precious time bobbing up and down on Turkey's choppy coastal waters, eating oily food and discussing how large a carpet would be needed to fill the Kendall-Humes' front room.

However, they still managed to complete a large part of their programme and determinedly set aside the whole of the last day of the holiday in their quest for a carpet. As they did not need Beyazik's car to go into town, they felt confident that for that day at least they could safely avoid their tormentors.

On the final morning they rose a little later than planned and after breakfast strolled down the tiny cobbled path together, Christopher in possession of the seventeenth edition of *Carpets – Fact and Fiction*, Margaret with a tape measure and five hundred pounds in travellers' cheques.

Once the schoolmaster and his wife had reached the bazaar they began to look around a myriad of little shops, wondering where they should begin their adventure. Fez-topped men tried to entice them to enter their tiny emporiums but the Roberts spent the first hour simply taking in the atmosphere.

"I'm ready to start the search now," shouted Margaret above the babble of voices around her.

"Then we've found you just in time," said the one voice they thought they had escaped.

"We were just about to –"

"Then follow me."

The Roberts' hearts sank as they were led by Ray Kendall-Hume out of the bazaar and back towards the town.

"Take my advice, and you'll end up with one hell of a bargain," Kendall-Hume assured them both. "I've picked up some real beauties in my time from every corner of the globe at prices you wouldn't believe. I am happy to let you take full advantage of my expertise at no extra charge."

"I don't know how you could stand the noise and smell of that bazaar," said Melody, obviously glad to be back among the familiar signs of Gucci, Lacoste and Saint Laurent.

"We rather like . . ."

"Rescued in the nick of time," said Ray Kendall-Hume. "And the place I'm told you have to start and finish at if you want to purchase a serious carpet is Osman's."

Margaret recalled the name from her carpet book: "Only to be visited if money is no object and you know exactly what you are looking for." The vital last morning was to be wasted, she reflected as she pushed open the large glass doors of Osman's to enter a ground-floor area the size of a tennis court. The room was covered in carpets on the floor, the walls, the windowsills, and even the tables. Anywhere a carpet could be laid out, a carpet was there to be seen. Although the Roberts realised immediately that nothing on show could possibly be in their price range, the sheer beauty of the display entranced them.

Margaret walked slowly round the room, mentally measuring the small carpets so she could anticipate the sort of thing they might look for once they had escaped.

A tall, elegant man, hands raised as if in prayer and dressed immaculately in a tailored worsted suit that could have been made in Savile Row, advanced to greet them.

"Good morning, sir," he said to Mr Kendall-Hume, selecting the serious spender without difficulty. "Can I be of assistance?"

"You certainly can," replied Kendall-Hume. "I want to be shown your finest carpets, but I do not intend to pay your finest prices."

The dealer smiled politely and clapped his hands. Six small carpets were brought in by three assistants who rolled them out in the centre of the room. Margaret fell in love with a muted green-based carpet with a pattern of tiny red squares woven around the borders. The pattern was so intricate she could not take her eyes off it. She measured the carpet out of interest: seven by three exactly.

"You have excellent taste, madam," said the dealer. Margaret, colouring slightly, quickly stood up, took a pace backwards and hid the tape measure behind her back.

"How do you feel about that lot, pet?" asked Kendall-Hume, sweeping a hand across the six carpets.

"None of them are big enough," Melody replied, giving them only a fleeting glance.

The dealer clapped his hands a second time and the exhibits were rolled up and taken away. Four larger ones soon replaced them.

"Would you care for some coffee?" the dealer asked Mr Kendall-Hume as the new carpets lay unfurled at their feet.

"Haven't the time," said Kendall-Hume shortly. "Here to buy a carpet. If I want a coffee, I can always go to a coffee shop," he said with a chuckle. Melody smiled her complicity.

"Well, I would like some coffee," declared Margaret, determined to rebel at some point on the holiday.

"Delighted, madam," said the dealer, and one of the assistants disappeared to carry out her wishes while the Kendall-Humes studied the new carpets.

The coffee arrived a few moments later. She thanked the young assistant and began to sip the thick black liquid slowly. Delicious, she thought, and smiled her acknowledgment to the dealer.

"Still not large enough," Mrs Kendall-Hume insisted. The dealer gave a slight sigh and clapped his hands yet again. Once more the assistants began to roll up the rejected goods. He then addressed one of his staff in Turkish. The assistant looked doubtfully at his mentor but the dealer gave a firm nod and waved him away. The assistant returned a little later with a small platoon of lesser assistants carrying two carpets, both of which when unfolded took up most of the shop floor. Margaret liked them even less than the ones she had just been shown, but as her opinion was not sought she did not offer it.

"That's more like it," said Ray Kendall-Hume. "Just about the right size for the lounge, wouldn't you say, Melody?"

"Perfect," his wife replied, making no attempt to measure either of the carpets.

"I'm glad we agree," said Ray Kendall-Hume. "But which one, my pet? The faded red and blue, or the bright yellow and orange?"

"The yellow and orange one," said Melody without hesitation. "I like the pattern of brightly coloured birds running round the outside." Christopher thought he saw the dealer wince.

"So now all we have left to do is agree on a price," said Kendall-Hume. "You'd better sit down, pet, as this may take a while."

"I hope not," said Mrs Kendall-Hume, resolutely standing. The Roberts remained mute.

"Unfortunately, sir," began the dealer, "your wife has selected one of the finest carpets in our collection and so I fear there can be little room for any re-adjustment."

"How much?" said Kendall-Hume.

"You see, sir, this carpet was woven in Demirdji, in the province of Izmir, by over a hundred seamstresses and it took them more than a year to complete."

"Don't give me that baloney," said Kendall-Hume, winking at Christopher. "Just tell me how much I'm expected to pay."

"I feel it my duty to point out, sir, that this carpet shouldn't be here at all," said the Turk plaintively. "It was originally made for an Arab prince who failed to complete the transaction when the price of oil collapsed."

"But he must have agreed on a price at the time?"

"I cannot reveal the exact figure, sir. It embarrasses me to mention it."

"It wouldn't embarrass me," said Kendall-Hume. "Come on, what's the price?" he insisted.

"Which currency would you prefer to trade in?" the Turk asked.

"Pounds."

The dealer removed a slim calculator from his jacket pocket, programmed some numbers into it, then looked unhappily towards the Kendall-Humes.

Christopher and Margaret remained silent, like schoolchildren fearing the headmaster might ask them a question to which they could not possibly know the answer.

"Come on, come on, how much were you hoping to sting me for?"

"I think you must prepare yourself for a shock, sir," said the dealer.

"How much?" repeated Kendall-Hume, impatiently.

"Twenty-five thousand."

"Pounds?"

"Pounds."

"You must be joking," said Kendall-Hume, walking round the carpet and ending up standing next to Margaret. "You're about to find out why I'm considered the scourge of the East Midlands car trade," he whispered to her. "I wouldn't pay more than fifteen thousand for that carpet." He turned back to face the dealer. "Even if my life depended on it."

"Then I fear your time has been wasted, sir," the Turk replied. "For this is a carpet intended only for the *cognoscenti*. Perhaps madam might reconsider the red and blue?"

"Certainly not," said Kendall-Hume. "The colour's all faded. Can't you see? You obviously left it in the window too long, and the sun has got at it. No, you'll have to reconsider your price if you want the orange and yellow one to end up in the home of a connoisseur."

The dealer sighed as his fingers tapped the calculator again.

While the transaction continued, Melody looked on vacantly, occasionally gazing out of the window towards the bay.

"I could not drop a penny below twenty-three thousand pounds."

"I'd be willing to go as high as eighteen thousand," said Kendall-Hume, "but not a penny more."

The Roberts watched the dealer tap the numbers into the calculator.

"That would not even cover the cost of what I paid for it myself," he said sadly, staring down at the little glowing figures.

"You're pushing me, but don't push me too far. Nineteen thousand," said Mr Kendall-Hume. "That's my final offer."

"Twenty thousand pounds is the lowest figure I could consider," replied the dealer. "A give-away price on my mother's grave."

Kendall-Hume took out his wallet and placed it on the table by the side of the dealer.

"Nineteen thousand pounds and you've got yourself a deal," he said.

"But how will I feed my children?" asked the dealer, his arms raised above his head.

"The same way I feed mine," said Kendall-Hume, laughing. "By making a fair profit."

The dealer paused as if re-considering, then said, "I can't do it, sir. I'm sorry. We must show you some other carpets." The assistants came forward on cue.

"No, that's the one I want," said Mrs Kendall-Hume. "Don't quarrel over a thousand pounds, pet."

"Take my word for it, madam," the dealer said, turning towards Mrs Kendall-Hume. "My family would starve if we only did business with customers like your husband."

"Okay, you get the twenty thousand, but on one condition."

"Condition?"

"My receipt must show that the bill was for ten thousand pounds. Otherwise I'll only end up paying the difference in customs duty."

The dealer bowed low as if to indicate he did not find the request an unusual one.

Mr Kendall-Hume opened his wallet and withdrew ten thousand pounds in travellers' cheques and ten thousand pounds in cash.

"As you can see," he said, grinning, "I came prepared." He removed another five thousand pounds and, waving it at the dealer, added, "and I would have been willing to pay far more."

The dealer shrugged. "You drive a hard bargain, sir. But you will not hear me complain now the deal has been struck."

The vast carpet was folded, wrapped and a receipt for ten thousand pounds made out while the travellers' cheques and cash were paid over.

The Roberts had not uttered a word for twenty minutes. When they saw the cash change hands it crossed Margaret's mind that it was more money than the two of them earned in a year.

"Time to get back to the yacht," said Kendall-Hume. "Do join us for lunch if you choose a carpet in time."

"Thank you," said the Roberts in unison. They waited until the Kendall-Humes were out of sight, two assistants bearing the orange and yellow carpet in their wake, before they thanked the dealer for the coffee and in turn began to make their move towards the door.

"What sort of carpet were you looking for?" asked the dealer.

"I fear your prices are way beyond us," said Christopher politely. "But thank you."

"Well, let me at least find out. Have you or your wife seen a carpet you liked?"

"Yes," replied Margaret, "the small carpet, but . . ."

"Ah, yes," said the dealer. "I remember madam's eyes when she saw the Hereke."

He left them, to return a few moments later with the little soft-toned, green-based carpet with the tiny red squares that the Kendall-Humes had so firmly rejected. Not waiting for assistance he rolled it out himself for the Roberts in inspect more carefully.

Margaret thought it looked even more magnificent the second time and feared that she could never hope to find its equal in the few hours left to them.

"Perfect," she admitted, quite unashamedly.

"Then we have only the price to discuss," said the dealer kindly. "How much were you wanting to spend, madam?"

"We had planned to spend three hundred pounds," said Christopher, jumping in. Margaret was unable to hide her surprise.

"But we agreed –" she began.

"Thank you, my dear, I think I should deal with this matter."

The dealer smiled and returned to the bargaining.

"I would have to charge you six hundred pounds," he said. "Anything less would be robbery."

"Four hundred pounds is my final offer," said

Christopher, trying to sound in control.

"Five hundred pounds would have to be my bottom price," said the dealer.

"I'll take it!" cried Christopher.

An assistant began waving his arms and talking to the dealer noisily in his native tongue. The owner raised a hand to dismiss the young man's protests, while the Roberts looked on anxiously.

"My son," explained the dealer, "is not happy with the arrangement, but I am delighted that the little carpet will reside in the home of a couple who will so obviously appreciate its true worth."

"Thank you," said Christopher quietly.

"Will you also require a bill of a different price?"

"No, thank you," said Christopher, handing over ten fifty-pound notes and then waiting until the carpet was wrapped and he was presented with the correct receipt.

As he watched the Roberts leave his shop clinging on to their purchase, the dealer smiled to himself.

When they arrived at the quayside, the Kendall-Humes' boat was already half way across the bay heading towards the quiet beach. The Roberts sighed their combined relief and returned to the bazaar for lunch.

It was while they were waiting for their baggage to appear on the carousel at Heathrow Airport that Christopher felt a tap on his shoulder. He turned round to face a beaming Ray Kendall-Hume.

"I wonder if you could do me a favour, old boy?"

"I will if I can," said Christopher, who still

had not fully recovered from their last encounter.

"It's simple enough," said Kendall-Hume. "The old girl and I have brought back far too many presents and I wondered if you could take one of them through customs. Otherwise we're likely to be held up all night."

Melody, standing behind an already laden trolley, smiled at the two men benignly.

"You would still have to pay any duty that was due on it," said Christopher firmly.

"I wouldn't dream of doing otherwise," said Kendall-Hume, struggling with a massive package before pushing it on the Roberts' trolley. Christopher wanted to protest as Kendall-Hume peeled off two thousand pounds and handed the money and the receipt over to the schoolmaster.

"What do we do if they claim your carpet is worth a lot more than ten thousand pounds?" asked Margaret anxiously, coming to stand by her husband's side.

"Pay the difference and I'll refund you immediately. But I assure you it's most unlikely to arise."

"I hope you're right."

"Of course I'm right," said Kendall-Hume. "Don't worry, I've done this sort of thing before. And I won't forget your help when it comes to the next school appeal," he added, leaving them with the huge parcel.

Once Christopher and Margaret had located their own bags, they collected the second trolley and took their place in the red "Something to Declare" queue.

"Are you in possession of any items over five

hundred pounds in value?" asked the young customs official politely.

"Yes," said Christopher. "We purchased two carpets when we were on holiday in Turkey." He handed over the two bills.

The customs official studied the receipts carefully, then asked if he might be allowed to see the carpets for himself.

"Certainly," said Christopher, and began the task of undoing the larger package while Margaret worked on the smaller one.

"I shall need to have these looked at by an expert," said the official once the parcels were unwrapped. "It shouldn't take more than a few minutes." The carpets were soon taken away.

The "few minutes" turned out to be over fifteen and Christopher and Margaret were soon regretting their decision to assist the Kendall-Humes, whatever the needs of the school appeal. They began to indulge in irrelevant small-talk that wouldn't have fooled the most amateur of sleuths.

At last the customs official returned.

"I wonder if you would be kind enough to have a word with my colleague in private?" he asked.

"Is that really necessary?" asked Christopher, reddening.

"I'm afraid so, sir."

"We shouldn't have agreed to it in the first place," whispered Margaret. "We've never been in any trouble with the authorities before."

"Don't fret, dear. It will be all over in a few minutes, you'll see," said Christopher, not sure that he believed his own words. They followed the young man out through the back and into a small room.

"Good afternoon, sir," said a white-haired man with several gold rings around the cuff of his sleeve. "I am sorry to have kept you waiting but we have had your carpets looked at by our expert and he feels sure a mistake must have been made."

Christopher wanted to protest but he couldn't get a word out.

"A mistake?" managed Margaret.

"Yes, madam. The bills you presented don't make any sense to him."

"Don't make any sense?"

"No, madam," said the senior customs officer. "I repeat, we feel certain a mistake has been made."

"What kind of mistake?" asked Christopher, at last finding his voice.

"Well, you have come forward and declared two carpets, one at a price of ten thousand pounds and one at a price of five hundred pounds, according to these receipts."

"Yes?"

"Every year hundreds of people return to England with Turkish carpets, so we have some experience in these matters. Our adviser feels certain that the bills have been incorrectly made out."

"I don't begin to understand . . ." said Christopher.

"Well," explained the senior officer, "the large carpet, we are assured, has been spun with a crude distaff and has only two hundred ghiordes, or knots, per square inch. Despite its size we estimate it to be valued around five thousand pounds. The small carpet, on the other hand, we estimate to have nine hundred knots per square inch and is a fine example of a silk hand-woven traditional

Hereke and undoubtedly would have been a bargain at five hundred pounds. As both carpets come from the same shop, we assume it must be a clerical error."

The Roberts remained speechless.

"It doesn't make any difference to the duty you will have to pay, but we felt sure you would want to know, for insurance purposes."

Still the Roberts said nothing.

"As you're allowed five hundred pounds before paying any duty, the excise will still be two thousand pounds."

Christopher quickly handed over the Kendall-Humes' wad of notes. The senior officer counted them while his junior carefully re-wrapped the two carpets.

"Thank you," said Christopher, as they were handed back the parcels and a receipt for the two thousand pounds.

The Roberts quickly bundled the large package on to its trolley before wheeling it through the concourse and on to the pavement outside where the Kendall-Humes impatiently awaited them.

"You were in there a long time," said Kendall-Hume. "Any problems?"

"No, they were just assessing the value of the carpets."

"Any extra charge?" Kendall-Hume asked apprehensively.

"No, your two thousand pounds covered everything," said Christopher, passing over the receipt.

"Then we got away with it, old fellow. Well done. One hell of a bargain to add to my collection." Kendall-Hume turned to bundle the large package into the boot of his Mercedes before locking it and taking his place behind the steering wheel. "Well done," he repeated through the open window, as the car drove off. "I won't forget the school appeal."

The Roberts stood and watched as the silver grey car joined a line of traffic leaving the airport.

"Why didn't you tell Mr Kendall-Hume the real value of his carpet?" asked Margaret once they were seated in the bus.

"I did give it some considerable thought but I came to the conclusion that the *truth* was the last thing Kendall-Hume wanted to be told."

"But don't you feel any guilt? After all, we've stolen –"

"Not at all, my dear. We haven't stolen anything. But we did get one hell of a 'steal'."

Colonel Bullfrog

COLONEL BULLFROG

THERE is one cathedral in England that has never found it necessary to launch a national appeal.

When the Colonel woke he found himself tied to a stake where the ambush had taken place. He could feel a numb sensation in his leg. The last thing he could recall was the bayonet entering his thigh. All he was aware of now were ants crawling up the leg on an endless march towards the wound.

It would have been better to have remained unconscious, he decided.

Then someone undid the knots and he collapsed head first into the mud. It would be better still to be dead, he concluded. The Colonel somehow got to his knees and crawled over to the stake next to him. Tied to it was a corporal who must have been dead for several hours. Ants were crawling into his mouth. The Colonel tore off a strip from the man's shirt, washed it in a large puddle nearby and cleaned the wound in his leg as best he could before binding it tightly.

That was February 17th, 1943, a date that would be etched on the Colonel's memory for the rest of his life.

That same morning the Japanese received orders that the newly captured Allied prisoners were to be moved at dawn. Many were to die on the march and even more had perished before the trek began. Colonel Richard Moore was determined not to be counted among them.

Twenty-nine days later, one hundred and seventeen of the original seven hundred and thirty-two Allied troops reached Tonchan. Any man whose travels had previously not taken him beyond Rome could hardly have been prepared for such an experience as Tonchan. This heavily guarded prisoner-of-war camp, some three hundred miles north of Singapore and hidden in the deepest equatorial jungle, offered no possibility of freedom. Anyone who contemplated escape could not hope to survive in the jungle for more than a few days, while those who remained discovered the odds were not a lot shorter.

When the Colonel first arrived, Major Sakata, the camp commandant, informed him that he was the senior ranking officer and would therefore be held responsible for the welfare of all Allied troops.

Colonel Moore had stared down at the Japanese officer. Sakata must have been a foot shorter than himself but after that twenty-eight-day march the British soldier couldn't have weighed much more than the diminutive Major.

Moore's first act on leaving the commandant's office was to call together all the Allied officers. He discovered there was a good cross-section from

Britain, Australia, New Zealand and America but few could have been described as fit. Men were dying daily from malaria, dysentery and malnutrition. He was suddenly aware what the expression "dying like flies" meant.

The Colonel learned from his staff officers that for the previous two years of the camp's existence they had been ordered to build bamboo huts for the Japanese officers. These had had to be completed before they had been allowed to start on a hospital for their own men and only recently huts for themselves. Many prisoners had died during those two years, not from illness but from the atrocities some Japanese perpetrated on a daily basis. Major Sakata, known because of his skinny arms as "Chopsticks", was, however, not considered to be the villain. His second-in-command, Lieutenant Takasaki (the Undertaker), and Sergeant Ayut (the Pig) were of a different mould and to be avoided at all cost, his men warned him.

It took the Colonel only a few days to discover why.

He decided his first task was to try to raise the battered morale of his troops. As there was no padre among those officers who had been captured he began each day by conducting a short service of prayer. Once the service was over the men would start work on the railway that ran alongside the camp. Each arduous day consisted of laying tracks to help Japanese soldiers get to the front more quickly so they could in turn kill and capture more Allied troops. Any prisoner suspected of undermining this work was found guilty of sabotage and put to death without trial. Lieutenant Takasaki considered taking an unscheduled five-minute break to be sabotage.

At lunch prisoners were allowed twenty minutes off to share a bowl of rice – usually with maggots – and, if they were lucky, a mug of water. Although the men returned to the camp each night exhausted, the Colonel still set about organising squads to be responsible for the cleanliness of their huts and the state of the latrines.

After only a few months, the Colonel was able to organise a football match between the British and the Americans, and following its success even set up a camp league. But he was even more delighted when the men turned up for karate lessons under Sergeant Hawke, a thick-set Australian, who had a Black Belt and for good measure also played the mouth-organ. The tiny instrument had survived the march through the jungle but everyone assumed it would be discovered before long and confiscated.

Each day Moore renewed his determination not to allow the Japanese to believe for one moment that the Allies were beaten – despite the fact that while he was at Tonchan he lost another twenty pounds in weight, and at least one man under his command every day.

To the Colonel's surprise the camp commandant, despite the Japanese national belief that any soldier who allowed himself to be captured ought to be treated as a deserter, did not place too many unnecessary obstacles in his path.

"You are like the British Bullfrog," Major Sakata suggested one evening as he watched the Colonel carving cricket bails out of bamboo. It was one of the rare occasions when the Colonel managed a smile.

His real problems continued to come from Lieutenant Takasaki and his henchmen, who considered captured Allied prisoners fit only to be considered as traitors. Takasaki was always careful how he treated the Colonel personally, but felt no such reservations when dealing with the other ranks, with the result that Allied soldiers often ended up with their meagre rations confiscated, a rifle butt in the stomach, or even left bound to a tree for days on end.

Whenever the Colonel made an official complaint to the commandant, Major Sakata listened sympathetically and even made an effort to weed out the main offenders. Moore's happiest moment at Tonchan was to witness the Undertaker and the Pig boarding the train for the front line. No one attempted to sabotage that journey. The commandant replaced them with Sergeant Akida and Corporal Sushi, known by the prisoners almost affectionately as "Sweet and Sour Pork". However, the Japanese High Command sent a new Number Two to the camp, a Lieutenant Osawa, who quickly became known as "The Devil" since he perpetrated atrocities that made the Undertaker and the Pig look like church fête organisers.

As the months passed the Colonel and the commandant's mutual respect grew. Sakata even confided to his English prisoner that he had requested that he be sent to the front line and join the real war. "And if," the Major added, "the High Command grants my request, there will be only two NCOs I would want to accompany me."

Colonel Moore knew the Major had Sweet and Sour Pork in mind, and was fearful what might become of his men if the only three Japanese he could work with were posted back to active duties to leave Lieutenant Osawa in command of the camp.

Colonel Moore realised that something quite extraordinary must have taken place for Major Sakata to come to his hut, because he had never done so before. The Colonel put his bowl of rice back down on the table and asked the three Allied officers who were sharing breakfast with him to wait outside.

The Major stood to attention and saluted.

The Colonel pushed himself to his full six feet, returned the salute and stared down into Sakata's eyes.

"The war is over," said the Japanese officer. For a brief moment Moore feared the worst. "Japan has surrendered unconditionally. You, sir," Sakata said quietly, "are now in command of the camp."

The Colonel immediately ordered all Japanese officers to be placed under arrest in the commandant's quarters. While his orders were being carried out he personally went in search of The Devil. Moore marched across the parade ground and headed towards the officers' quarters. He located the second-in-command's hut, walked up the steps and threw open Osawa's door. The sight that met the new commandant's eyes was one he would never forget. The Colonel had read of ceremonial hara-kiri without any real idea of what the final act consisted. Lieutenant Osawa must have cut himself a hundred times before he eventually died. The blood, the stench and the sight of the mutilated body would have caused a Gurkha to be sick. Only the head was there to confirm that the remains had once belonged to a human being.

The Colonel ordered Osawa to be buried outside the gates of the camp.

When the surrender of Japan was finally signed on board the US *Missouri* in Tokyo Bay, all at Tonchan PoW camp listened to the ceremony on the single camp radio. Colonel Moore then called a full parade on the camp square. For the first time in two and a half years he wore his dress uniform which made him look like a pierrot who had turned up at a formal party. He accepted the Japanese flag of surrender from Major Sakata on behalf of the Allies, then made the defeated enemy raise the American and British flags to the sound of both national anthems played in turn by Sergeant Hawke on his mouth-organ.

The Colonel then held a short service of thanksgiving which he conducted in the presence of all the Allied and Japanese soldiers.

Once command had changed hands Colonel Moore waited as week followed pointless week for news that he would be sent home. Many of his men had been given their orders to start the ten-thousand-mile journey back to England via Bangkok and Calcutta, but no such orders came for the Colonel and he waited in vain to be sent his repatriation papers.

Then, in January 1946, a smartly dressed young

Guards officer arrived at the camp with orders to see the Colonel. He was conducted to the commandant's office and saluted before shaking hands. Richard Moore stared at the young captain who, from his healthy complexion, had obviously arrived in the Far East long after the Japanese had surrendered. The captain handed over a letter to the Colonel.

"Home at last," said the older man breezily, as he ripped open the envelope, only to discover that it would be years before he could hope to exchange the paddy fields of Tonchan for the green fields of Lincolnshire.

The letter requested that the Colonel travel to Tokyo and represent Britain on the forthcoming war tribunal which was to be conducted in the Japanese capital. Captain Ross of the Coldstream Guards would take over his command at Tonchan.

The tribunal was to consist of twelve officers under the chairmanship of General Matthew Tomkins. Moore was to be the sole British representative and was to report directly to the General, "as soon as you find it convenient". Further details would be supplied to him on his arrival in Tokyo. The letter ended: "If for any reason you should require my help in your deliberations, do not hesitate to contact me personally." There followed the signature of Clement Attlee.

Staff officers are not in the habit of disobeying Prime Ministers, so the Colonel resigned himself to a prolonged stay in Japan.

It took several months to set up the tribunal and during that time Colonel Moore continued supervising the return of British troops to their homeland. The paperwork was endless and some of the men under his command were so frail that he found it necessary to build them up spiritually as well as physically before he could put them on boats to their various destinations. Some died long after the declaration of surrender had been ratified.

During this period of waiting, Colonel Moore used Major Sakata and the two NCOs in whom he had placed so much trust, Sergeant Akida and Corporal Sushi, as his liaison officers. This sudden change of command did not affect the relationship between the two senior officers, although Sakata admitted to the Colonel that he wished he had been killed in the defence of his country and not left to witness its humiliations. The Colonel found the Japanese remained well-disciplined while they waited to learn their fate, and most of them assumed death was the natural consequence of defeat.

The war tribunal held its first plenary session in Tokyo on April 19th, 1946. General Tomkins took over the fifth floor of the old Imperial Courthouse in the Ginza quarter of Tokyo – one of the few buildings that had survived the war intact. Tomkins, a squat, short-tempered man who was described by his own staff officer as a "pen-pusher from the Pentagon", arrived in Tokyo only a week before he began his first deliberations. The only rat-a-tat-tat this General had ever heard, the staff officer freely admitted to Colonel Moore, had come from the typewriter in his secretary's office. However, when it came to those on trial the General was in no doubt as to where the guilt lay and how the guilty should be punished.

"Hang every one of the little slit-eyed, yellow bastards," turned out to be one of Tomkins's favourite expressions.

Seated round a table in an old courtroom, the twelve-man tribunal conducted their deliberations. It was clear from the opening session that the General had no intention of considering "extenuating circumstances", "past record" or "humanitarian grounds". As the Colonel listened to Tomkins's views he began to fear for the lives of any innocent member of the armed forces who was brought in front of the General.

The Colonel quickly identified four Americans from the tribunal who, like himself, did not always concur with the General's sweeping judgments. Two were lawyers and the other two had been fighting soldiers recently involved in combat duty. The five men began to work together to counteract the General's most prejudiced decisions. During the following weeks they were able to persuade one or two others around the table to commute the sentences of hanging to life imprisonment for several Japanese who had been condemned for crimes they could not possibly have committed.

As each such case was debated, General Tomkins left the five men in no doubt as to his contempt for their views. "Goddam Nip sympathisers," he often suggested, and not always under his breath. As the General still held sway over the twelve-man tribunal, the Colonel's successes turned out to be few in number.

When the time came to determine the fate of

those who had been in command of the PoW camp at Tonchan the General demanded mass hanging for every Japanese officer involved without even the pretence of a proper trial. He showed no surprise when the usual five tribunal members raised their voices in protest. Colonel Moore spoke eloquently of having been a prisoner at Tonchan and petitioned in the defence of Major Sakata, Sergeant Akida and Corporal Sushi. He attempted to explain why hanging them would in its own way be as barbaric as any atrocity carried out by the Japanese. He insisted their sentence should be commuted to life imprisonment. The General yawned throughout the Colonel's remarks and, once Moore had completed his case, made no attempt to justify his position but simply called for a vote. To the General's surprise, the result was six-all; an American lawyer who previously had sided with the General raised his hand to join the Colonel's five. Without hesitation the General threw his casting vote in favour of the gallows. Tomkins leered down the table at Moore and said, "Time for lunch, I think, gentlemen. I don't know about you but I'm famished. And no one can say that this time we didn't give the little yellow bastards a fair hearing."

Colonel Moore rose from his place and without offering an opinion left the room.

He ran down the steps of the courthouse and instructed his driver to take him to British HQ in the centre of the city as quickly as possible. The short journey took them some time because of the mêlée of people that were always thronging the streets night and day. Once the Colonel arrived at his office he asked his secretary to place a call through to England. While she was carrying out his order Moore went to his green cabinet and thumbed through several files until he reached the one marked "Personal". He opened it and fished out the letter. He wanted to be certain that he had remembered the sentence accurately . . .

"If for any reason you should require my help in your deliberations, do not hesitate to contact me personally."

"He's coming to the phone, sir," the secretary said nervously. The Colonel walked over to the phone and waited. He found himself standing to attention when he heard the gentle, cultivated voice ask, "Is that you, Colonel?" It took Richard Moore less than ten minutes to explain the problem he faced and obtain the authority he needed.

Immediately he had completed his conversation he returned to the tribunal headquarters. He marched straight back into the conference room just as General Tomkins was settling down in his chair to start the afternoon proceedings.

The Colonel was the first to rise from his place when the General declared the tribunal to be in session. "I wonder if I might be allowed to open with a statement?" he requested.

"Be my guest," said Tomkins. "But make it brief. We've got a lot more of these Japs to get through yet."

Colonel Moore looked around the table at the other eleven men.

"Gentlemen," he began. "I hereby resign my position as the British representative on this commission."

General Tomkins was unable to stifle a smile.

"I do it," the Colonel continued, "reluctantly, but with the backing of my Prime Minister, to whom I spoke only a few moments ago." At this piece of information Tomkins's smile was replaced by a frown. "I shall be returning to England in order to make a full report to Mr Attlee and the British Cabinet on the manner in which this tribunal is being conducted."

"Now look here, sonny," began the General. "You can't –"

"I can, sir, and I will. Unlike you, I am unwilling to have the blood of innocent soldiers on my hands for the rest of my life."

"Now look here, sonny," the General repeated. "Let's at least talk this through before you do anything you might regret."

There was no break for the rest of that day, and by late afternoon Major Sakata, Sergeant Akida and Corporal Sushi had had their sentences commuted to life imprisonment.

Within a month, General Tomkins had been recalled by the Pentagon to be replaced by a distinguished American marine who had been decorated in combat during the First World War.

In the weeks that followed the new appointment the death sentences of two hundred and twenty-nine Japanese prisoners of war were commuted.

Colonel Moore returned to Lincolnshire on November 11th, 1948, having had enough of the realities of war and the hypocrisies of peace.

Just under two years later Richard Moore took holy orders and became a parish priest in the sleepy hamlet of Weddlebeach, in Suffolk. He enjoyed his calling and although he rarely mentioned his war-time experiences to his parishioners he often thought of his days in Japan.

"Blessed are the peacemakers for they shall . . ." the vicar began his sermon from the pulpit one Palm Sunday morning in the early 1960s, but he failed to complete the sentence.

His parishioners looked up anxiously only to see that a broad smile had spread across the vicar's face as he gazed down at someone seated in the third row.

The man he was staring at bowed his head in embarrassment and the vicar quickly continued with his sermon.

When the service was over Richard Moore waited by the east door to be sure his eyes had not deceived him. When they met face to face for the first time in fifteen years both men bowed and then shook hands.

The priest was delighted to learn over lunch that day back at the vicarage that Chopsticks Sakata had been released from prison after only five years, following the Allies' agreement with the newly installed Japanese government to release all prisoners who had not committed capital crimes. When the Colonel enquired after "Sweet and Sour Pork" the Major admitted that he had lost touch with Sergeant Akida (Sweet) but that Corporal Sushi (Sour) and he were working for the same electronics company. "And whenever we meet," he assured the priest, "we talk of the honourable man who saved our lives, 'the British Bullfrog'."

* * *

Over the years, the priest and his Japanese friend progressed in their chosen professions and regularly corresponded with each other. In 1971 Ari Sakata was put in charge of a large electronics factory in Osaka while eighteen months later Richard Moore became the Very Revd Richard Moore, Dean of Lincoln Cathedral.

"I read in the London *Times* that your cathedral is appealing for a new roof," wrote Sakata from his homeland in 1975.

"Nothing unusual about that," the Dean explained in his letter of reply. "There isn't a cathedral in England that doesn't suffer from dry rot or bomb damage. The former I fear is terminal; the latter at least has the chance of a cure."

A few weeks later the Dean received a cheque for ten thousand pounds from a not-unknown Japanese electronics company.

When in 1979 the Very Revd Richard Moore was appointed to the bishopric of Taunton, the new managing director of the largest electronics company in Japan flew over to attend his enthronement.

"I see you have another roof problem," commented Ari Sakata as he gazed up at the scaffolding surrounding the pulpit. "How much will it cost this time?"

"At least twenty-five thousand pounds a year," replied the Bishop without thought. "Just to make sure the roof doesn't fall in on the congregation during my sterner sermons." He sighed as he passed the evidence of reconstruction all around him. "As soon as I've settled into my new job I intend to launch a proper appeal to ensure my successor doesn't have to worry about the roof ever again."

The managing director nodded his understanding. A week later a cheque for twenty-five thousand pounds arrived on the churchman's desk.

The Bishop tried hard to express his grateful thanks. He knew he must never allow Chopsticks to feel that by his generosity he might have done the wrong thing as this would only insult his friend and undoubtedly end their relationship. Rewrite after rewrite was drafted to ensure that the final version of the long hand-written letter would have passed muster with the Foreign Office mandarin in charge of the Japanese desk. Finally the letter was posted.

As the years passed Richard Moore became fearful of writing to his old friend more than once a year as each letter elicited an even larger cheque. And, when towards the end of 1986 he did write, he made no reference to the Dean and Chapter's decision to designate 1988 as the cathedral's appeal year. Nor did he mention his own failing health, lest the old Japanese gentleman should feel in some way responsible, as his doctor had warned him that he could never expect to recover fully from those experiences at Tonchan.

The Bishop set about forming his appeal committee in January 1987. The Prince of Wales became the patron and the Lord Lieutenant of the county its chairman. In his opening address to the members of the appeal committee the Bishop instructed them that it was their duty to raise not less than three million pounds during 1988. Some apprehensive looks appeared on the faces around the table.

On August 11th, 1987, the Bishop of Taunton was umpiring a village cricket match when he suddenly collapsed from a heart attack. "See that the appeal brochures are printed in time for the next meeting," were his final words to the captain of the local team.

Bishop Moore's memorial service was held in Taunton Cathedral and conducted by the Archbishop of Canterbury. Not a seat could be found in the cathedral that day, and so many crowded into every pew that the west door was left open. Those who arrived late had to listen to the Archbishop's address relayed over loudspeakers placed around the market square.

Casual onlookers must have been puzzled by the presence of several elderly Japanese gentlemen dotted around the congregation.

When the service came to an end the Archbishop held a private meeting in the vestry of the cathedral with the chairman of the largest electronics company in the world.

"You must be Mr Sakata," said the Archbishop, warmly shaking the hand of a man who stepped forward from the small cluster of Japanese who were in attendance. "Thank you for taking the trouble to write and let me know that you would be coming. I am delighted to meet you at last. The Bishop always spoke of you with great affection and as a close friend – 'Chopsticks', if I remember."

Mr Sakata bowed low.

"And I also know that he always considered himself in your personal debt for such generosity over so many years."

"No, no, not me," replied the former Major. "I,

like my dear friend the late Bishop, am representative of higher authority."

The Archbishop looked puzzled.

"You see, sir," continued Mr Sakata, "I am only the chairman of the company. May I have the honour of introducing my President?"

Mr Sakata took a pace backwards to allow an even smaller figure, whom the Archbishop had originally assumed to be part of Mr Sakata's entourage, to step forward.

The President bowed low and, still without speaking, passed an envelope to the Archbishop.

"May I be allowed to open it?" the church leader asked, unaware of the Japanese custom of waiting until the giver has departed.

The little man bowed again.

The Archbishop slit open the envelope and removed a cheque for three million pounds.

"The late Bishop must have been a very close friend," was all he could think of saying.

"No, sir," the President replied. "I did not have that privilege."

"Then he must have done something incredible to be deserving of such a munificent gesture."

"He performed an act of honour over forty years ago and now I try inadequately to repay it."

"Then he would surely have remembered you," said the Archbishop.

"Is possible he would remember me but if so only as the sour half of 'Sweet and Sour Pork'."

There is one cathedral in England that has never found it necessary to launch a national appeal.

Checkmate

AS she entered the room every eye turned towards her.

When admiring a girl some men start with her head and work down. I start with the ankles and work up.

She wore black high-heeled velvet shoes and a tight-fitting black dress that stopped high enough above the knees to reveal the most perfectly tapering legs. As my eyes continued their upward sweep they paused to take in her narrow waist and slim athletic figure. But it was the oval face that I found captivating, slightly pouting lips and the largest blue eyes I've ever seen, crowned with a head of thick, black, short-cut hair that literally shone with lustre. Her entrance was all the more breathtaking because of the surroundings she had chosen. Heads would have turned at a diplomatic reception, a society cocktail party, even a charity ball, but at a chess tournament . . .

I followed her every movement, patronisingly unable to accept she could be a player. She walked slowly over to the club secretary's table and signed in to prove me wrong. She was handed a number to indicate her challenger for the opening match. Anyone who had not yet been allocated an opponent waited to see if she would take her place opposite their side of the board.

The player checked the number she had been given and made her way towards an elderly man who was seated in the far corner of the room, a former captain of the club now past his best.

As the club's new captain I had been responsible for instigating these round-robin matches. We meet on the last Friday of the month in a large club-like room on top of the Mason's Arms in the High Street. The landlord sees to it that thirty tables are set out for us and that food and drink are readily available. Three or four other clubs in the district send half a dozen opponents to play a couple of blitz games, giving us a chance to face rivals we would not normally play. The rules for the matches are simple enough – one minute on the clock is the maximum allowed for each move, so a game rarely lasts for more than an hour, and if a pawn hasn't been captured in thirty moves the game is automatically declared a draw. A short break for a drink between games, paid for by the loser, ensures that everyone has the chance to challenge two opponents during the evening.

A thin man wearing half-moon spectacles and a dark blue three-piece suit made his way over towards my board. We smiled and shook hands. My guess would have been a solicitor, but I was wrong as he turned out to be an accountant working for a stationery supplier in Woking.

I found it hard to concentrate on my opponent's well-rehearsed Moscow opening as my eyes kept leaving the board and wandering over to the girl in the black dress. On the one occasion our eyes did meet she gave me an enigmatic smile, but although I tried again I was unable to elicit the same response a second time. Despite being preoccupied I still managed to defeat the accountant, who seemed unaware that there were several ways out of a seven-pawn attack.

At the half-time break three other members of the club had offered her a drink before I even reached the bar. I knew I could not hope to play my second match against the girl as I would be expected to challenge one of the visiting team captains. In fact she ended up playing the accountant.

I defeated my new opponent in a little over forty minutes and, as a solicitous host, began to take an interest in the other matches that were still being played. I set out on a circuitous route that ensured I ended up at her table. I could see that the accountant already had the better of her and within moments of my arrival she had lost both her queen and the game.

I introduced myself and found that just shaking hands with her was a sexual experience. Weaving our way through the tables we strolled over to the bar together. Her name, she told me, was Amanda Curzon. I ordered Amanda the glass of red wine she requested and a half-pint of beer for myself. I began by commiserating with her over the defeat.

"How did you get on against him?" she asked.

"Just managed to beat him," I said. "But it was very close. How did your first game with our old captain turn out?"

"Stalemate," said Amanda. "But I think he was just being courteous."

"Last time I played him it ended up in stalemate," I told her.

She smiled. "Perhaps we ought to have a game some time?"

"I'll look forward to that," I said, as she finished her drink.

"Well, I must be off," she announced suddenly. "Have to catch the last train to Hounslow."

"Allow me to drive you," I said gallantly. "It's the least the host captain can be expected to do."

"But surely it's miles out of your way?"

"Not at all," I lied, Hounslow being about twenty minutes beyond my flat. I gulped down the last drop of my beer and helped Amanda on with her coat. Before leaving I thanked the landlord for the efficient organisation of the evening.

We then strolled into the car park. I opened the passenger door of my Scirocco to allow Amanda to climb in.

"A slight improvement on London Transport," she said as I slid into my side of the car. I smiled and headed out on the road northwards. That black dress that I described earlier goes even higher up the legs when a girl sits back in a Scirocco. It didn't seem to embarrass her.

"It's still very early," I ventured after a few inconsequential remarks about the club evening. "Have you time to drop in for a drink?"

"It would have to be a quick one," she replied, looking at her watch. "I've a busy day ahead of me tomorrow."

"Of course," I said, chatting on, hoping she

wouldn't notice a detour that could hardly be described as on the way to Hounslow.

"Do you work in town?" I asked.

"Yes. I'm a receptionist for a firm of estate agents in Berkeley Square."

"I'm surprised you're not a model."

"I used to be," she replied without further explanation. She seemed quite oblivious to the route I was taking as she chatted on about her holiday plans for Ibiza. Once we had arrived at my place I parked the car and led Amanda through my front gate and up to the flat. In the hall I helped her off with her coat before taking her through to the front room.

"What would you like to drink?" I asked.

"I'll stick to wine, if you've a bottle already open," she replied, as she walked slowly round, taking in the unusually tidy room. My mother must have dropped by during the morning, I thought gratefully.

"It's only a bachelor pad," I said, emphasising the word "bachelor" before going into the kitchen. To my relief I found there was an unopened bottle of wine in the larder. I joined Amanda with the bottle and two glasses a few moments later, to find her studying my chess board and fingering the delicate ivory pieces that were set out for a game I was playing by post.

"What a beautiful set," she volunteered as I handed her a glass of wine. "Where did you find it?"

"Mexico," I told her, not explaining that I had won it in a tournament while on holiday there. "I was only sorry we didn't have the chance to have a game ourselves."

She checked her watch. "Time for a quick one," she said, taking a seat behind the little white pieces.

I quickly took my place opposite her. She smiled, picked up a white and a black bishop and hid them behind her back. Her dress became even tighter and emphasised the shape of her breasts. She then placed both clenched fists in front of me. I touched her right hand and she turned it over and opened it to reveal a white bishop.

"Is there to be a wager of any kind?" I asked lightheartedly. She checked inside her evening bag.

"I only have a few pounds on me," she said.

"I'd be willing to play for lower stakes."

"What do you have in mind?" she asked.

"What can you offer?"

"What would you like?"

"Ten pounds if you win."

"And if I lose?"

"You take something off."

I regretted the words the moment I had said them and waited for her to slap my face and leave but she said simply, "There's not much harm in that if we only play one game."

I nodded my agreement and stared down at the board.

She wasn't a bad player – what the pros call a *patzer* – though her Roux opening was somewhat orthodox. I managed to make the game last twenty minutes while sacrificing several pieces without making it look too obvious. When I said "Checkmate", she kicked off both her shoes and laughed.

"Care for another drink?" I asked, not feeling too hopeful. "After all, it's not yet eleven."

"All right. Just a small one and then I must be off."

I went to the kitchen, returned a moment later clutching the bottle, and refilled her glass.

"I only wanted half a glass," she said, frowning.

"I was lucky to win," I said, ignoring her remark, "after your bishop captured my knight. Extremely close-run thing."

"Perhaps," she replied.

"Care for another game?" I ventured.

She hesitated.

"Double or quits?"

"What do you mean?"

"Twenty pounds or another garment?"

"Neither of us is going to lose much tonight, are we?"

She pulled up her chair as I turned the board round and we both began to put the ivory pieces back in place.

The second game took a little longer as I made a silly mistake early on, castling on my queen's side, and it took several moves to recover. However, I still managed to finish the game off in under thirty minutes and even found time to refill Amanda's glass when she wasn't looking.

She smiled at me as she hitched her dress up high enough to allow me to see the tops of her stockings. She undid the suspenders and slowly peeled the stockings off before dropping them on my side of the table.

"I nearly beat you that time," she said.

"Almost," I replied. "Want another chance to get even? Let's say fifty pounds this time," I suggested, trying to make the offer sound magnanimous.

"The stakes are getting higher for both of us," she replied as she reset the board. I began to wonder what might be going through her mind. Whatever it was, she foolishly sacrificed both her rooks early on and the game was over in a matter of minutes.

Once again she lifted her dress but this time well above her waist. My eyes were glued to her thighs as she undid the black suspender belt and held it high above my head before letting it drop and join her stockings on my side of the table.

"Once I had lost the second rook," she said, "I was never in with a chance."

"I agree. It would therefore only be fair to allow you one more chance," I said, quickly re-setting the board. "After all," I added, "you could win one hundred pounds this time." She smiled.

"I really ought to be going home," she said as she moved her queen's pawn two squares forward. She smiled that enigmatic smile again as I countered with my bishop's pawn.

It was the best game she had played all evening and her use of the Warsaw gambit kept me at the board for over thirty minutes. In fact I damn nearly lost early on because I found it hard to concentrate properly on her defence strategy. A couple of times Amanda chuckled when she thought she had got the better of me, but it became obvious she had not seen Karpov play the Sicilian defence and win from a seemingly impossible position.

"Checkmate," I finally declared.

"Damn," she said, and standing up turned her back on me. "You'll have to give me a hand." Trembling, I leaned over and slowly pulled the zip down until it reached the small of her back. Once again I wanted to touch the smooth, creamy skin. She swung round to face me, shrugged gracefully and the dress fell to the ground as if a statue were being unveiled. She leaned forward and brushed the side of my cheek with her hand, which had much the same effect as an electric shock. I emptied the last of the bottle of wine into her glass and left for the kitchen with the excuse of needing to refill my own. When I returned she hadn't moved. A gauzy black bra and pair of panties were now the only garments that I still hoped to see removed.

"I don't suppose you'd play one more game?" I asked, trying not to sound desperate.

"It's time you took me home," she said with a giggle.

I passed her another glass of wine. "Just one more," I begged. "But this time it must be for both garments."

She laughed. "Certainly not," she said. "I couldn't afford to lose."

"It would have to be the last game," I agreed. "But two hundred pounds this time and we play for both garments." I waited, hoping the size of the wager would tempt her. "The odds must surely be on your side. After all, you've nearly won three times."

She sipped her drink as if considering the proposition. "All right," she said. "One last fling."

Neither of us voiced our feeling as to what was certain to happen if she lost.

I could not stop myself trembling as I set the board up once again. I cleared my mind, hoping she hadn't noticed that I had drunk only one glass of wine all night. I was determined to finish this one off quickly.

I moved my queen's pawn one square forward. She retaliated, pushing her king's pawn up two squares. I knew exactly what my next move needed to be and because of it the game only lasted eleven minutes.

I have never been so comprehensively beaten in my life. Amanda was in a totally different class to me. She anticipated my every move and had gambits I had never encountered or even read of before.

It was her turn to say "Checkmate", which she delivered with the same enigmatic smile as before, adding, "You did say the odds were on my side this time."

I lowered my head in disbelief. When I looked up again, she had already slipped that beautiful black dress back on, and was stuffing her stockings and suspenders into her evening bag. A moment later she put on her shoes.

I took out my cheque book, filled in the name "Amanda Curzon" and added the figure "£200", the date and my signature. While I was doing this she replaced the little ivory pieces on the exact squares on which they had been when she had first entered the room.

She bent over and kissed me gently on the cheek. "Thank you," she said as she placed the cheque in her handbag. "We must play again some time." I was still staring at the re-set board in disbelief when I heard the front door close behind her.

"Wait a minute," I said, rushing to the door. "How will you get home?"

I was just in time to see her running down the

steps and towards the open door of a BMW. She climbed in, allowing me one more look at those long tapering legs. She smiled as the car door was closed behind her.

The accountant strolled round to the driver's side, got in, revved up the engine and drove the champion home.

The Wine Taster

THE WINE TASTER

THE first occasion I met Sefton Hamilton was in late August last year when my wife and I were dining with Henry and Suzanne Kennedy at their home in Warwick Square.

Hamilton was one of those unfortunate men who have inherited immense wealth but not a lot more. He was able quickly to convince us that he had little time to read and no time to attend the theatre or opera. However, this did not prevent him from holding opinions on every subject from Shaw to Pavarotti, from Gorbachev to Picasso. He remained puzzled, for instance, as to what the unemployed had to complain about when their dole packet was only just less than what he was currently paying the labourers on his estate. In any case, they only spent it on bingo and drinking, he assured us.

Drinking brings me to the other dinner guest that night – Freddie Barker, the President of the Wine Society, who sat opposite my wife and unlike Hamilton hardly uttered a word. Henry had assured me over the phone that Barker had not only managed to get the Society back on to a proper financial footing but was also acknowledged as a leading authority on his subject. I looked forward to picking up useful bits of inside knowledge. Whenever Barker was allowed to get a word in edgeways, he showed enough knowledge of the topic under discussion to convince me that he would be fascinating if only Hamilton would remain silent long enough for him to speak.

While our hostess produced as a starter a spinach soufflé that melted in the mouth, Henry moved round the table pouring each of us a glass of wine.

Barker sniffed his appreciatively. "Appropriate in bicentennial year that we should be drinking an Australian Chablis of such fine vintage. I feel sure their whites will soon be making the French look to their laurels."

"Australian?" said Hamilton in disbelief as he put down his glass. "How could a nation of beer-swiggers begin to understand the first thing about producing a half decent wine?"

"I think you'll find," began Barker, "that the Australians –"

"Bicentennial indeed," Hamilton continued. "Let's face it, they're only celebrating two hundred years of parole." No one laughed except Hamilton. "I'd still pack the rest of our criminals off there, given half a chance."

No one doubted him.

Hamilton sipped the wine tentatively, like a man who fears he is about to be poisoned, then began to explain why, in his considered view, judges were far too lenient with petty criminals. I found myself concentrating more on the food than the incessant flow of my neighbour's views.

I always enjoy Beef Wellington, and Suzanne can produce a pastry that doesn't flake when cut and meat that's so tender that once one has finished a first helping, Oliver Twist comes to mind. It certainly helped me to endure Hamilton's pontificating. Barker managed to pass an appreciative comment to Henry on the quality of the claret between Hamilton's opinions on the chances of Paddy Ashdown reviving the Liberal Party and the role of Arthur Scargill in the trade union movement, allowing no one the chance to reply.

"I don't allow my staff to belong to any union," Hamilton declared, gulping down his drink. "I run a closed shop." He laughed once more at his own joke and held his empty glass high in the air as if it would be filled by magic. In fact it was filled by Henry with a discretion that shamed Hamilton – not that he noticed. In the brief pause that followed, my wife suggested that perhaps the trade union movement had been born out of a response to a genuine social need.

"Balderdash, madam," said Hamilton. "With great respect, the trade unions have been the single most important factor in the decline of Britain as we know it. They've no interest in anybody but themselves. You only have to look at Ron Todd and the whole Ford fiasco to understand that."

Suzanne began to clear the plates away and I noticed she took the opportunity to nudge Henry, who quickly changed the subject.

Moments later a raspberry meringue glazed with a thick sauce appeared. It seemed a pity to cut such a creation but Suzanne carefully divided six generous helpings like a nanny feeding her charges while

Henry uncorked a 1981 Sauternes. Barker literally licked his lips in anticipation.

"And another thing," Hamilton was saying. "The Prime Minister has got far too many Wets in her Cabinet for my liking."

"With whom would you replace them?" asked Barker innocently.

Herod would have had little trouble in convincing the list of gentlemen Hamilton proffered that the slaughter of the innocents was merely an extension of the child care programme.

Once again I became more interested in Suzanne's culinary efforts, especially as she had allowed me an indulgence: Cheddar was to be served as the final course. I knew the moment I tasted it that it had been purchased from the Alvis Brothers' farm in Keynsham; we all have to be knowledgeable about something, and Cheddar is my speciality.

To accompany the cheese, Henry supplied a port which was to be the highlight of the evening. "Sandeman 1970," he said in an aside to Barker as he poured the first drops into the expert's glass.

"Yes, of course," said Barker, holding it to his nose. "I would have known it anywhere. Typical Sandeman warmth but with real body. I hope you've laid some down, Henry," he added. "You'll enjoy it even more in your old age."

"Think you're a bit of an authority on wines, do you?" said Hamilton, the first question he had asked all evening.

"Not exactly," began Barker, "but I –"

"You're all a bunch of humbugs, the lot of you,"

interrupted Hamilton. "You sniff and you swirl, you taste and you spit, then you spout a whole lot of gobbledegook and expect us to swallow it. Body and warmth be damned. You can't take me in that easily."

"No one was trying to," said Barker with feeling.

"You've been keen to put one over on us all evening," replied Hamilton, "with your 'Yes, of course, I'd have known it anywhere' routine. Come on, admit it."

"I didn't mean to suggest –" added Barker.

"I'll prove it, if you like," said Hamilton.

The five of us stared at the ungracious guest and, for the first time that evening, I wondered what could possibly be coming next.

"I have heard it said," continued Hamilton, "that Sefton Hall boasts one of the finest wine cellars in England. It was laid down by my father and his father before him, though I confess I haven't found the time to continue the tradition." Barker nodded in belief. "But my butler knows exactly what I like. I therefore invite you, sir, to join me for lunch on the Saturday after next, when I will produce four wines of the finest vintage for your consideration. And I offer you a wager," he added, looking straight at Barker. "Five hundred pounds to fifty a bottle – tempting odds, I'm sure you'll agree – that you will be unable to name any one of them." He stared belligerently at the distinguished President of the Wine Society.

"The sum is so large that I could not consider –"

"Unwilling to take up the challenge, eh, Barker? Then you are, sir, a coward as well as a humbug."

After the embarrassing pause that followed, Barker replied, "As you wish, sir. It appears I am left with no choice but to accept your challenge."

A satisfied grin appeared on the other man's face. "You must come along as a witness, Henry," he said, turning to our host. "And why don't you bring along that author johnny?" he added, pointing at me. "Then he'll really have something to write about for a change."

From Hamilton's manner it was obvious that the feelings of our wives were not to be taken into consideration. Mary gave me a wry smile.

Henry looked anxiously towards me, but I was quite content to be an observer of this unfolding drama. I nodded my assent.

"Good," said Hamilton, rising from his place, his napkin still tucked under his collar. "I look forward to seeing the three of you at Sefton Hall on Saturday week. Shall we say twelve thirty?" He bowed to Suzanne.

"I won't be able to join you, I'm afraid," she said, clearing up any lingering doubt she might have been included in the invitation. "I always have lunch with my mother on Saturdays."

Hamilton waved a hand to signify that it did not concern him one way or the other.

After the strange guest had left we sat in silence for some moments before Henry volunteered a statement. "I'm sorry about all that," he began. "His mother and my aunt are old friends and she's asked me on several occasions to have him over to dinner. It seems no one else will."

"Don't worry," said Barker eventually. "I'll do my best not to let you down. And in return for such excellent hospitality perhaps both of you would be kind enough to leave Saturday evening free? There is," he explained, "an inn near Sefton Hall I have wanted to visit for some time: the Hamilton Arms. The food, I'm assured, is more than adequate but the wine list is . . ." he hesitated, "considered by experts to be exceptional."

Henry and I both checked our diaries and readily accepted his invitation.

I thought a great deal about Sefton Hamilton during the next ten days and awaited our lunch with a mixture of apprehension and anticipation. On the Saturday morning Henry drove the three of us down to Sefton Park and we arrived a little after twelve thirty. Actually we passed through the massive wrought-iron gates at twelve thirty precisely, but did not reach the front door of the house until twelve thirty-seven.

The great oak door was opened before we had a chance to knock by a tall elegant man in a tail coat, wing collar and black tie. He informed us that he was Adams, the butler. He then escorted us to the morning room, where we were greeted by a large log fire. Above it hung a picture of a disapproving man who I presumed was Sefton Hamilton's grandfather. On the other walls was a massive tapestry of the Battle of Waterloo and an enormous oil of the Crimean War. Antique furniture littered the room and the one sculpture on display was of a Greek figure throwing a discus. Looking around, I reflected that only the telephone belonged to the present century.

Sefton Hamilton entered the room as a gale

might hit an unhappy seaside town. Immediately he stood with his back to the fire, blocking any heat we might have been appreciating.

"Whisky!" he bellowed as Adams appeared once again. "Barker?"

"Not for me," said Barker with a thin smile.

"Ah," said Hamilton. "Want to keep your taste buds at their most sensitive, eh?"

Barker did not reply. Before we went into lunch we learned that the estate was seven thousand acres in size and had some of the finest shooting outside of Scotland. The Hall had one hundred and twelve rooms, one or two of which Hamilton had not visited since he was a child. The roof itself, he assured us finally, was an acre and a half, a statistic that will long remain in my memory as it is the same size as my garden.

The longcase clock in the corner of the room struck one. "Time for the contest to begin," declared Hamilton, and marched out of the room like a general who assumes his troops will follow him without question. We did, all the way down thirty yards of corridor to the dining room. The four of us then took our places around a seventeenth-century oak table that could comfortably have seated twenty.

Adorning the centre of the table were two Georgian decanters and two unlabelled bottles. The first bottle was filled with a clear white wine, the first decanter with a red, the second bottle with a richer white and the second decanter with a tawny red substance. In front of the four wines were four white cards. By each lay a slim bundle of fifty-pound notes.

Hamilton took his place in the large chair at the top of the table while Barker and I sat opposite each other in the centre, facing the wine, leaving Henry to occupy the final place at the far end of the table.

The butler stood one pace behind his master's chair. He nodded and four footmen appeared, bearing the first course. A fish and prawn terrine was placed in front of each of us. Adams received a nod from his master before he picked up the first bottle and began to fill Barker's glass. Barker waited for the butler to go round the table and fill the other three glasses before he began his ritual.

First he swirled the wine round while at the same time studying it carefully. Then he sniffed it. He hesitated and a surprised look came over his face. He took a sip.

"Um," he said eventually. "I confess, quite a challenge." He sniffed it again just to be sure. Then he looked up and gave a smile of satisfaction. Hamilton stared at him, his mouth slightly open, although he remained unusually silent.

Barker took one more sip. "Montagny Tête de Cuvée 1985," he declared with the confidence of an expert, "bottled by Louis Latour." We all looked towards Hamilton who, in contrast, displayed an unhappy frown.

"You're right," said Hamilton. "It was bottled by Latour. But that's about as clever as telling us that Heinz bottle tomato sauce. And as my father died in 1984 I can assure you, sir, you are mistaken." He looked round at his butler to confirm the statement. Adams's face remained inscrutable. Barker turned over the card. It read: "Chevalier Montrachet Les Demorselles 1983". He stared at the card, obviously unable to believe his eyes.

"One down and three to go," Hamilton declared, oblivious to Barker's reaction. The footmen reappeared and took away the fish plates, to replace them a few moments later with lightly cooked grouse. While its accompaniments were being served Barker did not speak. He just stared at the other three decanters, not even hearing his host inform Henry who his guests were to be for the first shoot of the season the following week. I remember that the names corresponded roughly with the ones Hamilton had suggested for his ideal Cabinet.

Barker nibbled at the grouse as he waited for Adams to fill a glass from the first decanter. He had not finished his terrine after the opening failure, only taking the occasional sip of water.

"As Adams and I spent a considerable part of our morning selecting the wines for this little challenge, let us hope you can do better this time," said Hamilton, unable to hide his satisfaction. Barker once again began to swirl the wine round. He seemed to take longer this time, sniffing it several times before putting his glass to his lips and finally sipping from it.

A smile of instant recognition appeared on his face and he did not hesitate. "Château la Louvière 1978."

"This time you have the correct year, sir, but you have insulted the wine."

Immediately Barker turned the card over and read it out incredulously: Château Lafite 1978. Even I knew that to be one of the finest clarets one might ever hope to taste. Barker lapsed into a deep silence and continued to nibble at his food.

Hamilton appeared to be enjoying the wine almost as much as the half-time score. "One hundred pounds to me, nothing to the President of the Wine Society," he reminded us. Embarrassed, Henry and I tried to keep the conversation going until the third course had been served – a lemon and lime soufflé which could not compare in presentation or subtlety with any of Suzanne's offerings.

"Shall we move on to my third challenge?" asked Hamilton crisply.

Once again, Adams picked up a decanter and began to pour the wine. I was surprised to see that he spilled a little as he filled Barker's glass.

"Clumsy oaf," barked Hamilton.

"I do apologise, sir," said Adams. He removed the spilled drop from the wooden table with a napkin. As he did so he stared at Barker with a desperate look that I felt sure had nothing to do with the spilling of the wine. However, he remained mute as he continued to circle the table.

Once again Barker went through his ritual, the swirling, the sniffing and finally the tasting. This time he took even longer. Hamilton became impatient and drummed the great Jacobean table with his podgy fingers.

"It's a Sauternes," began Barker.

"Any half-wit could tell you that," said Hamilton. "I want to know the year and the vintage."

His guest hesitated.

"Château Guiraud 1976," he said flatly.

"At least you are consistent," said Hamilton. "You're always wrong."

Barker flicked over the card.

"Château d'Yquem 1980," he said in disbelief. It

was a vintage that I had only seen at the bottom of wine lists in expensive restaurants and had never had the privilege of tasting. It puzzled me greatly that Barker could have been wrong about the Mona Lisa of wines.

Barker quickly turned towards Hamilton to protest and must have seen Adams standing behind his master, all six foot three of the man trembling, at exactly the same time I did. I wanted Hamilton to leave the room so I could ask Adams what was making him so fearful, but the owner of Sefton Hall was now in full cry.

Meanwhile Barker gazed at the butler for a moment more and, sensing his discomfort, lowered his eyes and contributed nothing else to the conversation until the port was poured some twenty minutes later.

"Your last chance to avoid complete humiliation," said Hamilton.

A cheese board, displaying several varieties, was brought round and each guest selected his choice – I stuck to a Cheddar that I could have told Hamilton had not been made in Somerset. Meanwhile the port was poured by the butler, who was now as white as a sheet. I began to wonder if he was going to faint, but somehow he managed to fill all four glasses before returning to stand a pace behind his master's chair. Hamilton noticed nothing untoward.

Barker drank the port, not bothering with any of his previous preliminaries.

"Taylors," he began.

"Agreed," said Hamilton. "But as there are only three decent suppliers of port in the world, the year can be all that matters – as you, in your exalted position, must be well aware, Mr Barker."

Freddie nodded his agreement. "Nineteen seventy-five," he said firmly, then quickly flicked the card over.

"Taylors 1927", I read upside-down.

Once again Barker turned sharply towards his host, who was rocking with laughter. The butler stared back at his master's guest with haunted eyes. Barker hesitated only for a moment before removing a cheque book from his inside pocket. He filled in the name "Sefton Hamilton" and the figure of £200. He signed it and wordlessly passed the cheque along the table to his host.

"That was only half the bargain," said Hamilton, enjoying every moment of his triumph.

Barker rose, paused and said, "I am a humbug."

"You are indeed, sir," said Hamilton.

After spending three of the most unpleasant hours of my life, I managed to escape with Henry and Freddie Barker a little after four o'clock. As Henry drove away from Sefton Hall neither of us uttered a word. Perhaps we both felt that Barker should be allowed the first comment.

"I fear, gentlemen," he said eventually, "I shall not be good company for the next few hours, and so I will, with your permission, take a brisk walk and join you both for dinner at the Hamilton Arms around seven thirty. I have booked a table for eight o'clock." Without another word, Barker signalled that Henry should bring the car to a halt and we watched as he climbed out and headed off down a country lane. Henry did not drive on until his friend was well out of sight.

My sympathies were entirely with Barker, although I remained puzzled by the whole affair. How could the President of the Wine Society make such basic mistakes? After all, I could read one page of Dickens and know it wasn't Graham Greene.

Like Dr Watson, I felt I required a fuller explanation.

Barker found us sitting round the fire in the private bar at the Hamilton Arms a little after seven thirty that night. Following his exercise, he appeared in far better spirits. He chatted about nothing consequential and didn't once mention what had taken place at lunchtime.

It must have been a few minutes later, when I turned to check the old clock above the door, that I saw Hamilton's butler seated at the bar in earnest conversation with the innkeeper. I would have thought nothing of it had I not noticed the same terrified look that I had witnessed earlier in the afternoon as he pointed in our direction. The innkeeper appeared equally anxious, as if he had been found guilty of serving half-measures by a customs and excise officer.

He picked up some menus and walked over to our table.

"We've no need for those," said Barker. "Your reputation goes before you. We are in your hands. Whatever you suggest we will happily consume."

"Thank you, sir," he said and passed our host the wine list.

Barker studied the contents inside the leather-bound covers for some time before a large smile appeared on his face. "I think you had better select the wines as well," he said, "as I have a feeling you know the sort of thing I would expect."

"Of course, sir," said the innkeeper as Freddie passed back the wine list leaving me totally mystified, remembering that this was Barker's first visit to the inn.

The innkeeper left for the kitchens while we chatted away and didn't reappear for some fifteen minutes.

"Your table is ready, gentlemen," he said, and we followed him into an adjoining dining room. There were only a dozen tables but as ours was the last to be filled there was no doubting the inn's popularity.

The innkeeper had selected a light supper of consommé, followed by thin slices of duck, almost as if he had known that we would be unable to handle another heavy meal after our lunch at the Hall.

I was also surprised to find that all the wines he had chosen were served in decanters and I assumed that the innkeeper must therefore have selected the house wines. As each was poured and consumed I admit that, to my untutored palate, they seemed far superior to those which I had drunk at Sefton Hall earlier that day. Barker certainly seemed to linger over every mouthful and on one occasion said appreciatively, "This is the real McCoy."

At the end of the evening when our table had been cleared we sat back and enjoyed a magnificent port and smoked cigars.

It was at this point that Henry mentioned Hamilton for the first time.

"Are you going to let us into the mystery of what really happened at lunch today?" he asked.

"I'm still not altogether sure myself," came back Barker's reply, "but I am certain of one thing: Mr Hamilton's father was a man who knew his wines, while his son doesn't."

I would have pressed Barker further on the subject if the innkeeper had not arrived by his side at that moment.

"An excellent meal," Barker declared. "And as for the wine – quite exceptional."

"You are kind, sir," said the innkeeper, as he handed him the bill.

My curiosity got the better of me, I'm sorry to admit, and I glanced at the bottom of the slim strip of paper. I couldn't believe my eyes – the bill came to two hundred pounds.

To my surprise, Barker only commented, "Very reasonable, considering." He wrote out a cheque and passed it over to the innkeeper. "I have only tasted Château d'Yquem 1980 once before today;" he added, "and Taylors 1927 never."

The innkeeper smiled. "I hope you enjoyed them both, sir. I feel sure you wouldn't have wanted to see them wasted on a humbug."

Barker nodded his agreement.

I watched as the innkeeper left the dining room and returned to his place behind the bar.

He passed the cheque over to Adams the butler, who studied it for a moment, smiled and then tore it into little pieces.

A Chapter of Accidents

A CHAPTER OF ACCIDENTS

WE first met Patrick Travers on our annual winter holiday to Verbier. We were waiting at the ski lift that first Saturday morning when a man who must have been in his early forties stood aside to allow Caroline to take his place, so that we could travel up together. He explained that he had already completed two runs that morning and didn't mind waiting. I thanked him and thought nothing more of it.

As soon as we reach the top my wife and I always go our separate ways, she to the A-slope to join Marcel, who only instructs advanced skiers – she has been skiing since the age of seven – I to the B-slope and any instructor who is available – I took up skiing at the age of forty-one – and frankly the B-slope is still too advanced for me though I don't dare admit as much, especially to Caroline. We always meet up again at the ski lift after completing our different runs.

That evening we bumped into Travers at the hotel bar. Since he seemed to be on his own we invited him to join us for dinner. He proved to be an amusing companion and we passed a pleasant enough evening together. He flirted politely with my wife without ever overstepping the mark and she appeared to be flattered by his attentions. Over the years I have become used to men being attracted to Caroline and I never need reminding how lucky I am. During dinner we learned that Travers was a merchant banker with an office in the City and a flat in Eaton Square. He had come to Verbier every year since he had been taken on a school trip in the late Fifties, he told us. He still prided himself on being the first on the ski lift every morning, almost always beating the local blades up and down.

Travers appeared to be genuinely interested in the fact that I ran a small West End art gallery; as it turned out, he was something of a collector himself, specialising in minor Impressionists. He promised he would drop by and see my next exhibition when he was back in London.

I assured him that he would be most welcome but never gave it a second thought. In fact I only saw Travers a couple of times over the rest of the holiday, once talking to the wife of a friend of mine who owned a gallery that specialises in oriental rugs, and later I noticed him following Caroline expertly down the treacherous A-slope.

It was six weeks later, and some minutes before I could place him that night at my gallery. I had to rack that part of one's memory which recalls names, a skill politicians rely on every day.

"Good to see you, Edward," he said. "I saw the write-up you got in the *Independent* and remembered your kind invitation to the private view."

"Glad you could make it, Patrick," I replied, remembering just in time.

"I'm not a champagne man myself," he told me, "but I'll travel a long way to see a Vuillard."

"You think highly of him?"

"Oh yes. I would compare him favourably with Pissarro and Bonnard, and he still remains one of the most underrated of the Impressionists."

"I agree," I replied. "But my gallery has felt that way about Vuillard for some considerable time."

"How much is 'The Lady at the Window'?" he asked.

"Eighty thousand pounds," I said quietly.

"It reminds me of a picture of his in the Metropolitan," he said, as he studied the reproduction in the catalogue.

I was impressed, and told Travers that the Vuillard in New York had been painted within a month of the one he so admired.

He nodded. "And the small nude?"

"Forty-seven thousand," I told him.

"Mrs Hensell, the wife of his dealer and Vuillard's second mistress, if I'm not mistaken. The French are always so much more civilised about these things than we are. But my favourite painting in this exhibition," he continued, "compares surely with the finest of his work." He turned to face the large oil of a young girl playing a piano, her mother bending to turn a page of the score.

"Magnificent," he said. "Dare I ask how much?"

"Three hundred and seventy thousand pounds," I said, wondering if such a price tag put it out of Travers's bracket.

"What a super party, Edward," said a voice from behind my shoulder.

"Percy!" I cried, turning round. "I thought you said you wouldn't be able to make it."

"Yes I did, old fellow, but I decided I couldn't sit at home alone all the time, so I've come to drown my sorrows in champagne."

"Quite right too," I said. "Sorry to hear about Diana," I added as Percy moved on. When I turned back to continue my conversation with Patrick Travers he was nowhere to be seen. I searched around the room and spotted him standing in the far corner of the gallery chatting to my wife, a glass of champagne in his hand. She was wearing an off-the-shoulder green dress that I considered a little too modern. Travers's eyes seemed to be glued to a spot a few inches below the shoulders. I would have thought nothing of it had he spoken to anyone else that evening.

The next occasion on which I saw Travers was about a week later on returning from the bank with some petty cash. Once again he was standing in front of the Vuillard oil of mother and daughter at the piano.

"Good morning, Patrick," I said as I joined him.

"I can't seem to get that picture out of my mind," he declared, as he continued to stare at the two figures.

"Understandably."

"I don't suppose you would allow me to live with them for a week or two until I can finally make up my mind? Naturally I would be quite happy to leave a deposit."

"Of course," I said. "I would require a bank

reference as well and the deposit would be twenty-five thousand pounds."

He agreed to both requests without hesitation so I asked him where he would like the picture delivered. He handed me a card which revealed his address in Eaton Square. The following morning his bankers confirmed that three hundred and seventy thousand pounds would not be a problem for their client.

Within twenty-four hours the Vuillard had been taken round to his home and hung in the dining room on the ground floor. He phoned back in the afternoon to thank me and asked if Caroline and I would care to join him for dinner; he wanted, he said, a second opinion on how the painting looked.

With three hundred and seventy thousand pounds at stake I didn't feel it was an invitation I could reasonably turn down, and in any case Caroline seemed eager to accept, explaining that she was interested to see what his house was like.

We dined with Travers the following Thursday. We turned out to be the only guests, and I remember being surprised that there wasn't a Mrs Travers or at least a resident girlfriend. He was a thoughtful host and the meal he had arranged was superb. However, I considered at the time that he seemed a little too solicitous with Caroline, although she certainly gave the impression of enjoying his undivided attention. At one point I began to wonder if either of them would have noticed if I had disappeared into thin air.

When we left Eaton Square that night Travers told me that he had almost made up his mind about the picture, which made me feel the evening had served at least some purpose.

Six days later the painting was returned to the gallery with a note attached explaining that he no longer cared for it. Travers did not elaborate on his reasons, but simply ended by saying that he hoped to drop by some time and reconsider the other Vuillards. Disappointed, I returned his deposit, but realised that customers often do come back, sometimes months, even years later.

But Travers never did.

It was about a month later that I learned why he would never return. I was lunching at the large centre table at my club, as in most all-male establishments the table reserved for members who drift in on their own. Percy Fellows was the next to enter the dining room so he took a seat opposite me. I hadn't seen him to talk to since the private view of the Vuillard exhibition and we hadn't really had much of a conversation then. Percy was one of the most respected antique dealers in England and I had once even done a successful barter with him, a Charles II writing desk in exchange for a Dutch landscape by Utrillo.

I repeated how sorry I was to learn about Diana.

"It was always going to end in divorce," he explained. "She was in and out of every bedroom in London. I was beginning to look a complete cuckold, and that bloody man Travers was the last straw."

"Travers?" I said, not understanding.

"Patrick Travers, the man named in my divorce petition. Ever come across him?"

"I know the name," I said hesitantly, wanting to

hear more before I admitted to our slight acquaintanceship.

"Funny," he said. "Could have sworn I saw him at the private view."

"But what do you mean, he was the last straw?" I asked, trying to take his mind off the opening.

"Met the bloody fellow at Ascot, didn't we? Joined us for lunch, happily drank my champagne, ate my strawberries and cream and then before the week was out had bedded my wife. But that's not the half of it."

"The half of it?"

"The man had the nerve to come round to my shop and put down a large deposit on a Georgian table. Then he invites the two of us round to dinner to see how it looks. After he's had enough time to make love to Diana he returns them both slightly soiled. You don't look too well, old fellow," said Percy suddenly. "Something wrong with the food? Never been the same since Harry left for the Carlton. I've written to the wine committee about it several times but –"

"No, I'm fine," I said. "I just need a little fresh air. Please excuse me, Percy."

It was on the walk back from my club that I decided I would have to do something about Mr Travers.

The next morning I waited for the mail to arrive and checked any envelopes addressed to Caroline. Nothing seemed untoward but then I decided that Travers wouldn't have been foolish enough to commit anything to paper. I also began to eavesdrop on her telephone conversations, but he was not among the callers, at least not while I was at home. I even checked the mileometer on her Mini to see if she had driven any long distances, but then Eaton Square isn't all that far. It's often what you don't do that gives the game away, I decided: we didn't make love for a fortnight, and she didn't comment.

I continued to watch Caroline more carefully over the next fortnight but it became obvious to me that Travers must have tired of her about the same time as he had returned the Vuillard. This only made me more angry.

I then formed a plan of revenge that seemed quite extraordinary to me at the time and I assumed that in a matter of days I would get over it, even forget it. But I didn't. If anything, the idea grew into an obsession. I began to convince myself that it was my bounden duty to do away with Travers before he besmirched any more of my friends.

I have never in my life knowingly broken the law. Parking fines annoy me, dropped litter offends me and I pay my VAT on the same day the frightful buff envelope drops through the letterbox.

Nevertheless once I'd decided what had to be done I set about my task meticulously. At first I had considered shooting Travers until I discovered how hard it is to get a gun licence and that if I did the job properly, he would end up feeling very little pain, which wasn't what I had planned for him; then poisoning crossed my mind – but that requires a witnessed prescription and I still wouldn't be able to watch the long slow death I desired. Then strangling, which I decided would necessitate too much courage – and in any case he was a bigger man than me so *I* might end up being the one who was strangled. Then drowning, which could take years to get the man near any water and then I might not be able to hang around to make sure he went under for the third time. I even gave some thought to running over the damned man, but dropped that idea when I realised opportunity would be almost nil and besides, I wouldn't be left any time to check if he was dead. I was quickly becoming aware just how hard it is to kill someone – and get away with it.

I sat awake at night reading the biographies of murderers, but as they had all been caught and found guilty that didn't fill me with much confidence. I turned to detective novels which always seemed to allow for a degree of coincidence, luck and surprise that I was unwilling to risk, until I came across a rewarding line from Conan Doyle: "Any intended victim who has a regular routine immediately makes himself more vulnerable". And then I recalled one routine of which Travers was particularly proud. It required a further six-month wait on my part but that also gave me more time to perfect my plan. I used the enforced wait well because whenever Caroline was away for more than twenty-four hours, I booked in for a skiing lesson on the dry slope at Harrow.

I found it surprisingly easy to discover when Travers would be returning to Verbier, and I was able to organise the winter holiday so that our paths would cross for only three days, a period of time quite sufficient for me to commit my first crime.

Caroline and I arrived in Verbier on the second Friday in January. She had commented on the state of my nerves more than once over the Christmas period, and hoped the holiday would help me relax. I could hardly explain to her that it was the thought of the holiday that was making me so tense. It didn't help when she asked me on the plane to Switzerland if I thought Travers might be there this year.

On the first morning after our arrival we took the ski lift up at about ten thirty and, once we had reached the top, Caroline duly reported to Marcel. As she departed with him for the A-slope I returned to the B-slope to work on my own. As always we agreed to meet back at the ski lift or, if we missed each other, at least for lunch.

During the days that followed I went over and over the plan I had perfected in my mind and practised so diligently at Harrow until I felt sure it was foolproof. By the end of the first week I had convinced myself I was ready.

The night before Travers was due to arrive I was the last to leave the slopes. Even Caroline commented on how much my skiing had improved and she suggested to Marcel that I was ready for the A-slope with its sharper bends and steeper inclines.

"Next year, perhaps," I told her, trying to make light of it, and returned to the B-slope.

During the final morning I skied over the first mile of the course again and again, and became so preoccupied with my work that I quite forgot to join Caroline for lunch.

In the afternoon I checked and rechecked the placing of every red flag marking the run, and once

I was convinced the last skier had left the slope for the evening I collected about thirty of the flags and replaced them at intervals I had carefully worked out. My final task was to check the prepared patch before building a large mound of snow some twenty paces above the chosen spot. Once my preparations were complete I skied slowly down the mountain in the fading light.

"Are you trying to win an Olympic gold medal or something?" Caroline asked me when I eventually got back to our room. I closed the bathroom door so she couldn't expect a reply.

Travers checked in to the hotel an hour later.

I waited until the early evening before I joined him at the bar for a drink. He seemed a little nervous when he first saw me, but I quickly put him at ease. His old self-confidence soon returned, which only made me more determined to carry out my plan. I left him at the bar a few minutes before Caroline came down for dinner so that she would not see the two of us together. Innocent surprise would be necessary once the deed had been done.

"Unlike you to eat so little, especially as you missed your lunch," Caroline commented as we left the dining room that night.

I made no comment as we passed Travers seated at the bar, his hand on the knee of another innocent middle-aged woman.

I did not sleep for one second that night and I crept out of bed just before six the next morning, careful not to wake Caroline. Everything was laid out on the bathroom floor just as I had left it the night before. A few moments later I was dressed and ready. I walked down the back stairs of the hotel, avoiding the lift, and crept out by the "fire exit", realising for the first time what a thief must feel like. I had a woollen cap pulled well down over my ears and a pair of snow goggles covering my eyes: not even Caroline would have recognised me.

I arrived at the bottom of the ski lift forty minutes before it was due to open. As I stood alone behind the little shed that housed the electrical machinery to work the lift I realised that everything now depended on Travers's sticking to his routine. I wasn't sure I could go through with it if my plan had to be moved on to the following day. As I waited, I stamped my feet in the freshly fallen snow, and slapped my arms around my chest to keep warm. Every few moments I kept peering round the corner of the building in the hope that I would see him striding towards me. At last a speck appeared at the bottom of the hill by the side of the road, a pair of skis resting on the man's shoulders. But what if it didn't turn out to be Travers?

I stepped out from behind the shed a few moments later to join the warmly wrapped man. It *was* Travers and he could not hide his surprise at seeing me standing there. I started up a casual conversation about being unable to sleep, and how I thought I might as well put in a few runs before the rush began. Now all I needed was the ski lift to start up on time. A few minutes after seven an engineer arrived and the vast oily mechanism cranked into action.

We were the first two to take our places on those little seats before heading up and over the deep ravine. I kept turning back to check there was still no one else in sight.

"I usually manage to complete a full run even before the second person arrives," Travers told me when the lift had reached its highest point. I looked back again to be sure we were now well out of sight of the engineer working the lift, then peered down some two hundred feet and wondered what it would be like to land head first in the ravine. I began to feel dizzy and wished I hadn't looked down.

The ski lift jerked slowly on up the icy wire until we finally reached the landing point.

"Damn," I said, as we jumped off our little seats. "Marcel isn't here."

"Never is at this time," said Travers, making off towards the advanced slope. "Far too early for him."

"I don't suppose you would come down with me?" I said, calling after Travers.

He stopped and looked back suspiciously.

"Caroline thinks I'm ready to join you," I explained, "but I'm not so sure and would value a second opinion. I've broken my own record for the B-slope several times, but I wouldn't want to make a fool of myself in front of my wife."

"Well, I –"

"I'd ask Marcel if he were here. And in any case you're the best skier I know."

"Well, if you –" he began.

"Just the once, then you can spend the rest of your holiday on the A-slope. You could even treat the run as a warm-up."

"Might make a change, I suppose," he said.

"Just the once," I repeated. "That's all I'll need. Then you'll be able to tell me if I'm good enough."

"Shall we make a race of it?" he said, taking me

by surprise just as I began clamping on my skis. I couldn't complain; all the books on murder had warned me to be prepared for the unexpected. "That's one way we can find out if you're ready," he added cockily.

"If you insist. Don't forget, I'm older and less experienced than you," I reminded him. I checked my skis quickly because I knew I had to start off in front of him.

"But you know the B-course backwards," he retorted. " I've never even seen it before."

"I'll agree to a race, but only if you'll consider a wager," I replied.

For the first time I could see I had caught his interest. "How much?" he asked.

"Oh, nothing so vulgar as money," I said. "The winner gets to tell Caroline the truth."

"The truth?" he said, looking puzzled.

"Yes," I replied, and shot off down the hill before he could respond. I got a good start as I skied in and out of the red flags, but looking back over my shoulder I could see he had recovered quickly and was already chasing hard after me. I realised that it was vital for me to stay in front of him for the first third of the course, but I could already feel him cutting down my lead.

After half a mile of swerving and driving he shouted, "You'll have to go a lot faster than that if you hope to beat me." His arrogant boast only pushed me to stay ahead but I kept the lead only because of my advantage of knowing every twist and turn during that first mile. Once I was sure that I would reach the vital newly marked route before he could I began to relax. After all, I had practised over the next two hundred metres fifty times a day for the last ten days, but I was only too aware that this time was the only one that mattered.

I glanced over my shoulder to see he was now about thirty metres behind me. I began to slow slightly as we approached the prepared ice patch, hoping he wouldn't notice or would think I'd lost my nerve. I held back even more when I reached the top of the patch until I could almost feel the sound of his breathing. Then, quite suddenly, the moment before I would have hit the ice I ploughed my skis and came to a complete halt in the mound of snow I had built the previous night. Travers sailed past me at about forty miles an hour, and seconds later flew high into the air over the ravine with a scream I will never forget. I couldn't get myself to look over the edge as I knew he must have broken every bone in his body the moment he hit the snow some hundred feet below.

I carefully levelled the mound of snow that had saved my life and then clambered back up the mountain as fast as I could go, gathering the thirty flags that had heralded my false route. Then I skied from side to side replacing them in their correct positions on the B-slope, some one hundred metres above my carefully prepared ice patch. Once each one was back in place I skied on down the hill, feeling like an Olympic champion. When I reached the base of the slope I pulled up my hood to cover my head and didn't remove my snow goggles. I unstrapped my skis and walked casually towards the hotel. I re-entered the building by the rear door and was back in bed by seven forty.

I tried to control my breathing but it was some

time before my pulse had returned to normal. Caroline woke a few minutes later, turned over and put her arms round me.

"Ugh," she said, "you're frozen. Have you been sleeping without the covers on?"

I laughed. "You must have pulled them off during the night."

"Go and have a hot bath."

After I had had a quick bath we made love and I dressed a second time, double-checking that I had left no clues of my early flight before going down to breakfast.

As Caroline was pouring my second cup of coffee, I heard the ambulance siren at first coming from the town and then later returning.

"Hope it wasn't a bad accident," my wife said, as she continued to pour her coffee.

"What?" I said, a little too loudly, glancing up from the previous day's *Times*.

"The siren, silly. There must have been an accident on the mountain. Probably Travers," she said.

"Travers?" I said, even more loudly.

"Patrick Travers. I saw him at the bar last night. I didn't mention it to you because I know you don't care for him."

"But why Travers?" I asked nervously.

"Doesn't he always claim he's the first on the slope every morning? Even beats the instructors up to the top."

"Does he?" I said.

"You must remember. We were going up for the first time the day we met him when he was already on his third run."

"Was he?"

"You are being dim this morning, Edward. Did you get out of bed the wrong side?" she asked, laughing.

I didn't reply.

"Well, I only hope it *is* Travers," Caroline added, sipping her coffee. "I never did like the man."

"Why not?" I asked, somewhat taken aback.

"He once made a pass at me," she said casually.

I stared across at her, unable to speak.

"Aren't you going to ask what happened?"

"I'm so stunned I don't know what to say," I replied.

"He was all over me at the gallery that night and then invited me out to lunch after we had dinner with him. I told him to get lost," Caroline said. She touched me gently on the hand. "I've never mentioned it to you before because I thought it might have been the reason he returned the Vuillard, and that only made me feel guilty."

"But it's me who should feel guilty," I said, fumbling with a piece of toast.

"Oh, no, darling, you're not guilty of anything. In any case, if I ever decided to be unfaithful it wouldn't be with a lounge lizard like that. Good heavens no. Diana had already warned me what to expect from him. Not my style at all."

I sat there thinking of Travers on his way to a morgue, or even worse, still buried under the snow, knowing there was nothing I could do about it.

"You know, I think the time really has come for you to tackle the A-slope," Caroline said as we finished breakfast. "Your skiing has improved beyond words."

"Yes," I replied, more than a little preoccupied.

I hardly spoke another word as we made our way together to the foot of the mountain.

"Are you all right, darling?" Caroline asked as we travelled up side by side on the lift.

"Fine," I said, unable to look down into the ravine as we reached the highest point. Was Travers still down there, or already in the morgue?

"Stop looking like a frightened child. After all the work you've put in this week you're more than ready to join me," she said reassuringly.

I smiled weakly. When we reached the top, I jumped off the ski lift just a moment too early, and knew immediately I took my second step that I had sprained an ankle.

I received no sympathy from Caroline. She was convinced I was putting it on in order to avoid attempting the advanced run. She swept past me and sped on down the mountain while I returned in ignominy via the lift. When I reached the bottom I glanced towards the engineer but he didn't give me a second look. I hobbled over to the First Aid post and checked in. Caroline joined me a few minutes later.

I explained to her that the duty orderly thought it might be a fracture and it had been suggested I report to the hospital immediately.

Caroline frowned, removed her skis and went off to find a taxi to take us to the hospital. It wasn't a long journey but it was one the taxi driver evidently had done many times before from the way he took the slippery bends.

"I ought to be able to dine out on this for about a

year," Caroline promised me as we entered the double doors of the hospital.

"Would you be kind enough to wait outside, madam?" asked a male orderly as I was ushered into the X-ray room.

"Yes, but will I ever see my poor husband again?" she mocked as the door was closed in front of her.

I entered a room full of sophisticated machinery presided over by an expensively dressed doctor. I told him what I thought was wrong with me and he lifted the offending foot gently up on to an X-ray machine. Moments later he was studying the large negative.

"There's no fracture there," he assured me, pointing to the bone. "But if you are still in any pain it might be wise for me to bind the ankle up tightly." The doctor then pinned my X-ray next to five others hanging from a rail.

"Am I the sixth person already today?" I asked, looking up at the row of X-rays.

"No, no," he said, laughing. "The other five are all the same man. I think he must have tried to fly over the ravine, the fool."

"Over the ravine?"

"Yes, showing off, I suspect," he said as he began to bind my ankle. "We get one every year but this poor fellow broke both his legs and an arm, and will have a nasty scar on his face to remind him of his stupidity. Lucky to be alive in my opinion."

"Lucky to be alive?" I repeated weakly.

"Yes, but only because he didn't know what he was doing. My fourteen-year-old skis over that ravine and can land like a seagull on water. He, on the other hand," the doctor pointed to the X-rays, "won't be skiing again this holiday. In fact, he won't be walking for at least six months."

"Really?" I said.

"And as for you," he added, after he finished binding me up, "just rest the ankle in ice every three hours and change the bandage once a day. You should be back on the slopes again in a couple of days, three at the most."

"We're flying back this evening," I told him as I gingerly got to my feet.

"Good timing," he said, smiling.

I hobbled happily out of the X-ray room to find Caroline head down in *Elle*.

"You look pleased with yourself," she said, looking up.

"I am. It turns out to be nothing worse than two broken legs, a broken arm and a scar on the face."

"How stupid of me," said Caroline, "I thought it was a simple sprain."

"Not me," I told her. "Travers – the accident this morning, you remember? The ambulance. Still, they assure me he'll live," I added.

"Pity," she said, linking her arm through mine. "After all the trouble you took, I was rather hoping you'd succeed."

The Loophole

"THAT isn't the version I heard," said Philip.

One of the club members seated at the bar glanced round at the sound of raised voices, but when he saw who was involved only smiled and continued his conversation.

The Haslemere Golf Club was fairly crowded that Saturday morning. And just before lunch it was often difficult to find a seat in the spacious clubhouse.

Two of the members had already ordered their second round and settled themselves in the alcove overlooking the first hole long before the room began to fill up. Philip Masters and Michael Gilmour had finished their Saturday morning game earlier than usual and now seemed engrossed in conversation.

"And what did you hear?" asked Michael Gilmour quietly, but in a voice that carried.

"That you weren't altogether blameless in the matter."

"I most certainly was," said Michael. "What are you suggesting?"

"I'm not suggesting anything," said Philip. "But don't forget, you can't fool me. I employed you myself once and I've known you for far too long to accept everything you say at face value."

"I wasn't trying to fool anyone," said Michael. "It's common knowledge that I lost my job. I've never suggested otherwise."

"Agreed. But what isn't common knowledge is *how* you lost your job and why you haven't been able to find a new one."

"I haven't been able to find a new one for the simple reason jobs aren't that easy to come by at the moment. And by the way, it's not my fault you're a success story and a bloody millionaire."

"And it's not my fault that you're penniless and always out of work. The truth is that jobs are easy enough to come by for someone who can supply references from his last employer."

"Just what are you hinting at?" said Michael.

"I'm not hinting at anything."

Several members had stopped taking part in the conversation in front of them as they tried to listen to the one going on behind them.

"What I am saying," Philip continued, "is that no one will employ you for the simple reason that you can't find anyone who will supply you with a reference – and everybody knows it."

Everybody didn't know it, which explained why most people in the room were now trying to find out.

"I was made redundant," insisted Michael.

"In your case redundant was just a euphemism for sacked. No one pretended otherwise at the time."

"I was made redundant," repeated Michael, "for the simple reason that the company profits turned out to be a little disappointing this year."

"A little disappointing? That's rich. They were non-existent."

"Simply because we lost one or two of our major accounts to rivals."

"Rivals who, I'm informed, were only too happy to pay for a little inside information."

By now most members of the club had cut short their own conversations as they leaned, twisted, turned and bent in an effort to capture every word coming from the two men seated in the window alcove of the club room.

"The loss of those accounts was fully explained in the report to shareholders at this year's AGM," said Michael.

"But was it explained to those same shareholders how a former employee could afford to buy a new car only a matter of days after being sacked?" pursued Philip. "A second car, I might add." Philip took a sip of his tomato juice.

"It wasn't a new car," said Michael defensively. "It was a second-hand Mini and I bought it with part of my redundancy pay when I had to return the company car. And in any case, you know Carol needs her own car for the job at the bank."

"Frankly, I am amazed Carol has stuck it for so long as she has after all you've put her through."

"All I've put her through; what are you implying?" asked Michael.

"I am not *implying* anything," Philip retorted. "But the fact is that a certain young woman who shall remain nameless" – this piece of information seemed to disappoint most eavesdroppers – "also became redundant at about the same time, not to mention pregnant."

The barman had not been asked for a drink for nearly seven minutes, and by now there were few members still affecting not to be listening to the altercation between the two men. Some were even staring in open disbelief.

"But I hardly knew her," protested Michael.

"As I said, that's not the version I heard. And what's more I'm told the child bears a striking resemblance –"

"That's going too far –"

"Only if you have nothing to hide," said Philip grimly.

"You know I've nothing to hide."

"Not even the blonde hairs Carol found all over the back seat of the new Mini. The girl at work was a blonde, wasn't she?"

"Yes, but those hairs came from a golden retriever."

"You don't have a golden retriever."

"I know, but the dog belonged to the last owner."

"That bitch didn't belong to the last owner, and I refuse to believe Carol fell for that old chestnut."

"She believed it because it was the truth."

"The truth, I fear, is something you lost contact with a long time ago. You were sacked, first because you couldn't keep your hands off anything in a skirt under forty, and second, because you couldn't keep your fingers out of the till. I ought to know. Don't forget I had to get rid of you for the same reasons."

Michael jumped up, his cheeks almost the colour of Philip's tomato juice. He raised his clenched fist and was about to take a swing at Philip when Colonel Mather, the club president, appeared at his side.

"Good morning, sir," said Philip calmly, rising for the Colonel.

"Good morning, Philip," the Colonel barked. "Don't you think this little misunderstanding has gone quite far enough?"

"Little misunderstanding?" protested Michael. "Didn't you hear what he's been saying about me?"

"Every word, unfortunately, like any other member present," said the Colonel. Turning back to Philip, he added, "Perhaps you two should shake hands like good fellows and call it a day."

"Shake hands with that philandering, double-crossing shyster? Never," said Philip. "I tell you, Colonel, he's not fit to be a member of this club, and I can assure you that you've only heard half the story."

Before the Colonel could attempt another round of diplomacy Michael sprang on Philip and it took three men younger than the club president to prise them apart. The Colonel immediately ordered both men off the premises, warning them that their conduct would be reported to the house committee at its next monthly meeting. And until that meeting had taken place, they were both suspended.

The club secretary, Jeremy Howard, escorted the two men off the premises and watched Philip get into his Rolls-Royce and drive sedately down the drive and out through the gates. He had to wait on the steps of the club for several minutes before Michael departed in his Mini. He appeared to be sitting in the front seat writing something. When he had eventually passed through the club gates, the secretary turned on his heels and made his way back to the bar. What they did to each other after they left the grounds was none of his business.

Back in the clubhouse, the secretary found that the conversation had not returned to the likely winner of the President's Putter, the seeding of the Ladies' Handicap Cup, or who might be prevailed upon to sponsor the Youth Tournament that year.

"They seemed in a jolly enough mood when I passed them on the sixteenth hole earlier this morning," the club captain informed the Colonel.

The Colonel admitted to being mystified. He had known both men since the day they joined the club nearly fifteen years before. They weren't bad lads, he assured the captain; in fact he rather liked them. They had played a round of golf every Saturday morning for as long as anyone could remember, and never a cross word had been known to pass between them.

"Pity," said the Colonel. "I was hoping to ask Masters to sponsor the Youth Tournament this year."

"Good idea, but I can't see you pulling that off now."

"I can't imagine what they thought they were up to."

"Can it simply be that Philip is such a success story and Michael has fallen on hard times?" suggested the captain.

"No, there's more to it than that," replied the

Colonel. "This morning's little episode requires a fuller explanation," he added sagely.

Everyone in the club was aware that Philip Masters had built up his own business from scratch after he had left his first job as a kitchen salesman. "Ready-Fit Kitchens" had started in a shed at the end of Philip's garden and ended up in a factory on the other side of town which employed over three hundred people. After Ready-Fit went public the financial press speculated that Philip's shares alone had to be worth a couple of million. When five years later the company was taken over by the John Lewis Partnership, it became public knowledge that Philip had walked away from the deal with a cheque for seventeen million pounds and a five-year service contract that would have pleased a pop star. Some of the windfall had been spent on a magnificent Georgian house in sixty acres of woodland just outside Haslemere: he could even see the golf course from his bedroom. Philip had been married for over twenty years and his wife Sally was chairman of the regional branch of the Save the Children Fund and a JP. Their son had just won a place at St Anne's College, Oxford.

Michael was the boy's godfather.

Michael Gilmour could not have been a greater contrast. On leaving school, where Philip had been his closest friend, he had drifted from job to job. He started out as a trainee with Watneys, but lasted only a few months before moving on to work as a rep with a publishing company. Like Philip, he married his childhood sweetheart, Carol West, the daughter of a local doctor.

When their own daughter was born, Carol

complained about the hours Michael spent away from home so he left publishing and signed on as a distribution manager with a local soft drinks firm. He lasted for a couple of years until his deputy was promoted over him as area manager, at which decision Michael left in a huff. After his first spell on the dole, Michael joined a grain-packing company, but found he was allergic to corn and, having been supplied with a medical certificate to prove it, collected his first redundancy cheque. He then joined Philip as a Ready-Fit Kitchens rep but left without explanation within a month of the company being taken over. Another spell of unemployment followed before he took up the job of sales manager with a company that made microwave ovens. He seemed to have settled down at last until, without warning, he was made redundant. It was true that the company profits had been halved that year, while the company directors were sorry to see Michael go – or that was how it was expressed in their in-house magazine.

Carol was unable to hide her distress when Michael was made redundant for the fourth time. They could have done with the extra cash now that their daughter had been offered a place at art school.

Philip was the girl's godfather.

"What are you going to do about it?" asked Carol anxiously, when Michael had told her what had taken place at the club.

"There's only one thing I can do," he replied. "After all, I have my reputation to consider. I shall sue the bastard."

"That's a terrible way to talk about your oldest friend. And anyway we can't afford to go to law," said Carol. "Philip's a millionaire and we're penniless."

"Can't be helped," said Michael. "I'll have to go through with it, even if it means selling up everything."

"And even if the rest of your family has to suffer along with you?"

"None of us will suffer when he ends up paying my costs plus massive damages."

"But you could *lose*," said Carol. "Then we would end up with nothing – worse than nothing."

"That's not possible," said Michael. "He made the mistake of saying all those things in front of witnesses. There must have been over fifty members in the clubhouse this morning, including the president of the club and the editor of the local paper, and they couldn't have failed to hear every word."

Carol remained unconvinced, and she was relieved that during the next few days Michael didn't mention Philip's name once. She hoped that her husband had come to his senses and the whole affair was best forgotten.

But then the *Haslemere Chronicle* decided to print its version of the quarrel between Michael and Philip. Under the headline "Fight breaks out at golf club" came a carefully worded account of what had taken place on the previous Saturday. The editor of the *Haslemere Chronicle* knew only too well that the conversation itself was unprintable unless he also wanted to be sued, but he managed to include enough innuendo in the article to give a full flavour of what had happened that morning.

"That's the final straw," said Michael, when he finished reading the article for a third time. Carol realised that nothing she could say or do was going to stop her husband now.

The following Monday, Michael contacted a local solicitor, Reginald Lomax, who had been at school with them both. Armed with the article, Michael briefed Lomax on the conversation that the *Chronicle* had felt injudicious to publish in any great detail. Michael also gave Lomax his own detailed account of what had happened at the club that morning, and handed him four pages of handwritten notes to back his claims up.

Lomax studied the notes carefully.

"When did you write these?"

"In my car, immediately after we were suspended."

"That was circumspect of you," said Lomax. "Most circumspect." He stared quizzically at his client over the top of his half-moon spectacles. Michael made no comment. "Of course you must be aware that the law is an expensive pastime," Lomax continued. "Suing for slander will not come cheap, and even with evidence as strong as this" – he tapped the notes in front of him – "you could still lose. Slander depends so much on what other people remember or, more important, will admit to remembering."

"I'm well aware of that," said Michael. "But I'm determined to go through with it. There were over fifty people in the club within earshot that morning."

"So be it," said Lomax. "Then I shall require five thousand pounds in advance as a contingency fee to cover all the immediate costs and the preparations for a court case." For the first time Michael looked hesitant.

"Returnable, of course, but only if you win the case."

Michael removed his cheque book and wrote out a figure which, he reflected, would only just be covered by the remainder of his redundancy pay.

The writ for slander against Philip Masters was issued the next morning by Lomax, Davis and Lomax.

A week later the writ was accepted by another firm of solicitors in the same town, actually in the same building.

Back at the club, debate on the rights and wrongs of Gilmour v. Masters did not subside as the weeks passed.

Club members whispered furtively among themselves whether they might be called to give evidence at the trial. Several had already received letters from Lomax, Davis and Lomax requesting statements about what they could recall being said by the two men that morning. A good many pleaded amnesia or deafness but a few turned in graphic accounts of the quarrel. Encouraged, Michael pressed on, much to Carol's dismay.

One morning about a month later, after Carol had left for the bank, Michael Gilmour received a call from Reginald Lomax. The defendant's solicitors, he was informed, had requested a "without prejudice" consultation.

"Surely you're not surprised by that after all the evidence we've collected?" Michael replied.

"It's only a consultation," Lomax reminded him.

"Consultation or no consultation I won't settle for less than one hundred thousand pounds."

"Well, I don't even know that they –" began Lomax.

"I do, and I also know that for the last eleven weeks I haven't been able to even get an interview for a job because of that bastard," Michael said with contempt. "Nothing less than one hundred thousand pounds, do you hear me?"

"I think you are being a trifle optimistic, in the circumstances," said Lomax. "But I'll call you and let you know the other side's response as soon as the meeting has taken place."

Michael told Carol the good news that evening, but like Reginald Lomax she was sceptical. The ringing of the phone interrupted their discussion on the subject. Michael, with Carol standing by his side, listened carefully to Lomax's report. Philip, it seemed, was willing to settle for twenty-five thousand pounds and had agreed to paying both sides' costs.

Carol nodded her grateful acceptance, but Michael only repeated that Lomax was to hold out for nothing less than one hundred thousand. "Can't you see that Philip's already worked out what it's going to cost him if this case ends up in court? And he knows only too well that I won't give in."

Carol and Lomax remained unconvinced. "It's much more touch and go than you realise," the solicitor told him. "A High Court jury might consider the words were only meant as banter."

"Banter? But what about the fight that followed the banter?" said Michael.

"Started by you," Lomax pointed out. "Twenty-five thousand is a good figure in the circumstances," he added.

Michael refused to budge, and ended the conversation by repeating his demand for one hundred thousand pounds.

Two weeks passed before the other side offered fifty thousand in exchange for a quick settlement. This time Lomax was not surprised when Michael rejected the offer out of hand. "Quick settlement be damned. I've told you I won't consider less than a hundred thousand." Lomax knew by now that any plea for prudence was going to fall on deaf ears.

It took three more weeks and several more phone calls between solicitors before the other side accepted that they were going to have to pay the full one hundred thousand pounds. Reginald Lomax rang Michael to inform him of the news late one evening, trying to make it sound as if he had scored a personal triumph. He assured Michael that the necessary papers could be drawn up immediately and the settlement signed in a matter of days.

"Naturally all your costs will be covered," he added.

"Naturally," said Michael.

"So all that is left for you to do now is agree on a statement."

A short statement was penned and, with the agreement of both sides, issued to the *Haslemere Chronicle*. The paper printed the contents the following Friday on its front page. "The writ for slander between Gilmour and Masters," the

Chronicle reported, "has been withdrawn with the agreement of both sides but only after a substantial out-of-court settlement by the defendant. Philip Masters has withdrawn unreservedly what was said at the club that morning and has given an unconditional apology; he has also made a promise that he will never repeat the words used again. Mr Masters has paid the plaintiff's costs in full."

Philip wrote to the Colonel the same day, admitting perhaps he had had a little too much to drink on the morning in question. He regretted his impetuous outburst, apologised and assured the club's president it would never happen again.

Carol was the only one who seemed to be saddened by the outcome.

"What's the matter, darling?" asked Michael. "We've won, and what's more it's solved our financial problems."

"I know," said Carol, "but is it worth losing your closest friend for one hundred thousand pounds?"

On the following Saturday morning Michael was pleased to find an envelope among his morning post with the Golf Club crest on the flap. He opened it nervously and pulled out a single sheet of paper. It read:

Dear Mr Gilmour,

At the monthly committee meeting held last Wednesday Colonel Mather raised the matter of your behaviour in the clubhouse on the morning of Saturday, April 16th.

It was decided to minute the complaints of several members, but on this occasion only to issue a severe reprimand to you both. Should a similar incident occur in the future, loss of membership would be automatic.

The temporary suspension issued by Colonel Mather on April 16th is now lifted.

Yours sincerely,

Jeremy Howard

Jeremy Howard (Secretary)

"I'm off to do the shopping," shouted Carol from the top of the stairs. "What are your plans for the morning?"

"I'm going to have a round of golf," said Michael, folding up the letter.

"Good idea," said Carol to herself as she wondered whom Michael would find to play against in the future.

Quite a few members noticed Michael and Philip teeing up at the first hole that Saturday morning. The club captain commented to the Colonel that he was glad to observe that the quarrel had been sorted out to everyone's satisfaction.

"Not to mine," said the Colonel under his breath. "You can't get drunk on tomato juice."

"I wonder what the devil they can be talking about?" the club captain said as he stared at them both through the bay windows. The Colonel raised his binoculars to take a closer look at the two men.

"How could you possibly miss a four-foot putt, dummy?" asked Michael when they had reached the first green. "You must be drunk again."

"As you well know," replied Philip, "I never drink before dinner, and I therefore suggest that your allegation that I am drunk again is nothing less than slander."

"Yes, but where are your witnesses?" said Michael as they moved up on to the second tee. "I had over fifty, don't forget."

Both men laughed.

Their conversation ranged over many subjects as they played the first eight holes, never once touching on their past quarrel until they reached the ninth green, the farthest point from the club-house. They both checked to see there was no one within earshot. The nearest player was still putting out some two hundred yards behind them on the eighth hole. It was then that Michael removed a bulky brown envelope from his golf bag and handed it over to Philip.

"Thank you," said Philip, dropping the package into his own golf bag as he removed a putter. "As neat a little operation as I've been involved in for a long time," Philip added as he addressed the ball.

"I end up with forty thousand pounds," said Michael grinning, "while you lose nothing at all."

"Only because I pay tax at the highest rate and can therefore claim the loss as a legitimate business expense," said Philip, "and I wouldn't have been able to do that if I hadn't once employed you."

"And I, as a successful litigant, need pay no tax at all on damages received in a civil case."

"A loophole that even this Chancellor hasn't caught on to," said Philip.

"Even though it went to Reggie Lomax, I was sorry about the solicitors' fees," added Michael.

"No problem, old fellow. They're also one hundred per cent claimable against tax. So as you see, I didn't lose a penny and you ended up with forty thousand pounds tax free."

"And nobody the wiser," said Michael, laughing.

The Colonel put his binoculars back into their case.

"Had your eye on this year's winner of the President's Putter, Colonel?" asked the club captain.

"No," the Colonel replied. "The certain sponsor of this year's Youth Tournament."

Christina Rosenthal

THE rabbi knew he couldn't hope to begin on his sermon until he'd read the letter. He had been sitting at his desk in front of a blank sheet of paper for over an hour and still couldn't come up with a first sentence. Lately he had been unable to concentrate on a task he had carried out every Friday evening for the last thirty years. They must have realised by now that he was no longer up to it. He took the letter out of the envelope and slowly unfolded the pages. Then he pushed his half-moon spectacles up the bridge of his nose and started to read.

My dear Father,

"Jew boy! Jew boy! Jew boy!" were the first words I ever heard her say as I ran past her on the first lap of the race. She was standing behind the railing at the beginning of the home straight, hands cupped around her lips to be sure I couldn't miss the chant. She must have come from another school because I didn't recognise her, but it only took a fleeting glance to see that it was Greg Reynolds who was standing by her side.

After five years of having to tolerate his snide comments

and bullying at school all I wanted to retaliate with was, "Nazi, Nazi, Nazi," but you had always taught me to rise above such provocation.

I tried to put them both out of my mind as I moved into the second lap. I had dreamed for years of winning the mile in the West Mount High School championships, and I was determined not to let them do anything to stop me.

As I came into the back straight a second time I took a more careful look at her. She was standing amid a cluster of friends who were wearing the scarves of Marianapolis Convent. She must have been about sixteen, and as slim as a willow. I wonder if you would have chastised me had I only shouted, "No breasts, no breasts, no breasts," in the hope it might at least provoke the boy standing next to her into a fight. Then I would have been able to tell you truthfully that he had thrown the first punch but the moment you had learned that it was Greg Reynolds you would have realised how little provocation I needed.

As I reached the back straight I once again prepared myself for the chants. Chanting at track meetings had become fashionable in the late 1950s when "Zat-o-pek, Zat-o-pek, Zat-o-pek" had been roared in adulation across running stadiums around the world for the great Czech champion. Not for me was there to be the shout of "Ros-en-thal, Ros-en-thal, Ros-en-thal" as I came into earshot.

"Jew boy! Jew boy! Jew boy!" she said, sounding like a gramophone record that had got stuck. Her friend Greg, who would nowadays be described as a preppie, began laughing. I knew he had put her up to it, and how I would like to have removed that smug grin from his face. I reached the half-mile mark in two minutes seventeen seconds, comfortably inside the pace necessary to break the school record, and I felt that was the best way to put the taunting girl and that

fascist Reynolds in their place. I couldn't help thinking at the time how unfair it all was. I was a real Canadian, born and bred in this country, while she was just an immigrant. After all, you, Father, had escaped from Hamburg in 1937 and started with nothing. Her parents did not land on these shores until 1949, by which time you were a respected figure in the community.

I gritted my teeth and tried to concentrate. Zatopek had written in his autobiography that no runner can afford to lose his concentration during a race. When I reached the penultimate bend the inevitable chanting began again, but this time it only made me speed up and even more determined to break that record. Once I was back in the safety of the home straight I could hear some of my friends roaring, "Come on, Benjamin, you can do it," and the timekeeper called out, "Three twenty-three, three twenty-four, three twenty-five" as I passed the bell to begin the last lap.

I knew that the record – four thirty-two – was now well within my grasp and all those dark nights of winter training suddenly seemed worthwhile. As I reached the back straight I took the lead, and even felt that I could face the girl again. I summoned up my strength for one last effort. A quick glance over my shoulder confirmed I was already yards in front of any of my rivals, so it was only me against the clock. Then I heard the chanting, but this time it was even louder than before, "Jew boy! Jew boy! Jew boy!" It was louder because the two of them were now working in unison, and just as I came round the bend Reynolds raised his arm in a flagrant Nazi salute.

If I had only carried on for another twenty yards I would have reached the safety of the home straight and the cheers of my friends, the cup and the record. But they had made me so angry that I could no longer control myself.

I shot off the track and ran across the grass over the

long-jump pit and straight towards them. At least my crazy decision stopped their chanting because Reynolds lowered his arm and just stood there staring pathetically at me from behind the small railing that surrounded the outer perimeter of the track. I leaped right over it and landed in front of my adversary. With all the energy I had saved for the final straight I took an almighty swing at him. My fist landed an inch below his left eye and he buckled and fell to the ground by her side. Quickly she knelt down and, staring up, gave me a look of such hatred that no words could have matched it. Once I was sure Greg wasn't going to get up, I walked slowly back on to the track as the last of the runners were coming round the final bend.

"Last again, Jew boy," I heard her shout as I jogged down the home straight, so far behind the others that they didn't even bother to record my time.

How often since have you quoted me those words: "Still have I borne it with a patient shrug, for sufferance is the badge of all our tribe". Of course you were right, but I was only seventeen then, and even after I had learned the truth about Christina's father I still couldn't understand how anyone who had come from a defeated Germany, a Germany condemned by the rest of the world for its treatment of the Jews, could still behave in such a manner. And in those days I really believed her family were Nazis, but I remember you patiently explaining to me that her father had been an admiral in the German navy, and had won an Iron Cross for sinking Allied ships. Do you remember me asking how could you tolerate such a man, let alone allow him to settle down in our country?

You went on to assure me that Admiral von Braumer, who came from an old Roman Catholic family and probably despised the Nazis as much as we did, had acquitted himself honourably as an officer and a gentleman throughout his life as a German sailor. But I still couldn't accept your attitude, or didn't want to.

It didn't help, Father, that you always saw the other man's point of view, and even though Mother had died prematurely because of those bastards you could still find it in you to forgive.

If you had been born a Christian, you would have been a saint.

The rabbi put the letter down and rubbed his tired eyes before he turned over another page written in that fine script that he had taught his only son so many years before. Benjamin had always learned quickly, everything from the Hebrew scriptures to a complicated algebraic equation. The old man had even begun to hope the boy might become a rabbi.

Do you remember my asking you that evening why people couldn't understand that the world had changed? Didn't the girl realise that she was no better than we were? I shall never forget your reply. She is, you said, far better than us, if the only way you can prove your superiority is to punch her friend in the face.

I returned to my room angered by your weakness. It was to be many years before I understood your strength.

When I wasn't pounding round that track I rarely had time for anything other than working for a scholarship to McGill, so it came as a surprise that her path crossed mine again so soon.

It must have been about a week later that I saw her at the local swimming pool. She was standing at the deep end, just under the diving board, when I came in. Her long fair hair was dancing on her shoulders, her bright eyes eagerly taking in everything going on around her. Greg was by her side. I was pleased to notice a deep purple patch remained under his left eye for all to see. I also remember chuckling to myself because she really did have the flattest chest I had ever seen on a sixteen-year-old girl, though I have to confess she had fantastic legs. Perhaps she's a freak, I thought. I turned to go in to the changing room – a split second before I hit the water. When I came up for breath there was no sign of who had pushed me in, just a group of grinning but innocent faces. I didn't need a law degree to work out who it must have been, but as you constantly reminded me, Father, without evidence there is no proof . . . I wouldn't have minded that much about being pushed into the pool if I hadn't been wearing my best suit – in truth, my only suit with long trousers, the one I wore on days I was going to the synagogue.

I climbed out of the water but didn't waste any time looking round for him. I knew Greg would be a long way off by then. I walked home through the back streets, avoiding taking the bus in case someone saw me and told you what a state I was in. As soon as I got home I crept past your study and on upstairs to my room, changing before you had the chance to discover what had taken place.

Old Isaac Cohen gave me a disapproving look when I turned up at the synagogue an hour later wearing a blazer and jeans.

I took the suit to the cleaners the next morning. It cost me three weeks' pocket money to be sure that you were never aware of what had happened at the swimming pool that day.

The rabbi picked up the picture of his seventeen-year-old son in that synagogue suit. He well remembered Benjamin turning up to his service in a blazer and jeans and Isaac Cohen's outspoken reprimand. The rabbi was thankful that Mr Atkins, the swimming instructor, had phoned to warn him of what had taken place that afternoon so at least he didn't add to Mr Cohen's harsh words. He continued gazing at the photograph for a long time before he returned to the letter.

The next occasion I saw Christina – by now I had found out her name – was at the end-of-term dance held in the school gymnasium. I thought I looked pretty cool in my neatly pressed suit until I saw Greg standing by her side in a smart new dinner jacket. I remember wondering at the time if I would ever be able to afford a dinner jacket. Greg had been offered a place at McGill and was announcing the fact to everyone who cared to listen, which made me all the more determined to win a scholarship there the following year.

I stared at Christina. She was wearing a long red dress that completely covered those beautiful legs. A thin gold belt emphasised her tiny waist and the only jewellery she wore was a simple gold necklace. I knew if I waited a moment longer I wouldn't have the courage to go through with it. I clenched my fists, walked over to where they were sitting, and as you had always taught me, Father, bowed slightly before I asked, "May I have the pleasure of this dance?"

She stared into my eyes. I swear if she had told me to go out and kill a thousand men before I dared ask her again I would have done it.

She didn't even speak, but Greg leaned over her shoulder and said, "Why don't you go and find yourself a nice Jewish girl?" I thought I saw her scowl at his remark, but I only blushed like someone who's been caught with their hands in the cookie jar. I didn't dance with anyone that night. I walked straight out of the gymnasium and ran home.

I was convinced then that I hated her.

That last week of term I broke the school record for the

mile. You were there to watch me but, thank heavens, she wasn't. That was the holiday we drove over to Ottawa to spend our summer vacation with Aunt Rebecca. I was told by a school friend that Christina had spent hers in Vancouver with a German family. At least Greg had not gone with her, the friend assured me.

You went on reminding me of the importance of a good education, but you didn't need to, because every time I saw Greg it made me more determined to win that scholarship.

I worked even harder in the summer of '65 when you explained that, for a Canadian, a place at McGill was like going to Harvard or Oxford and would clear a path for the rest of my days.

For the first time in my life running took second place.

Although I didn't see much of Christina that term she was often in my mind. A classmate told me that she and Greg were no longer seeing each other, but could give me no reason for this sudden change of heart. At the time I had a so-called girlfriend who always sat on the other side of the synagogue – Naomi Goldblatz, you remember her – but it was she who dated me.

As my exams drew nearer, I was grateful that you always found time to go over my essays and tests after I had finished them. What you couldn't know was that I inevitably returned to my own room to do them a third time. Often I would fall asleep at my desk. When I woke I would turn over the page and read on.

Even you, Father, who have not an ounce of vanity in you, found it hard to disguise from your congregation the pride you took in my eight straight "A's" and the award of a top scholarship to McGill. I wondered if Christina was aware of it. She must have been. My name was painted up on the Honours Board in fresh gold leaf the following week, so someone would have told her.

* * *

It must have been three months later when I was in my first term at McGill that I saw her next. Do you remember taking me to St Joan *at the Centaur Theatre? There she was, seated a few rows in front of us with her parents and a sophomore called Bob Richards. The admiral and his wife looked strait-laced and very stern but not unsympathetic. In the interval I watched her laughing and joking with them: she had obviously enjoyed herself. I hardly saw* St Joan, *and although I couldn't take my eyes off Christina she never once noticed me. I just wanted to be on the stage playing the Dauphin so she would have to look up at me.*

When the curtain came down she and Bob Richards left her parents and headed for the exit. I followed the two of them out of the foyer and into the car park, and watched them get into a Thunderbird. A Thunderbird! I remember thinking I might one day be able to afford a dinner jacket, but never a Thunderbird.

From that moment she was in my thoughts whenever I trained, wherever I worked and even when I slept. I found out everything I could about Bob Richards and discovered that he was liked by all who knew him.

For the first time in my life I hated being a Jew.

When I next saw Christina I dreaded what might happen. It was the start of the mile against the University of Vancouver and as a freshman I had been lucky to be selected for McGill. When I came out on to the track to warm up I saw her sitting in the third row of the stand alongside Richards. They were holding hands.

I was last off when the starter's gun fired but as we went into the back straight moved up into fifth position. It was the largest crowd I had ever run in front of, and when I reached the home straight I waited for the chant "Jew boy! Jew boy! Jew boy!" but nothing happened. I wondered if she had failed to notice that I was in the race. But she had noticed because as I came round the bend I could hear her voice clearly. "Come on, Benjamin, you've got to win!" she shouted.

I wanted to look back to make sure it was Christina who had called those words; it would be another quarter of a mile before I could pass her again. By the time I did so I had moved up into third place, and I could hear her clearly: "Come on, Benjamin, you can do it!"

I immediately took the lead because all I wanted to do was get back to her. I charged on without thought of who was behind me, and by the time I passed her the third time I was several yards ahead of the field. "You're going to win!" she shouted as I ran on to reach the bell in three minutes eight seconds, eleven seconds faster than I had ever done before. I remember thinking that they ought to put something in those training manuals about love being worth two to three seconds a lap.

I watched her all the way down the back straight and when I came into the final bend for the last time the crowd rose to their feet. I turned to search for her. She was jumping up and down shouting, "Look out! Look out!" which I didn't understand until I was overtaken on the inside by the Vancouver Number One string who the coach had warned me was renowned for his strong finish. I staggered over the line a few yards behind him in second place but went on running until I was safely inside the changing room. I sat alone by my locker. Four minutes seventeen, someone told me: six seconds faster than I had ever run before. It didn't help. I stood in the shower for a long time, trying to work out what could possibly have changed her attitude.

When I walked back on to the track only the ground staff were still around. I took one last look at the finishing line before I strolled over to the Forsyth Library. I felt unable to face the usual team get-together, so I tried to settle down to write an essay on the property rights of married women.

The library was almost empty that Saturday evening and I was well into my third page when I heard a voice say, "I hope I'm not interrupting you but you didn't come to Joe's." I looked up to see Christina standing on the other side of the table. Father, I didn't know what to say. I just stared up at the beautiful creature in her fashionable blue mini-skirt and tight-fitting sweater that emphasised the most perfect breasts, and said nothing.

"I was the one who shouted 'Jew boy' when you were still at High School. I've felt ashamed about it ever since. I wanted to apologise to you on the night of the prom dance but couldn't summon up the courage with Greg standing there." I nodded my understanding – I couldn't think of any words that seemed appropriate. "I never spoke to him again," she said. "But I don't suppose you even remember Greg."

I just smiled. "Care for coffee?" I asked, trying to sound as if I wouldn't mind if she replied, "I'm sorry, I must get back to Bob."

"I'd like that very much," she said.

I took her to the library coffee shop, which was about all I could afford at the time. She never bothered to explain what had happened to Bob Richards, and I never asked.

Christina seemed to know so much about me that I felt embarrassed. She asked me to forgive her for what she had shouted on the track that day two years before. She made no excuses, placed the blame on no one else, just asked to be forgiven.

Christina told me she was hoping to join me at McGill in September, to major in German. "Bit of a cheek," she admitted, "as it is *my native tongue."*

We spent the rest of that summer in each other's company. We saw St Joan *again, and even queued for a film called* Dr No *that was all the craze at the time. We worked together, we ate together, we played together, but we slept alone.*

I said little about Christina to you at the time, but I'd bet you knew already how much I loved her; I could never hide anything from you. And after all your teaching of forgiveness and understanding you could hardly disapprove.

The rabbi paused. His heart ached because he knew so much of what was still to come although he could not have foretold what would happen in the end. He had never thought he would live to regret his Orthodox upbringing but when Mrs Goldblatz first told him about Christina he had been unable to mask his disapproval. It will pass, given time, he told her. So much for wisdom.

Whenever I went to Christina's home I was always treated with courtesy but her family were unable to hide their disapproval. They uttered words they didn't believe in an attempt to show that they were not anti-semitic, and whenever I brought up the subject with Christina she told me I was over-reacting. We both knew I wasn't. They quite simply thought I was unworthy of their daughter. They were right, but it had nothing to do with my being Jewish.

I shall never forget the first time we made love. It was the day that Christina learned she had won a place at McGill.

We had gone to my room at three o'clock to change for a game of tennis. I took her in my arms for what I thought would be a brief moment and we didn't part until the next morning. Nothing had been planned. But how could it have been, when it was the first time for both of us?

I told her I would marry her – don't all men the first time? – only I meant it.

Then a few weeks later she missed her period. I begged

her not to panic, and we both waited for another month because she was fearful of going to see any doctor in Montreal.

If I had told you everything then, Father, perhaps my life would have taken a different course. But I didn't, and have only myself to blame.

I began to plan for a marriage that neither Christina's family nor you could possibly have found acceptable, but we didn't care. Love knows no parents, and certainly no religion. When she missed her second period I agreed Christina should tell her mother. I asked her if she would like me to be with her at the time, but she simply shook her head, and explained that she felt she had to face them on her own.

"I'll wait here until you return," I promised.

She smiled. "I'll be back even before you've had the time to change your mind about marrying me."

I sat in my room at McGill all that afternoon reading and pacing – mostly pacing – but she never came back, and I didn't go in search of her until it was dark. I crept round to her home, all the while trying to convince myself there must be some simple explanation as to why she hadn't returned.

When I reached her road I could see a light on in her bedroom but nowhere else in the house so I thought she must be alone. I marched through the gate and up to the front porch, knocked on the door and waited.

Her father answered the door.

"What do you want?" he asked, his eyes never leaving me for a moment.

"I love your daughter," I told him, "and I want to marry her."

"She will never marry a Jew," he said simply and closed the door. I remember that he didn't slam it; he just closed it, which made it somehow even worse.

I stood outside in the road staring up at her room for over an hour until the light went out. Then I walked home. I recall there was a light drizzle that night and few people were on the streets. I tried to work out what I should do next, although the situation seemed hopeless to me. I went to bed that night hoping for a miracle. I had forgotten that miracles are for Christians, not Jews.

By the next morning I had worked out a plan. I phoned Christina's home at eight and nearly put the phone down when I heard the voice at the other end.

"Mrs von Braumer," she said.

"Is Christina there?" I asked in a whisper.

"No, she's not," came back the controlled impersonal reply.

"When are you expecting her back?" I asked.

"Not for some time," she said, and then the phone went dead.

"Not for some time" turned out to be over a year. I wrote, telephoned, asked friends from school and university but could never find out where they had taken her.

Then one day, unannounced, she returned to Montreal accompanied by a husband and my child. I learned the bitter details from that font of all knowledge, Naomi Goldblatz, who had already seen all three of them.

I received a short note from Christina about a week later begging me not to make any attempt to contact her.

I had just begun my last year at McGill and like some eighteenth-century gentleman I honoured her wish to the letter and turned all my energies to the final exams. She still continued to preoccupy my thoughts and I considered myself lucky at the end of the year to be offered a place at Harvard Law School.

I left Montreal for Boston on September 12th, 1968.

You must have wondered why I never came home once

during those three years. I knew of your disapproval. Thanks to Mrs Goldblatz everyone was aware who the father of Christina's child was and I felt an enforced absence might make life a little easier for you.

The rabbi paused as he remembered Mrs Goldblatz letting him know what she had considered was "only her duty".

"You're an interfering old busybody," he had told her. By the following Saturday she had moved to another synagogue and let everyone in the town know why.

He was more angry with himself than with Benjamin. He should have visited Harvard to let his son know that his love for him had not changed. So much for his powers of forgiveness.

He took up the letter once again.

Throughout those years at law school I had plenty of friends of both sexes, but Christina was rarely out of my mind for more than a few hours at a time. I wrote over forty letters to her while I was in Boston, but didn't post one of them. I even phoned, but it was never her voice that answered. If it had been, I'm not even sure I would have said anything. I just wanted to hear her.

Were you ever curious about the women in my life? I had affairs with bright girls from Radcliffe who were reading law, history or science, and once with a shop assistant who never read anything. Can you imagine, in the very act of making love, always thinking of another woman? I seemed to be doing my work on autopilot, and even my passion for running became reduced to an hour's jogging a day.

Long before the end of my last year, leading law firms in New York, Chicago and Toronto were turning up to interview us. The Harvard tom-toms can be relied on to beat across the world, but even I was surprised by a visit from the senior partner of Graham Douglas & Wilkins of Toronto. It's not a firm known for its Jewish partners, but I liked the idea of their letterhead one day reading "Graham Douglas Wilkins & Rosenthal". Even her father would surely have been impressed by that.

At least if I lived and worked in Toronto, I convinced myself, it would be far enough away for me to forget her, and perhaps with luck find someone else I could feel that way about.

Graham Douglas & Wilkins found me a spacious apartment overlooking the park and started me off at a handsome salary. In return I worked all the hours God – whoever's God – made. If I thought they had pushed me at McGill or Harvard, Father, it turned out to be no more than a dry run for the real world. I didn't complain. The work was exciting, and the rewards beyond my expectation. Only now that I could afford a Thunderbird I didn't want one.

New girlfriends came, and went as soon as they talked of marriage. The Jewish ones usually raised the subject within a week, the Gentiles, I found, waited a little longer. I even began living with one of them, Rebecca Wertz, but that too ended – on a Thursday.

I was driving to the office that morning – it must have been a little after eight, which was late for me – when I saw Christina on the other side of the busy highway, a barrier separating us. She was standing at a bus stop holding the hand of a little boy, who must have been about five – my son.

The heavy morning traffic allowed me a little longer to stare in disbelief. I found that I wanted to look at them both at once. She wore a long lightweight coat that showed she had not lost her figure. Her face was serene and only reminded me why she was rarely out of my thoughts. Her son

– our son – was wrapped up in an oversize duffle coat and his head was covered by a baseball hat that informed me that he supported the Toronto Dolphins. Sadly, it really stopped me seeing what he looked like. You can't be in Toronto, I remember thinking, you're meant to be in Montreal. I watched them both in my side-mirror as they climbed on to a bus. That particular Thursday I must have been an appalling counsellor to every client who sought my advice.

For the next week I passed by that bus stop every morning within minutes of the time I had seen them standing there but never saw them again. I began to wonder if I had imagined the whole scene. Then I spotted Christina again when I was returning across the city, having visited a client. She was on her own and I braked hard as I watched her entering a shop on Bloor Street. This time I double-parked the car and walked quickly across the road feeling like a sleazy private detective who spends his life peeping through keyholes.

What I saw took me by surprise – not to find her in a beautiful dress shop, but to discover it was where she worked.

The moment I saw that she was serving a customer I hurried back to my car. Once I had reached my office I asked my secretary if she knew of a shop called "Willing's".

My secretary laughed. "You must pronounce it the German way, the W becomes a V," she explained, "thus 'Villing's'. If you were married you would know that it's the most expensive dress shop in town," she added.

"Do you know anything else about the place?" I asked, trying to sound casual.

"Not a lot," she said. "Only that it is owned by a wealthy German lady called Mrs Klaus Willing whom they often write about in the women's magazines."

I didn't need to ask my secretary any more questions and I won't trouble you, Father, with my detective work. But, armed with those snippets of information, it didn't take me long to discover where Christina lived, that her husband was an overseas director with BMW, and that they only had the one child.

The old rabbi breathed deeply as he glanced up at the clock on his desk, more out of habit than any desire to know the time. He paused for a moment before returning to the letter. He had been so proud of his lawyer son then; why hadn't he made the first step towards a reconciliation? How he would have liked to have seen his grandson.

My ultimate decision did not require an acute legal mind, just a little common sense – although a lawyer who advises himself undoubtedly has a fool for a client. Contact, I decided, had to be direct and a letter was the only method I felt Christina would find acceptable.

I wrote a simple message that Monday morning, then rewrote it several times before I telephoned "Fleet Deliveries" and asked them to hand it to her in person at the shop. When the young man left with the letter I wanted to follow him, just to be certain he had given it to the right person. I can still repeat it word for word.

Dear Christina,

You must know I live and work in Toronto. Can we meet? I will wait for you in the lounge of the Royal York Hotel every evening between six and seven this week. If you don't come be assured I will never trouble you again.

Benjamin

I arrived that evening nearly thirty minutes early. I remember taking a seat in a large impersonal lounge just off the main hall and ordering coffee.

"Will anyone be joining you, sir?" the waiter asked.

"I can't be sure," I told him. No one did join me, but I still hung around until seven forty.

By Thursday the waiter had stopped asking if anyone would be joining me as I sat alone and allowed yet another cup of coffee to grow cold. Every few minutes I checked my watch. Each time a woman with blonde hair entered the lounge my heart leaped but it was never the woman I hoped for.

It was just before seven on Friday that I finally saw Christina standing in the doorway. She wore a smart blue suit buttoned up almost to the neck and a white blouse that made her look as if she were on her way to a business conference. Her long fair hair was pulled back behind her ears to give an impression of severity, but however hard she tried she could not be other than beautiful. I stood and raised my arm. She walked quickly over and took the seat beside me. We didn't kiss or shake hands and for some time didn't even speak.

"Thank you for coming," I said.

"I shouldn't have, it was foolish."

Some time passed before either of us spoke again.

"Can I pour you a coffee?" I asked.

"Yes, thank you."

"Black?"

"Yes."

"You haven't changed."

How banal it all would have sounded to anyone eaves-dropping.

She sipped her coffee.

I should have taken her in my arms right then but I had no way of knowing that that was what she wanted. For several minutes we talked of inconsequential matters, always avoiding each other's eyes, until I suddenly said, "Do you realise that I still love you?"

Tears filled her eyes as she replied, "Of course I do. And I still feel the same about you now as I did the day we parted. And don't forget I have to see you every day, through Nicholas."

She leaned forward and spoke almost in a whisper. She told me about the meeting with her parents that had taken place more than five years before as if we had not been parted in between. Her father had shown no anger when he learned she was pregnant but the family still left for Vancouver the following morning. There they had stayed with the Willings, a family also from Munich, who were old friends of the von Braumers. Their son, Klaus, had always been besotted with Christina and didn't care about her being pregnant, or even the fact she felt nothing for him. He was confident that, given time, it would all work out for the best.

It didn't, because it couldn't. Christina had always known it would never work, however hard Klaus tried. They even left Montreal in an attempt to make a go of it. Klaus bought her the shop in Toronto and every luxury that money could afford, but it made no difference. Their marriage was an obvious sham. Yet they could not bring themselves to distress their families further with a divorce so they had led separate lives from the beginning.

As soon as Christina finished her story I touched her cheek and she took my hand and kissed it. From that moment on we saw each other every spare moment that could be stolen, day or night. It was the happiest year of my life, and I was unable to hide from anyone how I felt.

Our affair – for that's how the gossips were describing it – inevitably became public. However discreet we tried to be,

Toronto, I quickly discovered, is a very small place, full of people who took pleasure in informing those whom we also loved that we had been seen together regularly, even leaving my home in the early hours.

Then quite suddenly we were left with no choice in the matter: Christina told me she was pregnant again. Only this time it held no fears for either of us.

Once she had told Klaus the settlement went through as quickly as the best divorce lawyer at Graham Douglas & Wilkins could negotiate. We were married only a few days after the final papers were signed. We both regretted that Christina's parents felt unable to attend the wedding but I couldn't understand why you didn't come.

The rabbi still could not believe his own intolerance and short-sightedness. The demands on an Orthodox Jew should be waived if it meant losing one's only child. He had searched the Talmud in vain for any passage that would allow him to break his lifelong vows. In vain.

The only sad part of the divorce settlement was that Klaus was given custody of our child. He also demanded, in exchange for a quick divorce, that I not be allowed to see Nicholas before his twenty-first birthday, and that he should not be told that I was his real father. At the time it seemed a hard price to pay, even for such happiness. We both knew that we had been left with no choice but to accept his terms.

I used to wonder how each day could be so much better than the last. If I was apart from Christina for more than a few hours I always missed her. If the firm sent me out of town on business for a night I would phone her two, three, perhaps four times, and if it was for more than a night then she came with me. I remember you once describing your love for my mother and wondering at the time if I could ever hope to achieve such happiness.

We began to make plans for the birth of our child. William, if it was a boy – her choice; Deborah, if it was a girl – mine. I painted the spare room pink, assuming I had already won.

Christina had to stop me buying too many baby clothes, but I warned her that it didn't matter as we were going to have a dozen more children. Jews, I reminded her, believed in dynasties.

She attended her exercise classes regularly, dieted carefully, rested sensibly. I told her she was doing far more than was required of a mother, even of my daughter. I asked if I could be present when our child was born and her gynaecologist seemed reluctant at first, but then agreed. By the time the ninth month came the hospital must have thought from the amount of fuss I was making they were preparing for the birth of a royal prince.

I drove Christina into Women's College Hospital on the way to work last Tuesday. Although I went on to the office I found it impossible to concentrate. The hospital rang in the afternoon to say they thought the child would be born early that evening: obviously Deborah did not wish to disrupt the working hours of Graham Douglas & Wilkins. However, I still arrived at the hospital far too early. I sat on the end of Christina's bed until her contractions started coming every minute and then to my surprise they asked me to leave. They needed to rupture her membranes, a nurse explained. I asked her to remind the midwife that I wanted to be present to witness the birth.

I went out into the corridor and began pacing up and down, the way expectant fathers do in B-movies. Christina's gynaecologist arrived about half an hour later and gave me a huge smile. I noticed a cigar in his top pocket, obviously reserved for expectant fathers. "It's about to happen," was all he said.

A second doctor whom I had never seen before arrived a few minutes later and went quickly into her room. He only gave me a nod. I felt like a man in the dock waiting to hear the jury's verdict.

It must have been at least another fifteen minutes before I saw the unit being rushed down the corridor by a team of three young interns. They didn't even give me so much as a second glance as they disappeared into Christina's room.

I heard the screams that suddenly gave way to the plaintive cry of a new-born child. I thanked my God and hers. When the doctor came out of her room I remember noticing that the cigar had disappeared.

"It's a girl," he said quietly. I was overjoyed. "No need to repaint the bedroom immediately" flashed through my mind.

"Can I see Christina now?" I asked.

He took me by the arm and led me across the corridor and into his office.

"Would you like to sit down?" he asked. "I'm afraid I have some sad news."

"Is she all right?"

"I am sorry, so very sorry, to tell you that your wife is dead."

At first I didn't believe him, I refused to believe him. Why? Why? I wanted to scream.

"We did warn her," he added.

"Warn her? Warn her of what?"

"That her blood pressure might not stand up to it a second time."

Christina had never told me what the doctor went on to explain – that the birth of our first child had been complicated, and that the doctors had advised her against becoming pregnant again.

"Why hadn't she told me?" I demanded. Then I realised why. She had risked everything for me – foolish, selfish, thoughtless me – and I had ended up killing the one person I loved.

They allowed me to hold Deborah in my arms for just a moment before they put her into an incubator and told me it would be another twenty-four hours before she came off the danger list.

You will never know how much it meant to me, Father, that you came to the hospital so quickly. Christina's parents arrived later that evening. They were magnificent. He begged for my forgiveness – begged for my *forgiveness. It could never have happened, he kept repeating, if he hadn't been so stupid and prejudiced.*

His wife took my hand and asked if she might be allowed to see Deborah from time to time. Of course I agreed. They left just before midnight. I sat, walked, slept in that corridor for the next twenty-four hours until they told me that my daughter was off the danger list. She would have to remain in the hospital for a few more days, they explained, but she was now managing to suck milk from a bottle.

Christina's father kindly took over the funeral arrangements.

You must have wondered why I didn't appear and I owe you an explanation. I thought I would just drop into the hospital on my way to the funeral so that I could spend a few moments with Deborah. I had already transferred my love.

The doctor couldn't get the words out. It took a brave man to tell me that her heart had stopped beating a few minutes before my arrival. Even the senior surgeon was in tears. When I left the hospital the corridors were empty.

I want you to know, Father, that I love you with all my

heart, but I have no desire to spend the rest of my life without Christina or Deborah.

I only ask to be buried beside my wife and daughter and to be remembered as their husband and father. That way unthinking people might learn from our love. And when you finish this letter, remember only that I had such total happiness when I was with her that death holds no fears for me.

Your son,
Benjamin.

The old rabbi placed the letter down on the table in front of him. He had read it every day for the last ten years.

AS THE CROW FLIES

To James

CHARLIE

1900-1919

CHAPTER 1

"I don't offer you these for twopence," my Granpa would shout, holding up a cabbage in both hands, "I don't offer 'em for a penny, not even a ha'penny. No, I'll give 'em away for a farthin'."

Those were the first words I can remember. Even before I had learned to walk my eldest sister used to dump me in an orange box on the pavement next to Granpa's pitch just to be sure I could start my apprenticeship early.

"Only stakin' 'is claim," Granpa used to tell the customers as he pointed at me in the wooden box. In truth, the first word I ever spoke was "Granpa", the second "farthing", and I could repeat his whole sales patter word for word by my third birthday. Not that any of my family could be that certain of the exact day on which *I* was born, on account of the fact that my old man had spent the night in gaol and my mother had died even before I drew breath. Granpa thought it could well have been a Saturday, felt it most likely the month had been January, was confident the year was 1900, and knew it was in the reign of Queen Victoria. So we settled on Saturday, 20 January 1900.

I never knew my mother because, as I explained, she died on the day I was born. "Childbirth" our local priest called it, but I didn't really understand what he was on about until several years later when I came up against the problem again. Father O'Malley never stopped telling me that she was a saint if ever he'd seen one. My father – who couldn't have been described as a saint by anyone – worked on the docks by day, lived in the pub at night and came home in the early morning because it was the only place he could fall asleep without being disturbed.

The rest of my family was made up of three sisters – Sal, the eldest who was five and knew when she was born because it was in the middle of the night and had kept the old man awake, Grace who was three and didn't cause anyone to lose sleep, and red-headed Kitty who was eighteen months and never stopped bawling.

The head of the family was Granpa Charlie, whom I was named after. He slept in his own room on the ground floor of our home in Whitechapel Road, not only because he was the oldest but because he always paid the rent. The rest of us were herded all together in the room opposite. We had two other rooms on the ground floor, a sort of kitchen and what most people would have called a large cupboard, but which Grace liked to describe as the parlour.

There was a lavatory in the garden – no grass – which we shared with an Irish family who lived on the floor above us. They always seemed to go at three o'clock in the morning.

Granpa – who was a costermonger by trade – worked the pitch on the corner of Whitechapel Road. Once I was able to escape from my orange box and ferret around among the other barrows, I quickly discovered that he was reckoned by the locals to be the finest trader in the East End.

My dad, who, as I have already told you, was a docker by trade, never seemed to take that much interest in any of us and though he could sometimes earn as much as a pound a week, the money always seemed to end up in the Black Bull, where it was spent on pint after pint of ale, and gambled away on games of cribbage or dominoes in the company of our next-door neighbour, Bert Shorrocks, a man who never seemed to speak, just grunt.

In fact, if it hadn't been for Granpa I wouldn't even have been made to attend the local elementary school in Jubilee Street, and "attend" was the right word, because I didn't do a lot once I'd got there, other than bang the lid of my little desk and occasionally pull the pigtails of "Posh Porky", the girl who sat in front of me. Her real name was Rebecca Salmon and she was the daughter of Dan Salmon who owned the baker's shop on the corner of Brick Lane. Posh Porky knew exactly when and where she was born and never stopped reminding us all that she was nearly a year younger than anyone else in the class.

I couldn't wait for the bell to ring at four in the afternoon when class would end and I could bang my lid for the last time before running all the way down the Whitechapel Road to help out on the barrow.

On Saturdays as a special treat Granpa would allow me to go along with him to the early morning market in Covent Garden, where he would select the fruit and vegetables that we would later sell from his pitch, just opposite Mr Salmon's and Dunkley's, the fish and chippy that stood next to the baker's.

Although I couldn't wait to leave school once and for all so I could join Granpa permanently, if I ever played truant for as much as an hour he wouldn't take me to watch West Ham on Saturday afternoon or, worse, he'd stop me selling on the barrow in the morning.

"I 'oped you'd grow up to be more like Rebecca Salmon," he used to say. "That girl will go a long way –"

"The further the better," I would tell him, but he never laughed, just reminded me that she was always top in every subject.

" 'cept 'rithmetic," I replied with bravado, "where I beat her silly." You see, I could do any sum in my head that Rebecca Salmon had to write out in long-hand; it used to drive her potty.

My father never visited Jubilee Street Elementary once in all the years I was there, but Granpa used to pop along at least once a term and have a word with Mr Cartwright my teacher. Mr Cartwright told Granpa that with my head for figures I could end up an accountant or a clerk. He once said that he might even be able to "find me a position in the City". Which was a waste of time really, because all I wanted to do was join Granpa on the barrow.

I was seven before I worked out that the name down the side of Granpa's barrow – Charlie Trumper, the honest trader, founded in 1823 – was the same as mine. Dad's first name was George, and he had already made it clear on several occasions that when Granpa retired he had no intention of taking over from him as he didn't want to leave his mates on the docks.

I couldn't have been more pleased by his decision, and told Granpa that when I finally took over the barrow we wouldn't even have to change the name.

Granpa just groaned and said, "I don't want you to end up workin' in the East End, young 'un. You're far too good to be a barrow boy for the rest of your life." It made me sad to hear him speak like that; he didn't seem to understand that was all I wanted to do.

School dragged on for month after month, year after year, with Rebecca Salmon going up to collect prize after prize on Speech Day. What made the annual gathering even worse was we always had to listen to her recite the twenty-third psalm, standing up there on the stage in her white dress, white socks, black shoes. She even had a white bow in her long black hair.

"And I expect she wears a new pair of knickers every day," little Kitty whispered in my ear.

"And I'll bet you a guinea to a farthin' she's still a virgin," said Sal.

I burst out laughing because all the costermongers

in the Whitechapel Road always did whenever they heard that word, although I admit that at the time I didn't have a clue what a virgin was. Granpa told me to "shhh" and didn't smile again until I went up to get the arithmetic prize, a box of coloured crayons that were damned-all use to anyone. Still, it was them or a book.

Granpa clapped so loud as I returned to my place that some of the mums looked round and smiled, which made the old fellow even more determined to see that I stayed on at school until I was fourteen.

By the time I was ten, Granpa allowed me to lay out the morning wares on the barrow before going off to school for the day. Potatoes on the front, greens in the middle and soft fruits at the back was his golden rule.

"Never let 'em touch the fruit until they've 'anded over their money," he used to say. "'ard to bruise a 'tato, but even 'arder to sell a bunch of grapes that's been picked up and dropped a few times."

By the age of eleven I was collecting the money from the customers and handing them the change they were due. That's when I first learned about palming. Sometimes, after I'd given them back their money, the customer would open the palm of their hand and I would discover that one of the coins I had passed over had suddenly disappeared so I ended up having to give them even more bees and honey. I lost Granpa quite a bit of our weekly profit that way, until he taught me to say, "Twopence change, Mrs Smith," then hold up the coins for all to see before handing them over.

By twelve, I had learned how to bargain with the suppliers at Covent Garden while displaying a poker face, later selling the same produce to the customers back in Whitechapel with a grin that stretched from ear to ear. I also discovered that Granpa used to switch suppliers regularly, "just to be sure no one takes me for granted".

By thirteen, I had become his eyes and ears as I already knew the name of every worthwhile trader of fruit and vegetables in Covent Garden. I quickly sussed out which sellers just piled good fruit on top of bad, which dealers would attempt to hide a bruised apple and which suppliers would always try to short-measure you. Most important of all, back on the pitch I learnt which customers didn't pay their debts and so could never be allowed to have their names chalked up on the slate.

I remember that my chest swelled with pride the day Mrs Smelley, who owned a boarding house in the Commercial Road, told me that I was a chip off the old block and that in her opinion one day I might even be as good as my Granpa. I celebrated that night by ordering my first pint of beer and lighting up my first Woodbine. I didn't finish either of them.

I'll never forget that Saturday morning when Granpa first let me run the barrow on my own. For five hours he didn't once open his mouth to offer advice or even give an opinion and, when he checked the takings at the end of the day, although we were two shillings and fivepence light from a usual Saturday, he still handed over the sixpenny piece he always gave me at the end of the week.

I knew Granpa wanted me to stay on at school and improve my readin' and writin', but on the last Friday of term in December 1913 I walked out of the gates of Jubilee Street Elementary, with my father's blessing. He had always told me that education was a waste of time and he couldn't see the point of it. I agreed with him, even if Posh Porky had won a scholarship to some place called St Paul's, which in any case was miles away in Hammersmith. And who wants to go to school in Hammersmith when you can live in the East End?

Mrs Salmon obviously wanted her to because she told everyone who was held up in the bread queue of her daughter's "interlectual prowess", whatever that meant.

"Stuck-up snob," Grandpa used to whisper in my ear. "She's the sort of person who 'as a bowl of fruit in the 'ouse when no one's ill."

I felt much the same way about Posh Porky as Grandpa did about Mrs Salmon. Mr Salmon was all right, though. You see, he'd once been a costermonger himself, but that was before he married Miss Roach, the baker's daughter.

Every Saturday morning, while I was setting up the barrow, Mr Salmon used to disappear off to the Whitechapel synagogue leaving his wife to run the shop. While he was away she never stopped reminding us at the top of her voice that she wasn't a five by two.

Posh Porky seemed to be torn between going along with her old man to the synagogue and staying put at the shop, where she'd sit by the window and start scoffing cream buns the moment he was out of sight.

"Always a problem, a mixed marriage," Granpa would tell me. It was years before I worked out that he wasn't talking about the cream buns.

The day I left school I told Granpa he could lie in while I went off to Covent Garden to fill up the barrow, but he wouldn't hear of it. When we got to the market, for the first time he allowed me to bargain with the dealers. I quickly found one who agreed to supply me with a dozen apples for threepence as long as I could guarantee the same order every day for the next month. As Granpa Charlie and I always had an apple for breakfast, the arrangement sorted out our own needs and also gave me the chance to sample what we were selling to the customers.

From that moment on, every day was a Saturday and between us we could sometimes manage to put the profits up by as much as fourteen shillings a week.

After that, I was put on a weekly wage of five shillings – a veritable fortune – four of which I kept locked in a tin box under Granpa's bed until I had saved up my first guinea: a man what's got a guinea got security, Mr Salmon once told me as he stood outside his shop, thumbs in his waistcoat pockets, displaying a shiny gold watch and chain.

In the evenings, after Granpa had come home for supper and the old man had gone off to the pub, I soon became bored just sitting around listening to what my sisters had been up to all day; so I joined the Whitechapel Boys' Club. Table tennis Mondays, Wednesdays and Fridays; boxing Tuesdays, Thursdays and Saturdays. I never did get the hang of table tennis but I became quite a useful bantam-weight and once even represented the club against Bethnal Green.

Unlike my old man I didn't go much on pubs, the horses or cribbage but I still went on supporting West Ham most Saturday afternoons. I even made the occasional trip into the West End of an evening to see the latest music-hall star.

When Granpa asked me what I wanted for my fifteenth birthday I replied without a moment's hesitation, "My own barrow," and added that I'd nearly saved enough to get one. He just laughed and told me that his old one was well good enough for whenever the time came for me to take over. In any case, he warned me, it's what a rich man calls an asset and, he added for good measure, never invest in something new, especially when there's a war on.

Although Mr Salmon had already told me that we had declared war against the Germans almost a year ago – none of us having heard of Archduke Franz Ferdinand – we only found out how serious it was when a lot of young lads who had worked in the market began to disappear off to "the front" to be replaced by their younger brothers – and sometimes even sisters. On a Saturday morning there were often more lads down the East End dressed in khaki than in civvies.

My only other memory of that period was Schultz's,

the sausage-maker – a Saturday night treat for us, especially when he gave us a toothless grin and slipped an extra sausage in free. Lately he had always seemed to start the day with a broken window-pane, and then suddenly one morning the front of his shop was boarded up and we never saw Mr Schultz again. "Internment," my granpa whispered mysteriously.

My old man occasionally joined us on a Saturday morning, but only to get some cash off Granpa so that he could go to the Black Bull and spend it all with his mate Bert Shorrocks.

Week after week Granpa would fork out a bob, sometimes even a florin, which we both knew he couldn't afford. And what really annoyed me was that he never drank and certainly didn't go a bundle on gambling. That didn't stop my old man pocketing the money, touching his cap and then heading off towards the Black Bull.

This routine went on week after week, and might never have changed, until one Saturday morning a toffee-nosed lady who I had noticed standing on the corner for the past week, wearing a long black dress and carrying a parasol, strode over to our barrow, stopped and placed a white feather in Dad's lapel.

I've never seen him go so mad, far worse than the usual Saturday night when he had lost all his money gambling and came home so drunk that we all had to hide under the bed. He raised his clenched fist to the lady but she didn't flinch and even called him "coward" to his face. He screamed back at her some choice words that he usually saved for the rent collector. He then grabbed all her feathers and threw them in the gutter before storming off in the direction of the Black Bull. What's more, he didn't come home at midday, when Sal served us up a dinner of fish and chips. I never complained as I went off to watch West Ham that afternoon, having scoffed his portion of chips. He still wasn't back when I returned that night, and when I woke the next morning, his side of the bed hadn't been slept in. When Granpa brought us all home from midday mass there was still no sign of Dad, so I had a second night with the double bed all to myself.

"'e's probably spent another night in gaol," said Granpa on Monday morning as I pushed our barrow down the middle of the road, trying to avoid the horse shit from the buses that were dragged backwards and forwards, to and from the City along the Metropolitan Line.

As we passed Number 110, I spotted Mrs Shorrocks staring at me out of the window, sporting her usual black eye and a mass of different coloured bruises which she collected from Bert most Saturday nights.

"You can go and bail 'im out round noon," said Granpa. "'e should have sobered up by then."

I scowled at the thought of having to fork out the half-crown to cover his fine, which simply meant another day's profits down the drain.

A few minutes after twelve o'clock I reported to the police station. The duty sergeant told me that Bert Shorrocks was still in the cells and due up in front of the beak that afternoon, but they hadn't set eyes on my old man the whole weekend.

"Like a bad penny, you can be sure 'e'll turn up again," said Granpa with a chuckle.

But it was to be over a month before Dad "turned up" again. When I first saw him I couldn't believe my eyes – he was dressed from head to toe in khaki. You see, he had signed up with the second battalion of the Royal Fusiliers. He told us that he expected to be posted to the front at some time in the next few weeks but he would still be home by Christmas; an officer had told him that the bloody Huns would have been sent packing long before then.

Granpa shook his head and frowned, but I was so proud of my dad that for the rest of the day I just strutted around the market by his side. Even the lady who stood on the corner handing out white feathers gave him an approving nod. I scowled at her and promised Dad that if the Germans hadn't been sent packing by Christmas – I would leave the market and join up myself to help him finish off the job. I even went with him to the Black Bull that night, determined to spend my weekly wages on whatever he wanted. But no one would let him buy a drink so I ended up not spending a ha'penny. The next morning he had left us to rejoin his regiment, even before Granpa and I started out for the market.

The old man never wrote because he couldn't write, but everyone in the East End knew that if you didn't get one of those brown envelopes pushed under your door the member of your family who was away at the war must still be alive.

From time to time Mr Salmon used to read to me from his morning paper, but as he could never find a mention of the Royal Fusiliers I didn't discover what the old man was up to. I only prayed that he wasn't at some place called Ypres where, the paper warned us, casualties were heavy.

Christmas Day was fairly quiet for the family that year on account of the fact that the old man hadn't returned from the front as the officer had promised.

Sal, who was working shifts in a café on the Commercial Road, went back to work on Boxing Day, and Grace remained on duty at the London hospital throughout the so-called holiday, while Kitty mooched around checking on everyone else's presents before going back to bed. Kitty never seemed to be able to hold down a job for more than a week at a time, but somehow she was still better dressed than any of us. I suppose it must have been because a string of boyfriends seemed quite willing to spend their last penny on her before going off to the front. I couldn't imagine what she expected to tell them if they all came back on the same day.

Now and then, Kitty would volunteer to do a couple of hours' work on the barrow, but once she had eaten her way through the day's profits she would soon disappear. "Couldn't describe that one as an asset," Granpa used to say. Still, I didn't complain. I was sixteen without a care in the world and my only thoughts at that time were on how soon I could get hold of my own barrow.

Mr Salmon told me that he'd heard the best barrows were being sold off in the Old Kent Road, on account of the fact that so many young lads were heeding Kitchener's cry and joining up to fight for King and country. He felt sure there wouldn't be a better time to make what he called a good *metsieh*. I thanked the baker and begged him not to let Granpa know what I was about, as I wanted to close the *metsieh* before he found out.

The following Saturday morning I asked Granpa for a couple of hours off.

"Found yourself a girl, 'ave you? Because I only 'ope it's not the boozer."

"Neither," I told him with a grin. "But you'll be the first to find out, Granpa, I promise you." I touched my cap and strolled off in the direction of the Old Kent Road.

I crossed the Thames at Tower Bridge and walked further south than I had ever been before, and when I arrived at the rival market I couldn't believe my eyes. I'd never seen so many barrows. Lined up in rows, they were. Long ones, short ones, stubby ones, in all the colours of the rainbow and some of them displaying names that went back generations in the East End. I spent over an hour checking out all those that were for sale but the only one I kept coming back to had displayed in blue on gold down its sides, "The biggest barrow in the world".

The woman who was selling the magnificent object told me that it was only a month old and her old man, who had been killed by the Huns, had paid three quid for it: she wasn't going to let it go for anything less.

I explained to her that I only had a couple of quid to my name, but I'd be willing to pay off the rest before six months were up.

"We could all be dead in six months," she replied, shaking her head with an air of someone who'd heard those sort of stories before.

"Then I'll let you 'ave two quid and sixpence, with my granpa's barrow thrown in," I said without thinking.

"Who's your granpa?"

"Charlie Trumper," I told her with pride, though if the truth be known I hadn't expected her to have heard of him.

"Charlie Trumper's your granpa?"

"What of it?" I said defiantly.

"Then two quid and sixpence will do just fine for now, young un'," she said. "And see you pay the rest back before Christmas."

That was the first time I discovered what the word "reputation" meant. I handed over my life's savings and promised that I would give her the other nineteen and six before the year was up.

We shook hands on the deal and I grabbed the handles and began to push my first cock sparrow back over the bridge towards the Whitechapel Road. When Sal and Kitty first set eyes on my prize, they couldn't stop jumping up and down with excitement and even helped me to paint down one side, "Charlie Trumper, the honest trader, founded in 1823".

Once we had finished our efforts and long before the paint was dry, I wheeled the barrow triumphantly off towards the market. By the time I was in sight of Granpa's pitch my grin already stretched from ear to ear.

The crowd around the old fellow's barrow seemed larger than usual for a Saturday morning and I couldn't work out why there was such a hush the moment I showed up. "There's young Charlie," shouted a voice and several faces turned to stare at me. Sensing trouble, I let go of the handles of my new barrow and ran into the crowd. They quickly stood aside, making a path for me. When I had reached the front, the first thing I saw was Granpa lying on the pavement, his head propped up on a box of apples and his face as white as a sheet.

I ran to his side and fell on my knees. "It's Charlie, Granpa, it's me, I'm 'ere," I cried. "What do you want me to do? Just tell me what and I'll do it."

His tired eyelids blinked slowly. "Listen to me careful, lad," he said, between gasps of breath. "The barrow now belongs to you, so never let it or the pitch out of your sight for more than a few hours at a time."

"But it's your barrow and your pitch, Granpa. 'ow will you work without a barrow and a pitch?" I asked. But he was no longer listening.

Until that moment I never realised anyone I knew could die.

CHAPTER 2

Granpa Charlie's funeral was held on a cloudless morning in early February at the church of St Mary's and St Michael's on Jubilee Street. Once the choir had filed into their places there was standing room only, and even Mr Salmon, wearing a long black coat and deep-brimmed black hat, was among those who were to be found huddled at the back.

When Charlie wheeled the brand-new barrow on to his granpa's pitch the following morning, Mr Dunkley came out of the fish and chip shop to admire the new acquisition.

"It can carry almost twice as much as my granpa's old barrow," Charlie told him. "What's more, I only owe nineteen and six on it." But by the end of the week Charlie had discovered that his barrow was still half-full of stale food that nobody wanted. Even Sal and Kitty turned up their noses when he offered them such delicacies as black bananas and bruised apples. It took several weeks before the new trader was able to work out roughly the quantities he needed each morning to satisfy his customers' needs, and still longer to realise that those needs would vary from day to day.

It was a Saturday morning, after Charlie had collected his produce from the market and was on his way back to Whitechapel, that he heard the raucous cry.

"British troops slain on the Somme," shouted out the boy who stood on the corner of Covent Garden waving a paper high above his head.

Charlie parted with a halfpenny in exchange for the *Daily Chronicle,* then sat on the pavement and started to read, picking out the words he recognised. He learned of the death of thousands of British troops who had been involved in a combined operation with the French against Kaiser Bill's army. The ill-fated exchange had ended in disaster. General Haig had predicted an advance of four thousand yards a day, but it had ended in retreat. The cry of "We'll all be home for Christmas" now seemed an idle boast.

Charlie threw the paper in the gutter. No German would kill his dad, of that he felt certain, though lately he had begun to feel guilty about his own war efforts since Grace had signed up for a spell in the hospital tents, a mere half-mile behind the front line.

Although Grace wrote to Charlie every month, she was unable to supply any news on the whereabouts of their father. "There are half a million soldiers out here," she explained, "and cold, wet and hungry they all look alike." Sal continued her job as a waitress in the Commercial Road and spent all her spare time looking for a husband, while Kitty had no trouble in finding any amount of men who were happy to satisfy her every need. In fact, Kitty was the only one of the three who had enough time off during the day to help out on the barrow, but as she never got up until the sun rose and slipped away long before it had set, she still wasn't what Granpa would have called an asset.

It was to be weeks before young Charlie would stop turning his head to ask, "'ow many, Granpa?", "'ow much, Granpa?", "Is Mrs Ruggles good for credit, Granpa?" And only after he had paid back every penny of his debt on the new barrow and been left with hardly any spare cash to talk of did he begin to realise just how good a costermonger the old fellow must have been.

For the first few months they earned only a few pennies a week between them and Sal became convinced they would all end up in the workhouse if they kept failing to cough up the rent. She begged Charlie to sell Granpa's old barrow to raise another pound, but Charlie's reply was always the same – "Never" – before adding that he would rather starve and leave the relic to rot in the back yard than let another hand wheel it away.

Soon business began to look up, and the biggest barrow in the world even returned enough of a profit to allow Sal to buy a second-hand dress, Kitty a pair of shoes and Charlie a third-hand suit.

Although Charlie was still thin – now a flyweight – and not all that tall, once his seventeenth birthday had come and gone he noticed that the ladies on the corner of the Whitechapel Road, who were still placing white feathers on anyone wearing civilian clothes who looked as if they might be between the ages of eighteen and forty, were beginning to eye him like impatient vultures.

Charlie wasn't frightened of any Germans, but he still hoped that the war might come to an end quickly and that his father would return to Whitechapel and his routine of working at the docks during the day and drinking in the Black Bull at night. But with no letters and only restricted news in the papers even Mr Salmon couldn't tell him what was really happening at the front.

As the months passed, Charlie became more and more aware of his customers' needs and in turn they were discovering that his barrow was now offering better value for money than many of its rivals. Even Charlie felt things were on the up when Mrs Smelley's smiling face appeared, to buy more potatoes for her boarding house in one morning than he would normally have hoped to sell a regular customer in a month.

"I could deliver your order, Mrs Smelley, you know," he said, raising his cap. "Direct to your boarding 'ouse every Monday mornin'."

"No, thank you, Charlie," she replied. "I always like to see what I'm buyin'."

"Give me a chance to prove myself, Mrs Smelley, and then you wouldn't 'ave to come out in all weathers, when you suddenly discover you've taken more bookin's than you expected."

She stared directly at him. "Well, I'll give it a go for a couple of weeks," she said. "But if you ever let me down, Charlie Trumper – "

"You've got yourself a deal," said Charlie with a grin, and from that day Mrs Smelley was never seen shopping for fruit or vegetables in the market again.

Charlie decided that, following this initial success, he should extend his delivery service to other customers in the East End. Perhaps that way, he thought, he might even be able to double his income. The following morning, he wheeled out his Granpa's old barrow from the back yard, removed the cobwebs, gave it a lick of paint and put Kitty on to house-to-house calls taking orders, while he remained on his pitch in Whitechapel.

Within days Charlie had lost all the profit he had made in the past year and suddenly found himself back to square one. Kitty, it turned out, had no head for figures and, worse, fell for every sob story she was told, often ending up giving the food away. By the end of that month Charlie was almost wiped out and once again unable to pay the rent.

"So what you learn from such a bold step?" asked Dan Salmon as he stood on the doorstep of his shop, skull cap on the back of his head, thumbs lodged in the black waistcoat pockets that proudly displayed his half-hunter watch.

"Think twice before you employ members of your own family and never assume that anyone will pay their debts."

"Good," said Mr Salmon. "You learn fast. So how much you need to clear rent and see yourself past next month?"

"What are you getting at?" asked Charlie.

"How much?" repeated Mr Salmon.

"Five quid," said Charlie, lowering his head.

On Friday night after he had pulled down the blind Dan Salmon handed over five sovereigns to Charlie along with several wafers of matzos. "Pay back when possible, boychik, and don't ever tell the missus or we both end up in big trouble."

Charlie paid back his loan at a rate of five shillings a week and twenty weeks later he had returned the full amount. He would always remember handing over the final payment, because it was on the same day as the first big aeroplane raid over London and he spent most of that night hiding under his father's bed, with both Sal and Kitty clinging on to him for dear life.

The following morning Charlie read an account of the bombing in the *Daily Chronicle* and learned that over a hundred Londoners had been killed and some four hundred injured in the raid.

He dug his teeth into a morning apple before he dropped off Mrs Smelley's weekly order and returned to his pitch in the Whitechapel Road. Monday was always busy with everybody stocking up after the weekend and by the time he arrived back at Number 112 for his afternoon tea he was exhausted. Charlie was sticking a fork into his third of a pork pie when he heard a knock on the door.

"Who can that be?" said Kitty, as Sal served Charlie a second potato.

"There's only one way we're going to find out, my girl," said Charlie, not budging an inch.

Kitty reluctantly left the table only to return a moment later with her nose held high in the air. "It's that Becky Salmon. Says she 'desires to have a word with you'."

"Does she now? Then you had better show Miss Salmon into the parlour," said Charlie with a grin.

Kitty slouched off again while Charlie got up from the kitchen table carrying the remainder of the pie in his fingers. He strolled into the only other room that wasn't a bedroom. He lowered himself into an old leather chair and continued chewing while he waited. A moment later Posh Porky marched into the middle of the room and stood right in front of him. She didn't speak. He was slightly taken aback by the sheer size of the girl. Although she was two or three inches shorter than Charlie, she must have weighed at least a stone more than he did; a genuine heavyweight. She so obviously hadn't given up stuffing herself with Salmon's cream buns. Charlie stared at her gleaming white blouse and dark blue pleated skirt. Her smart blue blazer sported a golden eagle surrounded by words he had never seen before. A red ribbon sat uneasily in her short dark hair and Charlie noticed that her little black shoes and white socks were as spotless as ever.

He would have asked her to sit down but as he was occupying the only chair in the room he couldn't. He ordered Kitty to leave them alone. For a moment she stared defiantly at Charlie, but then left without another word.

"So what do you want?" asked Charlie once he heard the door close.

Rebecca Salmon began to tremble as she tried to get the words out. "I've come to see you because of what has happened to my parents." She enunciated each word slowly and carefully and, to Charlie's disgust, without any trace of an East End accent.

"So what 'as 'appened to your parents?" asked Charlie gruffly, hoping she wouldn't realise that his voice had only recently broken. Becky burst into tears. Charlie's only reaction was to stare out of the window because he wasn't quite sure what else to do.

Becky continued shaking as she began to speak again. "Tata was killed in the raid last night and Mummy has been taken to the London hospital." She stopped abruptly, adding no further explanation.

Charlie jumped out of his chair. "No one told me," he said as he began pacing round the room.

"There's no way that you could possibly have known," said Becky. "I haven't even told the assistants at the shop yet. They think he's off sick for the day."

"Do you want me to tell them?" asked Charlie. "Is that why you came round?"

"No," she said, raising her head slowly and pausing for a moment. "I want you to take over the shop."

Charlie was so stunned by this suggestion that although he stopped pacing he made no attempt to reply.

"My father always used to say that it wouldn't be that long before you had your own shop, so I thought . . ."

"But I don't know the first thing about baking," stammered Charlie as he fell back into his chair.

"Tata's two assistants know everything there is to know about the trade, and I suspect you'll know even more than they do within a few months. What that shop needs at this particular moment is a salesman. My father always considered that you were as good as old Granpa Charlie and everyone knows he was the best."

"But what about my barrow?"

"It's only a few yards away from the shop, so you could easily keep an eye on both." She hesitated before adding, "Unlike your delivery service."

"You knew about that?"

"Even know you tried to pay back the last five shillings a few minutes before my father went to the synagogue one Saturday. We had no secrets."

"So 'ow would it work?" asked Charlie, beginning to feel he was always a yard behind the girl.

"You run the barrow and the shop and we'll be fifty-fifty partners."

"And what will you do to earn your share?"

"I'll check the books every month and make sure that we pay our tax on time and don't break any council regulations."

"I've never paid any taxes before," said Charlie, "and who in 'ell's name cares about the council and their soppy regulations?"

Becky's dark eyes fixed on him for the first time. "People who one day hope to be running a serious business enterprise, Charlie Trumper, that's who."

"Fifty-fifty doesn't seem all that fair to me," said Charlie, still trying to get the upper hand.

"My shop is considerably more valuable than your barrow and it also derives a far larger income."

"Did, until your father died," said Charlie, regretting the words immediately he had spoken them.

Becky bowed her head again. "Are we to be partners or not?" she muttered.

"Sixty-forty," said Charlie.

She hesitated for a long moment, then suddenly thrust out her arm. Charlie rose from the chair and shook her hand vigorously to confirm that his first deal was closed.

After Dan Salmon's funeral, Charlie tried to read the *Daily Chronicle* every morning in the hope of discovering what the second battalion, Royal Fusiliers, were up to and where his father might be. He knew the regiment was fighting somewhere in France, but its exact location was never recorded in the paper, so Charlie was none the wiser.

The daily broadsheet began to have a double fascination for Charlie, as he started to take an interest in the advertisements displayed on almost every page. He couldn't believe that those nobs in the West End were willing to pay good money for things that seemed to him to be nothing more than unnecessary luxuries. However, it didn't stop Charlie wanting to taste Coca-Cola, the latest drink from America, at a cost of a penny a bottle; or to try the new safety razor from Gillette – despite the fact that he hadn't even started shaving – at sixpence for the holder and twopence for six blades: he felt sure his father, who had only ever used a cut-throat, would consider the whole idea sissy. And a woman's girdle at two guineas struck Charlie as quite ridiculous. Neither Sal nor Kitty would ever need one of those – although Posh Porky might soon enough, the way she was going.

So intrigued did Charlie become by these seemingly endless selling opportunities that he started to take a tram up to the West End on a Sunday morning just to see for himself. Having ridden on a horse-drawn vehicle to Chelsea, he would then walk slowly back east towards Mayfair, studying all the goods in the shop windows on the way. He also noted how people dressed and admired the motor vehicles that belched out fumes but didn't drop shit as they travelled down the middle of the road. He even began to wonder just how much it cost to rent a shop in Chelsea.

On the first Sunday in October 1917 Charlie took Sal up West with him – to show her the sights, he explained.

Charlie and his sister walked slowly from shop window to shop window, and he was unable to hide his excitement at every new discovery he came across. Men's clothes, hats, shoes, women's dresses, perfume, undergarments, even cakes and pastries could hold his attention for minutes on end.

"For Gawd's sake, let's get ourselves back to Whitechapel where we belong," said Sal. "Because one thing's for sure – I'm never going to feel at 'ome 'ere."

"But don't you understand?" said Charlie. "One day I'm going to own a shop in Chelsea."

"Don't talk daft," said Sal. "Even Dan Salmon couldn't 'ave afforded one of these."

Charlie didn't bother to reply.

When it came to how long Charlie would take to master the baking trade, Becky's judgment proved accurate. Within a month he knew almost as much about oven temperatures, controls, rising yeast and the correct mixture of flour to water as either of the two assistants, and as they were dealing with the same customers as Charlie was on his barrow, sales on both dropped only slightly during the first quarter.

Becky turned out to be as good as her word, keeping the accounts in what she described as "apple-pie order" and even opening a set of books for Trumper's barrow. By the end of their first three months as partners they declared a profit of four pounds eleven shillings, despite having a gas oven refitted at Salmon's and allowing Charlie to buy his first second-hand suit.

Sal continued working as a waitress in a café on the Commercial Road, but Charlie knew she couldn't wait to find someone willing to marry her – whatever physical shape he was in – just as long as I can sleep in a room of my own, she explained.

Grace never failed to send a letter on the first of every month, and somehow managed to sound cheerful despite being surrounded by death. She's just like her mother, Father O'Malley would tell his parishioners. Kitty still came and went as she pleased, borrowing money from both her sisters as well as Charlie, and never paying them back. Just like her father, the priest told the same parishioners.

"Like your new suit," said Mrs Smelley, when Charlie dropped off her weekly order that Monday afternoon. He blushed, raised his cap and pretended not to hear the compliment, as he dashed off to the baker's shop.

The second quarter promised to show a further profit on both Charlie's enterprises, and he warned Becky that he had his eye on the butcher's shop, since the owner's only boy had lost his life at Passchendaele. Becky cautioned him against rushing into another venture before they had discovered what their profit margins were like, and then only if the rather elderly assistants knew what they were up to. "Because one thing's for certain, Charlie Trumper," she told him as they sat down in the little room at the back of Salmon's to check the monthly accounts, "you don't know the first thing about butchery. 'Trumper, the Honest Trader, founded in 1823' still appeals to me," she added. "'Trumper, the Foolish Bankrupt, folded in 1917' doesn't."

Becky also commented on the new suit, but not until she had finished checking a lengthy column of figures. He was about to return the compliment by suggesting that she might have lost a little weight when she leaned across and helped herself to another jam tart.

She ran a sticky finger down the monthly balance-sheet, then checked the figures against the handwritten bank statement. A profit of eight pounds and fourteen shillings, she wrote in thick black ink neatly on the bottom line.

"At this rate we'll be millionaires by the time I'm forty," said Charlie with a grin.

"Forty, Charlie Trumper?" Becky repeated disdainfully. "Not exactly in a hurry, are you?"

"What do you mean?" asked Charlie.

"Just that I was rather hoping we might have achieved that long before then."

Charlie laughed loudly to cover the fact that he wasn't quite certain whether or not she was joking. Once Becky felt sure the ink was dry she closed the books and put them back in her satchel while Charlie prepared to lock up the baker's shop. As they stepped out on to the pavement Charlie bade his partner goodnight with an exaggerated bow. He then turned the key in the lock before starting his journey home. He whistled "It's a Long Way to Tipperary" out of tune as he pushed the few remains left over from the day towards the setting sun. Could he really make a million before he was forty, or had Becky just been teasing him?

As he reached Bert Shorrocks's place Charlie came to a sudden halt. Outside the front door of 112, dressed in a long black cassock, black hat, and with black bible in hand, stood Father O'Malley.

CHAPTER 3

Charlie sat in the carriage of a train bound for Edinburgh and thought about the actions he had taken during the past four days. Becky had described his decision as foolhardy. Sal hadn't bothered with the hardy. Mrs Smelley didn't think he should have gone until he had been called up, while Grace was still tending the wounded on the Western Front, so she didn't even know what he had done. As for Kitty, she just sulked and asked how she was expected to survive without him.

Private George Trumper had been killed on 2 November 1917 at Passchendaele, the letter had informed him: bravely, while charging the enemy lines at Polygon Wood. Over a thousand men had died that day attacking a ten-mile front from Messines to Passchendaele, so it wasn't surprising that the lieutenant's letter was short and to the point.

After a sleepless night, Charlie was the first to be found the following morning standing outside the recruiting office in Great Scotland Yard. The poster on the wall called for volunteers between the ages of eighteen and forty to join up and serve in "General Haig's" army.

Although not yet eighteen, Charlie prayed that they wouldn't reject him.

When the recruiting sergeant barked, "Name?" Charlie threw out his chest and almost shouted, "Trumper." He waited anxiously.

"Date of birth?" said the man with three white stripes on his arm.

"Twentieth of January, 1899," replied Charlie without hesitation, but his cheeks flushed as he delivered the words.

The recruiting sergeant looked up at him and winked. The letters and numbers were written on a buff form without comment. "Remove your cap, lad, and report to the medical officer."

A nurse led Charlie through to a cubicle where an elderly man in a long white coat made him strip to the waist, cough, stick out his tongue and breathe heavily before prodding him all over with a cold rubber object. He then proceeded to stare into Charlie's ears and eyes before going on to hit his kneecaps with a rubber stick. After taking his trousers and underpants off – for the first time ever in front of someone who wasn't a member of his family – he was told he had no transmittable diseases – whatever they were, thought Charlie.

He stared at himself in the mirror as they measured him. "Five foot nine and a quarter," said the orderly.

And still growing, Charlie wanted to add, as he pushed a mop of dark hair out of his eyes.

"Teeth in good condition, eyes brown," stated the elderly doctor. "Not much wrong with you," he added. The old man made a series of ticks down the right-hand side of the buff form before telling Charlie to report back to the chap with the three white stripes.

Charlie found himself waiting in another queue before coming face to face with the sergeant again.

"Right, lad, sign up here and we'll issue you with a travel warrant."

Charlie scrawled his signature on the spot above where the sergeant's finger rested. He couldn't help noticing that the man didn't have a thumb.

"The Honourable Artillery Company or Royal Fusiliers?" the sergeant asked.

"Royal Fusiliers," said Charlie. "That was my old man's regiment."

"Royal Fusiliers it is then," said the sergeant without a second thought, and put a tick in yet another box.

"When do I get my uniform?"

"Not until you get to Edinburgh, lad. Report to King's Cross at zero eight hundred hours tomorrow morning. Next."

Charlie returned to 112 Whitechapel Road to spend another sleepless night. His thoughts dotted from Sal to Grace and then on to Kitty and how two of his sisters would survive in his absence. He also began thinking about Rebecca Salmon and their bargain, but in the end his thoughts always returned to his father's grave on a foreign battlefield and the revenge he intended to inflict on any German who dared to cross his path. These sentiments remained with him until the morning light came shining through the windows.

Charlie put on his new suit, the one Mrs Smelley had commented on, his best shirt, his father's tie, a flat cap and his only pair of leather shoes. I'm meant to be fighting the Germans, not going to a wedding, he said out loud, as he looked at himself in the cracked mirror above the wash-basin. He had already written a note to Becky – with a little help from Father O'Malley – instructing her to sell the shop along with the two barrows if she possibly could and to hold on to his share of the money until he came back to Whitechapel. No one talked about Christmas any longer.

"And if you don't return?" Father O'Malley had asked, head slightly bowed. "What's to happen to your possessions then?"

"Divide anything that's left over equally between my three sisters," Charlie said.

Father O'Malley wrote out his former pupil's instructions and for the second time in as many days Charlie signed his name to an official document.

After Charlie had finished dressing, he found Sal and Kitty waiting for him by the front door, but he refused to allow them to accompany him to the station, despite their tearful protest. Both his sisters kissed him – another first – and Kitty had to have her hand prised out of his before

Charlie was able to pick up the brown paper parcel that contained all his worldly goods.

Alone, he walked to the market and entered the baker's shop for the last time. The two assistants swore that nothing would have changed by the time he returned. He left the shop only to find another barrow boy, who looked about a year younger than himself, was already selling chestnuts from his pitch. He walked slowly through the market in the direction of King's Cross, never once looking back.

He arrived at the Great Northern station half an hour earlier than he had been instructed and immediately reported to the sergeant who had signed him up on the previous day. "Right, Trumper, get yourself a cup of char, then 'ang about on platform three." Charlie couldn't remember when he had last been given an order, let alone obeyed one. Certainly not since his grandfather's death.

Platform three was already crowded with men in uniforms and civilian clothes, some chatting noisily, others standing silent and alone, each displaying his own particular sense of insecurity.

At eleven, three hours after they had been ordered to report, they were finally given instructions to board a train. Charlie grabbed a seat in the corner of an unlit carriage and stared out of the grimy window at a passing English countryside he had never seen before. A mouth-organ was being played in the corridor, all the popular melodies of the day slightly out of tune. As they travelled through city stations, some he hadn't even heard of – Peterborough, Grantham, Newark, York – crowds waved and cheered their heroes. In Durham the engine came to a halt to take on more coal and water. The recruiting sergeant told them all to disembark, stretch their legs and grab another cup of char, and added that if they were lucky they might even get something to eat.

Charlie walked along the platform munching a sticky bun to the sound of a military band playing "Land of Hope and Glory". The war was everywhere. Once they were back on the train there was yet more waving of handkerchiefs from pin-hatted ladies who would remain spinsters for the rest of their lives.

The train chugged on northwards, further and further away from the enemy, until it finally came to a halt at Waverley station in Edinburgh. As they stepped from the carriage a captain, three NCOs and a thousand women were waiting on the platform to welcome them.

Charlie heard the words, "Carry on, Sergeant-Major," and a moment later a man who must have been six feet six inches in height, and whose beer-barrel chest was covered in medal ribbons, took a pace forward.

"Let's 'ave you in line then," the giant shouted in an unintelligible accent. He quickly – but, Charlie was to learn later, by his own standards, slowly – organised the men into ranks of four before reporting back to someone who Charlie assumed must have been an officer. He saluted the man. "All present and correct, sir," he said and the smartest-dressed man Charlie had ever seen in his life returned the salute. He appeared slight standing next to the sergeant-major, although he must have been a shade over six feet himself. His uniform was immaculate, but paraded no medals, and the creases on his trousers were so sharp that Charlie wondered if they had ever been worn before. The young officer held a short leather stick in a gloved hand and occasionally thumped the side of his leg with it, as if he thought he were on horseback. Charlie's eyes settled on the officer's Sam Browne belt and brown leather shoes. They shone so brightly they reminded him of Rebecca Salmon.

"My name is Captain Trentham," the man informed the expectant band of untrained warriors, in an accent that Charlie suspected would have sounded more in place in Mayfair than at a railway station in Scotland. "I'm the battalion adjutant," he went on to explain, as he swayed from foot to foot, "and will be responsible for this intake for the period that you are billeted in Edinburgh. First we will march to the barracks, where you will be issued with supplies so that you can get yourselves bedded down. Supper will be served at nineteen hundred hours and lights out will be at twenty-one hundred hours. Tomorrow morning reveille will be sounded at zero five hundred, when you will rise and have breakfast before you begin your basic training at zero six hundred. This routine will last for the next twelve weeks. And I can promise you that it will be twelve weeks of absolute hell," he added, sounding as if the idea didn't altogether displease him. "During this period Sergeant-Major Philpott will be the senior warrant officer in charge of the unit. The sergeant-major fought on the Somme, where he was awarded the Military Medal, so he knows exactly what you can expect when we eventually end up in France and have to face the enemy. Listen to his every word carefully, because it might be the one thing that saves your life. Carry on, Sergeant-Major."

"Thank you, sir," said Sergeant-Major Philpott in a clipped bark.

The motley band stared in awe at the figure who would be in charge of their lives for the next three months. He was, after all, a man who had seen the enemy and come home to tell the tale.

"Right, let's be having you then," he said, and proceeded to lead his recruits – carrying everything from battered suitcases to brown paper parcels – through the streets of Edinburgh at the double, only to be sure that the locals didn't realise just how undisciplined this rabble really was. Despite their amateur appearance, passers-by still stopped to cheer and clap. Out of the corner of one eye Charlie couldn't help noticing that one of them was resting his only hand against his only leg. Some twenty minutes later, after a climb up the biggest hill Charlie had ever seen, one that literally took his breath away, they entered the barracks of Edinburgh Castle.

That evening Charlie hardly opened his mouth as he listened to the different accents of the men babbling around him. After a supper of pea soup – "One pea each," the duty corporal quipped – and bully beef, he was quartered – and learning new words by the minute – in a large gymnasium that temporarily housed four hundred beds, each a mere two feet in width and set only a foot apart. On a thin horsehair mattress rested one sheet, one pillow and one blanket. King's Regulations.

It was the first time Charlie had thought that 112 Whitechapel Road might be considered luxurious. Exhausted, he collapsed on to the unmade bed, fell asleep, but still woke the next morning at four thirty. This time, however, there was no market to go to, and certainly no choice as to whether he should select a Cox's or a Granny Smith for breakfast.

At five a lone bugle woke his companions from their drowsy slumber. Charlie was already up, washed and dressed when a man with two stripes on his sleeve marched in. He slammed the door behind him and shouted, "Up, up, up," as he kicked the end of any bed that still had a body supine on it. The raw recruits leapt up and formed a queue to wash in basins half full of freezing water, changed only after every third man. Some then went off to the latrines behind the back of the hall, which Charlie thought smelled worse than the middle of Whitechapel Road on a steaming summer's day.

Breakfast consisted of one ladle of porridge, half a cup of milk and a dry biscuit, but no one complained. The cheerful noise that emanated from that hall wouldn't have left any German in doubt that these recruits were all united against a common enemy.

At six, after their beds had been made and inspected, they all trudged out into the dark cold air and on to the parade ground, its surface covered in a thin film of snow.

"If this is bonny Scotland," Charlie heard a Cockney accent declare, "then I'm a bloody Dutchman." Charlie laughed for the first time since he had left Whitechapel and strolled over to a youth far smaller than himself who was rubbing his hands between his legs as he tried to keep warm.

"Where you from?" Charlie asked.

"Poplar, mate. And you?"

"Whitechapel."

"Bloody foreigner."

Charlie stared at his new companion. The youth couldn't have been an inch over five feet three, skinny with dark curly hair and flashing eyes that never seemed to be still, as if he were always on the lookout for trouble. His shiny, elbow-patched suit hung on him, making his shoulders look like a coathanger.

"Charlie Trumper's the name."

"Tommy Prescott," came back the reply. He stopped his exercises and thrust out a warm hand. Charlie shook it vigorously.

"Quiet in the ranks," hollered the sergeant-major. "Now let's get you formed up in columns of three. Tallest on the right, shortest on the left. Move." They parted.

For the next two hours they carried out what the sergeant-major described as "drill". The snow continued to drop unceasingly from the sky, but the sergeant-major showed no inclination to allow one flake to settle on his parade ground. They marched in column of fours, which Charlie later learned were called platoons, arms swinging to waist height, heads held high, one hundred and twenty paces to the minute. "Look lively, lads," and "Keep in step," were the words Charlie had shouted at him again and again. "The Bosche are also marching out there somewhere, and they can't wait to have a crack at you lot," the sergeant-major assured them as the snow continued to fall.

Had he been in Whitechapel, Charlie would have been happy to run up and down the market from five in the morning to seven at night and still box a few rounds at the club, drink a couple of pints of beer and carry out the same routine the next day without a second thought, but when at nine o'clock the sergeant-major gave them a ten-minute break for cocoa he collapsed on to the verge exhausted. Looking up, he found Tommy Prescott peering at him. "Fag?"

"No, thanks," said Charlie. "I don't smoke."

"What's your trade then?" asked Tommy, lighting up.

"I own a baker's shop on the corner of Whitechapel Road," replied Charlie, "and a –"

"Ring the other one, it's got bells on," interrupted

Tommy. "Next you'll be telling me your dad's Lord Mayor of London."

Charlie laughed. "Not exactly. So what do you do?"

"Work for a brewery, don't I? Whitbread and Co, Chiswell Street, EC1. I'm the one who puts the barrels on the carts, and then the shire 'orses pulls me round the East End so that I can deliver my wares. Pay's not good, but you can always drink yourself silly before you get back each night."

"So what made you join up?"

"Now that's a long story, that is," replied Tommy. "You see, to start with –"

"Right. Back on parade, you lot," shouted Sergeant-Major Philpott, and neither man had the breath to speak another word for the next two hours as they were marched up and down, up and down, until Charlie felt that when they eventually stopped his feet must surely fall off.

Lunch consisted of bread and cheese, neither of which Charlie would have dared to offer for sale to Mrs Smelley. As they munched hungrily he learned how Tommy at the age of eighteen had been given the choice of two years at His Majesty's pleasure or volunteering to fight for King and country. He tossed a coin and the King's head landed face up.

"Two years?" said Charlie. "But what for?"

"Nicking the odd barrel 'ere and there and making a side deal with one or two of the more crafty landlords. I'd been getting away with it for ages. An 'undred years ago they would 'ave 'anged me on the spot or sent me off to Australia, so I can't complain. After all, that's what I'm trained for, ain't it?"

"What do you mean?" asked Charlie.

"Well, my father was a professional pick-pocket, wasn't 'e? And 'is father before 'im. You should have seen Captain Trentham's face when 'e found out that I had chosen a spell in the Fusiliers rather than going back to gaol."

Twenty minutes was the time allocated for lunch and then the afternoon was taken up with being fitted with a uniform. Charlie, who turned out to be a regular size, was dealt with fairly quickly, but it took almost an hour to find anything that didn't make Tommy look as if he was entering a sack race.

Once they were back in the billet Charlie folded up his best suit and placed it under the bed next to the one Tommy had settled on, then swaggered around the room in his new uniform.

"Dead men's clothes," warned Tommy, as he looked up and studied Charlie's khaki jacket.

"What do you mean?"

"Been sent back from the front, 'asn't it? Cleaned and sewn up," said Tommy, pointing to a two-inch mend just above Charlie's heart. "About wide enough to thrust a bayonet through, I reckon," he added.

After another two-hour session on the now freezing parade ground they were released for supper.

"More bloody stale bread and cheese," said Tommy morosely, but Charlie was far too hungry to complain as he scooped up every last crumb with a wet finger. For the second night running he collapsed on his bed.

"Enjoyed our first day serving King and country, 'ave we?" asked the duty corporal of his charges, when at twenty-one hundred hours he turned down the gas lights in the barrack room.

"Yes, thank you, Corp," came back the sarcastic cry.

"Good," said the corporal, "because we're always gentle with you on the first day."

A groan went up that Charlie reckoned must have been heard in the middle of Edinburgh. Above the nervous chatter that continued once the corporal had left, Charlie could hear the last post being played on a bugle from the castle battlements. He fell asleep.

When Charlie woke the next morning he jumped out of bed immediately and was washed and dressed before anyone else had stirred. He had folded up his sheets and blankets and was polishing his boots by the time reveille sounded.

"Aren't we the early bird?" said Tommy, as he turned over. "But why bother, I ask myself, when all you're goin' to get for breakfast is a worm."

"If you're first in the queue at least it's an 'ot worm," said Charlie. "And in any case –"

"Feet on the floor. *On* the *floor*," the corporal bellowed, as he entered the billet and banged the frame on the end of every bed he passed with his cane.

"Of course," suggested Tommy, as he tried to stifle a yawn, "a man of property like yourself would need to be up early of a mornin', to make sure 'is workers were already on parade and not shirkin'."

"Stop talking you two and look sharpish," said the corporal. "And get yourselves dressed or you'll find yourself on fatigues."

"I am dressed, Corp," insisted Charlie.

"Don't answer me back, laddie, and don't call me 'Corp' unless you want a spell cleaning out the latrines." That threat was even enough to get Tommy's feet on the floor.

The second morning consisted of more drill accompanied by the ever-falling snow, which this time had a two-inch start on them, followed by another lunch of bread and cheese. The afternoon, however, was designated on company orders as 'Games and Recreation'. So it was a change of kit before jogging in step over to the gymnasium for physical jerks followed by boxing instruction.

Charlie, now a light middleweight, couldn't wait to get in the ring while Tommy somehow managed to keep himself out of the firing line, although both of them became aware of Captain Trentham's menacing presence as his swagger stick continually struck the side of his leg. He always seemed to be hanging about, keeping a watchful eye on them. The only smile that crossed his lips all afternoon was when he saw someone knocked out. And every time he came across Tommy he just scowled.

"I'm one of nature's seconds," Tommy told Charlie later that evening. "You've no doubt 'eard the expression 'seconds out'. Well, that's me," he explained as his friend lay on his bed, staring up at the ceiling.

"Do we ever escape from this place, Corp?" Tommy asked when the duty corporal entered the barracks a few minutes before lights out. "You know, for like good behaviour?"

"You'll be allowed out on Saturday night," said the corporal. "Three hours' restricted leave from six to nine, when you can do what you please. However, you will go no further than two miles from the barracks, you will behave in a manner that befits a Royal Fusilier and you will report back to the guardroom sober as a judge at one minute before nine. Sleep well, my lovelies." These were the corporal's final words before he went round the barracks turning down every one of the gas lights.

When Saturday night eventually came, two swollen-footed, limb-aching, shattered soldiers covered as much of the city as they possibly could in three hours with only five shillings each to spend, a problem that limited their discussions on which pub to select.

Despite this, Tommy seemed to know how to get more beer per penny out of any landlord than Charlie had ever dreamed possible, even when he couldn't understand what they were saying or make himself understood. While they were in their last port of call, the Volunteer, Tommy even disappeared out of the pub followed by the barmaid, a pert, slightly plump girl called Rose. Ten minutes later he was back.

"What were you doin' out there?" asked Charlie.

"What do you think, idiot?"

"But you were only away for ten minutes."

"Quite enough time," said Tommy. "Only officers need more than ten minutes for what I was up to."

During the following week they had their first rifle lesson, bayonet practice and even a session of map-reading. While Charlie quickly mastered the art of map-reading it was Tommy who took only a day to find his way round a rifle. By their third lesson he could strip the barrel and put the pieces back together again faster than the instructor.

On Wednesday morning of the second week Captain Trentham gave them their first lecture on the history of the Royal Fusiliers. Charlie might have quite enjoyed the lesson if Trentham hadn't left the impression that none of them was worthy of being in the same regiment as himself.

"Those of us who selected the Royal Fusiliers because of historic links or family ties may feel that allowing criminals to join our ranks simply because we're at war is hardly likely to advance the regiment's reputation," he said, looking pointedly in the direction of Tommy.

"Stuck-up snob," declared Tommy, just loud enough to reach every ear in the lecture theatre except the captain's. The ripple of laughter that followed brought a scowl to Trentham's face.

On Thursday afternoon Captain Trentham returned to the gym, but this time he was not striking the side of his leg with a swagger stick. He was kitted up in a white gym singlet, dark blue shorts and a thick white sweater, the new outfit just as neat and tidy as his uniform. He walked around watching the instructors putting the men through their paces and, as on his last visit, seemed to take a particular interest in what was going on in the boxing ring. For an hour the men were placed in pairs while they received basic instructions, first in defence and then attack. "Hold your guard up, laddie," were the words barked out again and again whenever fists reached chins.

By the time Charlie and Tommy climbed through the ropes, Tommy had made it clear to his friend that he hoped to get away with three minutes' shadow-boxing.

"Get stuck into each other, you two," shouted Trentham, but although Charlie started to jab away at Tommy's chest he made no attempt to inflict any real pain.

"If you don't get on with it, I'll take on both of you, one after the other," shouted Trentham.

"I'll bet 'e couldn't knock the cream off a custard puddin'," said Tommy, but this time his voice did carry, and to the instructor's dismay, Trentham immediately leapt up into the ring and said, "We'll see about that." He asked the coach to fit him up with a pair of boxing gloves.

"I'll have three rounds with each of these two men," Trentham said as a reluctant instructor laced up the captain's gloves. Everyone else in the gymnasium stopped to watch what was going on.

"You first. What's your name?" asked the captain, pointing to Tommy.

"Prescott, sir," said Tommy, with a grin.

"Ah yes, the convict," said Trentham, and removed the grin in the first minute, as Tommy danced around him trying to stay out of trouble. In the second round Trentham began to land the odd punch, but never hard enough to allow Tommy to go down. He saved that humiliation for the third round, when he knocked Tommy out with an uppercut that the lad from Poplar never saw. Tommy was carried out of the ring as Charlie was having his gloves laced up.

"Now it's your turn," said Trentham. "What's your name?"

"Trumper, sir."

"Well. Let's get on with it, Trumper," was all the captain said before advancing towards him.

For the first two minutes Charlie defended himself well, using the ropes and the corner as he ducked and dived, remembering every skill he had learned at the Whitechapel Boys' Club. He felt he might even have given the captain a good run for his money if it hadn't been for the damn man's obvious advantage of height and weight.

By the third minute Charlie had begun to gain confidence and even landed a punch or two, to the delight of the onlookers. As the round ticked to an end, he felt he had acquitted himself rather well. When the bell sounded he dropped his gloves and turned to go back to his corner. A second later the captain's clenched fist landed on the side of Charlie's nose. Everyone in that gymnasium heard the break as Charlie staggered against the ropes. No one murmured as the captain unlaced his gloves and climbed out of the ring. Never let your guard down was the only solace he offered.

When Tommy studied the state of his friend's face that night as Charlie lay on his bed, all he said was, "Sorry, mate, all my fault. Bloody man's a sadist. But don't worry, if the Germans don't get the bastard, I will."

Charlie could only manage a thin smile.

By Saturday they had both recovered sufficiently to fall in with the rest of the company for pay parade, waiting in a long queue to collect five shillings each from the paymaster. During their three hours off duty that night the pennies disappeared more quickly than the queue, but Tommy somehow continued to get better value for money than any other recruit.

By the beginning of the third week, Charlie could only just fit his swollen toes into the heavy leather boots the army had supplied him with, but looking down the rows of feet that adorned the barrack room floor each morning he could see that none of his comrades was any better off.

"Fatigues for you, my lad, that's for sure," shouted the corporal. Charlie shot him a glance, but the words were being directed at the occupant of the next bed.

"What for, Corp?" asked Tommy.

"For the state of your sheets. Just look at them. You might have had three women in there with you during the night."

"Only two, to be 'onest with you, Corp."

"Less of your lip, Prescott, and see that you report for latrines duty straight after breakfast."

"I've already been this morning, thank you, Corp."

"Shut up, Tommy," said Charlie. "You're only makin' things more difficult for yourself."

"I see you're gettin' to understand my problem," whispered Tommy. "It's just that the corp's worse than the bloody Germans."

"I can only 'ope so, lad, for your sake," came back the corporal's reply. "Because that's the one chance you've got of coming through this whole thing alive. Now get yourself off to the latrines – at the double."

Tommy disappeared, only to return an hour later smelling like a manure heap.

"You could kill off the entire German army without any of us having to fire a shot," said Charlie. "All you'd 'ave to do is stand in front of 'em and 'ope the wind was blowin' in the right direction."

It was during the fifth week – Christmas and the New Year having passed with little to celebrate – that Charlie was put in charge of the duty roster for his own section.

"They'll be makin' you a bleedin' colonel before you've finished," said Tommy.

"Don't be stupid," replied Charlie. "Everyone gets a chance at runnin' the section at some time durin' the twelve weeks."

"Can't see them takin' that risk with me," said Tommy. "I'd turn the rifles on the officers and my first shot would be aimed at that bastard Trentham."

Charlie found that he enjoyed the responsibility of having to organise the section for seven days and was only sorry when his week was up and the task was handed on to someone else.

By the sixth week, Charlie could strip and clean a rifle almost as quickly as Tommy, but it was his friend who turned out to be a crack shot and seemed to be able to hit anything that moved at two hundred yards. Even the sergeant-major was impressed.

"All those hours spent on rifle ranges at fairs might 'ave somethin' to do with it," admitted Tommy. "But what I want to know is, when do I get a crack at the Huns?"

"Sooner than you think, lad," promised the corporal.

"Must complete twelve weeks' trainin'," said Charlie. "That's King's Regulations. So we won't get the chance for at least another month."

"King's Regulations be damned," said Tommy. "I'm

told this war could be all over before I even get a shot at them."

"Not much 'ope of that," said the corporal, as Charlie reloaded and took aim.

"Trumper," barked a voice.

"Yes, sir," said Charlie, surprised to find the duty sergeant standing by his side.

"The adjutant wants to see you. Follow me."

"But, Sergeant, I haven't done anythin' – "

"Don't argue, lad, just follow me."

"It 'as to be the firin' squad," said Tommy. "And just because you wet your bed. Tell 'im I'll volunteer to be the one who pulls the trigger. That way at least you can be certain it'd be over quick."

Charlie unloaded his magazine, grounded his rifle and chased after the sergeant.

"Don't forget, you can insist on a blindfold. Just a pity you don't smoke," were Tommy's last words as Charlie disappeared across the parade ground at the double.

The sergeant came to a halt outside the adjutant's hut, and an out-of-breath Charlie caught up with him just as the door was opened by a colour-sergeant who turned to Charlie and said, "Stand to attention, lad, remain one pace behind me and don't speak unless you're spoken to. Understood?"

"Yes, Colour-Sergeant."

Charlie followed the colour-sergeant through the outer office until they reached another door marked "Capt Trentham, Adj". Charlie could feel his heart pumping away as the colour-sergeant knocked quietly on the door.

"Enter," said a bored voice and the two men marched in, took four paces forward and came to a halt in front of Captain Trentham.

The colour-sergeant saluted.

"Trumper, Private 7312087, reporting as ordered, sir," he bellowed, despite neither of them being more than a yard away from Captain Trentham.

The adjutant looked up from behind his desk.

"Ah, yes, Trumper. I remember, you're the baker's lad from Whitechapel." Charlie was about to correct him when Trentham turned away to stare out of the window, obviously not anticipating a reply. "The sergeant-major has had his eye on you for several weeks," Trentham continued, "and feels you'd be a good candidate for promotion to lance-corporal. I have my doubts, I must confess. However, I do accept that occasionally it's necessary to promote a volunteer in order to keep up morale in the ranks. I presume you will take on this responsibility, Trumper?" he added, still not bothering to look in Charlie's direction.

Charlie didn't know what to say.

"Yes, sir, thank you, sir," offered the colour-sergeant before bellowing, "About turn, quick march, left, right, left, right."

Ten seconds later Lance-Corporal Charlie Trumper of the Royal Fusiliers found himself back out on the parade ground.

"Lance-Corporal Trumper," said Tommy in disbelief after he had been told the news. "Does that mean I 'ave to call you 'sir'?"

"Don't be daft, Tommy. 'Corp' will do," Charlie said with a grin, as he sat on the end of the bed sewing a single stripe on to a sleeve of his uniform.

The following day Charlie's section of ten began to wish that he hadn't spent the previous fourteen years of his life visiting the early morning market. Their drill, their boots, their turn-out and their weapons training became the benchmark for the whole company, as Charlie drove them harder and harder. The highlight for Charlie, however, came in the eleventh week, when they left the barracks to travel to Glasgow where Tommy won the top prize for rifle shooting, beating all the officers and men from seven other regiments.

"You're a genius," said Charlie, after the colonel had presented his friend with the silver cup.

"Wonder if there's an 'alf good fence to be found in Glasgow," was all Tommy had to say on the subject.

* * *

The passing out parade was held on Saturday, 23 February 1918, which ended with Charlie marching his section up and down the parade ground keeping step with the regimental band, and for the first time feeling like a soldier – even if Tommy still resembled a sack of potatoes.

When the parade finally came to an end, Sergeant-Major Philpott congratulated them all and before dismissing the parade told the troops they could take the rest of the day off, but they must return to barracks and be tucked up in bed before midnight.

The assembled company was let loose on Edinburgh for the last time. Tommy took charge again as the lads of Number Eleven Platoon lurched from pub to pub becoming drunker and drunker, before finally ending up in their established local, the Volunteer, on Leith Walk.

Ten happy soldiers stood around the piano sinking pint after pint as they sang, "Pack up your troubles in your old kit bag" and repeating every other item in their limited repertoire. Tommy, who was accompanying them on the mouth-organ, noticed that Charlie couldn't take his eyes off Rose the barmaid who, although on the wrong side of thirty, never stopped flirting with the young recruits. Tommy broke away from the group to join his friend at the bar. "Fancy 'er, mate, do you?"

"Yep, but she's your girl," said Charlie as he continued to stare at the long-haired blonde who pretended to ignore their attentions. He noticed that she had one button of her blouse more than usual undone.

"I wouldn't say that," said Tommy. "In any case, I owe you one for that broken nose."

Charlie laughed when Tommy added, "So we'll 'ave to see what I can do about it." Tommy winked at Rose, then left Charlie to join her at the far end of the bar.

Charlie found that he couldn't get himself to look at them, although he was still able to see from their reflection in the mirror behind the bar that they were deep in conversation. Rose on a couple of occasions turned to look in his direction. A moment later Tommy was standing by his side.

"It's all fixed, Charlie," he said.

"What do you mean, fixed?"

"Exactly what I said. All you 'ave to do is go out to the shed at the back of the pub where they pile up them empty crates, and Rose should be with you in a jiffy."

Charlie sat glued to the bar stool.

"Well, get on with it," said Tommy, "before the bleedin' woman changes her mind."

Charlie slipped off his stool and out of a side door without looking back. He only hoped that no one was watching him, as he almost ran down the unlit passage and out of the back door. He stood alone in the corner of the yard feeling more than a little stupid as he stamped up and down to keep warm. A shiver went through him and he began to wish he were back in the bar. A few moments later he shivered again, sneezed and decided the time had come to return to his mates and forget it. He was walking towards the door just as Rose came bustling out.

"'ello, I'm Rose. Sorry I took so long, but a customer came in just as you darted off." He stared at her in the poor light that filtered through a tiny window above the door. Yet another button was undone, revealing the top of a black girdle.

"Charlie Trumper," said Charlie, offering her his hand.

"I know," she giggled. "Tommy told me all about you, said you were probably the best lay in the platoon."

"I think 'e might 'ave been exaggeratin'," said Charlie, turning bright red, as Rose reached out with both her hands, taking him in her arms. She kissed him first on his neck, then his face and finally his mouth. She then parted Charlie's lips expertly before her tongue began to play with his.

To begin with Charlie was not quite sure what was happening, but he liked the sensation so much that he just continued to hold on to her, and after a time even began to press his tongue against hers. It was Rose who was the first to break away.

"Not so hard, Charlie. Relax. Prizes are awarded for endurance, not for strength."

Charlie began to kiss her again, this time more gently as he felt the corner of a beer crate jab into his buttocks. He tentatively placed a hand on her left breast, and let it remain there, not quite sure what to do next as he tried to make himself slightly more comfortable. It didn't seem to matter that much, because Rose knew exactly what was expected of her and quickly undid the remaining buttons of her blouse, revealing ample breasts well worthy of her name. She lifted a leg up on to a pile of old beer crates, leaving Charlie faced with an expanse of bare pink thigh. He placed his free hand tentatively on the soft flesh. He wanted to run his fingers up as far as they would go, but he remained motionless, like a frozen frame in a black and white film.

Once again Rose took the lead, and removing her arms from around his neck started to undo the buttons on the front of his trousers. A moment later she slid her hand inside his underpants and started to rub. Charlie couldn't believe what was happening although he felt it was well worth getting a broken nose for.

Rose began to rub faster and faster and started to pull down her knickers with her free hand. Charlie felt more and more out of control until suddenly Rose stopped, pulled herself away and stared down the front of her dress. "If you're the best lay the platoon has to offer, I can only hope the Germans win this bloody war."

The following morning battalion orders were posted on the board. The new battalion of Fusiliers was now considered to be of fighting strength and was expected to join the Allies on the Western Front. Charlie wondered if the comradeship that had bound such a disparate bunch of lads together during the past three months was quite enough to make them capable of joining combat with the elite of the German army.

On the train journey back south they were cheered once

again as they passed through every station, and this time Charlie felt they were more worthy of the hatted ladies' respect. Finally that evening the engine pulled into Maidstone where they disembarked, and were put up for the night at the local barracks of the Royal West Kents.

At zero six hundred hours the following morning Captain Trentham gave them a full briefing: they were to be transported by ship to Boulogne, they learned, and after ten days' further training they would be expected to march on to Etaples, where they would join their regiment under the command of Lieutenant-Colonel Sir Danvers Hamilton DSO, who, they were assured, was preparing for a massive assault on the German defences. They spent the rest of the morning checking over their equipment before being herded up a gangplank and on to the waiting troop carrier.

After the ship's foghorn had blasted out six times, they set sail from Dover, one thousand men huddled together on the deck of HMS *Resolution* singing, "It's a Long Way to Tipperary".

"Ever been abroad before, Corp?" Tommy asked.

"No, not unless you count Scotland," replied Charlie.

"Neither 'ave I," said Tommy nervously. After a few more minutes he mumbled, "You frightened?"

"No, of course not," said Charlie. "Bleedin' terrified."

"Me too," said Tommy.

"Goodbye Piccadilly, farewell Leicester Square. It's a long, long way to . . ."

CHAPTER 4

Charlie felt seasick only a few minutes after the English coast was out of sight. "I've never been on a boat before," he admitted to Tommy, "unless you count the paddle steamer at Brighton." Over half the men around him spent the crossing bringing up what little food they had eaten for breakfast.

"No officers coughin' up as far as I can see," said Tommy.

"Perhaps that lot are used to sailin'."

"Or doing it in their cabins."

When at last the French coast came in sight, a cheer went up from the soldiers on deck. By then all they wanted to do was set foot on dry land. And dry it would have been if the heavens hadn't opened the moment the ship docked and the troops set foot on French soil. Once everyone had disembarked, the sergeant-major warned them to prepare for a fifteen-mile route-march.

Charlie kept his section squelching forward through the mud with songs from the music-halls, accompanied by Tommy on the mouth-organ. When they reached Etaples and had pitched their tents for the night, Charlie decided that perhaps the gymnasium in Edinburgh had been luxury after all.

Once the last post had been played two thousand eyes closed, as soldiers under canvas for the first time tried to sleep. Each platoon had placed two men on guard duty, with orders to change them every two hours, to ensure that no one went without rest. Charlie drew the four o'clock watch with Tommy.

After a restless night of tossing and turning on lumpy, wet French soil, Charlie was woken at four, and in turn kicked Tommy, who simply turned over and went straight back to sleep. Minutes later Charlie was outside the tent, buttoning up his jacket before continually slapping himself on the back in an effort to keep warm. As his eyes slowly became accustomed to the half-light, he began to make out row upon row of brown tents stretching as far as the eye could see.

"Mornin', Corp," said Tommy, when he appeared a little after four twenty. "Got a lucifer, by any chance?"

"No, I 'aven't. And what I need is an 'ot cocoa, or an 'ot somethin'."

"Whatever your command, Corp."

Tommy wandered off to the cookhouse tent and returned half an hour later with two hot cocoas and two dry biscuits.

"No sugar, I'm afraid," he told Charlie. "That's only for sergeants and above. I told them you were a general in disguise but they said that all the generals were back in London sound asleep in their beds."

Charlie smiled as he placed his frozen fingers round the hot mug and sipped slowly to be sure that the simple pleasure lasted.

Tommy surveyed the skyline. "So where are all these bleedin' Germans we've been told so much about?"

"'eaven knows," said Charlie. "But you can be sure they're out there somewhere, probably askin' each other where we are."

At six o'clock Charlie woke the rest of his section. They were up and ready for inspection, with the tent down and folded back into a small square by six thirty.

Another bugle signalled breakfast, and the men took their place in a queue that Charlie reckoned would have gladdened the heart of any barrow boy in the Whitechapel Road.

When Charlie eventually reached the front of the queue, he held out his billycan to receive a ladle of lumpy porridge and a stale piece of bread. Tommy winked at the boy in his long white jacket and blue check trousers. "And to think I've waited all these years to sample French cookin'."

"It gets worse the nearer you get to the front," the cook promised him.

For the next ten days they set up camp at Etaples, spending their mornings being marched over dunes, their afternoons being instructed in gas warfare and their evenings being told by Captain Trentham the different ways they could die.

On the eleventh day they gathered up their belongings, packed up their tents and were formed into companies so they could be addressed by the Commanding Officer of the Regiment.

Over a thousand men stood in a formed square on a muddy field somewhere in France, wondering if twelve weeks of training and ten days of "acclimatisation" could possibly have made them ready to face the might of the German forces.

"P'raps they've only had twelve weeks' trainin' as well," said Tommy, hopefully.

At exactly zero nine hundred hours Lieutenant-Colonel Sir Danvers Hamilton DSO trotted in on a jet black mare and brought his charger to a halt in the middle of the man-made square. He began to address the troops. Charlie's abiding memory of the speech was that for fifteen minutes the horse never moved.

"Welcome to France," Colonel Hamilton began, placing a monocle over his left eye. "I only wish it were a day trip you were on." A little laughter trickled out of the ranks. "However, I'm afraid we're not going to be given much time off until we've sent the Huns back to Germany where they belong, with their tails between their legs." This time cheering broke out in the ranks. "And never forget, it's an away match, and we're on a sticky wicket. Worse, the Germans don't understand the laws of cricket." More laughter, although Charlie suspected the colonel meant every word he said.

"Today," the colonel continued, "we march towards Ypres where we will set up camp before beginning a new and I believe final assault on the German front. This time I'm convinced we will break through the German lines, and the glorious Fusiliers will surely carry the honours of the day. Fortune be with you all, and God save the King."

More cheers were followed by a rendering of the National Anthem from the regimental band. The troops joined in lustily with heart and voice.

It took another five days of route-marching before they heard the first sound of artillery fire, could smell the trenches and therefore knew they must be approaching the front. Another day and they passed the large green tents of the Red Cross. Just before eleven that morning Charlie saw his first dead soldier, a lieutenant from the East Yorkshire Regiment.

"Well, I'll be damned," said Tommy. "Bullets can't tell the difference between officers and enlisted men."

Within another mile they had both witnessed so many stretchers, so many bodies and so many limbs no longer attached to bodies that no one had the stomach for jokes. The battalion, it became clear, had arrived at what the newspapers called the "Western Front". No war correspondent, however, could have described the gloom that pervaded the air, or the look of hopelessness ingrained on the faces of anyone who had been there for more than a few days.

Charlie stared out at the open fields that must once have been productive farmland. All that remained was the odd burnt-out farmhouse to mark the spot where civilisation had once existed. There was still no sign of the enemy. He tried to take in the surrounding countryside that was to be his home during the months that lay ahead – if he lived that long. Every soldier knew that average life expectancy at the front was seventeen days.

Charlie left his men resting in their tents while he set out to do his own private recce. First he came across the reserve trenches a few hundred yards in front of the hospital tents, known as the "hotel area" as they were a quarter of a mile behind the front line, where each soldier spent four days without a break before being allowed four days of rest in the reserve trenches. Charlie strolled on up to the front like some visiting tourist who was not involved in a war. He listened to the few men who had survived for more than a few weeks and talked of "Blighty" and prayed only for a "cushy wound" so they could be moved to the nearest hospital tent and, if they were among the lucky ones, eventually be sent home to England.

As the stray bullets whistled across no-man's-land, Charlie fell on his knees and crawled back to the reserve trenches, to brief his section on what they might expect once they were pushed forward another hundred yards.

The trenches, he told his men, stretched from horizon to horizon and at any one time could be occupied by ten thousand troops. In front of them, about twenty yards away, he had seen a barbed-wire fence some three feet high which an old corporal told him had already cost a thousand lives of those who had done nothing more than erect it. Beyond that lay no-man's-land, consisting of five hundred acres once owned by an innocent family, caught in the centre of someone else's war. Beyond that lay the Germans' barbed-wire, and beyond that still the Germans, waiting for them in their trenches.

Each army, it seemed, lay in its own sodden, rat-infested dug-outs for days, sometimes months, waiting for the other side to make a move. Less than a mile separated them. If a head popped up to study the terrain, a bullet followed from the other side. If the order was to advance, a man's chances of completing twenty yards would not have been considered worth chalking up on a bookie's blackboard. If you reached the wire there were two ways of dying; if you reached the German trenches, a dozen.

If you stayed still, you could die of cholera, chlorine gas, gangrene, typhoid or trench foot that soldiers stuck bayonets through to take away the pain. Almost as many men died behind the lines as did from going over the top, an old sergeant told Charlie, and it didn't help to know that the Germans were suffering the same problems a few hundred yards away.

Charlie tried to settle his ten men into a routine. They carried out their daily duties, bailed water out of their trenches and cleaned equipment. Charlie picked up rumours and counter-rumours of what the future might hold for them. He suspected that only the colonel seated in HQ, a mile behind the lines, really had much idea of what was going on.

Whenever it was Charlie's turn to spend four days in the advance trenches his section seemed to occupy most of their time filling their billycans with pints of water, as they struggled to bail out the gallons that dropped daily from the heavens. Sometimes the water in the trenches would reach Charlie's kneecaps.

"The only reason I didn't sign up for the navy was because I couldn't swim," Tommy grumbled. "And no one warned me I could drown just as easily in the army."

Even soaked, frozen and hungry, they somehow remained cheerful. For four weeks Charlie and his section endured such conditions, waiting for fresh orders that would allow them to advance. The only advance they learned of during that time was von Ludendorff's. The German general had caused the Allies to retreat some forty miles, losing 400,000 men while another 80,000 were captured. Captain Trentham was generally the bearer of such news, and what annoyed Charlie even more was that he always looked so smart, clean, and worse – warm and well fed.

Two men from his own section had already died without even seeing the enemy. Most soldiers would have been only too happy to go over the top, as they no longer believed they would survive a war some were saying would last for ever. The boredom was broken only by bayoneting rats, bailing more water out of the trench or having to listen to Tommy repeat the same old melodies on a now rusty mouth-organ.

It wasn't until the ninth week that orders finally came through and they were called back to the man-made square. The colonel, monocle in place, once again briefed them from his motionless horse. The Royal Fusiliers were to advance on the German lines the following morning, having been given the responsibility for breaking through their northern flank. The Irish Guards would give them support from the right flank, while the Welsh would advance from the left.

"Tomorrow will be a day of glory for the Fusiliers," Colonel Hamilton assured them. "Now you must rest, as the battle will commence at first light."

On returning to the trenches, Charlie was surprised to find that the thought of at last being involved in a real fight had put the men in better humour. Every rifle was stripped, cleaned, oiled, checked and then checked again, every bullet placed carefully into its magazine, every Lewis gun tested, oiled and re-tested and then the men finally shaved before they faced the enemy. Charlie's first experience of a razor was in near-freezing water.

No man finds it easy to sleep the night before a battle, Charlie had been told, and many used the time to write long letters to their loved ones at home; some even had the courage to make a will. Charlie wrote to Posh Porky – he wasn't sure why – asking her to take care of Sal, Grace and Kitty if he didn't return. Tommy wrote to no one, and not simply because he couldn't write. At midnight Charlie collected all the section's efforts and handed them in a bundle to the orderly officer.

Bayonets were carefully sharpened, then fixed; hearts began to beat faster as the minutes passed, and they waited in silence for the command to advance. Charlie's own feelings raced between terror and exhilaration, as he watched Captain Trentham strolling from platoon to platoon to deliver his final briefing. Charlie downed in one gulp the tot of rum that was handed out to all the men up and down the trenches just before a battle.

A Second Lieutenant Makepeace took his place behind Charlie's trench, another officer he had never met. He looked like a fresh-faced schoolboy and introduced himself to Charlie as one might do to a casual acquaintance at a cocktail party. He asked Charlie to gather the section together a few yards behind the line so he could address them. Ten cold, frightened men climbed out of their trench and listened to the young officer in cynical silence. The day had been specially chosen because the meteorologists had assured them that the sun would rise at five fifty-three and there would be no rain. The meteorologists would prove to be right about the sun, but as if to prove their fallibility at four eleven a steady drizzle began. "A German drizzle," Charlie suggested to his comrades. "And whose side is God on, anyway?"

Lieutenant Makepeace smiled thinly. They waited for a Verey pistol to be fired, like some referee blowing a whistle before hostilities could officially commence.

"And don't forget, 'bangers and mash' is the password," said Lieutenant Makepeace. "Send it down the line."

At five fifty-three, as a blood-red sun peeped over the horizon, a Verey pistol was fired and Charlie looked back to see the sky lit up behind him.

Lieutenant Makepeace leapt out of the trench and cried, "Follow me, men."

Charlie climbed out after him and, screaming at the top of his voice – more out of fear than bravado – charged towards the barbed-wire.

The lieutenant hadn't gone fifteen yards before the first bullet hit him, but somehow he still managed to carry on until he reached the wire. Charlie watched in horror as Makepeace fell across the barbed barrier and another burst of enemy bullets peppered his motionless body. Two brave men changed direction to rush to his aid, but neither of them even reached the wire. Charlie was only a yard behind them, and was about to charge through a gap in the barrier when Tommy overtook him. Charlie turned, smiled, and that was the last thing he remembered of the Battle of the Lys.

Two days later Charlie woke up in a hospital tent, some three hundred yards behind the line, to find a young girl in a dark blue uniform with a royal crest above her heart hovering over him. She was talking to him. He knew only because her lips were moving: he couldn't hear a word she said. Thank God, Charlie thought, I'm still alive, and surely now I'll be sent back to England. Once a soldier had been certified medically deaf he was always shipped home. King's Regulations.

Charlie's hearing was fully restored a week later and a smile appeared on his lips for the first time when he saw Grace standing by his side pouring him a cup of tea. They had granted her permission to move tents once she'd heard that an unconscious soldier named Trumper was lying down the line. She told her brother that he had been one of the lucky ones, blown up by a land-mine, and only lost a toe – not even a big one, she teased. He was disappointed by her news as the loss of the big one also meant you could go home.

"Otherwise only a few grazes and cuts. Nothing serious and very much alive. Ought to have you back at the front in a matter of days," she added sadly.

He slept. He woke. He wondered if Tommy had survived.

"Any news of Private Prescott?" Charlie asked the orderly officer after he had completed his rounds.

The lieutenant checked his clipboard and a frown came over his face. "He's been arrested. Looks as if he might have to face a court-martial."

"What? Why?"

"No idea," replied the young lieutenant, and moved on to the next bed.

The following day Charlie managed a little food, took

a few painful steps the day after and could run a week later. He was sent back to the front only twenty-one days after Lieutenant Makepeace had leapt up and shouted, "Follow me."

Once Charlie had returned to the relief trenches he quickly discovered that only three men in his section of ten had survived the charge, and there was no sign of Tommy. A new batch of soldiers had arrived from England that morning to take their places and begin the routine of four days on, four days off. They treated Charlie as if he were a veteran.

He had only been back for a few hours when company orders were posted showing that Colonel Hamilton wished to see Lance-Corporal Trumper at eleven hundred hours the following morning.

"Why would the commanding officer want to see me?" Charlie enquired of the duty sergeant.

"It usually means a court-martial or a decoration – the governor hasn't time for anything else. And never forget that he also means trouble, so watch your tongue when you're in his presence. I can tell you, he's got a very short fuse."

At ten fifty-five hours sharp Lance-Corporal Trumper stood trembling outside the colonel's tent, almost as fearful of his commanding officer as of going over the top. A few minutes later the company sergeant-major marched out of the tent to collect him.

"Stand to attention, salute and give your name, rank and serial number," barked CSM Philpott. "And remember, don't speak unless you're spoken to," he added sharply.

Charlie marched into the tent and came to a halt in front of the colonel's desk. He saluted and said, "Trumper, Lance-Corporal 7312087 reporting, sir." It was the first time he had seen the colonel sitting on a chair, not on a horse.

"Ah, Trumper," said Colonel Hamilton, looking up. "Good to have you back. Delighted by your speedy recovery."

"Thank you, sir," said Charlie, aware for the first time that only one of the colonel's eyes actually moved.

"However, there's been a problem involving a private from your section that I'm hoping you might be able to throw some light on."

"I'll 'elp if I can, sir."

"Good, because it seems," said the colonel, placing his monocle up to his left eye, "that Prescott" – he studied a buff form on the desk in front of him before continuing – "yes, Private Prescott, may have shot himself in the hand in order to avoid facing the enemy. According to Captain Trentham's report, he was picked up with a single bullet wound in his right hand while lying in the mud only a few yards in front of his own trench. On the face of it such an action appears to be a simple case of cowardice in the face of the enemy. However, I was not willing to order the setting up of a court-martial before I had heard your version of what took place that morning. After all, he was in your section. So I felt you might have something of substance to add to Captain Trentham's report."

"Yes, sir, I certainly do," Charlie said. He tried to compose himself and go over in his mind the details of what had taken place almost a month before. "Once the Verey pistol 'ad been fired Lieutenant Makepeace led the charge and I went over the top after 'im followed by the rest of my section. The lieutenant was the first to reach the wire but was immediately 'it by several bullets, and there were only two men ahead of me at the time. They bravely went to 'is aid, but fell even before they could reach 'im. As soon as I got to the wire I spotted a gap and ran through it, only to see Private Prescott overtake me as he charged on towards the enemy lines. It must have been then that I was blown up by the land-mine, which may well have knocked out Private Prescott as well."

"Can you be certain it was Private Prescott that overtook you?" asked the colonel, looking puzzled.

"In the 'eat of a battle, it's 'ard to remember every detail, sir, but I will never forget Prescott overtakin' me."

"Why's that?" asked the colonel.

"Because 'e's my mate, and it annoyed me at the time to see 'im get ahead of me."

Charlie thought he saw a faint smile come over the colonel's face.

"Is Prescott a close friend of yours?" the colonel asked, fixing his monocle on him.

"Yes, sir, 'e is, but that would not affect my judgment, and no one 'as the right to suggest it would."

"Do you realise who you are talkin' to?" bellowed the sergeant-major.

"Yes, Sergeant-Major," said Charlie. "A man interested in finding out the truth, and therefore seeing that justice is done. I'm not an educated man, sir, but I am an 'onest one."

"Corporal, you will report –" began the sergeant-major.

"Thank you, Sergeant-Major, that will be all," said the colonel. "And thank you, Corporal Trumper, for your clear and concise evidence. I shall not need to trouble you any further. You may now return to your platoon."

"Thank you, sir," said Charlie. He took a pace backwards, saluted, did an about-turn and marched out of the tent.

"Would you like me to 'andle this matter in my own way?" asked the sergeant-major.

"Yes, I would," replied Colonel Hamilton. "Promote Trumper to full corporal and release Private Prescott immediately."

Tommy returned to his platoon that afternoon, his left hand bandaged.

"You saved my life, Charlie."

"I only told the truth."

"I know, so did I. But the difference is, they believed you."

Charlie lay in his tent that night wondering why Captain Trentham was so determined to be rid of Tommy.

Could any man believe he had the right to send another to his death simply because he had once been to gaol?

Another month passed while they continued the old routines before company orders revealed that they were to march south to the Marne and prepare for a counter-attack against General von Ludendorff. Charlie's heart sank when he read the orders; he knew the odds against surviving two attacks were virtually unknown. He managed to spend the odd hour alone with Grace, who told him she had fallen for a Welsh corporal who had stood on a land-mine and ended up blind in one eye.

Love at first sight, quipped Charlie.

Midnight on Wednesday, 17 July 1918, and an eerie silence fell over no-man's-land. Charlie let those who could, sleep, and didn't attempt to wake anyone until three o'clock the next morning. Now an acting sergeant, he had a platoon of forty men to prepare for battle, all of whom still came under the overall command of Captain Trentham, who hadn't been seen since the day Tommy had been released.

At three thirty, a Lieutenant Harvey joined them behind the trenches, by which time they were all on full battle alert. Harvey, it turned out, had arrived at the front the previous Friday.

"This is a mad war," said Charlie after they had been introduced.

"Oh, I don't know," said Harvey lightly. "I can't wait to have a go at the Hun myself."

"The Germans 'aven't an 'ope in 'ell, as long as we go on producin' nutcases like 'im," whispered Tommy.

"By the way, sir, what's the password this time?" asked Charlie.

"Oh, sorry, quite forgot. Little Red Riding Hood," said the lieutenant.

They all waited. At zero four hundred hours they fixed bayonets and at zero four twenty-one the Verey pistol shot a red flame into the sky somewhere behind the lines and the air was filled with whistles blowing.

"Tally-ho," cried Lieutenant Harvey. He fired his pistol in the air and charged over the top as if he were chasing some errant fox. Once again, Charlie scrambled up and out of the trench only yards behind. The rest of the platoon followed as he stumbled through mud over barren land that no longer bore a single tree to protect them. To the left Charlie could see another platoon ahead of him. The unmistakable figure of the immaculate Captain Trentham brought up the rear. But it was Lieutenant Harvey who was still leading the charge as he hurdled elegantly over the wire and into no-man's-land. It made Charlie feel curiously confident that anyone could survive such stupidity. On and on Harvey went, as if somehow indestructible, or charmed. Charlie assumed that he must fall with every pace he took, as he watched the lieutenant treat the German wire as just another hurdle, before running on towards the enemy trenches as if they were the finishing line in some race being held at his public school. The man got within twenty yards of the tape before a hail of bullets finally brought him down. Charlie now found himself in front and began firing at the Germans as their heads popped up from behind the dug-outs.

He had never heard of anyone actually reaching the German trenches, so he wasn't sure what he was supposed to do next, and despite all the training he still found it hard to shoot on the run. When four Germans and their rifles came up at once he knew that he was never going to find out. He shot straight at the first one, who fell back into the trench, but by then he could only watch the other three take aim. He suddenly became aware of a volley of shots from behind him, and all three bodies fell back like tin ducks on a rifle range. He realised then that the winner of the shooting prize must still be on his feet.

Suddenly he was in the enemy's trench and staring down into a young German's eyes, a terrified boy even younger than himself. He hesitated only for a moment before thrusting his bayonet down the middle of the German's mouth. He pulled the blade out and drove it home once again, this time into the boy's heart, then ran on. Three of his men were now ahead of him, chasing a retreating enemy. At that moment Charlie spotted Tommy on his right flank pursuing two Germans up a hill. He disappeared into some trees and Charlie distinctly heard a single shot somewhere above the noise of battle. He turned and charged quickly off into the forest to rescue his friend, only to find a German splayed out on the ground and Tommy still running on up the hill. A breathless Charlie managed to catch him up when he came finally to a halt behind a tree.

"You were bloody magnificent, Tommy," said Charlie, throwing himself down by his side.

"Not 'alf as good as that officer, what was 'is name?"

"'arvey, Lieutenant 'arvey."

"In the end we were both saved by 'is pistol," said Tommy, brandishing the weapon. "More than can be said for that bastard Trentham."

"What do you mean?" said Charlie.

"He funked the German trenches, didn't 'e? Bolted off into the forest. Two Germans saw the coward and chased after 'im, so I followed. Finished off one of them, didn't I?"

"So where's Trentham now?"

"Somewhere up there," said Tommy, pointing over the brow of the hill. "'e'll be 'iding from that lone German, no doubt."

Charlie stared into the distance.

"So what now, Corp?"

"We 'ave to go after that German and kill 'im before he catches up with the captain."

"Why don't we just go 'ome, and 'ope he finds the captain before I do?" said Tommy.

But Charlie was already on his feet advancing up the hill.

Slowly they moved on up the slope, using the trees for protection, watching and listening until they had reached the top, and open ground.

"No sign of either of them," whispered Charlie.

"Agreed. So we'd better get back behind our lines, because if the Germans catch us I can't believe they'll invite us to join 'em for tea and crumpet."

Charlie took his bearings. Ahead of them was a little church not unlike the many they had passed on the long route-march from Etaples to the front.

"Maybe we'd better check that church first," he said. "But don't let's take any unnecessary risks."

"What the 'ell do you think we've been doin' for the last hour?" asked Tommy.

Inch by inch, foot by foot, they crawled across the open ground until they reached the vestry door. Charlie pushed it open slowly, expecting a volley of bullets to follow but the loudest sound they heard was the screech of the hinges. Once inside, Charlie crossed himself the way his grandfather always had when entering St Mary's and St Michael's in Jubilee Street. Tommy lit a cigarette.

Charlie remained cautious as he began to study the layout of the little church. It had already lost half its roof, courtesy of a German or English shell, while the rest of the nave and porch remained intact.

Charlie found himself mesmerised by the mosaic patterns that covered the inner walls, their tiny squares making up life-size portraits. He moved slowly round the perimeter staring at the seven disciples who had so far survived the ungodly war.

When he reached the altar he fell on his knees and bowed his head, a vision of Father O'Malley coming into his mind. It was then that the bullet flew past him, hitting the brass cross and sending the crucifix crashing to the ground. As Charlie dived for cover behind the altar, a second shot went off. He glanced round the corner of the altar and watched a German officer who had been hit in the side of the head slump through the curtains and out of a wooden box on to the stone floor. He must have died instantly.

"I only 'ope he 'ad time to make a full confession," said Tommy.

Charlie crawled out from behind the altar.

"For Gawd's sake, stay put, you fool, because someone else is in this church and I've got a funny feelin' it isn't just the Almighty."

They both heard a movement in the pulpit above them and Charlie quickly scurried back behind the altar.

"It's only me," said a voice they immediately recognised.

" 'o's me?" said Tommy, trying not to laugh.

"Captain Trentham. So whatever you do, don't fire."

"Then show yourself, and come down with your 'ands above your 'ead so that we can be certain you're 'o you say you are," Tommy said, enjoying every moment of his tormentor's embarrassment.

Trentham rose slowly from the top of the pulpit and began to descend the stone steps with his hands held high above his head. He proceeded down the aisle towards the fallen cross, that now lay in front of the altar, before stepping over the dead German officer and continuing until he came face to face with Tommy, who was still holding a pistol pointing straight at his heart.

"Sorry, sir," said Tommy, lowering the pistol. "I 'ad to be sure you weren't a German."

"Who spoke the King's English," said Trentham sarcastically.

"You did warn us against being taken in by that in one of your lectures, sir," said Tommy.

"Less of your lip, Prescott. And how did you get hold of an officer's pistol?"

"It belonged to Lieutenant 'arvey," interjected Charlie, "who dropped it when – "

"You bolted off into the forest," said Tommy, his eyes never leaving Trentham.

"I was pursuing two Germans who were attempting to escape."

"It looked the other way round to me," said Tommy. "And when we get back, I intend to let anyone know who cares to listen."

"It would be your word against mine," said Trentham. "In any case, both Germans are dead."

"Only thanks to me and try not to forget that the corp 'ere also witnessed everything what 'appened."

"Then you know my version of the events is the accurate one," said Trentham, turning directly to face Charlie.

"All I know is that we ought to be up in that tower, plannin' how we get back to our own lines, and not wastin' any more time quarrellin' down 'ere."

The captain nodded his agreement, turned, ran to the back of the church and up the stone stairs to the safety of the tower. Charlie quickly followed him. They both took look-out positions on opposite sides of the roof, and although Charlie could still hear the sound of the battle, he was quite unable to make out who was getting the better of it on the other side of the forest.

"Where's Prescott?" asked Trentham after a few minutes had passed.

"Don't know, sir," said Charlie. "I thought he was just behind me." It was several minutes before Tommy, wearing the dead German's *pickelhaube*, appeared at the top of the stone steps.

"Where have you been?" asked Trentham suspiciously.

"Searchin' the place from top to bottom in the 'ope that there might 'ave been some grub to be found, but I couldn't even find any communion wine."

"Take your position over there," said the captain, pointing to an arch that was not yet covered, "and keep a look-out. We'll stay put until it's pitch dark. By then I'll have worked out a plan to get us back behind our own lines."

The three men stared out across the French countryside as the light turned first murky, then grey and finally black.

"Shouldn't we be thinkin' of moving soon, Captain?" asked Charlie, after they had sat in pitch darkness for over an hour.

"We'll go when I'm good and ready," said Trentham, "and not before."

"Yes, sir," said Charlie, and sat shivering as he continued to stare out into the darkness for another forty minutes.

"Right, follow me," said Trentham without warning. He rose and led them both down the stone steps, coming to a halt at the entrance to the vestry door. He pulled the door open slowly. The noise of the hinges sounded to Charlie like a magazine emptying on a machine-gun. The three of them stared into the night and Charlie wondered if there was yet another German out there, rifle cocked, waiting. The captain checked his compass.

"First we must try to reach the safety of those trees at the top of the ridge," Trentham whispered. "Then I'll work out a route for getting us back behind our own lines."

By the time Charlie's eyes had become accustomed to the darkness he began to study the moon and, more importantly, the movement of the clouds.

"It's open ground to those trees," the captain continued, "so we can't risk a crossing until the moon disappears behind some cover. Then we'll each make a dash for the ridge separately. So, Prescott, when I give the order, you'll go first."

"Me?" said Tommy.

"Yes, you, Prescott. Then Corporal Trumper will follow the moment you've reached the trees."

"And I suppose you'll bring up the rear, if we're lucky enough to survive?" said Tommy.

"Don't be insubordinate with me," said Trentham. "Or you'll find this time that you will be court-martialled and end up in the gaol you were originally intended for."

"Not without a witness, I won't," said Tommy. "That much of King's Regulations I do understand."

"Shut up, Tommy," said Charlie.

They all waited in silence behind the vestry door until a large shadow moved slowly across the path and finally enveloped the church all the way to the trees.

"Go!" said the captain, tapping Prescott on the shoulder. Tommy bolted off like a greyhound released from the slips, and the two other men watched as he scampered across the open ground, until some twenty seconds later he reached the safety of the trees.

The same hand tapped Charlie on the shoulder a moment later, and off he ran, faster than he had ever run before, despite having to carry a rifle in one hand and a pack on his back. The grin didn't reappear on his face until he had reached Tommy's side.

They both turned to stare in the direction of the captain.

"What the 'ell's he waitin' for?" said Charlie.

"To see if we get ourselves killed would be my guess," said Tommy as the moon came back out.

They both waited but said nothing until the circular glow had disappeared behind another cloud, when finally the captain came scurrying towards them.

He stopped by their side, and leaning against a tree rested until he had got his breath back.

"Right," he eventually whispered, "we'll advance slowly down through the forest, stopping every few yards to listen for the enemy, while at the same time using the trees for cover. Remember, never move as much as a muscle if the moon is out, and never speak unless it's to answer a question put by me."

The three of them began to creep slowly down the hill, moving from tree to tree, but no more than a few yards at a time. Charlie had no idea he could be so alert to the slightest unfamiliar sound. It took the three of them over an hour to reach the bottom of the slope, where they came to a halt. All they could see in front of them was a vast mass of barren open ground.

"No-man's-land," whispered Trentham. "That means we'll have to spend the rest of our time flat on our bellies." He immediately sank down into the mud. "I'll lead," he said. "Trumper, you'll follow, and Prescott will bring up the rear."

"Well at least that proves 'e knows where 'e's goin'," whispered Tommy. "Because 'e must 'ave worked out exactly where the bullets will be comin' from, and 'o they're likely to 'it first."

Slowly, inch by inch, the three men advanced the half mile across no-man's-land, towards the Allied front line, pressing their faces back down into the mud whenever the moon reappeared from behind its unreliable screen.

Although Charlie could always see Trentham in front of him, Tommy was so silent in his wake that from time to time he had to look back just to be certain his friend was still there. A grin of flashing white teeth was all he got for his trouble.

During the first hour the three of them covered a mere hundred yards. Charlie could have wished for a more cloudy night. Stray bullets flying across their heads from both trenches ensured that they kept themselves low to the ground. Charlie found he was continually spitting out mud and once even came face to face with a German who couldn't blink.

Another inch, another foot, another yard – on they crawled through the wet, cold mud across a terrain that still belonged to no man. Suddenly Charlie heard a loud squeal from behind him. He turned angrily to remonstrate with Tommy, only to see a rat the size of a rabbit lying between his legs. Tommy had thrust a bayonet right through its belly.

"I think it fancied you, Corp. Couldn't have been for the sex if Rose is to be believed, so must have wanted you for dinner."

Charlie covered his mouth with his hands for fear the Germans might hear him laughing.

The moon slid out from behind a cloud and again lit up the open land. Once more the three men buried themselves in the mud and waited until another passing cloud allowed them to advance a few more yards. It was two more hours before they reached the barbed-wire perimeter that had been erected to stop the Germans breaking through.

Once they had reached the spiky barrier Trentham

changed direction and began to crawl along the German side of the fence searching for a breach in the wire between them and safety. Another eighty yards had to be traversed – to Charlie it felt more like a mile – before the captain eventually found a tiny gap which he was able to crawl through. They were now only fifty yards from the safety of their own lines.

Charlie was surprised to find the captain hanging back, even allowing him to crawl past.

"Damn," said Charlie under his breath, as the moon made another entrance on to the centre of the stage and left them lying motionless only a street's length away from safety. Once the light had been turned out again, slowly, inch by inch, Charlie continued his crab-like advance, now more fearful of a stray bullet from his own side than from the enemy's. At last he could hear voices, English voices. He never thought the day would come when he would welcome the sight of those trenches.

"We've made it," shouted Tommy, in a voice that might even have been heard by the Germans. Once again Charlie buried his face in the mud.

"Who goes there?" came back the riposte. Charlie could hear rifles being cocked up and down the trenches as sleepy men quickly came to life.

"Captain Trentham, Corporal Trumper and Private Prescott of the Royal Fusiliers," called out Charlie firmly.

"Password?" demanded the voice.

"Oh, God, what's the pass –?"

"Little Red Riding Hood," shouted Trentham from behind them.

"Advance and be recognised."

"Prescott first," said Trentham, and Tommy pushed himself up on to his knees and began to crawl slowly towards his own trenches. Charlie heard the sound of a bullet that came from behind him and a moment later watched in horror as Tommy collapsed on his stomach and lay motionless in the mud.

Charlie looked quickly back through the half-light

towards Trentham who said, "Bloody Huns. Keep down or the same thing might happen to you."

Charlie ignored the order and crawled quickly forward until he came to the prostrate body of his friend. Once he had reached his side he placed an arm around Tommy's shoulder. "There's only about twenty yards to go," he told him. "Man wounded," said Charlie in a loud whisper as he looked up towards the trenches.

"Prescott, don't move while the moon's out," ordered Trentham from behind them.

"How you feelin', mate?" asked Charlie as he tried to fathom the expression on his friend's face.

"Felt better to be 'onest," said Tommy.

"Quiet, you two," said Trentham.

"By the way, that was no German bullet," choked Tommy as a trickle of blood began to run out of his mouth. "So just make sure you get the bastard if I'm not given the chance to do the job myself."

"You'll be all right," said Charlie. "Nothin' and nobody could kill Tommy Prescott."

As a large black cloud covered the moon, a group of men jumped including two Red Cross orderlies who were carrying a stretcher over the top and ran towards them. They dropped the stretcher by Tommy's side and dragged him on to the canvas before jogging back towards the trench. Another volley of bullets came flying across from the German lines.

Once they had reached the safety of the dug-out, the orderlies dumped the stretcher unceremoniously on the ground. Charlie shouted at them, "Get 'im to the 'ospital tent – quickly for God's sake, quickly."

"Not much point, Corp," said the medical orderly. "'e's dead."

CHAPTER 5

"HQ is still waiting for your report, Trumper."

"I know, Sarge, I know."

"Any problems, lad?" asked the colour-sergeant, which Charlie recognised as a coded message for, "Can you write?"

"No problems, Sarge."

For the next hour he wrote out his thoughts slowly, then rewrote the simple account of what had taken place on 18 July 1918 during the second battle of the Marne.

Charlie read and re-read his banal offering, aware that although he extolled Tommy's courage during the battle he made no mention of Trentham fleeing from the enemy. The plain truth was that he hadn't witnessed what was going on behind him. He might well have formed his own opinion but he knew that would not bear cross-examination at some later date. And as for Tommy's death, what proof had he that one stray bullet among so many had come from the pistol of Captain Trentham? Even if Tommy had been right on both counts and Charlie voiced those opinions, it would only be his word against that of an officer and a gentleman.

The only thing he could do was make sure that Trentham received no praise from his pen for what had taken place on the battlefield that day. Feeling like a traitor, Charlie scribbled his signature on the bottom of the second page before handing in his report to the orderly officer.

Later that afternoon the duty sergeant allowed him an hour off to dig the grave in which they would bury Private

Prescott. As he knelt by its head he cursed the men on either side who could have been responsible for such a war.

Charlie listened to the chaplain intone the words, "Ashes to ashes, dust to dust", before the last post was played yet again. Then the burial party took a pace to the right and began digging the grave of another known soldier. A hundred thousand men sacrificed their lives on the Marne. Charlie could no longer accept that any victory was worth such a price.

He sat cross-legged at the foot of the grave, unaware of the passing of time as he hewed out a cross with his bayonet. Finally he stood and placed it at the head of the mound. On the centre of the cross he had carved the words, "Private Tommy Prescott".

A neutral moon returned that night to shine on a thousand freshly dug graves, and Charlie swore to whatever God cared to listen that he would not forget his father or Tommy, or, for that matter, Captain Trentham.

He fell asleep among his comrades. Reveille stirred him at first light, and after one last look at Tommy's grave he returned to his platoon, to be informed that the Commanding Officer would be addressing the troops at zero nine hundred hours.

An hour later he was standing to attention in a depleted square of those who had survived the battle. Colonel Hamilton told his men that the Prime Minister had described the second battle of the Marne as the greatest victory in the history of the war. Charlie found himself unable to raise a voice to join his cheering comrades.

"It was a proud and honourable day to be a Royal Fusilier," continued the colonel, his monocle still firmly in place. The regiment had won a VC, six MCs and nine MMs in the battle. Charlie felt indifferent as each of the decorated men was announced and his citation read out until he heard the name of Lieutenant Arthur Harvey who, the colonel told them, had led a charge of Number Eleven Platoon all the way up to the German trenches, thus allowing those behind him to carry on and break through the enemy's defences. For this he was posthumously awarded the Military Cross.

A moment later Charlie heard the colonel utter the name of Captain Guy Trentham. This gallant officer, the colonel assured the regiment, careless of his own safety, continued the attack after Lieutenant Harvey had fallen, killing several German soldiers before reaching their dugouts, where he wiped out a complete enemy unit single-handed. Having crossed the enemy's lines, he proceeded to chase two Germans into a nearby forest. He succeeded in killing both enemy soldiers before rescuing two Fusiliers from German hands. He then led them back to the safety of the Allied trenches. For this supreme act of courage Captain Trentham was also awarded the Military Cross.

Trentham stepped forward and the troops cheered as the colonel removed a silver cross from a leather case before pinning the medal on his chest.

One sergeant-major, three sergeants, two corporals and four privates then had their citations read out, each one named and his acts of heroism recalled in turn. But only one of them stepped forward to receive his medal.

"Among those unable to be with us today," continued the colonel, "is a young man who followed Lieutenant Harvey into the enemy trenches and then killed four, perhaps five German soldiers before later stalking and shooting another, finally killing a German officer before being tragically killed himself by a stray bullet when only yards from the safety of his own trenches." Once again the assembled gathering cheered.

Moments later the parade was dismissed and while others returned to their tents Charlie walked slowly back behind the lines until he reached the mass burial ground.

He knelt down by a familiar mound and after a moment's hesitation yanked out the cross that he had placed at the head of the grave.

Charlie unclipped a knife that hung from his belt and beside the name Tommy Prescott he carved the letters MM.

* * *

A fortnight later one thousand men, with a thousand legs, a thousand arms and a thousand eyes between them, were ordered home. Sergeant Charles Trumper of the Royal Fusiliers was detailed to accompany them, perhaps because no man had been known to survive three charges on the enemy's lines.

Their cheerfulness and delight at still being alive only made Charlie feel more guilty. After all, he had only lost one toe. On the journey back by land, sea and land, he helped the men dress, wash, eat and be led without complaint or remonstration.

At Dover they were greeted on the quayside by cheering crowds welcoming their heroes home. Trains had been laid on to despatch them to all parts of the country, so that for the rest of their lives they would be able to recall a few moments of honour, even glory. But not for Charlie. His papers only instructed him to travel on to Edinburgh where he was to help train the next group of recruits who would take their places on the Western Front.

On 11 November 1918, at eleven hundred hours, hostilities ceased and a grateful nation stood in silence for three minutes when, on a railway carriage in the forest of Compiègne, the Armistice was signed. When Charlie heard the news of victory he was training some raw recruits on a rifle range in Edinburgh. Some of them were unable to hide their disappointment at being cheated out of the chance of facing the enemy.

The war was over and the Empire had won – or that is how the politicians presented the result of the match between Britain and Germany.

"More than ten million men have died for their country, and some even before they had finished growing," Charlie wrote in a letter to his sister Sal. "And what has either side to show for such carnage?"

Sal wrote back to let him know how thankful she was he was still alive and went on to say that she had become engaged to a pilot from Canada. "We plan to marry in the next few weeks and go to live with his parents in Toronto. Next time you get a letter from me it will be from the other side of the world.

"Grace is still in France but expects to return to the London hospital some time in the New Year. She's been made a ward sister. I expect you know her Welsh corporal caught pneumonia. He died a few days after peace had been declared.

"Kitty disappeared off the face of the earth and then without warning turned up in Whitechapel with a man in a motor car; neither of them seemed to be hers but she looked very pleased with life."

Charlie couldn't understand his sister's PS: "Where will you live when you get back to the East End?"

Sergeant Charles Trumper was discharged from active service on 20 February 1919, one of the early ones: the missing toe had at last counted for something. He folded up his uniform, placed his helmet on top, boots by the side, marched across the parade ground and handed them in to the quartermaster.

"I hardly recognised you, Sarge, in that old suit and cap. Don't fit any longer, do they? You must have grown during your time with the Fussies."

Charlie looked down and checked the length of his trousers: they now hung a good inch above the laces of his boots.

"Must have grown durin' my time with the Fussies," he repeated, pondering the words.

"Bet your family will be glad to see you when you get back to civvy street."

"Whatever's left of them," said Charlie as he turned to go. His final task was to report to the paymaster's office and receive his last pay packet and travel voucher before relinquishing the King's shilling.

"Trumper, the orderly officer would like a word with you," said the sergeant-major, after Charlie had completed what he had assumed was his last duty.

Lieutenants Makepeace and Harvey would always be his duty officers, thought Charlie as he made his way back across the parade ground in the direction of the company offices. Some fresh-faced youth, who had not been properly introduced to the enemy, now had the nerve to try and take their place.

Charlie was about to salute the lieutenant when he remembered he was no longer in uniform, so he simply removed his cap.

"You wanted to see me, sir?"

"Yes, Trumper, a personal matter." The young officer touched a large box that lay on his desk. Charlie couldn't quite see what was inside.

"It appears, Trumper, that your friend Private Prescott made a will in which he left everything to you."

Charlie was unable to hide his surprise as the lieutenant pushed the box across the table.

"Would you be kind enough to check through its contents, and then sign for them?"

Another buff form was placed in front of him. Above the typed name of Private Thomas Prescott was a paragraph written in a bold large hand. An "X" was scrawled below it, witnessed by Sergeant-Major Philpott.

Charlie began to remove the objects from the box one by one. Tommy's mouth-organ, rusty and falling apart, seven pounds eleven shillings and sixpence in back pay, followed by a German officer's helmet. Next Charlie took out a small leather box and opened the lid to discover Tommy's Military Medal and the simple words "For bravery in the field" printed across the back. He removed the medal and held it in the palm of his hand.

"Must have been a jolly brave chap, Prescott," said the lieutenant. "Salt of the earth and all that."

"And all that," agreed Charlie.

"A religious man as well?"

"No, can't pretend 'e was," said Charlie, allowing himself a smile. "Why do you ask?"

"The picture," said the lieutenant, pointing back into

the box. Charlie leaned forward and stared down in disbelief at a painting of the Virgin Mary and Child. It was about eight inches square and framed in black teak. He took the portrait out and held it in his hands.

He gazed at the deep reds, purples and blues that dominated the central figure in the painting, feeling certain he'd seen the image somewhere before. It was several moments before he replaced the little oil in the box along with Tommy's other possessions.

Charlie put his cap back on and turned to go, the box under one arm, a brown paper parcel under the other and a ticket to London in his top pocket.

He marched out of the barracks to make his way to the station – he wondered how long it would be before he could walk at a normal pace. When he reached the guardroom he stopped and turned round for one last look at the parade ground. A set of raw recruits was marching up and down with a new drill instructor, who sounded every bit as determined as the late Sergeant-Major Philpott had been to see that the snow was never allowed to settle.

Charlie turned his back on the parade ground and began his journey to London. He was nineteen years of age and had only just qualified to receive the King's shilling; but now he was a couple of inches taller, shaved and had even come near to losing his virginity.

He'd done his bit, and at least felt able to agree with the Prime Minister on one matter. He had surely taken part in the war to end all wars.

The night sleeper from Edinburgh was full of men in uniform who eyed the civilian-clad Charlie with suspicion, as a man who hadn't yet served his country or, worse, was a "conshi".

"They'll be calling him up soon enough," said a corporal to his mate in a loud whisper from the far side of the carriage. Charlie smiled but didn't comment.

He slept intermittently, amused by the thought that he might have found it easier to rest in a damp, muddy trench with rats and cockroaches for companions. By the time the train pulled into King's Cross station at seven the following morning, he had a stiff neck and an aching back. He stretched himself before he picked up his large paper parcel along with Tommy's life possessions.

On the station he bought a sandwich and a cup of tea. He was surprised when the girl asked him for threepence. "Twopence for those what are in uniform," he was told with undisguised disdain. Charlie downed the tea and left the station without another word.

The roads were busier and more hectic than he remembered, but he still jumped confidently on a tram that had "City" printed across the front. He sat alone on a trestled wooden bench, wondering what changes he would find on his return to the East End. Did his shop flourish, was it simply ticking over, had it been sold, or even gone bankrupt? And what of the biggest barrow in the world?

He jumped off the tram at Poultry, deciding to walk the final mile. His pace quickened as the accents changed; City gents in long black coats and bowlers gave way to professional men in dark suits and trilbies, to be taken over by rough lads in ill-fitting clothes and caps, until Charlie finally arrived in the East End, where even the boaters had been abandoned by those under thirty.

As Charlie approached the Whitechapel Road, he stopped and stared at the frantic bustle taking place all around him. Hooks of meat, barrows of vegetables, trays of pies, urns of tea passed him in every direction.

But what of the baker's shop, and his grandfather's pitch? Would they be "all present and correct"? He pulled his cap down over his forehead and slipped quietly into the market.

When he reached the corner of the Whitechapel Road he wasn't sure he had come to the right place. The baker's shop was no longer there but had been replaced by a bespoke tailor who traded under the name of Jacob Cohen. Charlie pressed his nose against the window but couldn't recognise anyone who was working inside. He swung round to stare at the spot where the barrow of "Trumper, the honest trader" had stood for nearly a century, only to find a gaggle of youths warming themselves round a charcoal fire where a man was selling chestnuts at a penny a bag. Charlie parted with a penny and was handed a bagful, but no one even gave him a second glance. Perhaps Becky had sold everything as he instructed, he thought, as he left the market to carry on down Whitechapel Road where at least he would have a chance to catch up with one of his sisters, rest and gather his thoughts.

When he arrived outside Number 112 he was pleased to find that the front door had been repainted. God bless Sal. He pushed the door open and walked straight into the parlour, where he came face to face with an overweight, half-shaven man dressed in a vest and trousers who was brandishing an open razor.

"What's your game then?" asked the man, holding up the razor firmly.

"I live 'ere," said Charlie.

"Like 'ell you do. I took over this dump six months ago."

"But –"

"No buts," said the man and without warning gave Charlie a shove in the chest which propelled him back into the street. The door slammed behind him, and Charlie heard a key turn in the lock. Not certain what to do next, he was beginning to wish he had never come home.

" 'ello, Charlie. It is Charlie, isn't it?" said a voice from behind him. "So you're not dead after all."

He swung round to see Mrs Shorrocks standing by her front door.

"Dead?" said Charlie.

"Yes," replied Mrs Shorrocks. "Kitty told us you'd been killed on the Western Front and that was why she 'ad to sell 112. That was months ago – 'aven't seen 'er since. Didn't anyone tell you?"

"No, no one told me," said Charlie, at least glad to

find someone who recognised him. He stared at his old neighbour trying to puzzle out why she looked so different.

"'ow about some lunch, luv? You look starved."

"Thanks, Mrs Shorrocks."

"I've just got myself a packet of fish and chips from Dunkley's. You won't 'ave forgotten how good they are. A threepenny lot, a nice piece of cod soaked in vinegar and a bag full of chips."

Charlie followed Mrs Shorrocks into Number 110, joined her in the tiny kitchen and collapsed on to a wooden chair.

"Don't suppose you know what 'appened to my barrow or even Dan Salmon's shop?"

"Young Miss Rebecca sold 'em both. Must 'ave been a good nine months back, not that long after you left for the front, come to think of it." Mrs Shorrocks placed the bag of chips and the fish on a piece of paper in the middle of the table. "To be fair, Kitty told us you were listed as killed on the Marne and by the time anyone found out the truth it was too late."

"May as well 'ave been," said Charlie, "for all there is to come 'ome to."

"Oh, I don't know," said Mrs Shorrocks as she flicked the top off a bottle of ale, took a swig and then pushed it over to Charlie. "I 'ear there's a lot of barrows up for sale nowadays and some still goin' for bargain prices."

"Glad to 'ear it," said Charlie. "But first I must catch up with Posh Porky as I don't 'ave much capital left of my own." He paused to take his first mouthful of fish. "Any idea where she's got to?"

"Never see her round these parts nowadays, Charlie. She always was a bit 'igh and mighty for the likes of us, but I did 'ear mention that Kitty had been to see her at London University."

"London University, eh? Well, she's about to discover Charlie Trumper's very much alive, however 'igh and mighty she's become. And she'd better have a pretty convincing story as to what 'appened to my share of our money." He rose from the table and gathered up his belongings, leaving the last two chips for Mrs Shorrocks.

"Shall I open another bottle, Charlie?"

"Can't stop now, Mrs Shorrocks. But thanks for the beer and grub – and give my best to Mr Shorrocks."

"Bert?" she said. "'aven't you 'eard? 'e died of an 'eart attack over six months ago, poor man. I do miss 'im." It was then that Charlie realised what was different about his old neighbour: no black eye and no bruises.

He left the house and set out to find London University, and see if he could track down Rebecca Salmon. Had she, as he'd instructed if he were listed as dead, divided the proceeds of the sale between his three sisters – Sal, now in Canada, Grace, still somewhere in France, and Kitty, God knows where? In which case there would be no capital for him to start up again other than Tommy's back pay and a few pounds he'd managed to save himself. He asked the first policeman he saw the way to London University and was pointed in the direction of the Strand. He walked another half-mile until he reached an archway that had chiselled in the stone above it: KING'S COLLEGE. He strolled through the opening and knocked on a door marked Enquiries, walked in and asked the man behind the counter if they had a Rebecca Salmon registered at the college. The man checked a list and shook his head. "Not 'ere," he said. "But you could try the university registry in Malet Street."

After another penny tram ride Charlie was beginning to wonder where he would end up spending the night.

"Rebecca Salmon?" said a man who stood behind the desk of the university registry dressed in a corporal's uniform. "Doesn't ring no bells with me." He checked her name in a large directory he pulled out from under the desk. "Oh, yes, 'ere she is. Bedford College, 'istory of Art." He was unable to hide the scorn in his voice.

"Don't have an address for 'er, do you, Corp?" asked Charlie.

"Get some service in, lad, before you call me corp," said the older man. "In fact the sooner you join up the better."

Charlie felt he had suffered enough insults for one day and suddenly let rip, "Sergeant Trumper, 7312087. I'll call you corp and you'll call me sergeant. Do I make myself clear?"

"Yes, Sergeant," said the corporal, springing to attention.

"Now, what's that address?"

"She's in digs at 97 Chelsea Terrace, Sergeant."

"Thank you," said Charlie, and left the startled ex-serviceman staring after him as he began yet another journey across London.

A weary Charlie finally stepped off a tram on the corner of Chelsea Terrace a little after four o'clock. Had Becky got there before him, he wondered, even if she were only living in digs?

He walked slowly up the familiar road admiring the shops he had once dreamed of owning. Number 131 – antiques, full of mahogany furniture, tables and chairs all beautifully polished. Number 133, women's clothes and hosiery from Paris, with garments displayed in the window that Charlie didn't consider it was right for a man to be looking at. On to Number 135 – meat and poultry hanging from the rods at the back of the shop that looked so delicious Charlie almost forgot there was a food shortage. His eyes settled on a restaurant called Mr Scallini which had opened at 139. Charlie wondered if Italian food would ever catch on in London.

Number 141 – an old bookshop, musty, cobwebbed and with not a single customer to be seen. Then 143 – a bespoke tailor. Suits, waistcoats, shirts and collars could, the message painted on the window assured him, be purchased by the discerning gentleman. Number 145 – freshly baked bread, the smell of which was almost enough to draw one inside. He stared up and down the street in incredulity as he watched the finely dressed women going about their daily tasks, as if a world war had never taken place. No one seemed to have told them about ration books.

Charlie came to a halt outside 147 Chelsea Terrace. He gasped with delight at the sight that met his tired eyes – rows and rows of fresh fruit and vegetables that he would have been proud to sell. Two well-turned-out girls in green aprons and an even smarter-looking youth waited to serve a customer.

Charlie took a pace backwards and stared up at the name above the shop. He was greeted by a sign printed in blue on gold which read: "Charlie Trumper, the honest trader. Founded 1823."

BECKY

1918-1920

CHAPTER 6

"From 1480 to 1532," he said.

I checked through my notes to make sure I had the correct dates, aware I had been finding it hard to concentrate. It was the last lecture of the day, and all I could think about was getting back to Chelsea Terrace.

The artist under discussion that afternoon was Bernardino Luini. I had already decided that my degree thesis would be on the life of this underrated painter from Milan. Milan . . . just another reason to be thankful that the war was finally over. Now I could plan excursions to Rome, Florence, Venice and yes, Milan, and study Luini's work at first hand. Michelangelo, da Vinci, Bellini, Caravaggio, Bernini – half the world's art treasures in one country, and I hadn't been able to travel beyond the walls of the Victoria and Albert.

At four thirty a bell rang to mark the end of lectures for the day. I closed my books and watched Professor Tilsey as he pottered towards the door. I felt a little sorry for the old fellow. He had only been dragged out of retirement because so many young dons had left to fight on the Western Front. The death of Matthew Makepeace, the man who *should* have been lecturing that afternoon, "one of the most promising scholars of his generation", the old Professor used to tell us, was "an inestimable loss to the department and the university as a whole". I had to agree with him: Makepeace was one of the few men in England acknowledged as an authority on Luini. I had only attended three of his lectures before he had signed up to go to France . . . The irony of such a man being riddled with German bullets while stretched over a barbed-wire fence somewhere in the middle of France was not lost on me.

I was in my first year at Bedford. It seemed there was never enough time to catch up, and I badly needed Charlie to return and take the shop off my hands. I had written to him in Edinburgh when he was in Belgium, to Belgium when he was in France and to France the very moment he arrived back in Edinburgh. The King's mail never seemed to catch up with him, and now I didn't want Charlie to find out what I had been up to until I had the chance to witness his reaction for myself.

Jacob Cohen had promised to send Charlie over to Chelsea the moment he reappeared in the Whitechapel Road. It couldn't be too soon for me.

I picked up my books and stuffed them away in my old school satchel, the one my father – Tata – had given me when I won my open scholarship to St Paul's. The R.S. he had had so proudly stamped on the front was fading now, and the leather strap had almost worn through, so lately I had been carrying the satchel under my arm: Tata would never have considered buying me a new one while the old one still had a day's life left in it.

How strict Tata had always been with me as a child; even taken the strap to me on a couple of occasions, once for pinching "fress", or buns as Mother called them, behind his back – he didn't mind how much I took from the shop as long as I asked – and once for saying "Damn" when I cut my finger peeling an apple. Although I wasn't brought up in the Jewish faith – my mother wouldn't hear of it – he still passed on to me all those standards that were part of his own upbringing and would never tolerate what he from time to time described as my "unacceptable behaviour".

It was to be many years later that I learned of the strictures Tata had accepted once he had proposed marriage to my mother, a Roman Catholic. He adored her and never once complained in my presence of the fact that he always had to attend *shul* on his own. "Mixed marriage" seems such an outdated expression nowadays but at the turn of the century it must have been quite a sacrifice for both of them to make.

I loved St Paul's from the first day I walked through the gates, I suppose partly because no one told me off for working too hard. The only thing I didn't like was being called "Porky". It was a girl from the class above me, Daphne Harcourt-Browne, who later explained its double connotation. Daphne was a curly-headed blonde known as "Snooty", and although we were not natural friends, our predilection for cream buns brought us together – especially when she discovered that I had a never-ending source of supply. Daphne would happily have paid for them but I wouldn't allow her to as I wanted my classmates to think we were pals. On one occasion she even invited me to her home in Chelsea, but I didn't accept as I knew if I did I would only have to ask her back to my place in Whitechapel.

It was Daphne who gave me my first art book, *The Treasures of Italy*, in exchange for several cream wafers, and from that day on I knew I had stumbled across a subject I wanted to study for the rest of my life. I never asked Daphne but it always puzzled me why one of the pages at the front of the book had been torn out.

Daphne came from one of the best families in London, certainly from what I understood to be the upper classes, so once I left St Paul's I assumed we would never come across each other again. After all, Lowndes Square was hardly a natural habitat for me. Although to be fair neither was the East End while it remained full of such people as the Trumpers and Shorrocks.

And when it came to those Trumpers I could only agree with my father's judgment. Mary Trumper, by all accounts, must have been a saint. George Trumper was a man whose behaviour was unacceptable, not in the same class as his father, whom Tata used to describe as a "mensch". Young Charlie – who was always up to no good as far as I could see – nevertheless had what Tata called "a future". The magic must have skipped a generation, he suggested.

"The boy's not bad for a goy," he would tell me. "He'll run his own shop one day, maybe even more than one, believe me." I didn't give this observation a lot of thought until my father's death left me with no one else to whom I could turn.

Tata had complained often enough that he couldn't leave his two assistants at the shop for more than an hour before something was certain to go wrong. "No *saychel*," he would complain of those unwilling to take responsibility. "Can't think what would happen to the shop if I take one day off."

As Rabbi Glikstein read out the last rites at his *levoyah*, those words rang in my ears. My mother was still unconscious in hospital and they couldn't tell me when or if she might recover. Meanwhile I was to be foisted on my reluctant Aunt Harriet, whom I had only previously met at family gatherings. It turned out that she lived in some place called Romford and as she was due to take me back there the day after the funeral I had only been left with a few hours to make a decision. I tried to work out what my father would have done in the same circumstances and came to the conclusion that he would have taken what he so often called "a bold step".

By the time I got up the next morning, I had determined to sell the baker's shop to the highest bidder – unless Charlie Trumper were willing to take on the responsibility himself. Looking back, I certainly had my doubts about whether Charlie was capable of doing the job but in the end they were outweighed by Tata's high opinion of him.

During my lessons that morning I prepared a plan of action. As soon as school was over I took the train from Hammersmith to Whitechapel, then continued the rest of the journey on foot to Charlie's home.

Once at Number 112 I banged on the door with the palm of my hand and waited – I remember being surprised that the Trumpers didn't have a knocker. My call was eventually answered by one of those awful sisters, but I wasn't quite sure which one it was. I told her I needed to speak to Charlie, and wasn't surprised to be left standing on the doorstep while she disappeared back into the house. She returned a few minutes later and somewhat grudgingly led me into a little room at the back.

When I left twenty minutes later I felt I had come off with rather the worst of the bargain but another of my father's aphorisms came to mind: shnorrers no choosers.

The following day I signed up for an accountancy course as an "extra option". The lessons took place during the evening and then only after I had finished my regular school work for the day. To begin with I found the subject somewhat tedious, but as the weeks passed I became fascinated by how meticulously recording each transaction could prove to be so beneficial even to our little business. I had no idea so much money could be saved by simply understanding a balance-sheet, debt repayments and how to make claims against tax. My only worry was that I suspected Charlie had never bothered to pay any tax in the first place.

I even began to enjoy my weekly visits to Whitechapel, where I would be given the chance to show off my new-found skills. Although I remained resolute that my partnership with Charlie would come to an end the moment I was offered a place at university, I still believed that with his energy and drive, combined with my level-headed approach in all matters financial, we would surely have impressed my father and perhaps even Granpa Charlie.

As the time approached for me to concentrate on my matriculation, I decided to offer Charlie the opportunity to buy out my share of the partnership and even arranged for a qualified accountant to replace me in order that they could take over the book-keeping. Then, yet again, those Germans upset my best laid plans.

This time they killed Charlie's father, which was a silly mistake because it only made the young fool sign up to fight the lot of them on his own. Typically he didn't even bother to consult anyone. Off he went to Great Scotland Yard, in that frightful double-breasted suit, silly flat cap and flashy green tie, carrying all the worries of the Empire on his shoulders, leaving me to pick up the pieces. It was little wonder I lost so much weight over the next year, which my mother considered a small compensation for having to associate with the likes of Charlie Trumper.

To make matters worse, a few weeks after Charlie had boarded the train for Edinburgh, I was offered a place at London University.

Charlie had left me with only two choices: I could try to run the baker's shop myself and give up any thought of taking a degree, or I could sell out to the highest bidder. He had dropped me a note the day he left advising me to sell, so sell I did, but despite many hours spent traipsing round the East End I could only find one interested party: Mr Cohen, who had for some years conducted his tailor's business from above my father's shop and wanted to expand. He made me a fair offer in the circumstances and I even picked up another two pounds from one of the street traders for Charlie's huge barrow; but hard though I tried I couldn't find a buyer for Granpa Charlie's dreadful old nineteenth-century relic.

I immediately placed all the money I had collected on deposit in the Bow Building Society at 102 Cheapside for a period of one year at a rate of four per cent. I had had no intention of touching it while Charlie Trumper was still away at war, until some five months later Kitty Trumper visited me in Romford. She burst into tears and told me that Charlie had been killed on the Western Front. She added that she didn't know what would become of the family now that her brother was no longer around to take care of them. I immediately explained to her what my arrangement with Charlie had been, and that at least brought a smile to her face. She agreed to accompany me to the building society the next day so that we could withdraw Charlie's share of the money.

It was my intention to carry out Charlie's wishes and see that his share of the money was distributed equally between his three sisters. However, the under-manager of the society pointed out to us both in the politest possible terms that I was unable to withdraw one penny of the deposit until the first full year had been completed. He even produced the document I had signed to that effect, bringing to my attention the relevant clause. On learning this Kitty immediately leapt up, let out a stream of obscenities that caused the under-manager to turn scarlet, and then flounced out.

Later, I had cause to be grateful for that clause. I could so easily have divided Charlie's sixty per cent between Sal, Grace, and that awful Kitty, who had so obviously lied about her brother's death. I only became aware of the truth when in July Grace wrote from the front to let me know that Charlie was being sent home following the second battle of the Marne. I vowed there and then to give him his share of the money the day he set foot in England; I wanted to be rid of all those

Trumpers and their distracting problems once and for all.

I only wish Tata had lived to see me take up my place at Bedford College. His daughter at London University; Whitechapel would never have heard the end of it. But a German aeroplane put paid to that and crippled my mother into the bargain. As it turned out, Mother was still delighted to remind all her friends that I had been among the first women from the East End to sign the register.

After I had written my letter of acceptance to Bedford I began to look for digs nearer the university: I was determined to show some independence. My mother, whose heart had never fully recovered from the shock of losing Tata, retired to the suburbs to live with Aunt Harriet in Romford. She couldn't understand why I needed to lodge in London at all, but insisted that any accommodation I settled on had to be approved by the university authorities. She emphasised that I could only share rooms with someone Tata would have considered "acceptable". Mother never stopped telling me she didn't care for the lax morals that had become so fashionable since the outbreak of the war.

Although I had kept in contact with several school friends from St Paul's, I knew only one who was likely to have surplus accommodation in London, and I considered she might well turn out to be my one hope of not having to spend the rest of my life on a train somewhere between Romford and Regent's Park. I wrote to Daphne Harcourt-Browne the following day.

She replied inviting me round to tea at her little flat in Chelsea. When I first saw her again I was surprised to find that I was now a little taller than Daphne but that she had lost almost as much weight as I had. Daphne not only welcomed me with open arms but to my surprise expressed delight at the thought of my occupying one of her spare rooms. I insisted that I should pay her a rent of five shillings a week and also asked her, somewhat tentatively, if she felt able to come and have tea with my mother in Romford. Daphne seemed amused by the thought and travelled down to Essex with me on the following Tuesday.

My mother and aunt hardly uttered a word the entire afternoon. A monologue that centred on hunt balls, riding to hounds, polo and the disgraceful decline of the manners of Guards officers were hardly subjects about which they were often invited to give an opinion. By the time Aunt Harriet had served a second round of muffins I wasn't at all surprised to see my mother happily nodding her approval.

In fact, the only embarrassing moment the entire afternoon came when Daphne carried the tray out into the kitchen – something I suspected she had seldom done before – and spotted my final school report pinned to the pantry door. Mother smiled and added to my humiliation by reading its contents out loud: "Miss Salmon displays an uncommon capacity for hard work which, combined with an inquiring and intuitive mind, should augur well for her future at Bedford College. Signed Miss Potter, Headmistress."

"Ma certainly didn't bother to display my final report anywhere," was all Daphne had to say on the subject.

After I had moved into Chelsea Terrace, life for both of us quickly settled into a routine. Daphne flitted from party to party while I walked at a slightly faster pace from lecture hall to lecture hall, our two paths rarely crossing.

Despite my apprehension, Daphne turned out to be a wonderful companion to share digs with. Although she showed little interest in my academic life – her energies were spent in the pursuit of foxes and Guards officers – she was always brimful of common sense on every subject under the sun, not to mention having constant contact with a string of eligible young men who seemed to arrive in a never-ending convoy at the front door of 97 Chelsea Terrace.

Daphne treated them all with the same disdain, confiding in me that her one true love was still serving on the Western Front – not that she once mentioned his name in my presence.

Whenever I found time to break away from my books, she could always manage to supply a spare young officer to escort me to a concert, a play, even the occasional regimental dance. Although she never showed any interest in what I was up to at university, she often asked questions about the East End and seemed fascinated by my stories of Charlie Trumper and his barrow.

It might have continued like this indefinitely if I hadn't picked up a copy of the *Kensington News*, a paper Daphne took so she could find out what was showing at the local picture-house.

As I flicked through the pages one Friday evening an advertisement caught my eye. I studied the wording closely to be sure the shop was exactly where I thought it was, folded up the paper and left the flat to check for myself. I strolled down Chelsea Terrace to find the sign in the window of the local greengrocer's. I must have walked past it for days without noticing: "For sale. Apply John D. Wood, 6 Mount Street, London W1."

I remembered that Charlie had always wanted to know how prices in Chelsea compared with those in Whitechapel, so I decided to find out for him.

The following day, having asked some leading questions of our local newsagent – Mr Bales always seemed to know exactly what was going on in the terrace and was only too happy to share his knowledge with anyone who wanted to pass the time of day – I presented myself at the offices of John D. Wood in Mount Street. For some time I was left standing at the counter but eventually one of four assistants came over, introduced himself to me as Mr Palmer and asked how he could help.

After a closer inspection of the young man, I doubted that he could help anyone. He must have been about seventeen and was so pale and thin he looked as if a gust of wind might blow him away.

"I'd like to know some more details concerning Number 147 Chelsea Terrace," I said.

He managed to look both surprised and baffled at the same time.

"Number 147 Chelsea Terrace?"

"Number 147 Chelsea Terrace."

"Would madam please excuse me," he said and walked over to a filing cabinet, shrugging exaggeratedly as he passed one of his colleagues. I could see him thumb through several papers before returning to the counter with a single sheet; he made no attempt to invite me in or even to offer me a chair.

He placed the single sheet on the counter top and studied it closely.

"A greengrocer's shop," he said.

"Yes."

"The shop frontage," the young man went on to explain in a tired voice, "is twenty-two feet. The shop itself is a little under one thousand square feet, which includes a small flat on the first floor overlooking the park."

"What park?" I asked, not certain we were discussing the same property.

"Princess Gardens, madam," he said.

"That's a patch of grass a few feet by a few feet," I informed him, suddenly aware that Mr Palmer had never visited Chelsea Terrace in his life.

"The premises are freehold," he continued, not responding to my comment, but at least no longer leaning on the counter. "And the owner would allow vacant possession within thirty days of contracts being signed."

"What price is the owner asking for the property?" I asked. I was becoming more and more annoyed by being so obviously patronised.

"Our client, a Mrs Chapman –" continued the assistant.

"Wife of Able Seaman Chapman, late of HMS *Boxer*," I informed him. "Killed in action on 8 February 1918, leaving a daughter aged seven and a son aged five."

Mr Palmer had the grace to turn white.

"I also know that Mrs Chapman has arthritis which makes it almost impossible for her to climb those stairs to the little flat," I added for good measure.

He now looked considerably perplexed. "Yes," he said. "Well, yes."

"So how much is Mrs Chapman hoping the property will fetch?" I insisted. By now Mr Palmer's three colleagues had stopped what they were doing in order to follow our conversation.

"One hundred and fifty guineas is being asked for the freehold," stated the assistant, his eyes fixed on the bottom line of the schedule.

"One hundred and fifty guineas," I repeated in mock disbelief, without a clue as to what the property was really worth. "She must be living in cloud cuckoo land. Has she forgotten there's a war on? Offer her one hundred, Mr Palmer, and don't bother me again if she expects a penny more."

"Guineas?" he said hopefully.

"Pounds," I replied as I wrote out my name and address on the back of the particulars and left it on the counter. Mr Palmer seemed incapable of speech, and his mouth remained wide open as I turned and walked out of the office.

I made my way back to Chelsea only too aware that I had no intention of buying a shop in the terrace. In any case, I hadn't got one hundred pounds, or anything like it. I had just over forty pounds in the bank and not much prospect of raising another bean, but the silly man's attitude had made me so angry. Still, I decided, there wasn't much fear of Mrs Chapman accepting so insulting an offer.

Mrs Chapman accepted my offer the following morning. Blissfully unaware that I had no obligation to sign any agreement, I put down a ten-pound deposit the same afternoon. Mr Palmer explained that the money was not returnable, should I fail to complete the contract within thirty days.

"That won't be a problem," I told him with bravado, though I hadn't a clue how I would get hold of the balance of the cash.

For the following twenty-seven days I approached everyone I knew, from the Bow Building Society to distant aunts, even fellow-students, but none of them showed the slightest interest in backing a young woman undergraduate to the tune of sixty pounds in order that she could buy a fruit and vegetable shop.

"But it's a wonderful investment," I tried to explain to anyone who would listen. "What's more, Charlie Trumper comes with the deal, the finest fruit and vegetable man the East End has ever seen." I rarely got beyond this point in my sales patter before expressions of incredulity replaced polite interest.

After the first week I came to the reluctant conclusion that Charlie Trumper wasn't going to be pleased that I had sacrificed ten pounds of our money – six of his and four of mine – just to appease my female vanity. I decided I would carry the six-pound loss myself rather than admit to him I'd made such a fool of myself.

"But why didn't you talk it over with your mother or your aunt before you went ahead with something quite so drastic?" enquired Daphne on the twenty-sixth day. "After all, they both seemed so sensible to me."

"And be killed for my trouble? No, thank you," I told her sharply. "In any case, I'm not that sure they have sixty pounds between them. Even if they did, I don't think they'd be willing to invest a penny in Charlie Trumper."

At the end of the month I crept back round to John D. Wood to explain that the ninety pounds would not be forthcoming and they should feel free to place the property back on the market. I dreaded the "I knew as much" smirk that would appear on Mr Palmer's face once he learned my news.

"But your representative completed the transaction yesterday," Mr Palmer assured me, looking as if he would never understand what made me tick.

"My representative?" I said.

The assistant checked the file. "Yes, a Miss Daphne Harcourt-Browne of –"

"But why?" I asked.

"I hardly feel that I'm the person to answer that particular question," offered Mr Palmer, "as I've never set eyes on the lady before yesterday."

"Quite simple really," Daphne replied when I put the same question to her that evening. "If Charlie Trumper is half as good as you claim then I'll have made a very sound investment."

"Investment?"

"Yes. You see, I require that my capital plus four per cent interest should be returned within three years."

"Four per cent?"

"Correct. After all, that's the amount I am receiving on my War Loan Stock. On the other hand, should you fail to return my capital plus interest in full, I will require ten per cent of the profits from the fourth year onwards."

"But there may not be any profits."

"In which case I will automatically take over sixty per cent of the assets. Charlie will then own twenty-four per cent and you sixteen. Everything you need to know is in this document." She handed over several pages of tightly worded copy, the last page of which had a seven on the top. "All it now requires is your signature on the bottom line."

I read through the papers slowly while Daphne poured herself a sherry. She or her advisors seemed to have considered every eventuality.

"There's only one difference between you and Charlie Trumper," I told her, penning my signature between two pencilled crosses.

"And what's that?"

"You were born in a four-poster bed."

As I was quite unable to organise the shop myself and continue with my studies at the university, I quickly came to the conclusion that I would have to appoint a temporary manager. The fact that the three girls who were already employed at Number 147 just giggled whenever I gave any instructions, only made the appointment more pressing.

The following Saturday I began a tour of Chelsea, Fulham and Kensington, staring into shop windows up and down the three boroughs and watching young men going about their business in the hope of eventually finding the right person to run Trumper's.

After keeping an eye on several possible candidates who were working in local shops, I finally selected a young man who was an assistant at a fruiterer's in Kensington. One evening in November I waited for him to finish his day's work. I then followed him as he began his journey home.

The ginger-haired lad was heading towards the nearest bus stop when I managed to catch him up.

"Good evening, Mr Makins," I said.

"Hello?" He looked round startled and was obviously surprised to discover that an unintroduced young woman knew his name. He carried on walking.

"I own a greengrocer's shop in Chelsea

Terrace . . ." I said, keeping up with him stride for stride as he continued on towards the bus stop. He showed even more surprise but didn't say anything, only quickened his pace. ". . . and I'm looking for a new manager."

This piece of information caused Makins to slow down for the first time and look at me more carefully.

"Chapman's," he said. "Was it you who bought Chapman's?"

"Yes, but it's Trumper's now," I told him. "And I'm offering you the job as manager at a pound a week more than your present salary." Not that I had any idea what his present salary was.

It took several miles on the bus and a lot of questions still to be answered outside his front door before he invited me in to meet his mother. Bob Makins joined us two weeks later, as manager of Trumper's.

Despite this coup I was disappointed to find at the end of our first month that the shop had made a loss of over three pounds which meant I wasn't able to return a penny piece to Daphne.

"Don't be despondent," she told me. "Just keep going and there must still be an outside chance the penalty clause will never come into force, especially if on Mr Trumper's return he proves half as good as you claim he is."

During the previous six months I had been able to keep a more watchful eye on the whereabouts of the elusive Charlie, thanks to the help of a young officer Daphne had introduced me to who worked in the War Office. He always seemed to know exactly where Sergeant Charles Trumper of the Royal Fusiliers could be located at any time of the day or night. However, I still remained determined to have Trumper's running smoothly and declaring a profit long before Charlie set foot in the premises.

However I learned from Daphne's friend that my errant partner was to be discharged on 20 February

1919, leaving me with little or no time to balance the books. And worse, we had recently found it necessary to replace two of the three giggling girls who had sadly fallen victim to the Spanish flu epidemic, and sack the third for incompetence.

I tried to recall all the lessons Tata had taught me when I was a child. If a queue was long then you must serve the customers quickly, but if short you had to take your time: that way the shop would never be empty. People don't like to go into empty shops, he explained; it makes them feel insecure.

"On your awning," he would insist, "should be printed in bold lettering the words 'Dan Salmon, freshly baked bread, Founded 1879'. Repeat name and date at every opportunity; the sort of people who live in the East End like to know you've been around for some time. Queues and history: the British have always appreciated the value of both."

I tried to implement this philosophy, as I suspected Chelsea was no different from the East End. But in our case the blue awning read, "Charlie Trumper, the honest trader, founded 1823". For a few days I had even considered calling the shop Trumper and Salmon, but dropped that idea when I realised that would only tie me in with Charlie for life.

One of the big differences I discovered between the East and the West End was that in Whitechapel the names of debtors were chalked up on a slate, whereas in Chelsea they opened an account. To my surprise, bad debts turned out to be more common in Chelsea than in Whitechapel. By the following month I was still unable to pay anything back to Daphne. It was becoming daily more apparent that my only hope now rested with Charlie.

On the day he was due back I had lunch in the college dining hall with two friends from my year. I munched away at my apple and toyed with a piece of cheese as I tried to concentrate on their views on Karl

Marx. Once I had sucked my third of a pint of milk dry I picked up my books and returned to the lecture theatre. Despite being normally mesmerised by the subject of the early Renaissance artists, on this occasion I was grateful to see the professor stacking up his papers a few minutes before the lecture was scheduled to end.

The tram back to Chelsea seemed to take for ever, but at last it came to a halt on the corner of Chelsea Terrace.

I always enjoyed walking the full length of the street to check how the other shops were faring. First I had to pass the antique shop where Mr Rutherford resided. He always raised his hat when he saw me. Then there was the women's clothes shop at Number 133 with its dresses in the window that I felt I would never be able to afford. Next came Kendrick's, the butchers, where Daphne kept an account; and a few doors on from them was the Italian restaurant with its empty cloth-covered tables. I knew the proprietor must be struggling to make a living, because we could no longer afford to extend him any credit. Finally came the bookshop where dear Mr Sneddles tried to eke out a living. Although he hadn't sold a book in weeks he would happily sit at the counter engrossed in his beloved William Blake until it was time to turn the sign on the front door from "Open" to "Closed". I smiled as I passed by but he didn't see me.

I calculated that if Charlie's train had arrived at King's Cross on time that morning, he should have already reached Chelsea by now, even if he had had to cover the entire journey on foot.

I hesitated only for a moment as I approached the shop, then walked straight in. To my chagrin, Charlie was nowhere to be seen. I immediately asked Bob Makins if anyone had called in asking for me.

"No one, Miss Becky," Bob confirmed. "Don't worry, we all remember exactly what was expected of us if Mr Trumper shows up." His two new assistants, Patsy and Gladys, nodded their agreement.

I checked my watch – a few minutes past five – and decided that if Charlie hadn't turned up by now he was unlikely to appear before the next day. I frowned and told Bob he could start closing up. When six chimed on the clock above the door, I reluctantly asked him to push the blind back in, and to lock up while I checked over the day's takings.

"Strange that," said Bob as he arrived by my side at the front door clutching on to the shop door keys.

"Strange?"

"Yes. That man over there. He's been sitting on the bench for the last hour and has never once taken his eyes off the shop. I only hope there's nothing wrong with the poor fellow."

I glanced across the road. Charlie was sitting, arms folded, staring directly at me. When our eyes met he unfolded his arms, stood up and walked slowly over to join me.

Neither of us spoke for some time until he said "So what's the deal?"

CHAPTER 7

"How do you do, Mr Trumper? Pleased to make your acquaintance, I'm sure," said Bob Makins, rubbing his palm down a green apron before shaking his new master's outstretched hand.

Gladys and Patsy both stepped forward and gave Charlie a half-curtsey, which brought a smile to Becky's lips.

"There'll be no need for anything like that," said Charlie. "I'm up from Whitechapel and the only bowing and scraping you'll be doing in future will be for the customers."

"Yes, sir," said the girls in unison, which left Charlie speechless.

"Bob, will you take Mr Trumper's things up to his room?" Becky asked. "While I show him round the shop."

"Certainly, miss," said Bob, looking down at the brown paper parcel and the little box that Charlie had left on the floor by his side. "Is that all there is, Mr Trumper?" he asked in disbelief.

Charlie nodded.

He stared at the two assistants in their smart white blouses and green aprons. They were both standing behind the counter looking as if they weren't quite sure what to do next. "Off you go, both of you," said Becky. "But be sure you're in first thing tomorrow morning. Mr Trumper's a stickler when it comes to time-keeping."

The two girls collected their little felt bags and scurried

away as Charlie sat himself down on a stool next to a box of plums.

"Now we're alone," he said, "you can tell me 'ow all this came about."

"Well," replied Becky, "foolish pride was how it all began but . . ."

Long before she had come to the end of her story Charlie was saying, "You're a wonder, Becky Salmon, a positive wonder."

She continued to tell Charlie everything that had taken place during the past year and the only frown to appear on his forehead came when Charlie learned the details of Daphne's investment.

"So I've got just about two years and nine months to pay back the full sixty pounds plus interest?"

"Plus the first six months' losses," said Becky sheepishly.

"I repeat, Rebecca Salmon, you're a wonder. If I can't do something that simple then I'm not worthy to be called your partner."

A smile of relief crossed Becky's face.

"And do you live 'ere as well?" Charlie asked as he looked up the stairs.

"Certainly not. I share digs with an old school friend of mine, Daphne Harcourt-Browne. We're just up the road at 97."

"The girl who supplied you with the money?" asked Charlie.

Becky nodded.

"She must be a good friend," said Charlie.

Bob reappeared at the bottom of the stairs.

"I've put Mr Trumper's things in the bedroom and checked over the flat. Everything seems to be in order."

"Thank you, Bob," said Becky. "As there's nothing else you can do today, I'll see you in the morning."

"Will Mr Trumper be coming to the market, miss?"

"I doubt it," said Becky. "So why don't you do the

ordering for tomorrow as usual? I'm sure Mr Trumper will join you some time later in the week."

"Covent Garden?" asked Charlie.

"Yes, sir," said Bob.

"Well, if they 'aven't moved it I'll see you there at four thirty tomorrow morning."

Becky watched Bob turn white. "I don't suppose Mr Trumper will expect you to be there every morning at four thirty," she laughed. "Just until he's got back in the swing of things. Goodnight, Bob."

"Goodnight miss, goodnight sir," said Bob, who left the shop with a perplexed look on his face.

"What's all this 'sir' and 'miss' nonsense?" asked Charlie. "I'm only about a year older than Bob."

"So were many of the officers on the Western Front who you called 'sir'."

"But that's the point. I'm not an officer."

"No, but you are the boss. What's more, you're no longer in Whitechapel, Charlie. Come on, it's time you saw your rooms."

"Rooms?" said Charlie. "I've never had 'rooms' in my life. It's been just trenches, tents and gymnasiums lately."

"Well, you have now." Becky led her partner up the wooden staircase to the first floor and began a guided tour. "Kitchen," she said. "Small, but ought to serve your purposes. By the way, I've seen to it that there are enough knives, forks and crockery for three and I've told Gladys that it's also her responsibility to keep the flat clean and tidy. The front room," she announced, opening a door, "if one has the nerve to describe something quite this small as a front room."

Charlie stared at a sofa and three chairs, all obviously new. "What happened to all my old things?"

"Most of them were burnt on Armistice Day," admitted Becky. "But I managed to get a shilling for the horsehair chair, with the bed thrown in."

"And what about my granpa's barrow? You didn't burn that as well?"

"Certainly not. I tried to sell it, but no one was willing to offer me more than five shillings, so Bob uses it for picking up the produce from the market every morning."

"Good," said Charlie, with a look of relief.

Becky turned and moved on to the bathroom. "Sorry about the stain below the cold water tap," she said. "None of us could find anything that would shift it however much elbow grease we used. And I must warn you, the lavatory doesn't always flush."

"I've never 'ad a toilet inside the 'ouse before," said Charlie. "Very posh."

Becky continued on into the bedroom.

Charlie tried to take in everything at once, but his eyes settled on a coloured picture that had hung above his bed in Whitechapel Road and had once belonged to his mother. He felt there was something familiar about it. His eyes moved on to a chest of drawers, two chairs and a bed he had never seen before. He desperately wanted to show Becky how much he appreciated all she had done, and settled for bouncing up and down on the corner of the bed.

"Another first," said Charlie.

"Another first?"

"Yes, curtains. Granpa wouldn't allow them, you know. He used to say –"

"Yes, I remember," said Becky. "Kept you asleep in the morning, and prevented you from doing a proper day's work."

"Well, somethin' like that, except I'm not sure my granpa would 'ave known what the word 'prevented' meant," said Charlie as he began to unpack Tommy's little box. Becky's eyes fell on the picture of the Virgin Mary and Child the moment Charlie placed the little painting on the bed. She picked up the oil and began to study it more closely.

"Where did you get this, Charlie? It's exquisite."

"A friend of mine who died at the front left it to me," he replied matter-of-factly.

"Your friend had taste." Becky kept holding on to the picture. "Any idea who painted it?"

"No, I 'aven't." Charlie stared up at his mother's framed photo that Becky had hung on the wall. "Blimey," he said, "it's exactly the same picture."

"Not quite," said Becky, studying the magazine picture above his bed. "You see, your mother's is a photograph of a masterpiece by Bronzino, while your friend's painting, although it looks similar, is actually a damned good copy of the original." She checked her watch. "I must be off," she said without warning. "I've promised I'd be at the Queen's Hall by eight o'clock. Mozart."

"Mozart. Do I know 'im?"

"I'll arrange an introduction in the near future."

"So you won't be 'anging around to cook my first dinner then?" asked Charlie. "You see, I've still got so many questions I need to 'ave answered. So many things I want to find out about. To start with –"

"Sorry, Charlie. I mustn't be late. See you in the morning though – when I promise I'll answer all your questions."

"First thing?"

"Yes, but not by your standards," laughed Becky. "Some time round eight would be my guess."

"Do you like this fellow Mozart?" Charlie asked, as Becky felt his eyes studying her more closely.

"Well, to be honest I don't know a lot about him myself, but Guy likes him."

"Guy?" said Charlie.

"Yes, Guy. He's the young man who's taking me to the concert and I haven't known him long enough to be late. I'll tell you more about both of them tomorrow. Bye, Charlie."

On the walk back to Daphne's flat Becky couldn't help feeling a little guilty about deserting Charlie on his first night home and began to think perhaps it had been selfish of her to accept an invitation to go to a concert with Guy that night. But the battalion didn't give him that many evenings off during the week, and if she didn't see him when he was free it often turned out to be several days before they could spend another evening together.

As she opened the front door of 97, Becky could hear Daphne splashing around in the bath.

"Has he changed?" her friend shouted on hearing the door close.

"Who?" asked Becky, walking through to the bedroom.

"Charlie, of course," said Daphne, pushing open the bathroom door. She stood leaning against the tiled wall with a towel wrapped around her body. She was almost enveloped in a cloud of steam.

Becky considered the question for a moment. "He's changed, yes; a lot, in fact, except for his clothes and voice."

"What do you mean?"

"Well, the voice is the same – I'd recognise it anywhere. The clothes are the same – I'd recognise them anywhere. But he's not the same."

"Am I meant to understand all that?" asked Daphne, as she began to rub her hair vigorously.

"Well, as he pointed out to me, Bob Makins is only a year younger than he is, but Charlie seems about ten years older than either of us. It must be something that happens to men once they've served on the Western Front."

"You shouldn't be surprised by that, but what I want to know is: did the shop come as a surprise to him?"

"Yes, I think I can honestly say it did." Becky slipped out of her dress. "Don't suppose you've got a pair of stockings I could borrow, have you?"

"Third drawer down," said Daphne. "But in exchange I'd like to borrow your legs."

Becky laughed.

"What's he like to look at?" Daphne continued as she threw her wet towel on the bathroom floor.

Becky considered the question. "An inch, perhaps two, under six foot, every bit as large as his father, only in his case it's muscle, not fat. He's not exactly Douglas Fairbanks, but some might consider him handsome."

"He's beginning to sound my type," said Daphne as she rummaged around among her clothes to find something suitable.

"Hardly, my dear," said Becky. "I can't see Brigadier Harcourt-Browne welcoming Charlie Trumper to morning sherry before the Cottenham Hunt."

"You're such a snob, Rebecca Salmon," said Daphne, laughing. "We may share rooms, but don't forget you and Charlie originate from the same stable. Come to think of it, you only met Guy because of me."

"Too true," Becky said, "but surely I get a little credit for St Paul's and London University?"

"Not where I come from, you don't," said Daphne, as she checked her nails. "Can't stop and chatter with the working class now, darling," she continued. "Must be off. Henry Bromsgrove is taking me to a flapper dance in Chelsea. And wet as our Henry is, I do enjoy an invitation to stalk at his country home in Scotland every August. Tootle pip!"

As Becky drew her bath, she thought about Daphne's words, delivered with humour and affection but still highlighting the problems she faced when trying to cross the established social barriers for more than a few moments.

Daphne had indeed introduced her to Guy, only a few weeks before, when Daphne had persuaded her to make up a party to see *La Bohème* at Covent Garden. Becky could still recall that first meeting clearly. She had tried so hard not to like him as they shared a drink at the Crush Bar, especially after Daphne's warning about his reputation. She had tried not to stare too obviously at the slim young man who stood before her. His thick blond hair, deep blue eyes and effortless charm had probably captivated the hearts of a host of women that evening, but as Becky assumed that every girl received exactly the same treatment, she avoided allowing herself to be flattered by him.

The following evening Daphne asked her what she had thought of the young officer she had met at the Opera.

"Remind me of his name," said Becky.

"Oh, I see," said Daphne. "Affected you that badly, did he?"

"Yes," she admitted. "But so what? Can you see a

young man with a background like his taking any interest in a girl from Whitechapel?"

"Yes, I can actually, although I suspect he's only after one thing."

"Then you'd better warn him I'm not that sort of girl," said Becky.

"I don't think that's ever put him off in the past," replied Daphne. "However, to start with he's asking if you would care to accompany him to the theatre along with some friends from his regiment. How does that strike you?"

"I'd love to."

"I thought you might," said Daphne. "So I told him 'yes' without bothering to consult you."

Becky laughed but had to wait another five days before she actually saw the young officer again. After he had come to collect her at the flat they joined a party of junior officers and debutantes at the Haymarket Theatre to see *Pygmalion* by the fashionable playwright George Bernard Shaw. Becky enjoyed the new play despite a girl called Amanda giggling all the way through the first act and then refusing to hold a conversation with her during the interval.

Over dinner at the Café Royal, she sat next to Guy and told him everything about herself from her birth in Whitechapel through to winning a place at Bedford College the previous year.

After Becky had bade her farewells to the rest of the party, Guy drove her back to Chelsea and having said, "Goodnight, Miss Salmon," shook her by the hand.

Becky assumed that she would not be seeing the young officer again.

But Guy dropped her a note the next day, inviting her to a reception at the mess. This was followed a week later by a dinner, then a ball, and after that regular outings took place, culminating in an invitation to spend the weekend with his parents in Berkshire.

Daphne did her best to brief Becky fully on the family. The major, Guy's father, was a sweetie, she assured her, farmed seven hundred acres of dairy land in Berkshire, and was also Master of the Buckhurst Hunt.

It took Daphne several attempts to explain what "riding to hounds" actually meant, though she had to admit that even Eliza Doolittle would have been hard pushed to understand fully why they bothered with the exercise in the first place.

"Guy's mother, however, is not graced with the same generous instincts as the major," Daphne warned. "She is a snob of the first order." Becky's heart sank. "Second daughter of a baronet, who was created by Lloyd George for making things they stick on the end of tanks. Probably gave large donations to the Liberal Party at the same time, I'll be bound. Second generation, of course. They're always the worst." Daphne checked the seams on her stockings. "My family have been around for seventeen generations, don't you know, so we feel we haven't an awful lot to prove. We're quite aware that we don't possess a modicum of brain between us, but by God we're rich, and by Harry we're ancient. However, I fear the same cannot be said for Captain Guy Trentham."

CHAPTER 8

Becky woke the next morning before her alarm went off, and was up, dressed and had left the flat long before Daphne had even stirred. She couldn't wait to find out how Charlie was coping on his first day. As she walked towards 147 she noticed that the shop was already open, and a lone customer was receiving Charlie's undivided attention.

"Good mornin', partner," shouted Charlie from behind the counter as Becky stepped into the shop.

"Good morning," Becky replied. "I see you're determined to spend your first day just sitting back and watching how it all works."

Charlie, she was to discover, had begun serving customers before Gladys and Patsy had arrived, while poor Bob Makins looked as if he had already completed a full day's work.

"'aven't the time to chatter to the idle classes at the moment," said Charlie, his Cockney accent seeming broader than ever. "Any 'ope of catching up with you later this evening?"

"Of course," said Becky.

She checked her watch, waved goodbye and departed for her first lecture of the morning. She found it hard to concentrate on the history of the Renaissance era, and even slides of Raphael's work, reflected from a magic lantern on to a white sheet, couldn't fully arouse her interest. Her mind kept switching from the anxiety of having to spend a weekend with Guy's parents to the problems of Charlie making enough of a profit to clear their debt with Daphne. Becky admitted to herself that she felt more confident of the latter. She was relieved to see the black hand of the clock pass four thirty. Once again she ran to catch the tram on the corner of Portland Place – and continued to run after the trudging vehicle had deposited her in Chelsea Terrace.

A little queue had formed at Trumper's and Becky could hear Charlie's familiar old catch-phrases even before she reached the front door.

" 'alf a pound of your King Edward's, a juicy grapefruit from South Africa, and why don't I throw in a nice Cox's orange pippin, all for a bob, my luv?" Grand dames, ladies-in-waiting and nannies, all who would have turned their noses up had anyone else called them "luv", seemed to melt when Charlie uttered the word. It was only after the last customer had left that Becky was able to properly take in the changes Charlie had already made to the shop.

"Up all night, wasn't I?" he told her. "Removin' 'alf-empty boxes and unsaleable items. Ended up with all the colourful vegetables, your greens, all soft, placed at the back; while all your 'ardy unattractive variety you put up front. Potatoes, swedes, and turnips. It's a golden rule."

"Granpa Charlie –" she began with a smile, but stopped herself just in time.

Becky began to study the rearranged counters and had to agree that it was far more practical the way Charlie had insisted they should be laid out. And she certainly couldn't argue with the smiles on the faces of the customers.

Within a month, a queue stretching out on to the pavement became part of Charlie's daily routine and within two he was already talking to Becky of expanding.

"Where to?" she asked. "Your bedroom?"

"No room for vegetables up there," he replied with a grin. "Not since we've 'ad longer queues at Trumper's than what they 'ave outside *Pygmalion*. What's more, *we're* goin' to run for ever."

After she had checked and rechecked the takings for

the first quarter, Becky couldn't believe how much they had turned over; she decided perhaps the time had come for a little celebration.

"Why don't we all have dinner at that Italian restaurant?" suggested Daphne, after she had received a far larger cheque for the past three months than she had anticipated.

Becky thought it a wonderful idea, but was surprised to find how reluctant Guy was to fall in with her plans, and also how much trouble Daphne took getting herself ready for the occasion.

"We're not expecting to spend all the profits in one evening," Becky assured her.

"More's the pity," said Daphne. "Because it's beginning to look as if it might be the one chance I'm given to enforce the penalty clause. Not that I'm complaining. After all, Charlie will be quite a change from the usual chinless vicars' sons and stable boys with no legs that I have to endure most weekends."

"Be careful he doesn't end up eating you for dessert."

Becky had warned Charlie that the table had been booked for eight o'clock and made him promise he would wear his best suit. "My only suit," he reminded her.

Guy collected the two girls from Number 97 on the dot of eight, but seemed unusually morose as he accompanied them to the restaurant, arriving a few minutes after the appointed hour. They found Charlie sitting alone in the corner, fidgeting and looking as if it might be the first time he had ever been to a restaurant.

Becky introduced first Daphne to Charlie and then Charlie to Guy. The two men just stood and stared at each other like prizefighters.

"Of course, you were both in the same regiment," said Daphne. "But I don't suppose you ever came across each other," she added, staring at Charlie. Neither man commented on her observation.

If the evening started badly, it was only to become worse, as the four of them were quite unable to settle on any subject with which they had something in common. Charlie, far from being witty and sharp as he was with the customers in the shop, became surly and uncommunicative. If Becky could have reached his ankle she would have kicked him, and not simply because he kept putting a knife covered with peas in his mouth.

Guy's particular brand of sullen silence didn't help matters either, despite Daphne laughing away, bubbly as ever, whatever anyone said. By the time the bill was finally presented, Becky was only too relieved that the evening was coming to an end. She even had discreetly to leave a tip, because Charlie didn't seem to realise it was expected of him.

She left the restaurant at Guy's side and the two of them lost contact with Daphne and Charlie as they strolled back towards 97. She assumed that her companions were only a few paces behind, but stopped thinking about where they might be when Guy took her in his arms, kissed her gently and said, "Goodnight, my darling. And don't forget, we're going down to Ashurst for the weekend." How could she forget? Becky watched Guy look back furtively in the direction that Daphne and Charlie had been walking, but then without another word he hailed a hansom and instructed the cabbie to take him to the Fusiliers' barracks in Hounslow.

Becky unlocked the front door and sat down on the sofa to consider whether or not she should return to 147 and tell Charlie exactly what she thought of him. A few minutes later Daphne breezed into the room.

"Sorry about this evening," said Becky before her friend had had the chance to offer an opinion. "Charlie's usually a little more communicative than that. I can't think what came over him."

"Not easy for him to have dinner with an officer from his old regiment, I suspect," said Daphne.

"I'm sure you're right," said Becky. "But they'll end up friends, I feel sure of that."

Daphne stared down at Becky thoughtfully.

* * *

The following Saturday morning, Guy arrived at 97 Chelsea Terrace to collect Becky and drive her down to Ashurst. The moment he saw her in one of Daphne's stylish red dresses he remarked on how beautiful she looked, and he was so cheerful and chatty on the journey down to Berkshire that Becky even began to relax. They arrived in the village of Ashurst just before three and Guy turned to wink at her as he swung the car into the mile-long drive that led up to the Hall.

Becky hadn't expected the house to be quite that large.

A butler, under-butler, and two footmen were waiting on the top step to greet them. Guy brought the car to a halt on the gravelled drive and the butler stepped forward to remove Becky's two small cases from the boot, before handing them over to a footman who whisked them away. The butler then led Captain Guy and Becky at a sedate pace up the stone steps, into the front hall, and on up the wide wooden staircase to a bedroom on the first-floor landing.

"The Wellington Room, madam," he intoned as he opened the door for her.

"He's meant to have spent the night here once," explained Guy, as he strolled up the stairs beside her. "By the way, no need for you to feel lonely. I'm only next door, and much more alive than the late general."

Becky walked into a large comfortable room where she found a young girl in a long black dress with a white collar and cuffs unpacking her bags. The girl turned, curtsied and announced, "I'm Nellie, your maid. Please let me know if you need anything, ma'am."

Becky thanked her, walked over to the bay window and stared out on to the green acres that stretched as far as her eye could see. There was a knock on the door and Becky turned to find Guy entering the room before she had been given the chance to say, "Come in."

"Room all right, darling?"

"Just perfect," said Becky as the maid curtsied once again. Becky thought she detected a slight look of apprehension in the young girl's eyes as Guy walked across the room.

"Ready to meet Pa?" he asked.

"As ready as I'm ever likely to be," Becky admitted, as she accompanied Guy back downstairs to the morning room where a man in his early fifties stood in front of a blazing log fire waiting to greet them.

"Welcome to Ashurst Hall," said Major Trentham.

Becky smiled at her host and said, "Thank you."

The major was slightly shorter than his son, but had the same slim build and fair hair, though there were some strands of grey appearing at the side. But that was where the likeness ended. Whereas Guy's complexion was fresh and pale, Major Trentham's skin had the ruddiness of a man who had spent most of his life outdoors, and when Becky shook his hand she felt the roughness of someone who obviously worked on the land.

"Those fine London shoes won't be much good for what I have in mind," declared the major. "You'll have to borrow a pair of my wife's riding boots, or perhaps Nigel's wellingtons."

"Nigel?" Becky enquired.

"Trentham minor. Hasn't Guy told you about him? He's in his last year at Harrow, hoping to go on to Sandhurst – and outshine his brother, I'm told."

"I didn't know you had a –"

"The little brat isn't worthy of a mention," Guy interrupted with a half-smile, as his father guided them back through the hall to a cupboard below the stairs. Becky stared at the row of leather riding boots that were even more highly polished than her shoes.

"Take your pick, m'dear," said Major Trentham.

After a couple of attempts Becky found a pair that fitted perfectly, then followed Guy and his father out into the garden. It took the best part of the afternoon for Major Trentham to show his young guest round the seven-hundred-acre estate and by the time Becky returned she was more than ready for the hot punch that awaited them in a large silver tureen in the morning room.

The butler informed them that Mrs Trentham had

phoned to say that she had been held up at the vicarage and would be unable to join them for tea.

By the time Becky returned to her room in the early evening to take a bath and change for dinner, Mrs Trentham still hadn't made an appearance.

Daphne had loaned Becky two dresses for the occasion, and even an exquisite semi-circular diamond brooch about which Becky had felt a little apprehensive. But when she looked at herself in the mirror, all her fears were quickly forgotten.

When Becky heard eight o'clock chiming in chorus from the numerous clocks around the house she returned to the drawing room. The dress and the brooch had a perceptible and immediate effect on both men. There was still no sign of Guy's mother.

"What a charming dress, Miss Salmon," said the major.

"Thank you, Major Trentham," said Becky, as she warmed her hands by the fire before glancing around the room.

"My wife will be joining us in a moment," the major assured Becky, as the butler proffered her a glass of sherry on a silver tray.

"I did enjoy being shown round the estate."

"Hardly warrants that description, my dear," the major replied with a warm smile. "But I'm glad you enjoyed the walk," he added as his attention was diverted over her shoulder.

Becky swung round to see a tall, elegant lady, dressed in black from the nape of her neck to her ankles, enter the room. She walked slowly and sedately towards them.

"Mother," said Guy, stepping forward to give her a kiss on the cheek, "I should like you to meet Becky Salmon."

"How do you do?" said Becky.

"May I be permitted to enquire who removed my best riding boots from the hall cupboard?" asked Mrs Trentham, ignoring Becky's outstretched hand. "And then saw fit to return them covered in mud?"

"I did," said the major. "Otherwise Miss Salmon would have had to walk around the farm in a pair of high heels. Which might have proved unwise in the circumstances."

"It might have proved wiser for Miss Salmon to have come properly equipped with the right footwear in the first place."

"I'm so sorry . . ." began Becky.

"Where have you been all day, Mother?" asked Guy, jumping in. "We had rather hoped to see you earlier."

"Trying to sort out some of the problems that our new vicar seems quite unable to cope with," replied Mrs Trentham. "He has absolutely no idea of how to go about organising a harvest festival. I can't imagine what they are teaching them at Oxford nowadays."

"Theology, perhaps," suggested Major Trentham.

The butler cleared his throat. "Dinner is served, madam."

Mrs Trentham turned without another word and led them through into the dining room at a brisk pace. She placed Becky on the right of the major and opposite herself. Three knives, four forks and two spoons shone up at Becky from the large square table. She had no trouble in selecting which one she should start with, as the first course was soup but from then on she knew she would simply have to follow Mrs Trentham's lead.

Her hostess didn't address a word to Becky until the main course had been served. Instead she spoke to her husband of Nigel's efforts at Harrow – not very impressive; the new vicar – almost as bad; and Lady Lavinia Malim – a judge's widow who had recently taken residence in the village and had been causing even more trouble than usual.

Becky's mouth was full of pheasant when Mrs Trentham suddenly asked, "And which of the professions is your father associated with, Miss Salmon?"

"He's dead," Becky spluttered.

"Oh, I am sorry to hear that," she said indifferently.

"Am I to presume he died serving with his regiment at the front?"

"No, he didn't."

"Oh, so what *did* he do during the war?"

"He ran a baker's shop. In Whitechapel," added Becky, mindful of her father's warning: "If you ever try to disguise your background, it will only end in tears."

"Whitechapel?" Mrs Trentham queried. "If I'm not mistaken, isn't that a sweet little village, just outside Worcester?"

"No, Mrs Trentham, it's in the heart of the East End of London," said Becky, hoping that Guy would come to her rescue, but he seemed more preoccupied with sipping his glass of claret.

"Oh," said Mrs Trentham, her lips remaining in a straight line. "I remember once visiting the Bishop of Worcester's wife in a place called Whitechapel, but I confess I have never found it necessary to travel as far as the East End. I don't suppose they have a bishop there." She put down her knife and fork. "However," she continued, "my father, Sir Raymond Hardcastle – you may have heard of him, Miss Salmon –"

"No, I haven't actually," said Becky honestly.

Another disdainful look appeared on the face of Mrs Trentham, although it failed to stop her flow. "– Who was created a baronet for his services to King George V . . ."

"And what were those services?" asked Becky innocently, which caused Mrs Trentham to pause for a moment before explaining, "He played a small part in His Majesty's efforts to see that we were not overrun by the Germans."

"He's an arms dealer," said Major Trentham under his breath.

If Mrs Trentham heard the comment she chose to ignore it.

"Did you come out this year, Miss Salmon?" she asked icily.

"No, I didn't," said Becky. "I went up to university instead."

"I don't approve of such goings-on myself. Ladies shouldn't be educated beyond the three 'Rs' plus an adequate understanding of how to manage servants and survive having to watch a cricket match."

"But if you don't have servants –" began Becky, and would have continued if Mrs Trentham hadn't rung a silver bell that was by her right hand.

When the butler reappeared she said curtly, "We'll take coffee in the drawing room, Gibson." The butler's face registered a hint of surprise as Mrs Trentham rose and led everyone out of the dining room, down a long corridor and back into the drawing room where the fire no longer burned so vigorously.

"Care for some port or brandy, Miss Salmon?" asked Major Trentham, as Gibson poured out the coffee.

"No, thank you," said Becky quietly.

"Please excuse me," said Mrs Trentham, rising from the chair in which she had just sat down. "I seem to have developed a slight headache and will therefore retire to my room, if you'll forgive me."

"Yes, of course, my dear," said the major flatly.

As soon as his mother had left the room Guy walked quickly over to Becky, sat down, and took her hand. "She'll be better in the morning, when her migraine has cleared up, you'll see."

"I doubt it," replied Becky in a whisper, and turning to Major Trentham said, "Perhaps you'll excuse me as well. It's been a long day, and in any case I'm sure the two of you have a lot to catch up on."

Both men rose as Becky left the room and climbed the long staircase to her bedroom. She undressed quickly and, after washing in a basin of near freezing water, crept across the unheated room to slide between the sheets of her cold bed.

Becky was already half asleep when she heard the door handle turning. She blinked a few times and tried to focus on the far side of the room. The door opened slowly, but all she could make out was the figure of a man entering, then the door closing silently behind him.

"Who's that?" she whispered sharply.

"Only me," murmured Guy. "Thought I'd pop in and see how you were."

Becky pulled her top sheet up to her chin. "Goodnight, Guy," she said briskly.

"That's not very friendly," said Guy, who had already crossed the room and was now sitting on the end of her bed. "Just wanted to check that everything was all right. Felt you had rather a rough time of it tonight."

"I'm just fine, thank you," said Becky flatly. As he leaned over to kiss her she slid away from him so he ended up brushing her left ear.

"Perhaps this isn't the right time?"

"Or place," added Becky sliding even further away so that she was nearly falling out of the far side of the bed.

"I only wanted to kiss you goodnight."

Becky reluctantly allowed him to take her in his arms and kiss her on the lips, but he held on to her far longer than she had anticipated and eventually she had to push him away.

"Goodnight, Guy," she said firmly.

At first Guy didn't move, but then he rose slowly and said, "Perhaps another time." A moment later she heard the door close behind him.

Becky waited for a few moments before getting out of bed. She walked over to the door, turned the key in the lock and removed it before going back to bed. It was some time before she was able to sleep.

When Becky came down for breakfast the following morning she quickly discovered from Major Trentham that a restless night had not improved his wife's migraine: she had therefore decided to remain in bed until the pain had completely cleared.

Later, when the major and Guy went off to church,

leaving Becky to read the Sunday newspapers in the drawing room, she couldn't help noticing that the servants were whispering among themselves whenever she caught their eye.

Mrs Trentham appeared for lunch, but made no attempt to join in the conversation that was taking place at the other end of the table. Unexpectedly, just as the custard was being poured on to the summer pudding she asked, "And what was the vicar's text this morning?"

"Do unto others as you expect them to do unto you," the major replied with a slight edge to his voice.

"And how did you find the service at our local church, Miss Salmon?" asked Mrs Trentham, addressing Becky for the first time.

"I didn't . . ." began Becky.

"Ah, yes, of course, you are one of the chosen brethren."

"No, actually if anything I'm a Roman Catholic," said Becky.

"Oh," said Mrs Trentham, feigning surprise "I assumed, with the name of Salmon . . . in any case you wouldn't have enjoyed St Michael's. You see, it's very down to earth."

Becky wondered if every word Mrs Trentham uttered and every action she took was rehearsed in advance.

Once lunch had been cleared away Mrs Trentham disappeared again and Guy suggested that he and Becky should take a brisk walk. Becky went up to her room and changed into her oldest shoes, far too terrified to suggest she might borrow a pair of Mrs Trentham's wellingtons.

"Anything to get away from the house," Becky told him when she returned downstairs and didn't open her mouth again until she felt certain that Mrs Trentham was well out of earshot.

"What does she expect of me?" Becky finally asked.

"Oh, it's not that bad," Guy insisted, taking her hand. "You're overreacting. Pa's convinced she'll come round given time and in any case, if I have to choose between you and her I know exactly which one of you is more important to me."

Becky squeezed his hand. "Thank you, darling, but I'm still not certain I can go through another evening like the last one."

"We could always leave early and spend the rest of the day at your place," Guy said. Becky turned to look at him, unsure what he meant. He added quickly, "Better get back to the house or she'll only grumble that we left her alone all afternoon." They both quickened their pace.

A few minutes later they were climbing the stone steps at the front of the hall. As soon as Becky had changed back into her house shoes and checked her hair in the mirror on the hallstand, she rejoined Guy in the drawing room. She was surprised to find a large tea already laid out. She checked her watch: it was only three fifteen.

"I'm sorry you felt it necessary to keep everyone waiting, Guy," were the first words that Becky heard as she entered the room.

"Never known us to have tea this early before," offered the major, from the other side of the fireplace.

"Do you take tea, Miss Salmon?" Mrs Trentham asked, even managing to make her name sound like a petty offence.

"Yes, thank you," replied Becky.

"Perhaps you could call Becky by her first name," Guy suggested.

Mrs Trentham's eyes came to rest on her son. "I cannot abide this modern-day custom of addressing everyone by their Christian name, especially when one has only just been introduced. Darjeeling, Lapsang or Earl Grey, Miss Salmon?" she asked before anyone had been given a chance to react. She looked up expectantly for Becky's reply, but no answer was immediately forthcoming because Becky still hadn't quite recovered from the previous jibe. "Obviously you're not given that much choice in Whitechapel," Mrs Trentham added.

Becky considered picking up the pot and pouring the contents all over the woman, but somehow she managed to hold her temper, if only because she knew that making her lose it was exactly what Mrs Trentham was hoping to achieve.

After a further silence Mrs Trentham asked, "Do you have any brothers or sisters, Miss Salmon?"

"No, I'm an only child."

"Surprising, really."

"Why's that?" asked Becky innocently.

"I always thought the lower classes bred like rabbits," said Mrs Trentham, dropping another lump of sugar into her tea.

"Mother, really –" began Guy.

"Just my little joke," she said quickly. "Guy will take me so seriously at times, Miss Salmon. However, I well remember my father, Sir Raymond, once saying . . ."

"Not again," said the major.

". . . that the classes were not unlike water and wine. Under no circumstances should one attempt to mix them."

"But I thought it was Christ who managed to turn water into wine," said Becky.

Mrs Trentham chose to ignore this observation. "That's exactly why we have officers and other ranks in the first place; because God planned it that way."

"And do you think that God planned that there should be a war, in order that those same officers and other ranks could then slaughter each other indiscriminately?" asked Becky.

"I'm sure I don't know, Miss Salmon," Mrs Trentham replied. "You see, I don't have the advantage of being an intellectual like yourself. I am just a plain, simple woman who speaks her mind. But what I do know is that we *all* made sacrifices during the war."

"And what sacrifices did you make, Mrs Trentham?" Becky enquired.

"A considerable number, young lady," Mrs Trentham replied, stretching to her full height. "For a start, I had to go without a lot of things that were quite fundamental to one's very existence."

"Like an arm or a leg?" said Becky, quickly regretting her words the moment she realised that she had fallen into Mrs Trentham's trap.

Guy's mother rose from her chair, walked slowly over to the fireplace, where she tugged violently on the servants' bell-pull. "I do not have to sit around and be insulted in my own home," she said. As soon as Gibson reappeared she turned to him and added, "See that Alfred collects Miss Salmon's belongings from her room. She will be returning to London earlier than planned."

Becky remained silently by the fire not sure what she should do next. Mrs Trentham stood coolly staring at her until finally Becky walked over to the major, shook him by the hand and said, "I'll say goodbye, Major Trentham. I have a feeling we won't be seeing each other again."

"My loss, Miss Salmon," he said graciously before kissing her hand. Then Becky turned and walked slowly out of the drawing room without giving Mrs Trentham a second look. Guy followed Becky into the hall.

On their journey back to London Guy made every excuse he could think of for his mother's behaviour, but Becky knew he didn't really believe his own words. When the car came to a halt outside Number 97 Guy jumped out and opened the passenger door.

"May I come up?" he said. "There's something I still have to tell you."

"Not tonight," said Becky. "I need to think and I'd rather like to be on my own."

Guy sighed. "It's just that I wanted to tell you how much I love you and perhaps talk about our plans for the future."

"Plans that include your mother?"

"To hell with my mother," he replied. "Don't you realise how much I love you?"

Becky hesitated.

"Let's announce our engagement in *The Times* as soon as possible, and to hell with what she thinks. What do you say?"

She turned and threw her arms around him. "Oh, Guy, I do love you too, but you'd better not come up tonight. Not while Daphne is expected back at any moment. Another time perhaps?"

A look of disappointment crossed Guy's face. He kissed her before saying, "Goodnight." She opened the front door and ran up the stairs.

Becky unlocked the flat door to find that Daphne had not returned from the country. She sat alone on the sofa, not bothering to turn the gas up when the light faded. It was to be a further two hours before Daphne sailed in.

"How did it all go?" were the first words Daphne uttered as she entered the drawing room, a little surprised to find her friend sitting in the dark.

"A disaster."

"So it's all over?"

"No, not exactly," said Becky. "In fact I have a feeling Guy proposed to me."

"But did you accept?" asked Daphne.

"I rather think I did."

"And what do you intend to do about India?"

The following morning when Becky unpacked her overnight case, she was horrified to discover that the delicate brooch Daphne had lent her for the weekend was missing. She assumed she must have left it at Ashurst Hall.

As she had no desire to make contact with Mrs Trentham again, she dropped a note to Guy at his regimental mess to alert him of her anxiety. He replied the next day to assure her that he would check on Sunday when he planned to have lunch with his parents at Ashurst.

Becky spent the next five days worrying about whether Guy would be able to find the missing piece: thankfully Daphne didn't seem to have noticed its absence. Becky only hoped she could get the brooch back before her friend felt the desire to wear it again.

Guy wrote on Monday to say that despite an extensive search of the guest bedroom he had been unable to locate the missing brooch, and in any case Nellie had informed him that she distinctly remembered packing all of Becky's jewellery.

This piece of news puzzled Becky because she remembered packing her own case following her summary dismissal from Ashurst Hall. With considerable trepidation she sat up late into the night, waiting for Daphne to return from her long weekend in the country so that she could explain to her friend what had happened. She feared that it might be months, even years before she could save enough to replace what was probably a family heirloom.

By the time her flatmate breezed into Chelsea Terrace a few minutes after midnight, Becky had already drunk several cups of black coffee and almost lit up one of Daphne's cigarettes.

"You're up late, my darling," were Daphne's opening words. "Are exams that close?"

"No," said Becky, then blurted out the whole story of the missing diamond brooch. She finished by asking how long she thought it might take to repay her.

"About a week would be my guess," said Daphne.

"A week?" said Becky, looking puzzled.

"Yes. It was only stage jewellery – all the rage at the moment. If I remember correctly, it cost me every penny of three shillings."

A relieved Becky told Guy over dinner on Tuesday why finding the missing piece of jewellery was no longer of such importance.

The following Monday Guy brought the piece round to Chelsea Terrace, explaining that Nellie had found it under the bed in the Wellington Room.

CHAPTER 9

Becky began to notice small changes in Charlie's manner, at first subtle and then more obvious.

Daphne made no attempt to hide her involvement in what she described as: "The social discovery of the decade, my very own Charlie Doolittle. Why, only this weekend," she declared, "I took him down to Harcourt Hall, don't you know, and he was a wow. Even Mother thought he was fantastic."

"Your mother approves of Charlie Trumper?" said Becky in disbelief.

"Oh, yes, darling, but then you see Mummy realises that I have no intention of marrying Charlie."

"Be careful, I had no intention of marrying Guy."

"My darling, never forget you spring from the romantic classes, whereas I come from a more practical background, which is exactly why the aristocracy have survived for so long. No, I shall end up marrying a certain Percy Wiltshire and it's got nothing to do with destiny or the stars, it's just good old-fashioned common sense."

"But is Mr Wiltshire aware of your plans for his future?"

"Of course the Marquess of Wiltshire isn't. Even his mother hasn't told him yet."

"But what if Charlie were to fall in love with you?"

"That's not possible. You see, there's another woman in his life."

"Good heavens," said Becky. "And to think I've never met her."

The shop's six-monthly figures showed a considerable improvement on the first quarter's, as Daphne discovered to her cost when she received her next dividend. She told Becky that at this rate she couldn't hope to make any long-term profit from her loan. As for Becky herself, she spent less and less of her time thinking about Daphne, Charlie or the shop as the hour drew nearer for Guy's departure to India.

India . . . Becky hadn't slept the night she had learned of Guy's three-year posting and she certainly might have wished to discover something that would so disrupt their future from his lips and not Daphne's. In the past Becky had accepted, without question, that because of Guy's duties with the regiment it would not be possible for them to see each other on a regular basis; but as the time of his departure drew nearer she began to resent guard duty, night exercises and, most of all, any weekend operations in which the Fusiliers were expected to take part.

Becky had feared that Guy's attentions would cool after her distressing visit to Ashurst Hall, but if anything he became even more ardent and kept repeating how different it would all be once they were married.

But then, as if without warning, the months became weeks, the weeks days, until the dreaded circle Becky had pencilled around 3 February 1920 on the calendar by the side of her bed was suddenly upon them.

"Let's have dinner at the Café Royal, where we spent our first evening together," Guy suggested, the Monday before he was due to leave.

"No," said Becky. "I don't want to share you with a hundred strangers on our last evening." She hesitated before adding, "If you can face the thought of my cooking, I'd rather give you dinner at the flat. At least that way we can be on our own."

Guy smiled.

* * *

Once the shop seemed to be running smoothly Becky didn't drop in every day, but she couldn't resist a glance through the window whenever she passed Number 147. She was surprised to find that that particular Monday morning Charlie wasn't to be seen behind the counter.

"Over here," she heard a voice cry and turned to find Charlie sitting on the same bench opposite the shop where she had first spotted him the day he returned to London. She crossed the road to join him.

"What's this, taking early retirement before we've repaid the loan?"

"Certainly not. I'm working."

"Working? Please explain, Mr Trumper, how lounging about on a park bench on a Monday morning can be described as work?"

"It was Henry Ford who taught us that 'For every minute of action, there should be an hour of thought,'" said Charlie, with only a slight trace of his old Cockney accent; Becky also couldn't help noticing how he had pronounced Henry.

"And where are those Fordian-like thoughts taking you at this particular moment?" she asked.

"To that row of shops opposite."

"All of them?" Becky looked over at the block. "And what conclusion would Mr Ford have come to had he been sitting on this bench, pray?"

"That they represent thirty-six different ways of making money."

"I've never counted them, but I'll take your word for it."

"But what else do you see when you look across the road?"

Becky's eyes returned to Chelsea Terrace. "Lots of people walking up and down the pavement, mainly ladies with parasols, nannies pushing prams, and the odd child with a skipping rope or hoop." She paused. "Why, what do you see?"

"Two 'For Sale' signs."

"I confess I hadn't noticed them." Once again she looked across the road.

"That's because you're looking with a different pair of eyes," Charlie explained. "First there's Kendrick's the butcher. Well, we all know about him, don't we? Heart attack, been advised by his doctor to retire early or he can't hope to live much longer."

"And then there's Mr Rutherford," said Becky, spotting the second 'For Sale' sign.

"The antique dealer. Oh, yes, dear Julian wants to sell up and join his friend in New York, where society is a little more sympathetic when it comes to his particular proclivities – like that word?"

"How did you find – ?"

"Information," said Charlie, touching his nose. "The life-blood of any business."

"Another Fordian Principle?"

"No, much nearer home than that," admitted Charlie. "Daphne Harcourt-Browne."

Becky smiled. "So what are you going to do about it?"

"I'm going to get hold of them both, aren't I?"

"And how do you intend to do that?"

"With my cunning and your diligence."

"Are you being serious, Charlie Trumper?"

"Never more." Charlie turned to face her once again. "After all, why should Chelsea Terrace be any different from Whitechapel?"

"Just the odd decimal point, perhaps," suggested Becky.

"Then let's move that decimal point, Miss Salmon. Because the time has come for you to stop being a sleeping partner and start fulfilling your end of the bargain."

"But what about my exams?"

"Use the extra time you'll have now that your boyfriend has departed for India."

"He goes tomorrow, actually."

"Then I'll grant you a further day's leave. Isn't that

how officers describe a day off? Because tomorrow I want you to return to John D. Wood and make an appointment to see that pimply young assistant – what was his name?"

"Palmer," said Becky.

"Yes, Palmer," said Charlie. "Instruct him to negotiate a price on our behalf for both those shops, and warn him that we're also interested in anything else that might come up in Chelsea Terrace."

"Anything else in Chelsea Terrace?" said Becky, who had begun making notes on the back of her textbook.

"Yes, and we'll also need to raise nearly all the money it's going to cost to purchase the freeholds, so visit several banks and see that you get good terms. Don't consider anything above four per cent."

"Nothing above four per cent," repeated Becky. Looking up, she added, "But thirty-six shops, Charlie?"

"I know, it could take an awful long time."

In the Bedford College library, Becky tried to push Charlie's dreams of being the next Mr Selfridge to one side as she attempted to complete an essay on the influence of Bernini on seventeenth-century sculpture. But her mind kept switching from Bernini to Charlie and then back to Guy. Unable to grapple with the modern, Becky felt she was having even less success with the ancient so she came to the conclusion that her essay would have to be postponed until she could find more time to concentrate on the past.

During her lunch break she sat on the red brick wall outside the library, munching a Cox's orange pippin while continuing to think. She took one last bite before tossing the core into a nearby wastepaper-basket and everything else back into her satchel before beginning her journey westward to Chelsea.

Once she had reached the terrace her first stop was the butcher's shop, where she picked up a leg of lamb and told Mrs Kendrick how sorry she was to hear about her husband. When she paid the bill she noted that the assistants, though well trained, didn't show a great deal of initiative. Customers escaped with only what they had come in for, which Charlie would never have allowed them to do. She then joined the queue at Trumper's and drew Charlie to serve her.

"Something special, madam?"

"Two pounds of potatoes, one pound of button mushrooms, a cabbage and a melon."

"It's your lucky day, madam. The melon should be eaten this very evening," he said, just pressing the top lightly. "Can I interest madam in anything else? A few oranges, a grapefruit perhaps?"

"No, thank you, my good man."

"Then that'll be three shillings and fourpence, madam."

"But don't I get a Cox's orange pippin thrown in, like all the other girls?"

"No, sorry, madam, such privileges are reserved only for our regular customers. Mind you, I could be persuaded, if I was asked to share that melon with you tonight. Which would give me the chance to explain in detail my master plan for Chelsea Terrace, London, the world –"

"Can't tonight, Charlie. Guy's leaving for India in the morning."

"Of course, 'ow silly of me, sorry. I forgot." He sounded uncharacteristically flustered. "Tomorrow, perhaps?"

"Yes, why not?"

"Then as a special treat I'll take you *out* to dinner. Pick you up at eight?"

"It's a deal, partner," said Becky, hoping she sounded like Mae West.

Charlie was suddenly distracted by a large lady who had taken her place at the front of the queue.

"Ah, Lady Nourse," said Charlie, returning to his Cockney accent, "your usual swedes and turnips, or are we going to be a little more adventurous today, m'lady?"

Becky looked back to watch Lady Nourse, who wasn't a day under sixty, blush as her ample breast swelled with satisfaction.

Once she had returned to her flat, Becky quickly checked the drawing room over to be sure that it was clean and tidy. The maid had done a thorough job and as Daphne hadn't yet returned from one of her long weekends at Harcourt Hall there was little for her to do other than plumping up the odd cushion and drawing the curtains.

Becky decided to prepare as much of the evening meal as possible before having a bath. She was already regretting turning down Daphne's offer of the use of a cook and a couple of maids from Lowndes Square to help her out, but she was determined to have Guy to herself for a change, although she knew her mother wouldn't approve of having dinner with a male friend without Daphne or a chaperone to keep an eye on them.

Melon, followed by leg of lamb with potatoes, cabbage and some button mushrooms: surely that would have met with her mother's approval. But she suspected that approval would not have been extended to wasting hard-earned money on the bottle of Nuits-St-Georges 1912 that she had purchased from Mr Cuthbert at Number 101. Becky peeled the potatoes, basted the lamb and checked she had some mint before removing the stalk on the cabbage.

As she ran her bath she decided that in future she would have to purchase all her goods locally, to be sure that her information on what was taking place in the terrace was as up to date as Charlie's. Before going to undress she also checked there was still some brandy left over in the bottle she had been given the previous Christmas.

She lay soaking in a hot bath for some time as she thought through which banks she would approach and, more importantly, how she would present her case. The detailed figures of Trumper's income and a time schedule required for the repayment of any loan . . . Her mind drifted back from Charlie to Guy, and why it was that neither of them would ever talk about the other.

When Becky heard the bedroom clock chime the half-hour she leapt out of the bath in a panic, suddenly realising how much time her thoughts must have occupied and only too aware that Guy was certain to appear on the doorstep as the clock struck eight. The one thing you could guarantee with a soldier, Daphne had warned her, was that they always turned up on time.

Clothes were strewn all over both their bedroom floors as Becky emptied half Daphne's wardrobe and most of her own in a desperate attempt to find something to wear. In the end she chose the dress Daphne had worn at the Fusiliers' Ball, and never worn since. Once she had managed to do up the top button she checked herself in the mirror. Becky felt confident she would pass muster. The clock on the mantelpiece struck eight and the doorbell rang.

Guy, wearing a double-breasted regimental blazer and cavalry twills, entered the room carrying another bottle of wine as well as a dozen red roses. Once he had placed both offerings on the table, he took Becky in his arms.

"What a beautiful dress," he said. "I don't think I've seen it before."

"No, it's the first time I've worn it," said Becky, feeling guilty about not asking Daphne's permission to borrow it.

"No one to help you?" asked Guy, looking around.

"To be honest, Daphne volunteered to act as chaperone, but I didn't accept as I hadn't wanted to share you with anyone on our last evening together."

Guy smiled. "Can I do anything?"

"Yes, you could uncork the wine while I put the potatoes on."

"Trumper's potatoes?"

"Of course," replied Becky, as she walked back through into the kitchen and dropped the cabbage into a pot of boiling water. She hesitated for a moment before calling back, "You don't like Charlie, do you?"

Guy poured out a glass of wine for each of them but either hadn't heard what she had said, or made no attempt to respond.

"What's your day been like?" Becky asked when she returned to the drawing room and took the glass of wine he handed her.

"Packing endless trunks in preparation for tomorrow's journey," he replied. "They expect you to have four of everything in that bloody country."

"Everything?" Becky sipped the wine. "Um, good."

"Everything. And you, what have you been up to?"

"Talked to Charlie about his plans for taking over London without actually declaring war; dismissed Caravaggio as second-rate; and selected some button mushrooms, not to mention Trumper's deal of the day." As she finished speaking, Becky placed half a melon on Guy's mat and the other half in her place as he refilled their glasses.

Over a lingering dinner, Becky became more and more conscious that this would probably be their last evening together for the next three years. They talked of the theatre, the regiment, the problems in Ireland, Daphne, even the price of melons, but never India.

"You could always come and visit me," he said finally, bringing up the taboo subject himself as he poured her another glass of wine, nearly emptying the bottle.

"A day trip, perhaps?" she suggested, removing the empty dinner plates from the table and taking them back to the kitchen.

"I suspect even that will be possible at some time in the future."

Guy filled his own glass once again, then opened the bottle he had brought with him.

"What do you mean?"

"By aeroplane. After all, Alcock and Brown have crossed the Atlantic non-stop, so India must be any pioneer's next ambition."

"Perhaps I could sit on a wing," said Becky when she returned from the kitchen.

Guy laughed. "Don't worry. I'm sure three years will pass by in a flash, and then we can be married just as soon as I return." He raised his glass and watched her take another drink. For some time they didn't speak.

Becky rose from the table feeling a little giddy. "Must put the kettle on," she explained.

When she returned Becky didn't notice that her glass had been refilled. "Thank you for a wonderful evening," Guy said, and for a moment Becky was anxious that he might be thinking of leaving.

"Now I fear the time has come to do the washing-up, as you don't seem to have any staff around tonight and I left my batman back at barracks."

"No, don't let's bother with that." Becky hiccuped. "After all, I can spend a year on the washing-up, followed by a year on the drying and still put aside a year for stacking."

Guy's own laugh was interrupted by the rising whistle of the kettle.

"Won't be a minute. Why don't you pour yourself some brandy?" Becky added, as she disappeared back into the kitchen and selected two cups that didn't have chips in them. She returned with them full of strong hot coffee, and thought for a moment that the gaslight might have been turned down a little. She placed the two cups on the table next to the sofa. "The coffee's so hot that it will be a couple of minutes before we can drink it," she warned.

He passed her a brandy balloon that was half full. He raised his glass and waited. She hesitated, then took a sip before sitting down beside him. For some time again neither of them spoke and then suddenly he put down his glass, took her in his arms and this time began kissing her passionately, first on her lips, then on her neck and then on her bare shoulders. Becky only began to resist when she felt a hand move from her back on to one of her breasts.

Guy broke away and said, "I have a special surprise for you, darling, which I've been saving for tonight."

"What's that?"

"Our engagement is to be announced in *The Times* tomorrow."

For a moment Becky was so stunned she could only stare at Guy. "Oh, darling, how wonderful." She took him back in her arms and made no effort to resist when his hand returned to her breast. She broke away again. "But how will your mother react?"

"I don't give a damn how she reacts," said Guy, and once again began to kiss her neck. His hand moved to her other breast as her lips parted and their tongues touched.

She began to feel the buttons on the back of her dress being undone, slowly at first, then with more confidence before Guy released her again. She blushed as he removed his regimental blazer and tie and threw them over the back of the sofa, and began to wonder if she shouldn't make it clear they had already gone too far.

When Guy started to undo the front of his shirt she panicked for a moment: things were getting a little out of control.

Guy leaned forward and slipped the top of Becky's dress off her shoulders. Once he had returned to kissing her again, she felt his hand trying to undo the back of her bodice.

Becky felt she might be saved by the fact that neither of them knew where the fasteners were. However, it became abundantly clear that Guy had overcome such problems before, as he deftly undid the offending clips and hesitated only for a moment before transferring his attention to her legs. He stopped quite suddenly when he reached the top of her stockings, and looking into her eyes murmured, "I had only imagined until now what this would be like, but I had no idea you would be quite so beautiful."

"Thank you," said Becky, and sat bolt upright. Guy handed over her brandy and she took another sip, wondering if it might not be wise for her to make some excuse about the coffee going cold and slip back into the kitchen to make another pot.

"However there's still been a disappointment for me this evening," he added, one hand still on her thigh.

"A disappointment?" Becky put down her brandy glass. She was beginning to feel distinctly woozy.

"Yes," said Guy. "Your engagement ring."

"My engagement ring?"

"I ordered it from Garrard's over a month ago, and they promised it would be ready for me to collect by this evening. But only this afternoon they informed me that I wouldn't be able to pick it up until first thing tomorrow."

"It doesn't matter," said Becky.

"It does," said Guy. "I'd wanted to slip it on your finger tonight, so I do hope you can be at the station a little earlier than we had planned. I intend to fall on one knee and present it to you then."

Becky stood up and smiled as Guy quickly rose and took her in his arms. "I'll always love you, you know that, don't you?" Daphne's dress slipped off and fell to the floor. Guy took her by the hand and she led him into the bedroom.

He quickly pushed back the top sheet, jumped in and held up his arms. Once she had climbed in to join him Guy quickly removed the rest of her clothes and began kissing her all over her body before making love with an expertise that Becky suspected could only have come from considerable practice.

Although the act itself was painful, Becky was surprised how quickly the promised sensation was over and she clung on to Guy for what seemed an eternity. He kept repeating how much he cared for her which made Becky feel less guilty – after all, they were engaged.

Becky was half asleep when she thought she heard a door slam, and turned over, assuming it must have come from the flat above them. Guy hardly stirred. Quite suddenly the bedroom door was flung open, and Daphne appeared in front of them.

"So sorry, I didn't realise," she said in a whisper and closed the door quietly behind her. Becky looked across at her lover apprehensively.

He smiled and took her in his arms. "No need to worry about Daphne. She won't tell anyone." He stretched out an arm and pulled her towards him and they made love once again.

Waterloo station was already crowded with men in uniforms when Becky walked on to platform one. She was a couple of minutes late, so a little surprised not to find Guy waiting for her. Then she remembered that he'd have had to go to Albemarle Street to pick up the ring.

She checked the board: chalked up in white capital letters were the words "*Southampton Boat Train*, P & O to India, departure time 11.30". Becky continued to look anxiously up and down the platform before her eyes settled on a band of helpless girls. They were huddled together under the station clock, their shrill, strained voices all talking at once of hunt balls, polo and who was coming out that season – each of them only too aware that farewells must be said at the station because it wasn't the done thing for a girl to accompany an officer on the train to Southampton unless they were married or officially engaged. But *The Times* that morning would prove that she and Guy were engaged, thought Becky, so perhaps she would be invited to travel on as far as the coast . . .

She checked her watch yet again: eleven twenty-one. For the first time she began to feel slightly uneasy. Then suddenly she saw him striding across the platform towards her followed by a man dragging two cases, and a porter wheeling even more luggage.

Guy apologised, but gave no explanation as to why he was so late, only ordering his batman to place his trunks on the train and wait for him. For the next few minutes they talked of nothing in particular and Becky even felt he was a little distant, but she was well aware that there were several brother officers on the platform, also bidding their farewells, some even to their wives.

A whistle blew and Becky noticed a guard check his watch. Guy leaned forward, brushed her cheek with his lips, then suddenly turned away. She watched him as he stepped quickly on to the train, never once looking back, while all she could think of was their naked bodies lodged together in that tiny bed and Guy saying, "I'll always love you. You know that, don't you?"

A final whistle blew and a green flag was waved. Becky stood quite alone. She shivered from the gust of wind that came as the engine wound its snake-like path out of the station and began its journey to Southampton. The giggling girls also departed, but in another direction, towards their hansom cabs and chauffeur-driven cars.

Becky walked over to a booth on the corner of platform seven, purchased a copy of *The Times* for threepence, and checked, first quickly, then slowly, down the list of forthcoming weddings.

From Arbuthnot to Yelland there was no mention of a Trentham, or a Salmon.

CHAPTER 10

Even before the first course had been served Becky regretted accepting Charlie's invitation to dinner at Mr Scallini's, the only restaurant he knew. Charlie was trying so hard to be considerate, which only made her feel more guilty.

"I like your dress," he said, admiring the pastel-coloured frock she had borrowed from Daphne's wardrobe.

"Thank you."

A long pause followed.

"I'm sorry," he said. "I should have thought twice before inviting you out the same day as Captain Trentham was leaving for India."

"Our engagement will be announced in *The Times* tomorrow," she said, not looking up from her untouched bowl of soup.

"Congratulations," said Charlie without feeling.

"You don't like Guy, do you?"

"I never was much good with officers."

"But your paths had crossed during the war. In fact, you knew him before I did, didn't you?" said Becky without warning. Charlie didn't reply, so she added, "I sensed it the first time we all had dinner together."

"'Knew him' would be an exaggeration," said Charlie. "We served in the same regiment, but until that night we'd never eaten at the same table."

"But you fought in the same war."

"Along with four thousand other men from our regiment," said Charlie, refusing to be drawn.

"And he was a brave and respected officer?"

A waiter appeared uninvited by their side. "What would you like to drink with your fish, sir?"

"Champagne," said Charlie. "After all, we do have something to celebrate."

"Do we?" said Becky, unaware that he had used the ploy simply to change the subject.

"Our first year's results. Or have you forgotten that Daphne's already been paid back more than half her loan?"

Becky managed a smile, realising that while she had been worrying about Guy's departure for India, Charlie had been concentrating on solving her other problem. But despite this news the evening continued in silence, occasionally punctuated with comments from Charlie that didn't always receive a reply. She occasionally sipped the champagne, toyed with her fish, ordered no dessert, and could barely hide her relief when the bill was eventually presented.

Charlie paid the waiter and left a handsome tip. Daphne would have been proud of him, Becky thought.

As she rose from her chair, she felt the room starting to go round in circles.

"Are you all right?" asked Charlie, placing an arm around her shoulder.

"I'm fine, just fine," said Becky. "I'm not used to drinking so much wine two nights in a row."

"And you didn't eat much dinner either," said Charlie, guiding her out of the restaurant and into the cold night air.

They proceeded arm in arm along Chelsea Terrace and Becky couldn't help thinking any casual passer-by might have taken them for lovers. When they arrived at the entrance to Daphne's flat Charlie had to dig deep into Becky's bag to find her keys. Somehow he managed to get the door open, while at the same time keeping her propped up against the wall. But then Becky's legs gave way and he had to cling on to stop her from falling. He gathered her up and carried her in his arms to the first floor. When he reached her flat, he had to perform a contortion to open the door without actually dropping her. At last he staggered into the drawing room and lowered her on to the sofa. He stood up and took his bearings, not sure whether to leave her on the sofa or to investigate where her bedroom might be.

Charlie was about to leave when she slipped off on to the floor, muttering something incoherent, the only word of which he caught was "engaged".

He returned to Becky's side, but this time lifted her firmly up over his shoulder. He carried her towards a door which, when he opened it, he discovered led to a bedroom. He placed her gently on top of the bed. As he began to tiptoe back to the door, she turned and Charlie had to rush back and pull her on to the middle of the bed to prevent her falling off. He hesitated, then bent over to lift up her shoulders before undoing the buttons down the back of her dress with his free hand. Once he had reached the bottom button he lowered her back on the bed, then lifted up her legs high in the air with one hand before he pulled with the other, inch by inch, until her dress was off. He left her only for a moment while he placed the dress neatly over a chair.

"Charlie Trumper," he said in a whisper, looking down at her, "you're a blind man, and you've been blind for an awfully long time."

He pulled back the blanket and placed Becky between the sheets, the way he had seen nurses on the Western Front carry out the same operation with wounded men.

He tucked her in securely, making sure that the whole process could not repeat itself. His final action was to lean over and kiss her on the cheek.

You're not only blind, Charlie Trumper, you're a fool, he told himself as he closed the front door behind him.

"Be with you in a moment," said Charlie as he threw some potatoes on to the weighing machine, while Becky waited patiently in the corner of the shop.

"Anythin' else, madam?" he asked the customer at the

front of the queue. "A few tangerines, per'aps? Some apples? And I've got some lovely grapefruit straight from South Africa, only arrived in the market this mornin'."

"No, thank you, Mr Trumper, that will be all for today."

"Then that'll be two shillings and fivepence, Mrs Symonds. Bob, could you carry on serving the next customer while I 'ave a word with Miss Salmon?"

"Sergeant Trumper."

"Sir," was Charlie's instant reaction when he heard the resonant voice. He turned to face the tall man who stood in front of him, straight as a ramrod, dressed in a Harris tweed jacket, cavalry twill trousers and carrying a brown felt hat.

"I never forget a face," the man said, although Charlie would have remained perplexed if it hadn't been for the monocle.

"Good God," said Charlie, standing to attention.

"No, Colonel will do," the other man said, laughing. "And no need for any of that bull. Those days have long gone. Although it's been some time since we last met, Trumper."

"Nearly two years, sir."

"Seems longer than that to me," the colonel said wistfully. "You certainly turned out to be right about Prescott, didn't you? And you were a good friend to him."

"'e was a good friend to me."

"And a first class soldier. Deserved his MM."

"Couldn't agree with you more, sir."

"Would have got one yourself, Trumper, but the rations were up after Prescott. Afraid it was only 'mentioned in dispatches' for you."

"The right man got the medal."

"Terrible way to die, though. The thought of it still haunts me, you know," said the colonel. "Only yards from the tape."

"Not your fault, sir. If anyone's, it was mine."

"If it was anyone's fault, it was certainly not yours,"

said the colonel. "And best forgotten, I suspect," he added without explanation.

"So 'ow's the regiment comin' along?" asked Charlie. "Survivin' without me?"

"And without me, I'm afraid," said the colonel, placing some apples into the shopping bag he was carrying. "They've departed for India, but not before they put this old horse out to grass."

"I'm sorry to 'ear that, sir. Your 'ole life was the regiment."

"True, though even Fusiliers have to succumb to the Geddes's axe. To be honest with you, I'm an infantry man myself, always have been, and I never did get the hang of those newfangled tanks."

"If we'd only 'ad 'em a couple of years earlier, sir, they might 'ave saved a few lives."

"Played their part, I'm bound to admit," the colonel nodded. "Like to think I played my part as well." He touched the knot of his striped tie. "Will we be seeing you at the regimental dinner, Trumper?"

"I didn't even know there was one, sir."

"Twice annually. First one in January, men only, second one in May with the memsahibs, which is also a ball. Gives the comrades a chance to get together and have a chinwag about old times. Would be nice if you could be on parade, Trumper. You see, I'm the president of the ball committee this year and rather hoping for a respectable turn-out."

"Then count me in, sir."

"Good man. I'll see that the office gets in touch with you pronto, ten shillings a ticket, and all you can drink thrown in, which I'm sure will be no hardship for you," added the colonel, looking round the busy shop.

"And can I get you anythin' while you're 'ere, sir?" Charlie asked, suddenly aware a long queue was forming behind the colonel.

"No, no, your able assistant has already taken excellent care of me, and as you can see I have completed the memsahib's written instructions." He held up a thin slip of paper bearing a list with a row of ticks down one side.

"Then I'll look forward to seeing you on the night of the ball, sir," said Charlie.

The colonel nodded and then stepped out on to the pavement without another word.

Becky strolled over to join her partner, only too aware that he had quite forgotten that she had been waiting to have a word with him. "You're still standing to attention, Charlie," she teased.

"That was my commanding officer, Lieutenant-Colonel Sir Danvers Hamilton," said Charlie a little pompously. "Led us at the front, 'e did, a gentleman, and 'e remembered my name."

"Charlie, if you could only hear yourself. A gentleman he may be, but he's the one who's out of work, while you're running a thriving business. I know which I'd rather be."

"But 'e's the Commanding Officer. Don't you understand?"

"Was," said Becky. "And he was also quick to point out the regiment have gone to India without him."

"That doesn't change anythin'."

"Mark my words, Charlie Trumper, that man will end up calling you 'sir'."

Guy had been away almost a week, and sometimes Becky could now go a whole hour without thinking about him.

She had sat up most of the previous night composing a letter to him, although when she left for her morning lecture the following day she walked straight past the pillar-box. She had managed to convince herself that the blame for failing to complete the letter should be placed firmly on the shoulders of Mr Palmer.

Becky had been disappointed to find their engagement had not been announced in *The Times* the next day, and became quite desperate when it failed to appear on any other day during that week. When in desperation she phoned Garrard's on the following Monday they claimed they knew nothing of a ring ordered in the name of a Captain Trentham of the Royal Fusiliers. Becky decided she would wait a further week before she wrote to Guy. She felt there must be some simple explanation.

Guy was still very much on her mind when she entered the offices of John D. Wood in Mount Street. She palmed the flat bell on the counter and asked an enquiring assistant if she could speak to Mr Palmer.

"Mr Palmer? We don't have a Mr Palmer any longer," she was told. "He was called up nearly a year ago, miss. Can I be of any assistance?"

Becky gripped the counter. "All right then, I'd like to speak to one of the partners," she said firmly.

"May I know the nature of your enquiry?" asked the assistant.

"Yes," said Becky. "I've come to discuss the instructions for the sale of 131 and 135 Chelsea Terrace."

"Ah yes, and may I ask who it is enquiring?"

"Miss Rebecca Salmon."

"I won't be a moment," the young man promised her, but didn't return for several minutes. When he did he was accompanied by a much older man, who wore a long black coat and horn-rimmed spectacles. A silver chain dangled from his waistcoat pocket.

"Good morning, Miss Salmon," the older man said. "My name is Crowther. Perhaps you'd be good enough to join me." He raised the counter lid and ushered her through. Becky duly followed in his wake.

"Good weather for this time of the year, wouldn't you say, madam?"

Becky stared out of the window and watched the umbrellas bobbing up and down along the pavement, but decided not to comment on Mr Crowther's meteorological judgment.

Once they had reached a poky little room at the back of the building he announced with obvious pride, "This is my office. Won't you please be seated, Miss Salmon?" He gestured towards an uncomfortably low chair placed opposite his desk. He then sat down in his own high-backed chair. "I'm a partner of the firm," he explained, "but I must confess a very junior partner." He laughed at his own joke. "Now, how can I help you?"

"My colleague and I want to acquire Numbers 131 and 135 Chelsea Terrace," replied Becky.

"Quite so," said Mr Crowther, looking down at his file. "And on this occasion will Miss Daphne Harcourt-Browne –"

"Miss Harcourt-Browne will not be involved in this transaction and if, because of that, you feel unable to deal with Mr Trumper or myself, we shall be happy to approach the vendors direct." Becky held her breath.

"Oh, please don't misunderstand me, madam. I'm sure we will have no trouble in continuing to do business with you."

"Thank you."

"Now, let us start with Number 135," said Mr Crowther, pushing his spectacles back up his nose before he leafed through the file in front of him. "Ah, yes, dear Mr Kendrick, a first-class butcher, you know. Sadly he is now considering an early retirement."

Becky sighed, and Mr Crowther looked up at her over his spectacles.

"His doctor has told him that he has no choice if he hopes to live more than a few more months," she said.

"Quite so," said Mr Crowther, returning to his file. "Well, it seems that his asking price is one hundred and fifty pounds for the freehold, plus one hundred pounds for the goodwill of the business."

"And how much will he take?"

"I'm not quite sure I catch your drift, madam." The junior partner raised his eyebrows.

"Mr Crowther, before we waste another minute of each other's time I feel I should let you know in confidence that it is our intention to purchase, if the price is right, every shop that becomes available in Chelsea Terrace, with the long-term aim of owning the entire block, even if it takes us a lifetime to achieve. It is not my intention to visit your office regularly for the next twenty years for the sole purpose of shadow-boxing with you. By then I suspect you will be a senior partner, and both of us will have better things to do. Do I make myself clear?"

"Abundantly," said Mr Crowther, glancing at the note Palmer had attached to the sale of 147: the lad hadn't exaggerated in the forthright opinion of his client. He pushed his spectacles back up his nose.

"I think Mr Kendrick might be willing to accept one hundred and twenty-five pounds if you would also agree to a pension of twenty-five pounds a year until his death."

"But he might live for ever."

"I feel I should point out, madam, that it was you, not I, who referred to Mr Kendrick's present state of health." For the first time the junior partner leaned back in his chair.

"I have no desire to rob Mr Kendrick of his pension," Becky replied. "Please offer him one hundred pounds for the freehold of the shop and twenty pounds a year for a period of eight years as a pension. I'm flexible on the latter part of the transaction but not on the former. Is that understood, Mr Crowther?"

"It certainly is, madam."

"And if I'm to pay Mr Kendrick a pension I shall also expect him to be available to offer advice from time to time as and when we require it."

"Quite so," said Crowther, making a note of her request in the margin.

"So what can you tell me about 131?"

"Now that is a knotty problem," said Crowther, opening a second file. "I don't know if you are fully aware of the circumstances, madam, but . . ."

Becky decided not to help him on this occasion. She smiled sweetly.

"Um, well," continued the junior partner, "Mr Rutherford is off to New York with a friend to open an antique gallery, in somewhere called 'the Village'." He hesitated.

"And their partnership is of a somewhat unusual nature?" assisted Becky after a prolonged silence. "And he might prefer to spend the rest of his days in an apartment in New York, rather than a cell in Brixton."

"Quite so," said Mr Crowther, as a bead of perspiration appeared on his forehead. "And in this particular gentleman's case, he wishes to remove everything from the premises, as he feels his merchandise might well fetch a better price in Manhattan. Therefore all that he would leave for your consideration would be the freehold."

"Then can I presume in his case, there will be no pension?"

"I think we may safely presume that," said Crowther.

"And may we therefore expect his price to be a little more reasonable, remembering some of the pressures he is under?"

"I would have thought not," replied Mr Crowther, "as the shop in question is rather larger than most of the others in Chelsea –"

"One thousand, four hundred and twenty-two square feet, to be precise," said Becky, "compared with one thousand square feet at Number 147, which we acquired for –"

"A very reasonable price at the time, if I may be so bold as to suggest, Miss Salmon."

"However . . ."

"Quite so," said Mr Crowther. Another bead of sweat appeared on his forehead.

"So how much is he hoping to raise for the freehold, now that we have established that he won't be requiring a pension?"

"His asking price," said Mr Crowther, whose eyes had once again returned to the file, "is two hundred pounds. However, I suspect," he added before Becky had the chance to challenge him, "that if you were able to close the negotiations quickly, he might allow the property to go for as little as one hundred and seventy-five." His eyebrows arched. "I am given to understand that he is anxious to join his friend as quickly as possible."

"If he's that anxious to join his friend I suspect he will be only too happy to lower his price to one hundred and fifty for a quick sale, and he might even accept one hundred and sixty, despite it taking a few days longer."

"Quite so." Mr Crowther removed his handkerchief from his top pocket and mopped his brow. Becky couldn't help noticing that it was still raining outside. "Will there be anything else, madam?" he asked, the handkerchief having been returned to the safety of his pocket.

"Yes, Mr Crowther," said Becky. "I should like you to keep a watching brief on all the properties in Chelsea Terrace and approach either Mr Trumper or myself the moment you hear of anything likely to come on the market."

"Perhaps it might be helpful if I were to prepare a full assessment of the properties on the block, then let you and Mr Trumper have a comprehensive written report for your consideration?"

"That would be most useful," said Becky, hiding her surprise at this sudden piece of initiative.

She rose from her chair to make it clear she considered the meeting to be over.

As they walked back to the front desk, Mr Crowther ventured, "I am given to understand that Number 147 is proving most popular with the inhabitants of Chelsea."

"And how would you know that?" asked Becky, surprised for a second time.

"My wife," Mr Crowther explained, "refuses to shop for her fruit and vegetables anywhere else, despite the fact that we live in Fulham."

"A discerning lady, your wife," said Becky.

"Quite so," said Mr Crowther.

Becky assumed that the banks would react to her approach with much the same enthusiasm as the estate agent had. However, having selected eight she thought might be possibilities, she quickly discovered that there is a considerable difference between offering yourself as a buyer to prostrating oneself as a borrower. Every time she presented her plans – to someone so junior as to be most unlikely to be able to make a decision – she received only a dismissive shake of the head. This included the bank that already held the Trumper account. "In fact," as she recounted to Daphne later that evening, "one of the junior assistants at the Penny Bank even had the nerve to suggest that should I ever become a married woman then they'd be only too delighted to do business with my husband."

"Come up against the world of men for the first time, have we?" asked Daphne, dropping her magazine on the floor. "Their cliques, their clubs? A woman's place is in the kitchen, and, if you're half attractive, perhaps occasionally in the bedroom."

Becky nodded glumly as she placed the magazine back on a side table.

"It's an attitude of mind that's never worried me, I must confess," Daphne admitted as she pushed her feet into a pair of shoes with stylish pointed toes. "But then I wasn't born overly ambitious like you, my darling. However, perhaps it's time to throw you another lifeline."

"Lifeline?"

"Yes. You see, what you need to solve your problem is an old school tie."

"Wouldn't it look a bit silly on me?"

"Probably look rather fetching actually, but that's not the point. The dilemma you seem to be facing is your gender – not to mention Charlie's accent, although I've nearly cured the dear boy of that problem. However, one thing's for sure, they haven't yet found a way to change people's sex."

"Where is all this leading?" asked Becky innocently.

"You're so impatient, darling. Just like Charlie. You must allow us lesser mortals a little more time to explain what we're about."

Becky took a seat on the corner of the sofa and placed her hands in her lap.

"First you must realise that all bankers are frightful snobs," continued Daphne. "Otherwise they'd be out there like you, running their own businesses. So what you require, to have them eating out of your hand, is a respectable front man."

"Front man?"

"Yes. Someone who'll accompany you on your trips to the bank whenever it should prove necessary." Daphne rose and checked herself in the mirror before continuing. "Such a person may not be blessed with your brains, but then on the other hand he won't be encumbered by your gender or by Charlie's accent. What he *will* have, however, is an old school tie, and preferably a title of some kind to go with it. Bankers do like a 'Bart', but most important of all you must secure someone who has a definite need of cash. For services rendered, you understand."

"Do such people exist?" asked Becky in disbelief.

"They most certainly do. In fact, there are far more of that type around than there are those who are willing to do a day's work." Daphne smiled reassuringly. "Give me a week or two and I feel confident I'll be able to come up with a short list of three. You'll see."

"You're a wonder," said Becky.

"In return I shall expect a small favour from you."

"Anything."

"Never use that word when dealing with a praying mantis like myself, darling. However, my request on this occasion is quite simple, and well within your power to grant. If Charlie should ask you to accompany him to his regimental dinner and dance, you are to accept."

"Why?"

"Because Reggie Arbuthnot has been stupid enough to invite me to the blithering occasion and I can't refuse him if I'm to hope for a little stalking on his estate in Scotland come November." Becky laughed as Daphne added, "I don't mind being taken to the ball by Reggie, but I do object to having to leave with him. So, if we have reached an agreement, I'll supply you with your necessary chinless

Bart and all you have to do when Charlie asks you, is say 'yes'."

"Yes."

Charlie wasn't surprised when Becky agreed without hesitation to be escorted to the regimental ball. After all, Daphne had already explained the details of their agreement to him. But it did come as a shock that, when Becky took her seat at the table, his fellow-sergeants couldn't take their eyes off her.

The dinner had been laid out in a massive gymnasium, which prompted Charlie's mates to tell story after story of their early days of training in Edinburgh. However, there the comparison ended, because the food was of a far higher standard than Charlie remembered being offered in Scotland.

"Where's Daphne?" asked Becky, as a portion of apple pie liberally covered in custard was placed in front of her.

"Up there on the top table with all the nobs," said Charlie, pointing over his shoulder with his thumb. "Can't afford to be seen with the likes of us, can she?" he added with a grin.

Once the dinner was over there followed a series of toasts – to everyone, it seemed to Becky, except the King. Charlie explained that the regiment had been granted dispensation from the loyal toast by King William IV in 1836 as their allegiance to the crown was without question. However, they did raise their glasses to the armed forces, each battalion in turn, and finally to the regiment, coupled with the name of their former colonel, each toast ending in rousing cheers. Becky watched the reactions of the men seated around her at the table and came to realise for the first time how many of that generation considered themselves lucky simply to be alive.

The former Commanding Officer, Sir Danvers Hamilton Bt, CBE, DSO, monocle in place, made a moving speech about all their fellow-comrades who were for different reasons unable to be present that night. Becky saw Charlie visibly stiffen at the mention of his friend Tommy Prescott. Finally they all rose and toasted absent friends. Becky found herself unexpectedly moved.

Once the colonel had sat down the tables were cleared to one side so that dancing could begin. No sooner had the first note struck up from the regimental band than Daphne appeared from the other end of the room.

"Come on, Charlie. I haven't the time to wait for you to find your way up to the top table."

"Delighted, I'm sure, madam," said Charlie, when he rose from his seat, "but what has happened to Reggie what's-his-name?"

"Arbuthnot," she said. "I have left the silly man clinging on to a deb from Chelmsford. And quite dreadful she was, I can tell you."

"What was so 'dreadful' about her?" mimicked Charlie.

"I never thought the day would come," said Daphne, "when His Majesty would allow anyone from Essex to be presented at court. But worse than that was her age."

"Why? How old is she?" asked Charlie, as he waltzed Daphne confidently round the floor.

"I can't altogether be certain, but she had the nerve to introduce me to her widowed father."

Charlie burst out laughing.

"You're not supposed to find it funny, Charles Trumper, you're meant to show some sympathy. There's still so much you have to learn."

Becky watched Charlie as he danced smoothly round the floor. "That Daphne's a bit of all right," said the man sitting next to her, who had introduced himself as Sergeant Mike Parker and turned out to be a butcher from Camberwell who had served alongside Charlie on the Marne. Becky accepted his judgment without comment, and when he later bowed and asked Becky for the pleasure of the next dance she reluctantly accepted. He proceeded to march her around the ballroom floor as if she were a leg of mutton on the way to the refrigeration room. The only thing he managed to do in time with the music was to tread on her toes.

At last he returned Becky to the comparative safety of their beer-stained table. Becky sat in silence while she watched everyone enjoying themselves, hoping that no one else would ask her for the pleasure. Her thoughts returned to Guy, and the meeting that she could no longer avoid if in another two weeks . . .

"May I have the honour, miss?"

Every man round the table shot to attention as the Commanding Officer escorted Becky on to the dance floor.

She found Colonel Hamilton an accomplished dancer, and an amusing companion, without showing any of those tendencies to patronise her that the string of bank managers had recently displayed. After the dance was over he invited Becky to the top table and introduced her to his wife.

"I must warn you," Daphne told Charlie, glancing over her shoulder in the direction of the Colonel and Lady Hamilton. "It's going to be quite a challenge for you to keep pace with the ambitious Miss Salmon. But as long as you stick with me and pay attention we'll give her a damn good run for her money."

After a couple more dances Daphne informed Becky that she had more than done her duty and the time had come for them all to leave. Becky, for her part, was only too pleased to escape the attention of so many young officers who had seen her dance with the colonel.

"I've some good news for you," Daphne told the two of them as the hansom trundled down the King's Road in the direction of Chelsea Terrace, with Charlie still clinging on to his half-empty bottle of champagne.

"What's that, my girl?" he asked, after a burp.

"I'm not your girl," Daphne remonstrated. "I may be willing to invest in the lower classes, Charlie Trumper, but never forget I'm not without breeding."

"So what's your news?" asked Becky laughing.

"You've kept your part of the bargain, so I must keep to mine."

"What do you mean?" asked Charlie, half asleep.

"I can now produce my short list of three to be considered as your front man, and thus, I hope, solve your banking problem."

Charlie immediately sobered up.

"My first offer is the second son of an earl," began Daphne. "Penniless but presentable. My second is a Bart, who will take the exercise on for a professional fee, but my *pièce de résistance* is a viscount whose luck has run out at the tables in Deauville and now finds it necessary to involve himself in the odd piece of vulgar commercial work."

"When do we get to meet them?" asked Charlie, trying not to slur his words.

"As soon as you wish," promised Daphne. "Tomorrow –"

"That won't be necessary," said Becky quietly.

"Why not?" asked Daphne, surprised.

"Because I have already chosen the man who will front for us."

"Who've you got in mind, darling? The Prince of Wales?"

"No. Lieutenant-Colonel Sir Danvers Hamilton, Bart, DSO, CBE."

"But 'e's the bleedin' Colonel of the Regiment," said Charlie, dropping the bottle of champagne on the floor of the hansom cab. "It's impossible, 'e'd never agree."

"I can assure you he will."

"What makes you so confident?" asked Daphne.

"Because we have an appointment to see him tomorrow morning at eleven o'clock."

CHAPTER 11

Daphne waved her parasol as a hansom approached them. The driver brought the cab to a halt and raised his hat. "Where to, miss?"

"Number 172 Harley Street," she instructed, before the two women climbed aboard.

He raised his hat again, and with a gentle flick of his whip headed the horse off in the direction of Hyde Park Corner.

"Have you told Charlie yet?" Becky asked.

"No, I funked it," admitted Daphne.

They sat in silence as the cabbie guided the horse towards Marble Arch.

"Perhaps it won't be necessary to tell him anything."

"Let's hope not," said Becky.

There followed another prolonged silence until the horse trotted into Oxford Street.

"Is your doctor an understanding man?"

"He always has been in the past."

"My God, I'm frightened."

"Don't worry. It will be over soon, then at least you'll know one way or the other."

The cabbie came to a halt outside Number 172 Harley Street, and the two women got out. While Becky stroked the horse's mane Daphne paid the man sixpence. Becky turned when she heard the rap on the brass knocker and climbed the three steps to join her friend.

A nurse in a starched blue uniform, white cap and collar

answered their call, and asked the two ladies to follow her. They were led down a dark corridor, lit by a single gaslight, then ushered into an empty waiting room. Copies of *Punch* and *Tatler* were displayed in neat rows on a table in the middle of the room. A variety of comfortable but unrelated chairs circled the low table. They each took a seat, but neither spoke again until the nurse had left the room.

"I –" began Daphne.

"If –" said Becky simultaneously.

They both laughed, a forced sound that echoed in the high-ceilinged room.

"No, you first," said Becky.

"I just wanted to know how the colonel's shaping up."

"Took his briefing like a man," said Becky. "We're off to our first official meeting tomorrow. Child and Co in Fleet Street. I've told him to treat the whole exercise like a dress rehearsal, as I'm saving the one I think we have a real chance with for later in the week."

"And Charlie?"

"All a bit much for him. He can't stop thinking of the colonel as his commanding officer."

"It would have been the same for you, if Charlie had suggested that the man teaching you accountancy should drop in and check the weekly takings at 147."

"I'm avoiding that particular gentleman at the moment," said Becky. "I'm only just putting in enough academic work to avoid being reprimanded; lately my commendeds have become passes, while my passes are just not good enough. If I don't manage to get a degree at the end of all this there will be only one person to blame."

"You'll be one of the few women who's a Bachelor of Arts. Perhaps you should demand they change the degree to SA."

"SA?"

"Spinster of Arts."

They laughed at what they both knew to be a hoary chestnut, as they continued to avoid the real reason they were in that waiting room. Suddenly the door swung open and they looked up to see that the nurse had returned.

"The doctor will see you now."

"May I come as well?"

"Yes, I'm sure that will be all right."

Both women rose and followed the nurse further down the same corridor until they reached a white door with a small brass plate almost worn away with rubbing which read "Fergus Gould, MD". A gentle knock from the nurse elicited a "yes" and Daphne and Becky entered the room together.

"Good morning, good morning," said the doctor cheerfully in a soft Scottish burr, shaking hands with the two of them in turn. "Won't you please be seated? The tests have been completed and I have excellent news for you." He returned to the seat behind his desk and opened a file in front of him. They both smiled, the taller of the two relaxing for the first time in days.

"I'm happy to say that you are physically in perfect health, but as this is your first child" – he watched both women turn white – "you will have to behave rather more cautiously over the coming months. But as long as you do, I can see no reason why this birth should have any complications. May I be the first to congratulate you?"

"Oh, God, no," she said, nearly fainting. "I thought you said the news was excellent."

"Why, yes," replied Doctor Gould. "I assumed you would be delighted."

Her friend interjected. "You see, Doctor, there's a problem. She's not married."

"Oh, yes, I do see," said the doctor, his voice immediately changing tone. "I'm so sorry, I had no idea. Perhaps if you had told me at our first meeting –"

"No, I'm entirely to blame, Doctor Gould. I had simply hoped –"

"No, it is I who am to blame. How extremely tactless of me." Doctor Gould paused thoughtfully. "Although it remains illegal in this country, I am assured that there are excellent doctors in Sweden who –"

"That is not possible," said the pregnant woman. "You see, it's against everything my parents would have considered 'acceptable behaviour'."

"Good morning, Hadlow," said the colonel as he marched into the bank, handing the manager his topcoat, hat and cane.

"Good morning, Sir Danvers," replied the manager, passing the hat, coat and cane on to an assistant. "May I say how honoured we are that you thought our humble establishment worthy of your consideration."

Becky couldn't help reflecting that it was not quite the same greeting she had received when visiting another bank of similar standing only a few weeks before.

"Would you be kind enough to come through to my office?" the manager continued, putting his arm out as if he were guiding wayward traffic.

"Certainly, but first may I introduce Mr Trumper and Miss Salmon, both of whom are my associates in this venture."

"Delighted, I'm sure," the manager said as he pushed his glasses back up his nose before shaking hands with Charlie and Becky in turn.

Becky noticed that Charlie was unusually silent and kept pulling at his collar, which looked as though it might be half an inch too tight for comfort. However, after spending a morning in Savile Row the previous week being measured from head to foot for a new suit, he had refused to wait a moment longer when Daphne suggested he should be measured for a shirt, so in the end Daphne was left to guess his neck size.

"Coffee?" enquired the manager, once they had all settled in his office.

"No, thank you," said the colonel.

Becky would have liked a cup of coffee but realised that the manager had assumed Sir Danvers had spoken for all three of them. She bit her lip.

"Now, how can I be of assistance, Sir Danvers?" The manager nervously touched the knot of his tie.

"My associates and I currently own a property in Chelsea Terrace – Number 147 – which although a small venture at present is nevertheless progressing satisfactorily." The manager's smile remained in place. "We purchased the premises some eighteen months ago at a cost of one hundred pounds and that investment has shown a profit this year of a little over forty-three pounds."

"Very satisfactory," said the manager. "Of course, I have read your letter and the accounts you so kindly had sent over by messenger."

Charlie was tempted to tell him who the messenger had been.

"However, we feel the time has come to expand," continued the colonel. "And in order to do so we will require a bank that can show a little more initiative than the establishment with which we're presently dealing – as well as one that has its eye on the future. Our current bankers, I sometimes feel, are still living in the nineteenth century. Frankly, they are little more than holders of deposits, while what we are looking for is the service of a real bank."

"I understand."

"It's been worrying me –" said the colonel, suddenly breaking off and fixing his monocle to his left eye.

"Worrying you?" Mr Hadlow sat forward anxiously in his chair.

"Your tie."

"My tie?" The manager once again fingered the knot nervously.

"Yes, your tie. Don't tell me – the Buffs?"

"You are correct, Sir Danvers."

"Saw some action, did you, Hadlow?"

"Well, not exactly, Sir Danvers. My sight, you understand." Mr Hadlow began fiddling with his glasses.

"Bad luck, old chap," said the colonel, his monocle dropping back down. "Well, to continue. My colleagues and I are of a mind to expand, but I feel it would only be the honourable thing to let you know that we have an appointment with a rival establishment on Thursday afternoon."

"Thursday afternoon," repeated the manager, after dipping his quill pen once more into the ink-well on the front of his desk and adding this to the other pieces of information he had already recorded.

"But I had rather hoped it would not have gone unnoticed," continued the colonel, "that we chose to come and see you first."

"I'm most flattered," said Mr Hadlow. "And what terms were you hoping this bank might offer, Sir Danvers, that your own could not?"

The colonel paused for a moment and Becky glanced towards him alarmed, as she couldn't remember if she had briefed him on terms. Neither of them had expected to have reached quite this far at the first meeting.

The colonel cleared his throat. "We would naturally expect competitive terms, if we are to move our business to your bank, being aware of the long-term implications."

This answer seemed to impress Hadlow. He looked down at the figures in front of him and pronounced, "Well, I see you are requesting a loan of two hundred and fifty pounds for the purchase of 131 and 135 Chelsea Terrace, which, bearing in mind the state of your account, would require an overdraft facility" – he paused, appearing to be making a calculation – "of at least one hundred and seventy pounds."

"Correct, Hadlow. I see you have mastered our present predicament admirably."

The manager allowed himself a smile. "Given the circumstances, Sir Danvers, I feel we could indeed advance such a loan, if a charge of four per cent interest per annum would be acceptable to you and your colleagues."

Again the colonel hesitated, until he caught Becky's half-smile.

"Our present bankers provide us with a facility of three and a half per cent," said the colonel. "As I'm sure you know."

"But they are taking no risk," pointed out Mr Hadlow. "As well as refusing to allow you to be overdrawn more than fifty pounds. However," he added before the colonel could reply, "I feel in this particular case we might also offer three and a half per cent. How does that sound to you?"

The colonel did not comment until he had observed the expression on Becky's face. Her smile had widened to a grin.

"I think I speak for my colleagues, Hadlow, when I say we find your proposition acceptable, most acceptable."

Becky and Charlie nodded their agreement.

"Then I shall begin to process all the paperwork. It may take a few days, of course."

"Of course," said the colonel. "And I can tell you, Hadlow, that we look forward to a long and profitable association with your bank."

The manager somehow rose and bowed all in one movement, an action Becky felt even Sir Henry Irving would have found difficult to accomplish.

Mr Hadlow then proceeded to escort the colonel and his young associates to the front hall.

"Old Chubby Duckworth still with this outfit?" enquired the colonel.

"Lord Duckworth is indeed our chairman," murmured Mr Hadlow reverentially.

"Good man – served with him in South Africa. Royal Rifles. I shall, with your permission, mention our meeting to him, when I next see Chubby at the club."

"That would be most kind of you, Sir Danvers."

When they reached the door the manager dispensed with his assistant and helped the colonel on with his topcoat himself, then handed him his hat and cane before bidding farewell to his new customers. "Do feel free to call me at any time," were his final words as he bowed once again. He stood there until the three of them were out of sight.

Once they were back on the street the colonel marched quickly round the corner, coming to a halt behind the nearest tree. Becky and Charlie ran after him, not quite sure what he was up to.

"Are you feeling all right, sir?" Charlie asked, as soon as he had caught up.

"I'm fine, Trumper," replied the colonel. "Just fine. But I can tell you, I would rather face a bunch of marauding Afghan natives than go through that again. Still, how did I do?"

"You were magnificent," said Becky. "I swear, if you had taken off your shoes and told Hadlow to polish them, he would have removed his handkerchief and started rubbing little circles immediately."

The colonel smiled. "Oh, good. Thought it went all right, did you?"

"Perfect," said Becky. "You couldn't have done better. I shall go round to John D. Wood this afternoon and put down the deposit on both shops."

"Thank God for your briefing, Miss Salmon," said the colonel, standing his full height. "You know what? You would have made a damned fine staff officer."

Becky smiled. "I take that as a great compliment, Colonel."

"Don't you agree, Trumper? Some partner you've found yourself," he added.

"Yes, sir," said Charlie as the colonel began to stride off down the road. "But may I ask you something that's been worrying me?"

"Of course, Trumper, fire away."

"If you're a friend of the chairman of the bank," said Charlie, matching him stride for stride, "why didn't we go direct to him in the first place?"

The colonel came to a sudden halt. "My dear Trumper," he explained, "you don't visit the chairman of the bank when you require a loan of only two hundred and fifty pounds. Nevertheless, let it be said that I have every confidence that it will not be long before we shall need to seek him out. However, at this very moment other needs are more pressing."

"Other needs?" said Charlie.

"Yes, Trumper. I require a whisky, don't you know?" said the colonel, eyeing a sign flapping above a pub on the opposite side of the road. "And while we're at it, let's make it a double."

"How far gone are you?" asked Charlie, when the following day Becky came round to tell him the news.

"About three months." She avoided looking him directly in the eye.

"Why didn't you tell me earlier?" He sounded a little hurt as he turned the Open sign to Closed, and marched up the stairs.

"I hoped I wouldn't need to," said Becky as she followed him into the flat.

"You've written to tell Trentham, of course?"

"No. I keep meaning to, but I haven't got round to it yet." She began to tidy up the room rather than face him.

"Keep meaning to?" said Charlie. "You should have told the bastard weeks ago. He's the first person who ought to know. After all, he's the one who's responsible for the bleedin' mess, if you'll excuse the expression."

"It's not that easy, Charlie."

"Why not, for heaven's sake?"

"It would mean the end of his career, and Guy lives for the regiment. He's like your colonel: it would be unfair to ask him to give up being a soldier at the age of twenty-three."

"He's nothing like the colonel," said Charlie. "In any case, he's still young enough to settle down and do a day's work like the rest of us."

"He's married to the army, Charlie, not to me. Why ruin both our lives?"

"But he should still be told what has happened and at least be given the choice."

"He wouldn't be left with any choice, Charlie, surely you see that? He'd sail home on the next boat and marry me. He's an honourable man."

"An honourable man, is he?" said Charlie. "Well, if he's so honourable you can afford to promise me one thing."

"What's that?"

"You'll write to him tonight and tell him the truth."

Becky hesitated for some time before saying, "All right, I will."

"Tonight?"

"Yes, tonight."

"And you should also let his parents know while you're at it."

"No, I can't be expected to do that, Charlie," she said, facing him for the first time.

"So what's the reason this time? Some fear that their careers might be ruined?"

"No, but if I did his father would insist that Guy return home and marry me."

"And what's so wrong with that?"

"His mother would then claim that I had tricked her son into the whole thing, or worse –"

"Worse?"

"– that it wasn't even his child."

"And who'd believe her?"

"All those who wanted to."

"But that isn't fair," said Charlie.

"Life isn't, to quote my father. I had to grow up some time, Charlie. For you it was the Western Front."

"So what are we going to do now?"

"We?" said Becky.

"Yes, we. We're still partners, you know. Or had you forgotten?"

"To start with I'll have to find somewhere else to live; it wouldn't be fair on Daphne –"

"What a friend she's turned out to be," said Charlie.

"To both of us," said Becky as Charlie stood up, thrust his hands in his pockets, and began to march around the little room. It reminded Becky of when they had been at school together.

"I don't suppose . . ." said Charlie. It was his turn to be unable to look her in the face.

"Suppose? Suppose what?"

"I don't suppose . . ." he began again.

"Yes?"

"You'd consider marrying me?"

There was a long silence before a shocked Becky felt able to reply. "But what about Daphne?" she eventually said.

"Daphne? You surely never believed we had that sort of relationship? It's true she's been giving me night classes but not the type you think. In any case, there's only ever been one man in Daphne's life, and it's certainly not Charlie Trumper, for the simple reason she's known all along that there's only been one woman in mine."

"But –"

"And I've loved you for such a long time, Becky."

"Oh, my God," said Becky, placing her head in her hands.

"I'm sorry," said Charlie. "I thought you knew. Daphne told me women always know these things."

"I had no idea, Charlie. I've been so blind as well as stupid."

"I haven't looked at another woman since the day I came back from Edinburgh. I suppose I just 'oped you might love me a little," he said.

"I'll always love you a little, Charlie, but I'm afraid it's Guy I'm in love with."

"Lucky blighter. And to think I saw you first. Your father once chased me out of 'is shop, you know, when he 'eard me calling you 'Posh Porky' behind your back." Becky smiled. "You see, I've always been able to grab everything I really wanted in life, so 'ow did I let you get away?"

Becky was unable to look up at him.

"He's an officer, of course, and I'm not. That would explain it." Charlie had stopped pacing round the room and came to a halt in front of her.

"You're a general, Charlie."

"It's not the same, though, is it?"

CHAPTER 12

97 Chelsea Terrace,
London SW3

May 20th, 1920

My Darling Guy

This is the hardest letter I have ever had to write in my life. In fact, I'm not sure where to begin. Just over three months have passed since you left for India, and something has happened that I felt you would want to know about at once. I have just been to see Daphne's doctor in Harley Street and

Becky stopped, checked carefully over the few sentences she had written, groaned, scrumpled up the notepaper and dropped it in the wastepaper-basket that rested at her feet. She stood up, stretched and started to pace around the room in the hope that she might be able to dream up some new excuse for not continuing with her task. It was already twelve thirty so she could now go to bed, claiming that she had been too weary to carry on – only Becky knew that she wouldn't be able to sleep until the letter had been completed. She returned to her desk and tried to settle herself again before reconsidering the opening line. She picked up her pen.

97 Chelsea Terrace,
London SW3

May 20th, 1920

My Dear Guy,

I fear that this letter may come as something of a surprise, especially after all the irrelevant gossip that I was able to share with you only a month ago. I have been postponing writing anything of consequence to you in the hope that my fears would prove unfounded. Unhappily that has not proved to be the case, and circumstances have now overtaken me.

After spending the most wonderful time with you the night before you left for India, I then missed my period the following month, but did not trouble you with the problem immediately in the hope that

Oh no, thought Becky, and tore up her latest effort before once again dropping the scraps of paper into the wastepaper-basket. She traipsed off to the kitchen to make herself a pot of tea. After her second cup, she reluctantly returned to her writing desk and settled herself again.

97 Chelsea Terrace,
London SW3

May 20th, 1920

Dear Guy,

I do hope everything is going well for you in India, and that they are not working you too hard. I miss you more than I can express, but what with exams looming and Charlie seeing himself as the next Mr. Selfridge, these first three months since you left have just shot by. In fact I feel sure you'll be fascinated to learn that your old Commanding Officer, Lieutenant-Colonel Sir Danvers Hamilton, has become

"And by the way I'm pregnant," said Becky out loud, and tore up her third attempt. She replaced the top back on her pen, deciding the time had come to take a walk round the square. She picked up her coat from its hook in the hall, ran down the stairs and let herself out.

She strolled aimlessly up and down the deserted road, seemingly unaware of the hour. She was pleased to find that "Sold" signs now appeared in the windows of Numbers 131 and 135. She stopped outside the old antique shop for a moment, cupped her hands round her eyes and peered in through the window. To her horror she discovered that Mr Rutherford had removed absolutely everything, even the gas fittings and the mantelpiece that she had assumed were fixed to the wall. That'll teach me to study an offer document more carefully next time, she thought. She continued to stare at the empty space as a mouse scurried across the floorboards. "Perhaps we should open a pet shop," she said aloud.

"Beg pardon, miss."

Becky swung round to find a policeman rattling the door knob of 133, to be certain the premises were locked.

"Oh, good evening, Constable," said Becky sheepishly, feeling guilty without any reason.

"It's nearly two in the morning, miss. You just said, 'Good evening'."

"Oh, is it?" said Becky, looking at her watch. "Oh, yes, so it is. How silly of me. You see, I live at 97." Feeling some explanation was necessary, she added, "I couldn't sleep, so I decided to take a walk."

"Better join the force then. They'll be happy to keep you walking all night."

Becky laughed. "No, thank you, Constable. I think I'll just go back to my flat and try and get some sleep. Goodnight."

"Goodnight, miss," said the policeman, touching his helmet in a half-salute before checking the empty antique shop was also safely locked up.

Becky turned and walked determinedly back down

Chelsea Terrace, opened the front door of 97, climbed the staircase to the flat, took off her coat and returned immediately to the little writing desk. She paused only for a moment before picking up her pen and starting to write.

For once the words flowed easily because she now knew exactly what needed to be said.

97 Chelsea Terrace,
London SW3

May 20th, 1920

Dear Guy,

I have tried to think of a hundred different ways of letting you know what has happened to me since you left for India, and finally came to the conclusion that only the simple truth makes any sense.

I am now some fourteen weeks pregnant with your child, the idea of which fills me with great happiness but I confess more than a little apprehension. Happiness because you are the only man I have ever loved, and apprehension because of the implications such a piece of news might have on your future with the regiment.

I must tell you from the outset that I have no desire to harm that career in any way by forcing you into marriage. A commitment honoured only out of some feeling of guilt, which then caused you to spend the rest of your life participating in a sham after what happened between us on one occasion, must surely be unacceptable to either of us.

For my part, I make no secret of my total devotion to you, but if it is not reciprocated, I can never be a party to sacrificing such a promising career on the altar of hypocrisy.

But, my darling, be left in no doubt of my complete love for you and my abiding interest in your future and well-being, even to the point of denying your involvement in this affair, should that be the course you wish me to follow.

Guy, I will always adore you, and be assured of my utmost loyalty whatever decision you should come to.

With all my love

Becky

She was unable to control her tears as she read her words through a second time. As she folded the notepaper the bedroom door swung open and a sleepy Daphne appeared in front of her.

"You all right, darling?"

"Yes. Just felt a little queasy," explained Becky. "I decided that I needed a breath of fresh air." She deftly slipped the letter into an unmarked envelope.

"Now I'm up," said Daphne, "would you care for a cup of tea?"

"No, thank you. I've already had two cups."

"Well, I think I will." Daphne disappeared into the kitchen. Becky immediately picked up her pen again and wrote on the envelope:

Captain Guy Trentham, M.C.,
2nd Battalion Royal Fusiliers,
Wellington Barracks,
Poona,
INDIA

She had left the flat, posted the letter in the pillar-box on the corner of Chelsea Terrace and returned to Number 97 even before the kettle had boiled.

Although Charlie received the occasional letter from Sal in Canada to tell him of the arrival of his latest nephew or niece, and the odd infrequent call from Grace whenever she could get away from her hospital duties, a visit from Kitty was rare indeed. But when she came to the flat it was always with the same purpose.

"I only need a couple of quid, Charlie, just to see me through," explained Kitty as she lowered herself into the one comfortable chair only moments after she had entered the room.

Charlie stared at his sister. Although she was only eighteen months older than himself she already looked like a woman well into her thirties. Under the baggy shapeless cardigan there was no longer any sign of the figure that had attracted every wandering eye in the East End, and without make-up her face was already beginning to look splotchy and lined.

"It was only a pound last time," Charlie reminded her. "And that wasn't so long ago."

"But my man's left me since then, Charlie. I'm on my own again, without even a roof over my head. Come on, do us a favour."

He continued to stare at her, thankful that Becky was not yet back from her afternoon lecture, although he suspected Kitty only came when she could be sure the till was full and Becky was safely out of the way.

"I won't be a moment," he said after a long period of silence. He slipped out of the room and headed off downstairs to the shop. Once he was sure the assistants weren't looking, he removed two pounds ten shillings from the till. He walked resignedly back upstairs to the flat.

Kitty was already waiting by the door. Charlie handed over the three notes. She almost snatched the money before tucking the notes in her glove and leaving without another word.

Charlie followed her down the stairs and watched her remove a peach from the top of a neat pyramid in the corner of the shop before taking a bite, stepping out on to the pavement and hurrying off down the road.

Charlie would have to take responsibility for checking the till that night; no one must find out the exact amount he had given her.

"You'll end up having to buy this bench, Charlie Trumper," said Becky as she lowered herself down beside him.

"Not until I own every shop in the block, my lovely," he said, turning to look at her. "And how about you? When's the baby due?"

"About another five weeks, the doctor thinks."

"Got the flat all ready for the new arrival, have you?"

"Yes, thanks to Daphne letting me stay on."

"I miss her," said Charlie.

"So do I, although I've never seen her happier since Percy was discharged from the Scots Guards."

"Bet it won't be long before they're engaged."

"Let's hope not," said Becky, looking across the road.

Three Trumper signs, all in gold on blue, shone back at her. The fruit and vegetable shop continued to make an excellent return and Bob Makins seemed to have grown in stature over the past year. The butcher's had lost a little custom after Mr Kendrick retired, but had picked up again since Charlie had employed Mike Parker to take his place.

"Let's hope he's a better butcher than a dancer," Becky had remarked when Charlie told her the news of Sergeant Parker's appointment.

As for the grocer's, Charlie's new pride and joy, it had flourished from the first day, although as far as his staff could tell, their master seemed to be in all three shops at once.

"Stroke of genius," said Charlie, "turning that old antique shop into a grocer's."

"So now you consider yourself to be a grocer, do you?"

"Certainly not, I'm a plain fruit and vegetable man, and always will be."

"I wonder if that's what you'll tell the girls when you own the whole block."

"That could take some time yet. So how is the balance-sheet shaping up for the new shops?"

"They're both in the books to show a loss during their first year."

"But they could still make a profit, certainly break even." Charlie's voice rose in protest. "And the grocer's shop is set to –"

"Not so loud. I want Mr Hadlow and his colleagues at the bank to discover that we've done far better than we originally predicted."

"You're an evil woman, Rebecca Salmon, that's no mistake."

"You won't be saying that, Charlie Trumper, when you need me to go begging for your next loan."

"If you're so clever, then explain to me why I can't get hold of the bookshop," said Charlie, pointing across the road at Number 141, where a single light was the only proof the building was still inhabited. "The place hasn't seen a customer in weeks from what I can tell, and even when they do it's only because someone had gone in to find directions back to Brompton Road."

"I've no idea," said Becky, laughing. "I've already had a long chat to Mr Sneddles about buying the premises, but he just wasn't interested. You see, since his wife died, running the shop has become the only reason for him to carry on."

"But carry on doing what?" asked Charlie. "Dusting old books and stacking up ancient manuscripts?"

"He's happy just to sit around and read William Blake and his beloved war poets. As long as he sells a couple of books every month he's quite content to keep the shop open. Not everyone wants to be a millionaire, you know – as Daphne never stops reminding me."

"Possibly. So why not offer Mr Sneddles one hundred

and fifty guineas for the freehold, then charge him a rent of say ten guineas a year? That way it'll automatically fall into our hands the moment he dies."

"You're a hard man to please, Charlie Trumper, but if that's what you want, I'll give it a try."

"That is what I want, Rebecca Salmon, so get on with it."

"I'll do my best, although it may have slipped your notice that I'm about to have a baby while also trying to sit a bachelor's degree."

"That combination doesn't sound quite right to me. However, I still may need you to pull off another coup."

"Another coup?"

"Fothergill's."

"The corner shop."

"No less," said Charlie. "And you know how I feel about corner shops, Miss Salmon."

"I certainly do, Mr Trumper. I am also aware that you know nothing about the fine art business, let alone being an auctioneer."

"Not a lot, I admit," said Charlie. "But after a couple of visits to New Bond Street, where I watched how they earn a living at Sotheby's, followed by a short walk down the road to St James's to study their only real rivals, Christie's, I came to the conclusion that we might eventually be able to put that art degree of yours to some use."

Becky raised her eyebrows. "I can't wait to learn what you have planned for the rest of my life."

"Once you've finished that degree of yours," continued Charlie, ignoring the comment, "I want you to apply for a job at Sotheby's or Christie's, I don't mind which, where you can spend three to five years learning everything they're up to. The moment you consider that you're good and ready to leave, you could then poach anyone you felt was worth employing and return to run Number 1 Chelsea Terrace and open up a genuine rival to those two establishments."

"I'm still listening, Charlie Trumper."

"You see, Rebecca Salmon, you've got your father's

business acumen. I hope you liked that word. Combine that with the one thing you've always loved and also have a natural talent for, how can you fail?"

"Thank you for the compliment, but may I, while we're on the subject, ask where Mr Fothergill fits into your master plan?"

"He doesn't."

"What do you mean?"

"He's been losing money hand over fist for the past three years," said Charlie. "At the moment the value of the property and sale of his best stock would just about cover his losses, but that state of affairs can't last too much longer. So now you know what's expected of you."

"I certainly do. Mr Trumper."

When September had come and gone, even Becky began to accept that Guy had no intention of responding to her letter.

As late as August Daphne reported to them that she had bumped into Mrs Trentham at Goodwood. Guy's mother had claimed that her son was not only revelling in his duties in India but had every reason to expect an imminent announcement concerning his promotion to major. Daphne found herself only just able to keep her promise and remain silent about Becky's condition.

As the day of the birth drew nearer, Charlie made sure that Becky didn't waste any time shopping for food and even detailed one of the girls at Number 147 to help her keep the flat clean, so much so that Becky began to accuse them both of pampering her.

By the eighth month Becky didn't even bother to check the morning post, as Daphne's long-held view of Captain Trentham began to gain more credibility. She was surprised to find how quickly he faded from her memory, despite the fact that it was his child she was about to give birth to.

Becky also felt embarrassed that most people assumed Charlie was the father, and it wasn't helped by the fact that, whenever he was asked, he refused to deny it.

Meanwhile, Charlie still had his eye on a couple of

shops whose owners he felt might soon be willing to sell but Daphne wouldn't hear of any further business transactions until after the child had been born.

"I don't want Becky involved in any of your dubious business enterprises before she's had the child and completed her degree. Do I make myself clear?"

"Yes, ma'am," said Charlie, clicking his heels. He didn't mention that only the week before Becky had herself closed the deal with Mr Sneddles so that the bookshop would be theirs once the old man died. There was only one clause in the agreement that Charlie remained concerned about, because he wasn't quite sure how he would get rid of that number of books.

"Miss Becky has just phoned," whispered Bob into the boss's ear one afternoon when Charlie was serving in the shop. "Says could you go round immediately. Thinks the baby's about to arrive."

"But it's not due for another two weeks," said Charlie as he pulled off his apron.

"I'm sure I don't know about that Mr Trumper but all she said was to hurry."

"Has she sent for the midwife?" Charlie asked, deserting a half-laden customer before grabbing his coat.

"I've no idea, sir."

"Right, take charge of the shop, because I may not be back again today." Charlie left the smiling queue of customers and ran down the road to 97, flew up the stairs, pushed open the door and marched straight on into Becky's bedroom.

He sat down beside her on the bed and held her hand for some time before either of them spoke.

"Have you sent for the midwife?" he eventually asked.

"She certainly has," said a voice from behind them, as a vast woman entered the room. She wore an old brown raincoat that was too small for her and carried a black leather bag. From the heaving of her breasts she had obviously had a struggle climbing the stairs. "I'm Mrs

Westlake, attached to St Stephen's hospital," she declared. "I do hope I've got here in time." Becky nodded as the midwife turned her attention to Charlie. "Now you go away and boil me some water, and quickly." Her voice sounded as if she wasn't in the habit of being questioned. Without another word Charlie jumped off the end of the bed and left the room.

Mrs Westlake placed her large Gladstone bag on the floor and started by taking Becky's pulse.

"How long between the spasms?" she asked matter-of-factly.

"Down to twenty minutes," Becky replied.

"Excellent. Then we don't have much longer to wait."

Charlie appeared at the door carrying a bowl of hot water. "Anything else I can do?"

"Yes, there certainly is. I need every clean towel you can lay your hands on, and I wouldn't mind a cup of tea."

Charlie ran back out of the room.

"Husbands are always a nuisance on these occasions," Mrs Westlake declared. "One must simply keep them on the move."

Becky was about to explain to her about Charlie when another contraction gripped her.

"Breathe deeply and slowly, my dear," encouraged Mrs Westlake in a gentler voice, as Charlie came back with three towels and a kettle of hot water.

Without turning to see who it was, Mrs Westlake continued. "Leave the towels on the sideboard, pour the water in the largest bowl you've got, then put the kettle back on so that I've always got more hot water whenever I call for it."

Charlie disappeared again without a word.

"I wish I could get him to do that," gasped Becky admiringly.

"Oh, don't worry, my dear. I can't do a thing with my own husband and we've got seven children."

A couple of minutes later Charlie pushed open the door

with a foot and carried another bowl of steaming water over to the bedside.

"On the side table," said Mrs Westlake, pointing. "And try not to forget my tea. After that I shall still need more towels," she added.

Becky let out a loud groan.

"Hold my hand and keep breathing deeply," said the midwife.

Charlie soon reappeared with another kettle of water, and was immediately instructed to empty the bowl before refilling it with the new supply. After he had completed the task, Mrs Westlake said, "You can wait outside until I call for you."

Charlie left the room, gently pulling the door closed behind him.

He seemed to be making countless cups of tea, and carrying endless kettles of water, backward and forward, always arriving with the wrong one at the wrong time until finally he was shut out of the bedroom and left to pace up and down the kitchen fearing the worst. Then he heard the plaintive little cry.

Becky watched from her bed as the midwife held up her child by one leg and gave it a gentle smack on the bottom. "I always enjoy that," said Mrs Westlake. "Feels good to know you've brought something new into the world." She wrapped up the child in a tea-towel and handed the bundle back to its mother.

"It's – ?"

"A boy, I'm afraid," said the midwife. "So the world is unlikely to be advanced by one jot or tittle. You'll have to produce a daughter next time," she said, smiling broadly. "If he's still up to it, of course." She pointed a thumb towards the closed door.

"But he's – " Becky tried again.

"Useless, I know. Like all men." Mrs Westlake opened the bedroom door in search of Charlie. "It's all over, Mr Salmon. You can stop skulking around and come and have a look at your son."

Charlie came in so quickly that he nearly knocked the midwife over. He stood at the end of the bed and stared down at the tiny figure in Becky's arms.

"He's an ugly little fellow, isn't he?" said Charlie.

"Well, we know who to blame for that," said the midwife. "Let's just hope this one doesn't end up with a broken nose. In any case, as I've already explained to your wife, what you need next is a daughter. By the way, what are you going to call this one?"

"Daniel George," said Becky without hesitation. "After my father," she explained, looking up at Charlie.

"And mine," said Charlie, as he walked to the head of the bed and placed an arm round Becky.

"Well, I'll have to go now Mrs Salmon. But I shall be back first thing in the morning."

"No, it's Mrs Trumper actually," said Becky quietly. "Salmon was my maiden name."

"Oh," said the midwife, looking flustered for the first time. "They seem to have got the names muddled up on my call sheet. Oh, well, see you tomorrow, Mrs Trumper," she said as she closed the door.

"Mrs Trumper?" said Charlie.

"It's taken me an awful long time to come to my senses, wouldn't you say, Mr Trumper?"

DAPHNE

1918-1921

CHAPTER 13

When I opened the letter, I confess I didn't immediately recall who Becky Salmon was. But then I remembered that there had been an extremely bright, rather plump pupil by that name at St Paul's, who always seemed to have an endless supply of cream cakes. If I remember, the only thing I gave her in return was an art book that had been a Christmas present from an aunt in Cumberland.

In fact, by the time I had reached the upper sixth, the precocious little blighter was already in the lower sixth, despite there being a good two years difference in our age.

Having read her letter a second time, I couldn't imagine why the girl should want to see me, and concluded that the only way I was likely to find out was to invite her round to tea at my little place in Chelsea.

When I first saw Becky again I hardly recognised her. Not only had she lost a couple of stone, but she would have made an ideal model for one of those Pepsodent advertisements that one saw displayed on the front of every tram – you know, a fresh-faced girl showing off a gleaming set of perfect teeth. I had to admit I was quite envious.

Becky explained to me that all she needed was a room in London while she was up at the university. I was only too happy to oblige. After all, the mater had made it clear on several occasions how much she disapproved of my being in the flat on my own, and that she couldn't for the life of her fathom what was wrong with 26 Lowndes Square, our family's London residence. I couldn't wait to tell Ma, and Pa for that matter, the news that I had, as they so often requested, found myself an appropriate companion.

"But who is this girl?" enquired my mother, when I went down to Harcourt Hall for the weekend. "Anyone we know?"

"Don't think so, Ma," I replied. "An old school chum from St Paul's. Rather the academic type."

"Bluestockin', you mean?" my father chipped in.

"Yes, you've got the idea, Pa. She's attending some place called Bedford College to read the history of the Renaissance, or something like that."

"Didn't know girls could get degrees," my father said. "Must all be part of that damned little Welshman's ideas for a new Britain."

"You must stop describing Lloyd George in that way," my mother reprimanded him. "He is, after all, our Prime Minister."

"He may be yours, my dear, but he's certainly not mine. I blame it all on those suffragettes," my father added, producing one of his habitual non sequiturs.

"My dear, you blame most things on the suffragettes," my mother reminded him, "even last year's harvest. However," she continued, "coming back to this girl, she sounds to me as if she could have a very beneficial influence on you, Daphne. Where did you say her parents come from?"

"I didn't," I replied. "But I think her father was a businessman out East somewhere, and I'm going to take tea with her mother some time next week."

"Singapore possibly?" said Pa. "There's a lot of business goin' on out there, rubber and all that sort of thing."

"No, I don't think he was in rubber, Pa."

"Well, whatever, do bring the girl round for tea one afternoon," Ma insisted. "Or even down here for the weekend. Does she hunt?"

"No, I don't think so, Ma, but I'll certainly invite her to tea in the near future, so that you can both inspect her."

I must confess that I was equally amused by the idea of being asked along to tea with Becky's mother, so that she could be sure that I was the right sort of girl for *her* daughter. After all, I was fairly confident that I wasn't. I had never been east of the Aldwych before, as far as I could recollect, so I found the idea of going to Essex even more exciting than travelling abroad.

Luckily the journey to Romford was without incident, mainly because Hoskins, my father's chauffeur, knew the road well. It turned out he had originated from somewhere called Dagenham, which he informed me was even deeper inside the Essex jungle.

I had no notion until that day that such people existed. They were neither servants nor from the professional classes nor members of the gentry, and I can't pretend that I exactly fell in love with Romford. However, Mrs Salmon and her sister Miss Roach couldn't have been more hospitable. Becky's mother turned out to be a practical, sensible, God-fearing woman who could also produce an excellent spread for tea, so it was not an altogether wasted journey.

Becky moved into my flat the following week, and I was horrified when I discovered how hard the girl worked. She seemed to spend all day at that Bedford place, returning home only to nibble a sandwich, sip a glass of milk and then continue her studies until she fell asleep, long after I had gone to bed. I could never quite work out what it was all in aid of.

It was after her foolish visit to John D. Wood that I first learned about Charlie Trumper and his ambitions. All that fuss, simply because she had sold off his barrow without consulting him. I felt it nothing less than my duty to point out that two of my ancestors had been beheaded for trying to steal counties, and one sent to the Tower for high treason; well, at least, I reflected, I had a kinsman who had spent his final days in the vicinity of the East End.

As always, Becky knew she was right. "But it's only a hundred pounds," she kept repeating.

"Which you don't possess."

"I've got forty and I feel confident it's such a good investment that I ought to be able to raise the other sixty without much trouble. After all, Charlie could sell blocks of ice to the Eskimos."

"And how are you planning to run the shop in his absence?" I asked. "Between lectures perhaps?"

"Oh, don't be so frivolous, Daphne. Charlie will manage the shop just as soon as he gets back from the war. After all, it can't be long now."

"The war has been over for some weeks," I reminded her. "And there doesn't seem to be much sign of your Charlie."

"He's not my Charlie" was all she said.

Anyway, I kept a close eye on Becky during the next thirty days and it quickly became plain for anyone to see that she wasn't going to raise the money. However, she was far too proud to admit as much to me. I therefore decided the time had come to pay another visit to Romford.

"This is an unexpected pleasure, Miss Harcourt-Browne," Becky's mother assured me, when I arrived unannounced at their little house in Belle Vue Road. I should point out, in my own defence, that I would have informed Mrs Salmon of my imminent arrival if she had possessed a telephone. As I sought certain information that only she could supply before the thirty days were up – information that would save not only her daughter's face but also her finances – I was unwilling to put my trust in the postal service.

"Becky isn't in any trouble, I hope?" was Mrs Salmon's first reaction when she saw me standing on the doorstep.

"Certainly not," I assured her. "Never seen the girl in perkier form."

"It's just that since her father's death I do worry about her," Mrs Salmon explained. She limped just slightly as she guided me into a drawing room that was as spotless as the day I had first accepted their kind invitation to tea. A bowl of fruit rested on the table in the centre of the room. I only prayed that Mrs Salmon would never drop into Number 97 without giving me at least a year's notice.

"How can I be of assistance?" Mrs Salmon asked, moments after Miss Roach had been despatched to the kitchen to prepare tea.

"I am considering making a small investment on a greengrocer's shop in Chelsea," I told her. "I am assured by John D. Wood that it is a sound proposition, despite the current food shortage and the growing problems with trade unions – that is, as long as I can install a first-class manager."

Mrs Salmon's smile was replaced by a puzzled expression.

"Becky has sung the praises of someone called Charlie Trumper, and the purpose of my visit is to seek your opinion of the gentleman in question."

"Gentleman he certainly is not," said Mrs Salmon without hesitation. "An uneducated ruffian might be nearer the mark."

"Oh, what a disappointment," I said. "Especially as Becky led me to believe that your late husband thought rather highly of him."

"As a fruit and vegetable man he certainly did. In fact I'd go as far as to say that Mr Salmon used to consider that young Charlie might end up being as good as his grandfather."

"And how good was that?"

"Although I didn't mix with those sort of people, you understand," explained Mrs Salmon, "I was told, second-hand of course, that he was the finest Whitechapel had ever seen."

"Good," I said. "But is he also honest?"

"I have never heard otherwise," Mrs Salmon admitted. "And heaven knows, he's willing to work all the hours God gave, but he's hardly your type, I would have thought, Miss Harcourt-Browne."

"I was considering employing the man as a shop-keeper, Mrs Salmon, not inviting him to join me in the Royal Enclosure at Ascot." At that moment Miss Roach reappeared with a tray of tea – jam tarts and eclairs smothered in cream. They turned out to be so delicious that I stayed far longer than I had planned.

The following morning I paid a visit to John D. Wood and handed over a cheque for the remaining ninety pounds. I then visited my solicitor and had a contract drawn up, which when it was completed I didn't begin to understand.

Once Becky had found out what I had been up to I drove a hard bargain, because I knew the girl would resent my interference if I wasn't able to prove that I was getting something worthwhile out of the deal.

As soon as she had been convinced of that, Becky immediately handed over a further thirty pounds to help reduce the debt. She certainly took her new enterprise most seriously, because within days she had stolen a young man from a shop in Kensington to take over Trumper's until Charlie returned. She also continued to work hours I didn't even know existed. I could never get her to explain to me the point of rising before the sun did.

After Becky had settled into her new routine I even invited her to make up a foursome for the opera one night to see *La Bohème*. In the past she had shown no inclination to attend any of my outings, especially since her new responsibilities with the shop. But on this occasion I pleaded with her to join the group because a chum of mine had cancelled at the last minute and I desperately needed a spare girl.

"But I've nothing to wear," she said helplessly.

"Take your pick of anything of mine you fancy," I told her, and ushered her through to my bedroom.

I could see that she found such an offer almost irresistible. An hour later she re-emerged in a long turquoise dress that brought back memories of what it had originally looked like on the model.

"Who are your other guests?" Becky enquired.

"Algernon Fitzpatrick. He's Percy Wiltshire's best friend. You remember, the man who hasn't yet been told I'm going to marry him."

"And who makes up the party?"

"Guy Trentham. He's a captain in the Royal Fusiliers, an acceptable regiment, just," I added. "He's recently returned from the Western Front where it's said he had a rather good war. MC and all that. We come from the same village in Berkshire, and grew up together, although I confess we don't really have a lot in common. Extremely good-looking, but has the reputation of being a bit of a ladies' man, so beware."

La Bohème, I felt, had been a great success, even if Algernon wasn't able to give me much news about what Percy was up to. Guy couldn't take his eyes off Becky throughout the second act – not that she seemed to show the slightest interest in him.

However, to my surprise, as soon as we got back home, Becky couldn't stop talking about Guy – his looks, his sophistication, his charm and how solicitous he had been throughout the entire evening. Eventually I managed to get to bed, but not before I had assured Becky to her satisfaction that her feelings were undoubtedly reciprocated.

In fact, I became, unwittingly, Cupid for the budding romance. The following day I was asked by Guy to invite Miss Salmon to accompany him to a West End play. Becky accepted, of course, but then I had already assured Guy she would.

After their outing to the Haymarket, I seemed to bump into the two of them all the time, and began to fear that if the relationship became any more serious it could only, as my nanny used to say, end in tears. I began to regret having ever introduced them in the first place, although there was no doubt, to quote the modern expression: she was head over heels in love.

Despite this, for a few weeks equilibrium returned to the residents of 97 – and then Charlie was demobbed.

I wasn't formally introduced to the man for some time after his return, and when I was I had to admit they didn't make them like that in Berkshire. The occasion was a dinner we all shared at that awful little Italian restaurant just up the road from my flat.

To be fair, the evening was not what one might describe as a wow, partly because Guy made no effort to be sociable, but mainly because Becky didn't bother to bring Charlie into the conversation at all. I found myself asking and then answering most of the questions, and, as for Charlie, he appeared on first sighting to be somewhat gauche.

When we were all walking back to the flat after dinner, I suggested to him that we should leave Becky and Guy to themselves. When Charlie escorted me into his shop he couldn't resist stopping to explain how he had changed everything around since he had taken over. His enthusiasm would have convinced the most cynical investor, but what impressed me most was his knowledge of a business which until that moment I hadn't given a second thought to. It was then that I made the decision to assist Charlie with both his causes.

I wasn't in the least surprised to discover how he felt about Becky, but that for her part she was so infatuated with Guy she wasn't even aware of Charlie's existence. It was during one of his interminable monologues on the virtues of the girl that I began to form a plan for Charlie's future. I was determined that he must have a different type of education, perhaps not as formal as Becky's, but no less valuable for the future he had decided on.

I assured Charlie that Guy would soon become bored with Becky – as that had proved to be the invariable pattern with girls who had crossed his path in the past. I added that he must be patient and the apple would eventually fall into his lap. I also explained who Newton was.

I assumed that those tears to which Nanny had so often referred might indeed begin to flow soon after Becky was invited to spend the weekend with Guy's parents at Ashurst. I made sure that I was asked to join the Trenthams for afternoon tea on the Sunday, to give whatever moral support Becky might feel in need of.

I arrived a little after three forty, which I have always considered a proper hour for taking tea, only to find Mrs Trentham surrounded by silverware and crockery but sitting quite alone.

"Where are the starstruck lovers?" I enquired, as I entered the drawing room.

"If you're referring, in that coarse way of yours, Daphne, to my son and Miss Salmon, they have already departed for London."

"Together, I presume?" I asked.

"Yes, although for the life of me I can't imagine what the dear boy sees in her." Mrs Trentham poured me a cup of tea. "As for myself, I found her exceedingly common."

"Perhaps it could be her brains and looks," I volunteered as the major entered the room. I smiled at a man I had known since I was a child and had come to treat as an uncle. The one mystery about him as far as I was concerned was how he could possibly have fallen for someone like Ethel Hardcastle.

"Guy left too?" he asked.

"Yes, he's returned to London with Miss Salmon," said Mrs Trentham for a second time.

"Oh, pity really. She seemed such a grand girl."

"In a parochial type of way," said Mrs Trentham.

"I get the impression Guy rather dotes on her," I said, hoping for a reaction.

"Heaven forbid," said Mrs Trentham.

"I doubt if heaven will have a lot to do with it," I told her, as I warmed to the challenge.

"Then *I* shall," said Mrs Trentham. "I have no intention of letting my son marry the daughter of an East End street trader."

"I can't see why not," interjected the major. "After all, isn't that what your grandfather was?"

"Gerald, really. My grandfather founded and built up a highly successful business in Yorkshire, not the East End."

"Then I think that it's only the location we are discussing," said the major. "I well recall your father tellin' me, with some pride I might add, that his old dad had started Hardcastle's in the back of a shed somewhere near Huddersfield."

"Gerald – I feel sure he was exaggerating."

"Never struck me as the type of man who was prone to exaggerate," retorted the major. "On the contrary, rather blunt sort of fellow. Shrewd with it, I always considered."

"Then that must have been a considerable time ago," said Mrs Trentham.

"What's more, I suspect that we shall live to see the children of Rebecca Salmon doing a bloody sight better than the likes of us," added the major.

"Gerald, I do wish you wouldn't use the word 'bloody' so frequently. We're all being influenced by that socialist playwright Mr Shaw and his frightful *Pygmalion*, which seems to be nothing more than a play about Miss Salmon."

"Hardly," I told her. "After all, Becky will leave London University with a Bachelor of Arts degree, which is more than my whole family has managed between them in eleven centuries."

"That may well be the case," Mrs Trentham concurred, "but they are hardly the qualifications that I feel appropriate for advancing Guy's military career, especially now his regiment will be completing a tour of duty in India."

This piece of information came as a bolt out of the blue. I also felt pretty certain Becky knew nothing of it.

"And when he returns to these shores," continued Mrs Trentham, "I shall be looking for someone of good breeding, sufficient money and perhaps even a little intelligence to be his matrimonial partner. Gerald may have failed, by petty prejudice, to become Commanding Officer of the Regiment, but I will not allow the same thing to happen to Guy, of that I can assure you."

"I simply wasn't good enough," said the major gruffly. "Sir Danvers was far better qualified for the job, and in any case it was only you who ever wanted me to be commanding officer in the first place."

"Nevertheless, I feel after Guy's results at Sandhurst –"

"He managed to pass out in the top half," the major reminded her. "That can hardly be described as carrying off the Sword of Honour, my dear."

"But he was awarded the Military Cross on the field of battle and his citation –"

The major grunted in a manner that suggested that he had been trotted round this particular course several times before.

"And so you see," Mrs Trentham continued, "I have every confidence that Guy will in time become Commanding Officer of the Regiment and I don't mind telling you that I already have someone in mind who will assist him in that quest. After all, wives can make or break a career, don't you know, Daphne."

"At least on that I am able to concur fully, my dear," murmured her husband.

I travelled back to London somewhat relieved that, after such an encounter, Becky's relationship with Guy must surely come to an end. Certainly the more I had seen of the damn man the more I distrusted him.

When I returned to the flat later that evening, I found Becky sitting on the sofa, red-eyed and trembling. She told me her version of what had taken place at the weekend, which she considered had been a disaster, but added that she thought Guy had proposed to her.

I was about to mention India when she said, "She hates me."

"She doesn't yet appreciate you," was how I remembered phrasing my reply. "But I can tell you that the major thinks you're a grand girl."

"How kind of him," said Becky. "He showed me round the estate, you know."

"My dear, one does not describe seven hundred acres as an estate. A freeholding, perhaps, but certainly not an estate."

"Do you think Guy will stop seeing me after what took place at Ashurst?"

I wanted to say, I hope so, but managed to curb my tongue. "Not if the man has any character," I replied diplomatically.

And indeed Guy did see her the following week, and as far as I could determine never raised the subject of his mother or that unfortunate weekend again.

However, I still considered my long-term plan for Charlie and Becky was proceeding rather well, until I returned home after a long weekend to find one of my favourite dresses strewn across the drawing room floor. I followed a trail of clothes until I reached Becky's door, which I opened tentatively to find, to my horror, that even more of my garments lay by the side of her bed, along with Guy's. I had rather hoped Becky would have seen him for the bounder he was long before she had allowed it to reach the terminal stage.

Guy started out on his journey to India the following day, and as soon as he had taken his leave Becky began telling everyone who cared to listen that she was engaged to the creature, although there was no ring on her finger and no announcement in any paper to confirm her version of the story. "Guy's word is good enough for me," she asserted, which left one simply speechless.

I arrived home that night to find her asleep in my bed. Becky told me over breakfast that Charlie had put her there – without further explanation.

The following Sunday afternoon I invited myself back to tea with the Trenthams, only to learn from Guy's mother that she had been assured by her son that he had not been in contact with Miss Salmon since her premature departure from Ashurst some nine months before.

"But that isn't –" I began, but stopped in midsentence when I recalled my promise to Becky not to inform Guy's mother that they were still seeing each other.

A few weeks later Becky told me that she had missed her period. I swore that I would keep her secret but did not hesitate to inform Charlie the same day. When he heard the news he nearly went berserk. What made matters worse was that he had to go on pretending whenever he saw the girl that he wasn't aware of anything untoward.

"I swear if that bastard Trentham were back in England I'd kill him," Charlie kept repeating, as he went on one of his route-marches round the drawing room.

"If he were in England I can think of at least three girls whose fathers would happily carry out the job for you," I retorted.

"So what am I meant to do about it?" Charlie asked me at last.

"Not a lot," I advised. "I suspect time – and eight thousand miles – may well turn out to be your greatest allies."

The colonel also fell into the category of those who would have happily shot Guy Trentham, given half a chance, in his case because of the honour of the regiment and all that. He even murmured something sinister about going to see Major Trentham and giving it to him straight. I could have told him that the major wasn't the problem. However, I wasn't sure if the colonel, even with his vast experience of different types of enemy, had ever come up against anyone as formidable as Mrs Trentham.

It must have been around this time that Percy Wiltshire was finally discharged from the Scots Guards. Lately I had stopped worrying about his mother telephoning me. During those dreadful years between 1916 and 1919 I always assumed it would be a message to say that Percy had been killed on the Western Front, as his father and elder brother had been before him. It was to be years before I admitted to the dowager marchioness whenever she called how much I dreaded hearing her voice on the other end of the line.

Then quite suddenly Percy asked me to marry him. I fear from that moment on I became so preoccupied with our future together and being expected to visit so many of his family that I quite neglected my duty to Becky, even though I had allowed her to take over the flat. Then, almost before I could look round, she had given birth to little Daniel. I only prayed that she could face the inevitable stigma.

It was some months after the christening that I decided to pay a surprise visit to the flat on my way back from a weekend in the country with Percy's mother.

When the front door opened I was greeted by Charlie, a newspaper tucked under his arm while Becky, who was sitting on the sofa, appeared to be darning a sock. I looked down to watch Daniel crawling towards me at a rate of knots. I took the child in my arms before he had the chance to head off down the stairs and out into the world.

"How lovely to see you," Becky said, jumping up. "It's been ages. Let me make you some tea."

"Thank you," I said, "I only came round to make sure you are free on . . ." My eyes settled on a little oil that hung above the mantelpiece. "What a truly beautiful picture," I remarked.

"But you must have seen the painting many times before," Becky said. "After all, it was in Charlie's –"

"No, I've never seen it before," I replied, not sure what she was getting at.

CHAPTER 14

The day the gold-edged card arrived at Lowndes Square Daphne placed the invitation between the one requesting her presence in the Royal Enclosure at Ascot and the command to attend a Garden Party at Buckingham Palace. However, she considered that this particular invitation could well remain on the mantelpiece for all to gaze upon long after Ascot and the palace had been relegated to the wastepaper-basket.

Although Daphne had spent a week in Paris selecting three outfits for the three different occasions, the most striking of them was to be saved for Becky's degree ceremony which she now described to Percy as "the great event".

Her fiancé – though she hadn't yet become quite used to thinking of Percy in that way – also admitted that he had never been asked to such a ceremony before.

Brigadier Harcourt-Browne suggested that his daughter should have Hoskins drive them to the Senate House in the Rolls, and admitted to being a little envious at not having been invited himself.

When the morning finally dawned, Percy accompanied Daphne to lunch at the Ritz, and once they had been over the guest list and the hymns that would be sung at the service for the umpteenth time, they turned their attention to the details of the afternoon outing.

"I do hope we won't be asked any awkward questions," said Daphne. "Because one thing's for certain, I will not know the answers."

"Oh, I'm sure we won't be put to any trouble like that, old gel," said Percy. "Not that I've ever attended one of these shindigs before. We Wiltshires aren't exactly known for troubling the authorities on these matters," he added, laughing which so often came out sounding like a cough.

"You must get out of that habit, Percy. If you are going to laugh, laugh. If you're going to cough, cough."

"Anything you say, old gel."

"And do stop calling me 'old gel'. I'm only twenty-three, and my parents endowed me with a perfectly acceptable christian name."

"Anything you say, old gel," repeated Percy.

"You haven't been listening to a word I've said." Daphne checked her watch. "And now I do believe it's time we were on our way. Better not be late for this one."

"Quite right," he replied, and called a waiter to bring them their bill.

"Do you have any idea where we are going, Hoskins?" asked Daphne, as he opened the back door of the Rolls for her.

"Yes, m'lady, I took the liberty of going over the route when you and His Lordship were up in Scotland last month."

"Good thinking, Hoskins," said Percy. "Otherwise we might have been going round in circles for the rest of the afternoon, don't you know."

As Hoskins turned on the engine Daphne looked at the man she loved, and couldn't help thinking how lucky she had been in her choice. In truth she had chosen him at the age of sixteen, and never faltered in her belief that he was the right partner – even if he wasn't aware of the fact. She had always thought Percy quite wonderful, kind, considerate and gentle and, if not exactly handsome, certainly distinguished. She thanked God each night that he had escaped that fearful war with every limb intact. Once Percy had told her he was going off to France to serve with the Scots Guards, Daphne had spent three of the unhappiest years of her life. From that moment on she assumed every letter, every message, every call could only be to inform her of his death. Other men tried to court her in his absence, but they all failed as Daphne waited, not unlike Penelope, for her chosen partner to return. She would only accept that he was still alive when she saw him striding down the gangplank at Dover. Daphne would always treasure his first words the moment he saw her.

"Fancy seeing you here, old gel. Dashed coincidence don't you know."

Percy never talked of the example his father had set, though *The Times* had devoted half a page to the late marquess's obituary. In it they described his action on the Marne in the course of which he had single-handedly overrun a German battery as "one of the great VCs of the war". When a month later Percy's elder brother was killed at Ypres it came home to her just how many families were sharing the same dreadful experience. Now Percy had inherited the title: the twelfth Marquess of Wiltshire. From tenth to twelfth in a matter of weeks.

"Are you sure we're going in the right direction?" asked Daphne as the Rolls entered Shaftesbury Avenue.

"Yes, m'lady," replied Hoskins, who had obviously decided to address Daphne by the title even though she and Percy were not yet married.

Percy coughed again. "He's only helping you to get accustomed to the idea, old gel."

Daphne had been delighted when Percy told her that he had decided to resign his commission with the Scots Guards in order to take over the running of the family estates. Much as she admired him in that dark blue uniform with its four brass buttons evenly spaced, stirruped boots, and funny red, white and blue checked cap, it was a farmer she wanted to marry, not a soldier. A life spent in India, Africa and the colonies had never really appealed to her.

As they turned into Malet Street, they saw a throng of people making their way up some stone steps to enter a monumental building. "That must be the Senate House," she exclaimed, as if she had come across an undiscovered pyramid.

"Yes, m'lady," replied Hoskins.

"And do remember, Percy –" began Daphne.

"Yes, old gel?"

"– not to speak unless you're spoken to. On this occasion we are not exactly on home ground, and I object to either of us being made to look foolish. Now, did you remember the invitation and the special tickets that show our seat allocation?"

"I know I put them somewhere." He began to search around in his pockets.

"They're in the left-hand inside top pocket of your jacket, Your Lordship," said Hoskins as he brought the car to a halt.

"Yes, of course they are," said Percy. "Thank you, Hoskins."

"A pleasure, m'lord," Hoskins intoned.

"Just follow the crowd," instructed Daphne. "And look as if you do this sort of thing every week."

They passed several uniformed doorkeepers and ushers before a clerk checked their tickets, then guided them to row M.

"I've never been seated this far back in a theatre before," said Daphne.

"I've only tried to be this far away in a theatre once myself," admitted Percy. "And that was when the Germans were on centre stage." He coughed again.

The two remained sitting in silence as they stared in front of them, waiting for something to happen. The stage was bare but for fourteen chairs, two of which, placed at its centre, might almost have been described as thrones.

At two fifty-five, ten men and two women, all of whom were dressed in what looked to Daphne like long black dressing-gowns with purple scarves hanging from their necks, proceeded across the stage in a gentle crocodile before taking their allocated places. Only the two thrones remained unoccupied. On the stroke of three Daphne's attention was drawn to the Minstrels' Gallery, where a fanfare of trumpets struck up to announce the arrival of the Visitors, and all those present rose as the King and Queen entered to take their places in the centre of the Senate. Everyone remained standing until after the National Anthem had been played.

"The King looks very well, considering," said Percy, resuming his seat.

"Do be quiet," said Daphne. "No one else knows him."

An elderly man in a long black gown, the only person who remained standing, waited for everyone to settle before he took a pace forward, bowed to the royal couple and then proceeded to address the audience.

After the vice-chancellor, Sir Russell Russell-Wells, had been speaking for some considerable time Percy enquired of his fiancée, "How is a fellow expected to follow all this piffle when he gave up Latin as an option in his fourth half?"

"I only survived a year of the subject myself."

"Then you won't be much help either, old gel," admitted Percy in a whisper.

Someone seated in the row in front turned round to glare at them ferociously.

Throughout the remainder of the ceremony Daphne and Percy tried to remain silent, although Daphne did find it necessary from time to time to place a firm hand on Percy's knee as he continued to shift uncomfortably from side to side on the flat wooden chair.

"It's all right for the King," whispered Percy. "He's got a dam' great cushion to sit on."

At last the moment came for which they had both been bidden.

The vice-chancellor, who continued to call out a list of names from the Roll of Honour, had at last come to the Ts. He then declared, "Bachelor of Arts, Mrs Charles Trumper of Bedford College." The applause almost doubled, as it had done every time a woman had walked up the steps to receive her degree from the Visitor. Becky curtsied before the King as he placed what the programme described as a "hood of purple" over her gown and handed her a parchment scroll. She curtsied again and took two paces backwards before returning to her seat.

"Couldn't have done it better myself," said Percy as he joined in the applause. "And no prizes for guessing who tutored her through that little performance," he added. Daphne blushed as they remained in their places for some time to allow all the Us, Vs, Ws and Ys to receive their degrees, before being allowed to escape into the garden for tea.

"Can't see them anywhere," said Percy, as he turned a slow circle in the middle of the lawn.

"Nor I," said Daphne. "But keep looking. They're bound to be here somewhere."

"Good afternoon, Miss Harcourt-Browne."

Daphne spun round. "Oh, hello, Mrs Salmon, how super to see you. And what a simply charming hat, and dear Miss Roach. Percy, this is Becky's mother, Mrs Salmon, and her aunt, Miss Roach. My fiancé – "

"Delighted to meet you, Your Lordship," said Mrs Salmon, wondering if anyone from the Ladies Circle at Romford would believe her when she told them.

"You must be so proud of your daughter," said Percy.

"Yes, I am, Your Lordship," said Mrs Salmon.

Miss Roach stood like a statue and didn't offer an opinion.

"And where is our little scholar?" demanded Daphne.

"I'm here," said Becky. "But where have you been?" she asked, emerging from a group of new graduates.

"Looking for you."

The two girls threw their arms around each other.

"Have you seen my mother?"

"She was with us a moment ago," said Daphne, looking around.

"She's gone to find some sandwiches, I think," said Miss Roach.

"Typical of Mum," said Becky, laughing.

"Hello, Percy," said Charlie. "How are things?"

"Things are spiffing," said Percy, coughing. "And well done, Becky, I say," he added as Mrs Salmon returned carrying a large plate of sandwiches.

"If Becky has inherited her mother's common sense, Mrs Salmon," said Daphne as she selected a cucumber sandwich for Percy, "she ought to do well in the real world, because I suspect there won't be many of these left in fifteen minutes' time." She picked out one of the smoked salmon variety for herself. "Were you very nervous when you marched up on to that stage?" Daphne asked, turning her attention back to Becky.

"I certainly was," replied Becky. "And when the King placed the hood over my head, my legs almost gave way. Then, to make matters worse, the moment I returned to my place I discovered Charlie was crying."

"I was not," protested her husband.

Becky said nothing more as she linked her arm through his.

"I've rather taken to that purple hood thing," said Percy. "I think I'd look quite a swell were I to sport one of those at next year's Hunt Ball. What do you think, old gel?"

"You're expected to do rather a lot of hard work before you're allowed to adorn yourself with one of those, Percy."

They all turned to see who it was who had offered this opinion.

Percy lowered his head. "Your Majesty is, as always, quite correct. I might add, sir, that I fear, given my present record, I am unlikely ever to be considered for such a distinction."

The King smiled, then added, "In fact I'm bound to say, Percy, that you seem to have strayed somewhat from your usual habitat."

"A friend of Daphne's," explained Percy.

"Daphne, my dear, how lovely to see you," said the King. "And I haven't yet had the opportunity to congratulate you on your engagement."

"I received a kind note from the Queen only yesterday,

Your Majesty. We are honoured that you are both able to attend the wedding."

"Yes, simply delighted," said Percy. "And may I present Mrs Trumper, who was the recipient of the degree?" Becky shook hands with the King for a second time. "Her husband, Mr Charles Trumper, and Mrs Trumper's mother, Mrs Salmon; her aunt Miss Roach."

The King shook hands with all four before saying, "Well done, Mrs Trumper. I do hope you're going to put your degree to some useful purpose."

"I shall be joining the staff of Sotheby's, Your Majesty. As an apprentice in their fine art department."

"Capital. Then I can only wish you continued success, Mrs Trumper. I look forward to seeing you at the wedding, if not before, Percy." With a nod the King moved on to another group.

"Decent fellow," said Percy. "Good of him to come over like that."

"I had no idea you knew –" began Becky.

"Well," explained Percy, "to be honest, *my* great-great-great-great-grandfather tried to murder *his* great-great-great-great-grandfather, and had he succeeded our roles might well have been reversed. Despite that he's always been jolly understanding about the whole affair."

"So what happened to your great-great-great-great-grandfather?" asked Charlie.

"Exiled," said Percy. "And I'm bound to add, quite rightly. Otherwise the blighter would only have tried again."

"Good heavens," said Becky, laughing.

"What is it?" said Charlie.

"I've just worked out who Percy's great-great-great-great-grandfather was."

Daphne didn't get a chance to see Becky again before the marriage ceremony, as the last few weeks of preparation for her wedding seemed to be totally occupied. However, she did manage to keep abreast of the goings-on in Chelsea

Terrace, after bumping into the colonel and his wife at Lady Denham's reception in Onslow Square. The colonel was able to inform her, *sotto voce*, that Charlie was beginning to run up a rather large overdraft with the bank – "even if he had cleared every other outstanding creditor". Daphne smiled when she recalled that her last payment had been returned in typical Charlie fashion several months before it was due. "And I've just learned that the man has his eye on yet another shop," added the colonel.

"Which one this time?"

"The bakery – Number 145."

"Becky's father's old trade," said Daphne. "Are they confident of getting their hands on it?"

"Yes, I think so – although I fear Charlie's going to have to pay a little over the odds this time."

"Why's that?"

"The baker is right next door to the fruit and vegetable shop, and Mr Reynolds is only too aware just how much Charlie wants to buy him out. However, Charlie has tempted Mr Reynolds with an offer to remain as manager, plus a share of the profits."

"Hmmm. How long do you think that little arrangement will last?"

"Just as long as it takes for Charlie to master the bakery trade once again."

"And how about Becky?"

"She's started her job at Sotheby's. As a counter clerk."

"A counter clerk?" said Daphne on a rising note. "What was the point of taking all that trouble to get a degree if she ends up as a counter clerk?"

"Apparently everybody starts off that way at Sotheby's, whatever qualifications they bring to the job. Becky explained it all to me," replied the colonel. "It seems that you can be the son of the chairman, have worked in a major West End art gallery for several years, possess a degree or even have no qualifications at all, but you still start on the front desk. Once they discover you're any good you get promoted into a specialist department. Not unlike the army, actually."

"So which department does Becky have her eye on?"

"Seems she wants to join some old fellow called Pemberton who's the acknowledged expert on Renaissance paintings."

"My bet," said Daphne, "is that she'll last on the front desk for about a couple of weeks."

"Charlie doesn't share your low opinion of her," said the colonel.

"Oh, so how long does he give her?"

The colonel smiled. "Ten days at the most."

CHAPTER 15

When the morning mail arrived at Lowndes Square, Wentworth, the butler, would place the letters on a silver tray and take them to the brigadier in his study, where his master would remove those addressed to himself before handing the tray back to the butler. He, in turn, would deliver the remaining letters to the ladies of the house.

However, since the announcement of his daughter's engagement in *The Times*, and the subsequent sending out of over five hundred invitations for the forthcoming wedding, the brigadier had become bored with the sorting-out process and instructed Wentworth to reverse his route, so that he would be handed only those letters addressed to him.

Thus it was on a Monday morning in June 1921 that Wentworth knocked on Miss Daphne's bedroom door, entered when bidden and handed her a large bundle of mail. Once Daphne had extracted the letters addressed to her mother and herself she returned the few that remained to Wentworth, who bowed slightly and proceeded on his anti-clockwise route.

As soon as Wentworth had closed the door behind him Daphne climbed out of bed, placed the stack of letters on her dressing-table and wandered into the bathroom. A little after ten thirty, feeling ready for the rigours of the day, she returned to her dressing-table and began slitting open the letters. Acceptances and regrets had to be placed in separate piles before they could be ticked or crossed off on a master list; her mother would then be able to calculate the exact numbers to cater for and proceed to work on a seating plan. The breakdown of the thirty-one letters that particular morning produced twenty-two yeses, including a princess, a viscount, two other lords, an ambassador and dear Colonel and Lady Hamilton. There were also four noes, comprising two couples who would be abroad, an elderly uncle who was suffering from advanced diabetes and another whose daughter had been foolish enough to select the same day as Daphne on which to be married. Having ticked and crossed their names off the master list, Daphne turned her attention to the five remaining letters.

One turned out to be from her eighty-seven-year-old Aunt Agatha, who resided in Cumberland and had some time previously stated that she would not be attending the wedding as she felt the journey to London might prove too much of a strain. However, Aunt Agatha went on to suggest that perhaps Daphne should bring Percy up north to visit her just as soon as they returned from their honeymoon, as she wished to make his acquaintance.

"Certainly not," said Daphne out loud. "Once I am back in England I shall have far more important things to worry myself with than ageing aunts." She then read the PS:

> And while you are in Cumberland, my darling, it will be a good opportunity for you to advise me on my will, because I'm not sure which of the pictures to give to whom, especially the Canaletto, which I do feel deserves a good home.

Wicked old lady, thought Daphne, well aware that Aunt Agatha wrote an identical PS to every one of her relations, however distant, thus guaranteeing that she rarely spent a weekend alone.

The second letter was from Michael Fishlock and Co, the catering specialists, who enclosed an estimate for supplying tea to eight hundred guests in Vincent Square immediately preceding the wedding. Three hundred guineas seemed an outrageous sum to Daphne, but without a second thought she placed the estimate on one side, to be dealt with by her father at some later date. Two other letters addressed to her mother that were from friends and no concern of Daphne's were also placed on one side.

The fifth letter she saved until last, because the envelope was enriched by the most colourful stamps, the King's crown set in an oval on the right-hand corner above the words "Ten Annas".

She slit the envelope open slowly and extracted several sheets of heavy notepaper, the first of which was embossed with the crest and legend of the Royal Fusiliers.

"Dear Daphne", the letter began. She hurriedly turned to the last page in order to check the salutation which read, "Your friend, as always, Guy".

Returning to the first page, she glanced at the address before beginning to read Guy's words with apprehension.

Officers' Mess
2nd Battalion
Royal Fusiliers
Wellington Barracks
Poona
India

May 15th, 1921

Dear Daphne,

I hope you will forgive me for presuming on our long family friendship, but a problem has arisen of which I am sure you are only too aware, and unfortunately I now find that I must turn to you for help and guidance.

Some time ago I received a letter from your friend Rebecca Salmon

Daphne placed the unread pages back on her dressing-table, wishing that the letter had arrived a few days after she had set out on her honeymoon rather than before. She fiddled around with the guest list for some time, but realised she would eventually have to find out what Guy expected of her. She returned to his letter.

informing me that she was pregnant and that I was the father of her child.

Let me assure you from the outset that nothing could be further from the truth, as on the only occasion I remained overnight in your flat, Rebecca and I had no physical contact.

As a matter of record, it was she who insisted we had dinner together at 97, Chelsea Terrace that evening, despite the fact that I had already booked a table for us at the Ritz.

As the evening progressed, it became obvious that she was trying to get me drunk, and indeed when I thought to leave. I confess I did feel a little queasy, and wasn't certain that I would be able to make the journey safely back to my barracks.

Rebecca immediately suggested that I remain overnight in order to "sleep it off". I use her exact words. Naturally I refused, until she pointed out that I could stay in your room as you were not expected to return from the country until the following afternoon – a fact which you later confirmed.

Indeed, I took up Rebecca's kind offer, and on retiring to bed, quickly fell into a deep sleep only to be awoken later by the banging of a door. To my horror I awoke to find you standing there in front of me. I was even more shocked to discover that Rebecca, quite unbeknown to me had crept into bed beside me.

You were naturally embarrassed and left immediately.

Without uttering another word I rose, dressed and returned to my barracks, arriving back in my own room by one-fifteen, at the latest.

On arriving at Waterloo station later in the morning to begin my journey to India I was, as you can imagine, somewhat surprised to find Rebecca waiting for me on the platform. I spent only a few moments with her but left her in no doubt as to how I felt about the trick she had played on me the previous evening. I then shook her by the hand and boarded the boat train for Southampton, never for one moment expecting to hear from her again. The next contact I had with Miss Salmon came a few months later when I received this unwarranted scurrilous letter, which brings me to the reason why I now need your assistance.

Daphne turned the page and stopped to look at herself in the mirror. She had no desire to find out what Guy expected of her. He had even forgotten in whose room he had been discovered. Yet it was only seconds before her eyes returned to the top of the next page and she began reading again.

No further action would have proved necessary had it not been for the fact that Lieutenant-Colonel Sir Danvers Hamilton took it upon himself to drop a note to my new Commanding Officer, Colonel Forbes, informing him of Miss Salmon's version of the story, which resulted in my being called upon to defend myself in front of a special enquiry made up of my brother officers.

Naturally, I told them exactly what had taken place that night, but because of Colonel Hamilton's continuing influence with the regiment some of them remained unwilling to accept my version of events. Fortunately my mother was able to write to Colonel Forbes a few weeks later to let him know that Miss Salmon had married her long-time lover, Charlie Trumper, and that he was not denying that the child that had been born out of wedlock was his. If the Colonel had not accepted my mother's word, I might have been forced to resign my commission immediately, but fortunately that injustice has been avoided.

However, since then my mother has informed me of your intention to visit India while you are on your honeymoon (on which my sincere congratulations). You are therefore almost certain to come across Colonel Forbes who, I fear, may well refer to this matter, as your name has already been mentioned in connection with the affair.

I therefore beg you to say nothing that might harm my career. In fact, if you felt able to confirm my story, the whole sorry business might finally be laid to rest.

Your friend, as always,

Guy.

Daphne placed the letter back on the dressing-table and began to brush her hair as she considered what should be done next. She did not want to discuss the problem with her mother or father and certainly had no desire to drag Percy into it. She also felt certain that Becky should not be made aware of Trentham's missive until she had thought out exactly what course of action needed to be taken. She was amazed at how short a memory Guy assumed she must have as he distanced himself from reality.

She put down the hairbrush and looked at herself in the mirror before returning to the letter for a second and then a third reading. Eventually she placed the letter back in the envelope and tried to dismiss its contents from her thoughts; but whatever distraction she turned her attention to, Guy's words continued to prey on her mind. It particularly aggravated her that he should imagine she was so gullible.

Suddenly Daphne realised from whom she should seek advice. She picked up the telephone, and after asking the operator for a Chelsea number, was delighted to find the colonel was still at home.

"I was just off to my club, Daphne," he told her. "But do let me know how I can be of help."

"I need to talk to you urgently but it's not something I feel I can discuss over the telephone," she explained.

"I understand," said the colonel, who paused for a moment before adding, "If you're free why don't you join me for lunch at the In and Out? I'll just change my booking to the Ladies Room."

Daphne accepted the offer gratefully, and once she had checked her make-up Hoskins drove her to Piccadilly, arriving at the Naval and Military a few minutes after one.

The colonel was standing in the entrance hall waiting to greet her. "This is a pleasant surprise," said Sir Danvers. "It's not every day I'm seen lunching with a beautiful young woman. It will do my reputation at the club no end of good. I shall wave at every brigadier and general I come across."

The fact that Daphne didn't laugh at the colonel's little aside brought about an immediate change in his demeanour. He took his guest gently by the arm and guided her through to the ladies' luncheon room. Once he had written out their order and handed it to a waitress, Daphne removed Guy's letter from her bag and without another word passed it over to her host.

The colonel fixed the monocle to his good eye and began to read, occasionally looking up at Daphne, only to observe that she hadn't touched the Brown Windsor soup that had been placed in front of her.

"Rum business this," he said, as he placed the letter in its envelope and handed it back to Daphne.

"I agree, but what do you suggest I do?"

"Well, one thing's for certain, my dear, you can't discuss the contents with Charlie or Becky. I also don't see how you can avoid letting Trentham know that should the question of who fathered the child be put to you directly you would feel beholden to tell the truth." He paused and took a sip of his soup. "I swear I'll never speak to Mrs

Trentham again as long as I live," he added without explanation.

Daphne was taken aback by this remark; until that moment she had not been aware that he had ever come across the woman.

"Perhaps we should use our combined efforts to come up with a suitable reply, my dear?" the colonel suggested after some further thought. He broke off to allow a waitress to serve up two helpings of the club's dish of the day.

"If you felt able to help, I would be eternally grateful," said Daphne nervously. "But first I think I ought to tell you everything I know."

The colonel nodded.

"As I'm sure you're only too aware it is I who am to blame for the two of them meeting in the first place . . ."

By the time Daphne had come to the end of her story the colonel's plate was empty.

"I knew most of that already," he admitted as he touched his lips with a napkin. "But you still managed to fill in one or two important gaps for me. I confess I had no idea Trentham was that much of a bounder. Looking back on it, I should have insisted on further corroboration before I agreed to allow his name being put forward for an MC." He rose. "Now, if you'll be good enough to amuse yourself for a few minutes by reading a magazine in the coffee room, I'll see what I can come up with as a first draft."

"I'm sorry to be such a nuisance," said Daphne.

"Don't be silly. I'm flattered that you consider me worthy of your confidence." The colonel stood up and strode off into the writing room.

He didn't reappear for nearly an hour, by which time Daphne was re-reading advertisements for nannies in the *Lady*.

She hastily dropped the magazine back on the table and sat bolt upright in her chair. The colonel handed over the results of his labours, which Daphne studied for several minutes before speaking.

"God knows what Guy would do if I were to write such a letter," she said at last.

"He'll resign his commission, my dear, it's as simple as that. And none too soon, in my opinion." The colonel frowned. "It's high time Trentham was made aware of the consequences of his misdeeds, not least because of the responsibilities he still has to Becky and the child."

"But now that she's happily married that's hardly fair on Charlie," Daphne pleaded.

"Have you seen Daniel lately?" asked the colonel, lowering his voice.

"A few months ago, why?"

"Then you'd better take another look, because there aren't many Trumpers, or Salmons for that matter, who have blond hair, a Roman nose and deep blue eyes. I fear the more obvious replicas are to be found in Ashurst, Berkshire. In any case, Becky and Charlie will eventually have to tell the child the truth or they'll only store up more trouble for themselves at some later date. Send the letter," he said, tapping his fingers on the side table, "that's my advice."

Once Daphne had returned home to Lowndes Square she went straight up to her room. She sat down at her writing desk and, pausing only for a moment, began to copy out the colonel's words.

When she had completed her task Daphne re-read the one paragraph of the colonel's deliberations that she had left out and prayed that his gloomy prognosis would not prove to be accurate.

Once she had completed her own version she tore up the colonel's transcript and rang for Wentworth.

"Just one letter to be posted," was all she said.

The preparations for the wedding became so frantic that once Daphne had passed over the letter to Wentworth she quite forgot about the problems of Guy Trentham. What with selecting the bridesmaids without offending half her family, enduring endless dress fittings that never ran to time, studying seating arrangements so as to be certain that those members of the family who hadn't spoken to each other in years were not placed at the same table – or for that matter in the same pew as each other – and finally having to cope with a future mother-in-law, the dowager marchioness, who, having married off three of her own daughters, always had three opinions to offer on every subject, she felt quite exhausted.

With only a week to go Daphne suggested to Percy that they should pop along to the nearest register office and get the whole thing over with as quickly as possible – and preferably without bothering to tell anyone else.

"Anything you say, old gel," said Percy, who had long ago stopped listening to anyone on the subject of marriage.

On 16 July 1921 Daphne woke at five forty-three feeling drained but by the time she stepped out into the sunshine in Lowndes Square at one forty-five she was exhilarated and actually looking forward to the occasion.

Her father helped her up the steps into an open carriage that her grandmother and mother had travelled in on the day they were married. A little crowd of servants and well-wishers cheered the bride as she began her journey to Westminster, while others waved from the pavement. Officers saluted, toffs blew her a kiss and would-be brides sighed as she passed by.

Daphne, on her father's arm, entered the church by the north door a few minutes after Big Ben had struck two, then proceeded slowly down the aisle to the accompaniment of Mendelssohn's Wedding March. She paused only for a moment before joining Percy, curtseying to the King and Queen, who sat alone in their private pews beside the altar. After all those months of waiting the service seemed over in moments. As the organ struck up "Rejoice, rejoice" and the married couple were bidden to an anteroom to sign the register, Daphne's only reaction was to want to go through the entire ceremony again.

Husband and wife left the church to a thunderous peal

of bells and strolled on through the streets of Westminster in the bright afternoon sun. Once they had arrived at the large marquee that had been set up on the lawn in Vincent Square, they began to welcome their guests.

Trying to have a word with every one of them resulted in Daphne almost failing to sample a piece of her own wedding cake, and no sooner had she taken a bite than the dowager marchioness swept up to announce that if they didn't get on with the speeches they might as well dispense with any hope of sailing on the last tide.

Algernon Fitzpatrick praised the bridesmaids and toasted the bride and groom. Percy made a surprisingly witty and well-received reply. Daphne was then ushered off to 45 Vincent Square, the home of a distant uncle, so that she could change into her going-away outfit.

Once again the crowds flocked out on to the pavement to throw rice and rose petals, while Hoskins waited to despatch the newly-weds off to Southampton.

Thirty minutes later Hoskins was motoring peacefully down the A307 past Kew Gardens, leaving the wedding guests behind them to continue their celebrations without the bride and groom.

"Well, now you're stuck with me for life, Percy Wiltshire," Daphne told her husband.

"That, I suspect, was ordained by our mothers before we even met," said Percy. "Silly, really."

"Silly?"

"Yes. I could have stopped all their plotting years ago, by simply telling them that I never wanted to marry anyone else in the first place."

Daphne was giving the honeymoon serious thought for the first time when Hoskins brought the Rolls to a halt on the dockside a good two hours before the *Mauretania* was due even to turn her pistons. With the help of several porters Hoskins unloaded two trunks from the boot of the car – fourteen having been sent down the previous day – while Daphne and Percy headed towards the gangplank where the ship's purser was awaiting them.

Just as the purser stepped forward to greet the marquess and his bride someone from the crowd shouted, "Good luck, Your Lordship! And I'd like to say on behalf of the missus and myself that the marchioness looks a bit of all right."

They both turned and burst out laughing when they saw Charlie and Becky, still in their wedding outfits, standing among the crowd.

The purser guided the four of them up the gangplank and into the Nelson stateroom, where they found yet another bottle of champagne waiting to be opened.

"How did you manage to get here ahead of us?" asked Daphne.

"Well," said Charlie in a broad Cockney accent, "we may not 'ave a Rolls-Royce, my lady, but we still managed to overtake 'oskins in our little two-seater just the other side of Winchester, didn't we?"

They all laughed except Becky who couldn't take her eyes off the little diamond brooch that looked exquisite on the lapel of Daphne's suit.

Three toots on the foghorn, and the purser suggested that the Trumpers might care to leave the ship, assuming it was not their intention to accompany the Wiltshires to New York.

"See you in a year or so's time," shouted Charlie, as he turned to wave at them from the gangplank.

"By then we will have travelled right round the world, old gel," Percy confided to his wife.

Daphne waved. "Yes, and by the time we get back heaven knows what those two will have been up to."

COLONEL HAMILTON

1920-1922

CHAPTER 16

I'm usually good on faces, and the moment I saw the man weighing those potatoes I knew at once that I recognised him. Then I recalled the sign above the shop door. Of course, Trumper, Corporal C. No, he ended up a sergeant, if I remember correctly. And what was his friend called, the one who got the MM? Ah, yes, Prescott, Private T. Explanation of death not altogether satisfactory. Funny the details one's mind considers worthy of retention.

When I arrived back home for lunch I told the memsahib I'd seen Sergeant Trumper again, but she didn't show a great deal of interest until I handed over the fruit and vegetables. It was then that she asked me where I'd bought them. "Trumper's," I told her. She nodded, making a note of the name without further explanation.

The following day I duly instructed the regimental secretary to send Trumper two tickets for the annual dinner and dance, then didn't give the man another thought until I spotted the two of them sitting at the sergeants' table on the night of the ball. I say "the two of them", because Trumper was accompanied by an extremely attractive girl. Yet for most of the evening he seemed to ignore the lady in favour of someone whose name I didn't catch, a young woman I might add who had previously been seated a few places away from me on the top table. When the adjutant asked Elizabeth for a dance I took my chance, I can tell you.

I marched right across the dance floor, aware that half the battalion had their eyes on me, bowed to the lady in question and asked her for the honour. Her name, I discovered, was Miss Salmon, and she danced like an officer's wife. Bright as a button she was too, and gay with it. I just can't imagine what Trumper thought he was up to, and if it had been any of my business I would have told him so.

After the dance was over I took Miss Salmon up to meet Elizabeth, who seemed equally enchanted. Later the memsahib told me that she had learned the girl was engaged to a Captain Trentham of the regiment, who was now serving in India. Trentham, Trentham . . . I remembered that there was a young officer in the battalion by that name – won an MC on the Marne – but there was something else about him that I couldn't immediately recall. Poor girl, I thought, because I had put Elizabeth through the same sort of ordeal when they posted me to Afghanistan in 1882. Lost an eye to those bloody Afghans and nearly lost the only woman I've ever loved at the same time. Still, it's bad form to marry before you're a captain – or after you're a major, for that matter.

On the way home, Elizabeth warned me that she had invited Miss Salmon and Trumper round to Tregunter Road the following morning.

"Why?" I asked.

"It seems they have a proposition to put to you."

They arrived at our little house in Tregunter Road even before the grandfather clock had finished chiming eleven and I settled them down in the drawing room before saying to Trumper, "So what's all this about, Sergeant?" He made no attempt to reply – it was Miss Salmon who turned out to be the spokesman for the two of them. Without a wasted word she set about presenting a most convincing case for my joining their little enterprise, in a non-executive capacity you understand, on a salary of one hundred pounds per annum. Although I didn't consider the proposition was quite up my street, I was touched by their confidence in me and promised I would give their proposal a great deal of thought. Indeed I said I would write to them and let them know my decision in the near future.

Elizabeth fully concurred with my judgment but felt the least I could do was conduct a little field reconnaissance of my own before I decided finally to turn down the offer.

For the next week I made sure I was somewhere in the vicinity of 147 Chelsea Terrace every working day. I quite often sat on a bench opposite the shop, from where without being seen I could watch how they went about their business. I chose different times of the day to carry out my observation, for obvious reasons. Sometimes I would appear first thing in the morning, at others during the busiest hour, then again perhaps later in the afternoon. On one occasion I even watched them close up for the day, when I quickly discovered that Sergeant Trumper was no clock-watcher: Number 147 turned out to be the last shop in the row to close its doors to the public. I don't mind telling you that both Trumper and Miss Salmon made a most favourable impression on me. A rare couple, I told Elizabeth after my final recce.

I had been sounded out some weeks before by the curator of the Imperial War Museum regarding an invitation to become a member of their council, but frankly Trumper's offer was the only other approach I'd received since hanging up my spurs the previous year. As the curator had made no reference to remuneration I assumed there wasn't any, and from the recent council papers they had sent me to browse through it looked as if their demands wouldn't exercise my time for more than about an hour a week.

After considerable soul-searching, a chat with Miss Daphne Harcourt-Browne and encouraging noises from Elizabeth – who didn't take to having me hanging about the house all hours of the day – I dropped Miss Salmon a note to let them know I was their man.

The following morning I discovered exactly what I had let myself in for when the aforementioned lady reappeared in Tregunter Road to brief me on my first assignment. Jolly good she was too, as thorough as any staff officer I ever had under my command, I can tell you.

Becky – she had told me that I should stop calling her "Miss Salmon" now that we were "partners" – said that I should treat our first visit to Child's of Fleet Street as a "dry run", because the fish she really wanted to land wasn't being lined up until the following week. That was when we would "move in for the kill". She kept using expressions I simply couldn't make head or tail of.

I can tell you that I came out in a muck sweat on the morning of our meeting with that first bank, and if the truth be known I nearly pulled out of the front line even before the order had been given to charge. Had it not been for the sight of those two expectant young faces waiting for me outside the bank I swear I might have withdrawn from the whole campaign.

Well, despite my misgivings, we walked out of the bank less than an hour later having successfully carried out our first sortie, and I think I can safely say, in all honesty, that I didn't let the side down. Not that I thought a lot of Hadlow, who struck me as an odd sort of cove, but then the Buffs were never what one might describe as a first-class outfit. More to the point, the damn man had never seen the whites of their eyes, which in my opinion always sorts a fellow out.

From that moment I kept a close eye on Trumper's activities, insisting on a weekly meeting at the shop so I could keep myself up to date on what was happening. I even felt able to offer the odd word of advice or encouragement from time to time. A fellow doesn't like to accept remuneration unless he feels he's pulling his weight.

To begin with everything seemed to be going swimmingly; in fact the quarterly accounts were downright impressive. Then late in May of 1920 Trumper requested a private meeting. I knew he had got his eyes fixed on another establishment in Chelsea Terrace and the account was a bit stretched so I assumed that was what he wanted to discuss with me.

I agreed to visit Trumper at his flat, as he never appeared completely at ease whenever I invited him round to my club or to Tregunter Road. When I arrived that evening I found him in quite a state, and assumed something must have been troubling him at one of our three establishments, but he assured me that was not the case.

"Well, out with it then, Trumper," I said.

"It's not that easy, to be honest, sir," he replied, so I remained silent in the hope that it might help him relax and get whatever it was off his chest.

"It's Becky, sir," he blurted out eventually.

"First-class girl," I assured him.

"Yes, sir, I agree. But I'm afraid she's pregnant."

I confess that I had already learned this news some days before from Becky herself but as I had given the lady my word not to tell anyone, including Charlie, I feigned surprise. Although I realise times have changed, I knew Becky had been strictly brought up and in any case she had never struck me as that sort of girl, if you know what I mean.

"Of course, you'll want to know who the father is," Charlie added.

"I had assumed –" I began, but Charlie immediately shook his head.

"Not me," he said. "I only wish it was. Then at least I could marry her and wouldn't have to bother you with the problem."

"Then who is the culprit?" I asked.

He hesitated before saying, "Guy Trentham, sir."

"Captain Trentham? But he's in India, if I remember correctly."

"That's right, sir. And I've had the devil's own job persuading Becky to write and let him know what's happened; says it would only ruin his career."

"But if she doesn't tell him, it could well ruin her whole life," I suggested testily. "Just imagine the stigma of being an unmarried mother, not to mention having to bring up an illegitimate child. In any case, Trentham's bound to find out eventually, don't you know."

"He may never learn the truth from Becky, and I certainly don't have the sort of influence that would make him do the decent thing."

"Are you holding anything else back about Trentham that I ought to know about, Trumper?"

"No, sir."

Trumper replied a little too quickly for me to be totally convinced.

"Then you'll have to leave the problem of Trentham to me," I told him. "Meanwhile you get on with running the shops. But be sure to let me know the moment it's all out in the open so I don't go around looking as if I haven't a clue what's going on." I rose to leave.

"The whole world will know before much longer," Charlie said.

I had said "leave the problem to me" without the slightest idea of what I was going to do about it, but when I had returned home that night I discussed the whole affair with Elizabeth. She advised me to have a chat with Daphne, who she felt confident would know considerably more about what was going on than Charlie did. I suspected she was right.

Elizabeth and I duly invited Daphne to tea at Tregunter Road a couple of days later. She confirmed everything Charlie had said and was also able to fill in one or two missing pieces of the jigsaw.

In Daphne's opinion Trentham had been Becky's first serious romance, and certainly to her knowledge Becky had never slept with any other man before they had met, and only once with Trentham. Captain Trentham, she assured us, was unable to boast the same blameless reputation.

The rest of her news did not augur well for a simple solution, as it turned out that Guy's mother could not be relied on to insist that her son do the decent thing by Becky.

"But what about Trentham's father?" I asked. "Do you think I should have a word with him? Although we were in the same regiment we were never in the same battalion, don't you know."

"He's the only member of that family I really care for," Daphne admitted. "He's the MP for Berkshire West, a Liberal."

"Then that has to be my approach route," I replied. "I can't abide the man's politics, but that won't stop him from knowing the difference between right and wrong."

Yet another letter sent on club notepaper elicited an immediate reply from the major, inviting me to drinks at Chester Square the following Monday.

I arrived punctually at six, and was taken into the drawing room where I was greeted by a quite charming lady who introduced herself as Mrs Trentham. She was not at all what I expected after Daphne's description; in fact she was a rather handsome woman. She was profuse in her apologies: it seemed that her husband had been held up at the House of Commons by a running three-line whip, which even I knew meant he was unable to leave the Palace of Westminster on pain of death. I made an instant decision – wrongly I realise in retrospect – that this matter couldn't wait a moment longer and I must relay my message to the major through his wife.

"I find this is all rather embarrassing actually," I began.

"Do feel free to speak quite openly, Colonel. I can assure you that I am fully in my husband's confidence. We have no secrets from each other."

"Well, to be frank with you, Mrs Trentham, the matter I wish to touch on concerns your son Guy."

"I see," was all she said.

"And his fiancée, Miss Salmon."

"She is not, and never has been, his fiancée," said Mrs Trentham, her voice revealing a sudden edge.

"But I was given to understand –"

"That promises were made to Miss Salmon by my son? I can assure you, Colonel, that nothing could be further from the truth."

Slightly taken aback, I was unable to think of a diplomatic way of letting the lady know the real purpose behind my wanting to see her husband. So I simply said, "Whatever promises were or were not made, madam, I do feel that you and your husband should be aware that Miss Salmon is expecting a child."

"And what has that to do with me?" Mrs Trentham stared directly at me with no fear showing in her eyes.

"Simply that your son is undoubtedly the father."

"We only have her word for that, Colonel."

"That, madam, was unworthy of you," I told her. "I know Miss Salmon to be a thoroughly decent and honest girl. And in any case, if it were not your son, who else could it have possibly been?"

"Heaven knows," said Mrs Trentham. "Any number of men, I would have thought, judging by her reputation. After all, her father was an immigrant."

"So was the King's grandfather, madam," I reminded her. "But he still would have known how to conduct himself had he been faced with the same predicament."

"I'm sure I don't know what you mean, Colonel."

"I mean, madam, that your son must either marry Miss Salmon or at least resign from the regiment and make suitable arrangements to see the child is properly provided for."

"It seems I must make it clear to you once again, Colonel, that this sad state of affairs has nothing whatsoever to do with my son. I can assure you that Guy stopped seeing the girl some months before he sailed for India."

"I know that is not the case, madam, because –"

"Do you, Colonel? Then I must ask what exactly this whole business has to do with you in the first place?"

"Simply that Miss Salmon and Mr Trumper are both colleagues of mine," I explained.

"I see," she said. "Then I suspect you will not have to look much further to discover who is the real father."

"Madam, that was also uncalled for. Charlie Trumper is not –"

"I cannot see any purpose in continuing this conversation, Colonel," Mrs Trentham said, rising from her chair. She began to walk towards the door, not even bothering to glance in my direction. "I must warn you, Colonel, that should I hear this slander repeated in any quarter I shall not hesitate to instruct solicitors to take the necessary action to defend my son's good reputation."

Although shaken, I followed her into the hall, determined to see that the matter was not allowed to rest there. I now felt Major Trentham was my only hope. As Mrs Trentham opened the front door to show me out I said firmly, "May I presume, madam, that you will recount this conversation faithfully to your husband?"

"You may presume nothing, Colonel," were her final words as the front door was slammed in my face. The last occasion I received such treatment from a lady had been in Rangoon, and I'm bound to say that the girl in question had considerably more reason to be aggrieved.

When I repeated the conversation to Elizabeth – as accurately as I could recall – my wife pointed out to me in that clear, concise way of hers that I had been left with only three choices. The first was to write to Captain Trentham direct and demand he do the decent thing, the second would be to inform his commanding officer of everything I knew.

"And the third?" I asked.

"Never to refer to the subject again."

I considered her words carefully, and chose the middle course, dropping a note to Ralph Forbes – acquainting him with the facts, as I knew them – a first-class fellow who had succeeded me as commanding officer. I chose my words most judiciously, aware that if Mrs Trentham were to carry out her threat any legal action she took could only bring the regiment's good name into disrepute perhaps even ridicule. However, I did at the same time decide to keep a fatherly eye on Becky, as she now seemed to be burning the candle at both ends, not to mention in the middle. After all, the girl was trying to prepare for her exams, as well as act as an unpaid secretary and accountant to a thriving little business, while everyone who passed her in the street must have known that it could only be a matter of weeks before she was due to give birth.

As those weeks passed, it worried me that nothing seemed to be happening on the Trentham front despite the fact that I had received a reply from Forbes assuring me that he had set up a panel of enquiry. Certainly when I enquired further of Daphne or Charlie neither of them seemed to be any better informed than I was.

It was in mid October that year that Daniel George was born and I was touched that Becky invited me to be a godparent, along with Bob Makins and Daphne. I was even more delighted when I learned from Becky that she and Charlie were to be married the following week. It wouldn't stop wagging tongues, of course, but at least the child would be considered legitimate in the eyes of the law.

Elizabeth and I, along with Daphne, Percy, Mrs Salmon, Miss Roach and Bob Makins, attended the simple civic service at Chelsea Register Office, followed by a boisterous reception in Charlie's flat above the shop.

I began to think that perhaps everything had worked out for the best until some months later Daphne telephoned, asking to see me urgently. I took her to lunch at the club, where she produced a letter that she had received from Captain Trentham that morning. As I read his words I became painfully aware that Mrs Trentham must have learned of my own letter to Forbes warning him of the consequences of a breach of promise suit and immediately taken matters into her own hands. I felt the time had come to let her son know that he had not got away with it.

I left my guest to have coffee while I retired to the writing room and with the help of a stiff brandy began to compose an even stiffer letter, I can tell you. I felt my final effort covered all the necessary points in as diplomatic and realistic a way as was possible given the circumstances. Daphne thanked me, and promised she would send the letter on to Trentham verbatim.

I didn't have another conversation with her again until we met at her wedding a month later, and that was hardly an appropriate time to broach the subject of Captain Trentham.

After the service was over I strolled round to Vincent Square where the reception was being held. I kept a wary eye out for Mrs Trentham who I assumed had also been invited. I had no desire to hold a second conversation with that particular lady.

I was, however, delighted to catch up with Charlie and Becky in the large marquee that had been erected especially for the occasion. I have never seen the girl looking more radiant, and Charlie could almost have been described as suave standing there in his morning coat, grey cravat and topper. The fine half-hunter that hung from his waistcoat turned out to be a wedding gift from Becky, left to her by her father, she explained, although the rest of the outfit, Charlie reported, had to be returned to Moss Bros first thing the following morning.

"Has the time not come, Charlie," I suggested, "for you to purchase a morning coat of your own? After all, there are likely to be considerably more of these occasions in the future."

"Certainly not," he replied. "That would only be a waste of good money."

"May I enquire why?" I asked. "Surely the cost of a –"

"Because it is my intention to purchase a tailor's shop of my own," he interjected. "I've had my eye on Number 143 for some considerable time, and I hear from Mr Crowther that it might come on the market at any moment."

I couldn't argue with this piece of logic, although his next question baffled me completely.

"Have you ever heard of Marshall Field, Colonel?"

"Was he in the regiment?" I asked, racking my brain.

"No, he was not," replied Charlie with a grin. "Marshall Field is a department store in Chicago, where you can purchase anything you could ever want for the rest of your life. What's more they have two million square feet of selling space all under one roof."

I couldn't think of a more ghastly concept, but I

didn't attempt to stop the boy's enthusiastic flow. "The building takes up an entire block," he informed me. "Can you imagine a store that has twenty-eight entrances? According to the advertisements there's nothing you can't buy, from an automobile to an apple, and they have twenty-four varieties of both. They've revolutionised retailing in the States by being the first store to give full credit facilities. They also claim that if they don't have it they'll get it for you within a week. Field's motto is: 'Give the lady what she wants'."

"Are you suggesting that we should purchase Marshall Field in exchange for 147 Chelsea Terrace?" I asked ingenuously.

"Not immediately, Colonel. But if in time I was able to get my hands on every shop in Chelsea Terrace we could then carry out the same operation in London, and perhaps even remove the first line from their current cheeky advertisement."

I knew I was being set up so I duly asked what the line proclaimed.

"The biggest store in the world," Charlie replied.

"And how do *you* feel about all this?" I asked, turning my attention to Becky.

"In Charlie's case," she replied, "it would have to be the biggest barrow in the world."

CHAPTER 17

The first annual general meeting of Trumper's was held above the fruit and vegetable shop in the front room of 147 Chelsea Terrace. The colonel, Charlie and Becky sat round a small trestle table, not quite sure how to get things started until the colonel opened the proceedings.

"I know there are only three of us, but I still consider all our future meetings should be conducted in a professional manner." Charlie raised his eyebrows but made no attempt to stop the colonel's flow. "I have therefore taken the liberty," he began, "of setting out an agenda. Otherwise I find one can so easily forget to raise quite important issues." The colonel proceeded to pass both his colleagues a sheet of paper with five items neatly written in his own hand. "To that end the first item to come under discussion is headed 'financial report' and I'll begin by asking Becky to let us know how she sees the current fiscal position."

Becky had carefully written out her report word for word, having the previous month purchased two large leather-bound books, one red, one blue, from the stationer's at 137 and for the past fortnight having risen only minutes after Charlie had left for Covent Garden in order to be sure she could answer any questions that might arise at their first meeting. She opened up the cover of the red book and began to read slowly, occasionally referring to the blue book, which was just as large and authoritative-looking. This had the single word "Accounts" stamped in gold on the outside.

"In the year ending 31 December 1921 we showed a

turnover on the seven shops of one thousand three hundred and twelve pounds and four shillings, on which we declared a profit of two hundred and nineteen pounds eleven shillings, showing seventeen per cent profit on turnover. Our debt at the bank currently stands at seven hundred and seventy-one pounds, which includes our tax liability for the year, but the value of the seven shops remains in the books at one thousand two hundred and ninety pounds, which is the exact price we paid for them. This therefore does not reflect their current market value.

"I have made a breakdown of the figures on each of the shops for your consideration," said Becky, handing copies of her efforts to Charlie and the colonel, both of whom studied them carefully for several minutes before either spoke.

"Grocery is still our number one earner, I see," said the colonel, as he ran his monocle down the profit and loss column. "Hardware is only just breaking even, and the tailor's is actually eating into our profits."

"Yes," said Charlie. "I met up with a right holy friar when I bought that one."

"Holy friar?" said the colonel, perplexed.

"Liar," said Becky, not looking up from her book.

"Afraid so," said Charlie. "You see, I paid through the nose for the freehold, too much for the stock, then got myself landed with poor staff who weren't properly trained. But things have taken a turn for the better since Major Arnold took over."

The colonel smiled at the knowledge that the appointment of one of his former staff officers had been such an immediate success. Tom Arnold had returned to Savile Row soon after the war only to find that his old job as undermanager at Hawkes had been taken up by someone who had been demobbed a few months earlier than himself, and he was therefore expected to be satisfied with the status of senior assistant. He wasn't. When the colonel told him there just might be an opening for him at Trumper's, Arnold had jumped at the opportunity.

"I'm bound to say," said Becky, studying the figures, "that people seem to have a totally different moral attitude to paying their tailor than they would ever consider applying to any other tradesman. Just look at the debtors' column."

"Agreed," said Charlie. "And I fear we won't be able to show a great deal of improvement on that until Major Arnold has managed to find replacements for at least three members of his present staff. I don't expect him to declare a profit during the next six months, although I would hope they might be able to break even by the end of the third quarter."

"Good," said the colonel. "Now what about hardware? I see Number 129 declared a decent enough profit last year, so why should the figures have fallen back so badly this? They're down over sixty pounds on 1920, declaring a loss for the first time."

"I'm afraid there's a simple enough explanation," said Becky. "The money was stolen."

"Stolen?"

"I fear so," replied Charlie. "Becky began to notice as long ago as October of last year that the weekly receipts were falling, at first only by a little but then the amount grew as a pattern began to evolve."

"Have we discovered who the culprit is?"

"Yes, that was simple enough. We switched Bob Makins from grocery when one of the staff at hardware was on holiday, and he spotted the tea leaf in no time."

"Stop it, Charlie," said Becky. "Sorry, Colonel, thief."

"It turned out the manager, Reg Larkins, has a gambling problem," Charlie continued, "and was using our money to cover his debts. The bigger those debts became the more he needed to steal."

"You sacked Larkins, of course," said the colonel.

"The same day," said Charlie. "He turned rather nasty at the time and tried to deny that he'd ever taken a penny. But we haven't heard a word from him since and in the last three weeks we've even begun to show a small profit again.

However, I'm still looking for a new manager to take over as soon as possible. I've got my eye on a young man who works at Cudsons just off the Charing Cross Road."

"Good," said the colonel. "That covers last year's problems, Charlie, so now you can frighten us with your plans for the future."

Charlie opened the smart new leather case that Becky had given him on 20 January and took out the latest report from John D. Wood. He cleared his throat theatrically and Becky had to put a hand to her mouth to stifle a laugh.

"Mr Crowther," began Charlie, "has prepared a comprehensive survey of all the properties in Chelsea Terrace."

"For which, incidentally, he has charged us ten guineas," said Becky, checking the accounts book.

"I have no quarrel with that, if it turns out to be a good investment," said the colonel.

"It already has," said Charlie. He handed over copies of Crowther's report. "As you both already know, there are thirty-six shops in Chelsea Terrace, of which we currently own seven. In Crowther's opinion a further five could well become available during the next twelve months. However, as he points out, all the shopkeepers in Chelsea Terrace are now only too aware of my role as a buyer, which doesn't exactly help keep the price down."

"I suppose that was bound to happen sooner or later."

"I agree, Colonel," said Charlie, "but it's still far sooner than I'd hoped for. In fact, Syd Wrexall, the chairman of the Shops Committee, is becoming quite wary of us."

"Why Mr Wrexall in particular?" asked the colonel.

"He's the publican who owns the Musketeer on the other corner of Chelsea Terrace. He's started telling his customers that it's my long-term aim to buy up all the property in the block and drive out the small shopkeepers."

"He has a point," said Becky.

"Maybe, but I never expected him to form a co-operative with the sole purpose of stopping me purchasing certain properties. I was rather hoping to get my hands on the Musketeer itself in time but whenever the subject comes up he just says, 'Over my dead body'."

"That comes as rather a blow," said the colonel.

"Not at all," said Charlie. "No one can expect to go through life without facing a moment of crisis. The secret will be spotting Wrexall's when it comes and then moving in quickly. But it does mean for the time being that I'm occasionally going to have to pay over the odds if a shop owner decides the time has come to sell."

"Not a lot we can do about that I suspect," said the colonel.

"Except call their bluff from time to time," said Charlie.

"Call their bluff? I'm not sure I catch your drift."

"Well, we've had an approach from two shops recently with an interest in disposing of their freehold and I turned them both down out of hand."

"Why?"

"Simply because they were demanding such outrageous prices, not to mention Becky nagging me about our present overdraft."

"And have they reconsidered their position?"

"Yes and no," said Charlie. "One has already come back with a far more realistic demand, while the other is still holding out for his original price."

"Who is holding out?"

"Cuthbert's, Number 101, the wine and spirits merchant. But there's no need to make any sort of move in that direction for the time being, because Crowther says that Mr Cuthbert, the owner, has recently been looking at several properties in Pimlico, and he'll be able to keep us informed of any progress on that front. We can then make a sensible offer the moment Cuthbert commits himself."

"Well done, Crowther I say. By the way, where do you pick up all your information?" the colonel asked.

"Mr Bales the newsagent, and Syd Wrexall himself."

"But I thought you said Wrexall wasn't proving that helpful."

"He isn't," said Charlie, "but he'll still offer his opinion on any subject for the price of a pint, so Bob Makins has become a regular and learned never to complain about being short-measured. I even get a copy of the Shops Committee minutes before they do."

The colonel laughed. "And what about the auctioneers at Number 1? Have we still got our eye on them?"

"We most certainly have, Colonel. Mr Fothergill, the proprietor, continues to go deeper and deeper into debt, having had another bad year. But somehow he manages to keep his head above water, if only just, but I anticipate he will finally go under some time next year, at the latest the year after, when I will be standing on the quayside waiting to throw him a lifeline. Especially if Becky feels she is ready to leave Sotheby's by then."

"I'm still learning so much," confessed Becky. "I'd rather like to stay put for as long as I can. I've completed a year in Old Masters," she added, "and now I'm trying to get myself moved to Modern, or Impressionist as they've started calling that department. You see, I still feel I need to gain as much experience as possible before they work out what I'm up to. I attend every auction I can, from silverware to old books, but I'd be far happier if we could leave Number 1 until the last possible moment."

"But if Fothergill does go under for a third time, Becky, you're our lifeboat. So what if the shop were suddenly to come on the market?"

"I could just about handle it, I suppose. I've already got my eye on the man who ought to be our general manager. Simon Matthews. He's been with Sotheby's for the past twelve years and is disenchanted at being passed over once too often. There's also a bright young trainee who's been around for about three years who I think will be the pick of the next generation of auctioneers. He's only two years younger than the chairman's son so he might be only too happy to join us if we were able to make him an attractive offer."

"On the other hand, it may well suit us for Becky to

remain at Sotheby's for as long as possible," said Charlie. "Because Mr Crowther has identified a further problem we're going to have to face in the near future."

"Namely?" queried the colonel.

"On page nine of his report, Crowther points out that Numbers 25 to 99, a block of thirty-seven flats bang in the middle of Chelsea Terrace – one of which Daphne and Becky shared until a couple of years ago – may well come on the market in the not too distant future. They're currently owned by a charitable trust who are no longer satisfied with the return they receive on their investment, and Crowther says they're considering disposing of them. Now, remembering our long-term plan, it might be wise to purchase the block as soon as possible rather than risk waiting for years when we would have to pay a far higher price or, worse, never be able to get hold of them at all."

"Thirty-eight flats," said the colonel. "Hm, how much is Crowther expecting them to fetch?"

"His guess would be around the two-thousand-pound mark; they're currently only showing an income of two hundred and ten pounds a year and what with repairs and maintenance they're probably not even declaring a profit. If the property does come on the market, and we're able to afford them, Crowther also recommends that we only issue ten-year leases in future, and try to place any empty flats with staff from embassies or foreign visitors, who never make any fuss about having to move at a moment's notice."

"So the profit on the shops would end up having to pay for the flats," said Becky.

"I'm afraid so," said Charlie. "But with any luck it would only take me a couple of years, three at the outside, before I could have them showing a profit. Mind you, if the charity commissioners are involved, the paperwork could take that long."

"Nevertheless, remembering our current overdraft limit a demand on our resources like that may well require another lunch with Hadlow," said the colonel. "Still, I can see if we need to get hold of those flats I'm left with little choice. Might even take the opportunity to bump into Chubby Duckworth at the club and drop a word in his ear." The colonel paused. "To be fair to Hadlow, he's also come up with a couple of good ideas himself, both of which I feel are worthy of our consideration, and accordingly I have placed them next on the agenda."

Becky stopped writing and looked up.

"Let me begin by saying that Hadlow is most satisfied with the way our first two years' figures have worked out, but nevertheless he feels strongly that because of the state of our overdraft and for taxation reasons we should stop being a partnership and form ourselves into a company."

"Why?" asked Charlie. "What advantage could there possibly be in that?"

"It's the new Finance Bill that has just gone through the Commons," explained Becky. "The change in the tax laws could well be used to our advantage, because at the moment we're trading as seven different businesses and taxed accordingly, whereas if we were to put all our shops into one company we could run the losses of, say, the tailor's shop and hardware against any gains made by the grocery store and the butcher's, and thus reduce our tax burden. It could be especially beneficial in a bad year."

"That all makes good sense to me," said Charlie. "So let's go ahead and do it."

"Well, it's not quite that easy," said the colonel, placing his monocle to his good eye. "To start with, if we were to become a company Mr Hadlow is advising us to appoint some new directors to cover those areas in which we currently have little or no professional experience."

"Why would Hadlow expect us to do that?" asked Charlie sharply. "We've never needed anyone else to interfere with our business before."

"Because we're growing so rapidly, Charlie. We may need other people to advise us in the future, who can offer expertise we simply don't at present possess. The purchasing of the flats is a good example."

"But we have Mr Crowther for that."

"And perhaps he would feel a greater commitment to our cause if he were on the board." Charlie frowned. "I can well understand how you feel," continued the colonel. "It's your show, and you believe you don't need any outsiders to tell you how to run Trumper's. Well, even if we did form a company it would still be your show, because all the shares would be lodged in the names of you and Becky, and any assets would therefore remain totally under your control. But you would have the added advantage of non-executive directors to call on for advice."

"And to spend our money and overrule our decisions," said Charlie. "I just don't like the idea of outsiders telling me what to do."

"It wouldn't necessarily work like that," said Becky.

"I'm not convinced it will work at all."

"Charlie, you should listen to yourself sometimes. You're beginning to sound like a Luddite."

"Perhaps we should take a vote," said the colonel, trying to calm things down. "Just to see where we all stand."

"Vote? What on? Why? The shops belong to me."

Becky looked up. "To both of us, Charlie, and the colonel has more than earned his right to give an opinion."

"I'm sorry, Colonel, I didn't mean – "

"I know you didn't, Charlie, but Becky's right. If you want to realise your long-term aims you'll undoubtedly need some outside help. It just won't be possible to achieve such a dream all on your own."

"And it will with outside interferers?"

"Think of them as inside helpers," said the colonel.

"So what are we voting on?" asked Charlie touchily.

"Well," began Becky, "someone should propose a resolution that we turn ourselves into a company. If that is passed we could then invite the colonel to be chairman, who can in turn appoint you as managing director and myself as secretary. I think Mr Crowther should also be invited to join the board, along with a representative from the bank."

"I can see you've given this a lot of thought," said Charlie.

"That was my side of the bargain, if you remember our original deal correctly, Mr Trumper," Becky replied.

"We're not Marks and Spencer, you know."

"Not yet," said the colonel, with a smile. "Remember it's you, Charlie, who has taught us to think like this."

"I knew somehow it would all end up being my fault."

"So I propose the resolution that we form a company," said Becky. "Those in favour?"

Becky and the colonel each placed a hand in the air, and a few seconds later Charlie reluctantly raised his and added, "Now what?"

"My second proposal," said Becky, "is that Lieutenant-Colonel Sir Danvers Hamilton should be our first chairman."

This time Charlie's hand shot straight up.

"Thank you," said the colonel. "And my first action as chairman is to appoint Mr Trumper as managing director and Mrs Trumper as company secretary. And with your permission I shall approach Mr Crowther, and I think also Mr Hadlow, with a view to asking them to join the board."

"Agreed," said Becky, who was scribbling furiously in the minutes book as she tried to keep up.

"Any other business?" asked the colonel.

"May I suggest, Mr Chairman," said Becky – the colonel couldn't resist a smile – "that we fix a date for our first monthly meeting of the full board?"

"Any time suits me," said Charlie. "Because one thing's for certain, we won't be able to get them all round this table at any one time, unless of course you propose to hold the meetings at four thirty in the morning. At least that way we might find out who the real workers are."

The colonel laughed. "Well, that's another way you could guarantee that all your own resolutions are passed without us ever finding out, Charlie. But I must warn you, one will no longer constitute a quorum."

"A quorum?"

"The minimum number of people needed to pass a resolution," explained Becky.

"That used to be just me," said Charlie wistfully.

"That was probably true of Mr Marks before he met Mr Spencer," said the colonel, "so let's settle on our next meeting being a month today."

Becky and Charlie nodded.

"Now if there is no other business I will declare the meeting closed."

"There is," said Becky, "but I don't think such information should be minuted."

"The floor's all yours," said the chairman, looking puzzled.

Becky stretched across the table and took Charlie's hand. "It comes under miscellaneous expenses," she said. "You see, I'm going to have another baby."

For once Charlie was speechless. It was the colonel who eventually asked if there were a bottle of champagne anywhere near at hand.

"I'm afraid not," said Becky. "Charlie won't let me buy anything from wine and spirits until we own the shop."

"Quite understandably," said the colonel. "Then we shall just have to walk round to my place," he added, rising from his seat and picking up his umbrella. "That way Elizabeth can join the celebration. I declare the meeting closed."

A few moments later the three of them stepped out on to Chelsea Terrace just as the postman was entering the shop. Seeing Becky he handed her a letter.

"It can only have come from Daphne with all those stamps," she told them as she ripped the envelope open and began reading its contents.

"Come on, then, what's she been up to?" asked Charlie, as they walked towards Tregunter Road.

"She's covered America and China, and as far as I can tell India's next," Becky announced. "She's also put on half a stone and met a Mr Calvin Coolidge, whoever he is."

"The Vice-President of the United States," said Charlie.

"Is that so? And they still hope to be home sometime in August, so it won't be that long before we are able to learn everything firsthand." Becky looked up to discover that only the colonel was still by her side. "Where's Charlie?" They both turned round to see him staring up at a small town house that had a "For Sale" sign attached to the wall.

They walked back towards him. "What do you think?" he asked, continuing to stare at the property.

"What do you mean, 'what do I think'?"

"I suspect, my dear, what Charlie is enquiring of you is your opinion of the house."

Becky stared up at the little house that was on three floors and the front was covered in Virginia creeper.

"It's wonderful, quite wonderful."

"It's better than that," said Charlie, placing his thumbs in his waistcoat pockets. "It's ours, and also ideal for someone with a wife and three children who is the managing director of an expanding business in Chelsea."

"But I don't have a second child yet, let alone a third."

"Just planning ahead," said Charlie. "Something you taught me."

"But can we afford it?"

"No, of course we can't," he said. "But I'm confident that the value of property will soon be going up in this area, once people realise they will have their own department store within walking distance. In any case, it's too late now, because I put down the deposit this morning." He placed a hand in his jacket pocket and removed a key.

"But why didn't you consult me first?" asked Becky.

"Because I knew you'd only say we couldn't afford it, as you did with the second, third, fourth, fifth and every subsequent shop."

He walked towards the front door with Becky still a yard behind him.

"But –"

"I'll leave you two to sort things out," said the colonel. "Come over to my place and have that glass of champagne just as soon as you've finished looking over your new home."

The colonel continued on down Tregunter Road, swinging his umbrella in the morning sun, pleased with himself and the world, arriving back just in time for his first whisky of the day.

He imparted all his news to Elizabeth, who had many more questions about the baby and the house than about the present state of the company accounts or her husband's appointment as chairman. Having acquitted himself as best he could, the colonel asked his manservant to place a bottle of champagne in a bucket of ice. He then retired to his study to check through the morning mail while he awaited the Trumpers' arrival.

There were three letters unopened on his desk: a bill from his tailor – which reminded him of Becky's strictures on such matters – an invitation to the Ashburton Shield to be held at Bisley, an annual event he always enjoyed, and a letter from Daphne, which he rather expected might simply repeat the news that Becky had already relayed to him.

The envelope was postmarked Delhi. The colonel slit it open in anticipation. Daphne dutifully repeated how much she was enjoying the trip, but failed to mention her weight problem. She did, however, go on to say that she had some distressing news to impart concerning Guy Trentham. She wrote that while they were staying in Poona, Percy had come across him one evening at the officers' club dressed in civilian clothes. He had lost so much weight that her husband hardly recognised him. He informed Percy that he had been forced to resign his commission and there was only one person to blame for his downfall: a corporal who had lied about him in the past, and was happy to associate with known criminals. Guy was claiming that he had even caught the man stealing himself. Once he was back in England Trentham intended to . . .

The front door bell rang.

"Can you answer it, Danvers?" Elizabeth said, leaning over the banisters. "I'm upstairs arranging the flowers."

The colonel was still seething with anger when he opened the front door to find Charlie and Becky waiting on the top step in anticipation. He must have looked surprised to see them because Becky had to say, "Champagne, Chairman. Or have you already forgotten my physical state?"

"Ah, yes, sorry. My thoughts were some distance away." The colonel stuffed Daphne's letter into his jacket pocket. "The champagne should be at the perfect temperature by now," he added, as he ushered his guests through to the drawing room.

"Two and a quarter Trumpers have arrived," he barked back up the stairs to his wife.

CHAPTER 18

It always amused the colonel to watch Charlie spending so much of his time running from shop to shop, trying to keep a close eye on all his staff, while also attempting to concentrate his energy on any establishment that wasn't showing a worthwhile return. But whatever the various problems he faced, the colonel was only too aware that Charlie couldn't resist a spell of serving at the fruit and vegetable shop, which remained his pride and joy. Coat off, sleeves rolled up and Cockney accent at its broadest, Charlie was allowed an hour a day by Bob Makins to pretend he was back on the corner of Whitechapel Road peddling his wares from Granpa's barrow.

"'alf a pound of tomatoes, some runner beans, and your usual pound of carrots, Mrs Symonds, if I remember correctly."

"Thank you so much, Mr Trumper. And how's Mrs Trumper?"

"Never better."

"And when's the baby expected?"

"In about three months, the doctor thinks."

"Don't see you serving in the shop so much nowadays."

"Only when I know the important customers are around, my luv," said Charlie. "After all, you were one of my first."

"I was indeed. So have you signed the deal on the flats yet, Mr Trumper?"

Charlie stared at Mrs Symonds as he handed back her change, unable to hide his surprise. "The flats?"

"Yes, you know, Mr Trumper. Numbers 25 to 99."

"Why do you ask, Mrs Symonds?"

"Because you're not the only person who's showing an interest in them."

"How do you know that?"

"I know because I saw a young man holding a bunch of keys waiting outside the building for a client last Sunday morning."

Charlie recalled that the Symondses lived in a house on the far side of the terrace immediately opposite the main entrance to the flats.

"And did you recognise them?"

"No. I watched a car draw up but then my husband seemed to think his breakfast was more important than me being nosey, so I didn't see who it was who got out."

Charlie continued to stare at Mrs Symonds as she picked up her bag, waved a cheery goodbye and walked out of the shop.

Despite Mrs Symonds's bombshell and Syd Wrexall's efforts to contain him, Charlie went about plotting his next acquisition. Through the combination of Major Arnold's diligence, Mr Crowther's inside knowledge and Mr Hadlow's loans, by late July Charlie had secured the freehold on another shop in the terrace – Number 39, women's clothes. At the August board meeting Becky recommended that Major Arnold be promoted to deputy managing director of the company, with the task of keeping a watching brief on everything that was taking place in Chelsea Terrace.

Charlie had desperately needed an extra pair of eyes and ears for some time, and with Becky still working at Sotheby's during the day, Arnold had begun to fill that role to perfection. The colonel was delighted to ask Becky to minute the confirmation of the major's appointment. The monthly meeting continued very smoothly until the colonel asked, "Any other business?"

"Yes," said Charlie. "What's happening about the flats?"

"I put in a bid of two thousand pounds as instructed," said Crowther. "The agent said they would recommend their clients should accept the offer, but to date I've been unable to close the deal."

"Why?" asked Charlie.

"Because Savill's rang back this morning to let me know that they have received another offer far in excess of what they had anticipated for this particular piece of property. They thought I might want to alert the board to the present situation."

"They were right about that," said Charlie. "But how much is this other offer? That's what I want to know."

"Two thousand five hundred pounds," said Crowther.

It was several moments before anyone round the boardroom table offered an opinion.

"How on earth can they hope to show a return on that kind of investment?" Hadlow eventually asked.

"They can't," said Crowther.

"Offer them three thousand pounds."

"What did you say?" said the chairman, as they all turned to face Charlie.

"Offer them three thousand," Charlie repeated.

"But Charlie, we agreed that two thousand was a high enough price only a few weeks ago," Becky pointed out. "How can the flats suddenly be worth so much more?"

"They're worth whatever someone is willing to pay for them," Charlie replied. "So we've been left with no choice."

"But Mr Trumper –" began Hadlow.

"If we end up with the rest of the block but then fail to get our hands on those flats, everything I have worked for will go up the spout. I'm not willing to risk that for three thousand pounds – or, as I see it, five hundred."

"Yes, but can we afford such a large outlay just at this moment?" asked the colonel.

"Five of the shops are now showing a profit," said Becky, checking her inventory. "Two are breaking even and only one is actually losing money consistently."

"We must have the courage to go ahead," said Charlie.

"Buy the flats, knock 'em down and then we can build half a dozen shops in their place. We'll be making a return on them before anyone can say 'Bob's your uncle'."

Crowther gave them all a moment to allow Charlie's strategy to sink in, then asked, "So what are the board's instructions?"

"I propose that we offer three thousand pounds," said the colonel. "As the managing director has pointed out, we must take the long view, but only if the bank feels able to back us on this one. Mr Hadlow?"

"You can just about afford three thousand pounds at the moment," said the bank manager, checking over the figures. "But that would stretch your overdraft facility to the limit. It would also mean that you couldn't consider buying any more shops for the foreseeable future."

"We don't have a choice," said Charlie, looking straight at Crowther. "Someone else is after those flats and we can't at this stage allow a rival to get their hands on them."

"Well, if those are the board's instructions I shall attempt to close the deal later today, at three thousand pounds."

"I think that's precisely what the board would wish you to do," confirmed the chairman, as he checked around the table. "Well, if there's no other business, I declare the meeting closed."

Once the meeting had broken up, the colonel took Crowther and Hadlow on one side. "I don't like the sound of this flats business at all. An offer coming out of the blue like that requires a little more explanation."

"I agree," said Crowther. "My instinct tells me that it's Syd Wrexall and his Shops Committee trying to stop Charlie taking over the whole block before it's too late."

"No," said Charlie as he joined them. "It can't be Syd because he doesn't have a car," he added mysteriously. "In any case, Wrexall and his cronies would have reached their limit long before two thousand five hundred pounds."

"So do you think it's an outside contractor," asked

Hadlow, "who has his own plans for developing Chelsea Terrace?"

"More likely to be an investor who's worked out your long-term plan and is willing to hang on until we have no choice but to pay the earth for them," said Crowther.

"I don't know who or what it is," said Charlie. "All I'm certain of is that we've made the right decision to outbid them."

"Agreed," said the colonel. "And Crowther, let me know the moment you've closed the deal. Afraid I can't hang about now. I'm taking a rather special lady to lunch at my club."

"Anyone we know?" asked Charlie.

"Daphne Wiltshire."

"Do give her my love," said Becky. "Tell her we're both looking forward to having dinner with them next Wednesday."

The colonel raised his hat to Becky, and left his four colleagues to continue discussing their different theories as to who else could possibly be interested in the flats.

Because the board meeting had run on later than he anticipated the colonel only managed one whisky before Daphne was ushered through to join him in the Ladies Room. She had, indeed, put on a few pounds, but he didn't consider she looked any the worse for that.

He ordered a gin and tonic for his guest from the club steward, while she chatted about the gaiety of America and the heat of Africa, but he suspected that it was another continent entirely that Daphne really wanted to talk about.

"And how was India?" he eventually asked.

"Not so good, I'm afraid," said Daphne before pausing to sip her gin and tonic. "In fact, awful."

"Funny, I always found the natives rather friendly," said the colonel.

"It wasn't the natives who turned out to be the problem," replied Daphne.

"Trentham?"

"I fear so."

"Hadn't he received your letter?"

"Oh, yes, but events had long superseded that, Colonel. Now I only wish I had taken your advice and copied out your letter word for word warning him that if the question were ever put to me directly I would have to tell anyone who asked that Trentham was Daniel's father."

"Why? What has caused this change of heart?"

Daphne drained her glass in one gulp. "Sorry, Colonel, but I needed that. Well, when Percy and I arrived in Poona the first thing we were told by Ralph Forbes, the Commanding Officer of the Regiment, was that Trentham had resigned his commission."

"Yes, you mentioned as much in your letter." The colonel put his knife and fork down. "What I want to know is why."

"Some problem with the adjutant's wife, Percy later discovered, but no one was willing to go into any detail. Evidently the subject's taboo – not the sort of thing they care to discuss in the officers' mess."

"The unmitigated bastard. If only I –"

"I couldn't agree with you more, Colonel, but I must warn you that there's worse to come."

The colonel ordered another gin and tonic for his guest and a whisky for himself before Daphne continued.

"When I visited Ashurst last weekend, Major Trentham showed me the letter that Guy had sent to his mother explaining why he had been forced to resign his commission with the Fusiliers. He claimed this had come about because you had written to Colonel Forbes informing him that he, Guy, had been responsible for putting 'a tart from Whitechapel' in the family way. I saw the exact wording of the sentence."

The colonel's cheeks suffused scarlet with rage.

"'Whereas time has proved conclusively that Trumper was the father of the child all along.' Anyway, that's the story Trentham is putting about."

"Has the man no morals?"

"None, it would seem," said Daphne. "You see, the

letter went on to suggest that Charlie Trumper is now employing you in order to make sure that you keep your mouth shut. 'Thirty pieces of silver' was the precise expression he used."

"He deserves to be horsewhipped."

"Even Major Trentham might add 'Hear, hear' to that. But my greatest fear isn't for you or even Becky for that matter, but for Charlie himself."

"What are you getting at?"

"Before we left India, Trentham warned Percy when they were on their own at the Overseas Club that Trumper would regret this for the rest of his life."

"But why blame Charlie?"

"Percy asked the same question, and Guy informed him that it was obvious that Trumper had put you up to it in the first place simply to settle an old score."

"But that's not true."

"Percy explained as much, but he just wouldn't listen."

"And in any case what did he mean by 'to settle an old score'?"

"No idea, except that later that evening Guy kept asking me about a painting of the Virgin Mary and Child."

"Not the one that hangs in Charlie's front room?"

"The same, and when I finally admitted I had seen it he dropped the subject altogether."

"The man must have gone completely out of his senses."

"He seemed sane enough to me," said Daphne.

"Well, let's at least be thankful that he's stuck in India, so there's still a little time to consider what course of action we should take."

"Not that much time, I fear," said Daphne.

"How come?"

"Mrs Trentham tells me that Guy is expected to return to these shores some time next month."

After lunch with Daphne the colonel returned to Tregunter Road. He was fuming with anger when his butler opened the front door to let him in but he remained uncertain as to what he could actually do about it. The butler informed his master that a Mr Crowther awaited him in the study.

"Crowther? What can he possibly want?" mumbled the colonel to himself before straightening a print of the Isle of Skye that hung in the hall and joining him in the study.

"Good afternoon, Chairman," Crowther said as he rose from the colonel's chair. "You asked me to report back as soon as I had any news on the flats."

"Ah, yes, so I did," said the colonel. "You've closed the deal?"

"No, sir. I placed a bid of three thousand pounds with Savill's, as instructed, but then received a call from them about an hour later to inform me that the other side had raised their offer to four thousand."

"Four thousand," said the colonel in disbelief. "But who – ?"

"I said we were quite unable to match the sum, and even enquired discreetly who their client might be. They informed me that it was no secret whom they were representing. I felt I ought to let you know immediately, Chairman, as the name of Mrs Gerald Trentham meant nothing to me."

CHARLIE

1919-1926

CHAPTER 19

As I sat alone on that bench in Chelsea Terrace staring across at a shop with the name "Trumper's" painted over the awning, a thousand questions went through my mind. Then I saw Posh Porky – or, to be accurate, I thought it must be her, because if it was, during my absence she'd changed into a woman. What had happened to that flat chest, those spindly legs, not to mention the spotty face? If it hadn't been for those flashing brown eyes I might have remained in doubt.

She went straight into the shop and spoke to the man who had been acting as if he was the manager. I saw him shake his head; she then turned to the two girls behind the counter who reacted in the same way. She shrugged, before going over to the till, pulling out the tray and beginning to check the day's takings.

I had been watching the manager carry out his duties for over an hour before Becky arrived, and to be fair he was pretty good, although I had already spotted several little things that could have been done to help improve sales, not least among them moving the counter to the far end of the shop and setting up some of the produce in boxes out on the pavement so that the customers could be tempted to buy. "You must advertise your wares, not just hope people will come across them," my granpa used to say. However, I remained patiently on that bench until the staff began to empty the shelves prior to closing up the premises.

A few minutes later Becky came back out on to the pavement and looked up and down the street as if she was waiting for someone. Then the young man, who was now holding a padlock and key, joined her and nodded in my direction. Becky looked over towards the bench for the first time.

Once she had seen me I jumped up and crossed the road to join her. For some time neither of us spoke. I wanted to hug her, but we ended up just shaking hands rather formally, before I asked, "So what's the deal?"

"Couldn't find anyone else who would supply me with free cream buns," she told me, before going on to explain why she had sold the baker's shop and how we had come to own 147 Chelsea Terrace. When the staff had left for the night, she showed me round the flat. I couldn't believe my eyes – a bathroom with a toilet, a kitchen with crockery and cutlery, a front room with chairs and a table, and a bedroom – not to mention a bed that didn't look as if it would collapse when you sat down on it.

Once again I wanted to hug her, but I simply asked if she could stay and share dinner, as I had a hundred other questions that still needed answering.

"Sorry, not tonight," she said as I opened my parcel and began to unpack. "I'm off to a concert with a gentleman friend." No sooner had she added some remark about Tommy's picture than she smiled and left. Suddenly I was on my own again.

I took off my coat, rolled up my sleeves, went downstairs to the shop and for several hours moved things around until everything was exactly where I wanted it. By the time I had packed away the last box I was so exhausted that I only just stopped myself collapsing on the bed and grabbing some kip fully dressed. I didn't draw the curtains so as to be sure I would wake by four.

I dressed quickly the following morning, excited by the thought of returning to a market I hadn't seen for nearly two years. I arrived at the Garden a few minutes before Bob Makins, whom I quickly discovered knew his way around – without actually knowing his way about. I accepted that it would take me a few days before I could work out which dealers were being supplied by the most reliable farmers, who had the real contacts at the docks and ports, who struck the most sensible price day in, day out, and, most important of all, who would take care of you whenever there was any sort of real shortage. None of these problems seemed to worry Bob, as he strolled around the market in an uninterrupted, undemanding circle, collecting his wares.

I loved the shop from the moment we opened that first morning, my first morning. It took me a little time to get used to Bob and the girls calling me "sir" but it also took them almost as long to become used to where I'd put the counter and to having to place the boxes out on the pavement before the customers were awake. However, even Becky agreed that it was an inspiration to place our wares right under the noses of potential buyers, although she wasn't sure how the local authority would react when they found out.

"Hasn't Chelsea ever heard of passing trade?" I asked her.

Within a month I knew the name of every regular customer who patronised the shop, and within two I was aware of their likes, dislikes, passions and even the occasional fad that each imagined must be unique to them. After the staff had packed up at the end of each day I would often walk across the road and sit on the bench opposite and just watch the comings and goings in Chelsea Terrace SW3. It didn't take long to realise that an apple was an apple whoever wanted to take a bite out of it, and Chelsea Terrace was no different from Whitechapel when it came to understanding a customer's needs: I suppose that must have been the moment I thought about owning a second shop. Why not? Trumper's was the only establishment in Chelsea Terrace that regularly had a queue out on to the street.

Becky, meanwhile, continued her studies at the university and kept attempting to arrange for me to meet her gentleman friend. If the truth be known, I was trying to avoid Trentham altogether, as I had no desire to come in contact with the man I was convinced had killed Tommy.

Eventually I ran out of excuses and agreed to have dinner with them. When Becky entered the restaurant with Daphne and Trentham, I wished that I had never agreed to spend the evening with them in the first place. The feeling must have been mutual, for Trentham's face registered the same loathing I felt for him, although Becky's friend, Daphne, tried to be friendly. She was a pretty girl and it wouldn't have surprised me to find that a lot of men enjoyed that hearty laugh. But blue-eyed, curly-headed blondes never were my type. I pretended for form's sake that Trentham and I hadn't met before.

I spent one of the most miserable evenings of my life wanting to tell Becky everything I knew about the bastard, but aware as I watched them together that nothing I had to reveal could possibly have any influence on her. It didn't help when Becky scowled at me for no reason. I just lowered my head and scooped up some more peas.

Becky's roommate, Daphne Harcourt-Browne, continued to do her best, but even Charlie Chaplin would have failed to raise a smile with the three of us as an audience.

Shortly after eleven I called for the bill, and a few minutes later we all left the restaurant. I let Becky and Trentham walk ahead in the hope that it would give me a chance to slip away, but to my surprise double-barrelled Daphne hung back, claiming she wanted to find out what changes I'd made to the shop.

From her opening question as I unlocked the front door I realised she didn't miss much.

"You're in love with Becky, aren't you?" she asked quite matter-of-factly.

"Yes," I replied without guile, and went on to reveal my feelings in a way I would never have done to someone I knew well.

Her second question took me even more by surprise.

"And just how long have you known Guy Trentham?"

As we climbed the steps to my little flat I told her that we had served together on the Western Front, but because of the difference in our rank our paths had rarely crossed.

"Then why do you dislike him so much?" Daphne asked, after she had taken the seat opposite me.

I hesitated again but then in a sudden rush of uncontrollable anger I described what had happened to Tommy and myself when we were trying to reach the safety of our own lines, and how I was convinced that Guy Trentham had shot my closest friend.

When I'd finished we both sat in silence for some time before I added, "You must never let Becky know what I've just told you as I've no real proof."

She nodded her agreement and went on to tell me about the only man in her life, as if swopping one secret for another to bond our friendship. Her love for the man was so transparent that I couldn't fail to be touched. And when Daphne left around midnight she promised that she'd do everything in her power to speed up the demise of Guy Trentham. I remembered her using the word "demise", because I had to ask her what it meant. She told me, and thus I received my first tutorial – with the warning that Becky had a good start on me as she had not wasted the last ten years.

My second lesson was to discover why Becky had scowled at me so often during dinner. I would have protested at her cheek, but realised she was right.

I saw a lot of Daphne during the next few months, without Becky ever becoming aware of our true relationship. She taught me so much about the world of my new customers and even took me on trips to clothes shops, picture houses and to West End theatres to see plays that didn't have any dancing girls on the stage but I still enjoyed them. I only drew the line when she tried to get me to stop spending my Saturday afternoons watching West Ham in favour of some rugby team called the Quins. However, it was her introduction to the National Gallery and its five thousand canvases that was to start a love affair that was to prove as costly as any woman. It was to be only a few months before I was dragging her off to the latest exhibitions: Renoir, Manet and even a young Spaniard called Picasso who was beginning to attract attention among London's fashionable society. I began to hope that Becky would appreciate the change in me, but her eyes never once wavered from Captain Trentham.

On Daphne's further insistence I started reading two daily newspapers. She selected the *Daily Express* and the *News Chronicle*, and occasionally when she invited me round to Lowndes Square I even delved into one of her magazines, *Punch* or *Strand*. I began to discover who was who and who did what, and to whom. I even went to Sotheby's for the first time and watched an early Constable come under the hammer for a record price of nine hundred guineas. It was more money than Trumper's and all its fixtures and fittings were worth put together. I confess that neither that magnificent country scene nor any other painting I came across in a gallery or auction house compared with my pride in Tommy's picture of the Virgin Mary and Child, which still hung above my bed.

When in January 1920 Becky presented the first year's accounts, I began to realise my ambition to own a second shop no longer had to be a daydream. Then without warning two sites became available in the same month. I immediately instructed Becky that somehow she had to come up with the money to purchase them.

Daphne later warned me on the QT that Becky was having considerable trouble raising the necessary cash, and although I said nothing I was quite expecting her to tell me that it simply wasn't possible, especially as her mind seemed to be almost totally preoccupied with Trentham and the fact that he was about to be posted to India. When Becky announced the day he left that they had become officially engaged, I could have willingly cut his throat – and then mine – but Daphne assured me that there were several young ladies in London who had at one time or another entertained the illusion that they were about to marry Guy Trentham. However, Becky herself remained so confident of Trentham's intentions that I didn't know which of the two women to believe.

The following week my old commanding officer appeared on the premises with a shopping list to complete for his wife. I'll never forget the moment he took a purse from his jacket pocket and fumbled around for some loose change. Until then it had never occurred to me that a colonel might actually live in the real world. However, he left with a promise to put me down for two ten-bob tickets at the regimental ball; he turned out to be as good as his word.

My euphoria – another Harcourt-Browne word – at meeting up with the colonel again lasted for about twenty-four hours. Then Daphne told me Becky was expecting. My first reaction was to wish I'd killed Trentham on the Western Front instead of helping to save the bloody man's life. I assumed that he would return immediately from India in order to marry her before the child was born. I hated the idea of his coming back into our lives, but it was the only course of action a gentleman could possibly consider, otherwise the rest of Becky's life would be spent as a social outcast.

It was around this time that Daphne explained that if we hoped to raise some real money from the banks then we were definitely in need of a front man. Becky's sex was now militating – another of Daphne's words – against her, although she was kind enough *not* to mention my accent "militating" against me.

On the way home from the regimental ball Becky breezily informed Daphne that she had decided that the colonel was the obvious man to represent us whenever we had to go cap in hand seeking loans from one of the banks. I wasn't optimistic, but Becky insisted after her conversation with the colonel's wife that we at least go round to see him and present our case.

I fell in line and to my surprise we received a letter ten days later saying that he was our man.

A few days after that Becky admitted she was going to have a baby. From that moment on my consuming interest became in finding out what news Becky had of Trentham's intentions. I was horrified to discover that she hadn't even written to tell him her news, although she was almost four months pregnant. I made her swear that she would send a letter that night, even if she did refuse to consider threatening him with a breach of promise suit. The following day Daphne assured me that she had watched from the kitchen window as Becky posted the letter.

I made an appointment to see the colonel and briefed him on Becky's state before the whole world knew. He said somewhat mysteriously, "Leave Trentham to me."

Six weeks later Becky told me that she had still heard nothing from the man, and I sensed for the first time that her feelings for him were beginning to wane.

I even asked her to marry me, but she didn't take my proposal at all seriously although I had never been more sincere about anything in my life. I lay awake at night wondering what else I could possibly do to make her feel I was worthy of her.

As the weeks passed Daphne and I began to take more and more care of Becky, as daily she increasingly resembled a beached whale. There was still no word from India but long before the child was due she had stopped referring to Trentham by name.

When I first saw Daniel I wanted to be his father and was overjoyed when Becky said she hoped I still loved her.

Hoped I still loved her!

We were married a week later with the colonel, Bob Makins and Daphne agreeing to be godparents.

The following summer Daphne and Percy were themselves married, not at Chelsea Register Office but at St Margaret's, Westminster. I watched out for Mrs Trentham just to see what she looked like, but then I remembered that Percy had said she hadn't been invited.

Daniel grew like a weed, and I was touched that one of the first words he repeated again and again was "dad". Despite this I could only wonder how long it would be before we had to sit down and tell the boy the truth. "Bastard" is such a vicious slur for an innocent child to have to live with.

"We don't have to worry about that for some time yet," Becky kept insisting, but it didn't stop me being fearful of the eventual outcome if we remained silent on the subject for much longer, after all some people in the terrace already knew the truth.

Sal wrote from Toronto to congratulate me, as well as to inform me that she herself had stopped having babies. Two girls – Maureen and Babs – and two boys – David and Rex – seemed to her quite enough, even for a good Catholic. Her husband, she wrote, had been promoted to areas sales rep for E.P. Taylor so altogether they seemed to be doing rather well. She never made mention of England in her letters or of any desire to return to the country of her birth. As her only real memories of home must have been sleeping three to a bed, a drunken father and never having enough food for a second helping I couldn't really blame her.

She went on to chastise me for allowing Grace to be a far better letter-writer than I was. I couldn't claim the excuse of work, she added, as being a ward sister in a London teaching hospital left my sister with even less time than I had. After Becky had read the letter and nodded her agreement I made more of an effort over the next few months.

Kitty made periodic visits to Chelsea Terrace, but only with the purpose of talking me out of more money, her demands rising on each occasion. However, she always made certain that Becky was not around whenever she turned up. The sums she extracted, although exorbitant, were always just possible.

I begged Kitty to find a job, even offered her one myself, but she simply explained that she and work didn't seem to get along together. Our conversations rarely lasted for more than a few minutes because as soon as I'd handed over the cash she immediately sloped off. I realised that with every shop I opened it would become harder and harder to convince Kitty that she should settle down, and once Becky and I moved into our new home on Gilston Road her visits only became more frequent.

Despite Syd Wrexall's efforts to thwart my ambition of trying to buy up every shop that became available in the terrace – I was able to get hold of seven before I came across any real opposition – I now had my eyes on Numbers 25 to 99, a block of flats which I intended to purchase without Wrexall ever finding out what I was up to; not to mention my desire to get my hands on Number 1 Chelsea Terrace, which, given its position on the street, remained crucial as part of my long-term plan to own the entire block.

During 1922 everything seemed to be falling neatly into place and I began to look forward to Daphne's return from her honeymoon so I could tell her exactly what I had been up to in her absence.

The week after Daphne arrived back in England she invited us both to dinner at her new home in Eaton Square. I couldn't wait to hear all her news, knowing that she would be impressed to learn that we now owned eight shops, a new home in Gilston Road and at any moment would be adding a block of flats to the Trumper portfolio. However, I knew the question she would ask me as soon as I walked in their front door, so I had my reply ready: "It will take me about another ten years before I own the entire block – as long as you can guarantee no floods, pestilence or the outbreak of war."

Just before Becky and I set out for our reunion dinner an envelope was dropped through the letter-box of 11 Gilston Road.

Even as it lay on the mat I could recognise the bold hand. I ripped it open and began to read the colonel's words. When I had finished the letter I suddenly felt sick and could only wonder why he should want to resign.

CHAPTER 20

Charlie stood alone in the hall and decided not to mention the colonel's letter to Becky until after they had returned from their dinner with Daphne. Becky had been looking forward to the occasion for such a long time that he feared the colonel's unexplained resignation could only put a blight on the rest of the evening.

"You all right, darling?" asked Becky when she reached the bottom of the stairs. "You look a bit pale."

"I'm just fine," said Charlie, nervously tucking the letter into an inside pocket. "Come on or we'll be late, and that would never do." Charlie looked at his wife and noticed that she was wearing the pink dress with a massive bow on the front. He remembered helping her choose it. "You look ravishing," he told her. "That gown will make Daphne green with envy."

"You don't look so bad yourself."

"When I put on one of these penguin suits I always feel like the head waiter of the Ritz," admitted Charlie as Becky straightened his white tie.

"How could you possibly know when you've never been to the Ritz?" she said, laughing.

"At least the outfit came from my own shop this time," Charlie replied as he opened the front door for his wife.

"Ah, but have you paid the bill yet?"

As they drove over to Eaton Square Charlie found it difficult to concentrate on his wife's chatty conversation while he tried to fathom why the colonel could possibly want to resign just at the point when everything was going so well.

"So how do you feel I should go about it?" asked Becky.

"Whichever way you think best," began Charlie.

"You haven't been listening to a word I've said since we left the house, Charlie Trumper. And to think we've been married for two years."

"Sorry," said Charlie, as he parked his little Austin Seven behind the Silver Ghost that stood directly in front of 14 Eaton Square. "Wouldn't mind living here," Charlie added, as he opened the car door for his wife.

"Not quite yet," suggested Becky.

"Why not?"

"I've a feeling that Mr Hadlow might not feel able to sanction the necessary loan."

A butler opened the door for them even before they had reached the top step. "Wouldn't mind one of those either," said Charlie.

"Behave yourself," said Becky.

"Of course," he said. "I must remember my place."

The butler ushered them through to the drawing room where they found Daphne sipping a dry martini.

"Darlings," she said. Becky ran forward and threw her arms around her and they bumped into each other.

"Why didn't you tell me?" said Becky.

"My little secret." Daphne patted her stomach. "Still, you seem to be well ahead of me, as usual."

"Not by that much," said Becky. "So when's yours due?"

"Doctor Gould is predicting some time in January. Clarence if it's a boy, Clarissa if it's a girl."

Her guests both laughed.

"Don't you two dare snigger. Those are the names of Percy's most distinguished ancestors," she told them, just as her husband entered the room.

"True, by Jove," said Percy, "though I'm damned if I can remember what they actually did."

"Welcome home," said Charlie, shaking him by the hand.

"Thank you, Charlie," said Percy, who then kissed Becky on both cheeks. "I don't mind telling you I'm damned pleased to see you again." A servant handed him a whisky and soda. "Now, Becky, tell me everything you've been up to and don't spare me any details."

They sat down together on the sofa as Daphne joined Charlie, who was slowly circling the room studying the large portraits that hung on every wall.

"Percy's ancestors," said Daphne. "All painted by second-rate artists. I'd swap the lot of them for that picture of the Virgin Mary you have in your drawing room."

"Not this one, you wouldn't," said Charlie, as he stopped in front of the second Marquess of Wiltshire.

"Ah, yes, the Holbein," said Daphne. "You're right. But since then I'm afraid it's been downhill all the way."

"I wouldn't begin to know, M'Lady," said Charlie with a grin. "You see, my ancestors didn't go a bundle on portraits. Come to think of it, I don't suppose Holbein was commissioned by that many costermongers from the East End."

Daphne laughed. "That reminds me, Charlie, what's happened to your Cockney accent?"

"What was you 'oping for, Marchioness, a pound ov tomatoes and 'alf a grapefruit, or just a night on the razzle?"

"That's more like it. Mustn't let a few night classes go to our head."

"Shhh," said Charlie, looking over to his wife who was seated on the sofa. "Becky still doesn't know and I'm not saying anything until –"

"I understand," said Daphne. "And I promise you that she won't hear a thing from me. I haven't even told Percy." She glanced towards Becky who was still deep in conversation with her husband. "By the way, how long before – ?"

"Ten years would be my guess," said Charlie, delivering his prepared answer.

"Oh, I thought that these things usually took about

nine months," said Daphne. "Unless of course you're an elephant."

Charlie smiled, realising his mistake. "Another two months would be my guess. Tommy if it's a boy and Debbie if it's a girl. So with a bit of luck whatever Becky delivers let's hope it turns out to be the ideal partner for Clarence or Clarissa."

"A nice idea but the way the world is going at the moment," said Daphne, "I wouldn't be surprised if mine ended up as your sales assistants."

Despite Daphne bombarding him with questions Charlie still couldn't take his eyes off the Holbein. Eventually Daphne bribed him away by saying, "Come on, Charlie, let's go and have something to eat. I always seem to be famished nowadays."

Percy and Becky stood up and followed Daphne and Charlie towards the dining room.

Daphne led her guests down a long corridor and through into another room that was exactly the same size and proportion as the one they had just left. The six full-length canvases that hung from the walls were all by Reynolds. "And this time only the ugly one is a relation," Percy assured them as he took his place at one end of the table and gestured to a long grey figure of a lady that hung on the wall behind him. "And she would have found it exceedingly difficult to land a Wiltshire had she not been accompanied by an extremely handsome dowry."

They took their places at a table that had been laid for four but would have comfortably seated eight, and proceeded to eat a four-course dinner that could have happily fed sixteen. Liveried footmen stood behind each chair to ensure the slightest need was administered to. "Every good home should have one," whispered Charlie across the table to his wife.

The conversation over dinner gave the four of them a chance to catch up with everything that had taken place during the past year. By the time a second coffee had been poured Daphne and Becky left the two men to enjoy a cigar and Charlie couldn't help thinking that it was as if the Wiltshires had never been away in the first place.

"Glad the girls have left us alone," said Percy, "as I feel there is something less pleasant we ought perhaps to touch on."

Charlie puffed away at his first cigar, wondering what it must be like to suffer in this way every day.

"When Daphne and I were in India," Percy continued, "we came across that bounder Trentham." Charlie coughed as some smoke went down the wrong way and began to pay closer attention as his host revealed the conversation that had taken place between Trentham and himself. "His threat that he would 'get you, come what may' could have been no more than an idle boast, of course," said Percy, "but Daphne felt it best that you were put fully in the picture."

"But what can I possibly do about it?" Charlie knocked an extended column of ash into a silver saucer that had been placed in front of him just in time.

"Not a lot, I suspect," said Percy. "Except to remember that forewarned is forearmed. He's expected back in England at any moment, and his mother is now telling anyone who still cares to enquire that Guy was offered such an irresistible appointment in the City that he was willing to sacrifice his commission. I can't imagine that anyone really believes her and anyway most decent-minded people think the City's about the right place for the likes of Trentham."

"Do you think I ought to tell Becky?"

"No, I don't," said Percy. "In fact I never told Daphne about my second encounter with Trentham at the Overseas Club. So why bother Becky with the details? From what I've learned from her this evening she's got quite enough on her plate to be going on with."

"Not to mention the fact that she's about to give birth," added Charlie.

"Exactly," said Percy. "So let's leave it at that for the time being. Now, shall we go and join the ladies?"

Over a large brandy in yet another room filled with

ancestors including a small oil of Bonnie Prince Charlie, Becky listened to Daphne describe the Americans, whom she adored, but felt we should never have given the darlings away; the Africans, whom she considered delightful, but who ought to be given away as soon as was convenient; and the Indians, who she understood couldn't wait to be given away, according to the little man who kept arriving at Government House in a dishcloth.

"Are you by any chance referring to Gandhi?" asked Charlie, as he puffed away more confidently at his cigar. "I find him rather impressive."

On the way back to Gilston Road Becky chatted happily as she revealed all the gossip she had picked up from Daphne. It became obvious to Charlie that the two women had not touched on the subject of Trentham, or the threat he currently posed.

Charlie had a restless night, partly caused by having indulged in too much rich food and alcohol, but mainly because his mind kept switching from why the colonel should want to resign to the problem that had to be faced with Trentham's imminent return to England.

At four o'clock in the morning he rose and donned his oldest clothes before setting off to the market, something he still tried to do at least once a week, convinced there was no one at Trumper's who could work the Garden the way he did, until, quite recently, when a trader at the market called Ned Denning had managed to palm him off with a couple of boxes of overripe avocados and followed it up the next day by pressing Charlie into buying a box of oranges he'd never wanted in the first place. Charlie decided to get up very early on the third day and see if he could have the man removed from his job once and for all.

The following Monday Ned Denning joined Trumper's as the grocery shop's first general manager.

Charlie had a successful morning stocking up with provisions for both 131 and 147 and Bob Makins arrived an hour later to drive him and Ned back to Chelsea Terrace in their newly acquired van.

Once they arrived at the fruit and vegetable shop, Charlie helped unload and lay out the goods before returning home for breakfast a few minutes after seven. He still considered it was a little early to place a phone call through to the colonel.

Cook served him up eggs and bacon for breakfast which he shared with Daniel and his nanny. Becky didn't join them, as she had not yet recovered from the after-effects of Daphne's dinner party.

Charlie happily spent most of breakfast trying to answer Daniel's string of unrelated, never-ending questions until Nanny picked up the protesting child and carried him back upstairs to the playroom. Charlie flicked open the cover of his half-hunter to check the time. Although it was still only a few minutes before eight, he felt he couldn't wait any longer so he walked through to the hall, picked up the stem phone, unhooked the earpiece and asked the operator to connect him with Kensington 1729. A few moments later he was put through.

"Can I have a word with the colonel?"

"I'll tell him you're on the line, Mr Trumper," came back the reply. Charlie was amused by the thought that he was never going to be able to disguise his accent over the telephone.

"Good morning, Charlie," came back another accent that was also immediately recognisable.

"I wonder if I might come round and see you, sir?" Charlie asked.

"Of course," said the colonel. "But could you leave it until ten, old fellow? By then Elizabeth will have gone off to visit her sister in Camden Hill."

"I'll be there at ten on the dot," promised Charlie. After he had put the phone back on the hook, he decided to occupy the two hours by completing a full round of the shops. For a second time that morning and still before Becky had stirred, he left for Chelsea Terrace.

Charlie dug Major Arnold out of hardware before beginning a spot check on all eight establishments. As he passed the block of flats he began to explain in detail to his deputy the plans he had to replace the building with six new shops.

After they had left Number 129, Charlie confided in Arnold that he was worried about wines and spirits, which he considered was still not pulling its weight. This was despite their now being able to take advantage of the new delivery service that had originally been introduced only for fruit and vegetables. Charlie was proud that his was one of the first shops in London to take orders by telephone, then drop off the goods on the same day for account customers. It was another idea he had stolen from the Americans, and the more he read about what his opposite numbers were up to in the States the more he wanted to visit that country and see how they went about it first-hand.

He could still recall his first delivery service when he used his granpa's barrow for transport and Kitty as the delivery girl. Now he ran a smart blue three-horsepower van with the words, "Trumper, the honest trader, founded 1823", emblazoned in blue letters down both sides.

He stopped on the corner of Chelsea Terrace and stared at the one shop that would always dominate Chelsea with its massive bow window and great double door. He knew the time must almost be ripe for him to walk in and offer Mr Fothergill a large cheque to cover the auctioneer's debts: a former employee of Number 1 had recently assured Charlie that his bank balance was overdrawn by more than two thousand pounds.

Charlie marched into Number 1 to pay a far smaller bill and asked the girl behind the counter if they had finished reframing the Virgin Mary and Child, which was already three weeks overdue.

He didn't complain about the delay as it gave him another excuse to nose around. The paper was still peeling off the wall behind the reception area, and there was only one girl assistant left at the desk, which suggested to Charlie that the weekly wages were not always being met.

Mr Fothergill eventually appeared with the picture in

its new gilt frame and handed the little oil over to Charlie.

"Thank you," said Charlie as he once again studied the bold brushwork of reds and blues that made up the portrait and realised just how much he had missed it.

"Wonder what it's worth?" he asked Fothergill casually as he passed over a ten-shilling note.

"A few pounds at the most," the expert declared as he touched his bow tie. "After all, you can find countless examples of the subject by unknown artists right across the continent of Europe."

"I wonder," said Charlie as he checked his watch and stuffed the receipt into his pocket. He had allowed himself sufficient time for a relaxed walk across Princess Gardens and on to the colonel's residence, expecting to arrive a couple of minutes before ten. He bade Mr Fothergill "Good morning," and left.

Although it was still quite early, the pavements in Chelsea were already bustling with people and Charlie raised his hat to several customers he recognised.

"Good morning, Mr Trumper."

"Good morning, Mrs Symonds," said Charlie as he crossed the road to take a short cut through the garden.

He began to try and compose in his mind what he would say to the colonel once he'd discovered why the chairman felt it had been necessary to offer his resignation. Whatever the reason, Charlie was determined not to lose the old soldier. He closed the park gate behind him and started to walk along the man-made path.

He stood aside to allow a lady pushing a pram to pass him and gave a mock salute to an old soldier sitting on a park bench rolling a Woodbine. Once he had crossed the tiny patch of grass, he stepped into the Gilston Road, closing the gate behind him.

Charlie continued his walk towards Tregunter Road and began to quicken his pace. He smiled as he passed his little home, quite forgetting he still had the picture under his arm, his mind still preoccupied with the reason for the colonel's resignation.

Charlie turned immediately he heard the scream and a door slam somewhere behind him, more as a reflex than from any genuine desire to see what was going on. He stopped in his tracks as he watched a dishevelled figure dash out on to the road and then start running towards him.

Charlie stood mesmerised as the tramp-like figure drew closer and closer until the man came to a sudden halt only a few feet in front of him. For a matter of seconds the two men stood and stared at each other without uttering a word. Neither ruffian nor gentleman showed on a face half-obscured by rough stubble. And then recognition was quickly followed by disbelief.

Charlie couldn't accept that the unshaven, slovenly figure who stood before him wearing an old army greatcoat and a battered felt hat was the same man he had first seen on a station in Edinburgh some five years before.

Charlie's abiding memory of that moment was to be the three clean circles on both epaulettes of Trentham's greatcoat from which the three pips of a captain must recently have been removed.

Trentham's eyes dropped as he stared at the painting for a second and then suddenly, without warning, he lunged at Charlie, taking him by surprise, and wrested the picture from his grasp. He turned and started running back down the road in the direction he had come. Charlie immediately set off in pursuit and quickly began to make up ground on his assailant who was impeded by his heavy greatcoat, while having also to cling on to the picture.

Charlie was within a yard of his quarry and about to make a dive for Trentham's waist when he heard the second scream. He hesitated for a moment as he realised the desperate cry must be coming from his own home. He knew he had been left with no choice but to allow Trentham to escape with the picture as he changed direction and dashed up the steps of Number 11. He charged on into the drawing room to find the cook and nanny standing over Becky. She was lying flat out on the sofa screaming with pain.

Becky's eyes lit up when she saw Charlie. "The baby's coming," was all she said.

"Pick her up gently, Cook," said Charlie, "and help me get her to the car."

Together they carried Becky out of the house and down the path as Nanny ran ahead of them to open the car door so they could place her on the back seat. Charlie stared down at his wife. Her face was drained of colour and her eyes were glazed. She appeared to lose consciousness as he closed the car door.

Charlie jumped into the front of the car and shouted at Cook, who was already turning the handle to get the engine started.

"Ring my sister at Guy's hospital and explain we're on our way. And tell her to be prepared for an emergency."

The motor spluttered into action and Cook jumped to one side as Charlie drove the car out into the middle of the road, trying to keep a steady pace as he avoided pedestrians, bicycles, trams, horses and other cars as he crashed through the gears on his journey south towards the Thames.

He turned his head every few seconds to stare at his wife, not even sure if she were still alive. "Let them both live," he shouted at the top of his voice. He continued on down the Embankment as fast as he could manage, honking his horn and several times screaming at people who were casually crossing the road unaware of his plight. As he drove across Southwark Bridge he heard Becky groan for the first time.

"We'll soon be there, my darling," he promised. "Just hold on a little longer."

Once over the bridge he took the first left and maintained his speed until the great iron gates of Guy's came into view. As he swung into the courtyard and round the circular flower-bed he spotted Grace and two men in long white coats standing waiting, a stretcher by their side. Charlie brought the car to a halt almost on their toes.

The two men lifted Becky gently out and placed her on the stretcher before rushing her up the ramp and into the hospital. Charlie jumped out of the car and marched by the stretcher, holding Becky's hand as they climbed a flight of stairs, Grace running by his side explaining that Mr Armitage, the hospital's senior obstetrician, was waiting for them in an operating theatre on the first floor.

By the time Charlie reached the door of the theatre, Becky was already inside. They left him outside in the corridor on his own. He began to pace up and down, unaware of others bustling past him as they went about their work.

Grace came out a few minutes later to reassure him that Mr Armitage had everything under control and that Becky could not be in better hands. The baby was expected at any moment. She squeezed her brother's hand, then disappeared back into the theatre. Charlie continued his pacing, thinking only of his wife and their first child, the sight of Trentham already becoming a blur. He prayed for a boy, Tommy, who would be a brother for Daniel and perhaps one day even take over Trumper's. Pray God that Becky was not going through too much pain as she delivered their son. He paced on up and down that long green-walled corridor mumbling to himself, aware once again how much he loved her.

It was to be another hour before a tall, thickset man emerged from behind the closed doors, followed by Grace. Charlie turned to face them but as the surgeon had a mask over his face he had no way of knowing how the operation had gone. Mr Armitage removed the mask: the expression on his face answered Charlie's silent prayer.

"I managed to save your wife's life," he said, "but I am so very sorry, Mr Trumper, I could do nothing about your stillborn daughter."

CHAPTER 21

For several days after the operation Becky never left her room in the hospital.

Charlie later learned from Grace that although Mr Armitage had saved his wife's life it might still be weeks before she was fully recovered, especially since it had been explained to Becky that she could never have another child without risking her own life.

Charlie visited her every morning and evening, but it was over a fortnight before she was able to tell her husband how Guy Trentham had forced his way into the house and then threatened to kill her unless she told him where the picture was.

"Why? I simply can't understand why," said Charlie.

"Has the picture turned up anywhere?"

"No sign of it so far," he said, just as Daphne came in bearing a huge basket of provisions. She kissed Becky on the cheek before confirming that the fruit had been purchased at Trumper's that morning. Becky managed a smile as she munched her way through a peach. Daphne sat on the end of the bed and immediately launched into all her latest news.

She was able to let them know, following one of her periodic visits to the Trenthams, that Guy had disappeared off to Australia and that his mother was claiming he had never set foot in England in the first place, but travelled to Sydney direct from India.

"Via the Gilston Road," said Charlie.

"That's not what the police think," said Daphne.

"They remain convinced that he left England in 1920 and they can find no proof he ever returned."

"Well, we're certainly not going to enlighten them," said Charlie, taking his wife's hand.

"Why not?" asked Daphne.

"Because even I consider Australia far enough away for Trentham to be left to his own devices: in any case nothing can be gained from pursuing him now. If the Australians give him enough rope I'm sure he'll hang himself."

"But why Australia?" asked Becky.

"Mrs Trentham's telling everyone who cares to listen that Guy has been offered a partnership in a cattle brokers – far too good a position to turn down, even if it did mean having to resign his commission. The vicar is the only person I can find who believes the story." But even Daphne had no simple answer as to why Trentham should have been so keen to get his hands on the little oil painting.

The colonel and Elizabeth also visited Becky on several occasions and as he continually talked of the company's future and never once referred to his resignation letter, Charlie didn't press him on the subject.

It was to be Crowther who eventually enlightened Charlie as to who had purchased the flats.

Six weeks later Charlie drove his wife home to Gilston Road – at a more stately pace – Mr Armitage having suggested a quiet month resting before she considered returning to work. Charlie promised the surgeon that he would not allow Becky to do anything until he felt sure she had fully recovered.

The morning Becky returned home Charlie left her propped up in bed with a book and headed back to Chelsea Terrace where he went straight to the jewellery shop he had acquired in his wife's absence.

Charlie took a considerable time selecting a string of cultured pearls, a gold bracelet and a lady's Victorian watch, which he then instructed to be sent to Grace, to the staff nurse and to the nurse who had taken care of Becky during her unscheduled stay at Guy's. His next stop was the greengrocer's shop where he asked Bob to make up a basket of the finest fruit, while he personally selected a bottle of vintage wine from Number 101 to accompany it. "Send them both round to Mr Armitage at 7 Cadogan Square, London SW1, with my compliments," he added.

"Right away," said Bob. "Anything else while I'm at it?"

"Yes, I want you to repeat that order every Monday for the rest of his life."

It was about a month later in November 1922 that Charlie learned of the problems Arnold was facing with the simple task of replacing a shop assistant. In fact, selecting staff had become one of Arnold's biggest headaches of late, because for every job that became vacant fifty to a hundred people were applying to fill it. Arnold would then put together a shortlist as Charlie still insisted that it was he who interviewed the final candidates before any position was confirmed.

On that particular Monday, Arnold had already considered a number of girls for the position as sales assistant at the flower shop, following the retirement of one of the company's longest-serving employees.

"Although I've already shortlisted three for the job," said Arnold, "I thought you would be interested in one of the applicants I rejected. She didn't seem to have the appropriate qualifications for this particular position. However –"

Charlie glanced at the sheet of paper Arnold passed to him. "Joan Moore. Why would I – ?" began Charlie, as his eyes ran swiftly down her application. "Ah, I see," he said. "How very observant of you, Tom." He read a few more lines. "But I don't need a – well, on the other hand perhaps I do." He looked up. "Arrange for me to see Miss Moore within the next week."

The following Thursday Charlie interviewed Joan Moore for over an hour at his home in Gilston Road and his first impression was of a cheery, well-mannered if somewhat immature girl. However, before he offered her the position as lady's maid to Mrs Trumper he still had a couple of questions he felt needed answering.

"Did you apply for this job because you knew of the relationship between my wife and your former employer?" Charlie asked.

The girl looked him straight in the eyes. "Yes, sir, I did."

"And were you sacked by your previous employer?"

"Not exactly, sir, but when I left she refused to supply me with a reference."

"What reason did she give for that?"

"I was walkin' out with the second footman, 'aving failed to inform the butler who is in charge of the 'ousehold."

"And are you still walking out with the second footman?"

The girl hesitated. "Yes, sir," she said. "You see, we're 'oping to be married as soon as we've saved up enough."

"Good," said Charlie. "Then you can report for duty next Monday morning. Mr Arnold will deal with all the necessary arrangements."

When Charlie told Becky he had employed a lady's maid for her she laughed at first, then asked, "And what would I want with one of those?" Charlie told her exactly why she wanted "one of those". When he had finished all Becky said was, "You're an evil man, Charlie Trumper, that's for sure."

It was at the February board meeting in 1924 that Crowther warned his colleagues that Number 1 Chelsea Terrace might well come on the market earlier than anticipated.

"Why's that?" asked Charlie, a little anxiously.

"Your estimate of another two years before Fothergill would have to cave in is beginning to look prophetic."

"So how much does he want?"

"It's not quite as simple as that."

"Why not?"

"Because he's decided to auction the property himself."

"Auction it?" enquired Becky.

"Yes," said Crowther. "That way he avoids paying any fees to an outside agent."

"I see. So what are you expecting the property to fetch?" asked the colonel.

"Not an easy one to answer, that," replied Crowther. "It's four times the size of any other shop in the terrace, it's on five floors and it's even bigger than Syd Wrexall's pub on the other corner. It also has the largest shop frontage in Chelsea and a double entrance on the corner facing the Fulham Road. For all those reasons it's not that simple to estimate its value."

"Even so, could you try and put a figure on it?" asked the chairman.

"If you were to press me I'd say somewhere in the region of two thousand, but it could be as much as three, if anyone else were to show an interest."

"What about the stock?" asked Becky. "Do we know what's happening to that?"

"Yes, it's being sold along with the building."

"And what's it worth?" asked Charlie. "Roughly?"

"More Mrs Trumper's department than mine, I feel," said Crowther.

"It's no longer that impressive," said Becky. "A lot of Fothergill's best works have already gone through Sotheby's, and I suspect Christie's have seen just as many during the past year. However, I would still expect what's left over to fetch around a thousand pounds under the hammer."

"So the face value of the property and the stock together appears to be around the three thousand pound mark," suggested Hadlow.

"But Number 1 will go for a lot more than that," said Charlie.

"Why?" queried Hadlow.

"Because Mrs Trentham will be among the bidders."

"How can you be so sure?" asked the chairman.

"Because our lady's maid is still walking out with her second footman."

The rest of the board laughed, but all the chairman volunteered was, "Not again. First the flats, now this. When will it end?"

"Not until she's dead and buried, I suspect," said Charlie.

"Perhaps not even then," added Becky.

"If you're referring to the son," said the colonel, "I doubt if he can cause too much trouble from twelve thousand miles away. But as for the mother, hell hath no fury –" he said testily.

"Commonly misquoted," said Charlie.

"What's that?" asked the chairman.

"Congreve, Colonel. The lines run, 'Heav'n has no rage, like love to hatred turn'd, Nor Hell a fury, like a woman scorn'd.'" The Colonel's mouth remained open but he was speechless. "However," Charlie continued, "more to the point, I need to know what is the limit the board will allow me to bid for Number 1."

"I consider five thousand may well prove necessary given the circumstances," said Becky.

"But no more," said Hadlow, studying the balance sheet in front of him.

"Perhaps one bid over?" suggested Becky.

"I'm sorry, I don't understand," said Hadlow. "What does 'one bid over' mean?"

"Bids never go to the exact figure you anticipate, Mr Hadlow. Most people who attend an auction usually have a set figure in their minds which inevitably ends in round numbers, so if you go one above that figure you often end up securing the lot."

Even Charlie nodded, as Hadlow said in admiration, "Then I agree to one bid over."

"May I also suggest," said the colonel, "that Mrs Trumper should carry out the bidding, because with her experience –"

"That's kind of you, Colonel, but I shall nevertheless need the help of my husband," said Becky with a smile. "And, in fact, the whole board's, come to that. You see, I have already formulated a plan." She proceeded to brief her colleagues on what she had in mind.

"What fun," said the colonel when she had finished. "But will I also be allowed to attend the proceedings?"

"Oh, yes," said Becky. "All of you must be present, and, with the exception of Charlie and myself, you ought to be seated silently in the row directly behind Mrs Trentham a few minutes before the auction is due to commence."

"Bloody woman," said the colonel, before adding hastily, "I do apologise."

"True. But, more important, we must never forget that she is also an amateur," Becky added.

"What's the significance of that statement?" asked Hadlow.

"Sometimes amateurs get carried away by the occasion, and when that happens the professionals have no chance because the amateur often ends up going one bid too far. We must remember that it may well be the first auction Mrs Trentham has ever placed a bid at, even attended, and as she wants the premises every bit as much as we do, and has the advantage of superior resources, we will have to secure the lot by sheer cunning." No one seemed to disagree with this assessment.

Once the board meeting was over Becky took Charlie through her plan for the forthcoming auction in greater detail, and even made him attend Sotheby's one morning with orders to bid for three pieces of Dutch silver. He carried out his wife's instructions but ended up with a Georgian mustard pot he had never intended to buy in the first place.

"No better way of learning," Becky assured him. "Just be thankful that it wasn't a Rembrandt you were bidding for."

She continued to explain to Charlie the subtleties of auctions over dinner that night in far greater detail than she had with the board. Charlie learned that there were different signs you could give the auctioneer, so that rivals remained unaware that you were still bidding, while at the same time you could discover who was bidding against you.

"But isn't Mrs Trentham bound to spot you?" said Charlie after he had cut his wife a slice of bread. "After all, you'll be the only two left bidding by that stage."

"Not if you've already put her off balance before I enter the fray," said Becky.

"But the board agreed that you . . ."

"That I should be allowed to go one bid over five thousand."

"But –"

"No buts, Charlie," said Becky as she served her husband up another portion of Irish stew. "On the morning of the auction I want you on parade, dressed in your best suit and sitting in the seventh row on the gangway looking very pleased with yourself. You will then proceed to bid ostentatiously up to one over three thousand pounds. When Mrs Trentham goes to the next bid, as undoubtedly she will, you must stand up and flounce out of the room, looking defeated, while I continue the bidding in your absence."

"Not bad," said Charlie as he put his fork into a couple of peas. "But surely Mrs Trentham will work out exactly what you're up to?"

"Not a chance," said Becky. "Because I will have an agreed code with the auctioneer that she could never hope to spot, let alone to decipher."

"But will *I* understand what you are up to?"

"Oh, yes," said Becky, "because you'll know exactly what I'm doing when I use the glasses ploy."

"The glasses ploy? But you don't even wear glasses."

"I will be on the day of the auction, and when I'm wearing them you'll know I'm still bidding. If I take them off, I've finished bidding. So when you leave the room all the auctioneer will see when he looks in my direction is that I still have my glasses on. Mrs Trentham will think you've gone, and will, I suspect, be quite happy to let someone else continue with the bidding so long as she's confident they don't represent you."

"You're a gem, Mrs Trumper," said Charlie as he rose to clear away the plates. "But what if she sees you chatting to the auctioneer or, worse, finds out your code even before Mr Fothergill calls for the first bid?"

"She can't," said Becky. "I'll agree the code with Fothergill only minutes before the auction begins. In any case, it will be at that moment that you will make a grand entrance, and then only seconds after the other members of the board have taken their seats directly behind Mrs Trentham, so with a bit of luck she'll be so distracted by everything that's going on around her that she won't even notice me."

"I married a very clever girl," said Charlie.

"You never admitted as much when we were at Jubilee Street Elementary."

On the morning of the auction, Charlie confessed over breakfast that he was very nervous, despite Becky's appearing to be remarkably calm, especially after Joan had informed her mistress that the second footman had heard from the cook that Mrs Trentham had placed a limit of four thousand pounds on her bidding.

"I just wonder . . ." said Charlie.

"Whether she planted the sum in the cook's mind?" said Becky. "It's possible. After all, she's every bit as cunning as you are. But as long as we stick to our agreed plan – and remember everyone, even Mrs Trentham, has a limit – we can still beat her."

The auction was advertised to begin at ten a.m. A full twenty minutes before the bidding was due to commence Mrs Trentham entered the room and swept regally down the aisle. She took her place in the centre of the third row, and placed her handbag on one seat and a catalogue on the other to be certain that no one sat next to her. The colonel and his two colleagues entered the half-filled room at nine-fifty a.m. and, as instructed, filed into the seats immediately behind their adversary. Mrs Trentham appeared to show no interest in their presence. Five minutes later Charlie made his entrance. He strolled down the centre aisle, raised his hat to a lady he recognised, shook hands with one of his regular customers and finally took his place on the gangway at the end of the seventh row. He continued to chat noisily with his next-door neighbour about England's tour of Australia, explaining once again that he was not related to the great Australian batsman whose name he bore. The minute hand on the grandfather clock behind the auctioneer's box moved slowly towards the appointed hour.

Although the room was not much larger than Daphne's hall in Eaton Square, they had still somehow managed to pack in over a hundred chairs of different shapes and sizes. The walls were covered in a faded green baize that displayed several hook marks where pictures must have hung in the past and the carpet had become so threadbare that Charlie could see the floorboards in places. He began to feel that the cost of bringing Number 1 up to the standard he expected for all Trumper's shops was going to be greater than he had originally anticipated.

Glancing around, he estimated that over seventy people were now seated in the auction house, and wondered just how many had no interest in bidding themselves but had simply come to see the showdown between the Trumpers and Mrs Trentham.

Syd Wrexall, as the representative of the Shops Committee, was already in the front row, arms folded, trying to look composed, his vast bulk almost taking up two seats. Charlie suspected that he wouldn't go much beyond the second or third bid. He soon spotted Mrs Trentham seated in the third row, her gaze fixed directly on the grandfather clock.

Then, with two minutes to spare, Becky slipped into the auction house. Charlie was sitting on the edge of his seat waiting to carry out his instructions to the letter. He rose from his place and walked purposefully towards the exit. This time Mrs Trentham did glance round to see what Charlie was up to. Innocently he collected another bill of sale from the back of the room, then returned to his seat at a leisurely pace, stopping to talk to another shop owner who had obviously taken an hour off to watch the proceedings.

When Charlie returned to his place he didn't look in the direction of his wife, who he knew must now be hidden somewhere towards the back of the room. Nor did he once look at Mrs Trentham, although he could feel her eyes fixed on him.

As the clock chimed ten, Mr Fothergill – a tall thin man with a flower in his buttonhole and not a hair of his silver locks out of place – climbed the four steps of the circular wooden box. Charlie thought he looked an impressive figure as he towered over them. As soon as he had composed himself he rested a hand on the rim of the box and beamed at the packed audience, picked up his gavel and said, "Good morning, ladies and gentlemen." A silence fell over the room.

"This is a sale of the property known as Number 1, Chelsea Terrace, its fixtures, fittings and contents, which have been on view to the general public for the past two weeks. The highest bidder will be required to make a deposit of ten per cent immediately following the auction, then complete the final transaction within ninety days. Those are the terms as stated on your bill of sale, and I repeat them only so that there can be no misunderstanding."

Mr Fothergill cleared his throat and Charlie could feel his heart beat faster and faster. He watched the colonel clench a fist as Becky removed a pair of glasses out of her bag and placed them in her lap.

"I have an opening bid of one thousand pounds," Fothergill told the silent audience, many of whom were standing at the side of the room or leaning against the wall as there were now few seats vacant. Charlie kept his eyes fixed on the auctioneer. Mr Fothergill smiled in the direction of Mr Wrexall, whose arms remained folded in an attitude of determined resolution. "Do I see any advance on one thousand?"

"One thousand, five hundred," said Charlie, just a little too loudly. Those not involved in the intrigue looked around to see who it was who had made the bid. Several turned to their neighbours and began talking in noisy whispers.

"One thousand, five hundred," said the auctioneer. "Do I see two thousand?" Mr Wrexall unfolded his arms and raised a hand like a child in school determined to prove he knows the answer to one of teacher's questions.

"Two thousand, five hundred," said Charlie, even before Wrexall had lowered his hand.

"Two thousand, five hundred in the centre of the room. Do I see three thousand?"

Mr Wrexall's hand rose an inch from his knee, then fell back. A deep frown formed on his face. "Do I see three thousand?" Mr Fothergill asked for a second time. Charlie couldn't believe his luck. He was going to get Number 1 for two thousand, five hundred. Each second felt like a minute as he waited for the hammer to come down.

"Do I hear three thousand bid anywhere in the room?" said Mr Fothergill, sounding a little disappointed. "Then I am offering Number 1 Chelsea Terrace at two thousand, five hundred pounds for the first time . . ." Charlie held his breath. "For the second time." The auctioneer started to raise his gavel ". . . Three thousand pounds," Mr Fothergill announced with an audible sigh of relief, as Mrs Trentham's gloved hand settled back in her lap.

"Three thousand, five hundred," said Charlie as Mr Fothergill smiled in his direction, but as soon as he looked back towards Mrs Trentham she nodded to the auctioneer's enquiry of four thousand pounds.

Charlie allowed a second or two to pass before he stood up, straightened his tie and, looking grim, walked slowly down the centre of the aisle and out on to the street. He didn't see Becky put her glasses on, or the look of triumph that came over Mrs Trentham's face. "Do I see four thousand, five hundred pounds?" asked the auctioneer, and with only a glance towards where Becky was seated he said, "I do."

Fothergill returned to Mrs Trentham and asked, "Five thousand pounds, madam?" Her eyes quickly searched round the room, but it became obvious for all to see that she couldn't work out where the last bid had come from. Murmurs started to turn into chatter as everyone in the auction house began the game of searching for the bidder. Only Becky, safely in her back row seat, didn't move a muscle.

"Quiet, please," said the auctioneer. "I have a bid of four thousand, five hundred pounds. Do I see five thousand anywhere in the room?" His gaze returned to Mrs Trentham. She raised her hand slowly, but as she did so swung quickly round to see if she could spot who was bidding against her. But no one had moved when the auctioneer said, "Five thousand, five hundred. I now have a bid of five thousand, five hundred." Mr Fothergill surveyed his audience. "Are there any more bids?" He looked in Mrs Trentham's direction, but she in turn looked baffled, her hands motionless in her lap.

"Then it's five thousand, five hundred for the first time," said Mr Fothergill. "Five thousand, five hundred for a second time" – Becky pursed her lips to stop herself from breaking into a large grin – "and for a third and final time," he said, raising his gavel.

"Six thousand," said Mrs Trentham clearly, while at the same time waving her hand. A gasp went up around the room: Becky removed her glasses with a sigh, realising that her carefully worked-out ploy had failed even though Mrs Trentham had been made to pay triple the price any shop in the terrace had fetched in the past.

The auctioneer's eyes returned to the back of the room but the glasses were now clasped firmly in Becky's hand, so he transferred his gaze back to Mrs Trentham, who sat bolt upright, a smile of satisfaction on her face.

"At six thousand for the first time," said the auctioneer, his eyes searching the room. "Six thousand for the second time then, if there are no more bids, it's six thousand for the last time . . ." Once again the gavel was raised.

"Seven thousand pounds," said a voice from the back of the room. Everyone turned to see that Charlie had returned and was now standing in the aisle, his right hand high in the air.

The colonel looked round, and when he saw who the new bidder was began to perspire, something he didn't like to do in public. He removed a handkerchief from his top pocket and mopped his brow.

"I have a bid of seven thousand pounds," said a surprised Mr Fothergill.

"Eight thousand," said Mrs Trentham, staring straight at Charlie belligerently.

"Nine thousand," barked back Charlie.

The chatter in the room quickly turned into a babble. Becky wanted to jump up and push her husband back out into the street.

"Quiet, please," said Mr Fothergill. "Quiet!" he pleaded, almost shouting. The colonel was still mopping his brow, Mr Crowther's mouth was open wide enough to have caught any passing fly and Mr Hadlow's head was firmly buried in his hands.

"Ten thousand," said Mrs Trentham, who Becky could see, like her husband, was now totally out of control.

The auctioneer asked, "Do I see eleven thousand?"

Charlie had a worried look on his face but he simply wrinkled his brow, shook his head and placed his hands back in his pocket.

Becky sighed with relief and, unclasping her hands, nervously put her glasses back on.

"Eleven thousand," said Mr Fothergill, looking towards Becky, while pandemonium broke out once again as she rose to protest, having quickly removed her glasses. Charlie looked totally bemused.

Mrs Trentham's eyes had now come to rest on Becky, whom she had finally located. With a smile of satisfaction Mrs Trentham declared, "Twelve thousand pounds."

The auctioneer looked back towards Becky, who had placed her glasses in her bag and closed the catch with a snap. He glanced towards Charlie whose hands remained firmly in his pockets.

"The bid is at the front of the room at twelve thousand pounds. Is anyone else bidding?" asked the auctioneer.

Once again his eyes darted from Becky to Charlie before returning to Mrs Trentham. "Then at twelve thousand for the first time" – he looked around once more – "for the second time, for the third and final time . . ." His gavel came down with a thud. "I declare the property sold for twelve thousand pounds to Mrs Gerald Trentham."

Becky ran towards the door, but Charlie was already out on the pavement.

"What were you playing at, Charlie?" she demanded even before she caught up with him.

"I knew she would bid up to ten thousand pounds," said Charlie, "because that's the amount she still has on deposit at her bank."

"But how could you possibly know that?"

"Mrs Trentham's second footman passed on the information to me this morning. He will, by the way, be joining us as our butler."

At that moment the chairman walked out on to the pavement. "I must say, Rebecca, your plan was brilliant. Had me completely fooled."

"Me too," said Charlie.

"You took an awful risk, Charlie Trumper," said Becky, not letting her husband off the hook.

"Perhaps, but at least I knew what her limit was. I had no idea what you were playing at."

"I made a genuine mistake," said Becky. "When I put my glasses back on . . . what are you laughing at, Charlie Trumper?"

"Thank God for genuine amateurs."

"What do you mean?"

"Mrs Trentham thought you really were bidding, and she had been tricked, so she went one bid too far. In fact, she wasn't the only one who was carried away by the occasion. I even begin to feel sorry for –"

"For Mrs Trentham?"

"Certainly not," said Charlie. "For Mr Fothergill. He's about to spend ninety days in heaven before he comes down to earth with an almighty thump."

MRS TRENTHAM

1919-1927

CHAPTER 22

I don't believe anyone could describe me as a snob. However, I do believe that the maxim, "There's a place for everything, and everything in its place" applies equally well to human beings.

I was born in Yorkshire at the height of the Victorian Empire, and I think I can safely say that during that period in our island's history my family played a considerable role.

My father, Sir Raymond Hardcastle, was not only an inventor and industrialist of great imagination and skill, but he also built up one of the nation's most successful companies. At the same time he always treated his workers as if they were all part of the family, and indeed it was this example that he set, whenever he dealt with those less fortunate than himself, that has been the benchmark by which I have attempted to conduct my own life.

I have no brothers and just one elder sister, Amy. Although there were only a couple of years between us I cannot pretend that we were ever particularly close, perhaps because I was an outgoing, even vivacious child, while she was shy and reserved, to the point of being retiring, particularly whenever it came to contact with members of the opposite sex. Father and I tried to help her find an appropriate spouse, but it was to prove an impossible task, and even he gave up once Amy had passed her fortieth birthday. Instead she has usefully occupied her time since my mother's untimely death taking care of my beloved father in his old age – an arrangement, I might add, that has suited them both admirably.

I, on the other hand, had no problem in finding myself a husband. If I remember correctly, Gerald was the fourth or perhaps even the fifth suitor who went down on bended knee to ask for my hand in marriage. Gerald and I first met when I had been a house guest at Lord and Lady Fanshaw's country home in Norfolk. The Fanshaws were old friends of my father, and I had been seeing their younger son Anthony for some considerable time. As it turned out, I was warned that he was not going to inherit his father's land or title, so it seemed to me there was little purpose in letting the young man entertain any hopes of a lasting relationship. If I remember correctly, Father was not overwhelmed with my conduct and may even have chastised me at the time, but as I tried to explain to him, at length, although Gerald may not have been the most dashing of my paramours, he did have the distinct advantage of coming from a family that farmed land in three counties, not to mention an estate in Aberdeen.

We were married at St Mary's, Great Ashton, in July 1894 and our first son, Guy, was conceived a year later; one does like a proper period of time to elapse before one's firstborn takes his place in the world, thus giving no one cause for idle chatter.

My father always treated both my sister and myself as equals, although I was often given to believe that I was his favourite. Had it not been for his sense of fair play he would surely have left everything to me, because he simply doted on Guy, whereas in fact Amy will, on my father's demise, inherit half his vast fortune. Heaven knows what possible use she could make of such wealth, her only interests in life being gardening, crochet work and the occasional visit to the Scarborough festival.

But to return to Guy, everyone who came into contact with the boy during those formative years invariably commented on what a handsome child he was, and although I never allowed him to become spoilt, I did consider it nothing less than my duty to ensure that he was given the sort of start in life that would prepare him for the role I felt confident he was bound eventually to play. With that in mind, even before he'd been christened, he was registered with Aysgarth Preparatory School, and then Harrow, from where I assumed he would enter the Royal Military Academy. His grandfather spared no expense when it came to his education, and indeed, in the case of his elder grandson, was generous to a fault.

Six years later I gave birth to a second son, Nigel, who arrived somewhat prematurely, which may account for why he took rather longer to progress than his elder brother. Guy, meanwhile, was going through several private tutors, one or two of whom found him perhaps a little too boisterous. After all, what child doesn't at some time put toads in your bathwater or cut shoe-laces in half?

At the age of nine Guy duly proceeded to Aysgarth, and from there on to Harrow. The Reverend Prebendary Anthony Wood was his headmaster at the time and I reminded him that Guy was the seventh generation of Trenthams to have attended that school.

While at Harrow Guy excelled both in the combined cadet force – becoming a company sergeant-major in his final year – and in the boxing ring, where he beat every one of his opponents with the notable exception of the match against Radley, where he came up against a Nigerian, who I later learned was in his mid-twenties.

It saddened me that during his last term at school Guy was not made a monitor. I understood that he had become involved in so many other activities that it was not considered to be in his own best interests. Although

I might have hoped that his exam results would have been a little more satisfactory, I have always considered that he was one of those children who can be described as innately intelligent rather than academically clever. Despite a rather biased housemaster's report that suggested some of the marks Guy had been awarded in his final exams came as a surprise to him, my son still managed to secure his place at Sandhurst.

At the Academy Guy proved to be a first-class cadet and also found time to continue with his boxing, becoming the cadet middleweight champion. Two years later, in July 1916, he passed out in the top half of the Roll of Honour before going on to join his father's old regiment.

Gerald, I should point out, had left the Fusiliers on the death of his father in order that he might return to Berkshire and take over the running of the family estates. He had been a brevet colonel at the time of his forced retirement, and many considered that he was the natural successor to be the Commanding Officer of the Regiment. As it turned out, he was passed over for someone who wasn't even in the first battalion, a certain Danvers Hamilton. Although I had never met the gentleman in question, several brother officers expressed the view that his appointment had been a travesty of justice. However, I had every confidence that Guy would redeem the family honour and in time go on to command the regiment himself.

Although Gerald was not directly involved in the Great War he did nevertheless serve his country during those arduous years by allowing his name to be put forward as a parliamentary candidate for Berkshire West, a constituency that in the middle of the last century his grandfather had represented for the Liberals under Palmerston. He was returned unopposed in three elections and worked for his party diligently from the back benches, having made it clear to all concerned that he had no desire to hold office.

After Guy had received the King's Commission, he was despatched to Aldershot as a second lieutenant where he continued with his training in preparation for joining the regiment on the Western Front. On being awarded his second pip in less than a year he was transferred to Edinburgh and seconded to the second battalion a few weeks before they were ordered to sail for France.

Nigel, meanwhile, had just entered Harrow and was attempting to follow in his brother's footsteps – I fear, however, not with quite the same obvious flair. In fact during one of those interminable holidays they will give children nowadays he complained to me of being bullied. I told the boy to buckle down and remember that we were at war. I also pointed out that I could never recall Guy making a fuss on that particular score.

I watched my two sons closely during that long summer of 1917 and cannot pretend that Guy found Nigel an amiable companion while he was at home on leave; in fact he barely tolerated his company. I kept telling Nigel that he had to strive to gain his elder brother's respect, but this only resulted in Nigel running off to hide in the garden for hours on end.

During his leave that summer I advised Guy to visit his grandfather in Yorkshire and even found a first edition of *Songs of Innocence* to present him with, which I knew my father had long wanted to add to his collection. Guy returned a week later and confirmed that securing a William Blake the old man did not have had indeed put Granpa "in good salts".

Naturally, like any mother, during that particular inspiring period in our history I became anxious that Guy should be seen to acquit himself well in the face of the enemy, and eventually, God willing, return home in one piece. As it turned out, I think I can safely say that no mother, however proud, could have asked for more of a son.

Guy was promoted to the rank of captain at a very young age and, following the second battle of the Marne, was awarded the Military Cross. Others who read the citation felt he had been a touch unlucky not to have been put forward for the VC. I have resisted pointing out to them that any such recommendation would have had to be countersigned by his commanding officer in the field, and as he was a certain Danvers Hamilton, the injustice was readily explicable.

Soon after the Armistice was signed Guy returned home to serve a tour of duty at the Regimental Barracks in Hounslow. While he was on leave I asked Spink's to engrave both of his MCs, dress and miniature, with the initials G.F.T. Meanwhile, his brother Nigel was, after some influence being exercised by Gerald, finally accepted as a cadet at the Royal Military Academy.

During the time Guy was back in London, I feel certain he sowed a few wild oats – what young man of that age doesn't? – but he well understood that marriage before the age of thirty could only harm his chances of promotion.

Although he brought several young ladies down to Ashurst at the weekends, I knew none of them was serious and anyway, I already had my eye on a particular girl from the next village who had been known to the family for some considerable time. Despite being without a title she could trace her family back to the Norman Conquest. More important, they could walk on their own land from Ashurst to Hastings.

It thus came as a particularly unpleasant shock for me when Guy turned up one weekend accompanied by a girl called Rebecca Salmon, who, I found it hard to believe, was at that time sharing rooms with the Harcourt-Brownes' daughter.

As I have already made abundantly clear, I am not a snob. But Miss Salmon is, I fear, the type of girl who always manages to bring out the worst in me. Don't misunderstand me. I have nothing against anyone simply because they wish to be educated. In fact I'm basically in favour of such goings-on – in sensible proportions – but at the same time that doesn't allow one to assume one automatically has a right to a place in society. You see, I just can't abide anyone who pretends to be something that they obviously are not, and I sensed even before meeting Miss Salmon that she was coming down to Ashurst with one purpose in mind.

We all understood that Guy was having a fling while he was based in London – after all, Miss Salmon was that type of girl. Indeed, when the following weekend I had Guy to myself for a few moments I was able to warn him never to allow the likes of Miss Salmon to get their hooks into him, and that he must realise he would be a marvellous catch for someone from her background.

Guy laughed at such a suggestion and assured me that he had no long-term plans for the baker's daughter. In any case, he reminded me, he would be departing to serve with the Colours in Poona before too long, so marriage was out of the question. He must have sensed, however, that my fears were still not fully assuaged, because after further thought he added, "It may interest you to know, Mother, that Miss Salmon is presently walking out with a sergeant from the regiment with whom she has an understanding."

In fact two weeks later Guy appeared at Ashurst with a Miss Victoria Berkeley, a far more suitable choice whose mother I had known for years; indeed, if the girl hadn't had four other sisters and an impoverished archdeacon for a father, she might in time have suited admirably.

To be fair, after that single unfortunate occasion Guy never mentioned the name of Rebecca Salmon in my presence again, and as he sailed for India a few months later I assumed I had heard the last of the wretched girl.

When Nigel eventually left Sandhurst he didn't follow Guy into the regiment, as it had become abundantly clear during his two-year period at the Academy that he was not cut out to be a soldier. However, Gerald was able to secure him a position with a firm of stockbrokers in the City where one of his cousins was the senior partner. I have to admit that the reports that filtered back to me from time to time were not encouraging, but once I had mentioned to Gerald's cousin that I would eventually be needing someone to manage his grandfather's portfolio, Nigel started to progress slowly up the firm's ladder.

It must have been about six months later that Lieutenant-Colonel Sir Danvers Hamilton dropped Gerald that note through the letter-box at 19 Chester Square. The moment Gerald told me that Hamilton wanted a private word with him, I sensed trouble. Over the years I had come in contact with many of Gerald's brother-officers so I knew exactly how to handle them. Gerald, on the other hand, is quite naïve when it comes to matters of a personal nature, invariably giving the other fellow the benefit of the doubt. I immediately checked my husband's whip commitments in the Commons for the following week and arranged for Sir Danvers to visit us on the Monday evening at six, knowing only too well that, because of his commitments in the House, Gerald would almost certainly have to cancel the meeting at the last moment.

Gerald phoned soon after five on the day in question to say that he couldn't possibly get away and suggested the colonel might come on over to the House of Commons. I said I would see what I could do. An hour later Sir Danvers arrived at Chester Square. After I had apologised and explained my husband's absence I was able to convince him that he should convey his message to me. When the colonel informed me that Miss Salmon was going to have a child I naturally asked of what interest that could possibly be to Gerald or myself. He hesitated only for a moment before suggesting that Guy was the father. I realised immediately that if such a slander was allowed to spread abroad it might even reach the ears of his brother-officers in Poona and that could only do immense harm to my son's chances of further promotion. Any such suggestion I therefore dismissed as ridiculous, along with the colonel in the same breath.

It was during a rubber of bridge at Celia Littlechild's house a few weeks later that she let slip that she had employed a private detective called Harris to spy on her first husband, once she was convinced he was being unfaithful. After learning this piece of information I found myself quite unable to concentrate on the game, much to my partner's annoyance.

On returning home I looked up the name in the London directory. There he was: Max Harris, Private Detective – ex-Scotland Yard, all problems considered. After some minutes staring at the phone, I finally picked up the headpiece and asked the operator to get me Paddington 3720. I waited for several moments before anyone spoke.

"Harris," said a gruff voice without further explanation.

"Is that the detective agency?" I asked, nearly replacing the phone back on the hook before I had given the man a chance to reply.

"Yes, madam, it is," said the voice, sounding a little more enthusiastic.

"I may be in need of your help – for a friend, you understand," I said, feeling rather embarrassed.

"A friend," said the voice. "Yes, of course. Then perhaps we should meet."

"But not at your office," I insisted.

"I quite understand, madam. Would the St Agnes Hotel, Bury Street, South Kensington, four o'clock tomorrow afternoon suit?"

"Yes," I said and put the phone down, suddenly aware that he didn't know my name and I didn't know what he looked like.

When the following day I arrived at the St Agnes, a dreadful little place just off the Brompton Road, I walked round the block several times before I finally felt able to enter the lobby. A man of about thirty perhaps thirty-five was leaning on the reception desk. He straightened up the moment he saw me.

"Are you looking for a Mr Harris, by any chance?" he enquired.

I nodded and he quickly led us through to the tea room and ushered me into a seat in the furthest corner. Once he had sat down in the chair opposite me I began to study him more carefully. He must have been about five foot ten, stocky with dark brown hair and an even browner moustache. He wore a brown check Harris Tweed jacket, cream shirt and thin yellow tie. As I began to explain why I might be in need of his services I became distracted as he started to click the knuckles of his fingers, one by one, first the left hand and then the right. I wanted to get up and leave, and would have done so had I believed for a moment that finding anyone less obnoxious to carry out the task would have proved easy.

It also took me some considerable time to convince Harris that I was not looking for a divorce. At that first meeting I explained to him as much of my dilemma as I felt able. I was shocked when he demanded the extortionate fee of five shillings an hour just to begin his investigation. However, I did not feel I had been left with a great deal of choice in the matter. I agreed that he should start the following day and that we would meet again a week later.

Mr Harris's first report informed me that, in the view of those who spent most of their working hours at a pub in Chelsea called the Musketeer, Charlie Trumper was the father of Rebecca Salmon's child, and indeed when the suggestion was put to him directly he made no attempt to deny it. As if to prove the point, within days of the child's birth he and Miss Salmon were married – quietly in a register office.

Mr Harris had no trouble in obtaining a copy of the child's birth certificate. It confirmed that the child, Daniel George Trumper, was the son of Rebecca Salmon and Charlie George Trumper of 147 Chelsea Terrace. I also noted that the child had been named after both his grandparents. In my next letter to Guy I enclosed a copy of the birth certificate along with one or two other little snippets that Harris had supplied, such as details of the wedding and Colonel Hamilton's appointment as chairman of the Trumper board. I must confess that I assumed that was an end of the matter.

However, two weeks later I received a letter from Guy: I presume it must have crossed with mine in the post. He explained that Sir Danvers had been in communication with his commanding officer, Colonel Forbes, and because of Forbes's insistence that there might be a breach of promise suit pending Guy had been made to appear in front of a group of his fellow-officers to explain the relationship between himself and Miss Salmon.

I immediately sat down and wrote a long letter to Colonel Forbes – Guy was obviously not in a position to present the full evidence I had managed to secure. I included a further copy of the birth certificate so that he would be left in no doubt that my son could not have possibly been involved with the Salmon girl in any way. I added – without prejudice – that Colonel Hamilton was now employed as chairman of the board of Trumper's, a position from which he certainly derived some remuneration. The long information sheets now sent to me on a weekly basis by Mr Harris were, I had to admit, proving of considerable value.

For some little time matters returned to normal. Gerald busied himself with his parliamentary duties while I concentrated on nothing more demanding than the appointment of the new vicar's warden and my bridge circle.

The problem, however, went deeper than I had imagined, for quite by chance I discovered that we were no longer to be included on the guest list for Daphne Harcourt-Browne's marriage to the Marquess of Wiltshire. Of course, Percy would never have become the twelfth marquess had it not been for his father and brother sacrificing their lives on the Western Front. However, I learned from others who were present at the ceremony that Colonel Hamilton as well as the Trumpers were to be seen at St Margaret's, and at the reception afterwards.

During this period, Mr Harris continued to supply me with memoranda about the comings and goings of the Trumpers and their growing business empire. I must confess that I had no interest whatsoever in any of their commercial transactions: it was a world that remained totally alien to me but I didn't stop him going beyond his brief as it gave me a useful insight into Guy's adversaries.

A few weeks later I received a note from Colonel Forbes acknowledging my letter but otherwise I heard nothing further concerning Guy's unfortunate misrepresentation. I therefore assumed everything must be back on an even keel and that Colonel Hamilton's fabrication had been treated with the disdain it merited.

Then one morning in June the following year, Gerald was called away to the War Office on what he thought at the time must be another routine parliamentary briefing.

When my husband returned to Chester Square unexpectedly that afternoon he made me sit down and drink a large whisky before he explained that he had some unpleasant news to impart. I had rarely seen him looking so grim as I sat there silently wondering what could possibly be important enough to cause him to return home during the day.

"Guy has resigned his commission," announced Gerald tersely. "He will be returning to England just as soon as the necessary paperwork has been completed."

"Why?" I asked, quite stunned.

"No reason was given," Gerald replied. "I was called to the War Office this morning, and tipped off by Billy Cuthbert, a brother-Fusilier. He informed me privately that if Guy hadn't resigned he would undoubtedly have been cashiered."

During the time I waited for Guy's return to England I went over every snippet of information on the rapidly growing Trumper empire that Mr Harris was able to supply me with, however minute or seemingly insignificant it seemed at the time. Among the many pages of material that the detective sent, no doubt in order to justify his outrageous fees, I came across one item which I suspected might have been almost as important to the Trumpers as my son's reputation was to me.

I carried out all the necessary enquiries myself, and having checked over the property one Sunday morning I phoned Savill's on the Monday and made a bid of two thousand, five hundred pounds for the property in question. The agent rang back later in the week to say someone else – who I realised had to be Trumpers – had offered three thousand. "Then bid four thousand," I told him, before replacing the phone.

The estate agents were able to confirm later that afternoon that I was in possession of the freehold on 25 to 99 Chelsea Terrace, a block of thirty-seven flats. Trumper's representative, I was assured, would be informed immediately who their next-door neighbour was to be.

CHAPTER 23

Guy Trentham arrived back on the doorstep of 19 Chester Square on a chilly afternoon in September 1922, just after Gibson had cleared away afternoon tea. His mother would never forget the occasion, because when Guy was shown into the drawing room she hardly recognised him. Mrs Trentham had been writing a letter at her desk when Gibson announced, "Captain Guy."

She turned to see her son enter the room and walk straight over to the fireplace where he stood, legs astride, with his back to the coals. His glazed eyes stared in front of him but he didn't speak.

Mrs Trentham was only thankful that her husband was taking part in a debate at the Commons that afternoon and was not expected back until after the ten o'clock vote that night.

Guy obviously hadn't shaved for several days. He could also have made excellent use of a scrubbing brush, while the suit he wore was barely recognisable as the one that only three years before had been tailored by Gieves. The dishevelled figure stood with his back to the blazing coal fire, his body visibly shivering, as he turned to face his mother. For the first time Mrs Trentham noticed that her son was holding a brown paper parcel under one arm.

Although she was not cold, Mrs Trentham also shuddered. She remained at her desk, feeling no desire to embrace her first-born, or be the one who broke the silence between them.

"What have you been told, Mother?" Guy uttered at last, his voice shaky and uncertain.

"Nothing of any real substance." She looked up at him quizzically. "Other than that you have resigned your commission, and that had you not done so you would have been cashiered."

"That much is true," he admitted, at last releasing the parcel he had been clutching and placing it on the table beside him. "But only because they conspired against me."

"They?"

"Yes, Colonel Hamilton, Trumper and the girl."

"Colonel Forbes preferred the word of Miss Salmon even after I had written to him?" asked Mrs Trentham icily.

"Yes – yes, he did. After all, Colonel Hamilton still has a lot of friends in the regiment and some of them were only too happy to carry out his bidding if it meant a rival might be eliminated."

She watched him for a moment as he swayed nervously from foot to foot. "But I thought the matter had been finally settled. After all, the birth certificate –"

"That might have been the case had it been signed by Charlie Trumper as well as the girl, but the certificate only bore the single signature – hers. What made matters worse, Colonel Hamilton advised Miss Salmon to threaten a breach of promise suit naming me as the father. Had she done so, of course, despite my being innocent of any charge they could lay at my door, the good name of the regiment would have suffered irredeemably. I therefore felt I'd been left with no choice but to take the honourable course and resign my commission." His voice became even more bitter. "And all because Trumper feared that the truth might come out."

"What are you talking about, Guy?"

He avoided his mother's direct gaze as he moved from the fireplace to the drinks cabinet where he poured himself a large whisky. He left the soda siphon untouched and took a long swallow. His mother waited in silence for him to continue.

"After the second battle of the Marne I was ordered by Colonel Hamilton to set up an enquiry into Trumper's cowardice in the field," said Guy as he moved back to the fireplace. "Many thought he should have been court-martialled, but the only other witness, a Private Prescott, was himself killed by a stray bullet when only yards from the safety of our own trenches. I had foolishly allowed myself to lead Prescott and Trumper back towards our lines, and when Prescott fell I looked round to see a smile on Trumper's face. All he said was, 'Bad luck, Captain, now you haven't got your witness, have you?' "

"Did you tell anyone about this at the time?"

Guy returned to the drinks cabinet to refill his glass. "Who could I tell without Prescott to back me up? The least I could do was to make sure that he was awarded a posthumous Military Medal. Even if it meant letting Trumper off the hook. Later, I discovered Trumper wouldn't even confirm my version of what had happened on the battlefield which nearly prevented my being awarded the MC."

"And now that he's succeeded in forcing you to resign your commission, it can only be your word against his."

"That would have been the case if Trumper had not made one foolish mistake which could still cause his downfall."

"What are you talking about?"

"Well," continued Guy, his manner slightly more composed, "while the battle was at its height I came to the rescue of the two men in question. I found them hiding in a bombed-out church. I made the decision to remain there until nightfall, when it was my intention to lead them back to the safety of our own trenches. While we were waiting on the roof for the sun to go down and Trumper was under the impression that I was asleep, I saw him slope off back to the chancel and remove a magnificent picture of the Virgin Mary from behind the altar. I continued to watch him as he placed the little oil in his haversack. I said nothing at the time because I realised that this was the proof I needed of his duplicity; after all, the picture could always be returned to the church at some later date. Once we were back behind our own lines I immediately had Trumper's equipment searched so I could have him arrested for the theft. But to my surprise it was nowhere to be found."

"So how can that be of any use to you now?"

"Because the picture has subsequently reappeared."

"Reappeared?"

"Yes," said Guy, his voice rising. "Daphne Harcourt-Browne told me that she had spotted the painting on the drawing room wall in Trumper's house, and was even able to give me a detailed description of it. There was no doubt in my mind that it was the same portrait of the Virgin Mary and Child that he had earlier stolen from the church."

"But there's little anyone can do about that while the painting is still hanging in his home."

"It isn't any longer. Which is the reason I'm disguised like this."

"You must stop talking in riddles," said his mother. "Explain yourself properly, Guy."

"This morning I visited Trumper's home, and told the housekeeper that I had served alongside her master on the Western Front."

"Was that wise, Guy?"

"I told her my name was Fowler, Corporal Denis Fowler, and I had been trying to get in touch with Charlie for some time. I knew he wasn't around because I'd seen him go into one of his shops on Chelsea Terrace only a few minutes before. The maid – who stared at me suspiciously – asked if I would wait in the hall while she went upstairs to tell Mrs Trumper I was there. That gave me easily enough time to slip into the front room and remove the picture from where Daphne had told me it was hanging. I was out of the house even before they could possibly have worked out what I was up to."

"But surely they will report the theft to the police and you will be arrested."

"Not a chance," said Guy as he picked up the brown

paper parcel from the table and started to unwrap it. "The last thing Trumper will want the police to get their hands on is this." He passed the picture over to his mother.

Mrs Trentham stared at the little oil. "From now on you can leave Mr Trumper to me," she said without explanation. Guy smiled for the first time since he had set foot in the house. "However," she continued, "we must concentrate on the more immediate problem of what we are going to do about your future. I'm still confident I can get you a position in the City. I have already spoken to –"

"That won't work, Mother, and you know it. There's no future for me in England for the time being. Or, at least, not until my name has been cleared. In any case, I don't want to hang around London explaining to your bridge circle why I'm no longer with the regiment in India. No, I'll have to go abroad until things have quietened down a little."

"Then I'll need some more time to think," Guy's mother replied. "Meanwhile, go up and have a bath and shave, and while you're at it find yourself some clean clothes and I'll work out what has to be done."

As soon as Guy had left the room Mrs Trentham returned to her writing desk and locked the little picture in the bottom left-hand drawer. She placed the key in her bag, then began to concentrate on the more immediate problem of what should be done to protect the Trentham name.

As she stared out of the window a plan began to form in her mind which, although it would require using even more of her dwindling resources, might at least give her the breathing space she required to expose Trumper for the thief and liar he was, and at the same time to exonerate her son.

Mrs Trentham reckoned she only had about fifty pounds in cash in the safe-deposit box in her bedroom, but she still possessed sixteen thousand of the twenty thousand that her father had settled on her the day she was married. "Always there in case of some unforeseen emergency," he had told her prophetically.

Mrs Trentham took out a piece of writing paper from her drawer and began to make some notes. She was only too aware that once her son left Chester Square that night she might not see him again for some considerable time. Forty minutes later she studied her efforts:

£50 (cash)
Sydney
Max Harris
Greatcoat
£5,000 (cheque)
Bentley's
Picture
Local police

Her thoughts were interrupted by the return of Guy looking a little more like the son she remembered. A blazer and cavalry twills had replaced the crumpled suit and the skin, although pale, was at least cleanshaven. Mrs Trentham folded up the piece of paper, having finally decided on exactly what course of action needed to be taken.

"Now, sit down and listen carefully," she said.

Guy Trentham left Chester Square a few minutes after nine o'clock, an hour before his father was due to return from the Commons. He had fifty-three pounds in cash along with a cheque for five thousand pounds lodged in an inside pocket. He had agreed that he would write to his father the moment he landed in Sydney, explaining why he had travelled direct to Australia. His mother had vowed that while he was away she would do everything in her power to clear her son's name, so that he might eventually return to England vindicated and take up his rightful place as head of the family.

The only two servants who had seen Captain Trentham that evening were instructed by their mistress not to mention his visit to anyone, especially her husband, on pain of losing their positions in the household.

Mrs Trentham's final task before her husband returned home that night was to phone the local police. A Constable Wrigley dealt with the reported theft.

During those weeks of waiting for her son's letter to arrive, Mrs Trentham did not sit around idly. The day after Guy sailed to Australia she made one of her periodic visits to the St Agnes Hotel – a rewrapped parcel under one arm – and handed over her prize to Mr Harris before giving him a series of detailed instructions.

Two days later the detective was able to confirm that the portrait of the Virgin Mary and Child had been left with Bentley's the pawnbroker, and could not be sold for at least five years when the date on the pawn ticket would have expired. He handed over a photo of the picture and the receipt to prove it. Mrs Trentham placed the photo in her handbag but didn't bother to ask Harris what had become of the five pounds he had been paid for the picture.

"Good," she said, placing her handbag by the side of her chair. "In fact highly satisfactory."

"So would you like me to point the right man at Scotland Yard in the direction of Bentley's?" asked Harris.

"Certainly not," said Mrs Trentham. "I need you to carry out a little research on the picture before anyone else will set eyes on it, and then if my information proves correct the next occasion that painting will be seen by the public will be when it comes under the hammer at Sotheby's."

CHAPTER 24

"Good morning, madam. I do apologise for having to bother you in this way."

"It's no bother," said Mrs Trentham to the police officer whom Gibson had announced as Inspector Richards.

"It's not you I was hoping to see actually, Mrs Trentham," explained the inspector. "It's your son, Captain Guy Trentham."

"Then you'll have a very long journey ahead of you, Inspector."

"I'm not sure I understand you, madam."

"My son," said Mrs Trentham, "is taking care of our family interests in Australia, where he is a partner in a large firm of cattle brokers."

Richards was unable to hide his surprise. "And how long has he been out there, madam?"

"For some considerable time, Inspector."

"Could you be more precise?"

"Captain Trentham left England for India in February 1920, to complete his tour of duty with the regiment. He won the MC at the second battle of the Marne, you know." She nodded towards the mantelpiece. The inspector looked suitably impressed. "Of course," Mrs Trentham continued, "it was never his intention to remain in the army, as we had always planned that he would have a spell in the colonies before returning to run our estates in Berkshire."

"But did he come back to England before taking up this position in Australia?"

"Sadly not, Inspector," said Mrs Trentham. "Once he had resigned his commission he travelled directly to Australia to take up his new responsibilities. My husband, who as I am sure you know is the Member of Parliament for Berkshire West, would be able to confirm the exact dates for you."

"I don't feel it will be necessary to bother him on this occasion, madam."

"And why, may I ask, did you wish to see my son in the first place?"

"We are following up enquiries concerning the theft of a painting in Chelsea."

Mrs Trentham offered no comment so the detective continued. "Someone who fits your son's description was seen in the vicinity wearing an old army greatcoat. We hoped he might therefore be able to help us with our enquiries."

"And when was this crime committed?"

"Last September, madam, and as the painting has not yet been recovered we are still pursuing the matter –" Mrs Trentham kept her head slightly bowed as she learned this piece of information and continued to listen carefully. "– but we are now given to understand that the owner will not be preferring charges, so I expect the file should be closed on this one fairly shortly. This your son?" The inspector pointed to a photograph of Guy in full dress uniform that rested on a side table.

"It is indeed, Inspector."

"Doesn't exactly fit the description we were given," said the policeman, looking slightly puzzled. "In any case, as you say, he must have been in Australia at the time. A cast-iron alibi." The inspector smiled ingratiatingly but Mrs Trentham's expression didn't alter.

"You're not suggesting that my son was in any way involved in this theft, are you?" she asked coldly.

"Certainly not, madam. It's just that we've come across

a greatcoat which Gieves, the Savile Row tailors, have confirmed they made for a Captain Trentham. We found an old soldier wearing it who . . ."

"Then you must have also found your thief," said Mrs Trentham with disdain.

"Hardly, madam. You see, the gentleman in question has only one leg."

Mrs Trentham still showed no concern. "Then I suggest you ring Chelsea police station," she said, "as I feel sure they will be able to enlighten you further on the matter."

"But I'm from Chelsea police station myself," replied the inspector, looking even more puzzled.

Mrs Trentham rose from the sofa and walked slowly over to her desk, pulled open a drawer and removed a single sheet of paper. She handed it to the inspector. His face reddened as he began to take in the contents. When he had finished reading the document he passed the piece of paper back.

"I do apologise, madam. I had no idea that you had reported the loss of the greatcoat the same day. I shall have a word with young Constable Wrigley just as soon as I get back to the station." Mrs Trentham showed no reaction to the policeman's embarrassment. "Well, I won't take up any more of your time," he said. "I'll just show myself out."

Mrs Trentham waited until she heard the door close behind him before picking up the phone and asking for a Paddington number.

She made only one request of the detective before replacing the receiver.

Mrs Trentham knew that Guy must have arrived safely in Australia when her cheque was cleared by Coutts and Co through a bank in Sydney. The promised letter to his father arrived on the doormat a further six weeks after that. When Gerald imparted to her the contents of the letter explaining that Guy had joined a firm of cattle brokers she feigned surprise at her son's uncharacteristic action, but her husband didn't seem to show a great deal of interest either way.

During the following months Harris's reports continued to show that Trumper's newly formed company was going from strength to strength, but it still brought a smile to Mrs Trentham's lips when she recalled how for a mere four thousand pounds she had stopped Charles Trumper right in his tracks.

The same smile was not to return to Mrs Trentham's face again until she received a letter from Savill's sometime later presenting her with an opportunity to repeat for Rebecca Trumper the same acute frustration as she had managed in the past for Charlie Trumper, even if this time the cost to herself might be a little higher. She checked her bank balance, satisfied that it would prove more than adequate for the purpose she had in mind.

Over the years Savill's had kept Mrs Trentham well informed of any shops that came up for sale in Chelsea Terrace but she made no attempt to stop Trumper from purchasing them, reasoning that her possession of the flats would be quite adequate to ruin any long-term plans he might have for the whole terrace. However, when the details of Number 1 Chelsea Terrace were sent to her she realised that here the circumstances were entirely different. Not only was Number 1 the corner shop, facing as it did towards the Fulham Road, and the largest property on the block, it was also an established if somewhat run-down fine art dealer and auctioneer. It was the obvious outlet for all those years of preparation Mrs Trumper had put in at Bedford College and more recently at Sotheby's.

A letter accompanying the bill of sale asked if Mrs Trentham wished to be represented at the auction that Mr Fothergill, the present owner, was proposing to conduct himself.

She wrote back the same day, thanking Savill's but explaining that she would prefer to carry out her own bidding and would be further obliged if they could furnish her with an estimate of how much the property might be expected to fetch.

Savill's reply contained several ifs and buts, as in their view the property was unique. They also pointed out that they were not qualified to offer an opinion as to the value of the stock. However, they settled on an upper estimate in the region of four thousand pounds.

During the following weeks Mrs Trentham was to be found regularly seated in the back row of Christie's, silently watching the various auctions as they were conducted. She never nodded or raised a hand herself. She wanted to be certain that when the time came for her to bid she would be thoroughly familiar with the protocol of such occasions.

On the morning of the sale of Number 1 Chelsea Terrace Mrs Trentham entered the auctioneer's wearing a long dark red dress that swept along the ground. She selected a place in the third row and was seated some twenty minutes before the bidding was due to commence. Her eyes never remained still as she watched the different players enter the room and take their places. Mr Wrexall arrived a few minutes after she had, taking a seat in the middle of the front row. He looked grim but determined. He was exactly as Mr Harris had described him, mid-forties, heavily built and balding. Being so badly overweight he looked considerably older than his years, she considered. His flesh was swarthy and whenever he lowered his head several more chins appeared. It was then that Mrs Trentham decided that should she fail to secure Number 1 Chelsea Terrace a meeting with Mr Wrexall might prove advantageous.

At nine fifty precisely Colonel Hamilton led his two colleagues down the aisle and filed into the vacant seats immediately behind Mrs Trentham. Although she glanced at the colonel he made no effort to acknowledge her presence. At nine fifty there was still no sign of either Mr or Mrs Trumper.

Savill's had warned Mrs Trentham that Trumper might be represented by an outside agent, but from all she had gathered about the man over the years she couldn't believe he would allow anyone else to carry out the bidding for him. She was not to be disappointed, for when the clock behind the auctioneer's box showed five minutes before the hour, in he strode. Although he was a few years older than he had been at the time of the photograph she held in her hand, she was in no doubt that it was Charlie Trumper. He wore a smart, well-tailored suit that helped disguise the fact that he was beginning to have a weight problem. A smile rarely left his lips though she had plans to remove it. He seemed to want everyone to know he had arrived, as he shook hands and chatted with several people before taking a reserved seat on the aisle about four rows behind her. Mrs Trentham half turned her chair so she could observe both Trumper and the auctioneer without having continually to look round.

Suddenly Mr Trumper rose and made his way towards the back of the room, only to pick up a bill of sale from the table at the entrance before returning to his reserved place on the aisle. Mrs Trentham suspected that this performance had been carried out for some specific reason. Her eyes raked each row and although she could see nothing untoward she nevertheless felt uneasy.

By the time Mr Fothergill had climbed the steps of the auctioneer's box the room was already full. Yet despite almost every place having been taken Mrs Trentham was still unable to see if Mrs Trumper was seated among the large gathering.

From the moment Mr Fothergill called for the first bid the auction did not proceed as Mrs Trentham had imagined, or indeed planned. Nothing she had experienced at Christie's during the previous month could have prepared her for the final outcome – Mr Fothergill announcing a mere six minutes later, "Sold for twelve thousand pounds to Mrs Gerald Trentham."

She was angry at having made such a public spectacle of herself, even if she had secured the fine art shop and dealt a satisfying blow to Rebecca Trumper. It had certainly been done at a considerable cost, and now she wasn't even certain she had enough money to cover the full amount she had committed herself to.

After eighty days of soul-searching, in which she considered approaching her husband and even her father to make up the shortfall, Mrs Trentham finally decided to sacrifice the one thousand and two hundred pounds deposit, retreat, and lick her wounds. The alternative was to admit to her husband exactly what had taken place at Number 1 Chelsea Terrace that day.

There was one compensation, however. She would no longer need to use Sotheby's when the time came to dispose of the stolen painting.

As the months passed, Mrs Trentham received regular letters from her son, first from Sydney, then later from Melbourne, informing her of his progress. They often requested her to send more money. The larger the partnership grew, Guy explained, the more he needed extra capital to secure his share of the equity. Overall some six thousand pounds found its way across the Pacific Ocean to a bank in Sydney during a period of four years, none of which Mrs Trentham resented giving since Guy appeared to be making such a success of his new profession. She also felt confident that once she could expose Charles Trumper for the thief and liar he was, her son could return to England with his reputation vindicated, even in the eyes of his father.

Then suddenly, just at the point when Mrs Trentham had begun to believe that the time might be right to put the next stage of her plan into action, a cable arrived from Melbourne. The address from which the missive had been sent left Mrs Trentham with no choice but to leave for that distant city without delay.

When, over dinner that night, she informed Gerald that she intended to depart for the Antipodes on the first possible tide her news was greeted with polite indifference. This came as no surprise, as Guy's name had rarely passed her husband's lips since that day he had visited the War Office over four years before. In fact, the only sign that still remained of their firstborn's existence at either Ashurst Hall or Chester Square was the one picture of him in full dress uniform that stood on her bedroom table and the MC that Gerald had allowed to remain on the mantelpiece.

As far as Gerald was concerned, Nigel was their only child.

Gerald Trentham was well aware that his wife told all his and her friends that Guy was a successful partner in a large firm of cattle brokers that had offices right across Australia. However, he had long ago stopped believing such stories, and had lately even stopped listening to them. Whenever the occasional envelope, in that all too familiar hand, dropped through the letter-box at Chester Square, Gerald Trentham made no enquiry as to his elder son's progress.

The next ship scheduled to sail for Australia was the SS *Orontes*, which was due out of Southampton on the following Monday. Mrs Trentham cabled back to an address in Melbourne to let them know her estimated time of arrival.

The five-week trip across two oceans seemed interminable to Mrs Trentham, especially as for most of the time she chose to remain in her cabin, having no desire to strike up a casual acquaintanceship with anyone on board – or, worse, bump into someone who actually knew her. She turned down several invitations to join the captain's table for dinner.

Once the ship had docked at Sydney, Mrs Trentham only rested overnight in that city before travelling on to Melbourne. On arrival at Spencer Street station she took a taxi directly to the Royal Victoria hospital where the sister in charge told her matter-of-factly that her son had only another week to live.

They allowed her to see him immediately, and a police officer escorted her to the special isolation wing. She stood by his bedside, staring down in disbelief at a face she could barely recognise. Guy's hair was so thin and grey and the lines on his face so deep that Mrs Trentham felt she might have been at her husband's death-bed.

A doctor told her that such a condition was not uncommon once the verdict had been delivered and the person concerned realised there was no hope of a reprieve. After standing at the end of the bed for nearly an hour she left without having been able to elicit a word from her son. At no time did she allow any of the hospital staff to become aware of her true feelings.

That evening Mrs Trentham booked herself into a quiet country club on the outskirts of Melbourne. She made only one enquiry of the young expatriate owner, a Mr Sinclair-Smith, before retiring to her room.

The next morning she presented herself at the offices of the oldest firm of solicitors in Melbourne, Asgarth, Jenkins and Co. A young man she considered far too familiar asked "what was her problem".

"I wish to have a word with your senior partner," Mrs Trentham replied.

"Then you'll have to take a seat in the waiting room," he told her.

Mrs Trentham sat alone for some time before Mr Asgarth was free to see her.

The senior partner, an elderly man who from his dress might have been conducting his practice in Lincoln's Inn Fields rather than Victoria Street, Melbourne, listened in silence to her sad story and agreed to deal with any problems that might arise from handling Guy Trentham's estate. To that end he promised to lodge an immediate application for permission to have the body transported back to England.

Mrs Trentham visited her son in hospital every day of that week before he died. Although little conversation passed between them, she did learn of one problem that would have to be dealt with before she could hope to travel back to England.

On the Wednesday afternoon Mrs Trentham returned to the offices of Asgarth, Jenkins and Co to seek the advice of the senior partner on what could be done following her latest discovery. The elderly lawyer ushered his client to a chair before he listened carefully to her revelation. He made the occasional note on a pad in front of him. When Mrs Trentham had finished he did not offer an opinion for some considerable time.

"There will have to be a change of name," he suggested, "if no one else is to find out what you have in mind."

"And we must also be sure that there is no way of tracing who her father was at some time in the future," said Mrs Trentham.

The old solicitor frowned. "That will require you to place considerable trust in" – he checked the scribbled name in front of him – "Miss Benson."

"Pay Miss Benson whatever it takes to assure her silence," said Mrs Trentham. "Coutts in London will handle all the financial details."

The senior partner nodded and by dint of remaining at his desk until nearly midnight for the next four days he managed to complete all the paperwork necessary to fulfil his client's requirements only hours before Mrs Trentham was due to return to London.

Guy Trentham was certified as dead by the doctor in attendance at three minutes past six on the morning of 23 April 1927, and the following day Mrs Trentham began her sombre journey back to England, accompanied by his coffin. She was relieved that only two people on that continent knew as much as she did, one an elderly gentleman only months away from retirement, the other a woman who could now spend the rest of her life in a style she would never have believed possible only a few days before.

Mrs Trentham cabled her husband with the minimum information she considered necessary before sailing back to Southampton as silently and as anonymously as she had come. Once she had set foot on English soil Mrs Trentham was driven directly to her home in Chester Square. She briefed her husband on the details of the tragedy, and he reluctantly accepted that an announcement should be placed in *The Times* the following day. It read:

The death is announced of Captain Guy Trentham MC, tragically from tuberculosis after suffering a long illness. The funeral will take place at St Mary's, Ashurst, Berkshire, on Tuesday, 8 June 1927.

The local vicar conducted the ceremony for the dear departed. His death, he assured the congregation, was a tragedy for all who knew him.

Guy Trentham was laid to rest in the plot originally reserved for his father. Major and Mrs Trentham, relations, friends of the family, parishioners and servants left the burial ground with their heads bowed low.

During the days that followed Mrs Trentham received over a hundred letters of condolence, one or two of which pointed out that she could at least be consoled with the knowledge that there was a second son to take Guy's place.

The next day Nigel's photograph replaced his elder brother's on the bedside table.

CHARLIE

1926-1945

CHAPTER 25

I was walking down Chelsea Terrace with Tom Arnold on our Monday morning round when he first offered an opinion.

"It will never happen," I said.

"You could be right, sir, but at the moment a lot of the shopkeepers are beginning to panic."

"Bunch of cowards," I told him. "With nearly a million already unemployed there'll be only a handful who would be foolish enough to consider an all-out strike."

"Perhaps, but the Shops Committee is still advising its members to board up their windows."

"Syd Wrexall would advise his members to board up their windows if a pekinese put a leg up against the front door of the Musketeer. What's more, the bloody animal wouldn't even have to piss."

A smile flickered across Tom's lips. "So you're prepared for a fight, Mr Trumper?"

"You bet I am. I'll back Mr Churchill all the way on this one." I stopped to check the window of hats and scarves. "How many people do we currently employ?"

"Seventy-one."

"And how many of those do you reckon are considering strike action?"

"Half a dozen, ten at the most would be my bet – and then only those who are members of the Shop-workers' Union. But there could still be the problem for some of our employees who wouldn't find it easy to get to work because of a public transport stoppage."

"Then give me all the names of those you're not sure of by this evening and I'll have a word with every one of them during the week. At least that way I might be able to convince one or two of them about their long-term future with the company."

"What about the company's long-term future if the strikes were to go ahead?"

"When will you get it into your head, Tom, that nothing is going to happen that will affect Trumper's?"

"Syd Wrexall thinks –"

"I can assure you that's the one thing he doesn't do."

"– thinks that at least three shops will come on the market during the next month, and if there were to be a general strike there might be a whole lot more suddenly available. The miners are persuading –"

"They're not persuading Charlie Trumper," I told him. "So let me know the moment you hear of anyone who wants to sell, because I'm still a buyer."

"While everyone else is a seller?"

"That's exactly when you *should* buy," I replied. "The time to get on a tram is when everyone else is getting off. So let me have those names, Tom. Meanwhile, I'm going to the bank." I strode off in the direction of Knightsbridge.

In the privacy of his new Brompton Road office Hadlow informed me that Trumper's were now holding a little over twelve thousand pounds on deposit: an adequate buttress, he considered, were there to be a general strike.

"Not you as well," I said in exasperation. "The strike will never take place. Even if it does, I predict it'll be over in a matter of days."

"Like the last war?" said Hadlow as he peered back at me over his half-moon spectacles. "I am by nature a cautious man, Mr Trumper –"

"Well, I'm not," I said, interrupting him. "So be

prepared to see that cash being put to good use."

"I have already earmarked around half the sum, should Mrs Trentham fail to take up her option on Number 1," he reminded me. "She still has" – he turned to check the calendar on the wall – "thirty-two days left to do so."

"Then I would suggest this is going to be a month for keeping our nerve."

"If the market were to collapse, it might be wise not to risk everything. Don't you think, Mr Trumper?"

"No, I don't, but that's why I'm –" I began, only just managing to stop myself venting my true feelings.

"It is indeed," replied Hadlow, making me feel even more embarrassed. "And that is also the reason I have backed you so wholeheartedly in the past," he added magnanimously.

As the days passed I had to admit that a general strike did look more and more likely. The air of uncertainty and lack of confidence in the future meant that first one shop and then another found its way on to the market.

I purchased the first two at knock-down prices, on the condition that the settlement was immediate, and thanks to the speed with which Crowther completed the paperwork and Hadlow released the cash, I was even able to add boots and shoes, followed by the chemist's, to my side of the ledger.

When the general strike finally began – on Tuesday, 4 May 1926 – the colonel and I were out on the streets at first light. We checked over every one of our properties from the north end to the south. All Syd Wrexall's committee members had already boarded up their shops, which I considered tantamount to giving in to the strikers. I did agree, however, to the colonel's plan for "operation lock-up", which on a given signal from me allowed Tom Arnold to have all thirteen shops locked and bolted within three minutes. On the previous Saturday I had watched Tom carry out several "practice runs", as he called them, to the amusement of the passers-by.

Although on the first morning of the strike the weather was fine and the streets were crowded the only concession I made to the milling throng was to keep all foodstuff from Numbers 147 and 131 off the pavements.

At eight Tom Arnold reported to me that only five employees had failed to turn up for work, despite spectacular traffic jams causing public transport to be held up for hours on end, and even one of those was genuinely ill.

As the colonel and I strolled up and down Chelsea Terrace we were met by the occasional insult but I didn't sense any real mood of violence and, everything considered, most people were surprisingly good-humoured. Some of the lads even started playing football in the street.

The first sign of any real unrest came on the second morning, when a brick was hurled through the front window of Number 5, jewellery and watches. I saw two or three young thugs grab whatever they could from the main window display before running off down the terrace. The crowd became restless and began shouting slogans so I gave the signal to Tom Arnold, who was about fifty yards up the road, and he immediately blew six blasts on his whistle. Within the three minutes the colonel had stipulated every one of our shops was locked and bolted. I stood my ground while the police moved in and several people were arrested. Although there was a lot of hot air blowing about, within an hour I was able to instruct Tom that the shops could be reopened and that we should continue serving customers as if nothing had happened. Within three hours hardware had replaced the window of Number 5 – not that it was a morning for buying jewellery.

By the Thursday, only three people failed to turn up for work, but I counted four more shops in the terrace that had been boarded up. The streets seemed a lot calmer. Over a snatched breakfast I learned from Becky that there would be no copy of *The Times* that morning because the printers were on strike, but in defiance the government had brought out their own paper, the *British Gazette*, a brainchild of Mr Churchill, which informed its readers that the railway and transport workers were now returning to work in their droves. Despite this, Norman Cosgrave, the fishmonger at Number 11, told me that he'd had enough, and asked how much I was prepared to offer him for his business. Having agreed on a price in the morning we walked over to the bank that same afternoon to close the deal. One phone call made sure that Crowther had the necessary documents typed up, and Hadlow had filled in a cheque by the time we arrived, so all that was required of me was a signature. When I returned to Chelsea Terrace I immediately put Tom Arnold in charge of the fishmonger's until he could find the right manager to take Cosgrave's place. I never said anything to him at the time, but it was to be several weeks after Tom had handed over to a lad from Billingsgate before he finally rid himself of the lingering smell.

The general strike officially ended on the ninth morning, and by the last day of the month I had acquired another seven shops in all. I seemed to be running constantly backwards and forwards to the bank, but at least every one of my acquisitions was at a price that allowed Hadlow an accompanying smile, even if he warned me that funds were running low.

At our next board meeting, I was able to report that Trumper's now owned twenty shops in Chelsea Terrace, which was more than the Shops Committee membership combined. However Hadlow did express a view to the board that we should now embark on a long period of consolidation if we wanted our recently acquired properties to attain the same quality and standard as the original thirteen. I made only one other proposal of any significance at that meeting, which received the unanimous backing of my colleagues – that Tom Arnold be invited to join the board.

I still couldn't resist spending the odd hour sitting on the bench opposite Number 147 and watching the transformation of Chelsea Terrace as it took place before my eyes. For the first time I could differentiate between those shops I owned and those that I still needed to acquire, which included the fourteen owned by Wrexall's committee members – not forgetting either the prestigious Number 1 or the Musketeer.

Seventy-two days had passed since the auction, and although Mr Fothergill still purchased his fruit and vegetables regularly from Number 147 he never uttered a word to me as to whether or not Mrs Trentham had fulfilled her contract. Joan Moore informed my wife that her former mistress had recently received a visit from Mr Fothergill, and although the cook had not been able to hear all the conversation there had definitely been raised voices.

When Daphne came to visit me at the shop the following week I enquired if she had any inside information on what Mrs Trentham was up to.

"Stop worrying about the damned woman," was all Daphne had to say on the subject. "In any case," she added, "the ninety days will be up soon enough, and frankly, you should be more worried about your Part II than Mrs Trentham's financial problems."

"I agree. But if I go on at this rate, I won't have completed the necessary work before next year," I said, having selected twelve perfect plums for her before placing them on the weighing machine.

"You're always in such a hurry, Charlie. Why do things always have to be finished by a certain date?"

"Because that's what keeps me going."

"But Becky will be just as impressed by your achievement if you manage to finish a year later."

"It wouldn't be the same," I told her. "I'll just have to work harder."

"There are only a given number of hours in each day," Daphne reminded him. "Even for you."

"Well, that's one thing I can't be blamed for."

Daphne laughed. "How's Becky's thesis on Luini coming along?"

"She's completed the bloody thing. Just about to check over the final draft of thirty thousand words, so she's still well ahead of me. But what with the general strike and acquiring all the new properties, not to mention Mrs Trentham, I haven't even had time to take Daniel to see West Ham this season." Charlie started placing her order in a large brown paper bag.

"Has Becky discovered what you're up to yet?" Daphne asked, passing over a ten-shilling note.

"No, and I make sure I only disappear completely whenever she's working late at Sotheby's or off cataloguing some grand collection. She still hasn't noticed that I get up every morning at four thirty, which is when I put in the real work." I passed over the bag and seven and tenpence change.

"Proper little Trollope, aren't we?" remarked Daphne. "By the way, I still haven't let Percy in on our secret, but I can't wait to see the expression on their faces when –"

"Shh, not a word . . ."

When you have been chasing something for a long time it's strange how the final prize so often lands in your lap just when you least expect it.

I was serving at Number 147 that morning. It always annoyed Bob Makins to see me roll up my sleeves, but I do enjoy a little chat with my old customers, and lately it was about the only chance I had to catch up on the gossip, as well as an occasional insight into what the customers really thought of my other shops. However, I confess that by the time I served Mr Fothergill the queue stretched nearly all the way to the grocery shop which I knew Bob still regarded as a rival.

"Good morning," I said, when Mr Fothergill reached the front of the queue. "And what can I offer you today, sir? I've got some lovely –"

"I wondered if we could have a word in private, Mr Trumper?"

I was so taken by surprise that I didn't reply immediately. I knew Mrs Trentham still had another nine days to go before she had to complete her contract and I had assumed I would hear nothing before then. After all, she must have had her own Hadlows and Crowthers to do all the paperwork.

"I'm afraid the storeroom is the only place available at the moment," I warned. I removed my green overall, rolled down my sleeves and replaced my jacket. "You see, my manager now occupies the flat above," I explained as I led the auctioneer through to the back of the shop.

I offered him a seat on an upturned orange box while pulling up another box opposite him. We faced each other, just a few feet apart, like rival chess players. Strange surroundings, I considered, to discuss the biggest deal of my life. I tried to remain calm.

"I'll come to the point straight away," said Fothergill. "Mrs Trentham has not been in touch for several weeks and lately she has been refusing to answer my calls. What's more, Savill's have made it abundantly clear that they have had no instruction to complete the transaction on her behalf. They have gone as far as to say that they are now given to understand that she is no longer interested in the property."

"Still, you got your one thousand, two hundred pounds deposit," I reminded him, trying to stifle a grin.

"I don't deny it," replied Fothergill. "But I have

since made other commitments, and what with the general strike –"

"Hard times, I agree," I told him. I felt the palms of my hands begin to sweat.

"But you've never hidden your desire to be the owner of Number 1."

"True enough, but since the auction I've been buying up several other properties with the cash I had originally put on one side for your shop."

"I know, Mr Trumper. But I would now be willing to settle for a far more reasonable price –"

"And three thousand, five hundred pounds is what I was willing to bid, as no doubt you recall."

"Nine thousand was your final bid, if I remember correctly."

"Tactics, Mr Fothergill, nothing more than tactics. I never had any intention of paying nine thousand, as I feel sure you are only too aware."

"But your wife bid five thousand, five hundred pounds, even forgetting her later bid of eleven thousand."

"I can't disagree with that," I told him, dropping back into my Cockney accent. "But if you 'ad ever married, Mr Fothergill, you would know only too well why we in the East End always refer to them as the trouble and strife."

"I'd let the property go for seven thousand pounds," he said. "But only to you."

"You'd let the property go for five thousand," I replied, "to anyone who'd cough up."

"Never," said Fothergill.

"In nine days' time would be my bet, but I'll tell you what I'll do," I added, leaning forward and nearly falling off my box. "I'll honour my wife's commitment of five thousand, five 'undred pounds, which I confess was the limit the board 'ad allowed us to go to, but only if you 'ave all the paperwork ready for me to sign before midnight." Mr Fothergill opened his mouth indignantly. "Of course," I added before he could protest, "it shouldn't be too much work for you. After all, the contract's been sitting on your desk for the last eighty-one days. All you have to do is change the name and knock off the odd nought. Well, if you'll excuse me, Mr Fothergill, I must be getting back to my customers."

"I have never been treated in such a cavalier way before, sir," declared Mr Fothergill, jumping up angrily. He turned and marched out, leaving me sitting in the storeroom on my own.

"I have never thought of myself as a cavalier," I told the upturned orange box. "More of a roundhead, I would have said."

Once I had read another chapter of *Through the Looking-Glass* to Daniel and waited for him to fall asleep, I went downstairs to join Becky for dinner. While she served me a bowl of soup I told her the details of my conversation with Fothergill.

"Pity," was her immediate reaction. "I only wish he'd approached me in the first place. Now we may never get our hands on Number 1" – a sentiment she repeated just before climbing into bed. I turned down the gaslight beside me, thinking that perhaps Becky could be right. I was just beginning to feel drowsy when I heard the front door bell sound.

"It's past eleven thirty," Becky said sleepily. "Who could that possibly be?"

"A man who understands deadlines?" I suggested as I turned the gaslight back up. I climbed out of bed, donned my dressing-gown and went downstairs to answer the door.

"Do come through to my study, Peregrine," I said, after I had welcomed Mr Fothergill.

"Thank you, Charles," he replied. I only just stopped myself laughing as I moved a copy of *Mathematics, Part Two* from my desk, so that I could get to the drawer that housed the company cheques.

"Five thousand, five hundred, if I remember correctly," I said, as I unscrewed the top of my pen and checked the clock on the mantelpiece. At eleven thirty-seven I handed over the full and final settlement to Mr Fothergill in exchange for the freehold of Number 1 Chelsea Terrace.

We shook hands on the deal and I showed the former auctioneer out. Once I had climbed back up the stairs and returned to the bedroom I found to my surprise that Becky was sitting at her writing desk.

"What are you up to?" I demanded.

"Writing my letter of resignation to Sotheby's."

Tom Arnold began going through Number 1 with far more than a fine-tooth comb in preparation for Becky joining us a month later as managing director of Trumper's Auctioneers and Fine Art Specialists. He realised that I considered our new acquisition should quickly become the flagship of the entire Trumper empire, even if – to the dismay of Hadlow – the costs were beginning to resemble those of a battleship.

Becky completed her notice at Sotheby's on Friday, 16 July 1926. She walked into Trumper's, *née* Fothergill's, the following morning at seven o'clock to take over the responsibility of refurbishing the building, at the same time releasing Tom so that he could get back to his normal duties. She immediately set about turning the basement of Number 1 into a storeroom, with the main reception remaining on the ground floor and the auction room on the first floor.

Becky and her team of specialists were to be housed on the second and third floors while the top floor, which had previously been Mr Fothergill's flat, became the company's administrative offices, with a room left over that turned out to be ideal for board meetings.

The full board met for the first time at Number 1 Chelsea Terrace on 17 October 1926.

Within three months of leaving Sotheby's Becky had "stolen" seven of the eleven staff she had wanted to join her and picked up another four from Bonham's and Phillips. At her first board meeting she warned us all that it could take anything up to three years to clear the debts incurred by the purchase and refurbishment of Number 1, and it might even be another three before she could be sure they would be making a serious contribution to the group's profits.

"Not like my first shop," I informed the board. "Made a profit within three weeks, you know, Chairman."

"Stop looking so pleased with yourself, Charlie Trumper, and try to remember I'm not selling potatoes," my wife told me.

"Oh, I don't know," I replied and on 21 October 1926, to celebrate our sixth wedding anniversary, I presented my wife with an oil painting by Van Gogh called *The Potato Eaters.*

Mr Reed of the Lefevre Gallery, who had been a personal friend of the artist, claimed it was almost as good an example as the one that hung in the Rijksmuseum. I had to agree even if I felt the asking price a little extravagant, but after some bargaining we settled on a price of six hundred guineas.

For some considerable time everything seemed to go quiet on the Mrs Trentham front. This state of affairs always worried me, because I assumed she must be up to no good. Whenever a shop came up for sale I expected her to be bidding against me, and if there was ever any trouble in the terrace I wondered if somehow she might be behind it. Becky agreed with Daphne that I was becoming paranoid, until Arnold told me he had been having a drink at the pub when Wrexall had received a call from Mrs Trentham. Arnold was unable to report anything of significance because Syd went into a back room to take it. After that my wife was willing to admit that the passing of time had obviously not lessened Mrs Trentham's desire for revenge.

It was some time in March that Joan informed us that her former mistress had spent two days packing before being driven to Southampton where she boarded a liner for Australia. Daphne was able to confirm this piece of information when she came round to dinner at Gilston Road the following week.

"So one can only assume, darlings, that she's paying a visit to that dreadful son of hers."

"In the past she's been only too willing to give lengthy reports on the bloody man's progress to anyone and everyone who cared to listen, so why's she not letting us know what she's up to this time?"

"Can't imagine," said Daphne.

"Do you think it's possible Guy might be planning to return to England now that things have settled down a little?"

"I doubt it." Daphne's brow furrowed. "Otherwise the ship would have been sailing in the opposite direction, wouldn't it? In any case, if his father's feelings are anything to go by, should Guy ever dare to show his face at Ashurst Hall he won't exactly be treated like the prodigal son."

"Something's still not quite right," I told her. "This veil of secrecy Mrs Trentham's been going in for lately requires some explanation."

It was three months later, in June 1927, that the colonel drew my attention to the announcement in *The Times* of Guy Trentham's death. "What a terrible way to die," was his only comment.

Daphne attended the funeral at Ashurst parish church – because, as she explained later, she wanted to see the coffin lowered into the grave before she was finally convinced that Guy Trentham was no longer among us.

Percy informed me later that he had only just been

able to restrain her from joining the gravediggers as they filled up the hole with good English sods. However, Daphne told us that she remained sceptical about the cause of death, despite the absence of any proof to the contrary.

"At least you'll have no more trouble from that quarter," were Percy's final words on the subject.

I scowled. "They'll have to bury Mrs Trentham alongside him before I'll believe that."

CHAPTER 26

In 1929 the Trumpers moved to a larger house in the Little Boltons. Daphne assured them that although it was "the Little", at least it was a step in the right direction. With a glance at Becky she added, "However, it's still a considerable way from being Eaton Square, darlings."

The house-warming party the Trumpers gave held a double significance for Becky, because the following day she was to be presented with her Master of Arts degree. When Percy teased her about the length of time she had taken to complete the thesis on her unrequited lover, Bernardino Luini, she cited her husband as the co-respondent.

Charlie made no attempt to defend himself, just poured Percy another brandy before clipping off the end of a cigar.

"Hoskins will be driving us to the ceremony," Daphne announced, "so we'll see you there. That is, assuming on this occasion they've been considerate enough to allow us to be seated in the first thirty rows."

Charlie was pleased to find that Daphne and Percy had been placed only a row behind them so this time were close enough to the stage to follow the entire proceedings.

"Who are they?" demanded Daniel, when fourteen dignified old gentlemen walked on to the platform wearing long black gowns and purple hoods, and took their places in the empty chairs.

"The Senate," explained Becky to her eight-year-old son. "They recommend who shall be awarded degrees. But you mustn't ask too many questions, Daniel, or you'll only annoy all the people sitting around us."

At that point, the vice-chancellor rose to present the scrolls.

"I'm afraid we'll have to sit through all the BAs before they reach me," said Becky.

"Do stop being so pompous, darling," said Daphne. "Some of us can remember when you considered being awarded a degree was the most important day in your life."

"Why hasn't Daddy got a degree?" asked Daniel as he picked up Becky's programme off the floor. "He's just as clever as you are, Mummy."

"True," said Becky. "But his daddy didn't make him stay at school as long as mine did."

Charlie leaned across. "But his granpa taught him instead how to sell fruit and vegetables, so he could do something useful for the rest of his life."

Daniel was silenced for a moment, as he weighed the value of these two contrary opinions.

"The ceremony's going to take an awfully long time if it keeps going at this rate," whispered Becky when after half an hour they had only reached the Ps.

"We can wait," whispered Daphne cheerfully. "Percy and I haven't a lot planned before Goodwood."

"Oh, look, Mummy," said Daniel. "I've found another Arnold, another Moore and another Trumper on my list."

"They're all fairly common names," said Becky, not bothering to check the programme as she placed Daniel on the edge of her seat.

"Wonder what he looks like?" asked Daniel. "Do all Trumpers look the same, Mummy?"

"No, silly, they come in all shapes and sizes."

"But he's got the same first initial as Dad," Daniel said, loudly enough for everyone in the three rows in front of them to feel they were now part of the conversation.

"Shh," said Becky, as one or two people turned round and stared in their direction.

"Bachelor of Arts," declared the vice-chancellor.

"Mathematics Second Class, Charles George Trumper."

"And he even looks like your dad," said Charlie as he rose from his place and walked up to receive his degree from the vice-chancellor. The applause increased once the assembled gathering became aware of the age of this particular graduate. Becky's mouth opened wide in disbelief, Percy rubbed his glasses, while Daphne showed no surprise at all.

"How long have you known?" demanded Becky through clenched teeth.

"He registered at Birkbeck College the day after you were awarded your degree."

"But when has he found the time?"

"It's taken him nearly eight years and an awful lot of early mornings while you were sound asleep."

By the end of her second year Becky's financial forecasts for Number 1 were beginning to look a little too optimistic. As each month passed by the overdraft seemed to remain constant, and it was not until the twenty-seventh month that she first began to make small inroads on the capital debt.

She complained to the board that although the managing director was continually helping with the turnover he was not actually contributing to the profits, because he always assumed he could purchase their most sought-after items at the buy-in cost.

"But we are at the same time building a major art collection, Mrs Trumper," he reminded her.

"And saving a great deal on tax while also making a sound investment," Hadlow pointed out. "Might even prove useful as collateral at some later date."

"Perhaps, but in the meantime it doesn't help my balance sheet, Chairman, if the managing director is always making off with my most saleable stock – and it certainly doesn't help that he's worked out the auctioneer's code so that he always knows what our reserve price is."

"You must look upon yourself as part of the company

and not as an individual, Mrs Trumper," said Charlie with a grin, adding, "though I confess it might have been a lot cheaper if we had left you at Sotheby's in the first place."

"Not to be minuted," said the chairman sternly. "By the way, what is this auctioneer's code?"

"A series of letters from a chosen word or words that indicate numbers; for example, Charlie would be C-1, H-2, A-3, but if any letter is repeated then it has to be ignored. So once you've worked out the two words we are substituting for one to zero and can get your hands on our master catalogue you will always know the reserve price we have set for each painting."

"So why don't you change the words from time to time?"

"Because once you've mastered the code, you can always work out the new words. In any case, it takes hours of practice to glance down at QNHH, and know immediately it's . . ."

"One thousand three hundred pounds," said Charlie with a smile of satisfaction.

While Becky had been trying to build up Number 1, Charlie had captured four more shops, including the barber and the newsagent, without any further interference from Mrs Trentham. As he told his fellow-directors, "I no longer believe she possesses the finances to challenge us."

"Until her father dies," Becky pointed out. "Once she inherits that fortune she could challenge Mr Selfridge and then there will be nothing Charlie can do about it."

Charlie agreed, but went on to assure the board that he had plans to get his hands on the rest of the block long before that eventuality. "No reason to believe the man hasn't got a good few years left in him yet."

"Which reminds me," said the colonel, "I'll be sixty-five next May, and feel that would be an appropriate time for me to step down as chairman."

Charlie and Becky were stunned by this sudden announcement, as neither of them had ever given a moment's thought as to when the colonel might retire.

"Couldn't you at least stay on until you're seventy?" asked Charlie quietly.

"No, Charlie, though it's kind of you to suggest it. You see, I've promised Elizabeth that we will spend our last few years on her beloved Isle of Skye. In any case, I think it's time you became chairman."

The colonel officially retired the following May. Charlie threw a party for him at the Savoy to which he invited every member of staff along with their husbands or wives. He laid on a five-course dinner with three wines for an evening that he hoped the colonel would never forget.

When the meal came to an end, Charlie rose from his place to toast the first chairman of Trumper's, before presenting him with a silver barrow which held a bottle of Glenlivet, the colonel's favourite brand of whisky. The staff all banged on their tables and demanded the outgoing chairman should reply.

The colonel rose, still straight as a ramrod, and began by thanking everyone present for their good wishes for his retirement. He went on to remind those present that when he had first joined Mr Trumper and Miss Salmon in 1920 they only possessed one shop in Chelsea Terrace, Number 147. It sold fruit and vegetables, and they had acquired it for the princely sum of one hundred pounds. Charlie could see as he glanced around the tables that many of the younger staff – and Daniel who was wearing long trousers for the first time – just didn't believe the old soldier.

"Now," the colonel continued, "we have twenty-four shops and a staff of one hundred and seventy-two. I told my wife all those years ago that I hoped I would live to see Charlie" – there was a ripple of laughter – "Mr Trumper, own the whole block, and build the biggest barrow in the world. Now I'm convinced I will." Turning to Charlie he raised his glass and said, "And I wish you luck, sir."

They cheered when he resumed his seat as chairman for the last time.

Charlie rose to reply. "Chairman," he began, "let no one in this room be in any doubt that Becky and I could not have built up Trumper's to the position it enjoys today without your support. In fact, if the truth be known, we wouldn't even have been able to purchase shops numbers two and three. I am proud to follow you and be the company's second chairman, and whenever I make a decision of any real importance I shall always imagine you are looking over my shoulder. The last proposal you made as chairman of the company will take effect from tomorrow. Tom Arnold will become managing director and Ned Denning and Bob Makins will join the board. Because it will always be Trumper's policy to promote from within.

"You are the new generation," said Charlie as he looked out into the ballroom at his staff, "and this is the first occasion at which we have all been together under the same roof. So let us set a date tonight for when we will all *work* under one roof, Trumper's of Chelsea Terrace. I give you – 1940."

The entire staff rose as one and all cried "1940" and cheered their new chairman. As Charlie sat down the conductor raised his baton to indicate that the dancing would begin.

The colonel rose from his place and invited Becky to join him for the opening waltz. He accompanied her on to an empty dance floor.

"Do you remember when you first asked me to dance?" said Becky.

"I certainly do," said the colonel. "And to quote Mr Hardy, 'That's another fine mess you've got us into.'"

"Blame him," said Becky as Charlie glided by, leading Elizabeth Hamilton around the dance floor.

The colonel smiled. "What a speech they'll make when Charlie retires," he said wistfully to Becky. "And I can't imagine who will dare follow him."

"A woman, perhaps?"

CHAPTER 27

The Silver Jubilee of King George V and Queen Mary in 1935 was celebrated by everyone at Trumper's. There were coloured posters and pictures of the royal couple in every shop window, and Tom Arnold ran a competition to see which shop could come up with the most imaginative display to commemorate the occasion.

Charlie took charge of Number 147, which he still looked upon as his personal fiefdom, and with the help of Bob Makins's daughter, who was in her first year at the Chelsea School of Art, they produced a model of the King and Queen made up of every fruit and vegetable that hailed from the British Empire.

Charlie was livid when the judges, the colonel along with the Marquess and Marchioness of Wiltshire, awarded Number 147 second place behind the flower shop, which was doing a roaring trade selling bunches of red, white and blue chrysanthemums; what had put them in first place was a vast map of the world made up entirely of flowers, with the British Empire set in red roses.

Charlie gave all the staff the day off and he escorted Becky and Daniel up the Mall at four thirty in the morning so that they could find a good vantage point to watch the King and Queen proceed from Buckingham Palace to St Paul's Cathedral, where a service of thanksgiving was to be conducted.

They arrived at the Mall only to discover that thousands of people were already covering every inch of the pavements with sleeping-bags, blankets and even tents, some having already begun their breakfast or simply fixed themselves to the spot.

The hours of waiting passed quickly as Charlie made friends with visitors who had travelled from all over the Empire. When the procession finally began, Daniel was speechless with delight as he watched the different soldiers from India, Africa, Australia, Canada and thirty-six other nations march past him. When the King and Queen drove by in the royal carriage Charlie stood to attention and removed his hat, an action he repeated when the Royal Fusiliers marched past playing their regimental anthem. Once they had all disappeared out of sight, he thought enviously of Daphne and Percy, who had been invited to attend the service at St Paul's.

After the King and Queen had returned to Buckingham Palace – well in time for their lunch, as Daniel explained to those around him – the Trumpers began their journey home. On the way back they passed Chelsea Terrace where Daniel spotted the big "2nd place" in the window of Number 147.

"Why's that there, Dad?" he immediately demanded. His mother took great delight in explaining to her son how the competition had worked.

"Where did you come, Mum?"

"Sixteenth out of twenty-six," said Charlie. "And then only because all three judges were long-standing friends."

Eight months later the King was dead.

Charlie hoped that with the accession of Edward VIII, a new era would begin, and decided that the time was well overdue for him to make a pilgrimage to America.

He warned the board of his proposed trip at their next meeting.

"Any real problems for me to worry about while I'm away?" the chairman asked his managing director.

"I'm still looking for a new manager at jewellery and

a couple of assistants for women's clothes," replied Arnold. "Otherwise it's fairly peaceful at the moment."

Confident that Tom Arnold and the board could hold the fort for the month they planned to be away, Charlie was finally convinced he should go when he read of the preparation for the launching of the *Queen Mary*. He booked a cabin for two on its maiden voyage.

Becky spent five glorious days on the *Queen* during the journey over, and was delighted to find that even her husband began to relax once he realised he had no way of getting in touch with Tom Arnold, or even Daniel, who was settling into his first boarding school. In fact, once Charlie accepted that he couldn't bother anyone he seemed thoroughly to enjoy himself as he discovered the various facilities that the liner had to offer a slightly overweight, unfit middle-aged man.

The great *Queen* sailed into the port of New York on the Monday morning to be greeted by a crowd of thousands; Charlie could only wonder how different it must have been for the Pilgrim Fathers bobbing along in the *Mayflower*, with no welcoming party and unsure of what to expect from the natives. In truth, Charlie wasn't quite sure what to expect from the natives either.

Charlie had booked in to the Waldorf Astoria Hotel, on the recommendation of Daphne, but once he and Becky had unpacked their suitcases, there was no longer any necessity to sit around and relax. He rose the following morning at four thirty and, browsing through the *New York Times*, learned of the name of Mrs Wallis Simpson for the first time. Once he had devoured the newspapers, Charlie left the Waldorf Astoria and strolled up and down Fifth Avenue studying the different displays in the shop windows. He quickly became absorbed by how inventive and original the Manhattaners were compared with their opposite numbers in Oxford Street.

As soon as the shops opened at nine, he was able to explore everything in greater detail. This time he walked up and down the aisles of the fashionable stores that made up most street corners. He checked their stock, watched the assistants and even followed certain customers around the store to see what they purchased. After each of those first three days in New York he arrived back at the hotel in the evening exhausted.

It was not until the third morning that Charlie, having completed Fifth Avenue and Madison, moved on down to Lexington, where he discovered Bloomingdale's, and from that moment Becky realised that she had lost her husband for the rest of their stay in New York.

Throughout the first two hours Charlie did nothing more than travel up and down the escalators until he had completely mastered the layout of the building. He then began to study each floor, department by department, making copious notes. On the ground floor they sold perfume, leather goods, jewellery; on the first floor, scarves, hats, gloves, stationery; on the second floor were men's clothes and on the third floor women's clothes; on the fourth floor, household goods and on up and up until he discovered that the company offices were on the twelfth floor, discreetly hidden behind a "No Entry" sign. Charlie longed to discover how that floor was laid out, but had no means of finding out.

On the fourth day he made a close study of how each of the counters was positioned, and began to draw their individual layouts. As he proceeded up the escalator to the third floor that morning, he found two athletic young men blocking his way. Charlie had no choice but to stop or try to go back down the escalator the wrong way.

"Something wrong?"

"We're not sure, sir," said one of the thickset men. "We are store detectives and wondered if you would be kind enough to come along with us."

"Delighted," said Charlie, unable to work out what their problem might be.

He was whisked up in a lift to the one floor he'd never had a chance to look round and led down a long corridor through an unmarked door and on into a bare room. There were no pictures on the wall, no carpet on the floor, and the only furniture consisted of three wooden chairs and a table. They left him alone. Moments later two older men came in to join him.

"I wonder if you would mind answering a few questions for us, sir?" began the taller of the two.

"Certainly," said Charlie, puzzled by the strange treatment he was receiving.

"Where do you come from?" asked the first.

"England."

"And how did you get here?" asked the second.

"On the maiden voyage of the *Queen Mary*." He could see that they both showed signs of nervousness when they learned this piece of information.

"Then why, sir, have you been walking all over the store for two days, making notes, but not attempted to purchase a single item?"

Charlie burst out laughing. "Because I own twenty-six shops of my own in London," he explained. "I was simply comparing the way you do things in America to the way I conduct my business in England."

The two men began to whisper to each other nervously.

"May I ask your name, sir?"

"Tru.nper, Charlie Trumper."

One of the men rose to his feet and left. Charlie had the distinct feeling that they found his story hard to believe. It brought back memories of when he had told Tommy about his first shop. The man who remained seated opposite him still did not offer an opinion, so the two of them sat silently opposite each other for several minutes before the door burst open and in walked a tall, elegantly dressed gentleman in a dark brown suit, brown shoes and a golden cravat. He almost ran forward, arms outstretched to engulf Charlie.

"I must apologise, Mr Trumper," were his opening words. "We had no idea you were in New York, let alone on the premises. My name is John Bloomingdale, and this is my little store which I hear you've been checking out."

"I certainly have," said Charlie.

Before he could say another word, Mr Bloomingdale added, "That's only fair, because I also checked over your famous barrows in Chelsea Terrace, and took one or two great ideas away with me."

"From Trumper's?" said Charlie in disbelief.

"Oh, certainly. Didn't you see the flag of America in our front window with all forty-eight states represented by different coloured flowers?"

"Well, yes," began Charlie, "but . . ."

"Stolen from you when my wife and I made a trip to see the Silver Jubilee. So consider me at your service, sir."

The two detectives were now smiling.

That night Becky and Charlie joined the Bloomingdales at their brownstone house on Sixty-First and Madison for dinner and John Bloomingdale answered Charlie's many questions until the early hours.

The following day Charlie was given an official tour of "my little store" by its owner while Patty Bloomingdale introduced Becky to the Metropolitan Museum of Art and the Frick, pumping her with endless questions about Mrs Simpson, to which Becky was unable to offer any answers as she had never heard of the lady before they'd set foot in America.

The Trumpers were sorry to say goodbye to the Bloomingdales before they continued their journey on to Chicago by train, where they had been booked into the Stevens. On their arrival in the windy city they found their room had been upgraded to a suite and Mr Joseph Field, of Marshall Field, had left a handwritten note hoping that they would be able to join them for a meal the following evening.

Over dinner in the Fields' home on Lake Shore Drive, Charlie reminded Mr Field of his advertisement describing his store as one of the biggest in the world, and warned him that Chelsea Terrace was seven feet longer.

"Ah, but will they let you build on twenty-one floors, Mr Trumper?"

"Twenty-two," countered Charlie, without the slightest

idea of what the London County Council were likely to permit.

The next day Charlie added to his growing knowledge of a major store by seeing Marshall Field's from the inside. He particularly admired the way the staff appeared to work as a team, all the girls dressed in smart green outfits with a gold "MF" on their lapels and all the floor walkers in grey suits, while the managers wore dark blue double-breasted blazers.

"Makes it easy for a customer to spot a member of my staff when they're in need of someone to help them, especially when the store becomes overcrowded," explained Mr Field.

While Charlie became engrossed in the workings of Marshall Field, Becky spent countless hours at the Chicago Art Institute, and came away particularly admiring the works of Wyeth and Remington, whom she felt should be given exhibitions in London. She was to return to England with one example of each artist tucked into newly acquired suitcases, but the British public never saw either the oil or the sculpture until years later, because once they had been unpacked Charlie wouldn't let them out of the house.

By the end of the month they were both exhausted, and sure of only one thing: they wanted to return to America again and again, though they feared they could never match the hospitality they had received, should either the Fields or the Bloomingdales ever decide to turn up in Chelsea Terrace. However, Joseph Field requested a small favour of Charlie which he promised he would deal with personally the moment he got back to London.

The rumours of the King's affair with Mrs Simpson that Charlie had seen chronicled in such detail by the American press were now beginning to reach the ears of the English, and Charlie was saddened when the King finally felt it necessary to announce his abdication. The unexpected responsibility was suddenly placed on the unprepared shoulders of the Duke of York, who became King George VI.

The other piece of news that Charlie followed on the front pages was the rise to power of Adolf Hitler in Nazi Germany. He could never understand why the Prime Minister, Mr Chamberlain, didn't use a little street sense and give the man a good thump on the nose.

"Neville Chamberlain's not a barrow boy from the East End," Becky explained to her husband over breakfast. "He's the Prime Minister."

"More's the pity," said Charlie. "Because that's exactly what would happen to Herr Hitler if he ever dared show his face in Whitechapel."

Tom Arnold didn't have a great deal to report to Charlie on his return, but he quickly became aware of the effect that the visit to America had had on his chairman by the ceaseless rat-tat-tat of orders and ideas that came flying at him from all directions during the days that followed.

"The Shops Committee," Arnold warned the chairman at their Monday morning meeting, after Charlie had finished extolling the virtues of America once again, "is now talking seriously of the effect a war with Germany might have on business."

"That lot would," said Charlie, taking a seat behind his desk. "Appeasers to a man. In any case, Germany won't declare war on any of Britain's allies – they wouldn't dare. After all, they can't have forgotten the hiding we gave them last time. So what other problems are we facing?"

"At a more mundane level," replied Tom from the other side of the desk, "I still haven't found the right person to manage the jewellery shop since Jack Slade's retirement."

"Then start advertising in the trade magazines and let me see anyone who appears suitable. Anything else?"

"Yes, a Mr Ben Schubert has been asking to see you."

"And what does he want?"

"He's a Jewish refugee from Germany, but he refused to say why he needed to see you."

"Then make an appointment for him when he gets back in touch with you."

"But he's sitting in the waiting room outside your office right now."

"In the waiting room?" said Charlie in disbelief.

"Yes. He turns up every morning and just sits there in silence."

"But didn't you explain to him I was in America?"

"Yes, I did," said Tom. "But it didn't seem to make a blind bit of difference."

"Sufferance is the badge of all our tribe," murmured Charlie. "Show the man in."

A small, bent, tired-looking figure whom Charlie suspected was not much older than himself entered the office and waited to be offered a seat. Charlie rose from behind his desk and ushered his visitor into an armchair near the fireplace before asking him how he could help.

Mr Schubert spent some time explaining to Charlie how he had escaped from Hamburg with his wife and two daughters, after so many of his friends had been sent off to concentration camps, never to be heard of again.

Charlie listened to Mr Schubert's account of his experiences at the hands of the Nazis without uttering a word. The man's escape and his description of what was taking place in Germany could have come straight off the pages of a John Buchan novel and was far more vivid than any newspaper report of recent months.

"How can I help?" asked Charlie when Mr Schubert appeared to have finished his sad tale.

The refugee smiled for the first time, revealing two gold teeth. He picked up the little briefcase by his side, placed it on Charlie's desk and then slowly opened it. Charlie stared down at the finest array of stones he had ever seen, diamonds and amethysts, some of them in the most magnificent settings. His visitor then removed what turned out to be nothing more than a thin tray to reveal loose stones, more rubies, topaz, diamonds, pearls and jade filling every inch of the deep box.

"They are but a tiny sample of what I had to leave behind, in a business that was built up by my father and his father before him. Now I must sell everything that is left to be sure that my family doesn't starve."

"You were in the jewellery business?"

"Twenty-six years," replied Mr Schubert. "Man and boy."

"And how much are you hoping to get for this lot?" Charlie pointed to the open case.

"Three thousand pounds," Mr Schubert said without hesitation. "That is far less than they are worth, but I am no longer left with the time or the will to bargain."

Charlie pulled open the drawer by his right hand, removed a cheque book and wrote out the words "Pay Mr Schubert three thousand pounds". He pushed it across the desk.

"But you have not checked their value," said Mr Schubert.

"Not necessary," said Charlie, as he rose from his chair. "Because you're going to sell them as the new manager of my jewellery shop. Which also means that you'll have to explain to me personally if they don't fetch the price you claim they are worth. Once you've repaid the advance, then we'll discuss your commission."

A smile came over Mr Schubert's face. "They teach you well in the East End, Mr Trumper."

"There are a lot of you down there to keep us on our toes," replied Charlie with a grin. "And don't forget, my father-in-law was one."

Ben Schubert stood up and hugged his new boss.

What Charlie hadn't anticipated was just how many Jewish refugees would find their way to Trumper's the Jeweller, closing deals with Mr Schubert that ensured Charlie never had to worry about the jewellery side of the business again.

It must have been about a week later that Tom Arnold entered the chairman's office without knocking. Charlie could see what an agitated state his managing director was in so he simply asked, "What's the problem, Tom?"

"Shoplifting."

"Where?"

"Number 133 – women's clothes."

"What's been stolen?"

"Two pairs of shoes and a skirt."

"Then follow the standard procedure as laid down in company regulations. First thing you do is call in the police."

"It's not that easy."

"Of course it's that easy. A thief is a thief."

"But she's claiming –"

"That her mother is ninety and dying of cancer, not to mention the fact that her children are all crippled?"

"No, that she's your sister."

Charlie rocked back in his chair, paused for a moment and then sighed heavily. "What have you done?"

"Nothing yet. I told the manager to hold on to her while I had a word with you."

"Then let's get on with it," said Charlie. He rose from behind his desk and began to march towards the door.

Neither man spoke again until they had reached Number 133 where an agitated manager was waiting for them by the front door.

"Sorry, Chairman," were Jim Grey's opening words.

"There's nothing for you to be sorry about, Jim," said Charlie as he was led through to the back room where they found Kitty sitting at a table, compact in hand, checking her lipstick in a hand mirror.

The moment she saw Charlie she clicked the compact lid closed and dropped it into her bag. On the table in front of her lay two pairs of fashionable leather shoes and a purple pleated skirt. Kitty clearly still liked the best as her selection was all from the top price range. She smiled up at her brother. The lipstick didn't help.

"Now that the big boss himself has arrived you'll find out exactly 'o I am," said Kitty, glaring at Jim Grey.

"You're a thief," said Charlie. "That's what you are."

"Come on, Charlie, you can afford it." Her voice showed no sign of remorse.

"That's not the point, Kitty. If I –"

"If you put me up in front of the beak claimin' I'm a tea leaf the press'll 'ave a field day. You wouldn't dare 'ave me arrested, Charlie, and you know it."

"Not this time, perhaps," said Charlie, "but it's the last occasion, that I promise you." He turned to the manager and added, "If this lady ever tries to leave again without paying for something, call in the police and see that she is charged without any reference to me. Do I make myself clear, Mr Grey?"

"Yes, sir."

"Yes, sir, no, sir, three bags full, sir. Don't worry yourself, Charlie, I won't be botherin' you again."

Charlie looked unconvinced.

"You see, I'm off to Canada next week where it seems there's at least one member of our family who actually cares about what happens to me."

Charlie was about to protest when Kitty picked up the skirt and both pairs of shoes and dropped them in the bag. She walked straight past the three men.

"Just a moment," said Tom Arnold.

"Bugger off," said Kitty over her shoulder as she marched through the shop.

Tom turned towards the chairman who stood and watched his sister as she stepped out on to the pavement without even looking back.

"Don't bother yourself, Tom. It's cheap at the price."

On 30 September 1938 the Prime Minister returned from Munich where he had been in talks with the German Chancellor. Charlie remained unconvinced by the Peace in our Time, Peace with Honour document that Chamberlain kept waving in front of the cameras, because after listening to Ben Schubert's first-hand description of what was taking place in the Third Reich he had become convinced that war with Germany was inevitable. Introducing conscription for those over twenty had already been debated in Parliament, and with Daniel in his last year at St Paul's waiting to sit his university entrance papers, Charlie couldn't bear the thought of losing a son to another war with the Germans. When a few weeks later Daniel was awarded a scholarship to Trinity College, Cambridge it only added to his fears.

Hitler marched into Poland on 1 September 1939 and Charlie realised that Ben Schubert's stories had not been exaggerated. Two days later Britain was at war.

For the first few weeks after the declaration of hostilities there was a lull, almost an anticlimax, and if it hadn't been for the increased number of men in uniforms marching up and down Chelsea Terrace and a drop in sales Charlie might have been forgiven for not realising Britain was engaged in a war at all.

During this time only the restaurant came up for sale. Charlie offered Mr Scallini a fair price, which he accepted without question before fleeing back to his native Florence. He was luckier than some, who were interned for no more reason than that they possessed a German or an Italian name. Charlie immediately locked up the restaurant because he wasn't sure what he could do with the premises – eating out was hardly a top priority for Londoners in 1940. Once the Scallini lease had been transferred only the antiquarian bookshop and the syndicate chaired by Mr Wrexall still remained in other traders' hands; but the significance of Mrs Trentham's large block of unoccupied flats became more obvious for all to see as each day went by.

On 7 September 1940 the false lull ended when the Luftwaffe carried out its first mass raid on the capital. After that Londoners started to emigrate to the country in droves. Charlie still refused to budge, and even ordered that "Business as usual" signs be placed in every one of his shop windows. In fact, the only concessions he made to Herr Hitler were to move his bedroom to the basement and have all the curtains changed to black drape.

Two months later, in the middle of the night, Charlie was woken by a duty constable to be told that the first bomb had fallen on Chelsea Terrace. He ran all the way from the Little Boltons down Tregunter Road in his dressing-gown and slippers to inspect the damage.

"Anyone killed?" he asked while on the move.

"Not that we know of," replied the constable, trying to keep up with him.

"Which shop did the bomb land on?"

"Can't tell you the answer to that, Mr Trumper. All I know is that it looks as if the whole of Chelsea Terrace is on fire."

As Charlie turned the corner of Fulham Road he was confronted by bright flames and dark smoke soaring up into the sky. The bomb had landed right in the middle of Mrs Trentham's flats, completely demolishing them, while at the same time shattering three of Charlie's shop windows and badly damaging the roof of Hats and Scarves.

By the time the fire brigade finally departed from the terrace all that was left of the flats was a grey, smouldering, bombed-out shell, right in the middle of the block. As the weeks passed, Charlie became only too aware of the obvious – Mrs Trentham had no intention of doing anything about the heap of rubble that now dominated the centre of Chelsea Terrace.

In May 1940 Mr Churchill took over from Mr Chamberlain as Prime Minister which gave Charlie a little more confidence about the future. He even talked to Becky of joining up again.

"Have you looked at yourself in the mirror lately?" asked his wife, laughing.

"I could get fit again, I know I could," said Charlie, pulling in his stomach. "In any case they don't only need troops for the front line."

"You can do a far more worthwhile job by keeping those shops open and stocked up for the general public."

"Arnold could do that just as well as me," said Charlie. "What's more, he's fifteen years older than I am."

However, Charlie reluctantly came to the conclusion

that Becky was right when Daphne came round to tell them that Percy had rejoined his old regiment. "Thank God they've told him he's too old to serve abroad this time," she confided in them. "So he's landed a desk job at the War Office."

The following afternoon, while Charlie was carrying out an inspection of repairs after another night of bombing, Tom Arnold warned him that Syd Wrexall's committee had begun to make noises about selling the remaining eleven of their shops, as well as the Musketeer itself.

"There's no hurry to do anything about them," said Charlie. "He'll be giving those shops away within a year."

"But by then Mrs Trentham could have bought them all at a knock-down price."

"Not while there's a war on, she won't. In any case, the damn woman knows only too well that I can't do a lot while that bloody great crater remains in the middle of Chelsea Terrace."

"Oh, hell," said Tom as the klaxon whine of the siren started up. "They must be on their way again."

"They certainly are," said Charlie, as he looked towards the sky. "You'd better get all the staff into the basement – sharpish." Charlie ran out on to the street, to find an ARP man cycling down the middle of the road, shouting instructions that everyone should head for the nearest Underground as quickly as possible. Tom Arnold had trained his managers to lock up the shops and have all the staff and customers safely in the basement with their torches and a small supply of food within five minutes. It always put Charlie in mind of the general strike. As they sat in the large storeroom under Number 1 waiting for the all-clear Charlie looked around the gathering of his fellow-Londoners and became aware of just how many of his best young men had already left Trumper's to join up; he was now down to fewer than two-thirds of his permanent staff, the majority of whom were women.

Some cradled young children in their arms, while others tried to sleep. Two regulars in a corner continued a game of chess as if the war were no more than an inconvenience. A couple of young girls practised the latest dance step on a small space left unoccupied in the centre of the basement, while others just slept.

They could all hear the bombs falling above them, and Becky told Charlie she felt sure one had landed nearby. "On Syd Wrexall's pub, perhaps?" said Charlie, trying to hide a grin. "That'll teach him to serve short measures." The all-clear klaxon eventually sounded, and they emerged back into an evening air filled with dust and ashes.

"You were right about Syd Wrexall's pub," said Becky, looking at the far corner of the block, but Charlie's eyes were not fixed on the Musketeer.

Becky's gaze eventually turned to where Charlie was staring. A bomb had landed right in the middle of his fruit and vegetable shop.

"The bastards," he said. "They've gone too far this time. Now I will join up."

"But what good will that do?"

"I don't know," said Charlie, "but at least I'll feel I'm involved in this war and not just sitting around watching."

"And what about the shops? Who's going to take charge of them?"

"Arnold can take care of them while I'm away."

"But what about Daniel and myself? Can Tom take care of us while you're away?" she asked, her voice rising.

Charlie was silent for a moment while he considered Becky's plea. "Daniel's old enough to take care of himself, and you'll have your time fully occupied seeing that Trumper's keeps its head above water. So don't say another word, Becky, because I've made up my mind."

After that nothing his wife could say or do would dissuade Charlie from signing up. To her surprise the Fusiliers were only too happy to accept their old sergeant back in the ranks, and immediately sent him off to a training camp near Cardiff.

With Tom Arnold looking anxiously on, Charlie kissed

his wife, hugged his son and shook hands with his managing director before waving goodbye to all three of them.

As he travelled down to Cardiff in a train full of fresh-faced eager youths not much older than Daniel – most of whom insisted on calling him "sir" – Charlie felt like an old man. A battered truck met the new recruits at the station and delivered them safely into barracks.

"Nice to have you back, Trumper," said a voice, as he stepped on to the parade ground for the first time in more than twenty years.

"Stan Russell. Good heavens, are you the company sergeant-major now? You were only a lance-corporal when –"

"I am, sir," Stan said. His voice dropped to a whisper. "And I'll see to it that you don't get the same treatment as the others, me old mate."

"No, you'd better not do that, Stan. I need worse than the same treatment," said Charlie, placing both hands on his stomach.

Although the senior NCOs were gentler on Charlie than they were on the raw recruits, he still found the first week of basic training a painful reminder of how little exercise he had done over the previous twenty years. When he became hungry he quickly discovered that what the NAAFI had to offer could hardly be described as appetising, while trying to get to sleep each night on a bed of unrelenting springs held together by a two-inch horsehair mattress made him less than delighted with Herr Hitler.

By the end of the second week Charlie was made up to corporal and told that if he wanted to stay on in Cardiff as an instructor they would immediately commission him as a training officer, with the rank of captain.

"The Germans are expected in Cardiff, are they, boyo?" asked Charlie. "I had no idea they played rugby football."

His exact words on the subject were relayed back to the commanding officer, so Charlie continued as a corporal, completing his basic training. By the eighth week he had been promoted to sergeant and given his own platoon to knock into shape, ready for wherever it was they were going to be sent. From that moment on there wasn't a competition, from the rifle range to the boxing ring, that his men were allowed to lose, and "Trumper's Terriers" set the standard for the rest of the battalion for the remaining four weeks.

With only ten days left before they completed their training, Stan Russell informed Charlie that the battalion was destined for Africa, where they would join Wavell in the desert. Charlie was delighted by the news, as he had long admired the reputation of the Poet General.

Sergeant Trumper spent most of that final week helping his lads write letters to their families and girlfriends. He didn't intend to put pen to paper himself until the last moment. With a week to go he admitted to Stan that he wasn't ready to take on the Germans in anything much more than a verbal battle.

He was in the middle of a Bren demonstration with his platoon, explaining cocking and reloading, when a red-faced lieutenant came running up.

"Trumper."

"Sir," said Charlie, leaping to attention.

"The commanding officer wants to see you immediately."

"Yes, sir," said Charlie. He instructed his corporal to carry on with the lesson and then chased after the lieutenant.

"Why are we running so fast?" asked Charlie.

"Because the commanding officer was running when he came looking for me."

"Then it has to be at least high treason," said Charlie.

"Heaven knows what it is, Sergeant, but you'll find out soon enough," said the lieutenant, as they arrived outside the CO's door. The lieutenant, closely followed by Charlie, entered the colonel's office without knocking.

"7312087 Sergeant Trumper reporting –"

"You can cut all that bullshit out, Trumper," said the

colonel, as Charlie watched the commanding officer pacing up and down, slapping his side with a swagger stick. "My car is waiting for you at the gate. You are to go straight to London."

"London, sir?"

"Yes, Trumper, London. Mr Churchill's just been on the blower. Wants to see you soonest."

CHAPTER 28

The colonel's driver did everything in his power to get Sergeant Trumper to London as quickly as possible. He pressed his foot to the floor again and again as he tried to keep the speedometer above eighty. However, as they were continually held up en route by convoys of troops, transportation lorries, and even at one point Warrior tanks, the task was daunting. When Charlie finally reached Chiswick on the outskirts of London they were then faced with the blackout, followed by an air-raid, followed by the all-clear, followed by countless more road blocks all the way to Downing Street.

Despite having six hours to ponder as to why Mr Churchill could possibly want to see him, when the car came to a halt outside Number 10 Charlie was no nearer a conclusion than he had been when he left the barracks at Cardiff earlier that afternoon.

When he explained to the policeman on the door who he was, the constable checked his clipboard, then gave a sharp rap on the brass knocker before inviting Sergeant Trumper to step into the hall. Charlie's first reaction on being inside Number 10 was surprise at discovering how small the house was compared with Daphne's home in Eaton Square.

A young Wren officer came forward to greet the middle-aged sergeant before ushering him through to an anteroom.

"The Prime Minister has the American ambassador

with him at the moment," she explained. "But he doesn't expect his meeting with Mr Kennedy to last much longer."

"Thank you," said Charlie.

"Would you like a cup of tea?"

"No, thank you." Charlie was too nervous to think about drinking tea. As she closed the door, he picked up a copy of *Lilliput* from a side table and leafed through the pages, but didn't attempt to take in the words.

After he had thumbed through every magazine on the table – and they were even more out of date at Number 10 than at his dentist – he began to take an interest in the pictures on the wall. Wellington, Palmerston and Disraeli; all inferior portraits that Becky would not have bothered to offer for sale at Number 1. Becky. Good heavens, he thought, she doesn't even know I'm in London. He stared at the telephone that rested on the sideboard, aware that he couldn't possibly call her from Number 10. In frustration he began to pace round the room feeling like a patient waiting for the doctor to tell him if the diagnosis was terminal. Suddenly the door swung open and the Wren reappeared.

"The Prime Minister will see you now, Mr Trumper," she said, then proceeded to lead him up a narrow staircase, past the framed photographs of former Prime Ministers. By the time he reached Chamberlain he found himself on the landing facing a man of five feet nine inches in height who stood, arms on hips, legs apart, staring defiantly at him.

"Trumper," said Churchill, thrusting out his hand. "Good of you to come at such short notice. Hope I didn't tear you away from anything important."

Just a Bren lesson, thought Charlie, but decided not to mention the fact as he followed the shambling figure through to his study. Churchill waved his guest into a comfortable winged chair near a roaring fire; Charlie looked at the burning logs and remembered the Prime Minister's strictures to the nation on wasting coal.

"You must be wondering what this is all about," the

Prime Minister said, as he lit up a cigar and opened a file that was resting on his knee. He started to read.

"Yes, sir," said Charlie, but his reply failed to elicit any explanation. Churchill continued to read from the copious notes in front of him.

"I see we have something in common."

"We do, Prime Minister?"

"We both served in the Great War."

"The war to end all wars."

"Yes, wrong again, wasn't he?" said Churchill. "But then he was a politician." The Prime Minister chuckled before continuing to read from the files. Suddenly he looked up. "However, we both have a far more important role to play in *this* war, Trumper, and I can't waste your time on teaching recruits Bren lessons in Cardiff."

The damn man knew all along, thought Charlie.

"When a nation is at war, Trumper," said the Prime Minister, closing the file, "people imagine victory will be guaranteed so long as we have more troops and better equipment than the enemy. But battles can be lost or won by something that the generals in the field have no control over. A little cog that stops the wheels going round smoothly. Only today I've had to set up a new department in the War Office to deal with code-breaking. I've stolen the two best professors they have at Cambridge, along with their assistants, to help solve the problem. Invaluable cogs, Trumper."

"Yes, sir," said Charlie, without a clue as to what the old man was talking about.

"And I have a problem with another of those cogs, Trumper, and my advisors tell me you're the best man to come up with a solution."

"Thank you, sir."

"Food, Trumper, and more important its distribution. I understand from Lord Woolton, the minister in charge, that supplies are fast running out. We can't even get enough potatoes shipped over from Ireland. So one of the biggest problems I'm facing at this moment is how to keep the nation's stomach full while waging a war on the enemy's shores and at the same time keeping our supply routes open. The minister tells me that when the food arrives in the ports it can often be weeks before the damn stuff is moved, and sometimes even then it ends up in the wrong place.

"Added to this," continued the Prime Minister, "our farmers are complaining that they can't do the job properly because we're recruiting their best men for the armed forces, and they're not receiving any back-up from the government in exchange." He paused for a moment to relight his cigar. "So what I'm looking for is a man who has spent his life buying, selling and distributing food, someone who has lived in the market place and whom the farmers and the suppliers will both respect. In short, Trumper, I need you. I want you to join Woolton as his right-hand man, and see that we get the supplies, and then that those supplies are distributed to the right quarters. Can't think of a more important job. I hope you'll be willing to take on the challenge."

The desire to get started must have shown in Charlie's eyes, because the Prime Minister didn't even bother to wait for his reply. "Good, I can see you've got the basic idea. I'd like you to report to the Ministry of Food at eight tomorrow morning. A car will come to pick you up from your home at seven forty-five."

"Thank you, sir," said Charlie, not bothering to explain to the Prime Minister that if a car did turn up at seven forty-five the driver would have missed him by over three hours.

"And, Trumper, I'm going to make you up to a brigadier so you've got some clout."

"I'd prefer to remain plain Charlie Trumper."

"Why?"

"I might at some time find it necessary to be rude to a general."

The Prime Minister removed his cigar and roared with laughter before he accompanied his guest to the door. "And,

Trumper," he said, placing a hand on Charlie's shoulder, "should the need ever arise, don't hesitate to contact me direct, if you think it could make the difference. Night or day. I don't bother with sleep, you know."

"Thank you, sir," said Charlie, as he proceeded down the staircase.

"Good luck, Trumper, and see you feed the people."

The Wren escorted Charlie back to his car and saluted him as he took his place in the front seat, which surprised Charlie because he was still dressed as a sergeant.

He asked the driver to take him to the Little Boltons via Chelsea Terrace. As they travelled slowly through the streets of the West End, it saddened him to find old familiar landmarks so badly damaged by the Luftwaffe, although he realised no one in London had escaped the Germans' relentless air bombardment.

When he arrived home, Becky opened the front door and threw her arms around her husband. "What did Mr Churchill want?" was her first question.

"How did you know I was seeing the Prime Minister?"

"Number 10 rang here first to ask where they could get hold of you. So what did he want?"

"Someone who can deliver his fruit and veg on a regular basis."

Charlie liked his new boss from the moment they met. Although James Woolton had come to the Ministry of Food with the reputation of being a brilliant businessman, he admitted that he was not an expert in Charlie's particular field but said his department was there to see that Charlie was given every assistance he required.

Charlie was allocated a large office on the same corridor as the minister and supplied with a staff of fourteen headed by a young personal assistant called Arthur Selwyn who hadn't been long down from Oxford.

Charlie soon learnt that Selwyn had a brain as sharp as a razor, and although he had no experience of Charlie's world he only ever needed to be told something once.

The navy supplied Charlie with a personal secretary called Jessica Allen, who appeared to be willing to work the same hours as him. Charlie wondered why such an attractive, intelligent girl appeared to have no social life until he studied her file more carefully and discovered that her young fiancé had been killed on the beach at Dunkirk.

Charlie quickly returned to his old routine of coming into the office at four thirty, even before the cleaners had arrived, which allowed him to read through his papers until eight without fear of being disturbed.

Because of the special nature of his assignment and the obvious support of his minister, doors opened whenever he appeared. Within a month most of his staff were coming in by five, although Selwyn turned out to be the only one of them who also had the stamina to stick with him through the night.

For that first month Charlie did nothing but read reports and listen to Selwyn's detailed assessment of the problems they had been facing for the best part of a year, while occasionally popping in to see the minister to clarify a point that he didn't fully understand.

During the second month Charlie decided to visit every major port in the kingdom to find out what was holding up the distribution of food, food that was sometimes simply being left to rot for days on end in the storehouses on the docksides throughout the country. When he reached Liverpool he quickly discovered that supplies were rightly not getting priority over tanks or men when it came to movement, so he requested that his ministry should operate a fleet of its own vehicles, with no purpose other than to distribute food supplies across the nation.

Woolton somehow managed to come up with sixty-two trucks, most of them, he admitted, rejects from war surplus. "Not unlike me," Charlie admitted. However, the minister still couldn't spare the men to drive them.

"If men aren't available, Minister, I need two hundred women," Charlie suggested, and despite the cartoonists' gentle jibes about women drivers it only took another month before the food started to move out of the docks within hours of its arrival.

The dockers themselves responded well to the women drivers, while trade union leaders never found out that Charlie spoke to them with one accent while using quite another when he was back at the ministry.

Once Charlie had begun to solve the distribution problem, he came up against two more dilemmas. On the one hand, the farmers were complaining that they couldn't produce enough food at home because the armed forces were taking away all their best men; on the other, Charlie found he just wasn't getting enough supplies coming in from abroad because of the success of the German U-boat campaign.

He came up with two solutions for Woolton's consideration. "You supplied me with lorry girls, now you must give me land girls," Charlie told him. "I need five thousand this time, because that's what the farmers are saying they're short of."

The next day Woolton was interviewed on the BBC and made a special appeal to the nation for land girls. Five hundred applied in the first twenty-four hours, and the minister had the five thousand Charlie requested within ten weeks. Charlie allowed the applications to continue pouring in until he had seven thousand, and could clearly identify a smile on the face of the president of the National Farmers' Union.

Over the second problem of lack of supplies, Charlie advised Woolton to buy rice as a substitute staple diet because of the hardship the nation was facing with a potato shortage. "But where do we find such a commodity?" asked Woolton. "China and the Far East is much too hazardous a journey for us even to consider right now."

"I'm aware of that," said Charlie, "but I know a supplier in Egypt who could let us have a million tons a month."

"Can he be trusted?"

"Certainly not," said Charlie. "But his brother still works in the East End, and if we were to intern him for a few months I reckon I could pull off some sort of deal with the family."

"If the press ever found out what we were up to, Charlie, they'd have my guts for garters."

"*I'm* not going to tell them, Minister."

The following day Eli Calil found himself interned in Brixton Prison while Charlie flew off to Cairo to close a deal with his brother for a million tons of rice per month, rice that had been originally earmarked for the Italians.

Charlie agreed with Nasim Calil that the payments could be made half in pounds sterling and half in piastres, and, as long as the shipments always arrived on time, no paperwork concerning the money needed be evident at the Cairo end. Failing this, Calil's government would be informed of the full details of their transaction.

"Very fair, Charlie, but then you always were. But what about my brother Eli?" asked Nasim Calil.

"We'll release him at the end of the war but then only if every shipment is delivered on time."

"Also most considerate," Nasim replied. "A couple of years in gaol will do Eli no harm. He is, after all, one of the few members of my family who hasn't yet been detained at His Majesty's pleasure."

Charlie tried to spend at least a couple of hours a week with Tom Arnold so that he could be kept up to date on what was happening in Chelsea Terrace. Tom had to report that Trumper's was now losing money steadily and he had found it necessary to close five of the premises and board up another four; this saddened Charlie because Syd Wrexall had recently written to him offering his entire group of shops and the bombed-out corner pub for only six thousand pounds, a sum Wrexall was claiming Charlie had once made him a firm offer on. All Charlie had to do now, Wrexall reminded Arnold in an accompanying letter, was to sign the cheque.

Charlie studied the contract that Wrexall had enclosed and said, "I made that offer long before the outbreak of war. Send all the documents back. I'm confident he'll let those shops go for around four thousand by this time next year. But try and keep him happy, Tom."

"That might prove a little difficult," replied Tom. "Since that bomb landed on the Musketeer Syd's gone off to live in Cheshire. He's now the landlord of a country pub in some place called Hatherton."

Charlie had to leave Tom and travel on down to Southampton where Calil's first shipment of rice had arrived. His lorry girls had gone to pick up the bags, but the manager of the port was refusing to release them without proper signed documentation. It was a trip Charlie could have well done without, and one he certainly didn't intend to make every month.

When he arrived on the dockside he quickly discovered that there was no problem with the trade unions, who were quite willing to unload the entire cargo, or with his girls, who were just sitting on the mudguards of their lorries waiting to take delivery.

Over a pint at the local pub, Alf Redwood, the dockers' leader, warned Charlie that Mr Simkins, the general manager of the Docks and Harbour Board, was a stickler when it came to paperwork and liked everything done by the book.

"Does he?" said Charlie. "Then I'll have to stick by the book, won't I?" After paying for his round, he walked over to the administration block where he asked to see Mr Simkins.

"He's rather busy at the moment," said a receptionist, not bothering to look up from painting her nails. Charlie walked straight past her and into Simkins's office, to find a thin, balding man sitting alone behind a very large desk dipping a biscuit into a cup of tea.

"And who are you?" asked the port's official, taken so completely by surprise that he dropped his biscuit into the tea.

"Charlie Trumper. And I'm here to find out why you won't release my rice."

"I don't have the proper authority," said Simkins, as he tried to rescue his biscuit which was now floating on the top of his morning beverage. "No official papers have come from Cairo, and your forms from London are inadequate, quite inadequate." He gave Charlie a smile of satisfaction.

"But it could take days for me to get the necessary paperwork sorted out."

"That's not my problem."

"But we're at war, man."

"Which is why we must all try to keep to the regulations. I'm sure the Germans do."

"I don't give a damn what the Germans do," said Charlie. "I've got a million tons of rice coming through this port every month, and I want to distribute every last grain of it as quickly as possible. Do I make myself clear?"

"You certainly do, Mr Trumper, but I shall still require the official papers correctly completed before you get your rice."

"I order you to release that rice immediately," said Charlie, barking at him for the first time.

"No need to raise your voice, Mr Trumper, because as I've already explained you don't have the authority to order me to do anything. This is the Docks and Harbour Board and it doesn't, as I'm sure you know, come under the Ministry of Food. I should go back to London, and this time do try a little harder to see that we get the correct forms properly filled in."

Charlie felt he was too old to hit the man, so he simply picked up the telephone on Simkins's desk and asked for a number.

"What are you doing?" demanded Simkins. "That's my telephone – you don't have the proper authority to use my telephone."

Charlie clung on to the phone and turned his back on

Simkins. When he heard the voice on the other end of the line, he said, "It's Charlie Trumper. Can you put me through to the Prime Minister?"

Simkins's cheeks turned first red, then white, as the blood drained quickly from his face. "There's really no need –" he began.

"Good morning, sir," said Charlie. "I'm down in Southampton. The rice problem I mentioned to you last night. There turns out to be a bit of a hold-up at this end. I don't seem to be able –"

Simkins was now frantically waving his hands like a semaphore sailor in an attempt to gain Charlie's attention, while at the same time nodding his head energetically up and down.

"I've got a million tons coming in every month, Prime Minister, and the girls are just sitting on their –"

"It will be all right," whispered Simkins as he began to circle Charlie. "It will be all right, I can assure you."

"Do you want to speak to the man in charge yourself, sir?"

"No, no," said Simkins. "That won't be necessary. I have all the forms, all the forms you need, all the forms."

"I'll let him know, sir," said Charlie, pausing for a moment. "I'm due back in London this evening. Yes, sir, yes, I'll brief you the moment I return. Goodbye, Prime Minister."

"Goodbye," said Becky as she put down the telephone. "And no doubt you'll tell me what all that was about when you do get home tonight."

The minister roared with laughter when Charlie repeated the whole story to him and Jessica Allen later that evening.

"You know, the Prime Minister would have been quite happy to speak to the man if you had wanted him to," said Woolton.

"If he'd done that Simkins would have had a heart

attack," said Charlie. "And then my rice, not to mention my drivers, would have been stuck in that port for ever. In any case, with the food shortage the way it is I wouldn't have wanted the wretched man to waste another of his biscuits."

Charlie was in Carlisle attending a farmers' conference when an urgent call came through for him from London.

"Who is it?" he asked as he tried to concentrate on a delegate who was explaining the problems of increasing turnip yields.

"The Marchioness of Wiltshire," whispered Arthur Selwyn.

"Then I'll take it," said Charlie, and left the conference room to return to his bedroom where the hotel operator put the call through.

"Daphne, what can I do for you, my luv?"

"No, darling, it's what I can do for you, as usual. Have you read your *Times* this morning?"

"Glanced at the headlines. Why?" asked Charlie.

"Then you'd better check the obituaries page more carefully. In particular, the last line of one of them. I won't waste any more of your time, darling, as the Prime Minister keeps reminding us just what a vital role you're playing in winning the war."

Charlie laughed as the line went dead.

"Anything I can do to help?" asked Selwyn.

"Yes, Arthur, I need a copy of today's *Times*."

When Selwyn returned with a copy of the morning paper, Charlie flicked quickly through the pages until he came to the obituaries: Admiral Sir Alexander Dexter, a First World War commander of outstanding tactical ability; J. T. Macpherson, the balloonist and author; and Sir Raymond Hardcastle, the industrialist . . .

Charlie skimmed through the bare details of Sir Raymond's career: born and educated in Yorkshire; built up his father's engineering firm at the turn of the century.

During the twenties Hardcastle's had expanded from a fledgling company into one of the great industrial forces in the north of England. In 1938 Hardcastle sold his shareholding to John Brown and Co for seven hundred and eighty thousand pounds. But Daphne was right – the last line was the only one that really concerned Charlie.

"Sir Raymond, whose wife died in 1914, is survived by two daughters, Miss Amy Hardcastle and Mrs Gerald Trentham."

Charlie picked up the telephone on the desk beside him and asked to be put through to a Chelsea number. A few moments later Tom Arnold came on the line.

"Where the hell did you say Wrexall was to be found?" was the only question Charlie asked.

"As I explained when you last enquired, Chairman, he now runs a pub in Cheshire, the Happy Poacher, in a village called Hatherton."

Charlie thanked his managing director and replaced the receiver without another word.

"Can I be of any assistance?" asked Selwyn drily.

"What's my programme for the rest of the day looking like, Arthur?"

"Well, they haven't quite finished with the turnips yet, then you're meant to be attending more sessions all afternoon. This evening you're proposing the health of the government at the conference dinner before finally presenting the farmers' annual dairy awards tomorrow morning."

"Then pray I'm back in time for the dinner," said Charlie. He stood up and grabbed his overcoat.

"Do you want me to come with you?" asked Selwyn, trying to keep up with his master.

"No, thank you, Arthur. It's a personal matter. Just cover for me if I'm not back in time."

Charlie ran down the stairs and out into the yard. His driver was dozing peacefully behind the wheel.

Charlie jumped into his car and the slammed door woke him up. "Take me to Hatherton."

"Hatherton, sir?"

"Yes, Hatherton. Head south out of Carlisle, and by then I should be able to point you in the right direction." Charlie flicked open the road map, turned to the back and began running his finger down the Hs. There were five Hathertons listed but luckily just the one in Cheshire. The only other word Charlie uttered on the entire journey was "Faster," which he repeated several times. They passed through Lancaster, Preston and Warrington before coming to a halt outside the Happy Poacher half an hour before the pub was due to close for the afternoon.

Syd Wrexall's eyes nearly popped out of his head when Charlie strolled in the front door.

"A Scotch egg and a pint of your best bitter, landlord, and no short measures," Charlie said with a grin, placing a briefcase by his side.

"Fancy seeing you in these parts, Mr Trumper," declared Syd after he had shouted over his shoulder, "Hilda, one Scotch egg, and come and see who's 'ere."

"I was just on my way to a farmers' conference in Carlisle," explained Charlie. "Thought I'd drop by and have a pint and a snack with an old friend."

"That's right neighbourly of you," said Syd as he placed the pint of bitter on the counter in front of him. "Of course, we read about you in the papers a lot nowadays, and all the work you're doing with Lord Woolton for the war effort. You're becoming quite a celebrity."

"It's a fascinating job the Prime Minister has given me," said Charlie. "I can only hope that I'm doing some good," he added, hoping he sounded pompous enough.

"But what about your shops, Charlie? Who's taking care of them with you away so much of the time?"

"Arnold's back at base doing the best he can in the circumstances, but I'm afraid I've got four or five closed, not to mention those that were already boarded up. I can tell you, Syd, in confidence" – Charlie lowered his voice – "if things don't start brightening up before too long I shall soon be looking for a buyer myself." Wrexall's wife came bustling in carrying a plate of food.

"Hello, Mrs Wrexall," said Charlie, as she put down a Scotch egg and a plate of salad in front of him. "Good to see you again, and why don't you and your husband have a drink on me?"

"Don't mind if I do, Charlie. Can you see to it, Hilda?" he said, as he leaned over the bar conspiratorially. "Don't suppose you know anyone who'd be interested in purchasing the syndicate's shops, and the pub, for that matter?"

"Can't say I do," said Charlie. "If I remember rightly, Syd, you were asking an awful lot of money for the Musketeer which is now nothing more than a bomb site. Not to mention the state of the few shops the syndicate still have boarded up."

"I came down to your figure of six thousand, which I thought we had already shaken hands on, but Arnold told me you were no longer interested," said Syd as his wife placed two pints on the counter before going off to serve another customer.

"He told you that?" said Charlie, trying to sound surprised.

"Oh, yes," said Wrexall. "I accepted your offer of six thousand, even sent the signed contract for your approval, but he just returned the documents without so much as a by your leave."

"I don't believe it," said Charlie. "After I'd given my word, Syd. Why didn't you get in touch with me direct?"

"Not that easy nowadays," said Wrexall, "what with your new exalted position I didn't think you'd be available for the likes of me."

"Arnold had no right to do that," said Charlie. "He obviously didn't appreciate how long our relationship goes back. I do apologise, Syd, and remember, for you I'm always available. You don't still have the contract, by any chance?"

"Certainly do," said Wrexall. "And it'll prove I'm as good as my word." He disappeared, leaving Charlie to take a bite of Scotch egg and a slow swig of the local brew.

The publican returned a few minutes later and slammed down some documents on the bar top. "There you are, Charlie, true as I stand here."

Charlie studied the contract that he had been shown by Arnold some eighteen months before. It already bore the signature "Sydney Wrexall", with the figures "six thousand" written in after the words "for the consideration of – "

"All that it needed was the date and your signature," said Syd. "I never thought you'd do that to me, Charlie, after all these years."

"As you well know, Syd, I'm a man of my word. I'm only sorry my managing director wasn't properly acquainted with our personal arrangement." Charlie removed a wallet from his pocket, took out a cheque book, and wrote out the words Syd Wrexall on the top line and six thousand pounds on the line below before signing it with a flourish.

"You're a gentleman, Charlie, I always said you were. Didn't I always say he was, Hilda?"

Mrs Wrexall nodded enthusiastically as Charlie smiled, picked up the contract, placed all the papers inside his briefcase and then shook hands with the publican and his wife.

"How much is the damage?" he asked after he had drained the last drop of his beer.

"It's on the house," said Wrexall.

"But, Syd – "

"No, I insist, wouldn't dream of treating an old friend like a customer, Charlie. On the house," he repeated as the telephone rang and Hilda Wrexall went off to answer it.

"Well, I must be on my way," said Charlie. "Otherwise I'll be late for this conference, and I'm meant to be delivering another speech tonight. Nice to have done business with you, Syd." He had just reached the door of the pub as Mrs Wrexall came rushing back to the counter.

"There's a lady on the line for you, Syd. Calling long distance. Says her name is Mrs Trentham."

As the months passed Charlie became the master of his brief. No port director could be sure when he might burst into his office, no supplier was surprised when he demanded to check his invoices and the president of the National Farmers' Union positively purred whenever Charlie's name came up in conversation.

He never found it necessary to phone the Prime Minister, although Mr Churchill did phone him on one occasion. It was four forty-five in the morning when Charlie picked up the receiver on his desk.

"Good morning," he said.

"Trumper?"

"Yes, who's that?"

"Churchill."

"Good morning, Prime Minister. What can I do for you, sir?"

"Nothing. I was just checking that it was true what they say about you. By the way, thank you." The phone went dead.

Charlie even managed from time to time to have lunch with Daniel. The boy was now attached to the War Office, but would never talk about the work he was involved in. After he was promoted to captain, Charlie's only worry became what Becky's reaction would be if she ever saw him in uniform.

When Charlie visited Tom Arnold at the end of the month he learned that Mr Hadlow had retired as manager of the bank and his replacement, a Mr Paul Merrick, was not proving to be quite as amenable. "Says our overdraft is reaching unacceptable levels and perhaps it's time we did something about it," explained Tom.

"Does he?" said Charlie. "Then I shall obviously have to see this Mr Merrick and tell him a few home truths."

Although Trumper's now owned all the shops in Chelsea Terrace, with the exception of the bookshop, Charlie was still faced with the problem of Mrs Trentham and her bombed-out flats, not to mention the additional worry of Herr Hitler and his unfinished war: these he tended to place in roughly the same category, and nearly always in that order.

The war with Herr Hitler began to take a step in the right direction towards the end of 1942 with the victory of the eighth army at El Alamein. Charlie felt confident that Churchill was right when he declared that the tide had turned, as first Africa, then Italy, France and finally Germany were invaded.

But by then it was Mr Merrick who was insisting on seeing Charlie.

When Charlie entered Mr Merrick's office for the first time he was surprised to find how young Mr Hadlow's replacement was. It also took him a few moments to get used to a bank manager who didn't wear a waistcoat or a black tie. Paul Merrick was a shade taller than Charlie and every bit as broad in everything except his smile. Charlie quickly discovered that Mr Merrick had no small-talk.

"Are you aware, Mr Trumper, that your company account is overdrawn by some forty-seven thousand pounds and your present income doesn't even cover . . ."

"But the property must be worth four or five times that amount."

"Only if you're able to find someone who's willing to buy it."

"But I'm not a seller."

"You may be left with no choice, Mr Trumper, if the bank decides to foreclose on you."

"Then I'll just have to change banks, won't I?" said Charlie.

"You have obviously not had the time recently to read the minutes of your own board meetings because when they last met, your managing director Mr Arnold reported that he had visited six banks in the past month and none of them had showed the slightest interest in taking over Trumper's account."

Merrick waited for his customer's response but as Charlie remained silent he continued. "Mr Crowther also explained to the board on that occasion that the problem you are now facing has been caused by property prices being lower now than they have been at any time since the 1930s."

"But that will change overnight once the war is over."

"Possibly, but that might not be for several years and you could be insolvent long before then . . ."

"More like twelve months would be my guess."

". . . especially if you continue to sign cheques to the value of six thousand pounds for property worth about half that amount."

"But if I hadn't . . ."

"You might not be in such a precarious position."

Charlie remained silent for some time. "So what do you expect me to do about it?" he asked finally.

"I require you to sign over all the properties and stock held by your company as collateral against the overdraft. I have already drawn up the necessary papers."

Merrick swivelled round a document that lay on the middle of his desk. "If you feel able to sign," he added, pointing to a dotted line near the bottom of the page marked by two pencil crosses, "I would be willing to extend your credit for a further twelve months."

"And if I refuse?"

"I'll be left with no choice but to issue an insolvency notice within twenty-eight days."

Charlie stared down at the document and saw that Becky had already signed on the line above his. Both men remained silent for some time as Charlie weighed up the alternatives. Then, without offering any further comment, Charlie took out his pen, scrawled a signature between the two pencilled crosses, swivelled the document back round, turned, and marched out of the room without another word.

The surrender of Germany was signed by General Jodl and accepted on behalf of the Allies by General Bedell Smith at Reims on 7 May 1945.

Charlie would have joined the VE Day celebrations in Trafalgar Square had Becky not reminded him that their overdraft had reached nearly sixty thousand pounds and Merrick was once again threatening them with bankruptcy.

"He's got his hands on the property and all our stock. What else does he expect me to do?" demanded Charlie.

"He's now suggesting that we sell the one thing that could clear the debt, and would even leave some capital over to see us through the next couple of years."

"And what's that?"

"Van Gogh's *The Potato Eaters*."

"Never!"

"But Charlie, the painting belongs to . . ."

Charlie made an appointment to see Lord Woolton the following morning and explained to the Minister he was now faced with his own problems that required his immediate attention. He therefore asked, now the war in Europe was over, if he could be released from his present duties.

Lord Woolton fully understood Charlie's dilemma, and made it clear how sad he and all at the department would be to see him go.

When Charlie left his office a month later the only thing he took with him was Jessica Allen.

Charlie's problems didn't ease up during 1945 as property prices continued to fall and inflation continued to rise. He was nevertheless touched when, after peace had been declared with Japan, and after Winston Churchill's General Election defeat, the former Prime Minister held a dinner in his honour, before he left Number 10. Daphne admitted that she had never entered the building, and told Becky that she wasn't even sure she wanted to. Percy admitted he wanted to, and was envious.

There were several leading cabinet ministers present for the occasion. Becky was placed between Churchill and the rising young star Rab Butler, while Charlie was seated next to Mrs Churchill and Lady Woolton. Becky watched her husband as he chatted in a relaxed way with the Prime

Minister and Lord Woolton, and had to smile when Charlie had the nerve to offer the old man a cigar he had specially selected that afternoon from Number 139. No one in that room could possibly have guessed that they were on the verge of bankruptcy.

When the evening finally came to an end, Becky thanked the Prime Minister, who in turn thanked her.

"What for?" asked Becky.

"Taking telephone calls in my name, and making excellent decisions on my behalf," he said, as he accompanied them both down the long corridor to the front hall.

"I had no idea you knew," said Charlie, turning scarlet.

"Knew? Woolton told the entire cabinet the next day. Never seen them laugh so much."

When the Prime Minister reached the front door of Number 10, he gave Becky a slight bow and said, "Goodnight, Lady Trumper."

"You know what that means, don't you?" said Charlie as he drove out of Downing Street and turned right into Whitehall.

"That you're about to get a knighthood?"

"Yes, but more important, we're going to have to sell the Van Gogh."

DANIEL

1931-1947

CHAPTER 29

"You're a little bastard," remains my first memory. I was five and three-quarters at the time and the words were being shouted by a small girl on the far side of the playground as she pointed at me and danced up and down. The rest of the class stopped and stared, until I ran across and pinned her against the wall.

"What does it mean?" I demanded, squeezing her arms.

She burst into tears and said, "I don't know. I just heard my mum tell my dad that you were a little bastard."

"I know what the word means," said a voice from behind me. I turned round to find myself surrounded by the rest of the pupils from my class, but I was quite unable to work out who had spoken.

"What does it mean?" I said again, even louder.

"Give me sixpence and I'll tell you."

I stared up at Neil Watson, the form bully who always sat in the row behind me.

"I've only got threepence."

He considered the offer for some time before saying, "All right then, I'll tell you for threepence."

He walked up to me, thrust out the palm of his hand, and waited until I'd slowly unwrapped my handkerchief and passed over my entire pocket money for the week. He then cupped his hands and whispered into my ear, "You don't have a father."

"It's not true!" I shouted, and started punching him on the chest. But he was far bigger than me and only laughed at my feeble efforts. The bell sounded for the end of break and everyone ran back to class, several of them laughing and shouting in unison, "Daniel's a little bastard."

Nanny came to pick me up from school that afternoon and when I was sure none of my classmates could overhear me I asked her what the word meant. She only said, "What a disgraceful question, Daniel, and I can only hope that it's not the sort of thing they're teaching you at St David's. Please don't let me ever hear you mention the word again."

Over tea in the kitchen, when Nanny had left to go and run my bath, I asked Cook to tell me what bastard meant. All she said was, "I'm sure I don't know, Master Daniel, and I would advise you not to ask anyone else."

I didn't dare ask my mother or father in case what Neil Watson had said turned out to be true, and I lay awake all night wondering how I could find out.

Then I remembered that a long time ago my mother had gone into hospital and was meant to come back with a brother or sister for me, and didn't. I wondered if that's what made you a bastard.

About a week later Nanny had taken me to visit Mummy at Guy's hospital but I can't recall that much about the outing, except that she looked very white and sad. I remember feeling very happy when she eventually came home.

The next episode in my life that I recall vividly was going to St Paul's School at the age of eleven. There I was made to work really hard for the first time in my life. At my prep school I came top in almost every subject without having to do much more than any other child, and although I was called "swot" or "swotty", it never worried me. At St Paul's there turned out to be lots of boys who were clever, but none of them could touch me when it came to maths. I not only enjoyed a subject so many of my classmates seemed to dread but the marks I was awarded in the end of term exams appeared always to delight my mum and dad. I couldn't wait for the next algebraic equation, a further geometric puzzle or the challenge of solving an arithmetic test in my head while others in the form sucked their pencils as they considered pages of longhand figures.

I did quite well in other subjects and although I was not much good at games I took up the cello and was invited to join the school orchestra, but my form master said none of this was important because I was obviously going to be a mathematician for the rest of my life. I didn't understand what he meant at the time, as I knew Dad had left school at fourteen to run my great-grandfather's fruit and vegetable barrow in Whitechapel, and even though Mum had gone to London University she still had to work at Number 1 Chelsea Terrace to keep Dad "in the style to which he'd become accustomed". Or that's what I used to hear Mum telling him at breakfast from time to time.

It must have been around that time that I discovered what the word "bastard" really meant. We were reading *King John* out loud in class, so I was able to ask Mr Quilter, my English master, without drawing too much attention to the question. One or two of the boys looked round and sniggered, but this time there were no pointed fingers or whispers, and when I was told the meaning I remember thinking Neil Watson hadn't been that far off the mark in the first place. But of course such an accusation could not be levelled at me, because my very first memories had involved my mum and dad being together. They had always been Mr and Mrs Trumper.

I suppose I would have dismissed the whole memory of that early incident if I hadn't come down to the kitchen one night for a glass of milk and overheard Joan Moore talking to Harold the butler.

"Young Daniel's doing well at school," said Harold. "Must have his mother's brains."

"True, but let's pray that he never finds out the truth about his father." The words made me freeze to the stair rail. I continued to listen intently.

"Well, one thing's for certain," continued Harold, "Mrs Trentham's never going to admit the boy's her grandson, so heaven knows who'll end up with all that money."

"Not Captain Guy any longer, that's for sure," said Joan. "So perhaps that brat Nigel will be left the lot."

After that the conversation turned to who should lay up for breakfast so I crept back upstairs to my bedroom; but I didn't sleep. Although I sat on those steps for many hours during the next few months, patiently waiting for another vital piece of information that might fall from the servants' lips, the subject never arose between them again.

The only other occasion I could recall having heard the name "Trentham" had been some time before, when the Marchioness of Wiltshire, a close friend of my mother's, came to tea. I remained in the hall when my mother asked, "Did you go to Guy's funeral?"

"Yes, but it wasn't well attended by the good parishioners of Ashurst," the Marchioness assured her. "Those who remembered him well seemed to be treating the occasion more as if it were a blessed release."

"Was Sir Raymond present?"

"No, he was conspicuous by his absence," came back the reply. "Mrs Trentham claimed he was too old to travel, which only acted as a sad reminder that she still stands to inherit a fortune in the not too distant future."

New facts learned, but they still made little sense.

The name of Trentham arose in my presence once

more when I heard Daddy talking to Colonel Hamilton as he was leaving the house after a private meeting that had been held in his study. All Daddy said was, "However much we offer Mrs Trentham, she's never going to sell those flats to us."

The colonel vigorously nodded his agreement, but all he had to say on the subject was, "Bloody woman."

When both my parents were out of the house, I looked up "Trentham" in the telephone directory. There was only one listing: Major G. H. Trentham, MP, 19 Chester Square. I wasn't any the wiser.

When in 1939 Trinity College offered me the Newton Mathematics Prize Scholarship I thought Dad was going to burst, he was so proud. We all drove up to the university city for the weekend to check my future digs, before strolling round the colleges' cloisters and through Great Court.

The only cloud on this otherwise unblemished horizon was the thunderous one of Nazi Germany. Conscription for all those over twenty was being debated in Parliament, and I couldn't wait to play my part if Hitler dared to plant as much as a toe on Polish soil.

My first year at Cambridge went well, mainly because I was being tutored by Horace Bradford who, along with his wife Victoria, were considered to be the pick of the bunch among a highly talented group of mathematicians who were teaching at the university at that time. Although Mrs Bradford was rumoured to have won the Wrangler's Prize for coming out top of her year, her husband explained that she was not given the prestigious award, simply because she was a woman. The man who came second was deemed to have come first, a piece of information that made my mother puce with anger.

Mrs Bradford rejoiced in the fact that my mother had been awarded her degree from London University in 1921, while Cambridge still refused to acknowledge hers even existed in 1939.

At the end of my first year I, like many Trinity undergraduates, applied to join the army, but my tutor asked me if I would like to work with him and his wife at the War Office in a new department that would be specialising in code-breaking.

I accepted the offer without a second thought, relishing the prospect of spending my time sitting in a dingy little back room somewhere in Bletchley Park attempting to break German codes. I felt a little guilty that I was going to be one of the few people in uniform who was actually enjoying the war. Dad gave me enough money to buy an old MG which meant I could get up to London from time to time to see him and Mum.

Occasionally I managed to grab an hour for lunch with him over at the Ministry of Food, but Dad would only eat bread and cheese accompanied by a glass of milk as an example to the rest of his team. This may have been considered edifying but it certainly wasn't nourishing, Mr Selwyn warned me, adding that my father even had the minister at it.

"But not Mr Churchill?" I suggested.

"He's next on his list, I'm told."

In 1943 I was made up to captain, which was simply the War Office acknowledging the work we were all doing in our fledgling department. Of course, my father was delighted but I was sorry that I couldn't share with my parents our excitement when we broke the code used by the German U-boat commanders. It still baffles me to this day why they continued to go on using the four-wheel Enigma key long after we'd made our discovery. The code was a mathematician's dream that we finally broke on the back of a menu at Lyons Corner House just off Piccadilly. The waitress serving at our table described me as a vandal. I laughed, and remember thinking that I would take the rest of the day off and go and surprise my mother by letting her see what I looked like in my captain's uniform. I thought I looked rather swish, but when she opened the front door to greet me I was shocked by her response. She stared at me as if she'd seen a ghost. Although she recovered quickly enough, that first reaction on seeing me in uniform became just another clue in an ever more complex puzzle, a puzzle that was never far from the back of my thoughts.

The next clue came in the bottom line of an obituary, to which I wasn't paying much attention until I discovered that a Mrs Trentham would be coming into a fortune; not an important clue in itself, until I reread the entry and learned that she was the daughter of someone called Sir Raymond Hardcastle, a name that allowed me to fill in several little boxes that went in both directions. But what puzzled me was there being no mention of a Guy Trentham among the surviving relatives.

Sometimes I wish I hadn't been born with the kind of mind that enjoyed breaking codes and meddling with mathematical formulae. But somehow "bastard", "Trentham", "hospital", "Captain Guy", "flats", "Sir Raymond", "that brat Nigel", "funeral", and Mother turning white when she saw me dressed in a captain's uniform seemed to have some linear connection. Although I realised I would need even more clues before logic would lead me to the correct solution.

Then suddenly I worked out to whom they must have been referring when the Marchioness had come to tea all those years before, and told Mother that she had just attended Guy's funeral. It must have been Captain Guy's burial that had taken place. But why was that so significant?

The following Saturday morning I rose at an ungodly hour and travelled down to Ashurst, the village in which the Marchioness of Wiltshire had once lived – not a coincidence, I concluded. I arrived at the parish church a little after six, and as I had anticipated at that hour there was no one to be seen in the churchyard. I strolled around the graveyard checking the names: Yardley, Baxter, Flood, and Harcourt-Brownes aplenty. Some of the graves were overgrown with weeds, others were well cared for and even had fresh flowers at the head. I paused for a moment at the grave of my godmother's grandfather. There must have been over a hundred parishioners buried around the clock tower, but it didn't take that long to find the neatly kept Trentham family plot, only a few yards from the church vestry.

When I came across the most recent family gravestone I broke out in a cold sweat:

CAPTAIN GUY TRENTHAM, M.C.
1896–1927
After a long illness.
Sadly missed by all his family.

And so the mystery had come literally to a dead end, at the grave of the one man who surely could have answered all my questions had he still been alive.

When the war ended I returned to Trinity and was granted an extra year to complete my degree. Although my father and mother considered the highlight of the year to be my passing out as senior Wrangler with the offer of a prize fellowship at Trinity, I thought Dad's investiture at Buckingham Palace wasn't to be sneezed at.

The ceremony turned out to be a double delight because I was also able to witness my old tutor, Professor Bradford, being knighted for the role he had played in the field of code-breaking – although there was nothing for his wife, my mother noted. I remember feeling equally outraged on Doctor Bradford's behalf. Dad may have played his part in filling the stomachs of the British people, but as Churchill had stated in the House of Commons our little team had probably cut down the length of the war by as much as a year.

We all met up afterwards for tea at the Ritz, and not unnaturally at some point during the afternoon the conversation switched to what career I proposed to follow now the war was over. To my father's abiding credit he had never once suggested that I should join him at Trumper's, especially as I knew how much he had longed for another son who might eventually take his place. In fact during the summer vacation I became even more conscious of my good fortune, as Father seemed to be preoccupied with the business and Mother was unable to hide her own anxieties about the future of Trumper's. But whenever I asked if I could help all she would say was: "Not to worry, it will all work out in the end."

Once I had returned to Cambridge, I persuaded myself that should I ever come across the name Trentham again I would no longer allow it to worry me. However, because the name was never mentioned freely in my presence it continued to nag away in the back of my mind. My father had always been such an open man that there was no simple explanation as to why on this one particular subject he remained so secretive – to such an extent, in fact, that I felt I just couldn't raise the subject with him myself.

I might have gone years without bothering to do anything more about the conundrum if I hadn't one morning picked up an extension to the phone in the Little Boltons and heard Tom Arnold, my father's right-hand man, say, "Well, at least we can be thankful that you got to Syd Wrexall before Mrs Trentham." I replaced the head set immediately, feeling that I now had to get to the bottom of the mystery once and for all – and what's more, without my parents finding out. Why does one always think the worst in these situations? Surely the final solution would turn out to be something quite innocuous.

Although I had never met Syd Wrexall I could still remember him as the landlord of the Musketeer, a pub that had stood proudly on the other end of Chelsea Terrace until a bomb had landed in the snug bar. During the war my father bought the freehold and later converted the building into an up-market furnishing department.

It didn't take a Dick Barton to discover that Mr Wrexall had left London during the war to become the landlord of a pub in a sleepy village called Hatherton, hidden away in the county of Cheshire.

I spent three days working out my strategy for Mr Wrexall, and only when I was convinced that I knew all the questions that needed to be asked did I feel confident enough to make the journey to Hatherton. I had to word every query I needed answering in such a way that they didn't appear to be questions; but I still waited for a further month before I drove up north, by which time I had grown a beard that was long enough for me to feel confident that Wrexall would not recognise me. Although I was unaware of having seen him in the past, I realised that it was possible Wrexall might have come across me as recently as three or four years ago, and would therefore have known who I was the moment I walked into his pub. I even purchased a modern pair of glasses to replace my old specs.

I chose a Monday to make the trip as I suspected it would be the quietest day of the week on which to have a pub lunch. Before I set out on the journey I telephoned the Happy Poacher to be sure Mr Wrexall would be on duty that day. His wife assured me that he would be around and I put the phone down before she could ask why I wanted to know.

During my journey up to Cheshire I rehearsed a

series of non-questions again and again. Having arrived in the village of Hatherton I parked my car down a side road some way from the pub before strolling into the Happy Poacher. I discovered three or four people standing at the bar chatting and another half-dozen enjoying a drink around a mean-looking fire. I took a seat at the end of the bar and ordered some shepherd's pie and a half-pint of best bitter from a buxom, middle-aged lady who I later discovered was the landlord's wife. It took only moments to work out who the landlord was, because the other customers all called him Syd, but I realised that I would still have to be patient as I listened to him chat about anybody and everybody, from Lady Docker to Richard Murdoch, as if they were all close friends.

"Same again, sir?" he asked eventually, as he returned to my end of the bar and picked up my empty glass.

"Yes, please," I said, relieved to find that he didn't appear to recognise me.

By the time he had come back with my beer there were only two or three of us left at the bar.

"From around these parts, are you, sir?" he asked, leaning on the counter.

"No," I said. "Only up for a couple of days on an inspection. I'm with the Ministry of Agriculture, Fisheries and Food."

"So what brings you to Hatherton?"

"I'm checking out all the farms in the area for foot and mouth disease."

"Oh, yes, I've read all about that in the papers," he said, toying with an empty glass.

"Care to join me, landlord?" I asked.

"Oh, thank you, sir. I'll have a whisky, if I may." He put his empty half-pint glass in the washing-up water below the counter and poured himself a double. He charged me half a crown, then asked how my findings were coming along.

"All clear so far," I told him. "But I've still got a few more farms in the north of the county to check out."

"I used to know someone in your department," he said.

"Oh, yes?"

"Sir Charles Trumper."

"Before my time," I said, taking a swig from my beer, "but they still talk about him back at the ministry. Must have been a tough customer if half the stories about him are true."

"Bloody right," said Wrexall. "And but for him I'd be a rich man."

"Really?"

"Oh, yes. You see, I used to own a little property in London before I moved up here. A pub, along with an interest in several shops in Chelsea Terrace, to be exact. He picked the lot up from me during the war for a mere six thousand. If I'd waited another twenty-four hours I could have sold them for twenty thousand, perhaps even thirty."

"But the war didn't end in twenty-four hours."

"Oh, no, I'm not suggesting for one moment that he did anything dishonest, but it always struck me as a little more than a coincidence that having not set eyes on him for years he should suddenly show up in this pub on that very morning."

Wrexall's glass was now empty.

"Same again for both of us?" I suggested, hoping that the investment of another half-crown might further loosen his tongue.

"That's very generous of you, sir," he responded, and when he returned he asked, "Where was I?"

"On that very morning . . ."

"Oh, yes, Sir Charles – Charlie, as I always called him. Well, he closed the deal right here at this bar, in under ten minutes, when blow me if another interested party didn't ring up and ask if the properties were still for sale. I had to tell the lady in question that I had just signed them away."

I avoided asking who "the lady" was, although I suspected I knew. "But that doesn't prove that she would have offered you twenty thousand pounds for them," I said.

"Oh, yes, she would," responded Wrexall. "That Mrs Trentham would have offered me anything to stop Sir Charles getting his hands on those shops."

"Great Scott," I said, once again avoiding the word "why?"

"Oh, yes, the Trumpers and the Trenthams have been at each other's throats for years, you know. She still owns a block of flats right in the middle of Chelsea Terrace. It's the only thing that's stopped him building his grand mausoleum, isn't it? What's more, when she tried to buy Number 1 Chelsea Terrace, Charlie completely outfoxed her, didn't he? Never seen anything like it in my life."

"But that must have been years ago," I said. "Amazing how people go on bearing grudges for so long."

"You're right, because to my knowledge this one's been going on since the early twenties, ever since her posh son was seen walking out with Miss Salmon."

I held my breath.

"She didn't approve of that, no, not Mrs Trentham. We all had that worked out at the Musketeer, and then when the son disappears off to India the Salmon girl suddenly ups sticks and marries Charlie. And that wasn't the end of the mystery"

"No?"

"Certainly not," said Wrexall. "Because none of us are sure to this day who the father was."

"The father?"

Wrexall hesitated. "I've gone too far. I'll say no more."

"Such a long time ago, I'm surprised anyone still

cares," I offered as my final effort before draining my glass.

"True enough," said Wrexall. "That's always been a bit of a mystery to me as well. But there's no telling with folks. Well, I must close up now, sir, or I'll have the law after me."

"Of course. And I must get back to those cattle."

Before I returned to Cambridge I sat in the car and wrote down every word I could remember the landlord saying. On the long journey back I tried to piece together the new clues and get them into some sort of order. Although Wrexall had supplied a lot of information I hadn't known before he had also begged a few more unanswered questions. The only thing I came away from that pub certain of was that I couldn't possibly stop now.

The next morning I decided to return to the War Office and ask Sir Horace's old secretary if she knew of any way that one could trace the background of a former serving officer.

"Name?" said the prim middle-aged woman who still kept her hair tied in a bun, a style left over from the war.

"Guy Trentham," I told her.

"Rank and regiment?"

"Captain and the Royal Fusiliers would be my guess."

She disappeared behind a closed door, but was back within fifteen minutes clutching a small brown file. She extracted a single sheet of paper and read aloud from it. "Captain Guy Trentham, MC. Served in the first war, further service in India, resigned his commission in 1922. No explanation given. No forwarding address."

"You're a genius," I said, and to her consternation kissed her on the forehead before leaving to return to Cambridge.

The more I discovered, the more I found I needed

to know, even though for the time being I seemed to have come to another dead-end.

For the next few weeks I concentrated on my job as a supervisor until my pupils had all safely departed for their Christmas vacation.

I returned to London for the three-week break and spent a happy family Christmas with my parents at the Little Boltons. Father seemed a lot more relaxed than he had been during the summer and even Mother appeared to have shed her unexplained anxieties.

However, another mystery arose during that holiday and as I was convinced it was in no way connected with the Trenthams, I didn't hesitate to ask my mother to solve it.

"What's happened to Dad's favourite picture?"

Her reply saddened me greatly and she begged me never to raise the subject of *The Potato Eaters* with my father.

The week before I was due to return to Cambridge I was strolling back down Beaufort Street towards the Little Boltons, when I spotted a Chelsea Pensioner in his blue serge uniform trying to cross the road.

"Allow me to help you," I offered.

"Thank you, sir," he said, looking up at me with a rheumy smile.

"And who did you serve with?" I asked casually.

"The Prince of Wales Own," he replied. "And you?"

"The Royal Fusiliers." We crossed the road together. "Got any of those, have you?"

"The Fussies," he said. "Oh, yes, Banger Smith who saw service in the Great War, and Sammy Tomkins who joined up later, twenty-two, twenty-three, if I remember, and was then invalided out after Tobruk."

"Banger Smith?" I said.

"Yes," replied the pensioner as we reached the other side of the road. "A right skiver, that one." He chuckled chestily. "But he still puts in a day a week at your regimental museum, if his stories are to be believed."

I was first to enter the small regimental museum the following day, only to be told by the curator that Banger Smith only came in on Thursdays, and even then, couldn't always be relied on. I glanced around a room filled with regimental mementoes, threadbare flags parading battle honours, a display case with uniforms, out-of-date implements of war from a bygone age and large maps covered in different coloured pins depicting how, where and when those honours had been won.

As the curator was only a few years older than me I didn't bother him with any questions about the First World War.

I returned the following Thursday when I found an old soldier seated in a corner of the museum pretending to be fully occupied.

"Banger Smith?"

The old contemptible couldn't have been an inch over five feet and made no attempt to get up off his chair. He looked at me warily.

"What of it?"

I produced a ten-bob note from my inside pocket.

He looked first at the note and then at me with an enquiring eye. "What are you after?"

"Can you remember a Captain Guy Trentham, by any chance?" I asked.

"You from the police?"

"No, I'm a solicitor dealing with his estate."

"I'll wager Captain Trentham didn't leave anything to anybody."

"I'm not at liberty to reveal that," I said. "But I don't suppose you know what happened to him after he left the Fusiliers? You see, there's no trace of him in regimental records since 1922."

"There wouldn't be, would there? He didn't

exactly leave the Fussies with the regimental band playing him off the parade ground. Bloody man should have been horse-whipped, in my opinion."

"Why?"

"You won't get a word out of me," he said. "Regimental secret," he added, touching the side of his nose.

"But have you any idea where he went after he left India?"

"Cost you more than ten bob, that will," said the old soldier, chuckling.

"What do you mean?"

"Buggered off to Australia, didn't he? Died out there, then got shipped back by his mother. Good riddance, is all I can say. I'd take his bloody picture off the wall if I had my way."

"His picture?"

"Yes. MCs next to the DSOs, top left-hand corner," he said, managing to raise an arm to point in that direction.

I walked slowly over to the corner Banger Smith had indicated, past the seven Fusilier VCs, several DSOs and on to the MCs. They were in chronological order: 1914 – three, 1915 – thirteen, 1916 – ten, 1917 – eleven, 1918 – seventeen. Captain Guy Trentham, the inscription read, had been awarded the MC after the second battle of the Marne on 18 July 1918.

I stared up at the picture of a young officer in captain's uniform and knew I would have to make a journey to Australia.

CHAPTER 30

"When were you thinking of going?"

"During the long vacation."

"Have you enough money to cover such a journey?"

"I've still got most of that five hundred pounds you gave me when I graduated. In any case, a bachelor with his own rooms in college is hardly in need of a vast private income." Daniel looked up as his mother entered the drawing room.

"Daniel's thinking of going to America this summer."

"How exciting," said Becky, placing some flowers on a side table next to the Remington. "Then you must try and see the Fields in Chicago and the Bloomingdales in New York, and if you have enough time you could also –"

"Actually," said Daniel, leaning against the mantelpiece, "I think I'll be trying to see Waterstone in Princeton and Stinstead at Berkeley."

"Do I know them?" Becky frowned as she looked up from her flower-arranging.

"I wouldn't have thought so, Mother. They're both college professors who teach maths, or math, as they call it."

Charlie laughed.

"Well, be sure you write to us regularly," said his mother. "I always like to know where you are and what you're up to."

"Of course I will, Mother," said Daniel, trying not to sound exasperated. "If you promise to remember that I'm now twenty-six years old."

Becky looked across at him with a smile. "Are you really, my dear?"

Daniel returned to Cambridge that night trying to work out how he could possibly keep in touch from America while he was in fact travelling to Australia. He disliked the thought of deceiving his mother, but knew it would have pained her even more to tell him the truth about Captain Trentham.

Matters weren't helped when Charlie sent him a first-class ticket for New York on the *Queen Mary* for the exact date he had mentioned. It cost one hundred and three pounds and included an open-ended return.

Daniel eventually came up with a solution. He worked out that if he took the *Queen Mary* bound for New York the week after term had ended, then continued his journey on the Twentieth Century Limited and the Super Chief across the States to San Francisco, he could pick up the SS *Aorangi* to Sydney with a day to spare. That would still give him four weeks in Australia before he would have to repeat the journey south to north, allowing him just enough time to arrive back in Southampton a few days before the Michaelmas term began.

As with everything on which Daniel embarked, he spent hours of research and preparation long before he even set off for Southampton. He allocated three days to the Australian High Commission Information Department in the Strand, and made sure he regularly sat next to a certain Dr Marcus Winters, a visiting professor from Adelaide, whenever he came to dine at Trinity High Table. Although the first secretary and deputy librarian at Australia House remained puzzled by some of Daniel's questions and Doctor Winters curious as to the motives of the young mathematician, by the end of the Trinity term Daniel felt confident that he had learned enough to ensure that his time wouldn't be wasted once he had set foot on the sub-continent. However, he realised the whole enterprise was still a huge gamble: if the first question he needed to be answered yielded the reply, "There's no way of finding that out."

Four days after the students had gone down and he had completed his supervision reports, Daniel was packed and ready. The following morning his mother arrived at the college to drive him to Southampton. On the journey down to the south coast he learned that Charlie had recently applied to the London County Council for outline planning permission to develop Chelsea Terrace as one gigantic department store.

"But what about those bombed-out flats?"

"The council have given the owners three months to proceed with an application to rebuild or they have threatened to issue a compulsory purchase order and put the site up for sale."

"Pity we just can't buy the flats ourselves," said Daniel, trying out one of his non-questions in the hope that it might elicit some response from his mother but she just continued to drive on down the A30 without offering an opinion.

It was ironic, Daniel reflected, that if only his mother had felt able to confide in him the reason Mrs Trentham wouldn't co-operate with his father she could have turned the car around and taken him back to Cambridge.

He returned to safer territory. "So how's Dad hoping to raise the cash for such a massive enterprise?"

"He can't make up his mind between a bank loan and going public."

"What sort of sum are you talking about?"

"Mr Merrick estimates around a hundred and fifty thousand pounds."

Daniel gave a low whistle.

"The bank are happy enough to loan us the full amount now that property prices have shot up," Becky continued, "but they're demanding everything we own as collateral including the property in Chelsea Terrace, the house, our art collection, and on top of that they want us to sign a personal guarantee and charge the company four per cent on the overdraft."

"Then perhaps the answer is to go public."

"It's not quite that easy. If we were to take that route the family might end up with only fifty-one per cent of the shares."

"Fifty-one per cent means you still control the company."

"Agreed," said Becky, "but should we ever need to raise some more capital at a future date, then further dilution would only mean we could well lose our majority shareholding. In any case, you know only too well how your father feels about outsiders being given too much of a say, let alone too large a stake. And his having to report regularly to even more non-executive directors, not to mention shareholders, could be a recipe for disaster. He's always run the business on instinct, while the Bank of England may well prefer a more orthodox approach."

"How quickly does the decision have to be made?"

"It should have been settled one way or the other by the time you get back from America."

"What about the future of Number 1?"

"There's a good chance I can knock it into shape. I've the right staff and enough contacts, so if we're granted the full planning permission we have applied for I believe we could, in time, give Sotheby's and Christie's a run for their money."

"Not if Dad keeps on stealing the best pictures –"

"True." Becky smiled. "But if he goes on the way he is now, our private collection will be worth more than the business, as selling my Van Gogh back to the Lefevre Gallery proved only too cruelly. He has the best amateur's eye I've ever come across – but don't ever tell him I said so."

Becky began to concentrate on the signs directing her to the docks and finally brought the car to a halt alongside the liner, but not quite so close as Daphne had once managed, if she remembered correctly.

Daniel sailed out of Southampton on the *Queen Mary* that evening, with his mother waving from the dockside.

While on board the great liner he wrote a long letter to his parents, which he posted five days later from Fifth Avenue. He then purchased a ticket on the Twentieth Century Limited for a Pullman to Chicago. The train pulled out of Penn station at eight the same night, Daniel having spent a total of six hours in Manhattan where his only other purchase was a guide book of America.

Once they had reached Chicago, the Pullman carriage was attached to the Super Chief which took him all the way to San Francisco.

During the four-day journey across America he began to regret he was going to Australia at all. As he passed through Kansas City, Newton City, La Junta, Albuquerque and Barstow, each city appeared more interesting than the last. Whenever the train pulled into a new station Daniel would leap off, buy a colourful postcard that indicated exactly where he was, fill in the white space with yet more information gained from the guide book before the train reached the next station. He would then post the filled-in card at the following stop and repeat the process. By the time the express had arrived at Oakland station, San Francisco, he had posted twenty-seven different cards back to his parents in the Little Boltons.

Once the bus had dropped him off in St Francis Square, Daniel booked himself into a small hotel near the harbour after checking the tariff was well within his budget. As he still had a thirty-six-hour wait before the SS *Aorangi* was due to depart, he travelled out to Berkeley and spent the whole of the second day with Professor Stinstead. He became so engrossed with Stinstead's research on tertiary calculus that he began to regret once again that he would not be staying longer, as he suspected he might learn far more by remaining at Berkeley than he would ever discover in Australia.

On the evening before he was due to sail, Daniel bought

twenty more postcards and sat up until one the following morning filling them in. By the twentieth his imagination had been stretched to its limit. The following morning, after he had settled his bill, he asked the head porter to post one of the postcards every three days until he returned. He handed over ten dollars and promised the porter that there would be a further ten when he came back to San Francisco, but only if the correct number of cards remained, as precisely when he would be back remained uncertain.

The senior porter was puzzled but pocketed the ten dollars, commenting in an aside to his young colleague on the desk that he had been asked to do far stranger things in the past, for far less.

By the time Daniel boarded the SS *Aorangi* his beard was no longer a rough stubble and his plan was as well prepared as it could be, given that his information had been gathered from the wrong side of the globe. During the voyage Daniel found himself seated at a large circular table with an Australian family who were on their way home from a holiday in the States. Over the next three weeks they added greatly to his store of knowledge, unaware that he was listening to every word they had to say with uncommon interest.

Daniel sailed into Sydney on the first Monday of August 1947. He stood out on the deck and watched the sun set behind Sydney Harbour Bridge as a pilot boat guided the liner slowly into the harbour. He suddenly felt very homesick and, not for the first time, wished he had never embarked on the trip. An hour later he had left the ship and booked himself into a guest-house which had been recommended to him by his travelling companions.

The owner of the guest-house, who introduced herself as Mrs Snell, turned out to be a big woman, with a big smile and a big laugh, who booked him into what she described as her de luxe room. Daniel was somewhat relieved that he hadn't ended up in one of her ordinary rooms, because when he lay down the double bed sagged in the centre, and when he turned over the springs followed him, clinging to the small of his back. Both taps in the wash-basin produced cold water in different shades of brown, and the one naked light that hung from the middle of the room was impossible to read by, unless he stood on a chair directly beneath it. Mrs Snell hadn't supplied a chair.

When Daniel was asked the next morning, after a breakfast of eggs, bacon, potatoes and fried bread whether he would be eating in or out, he said firmly, "Out," to the landlady's evident disappointment.

The first – and critical – call was to be made at the Immigration Office. If they had no information to assist him, he knew he might as well climb back on board the SS *Aorangi* that same evening. Daniel was beginning to feel that if that happened he wouldn't be too disappointed.

The massive brown building on Market Street that housed the official records of every person who had arrived in the colony since 1823 opened at ten o'clock. Although he arrived half an hour early Daniel still had to join one of the eight queues of people attempting to establish some fact about registered immigrants, which ensured that he didn't reach the counter for a further forty minutes.

When he eventually did get to the front of the queue he found himself looking at a ruddy-faced man in an open-necked blue shirt who was slumped behind the counter.

"I'm trying to trace an Englishman who came to Australia at some time between 1922 and 1925."

"Can't we do better than that, mate?"

"I fear not," said Daniel.

"You fear not, do you?" said the assistant. "Got a name, have you?"

"Oh, yes," said Daniel. "Guy Trentham."

"Trentham. How do you spell that?"

Daniel spelt the name out slowly for him.

"Right, mate. That'll be two pounds." Daniel extracted his wallet from inside his sports jacket and handed over the cash. "Sign here," the assistant said, swivelling a form round and placing his forefinger on the bottom line. "And come back Thursday."

"Thursday? But that's not for another three days."

"Glad they still teach you to count in England," said the assistant. "Next."

Daniel left the building with no information, merely a receipt for his two pounds. Once back out on the pavement, he picked up a copy of the *Sydney Morning Herald* and began to look for a café near the harbour at which to have lunch. He selected a small restaurant that was packed with young people. A waiter led him across a noisy, crowded room and seated him at a little table in the corner. He had nearly finished reading the paper by the time a waitress arrived with the salad he had ordered. He pushed the paper on one side, surprised to have found that there hadn't been one piece of news about what was taking place back in England.

As he munched away at a lettuce leaf and wondered how he could best use the unscheduled hold-up constructively, a girl on the next table leaned across and asked if she could borrow the sugar.

"Of course, allow me," said Daniel, handing over the shaker. He wouldn't have given the girl a second glance had he not noticed that she was reading *Principia Mathematica*, by A. N. Whitehead and Bertrand Russell.

"Are you a mathematics student, by any chance?" he asked once he had passed the sugar across.

"Yes," she said, not looking back in his direction.

"I only asked," said Daniel, feeling the question might have been construed as impolite, "because I teach the subject."

"Of course you do," she said, not bothering to turn round. "Oxford, I'm sure."

"Cambridge, actually."

This piece of information did make the girl glance across and study Daniel more carefully. "Then can you explain Simpson's Rule to me?" she asked abruptly.

Daniel unfolded his paper napkin, took out a fountain pen and drew some diagrams to illustrate the rule, stage by stage, something he hadn't done since he'd left St Paul's.

She checked what he had produced against the diagram

in her book, smiled and said, "Fair dinkum, you really do teach maths," which took Daniel a little by surprise as he wasn't sure what fair dinkum meant, but as it was accompanied by a smile he assumed it was some form of approval. He was taken even more by surprise when the girl picked up her plate of egg and beans, moved across and sat down next to him.

"I'm Jackie," she said. "A bushwhacker from Perth."

"I'm Daniel," he replied. "And I'm . . ."

"A Pom from Cambridge. You've already told me, remember?"

It was Daniel's turn to look more carefully at the young woman who sat opposite him. Jackie appeared to be about twenty. She had short blonde hair and a turned-up nose. Her clothes consisted of shorts and a yellow T-shirt that bore the legend "PERTH" right across her chest. She was quite unlike any undergraduate he had ever come across at Trinity.

"Are you up at university?" he enquired.

"Yeah. Second year, Perth. So what brings you to Sydney, Dan?"

Daniel couldn't think of an immediate response, but it hardly mattered that much because Jackie was already explaining why she was in the capital of New South Wales long before he had been given a chance to reply. In fact Jackie did most of the talking until their bills arrived. Daniel insisted on paying.

"Good on you," said Jackie. "So what are you doing tonight?"

"Haven't got anything particular planned."

"Great, because I was thinking of going to the Theatre Royal," she told him. "Why don't you join me?"

"Oh, what's playing?" asked Daniel, unable to hide his surprise at being picked up for the first time in his life.

"Noël Coward's *Tonight at Eight-Thirty* with Cyril Ritchard and Madge Elliott."

"Sounds promising," said Daniel non-committally.

"Great. Then I'll see you in the foyer at ten to eight,

Dan. And don't be late." She picked up her rucksack, threw it on her back, strapped up the buckle and in seconds was gone.

Daniel watched her leaving the café before he could think of an excuse for not agreeing to her suggestion. He decided it would be churlish not to turn up at the theatre, and in any case he had to admit he had rather enjoyed Jackie's company. He checked his watch and decided to spend the rest of the afternoon looking round the city.

When Daniel arrived at the Theatre Royal that evening, a few minutes before seven forty, he purchased two six-shilling tickets for the stalls then hung around in the foyer waiting for his guest – or was she his host? When the five-minute bell sounded Jackie still hadn't arrived and Daniel began to realise that he had been looking forward to seeing her again rather more than he cared to admit. There was still no sign of his lunch-time companion when the two-minute bell rang, so Daniel assumed that he would be seeing the play on his own. With only a minute to spare before the curtain went up, he felt a hand link through his arm and heard a voice say, "Hello, Dan. I didn't think you'd turn up." Another first, he had never taken a girl to the theatre who was wearing shorts.

Daniel smiled. Although he enjoyed the play, he found he enjoyed Jackie's company during the interval, after the show and then later over a meal at Romano's – a little Italian restaurant she seemed acquainted with – even more. He had never come across anyone who, after only knowing him for a few hours, could be so open and friendly. They discussed everything from mathematics to Clark Gable, and Jackie was never without a definite opinion, whatever the subject.

"May I walk you back to your hotel?" Daniel asked when they eventually left the restaurant.

"I don't have one," Jackie replied with a grin, and throwing the rucksack over her shoulder added, "so I may as well walk you back to yours."

"Why not?" said Daniel. "I expect Mrs Snell will be able to supply another room for the night."

"Let's hope not," said Jackie.

When Mrs Snell opened the door, after Jackie had pressed the night bell several times, she told them, "I hadn't realised there would be two of you. That will mean extra, of course."

"But we're not –" began Daniel.

"Thank you," said Jackie, seizing the key from Mrs Snell as the landlady gave Daniel a wink.

Once they were in Daniel's little room, Jackie removed her rucksack and said, "Don't worry about me, Dan, I'll sleep on the floor."

He didn't know what to say in reply, and without uttering another word went off into the bathroom, changed into his pyjamas and cleaned his teeth. He reopened the bedroom door and walked quietly over to his bed without even glancing in Jackie's direction. A few moments later he heard the bedroom door close, so he crept out of bed again, tiptoed over to the door and turned out the light before slipping back under the sheets. A few more minutes passed before he heard the bedroom door reopen. He closed his eyes pretending to be asleep. A moment later he felt a body slide in next to his and two arms encircle him.

"Oh, Daniel" – in the darkness Jackie's voice took on an exaggerated English accent – "do let's get rid of these frightful pyjamas." As she pulled at the cotton cord on his pyjama bottoms, he turned over to protest, only to find himself pressed up against her naked body. Daniel didn't utter a word as he lay there, eyes closed, doing almost nothing as Jackie began to move her hands slowly up and down his legs. He became utterly exhilarated, and soon after exhausted, unsure quite what had taken place. But he had certainly enjoyed every moment.

"You know, I do believe you're a virgin," Jackie said, when he eventually opened his eyes.

"No," he corrected. "*Was* a virgin."

"I'm afraid you still are," said Jackie. "Strictly speaking. But don't get worked up about it; I promise we'll have that sorted out by the morning. By the way, next time, Dan, you are allowed to join in."

Daniel spent most of the next three days in bed being tutored by a second-year undergraduate from the University of Perth. By the second morning he had discovered just how beautiful a woman's body could be. By the third evening Jackie let out a little moan that led him to believe that although he might not have graduated he was no longer a freshman.

He was sad when Jackie told him the time had come for her to return to Perth. She threw her rucksack over her shoulder for the last time, and after he had accompanied her to the station Daniel watched the train pull away from the platform as she began her journey back to Western Australia.

"If I ever get to Cambridge, Dan, I'll look you up," were the last words he remembered her saying.

"I do hope so," he said, feeling there were several members of Trinity High Table who would have benefited from a few days of Jackie's expert tuition.

On the Thursday morning Daniel reported back to the Immigration Department as instructed, and after another hour's wait in the inevitable queue, handed his receipt over to the assistant who was still slumped across the counter wearing the same shirt.

"Oh, yes, Guy Trentham, I remember. I discovered his particulars a few minutes after you'd left," the clerk told him. "Pity you didn't come back earlier."

"Then I can only thank you."

"Thank me, what for?" asked the assistant, suspiciously.

Daniel took the little green card the assistant handed to him. "For three of the happiest days of my life."

"What are you getting at, mate?" said the other man; but Daniel was already out of earshot.

He sat alone on the steps outside the tall colonial building and studied the official card. As he feared, it revealed very little:

Name:	Guy Trentham (registered as immigrant)
	18 November 1922
Occupation:	Land agent
Address:	117 Manley Drive
	Sydney

Daniel soon located Manley Drive on the city map which Jackie had left with him, and took a bus to the north side of Sydney where he was dropped off in a leafy suburb overlooking the harbour. The houses, although fairly large, looked a little run-down, leaving Daniel with the impression that the suburb might at some time in the past have been a fashionable area.

When he rang the bell of what could have been a former colonial guest-house, the door was answered by a young man wearing shorts and a singlet. Daniel was coming to accept that this was the national dress.

"It's a long shot, I know," Daniel began, "but I'm trying to trace someone who may have lived in this house in 1922."

"Bit before my time," said the youth cheerily. "Better come in and talk to my Aunt Sylvia – she'll be your best bet."

Daniel followed the young man through the hall into a drawing room that looked as if it hadn't been tidied for several days and out on to the verandah, which showed indications of having once been painted white. There, seated in a rocking chair, was a woman who might have been a shade under fifty but whose dyed hair and over-made-up face made it impossible for Daniel to be at all sure of her age. She continued to rock backwards and forwards, eyes closed, enjoying the morning sun.

"I'm sorry to bother you –"

"I'm not asleep," said the woman, her eyes opening to

take in the intruder. She stared suspiciously up at him. "Who are you? You look familiar."

"My name is Daniel Trumper," he told her. "I'm trying to trace someone who may have stayed here in 1922."

She began to laugh. "Twenty-five years ago. You're a bit of an optimist, I must say."

"His name was Guy Trentham."

She sat up with a start and stared straight at him. "You're his son, aren't you?" Daniel went ice cold. "I'll never forget that smooth-tongued phoney's face if I live to be a hundred."

The truth was no longer possible to deny, even to himself.

"So have you come back after all these years to clear up his debts?"

"I don't understand –" said Daniel.

"Scarpered with nearly a year's rent owing, didn't he? Always writing to his mother back in England for more money, but when it came I never saw any of it. I suppose he thought that bedding me was payment enough, so I'm not likely to forget the bastard, am I? Especially after what happened to him."

"Does that mean you know where he went after he left this house?"

She hesitated for some time looking as if she was trying to make up her mind. She turned to look out of the window while Daniel waited. "The last I heard," she said after a long pause, "was that he got a job working as a bookie's runner up in Melbourne, but that was before –"

"Before – ?" queried Daniel.

She stared up at him again with quizzical eyes.

"No," she said, "you'd better find that out for yourself because I wouldn't want to be the one who tells you. But if you want my advice, you'll take the first boat back to England and not bother yourself with Melbourne."

"But you may turn out to be the only person who can help me."

"I was taken for a ride by your father once so I'm not

going to wait around to be conned by his son, that's for sure. Show him the door, Kevin."

Daniel's heart sank. He thanked the woman for seeing him and left without another word. Once back on the street he took the bus into Sydney and walked the rest of the journey to the guest-house. He spent a lonely night missing Jackie while wondering why his father had behaved so badly when he came to Sydney, and whether he should heed "Aunt Sylvia's" advice.

The following morning Daniel left Mrs Snell and her big smile, but not before she had presented him with a big bill. He settled it without complaint and made his way to the railway station.

When the train from Sydney pulled into Spencer Street station in Melbourne that evening, Daniel's first action was to check the local telephone directory, just in case there was a Trentham listed, but there was none. Next he telephoned every bookmaker who was registered in the city, but it was not until he spoke to the ninth that Daniel came across anyone to whom the name meant anything.

"Sounds familiar," said a voice on the other end of the line. "But can't remember why. You could try Brad Morris, though. He ran this office around that time, so he may be able to help you. You'll find his number in the book."

Daniel looked up his number. When he was put through to Mr Morris his conversation with the old man was so short that it didn't require a second coin.

"Does the name Guy Trentham mean anything to you?" he asked once again.

"The Englishman?"

"Yes," Daniel replied, feeling his pulse quicken.

"Spoke with a posh accent and told everyone he was a major?"

"Might well have done."

"Then try the gaolhouse, because that's where he finished up." Daniel would have asked why but the line had already gone dead.

He was still shaking from head to toe when he dragged

his trunk out of the station and checked into the Railway Hotel on the other side of the road. Once again, he lay on a single bed, in a small dark room, trying to make up his mind whether he should continue with his enquiries or simply avoid the truth and do as Sylvia had advised, "take the first boat back to England".

He fell asleep in the early evening, but woke again in the middle of the night, to find he was still fully dressed. By the time the early morning sun shone through the window he had made up his mind. He didn't want to know, he didn't need to know, and he would return to England immediately.

But first he decided to have a bath, and a change of clothes, and by the time he had done that he had also changed his mind.

Daniel came down to the lobby half an hour later and asked the receptionist where the main police station was located. The man behind the desk directed him down the road to Bourke Street.

"Was your room that bad?" he enquired.

Daniel gave a false laugh. He set off slowly and full of apprehension in the direction he had been shown. It took him only a few minutes to reach Bourke Street but he circled the block several times before he finally climbed the stone steps of the police station and entered the building.

The young duty sergeant showed no recognition when he heard the name of Trentham and simply enquired who it was who wanted to know.

"A relation of his from England," replied Daniel. The sergeant left him at the counter and walked over to the far side of the room to speak to a senior officer seated behind a desk who was patiently turning over photographs. The officer stopped what he was doing and listened carefully, then appeared to ask the sergeant something. In response the sergeant turned and pointed at Daniel. Bastard, thought Daniel. You're a little bastard. A moment later the sergeant returned to the front desk.

"We've closed the file on Trentham," he said. "Any

further enquiries would have to be made at the Prison Department."

Daniel almost lost his voice, but somehow managed, "Where's that?"

"Seventh floor," he said, pointing up.

When he stepped out of the lift on the seventh floor Daniel was confronted by a larger-than-life poster showing a warm-faced man bearing the name Hector Watts, Inspector-General of Prisons.

Daniel walked over to the enquiry desk and asked if he could see Mr Watts.

"Do you have an appointment?"

"No," said Daniel.

"Then I doubt –"

"Would you be kind enough to explain to the inspector-general that I have travelled from England especially to see him?"

Daniel was kept waiting for only a few moments before he was shown up to the eighth floor. The same warm smile that appeared in the picture now beamed down at him in reality, even if the lines in the face were a little deeper. Daniel judged Hector Watts to be near his sixtieth birthday and, although overweight, he still looked as if he could take care of himself.

"Which part of England do you come from?" Watts asked.

"Cambridge," Daniel told him. "I teach mathematics at the university."

"I'm from Glasgow myself," Watts said. "Which won't come as a surprise to you, with my name and accent. So, please have a seat and tell me what I can do for you."

"I'm trying to trace a Guy Trentham, and the Police Department have referred me to you."

"Oh, yes, I remember that name. But why do I remember it?" The Scotsman rose from his desk and went over to a row of filing cabinets that lined the wall behind him. He pulled open the one marked "STV", and extracted a large box file.

"Trentham," he repeated, as he thumbed through the papers inside the box, before finally removing two sheets. He returned to his desk and, having placed the sheets in front of him, began reading. After he had absorbed the details, he looked up and studied Daniel more carefully.

"Been here long, have you, laddie?"

"Arrived in Sydney less than a week ago," said Daniel, puzzled by the question.

"And never been to Melbourne before?"

"No, never."

"So what's the reason for your enquiry?"

"I wanted to find out anything I could about Captain Guy Trentham."

"Why?" asked the inspector-general. "Are you a journo?"

"No," said Daniel, "I'm a teacher but –"

"Then you must have had a very good reason for travelling this far."

"Curiosity, I suppose," said Daniel. "You see, although I never knew him, Guy Trentham was my father."

The head of the prison service looked down at the names listed on the sheet as next of kin: wife, Anna Helen (deceased), one daughter, Margaret Ethel. There was no mention of a son. He looked back up at Daniel and, after a few moments of contemplation, came to a decision.

"I'm sorry to tell you, Mr Trentham, that your father died while he was in police custody."

Daniel was stunned, and began shaking.

Watts looked across his desk and added, "I'm sorry to have to give you such unhappy news, especially when you've travelled all this way."

"What was the cause of his death?" Daniel whispered.

The inspector-general turned the page, checked the bottom line of the charge sheet in front of him and re-read the words: Hanged by the neck until dead. He looked back up at Daniel.

"A heart attack," he said.

CHAPTER 31

Daniel took the sleeper back to Sydney but he didn't sleep. All he wanted to do was get as far away from Melbourne as he possibly could. As every mile slipped by he relaxed a little more, and after a time was even able to eat half a sandwich from the buffet car. When the train pulled into the station of Australia's largest city he jumped off, loaded his trunk into a taxi and headed straight for the port. He booked himself on the first boat sailing to the west coast of America.

The tiny tramp steamer, only licensed to carry four passengers, sailed at midnight for San Francisco, and Daniel wasn't allowed on board until he had handed over to the captain the full fare in cash, leaving himself just enough to get back to England – as long as he wasn't stranded anywhere on the way.

During that bobbing, swaying, endless crossing back to America, Daniel spent most of his time lying on a bunk, which gave him easily enough time to consider what he should do with the information he now possessed. He also tried to come to terms with the anxieties his mother must have suffered over the years and what a fine man his step-father was. How he hated the word step-father. He would never think of Charlie that way. If only they had taken him into their confidence from the beginning he could surely have used his talents to help rather than waste so much of his energy trying to find out the truth. But he was now even more painfully aware that he couldn't let them become aware what he had discovered, as he probably knew more than they did.

Daniel doubted that his mother realised that Trentham had died in gaol leaving a string of disgruntled debtors across Victoria and New South Wales. Certainly there had been no indication of that on the gravestone in Ashurst.

As he stood on the deck and watched the little boat bob along on its chosen course under the Golden Gate and into the bay, Daniel finally felt a plan beginning to take shape.

Once he had cleared immigration he took a bus into the centre of San Francisco and booked himself back into the hotel at which he had stayed before travelling on to Australia. The porter produced two remaining cards and Daniel handed over the promised ten-dollar note. He scribbled something new and posted them both before boarding the Transcontinental Express destined for New York.

With each hour and each day of solitude his ideas continued to develop although it still worried him how much more information his mother must have that he still daren't ask her about. But now at least he was certain that his father was Guy Trentham and had left India or England in disgrace. The fearsome Mrs Trentham must therefore be his grandmother, who had for some unfathomable reason blamed Charlie for what had happened to her son.

On arriving in New York Daniel was exasperated to find that the *Queen Mary* had sailed for England the previous day. He transferred his ticket to the *Queen Elizabeth*, leaving himself with only a few dollars in cash. His final action on American soil was to telegraph his mother with an estimated time of arrival at Southampton.

Daniel began to relax for the first time once he could no longer see the Statue of Liberty from the stern of the ocean liner. Mrs Trentham, however, remained constantly in his thoughts during the five-day journey. He couldn't think of her as his grandmother and when the time came to disembark at Southampton he felt he needed several more questions answered by his mother before he would be ready to carry out his plan.

As he walked down the gangplank and back on to English soil he noticed that the leaves on the trees had turned from green to gold in his absence. He intended to have solved the problem of Mrs Trentham before they had fallen.

His mother was there on the dockside waiting to greet him. Daniel had never been more happy to see her, giving her such a warm hug that she was unable to hide her surprise. On the drive back to London he learned the sad news that his other grandmother had died while he had been in America and although his mother had received several postcards she couldn't remember the name of either of the professors he had said he was visiting so she had been unable to contact him to pass on the news. However, she had enjoyed receiving so many postcards.

"There are some more still on their way, I suspect," said Daniel, feeling guilty for the first time.

"Will you have time to spend a few days with us before you return to Cambridge?"

"Yes. I'm back a little earlier than I expected, so you could be stuck with me for a few weeks."

"Oh, your father will be pleased to hear that."

Daniel wondered how long it would be before he could hear anyone say "your father" without a vision of Guy Trentham forming in his mind.

"What decision did you come to about raising the money for the new building?"

"We've decided to go public," said his mother. "In the end it was a case of simple arithmetic. The architect has completed the outline plan, and of course your father wants the best of everything, so I'm afraid the final cost is likely to be nearer a half a million pounds."

"And are you still able to keep fifty-one per cent of the new company?"

"Only just, because based on those figures it's going to be tight. We could even end up having to pawn your great-grandfather's barrow."

"And the flats – any news of them?" Daniel was gazing

out of the car window for his mother's reaction in the reflection of the glass. She seemed to hesitate for a moment.

"The owners are carrying out the council's instructions and have already begun knocking down what remains of them."

"Does that mean Dad is going to be granted his planning permission?"

"I hope so, but it now looks as if it might take a little longer than we'd originally thought as a local resident – a Mr Simpson on behalf of the Save the Small Shops Federation – has lodged an objection to our scheme with the council. So please don't ask about it when you see your father. The very mention of the flats brings him close to apoplexy."

And I presume it's Mrs Trentham who is behind this Mr Simpson? was all Daniel wanted to say but simply asked, "And how's the wicked Daphne?"

"Still trying to get Clarissa married off to the right man, and Clarence into the right regiment."

"Nothing less than a royal duke for one and a commission in the Scots Guards for the other would be my guess."

"That's about right," agreed his mother. "She also expects Clarissa to produce a girl fairly quickly so she can marry her off to the future Prince of Wales."

"But Princess Elizabeth has only just announced her engagement."

"I am aware of that, but we all know how Daphne does like to plan ahead."

Daniel adhered to his mother's wishes and made no mention of the flats when he discussed with Charlie the launching of the new company over dinner that night. He also noticed that a picture entitled *Apples and Pears* by an artist called Courbet had replaced the Van Gogh that had hung in the hall. Something else he didn't comment on.

Daniel spent the following day at the planning department of the LCC (Enquiries) at County Hall. Although a clerk supplied him with all the relevant papers he was quick to point out, to Daniel's frustration, that he could not remove any original documents from the building.

In consequence he spent the morning repeatedly going over the papers, making verbatim notes of the relevant clauses and then committing them to memory so it wouldn't prove necessary to carry anything around on paper. The last thing he wanted was for his parents to stumble across any notes he had made by accident. By five o'clock, when they locked the front door behind him, Daniel felt confident he could recall every relevant detail.

He left County Hall, sat on a low parapet overlooking the Thames and repeated the salient facts to himself.

Trumper's, he had discovered, had applied to build a major department store that would encompass the entire block known as Chelsea Terrace. There would be two towers of twelve storeys in height. Each tower would consist of eight hundred thousand square feet of floor space. On top of that would be a further five floors of offices and walkways that would span the two towers and join the twin structures together. Outline planning permission for the entire scheme had been granted by the LCC. However, an appeal had been lodged by a Mr Martin Simpson of the Save the Small Shops Federation against the five floors that would bring together the two main structures over an empty site in the centre of the terrace. It didn't take a great deal of hypothesising to decide who was making sure Mr Simpson was getting the necessary financial backing.

At the same time Mrs Trentham herself had been given outline planning permission to build a block of flats to be used specifically for low-rent accommodation. Daniel went over in his mind her detailed planning application which had showed that the flats would be built of rough-hewn concrete, with the minimum of internal or external facilities – the expression "Jerry-built" immediately sprang to mind. It wasn't hard for Daniel to work out that Mrs Trentham's purpose was to build the ugliest edifice the council would allow her to get away with, right in the middle of Charlie's proposed palace.

Daniel looked down to check his memory against the notes. He hadn't forgotten anything, so he tore the crib sheet into tiny pieces and dropped them into a litter bin on the corner of Westminster Bridge, then returned home to the Little Boltons.

Daniel's next move was to telephone David Oldcrest, the resident law tutor at Trinity who specialised in town and country planning. His colleague spent over an hour explaining to Daniel that, what with appeals and counter-appeals that could go all the way up to the House of Lords, permission for such a building as Trumper Towers might not be granted for several years. By the time a decision had been made Dr Oldcrest reckoned that only the lawyers would have ended up making any money.

Daniel thanked his friend and having considered the problem he now faced came to the conclusion that the success or failure of Charlie's ambitions rested entirely in the hands of Mrs Trentham. That was unless he could . . .

For the next couple of weeks he spent a considerable amount of his time in a telephone box on the corner of Chester Square, without ever once making a call. For the remainder of each day, he followed an immaculately dressed lady of obvious self-confidence and presence around the capital, trying not to be seen but often attempting to steal a glimpse of what she looked like, how she behaved, and the kind of world she lived in.

He quickly discovered that only three things appeared to be sacrosanct to the occupant of Number 19 Chester Square. First, there were the meetings with her lawyers in Lincoln's Inn Fields – which seemed to take place every two or three days, though not on a regular basis. Second came her bridge gatherings, which were always at two o'clock, three days a week: on Monday at 9 Cadogan Place, on Wednesday at 117 Sloane Avenue and on Friday at her own home in Chester Square. The same group of elderly women appeared to arrive at all three establishments. Third was the occasional visit to a seedy hotel in South Kensington where she sat in the darkest corner of the tea room and held a conversation with a man who looked to Daniel a most unlikely companion for the daughter of Sir Raymond Hardcastle. Certainly she did not treat him as a friend, even an associate, and Daniel was unable to work out what they could possibly have in common.

After a further week he decided that his plan could only be executed on the last Friday before he returned to Cambridge. Accordingly he spent a morning with a tailor who specialised in army uniforms. During the afternoon he set about writing a script which he later that evening rehearsed. He then made several telephone calls, including one to Spink's, the medal specialists, who felt confident they could have his order made up in time. On the last two mornings – but only after he was sure his parents were safely out of the house – he carried out a full dress rehearsal in the privacy of his bedroom.

Daniel needed to be certain that not only would Mrs Trentham be taken by surprise but also she would remain off balance for at least the twenty minutes he felt would prove necessary to see the whole exercise through.

That Friday over breakfast, Daniel confirmed that neither of his parents was expected to return home until after six that evening. He readily agreed that they should all have dinner together as he was returning to Cambridge the following day. He hung around patiently waiting for his father to leave for Chelsea Terrace, but then had to wait another half-hour before he could depart himself because his mother was held up by a phone call just as she was on her way out. Daniel left the bedroom door open and marched around in endless circles.

At last his mother's conversation came to an end and she left for work. Twenty minutes later Daniel strolled out of the house carrying a small suitcase containing the uniform he had obtained from Johns and Pegg the previous day. Cautiously he walked three blocks in the wrong direction before hailing a taxi.

On arrival at the Royal Fusiliers Museum Daniel spent

a few minutes checking the picture of his father that hung on the wall. The hair was wavier than his own, and looked from the sepia photo to be a touch fairer. He suddenly feared he might not be able to remember the exact details. Daniel waited until the curator's back was turned, then, despite feeling a tinge of guilt, quickly removed the little photograph and placed it in his briefcase.

He took another taxi to a barber in Kensington, who was only too delighted to bleach the gentleman's hair, switch his parting and even to add a wave or two, creating as near as possible a duplicate of the sepia photograph from which he had been asked to work. Every few minutes Daniel checked the changing process in the mirror, and once he believed the effect was as close as could be achieved he paid the bill and left. The next cabbie he directed to Spink's, the medal specialists in King Street, St James. On arrival he purchased for cash the four ribbons that he had ordered over the phone; to his relief the young assistant did not enquire if he was entitled to wear them. Another taxi took him from St James to the Dorchester Hotel. There he booked himself into a single room and informed the girl on the desk that he intended to check out of the hotel by six that night. She handed him a key marked 309. Daniel politely refused the porter's offer to carry his case and merely asked for directions to the lift.

Once safely in his room he locked the door and laid the contents of his suitcase carefully on the bed. The moment he had finished changing from his suit into the uniform he fixed the row of ribbons above the left-hand breast pocket exactly as they were in the photograph and finally checked the effect in the long mirror attached to the bathroom door. He was every inch a First World War captain of the Royal Fusiliers, and the purple and silver ribbon of the MC and the two campaign medals simply added the finishing touch.

Having checked over every last detail against the stolen photograph Daniel began to feel unsure of himself for the first time. But if he didn't go through with it . . . He sat on the end of the bed, checking his watch every few minutes. An hour passed before he stood up, took a deep breath and pulled on his long trenchcoat – almost the only article of clothing he had the right to wear – locked the door behind him and went down to the lobby. Once he had pushed his way through the swing doors, he hailed another taxi which took him to Chester Square. He paid off the cabbie and checked his watch. Three forty-seven. He estimated that he still had at least another twenty minutes before the bridge party would begin to break up.

From his now familiar telephone box on the corner of the square Daniel watched as the ladies began to depart from Number 19. Once he had counted eleven of them leave the house he felt confident that Mrs Trentham must, servants apart, now be on her own; he already knew from the parliamentary timetable detailed in the *Daily Telegraph* that morning that Mrs Trentham's husband would not be expected back in Chester Square until after six that night. He waited for another five minutes before he came out of the telephone box and marched quickly across the road. He knew that if he hesitated, even for a moment, he would surely lose his nerve. He rapped firmly on the knocker and waited for what felt like hours before the butler finally answered.

"Can I help you, sir?"

"Good afternoon, Gibson. I have an appointment with Mrs Trentham at four fifteen."

"Yes, of course, sir," said Gibson. As Daniel had anticipated, the butler would assume that someone who knew his name must indeed have an appointment. "Please come this way, sir," he said before taking Daniel's trenchcoat. When they reached the door of the drawing room Gibson enquired, "May I say who is calling?"

"Captain Daniel Trentham."

The butler seemed momentarily taken aback but opened the door of the drawing room and announced, "Captain Daniel Trentham, madam."

Mrs Trentham was standing by the window when

Daniel entered the room. She swung round, stared at the young man, took a couple of paces forward, hesitated and then fell heavily on to the sofa.

For God's sake don't faint, was Daniel's first reaction as he stood in the centre of the carpet facing his grandmother.

"Who are you?" she whispered at last.

"Don't let's play games, Grandmother. You know very well who I am," said Daniel, hoping he sounded confident.

"She sent you, didn't she?"

"If you are referring to my mother, no, she did not. In fact she doesn't even know I'm here."

Mrs Trentham's mouth opened in protest, but she did not speak. Daniel swayed from foot to foot during what seemed to him to be an unbearably long silence. His eye began to focus on an MC that stood on the mantelpiece.

"So what do you want?" she asked.

"I've come to make a deal with you, Grandmother."

"What do you mean, a deal? You're in no position to make any deals."

"Oh, I think I am, Grandmother. You see, I've just come back from a trip to Australia." He paused. "Which turned out to be very revealing."

Mrs Trentham flinched, but her eyes did not leave him for a moment.

"And what I learned about my father while I was there doesn't bear repeating. I won't go into any details, as I suspect you know every bit as much as I do."

Her eyes remained fixed on him and she slowly began to show signs of recovery.

"Unless, of course, you want to know where they had planned to bury my father originally, because it certainly wasn't in the family plot at Ashurst parish church."

"What do you want?" she repeated.

"As I said, Grandmother, I've come to make a deal."

"I'm listening."

"I want you to abandon your plans for building those dreadful flats in Chelsea Terrace, and at the same time withdraw any objections you may have to the detailed planning permission Trumper's have applied for."

"Never."

"Then I fear the time may have come for the world to be informed of the real reason for your vendetta against my mother."

"But that would harm your mother every bit as much as me."

"Oh, I don't think so, Grandmother," said Daniel. "Especially when the press find out that your son resigned his commission with far from glowing testimonials, and later died in Melbourne in even less auspicious circumstances – despite the fact he was finally laid to rest in a sleepy village in Berkshire after you had shipped the body home, telling your friends that he had been a successful cattle broker and died tragically of tuberculosis."

"But that's blackmail."

"Oh, no, Grandmother, just a troubled son, desperate to discover what had really happened to his long-lost father and shocked when he found out the truth behind the Trentham family secret. I think the press would describe such an incident quite simply as 'an internal feud'. One thing's for certain – my mother would come out smelling of roses, though I'm not sure how many people would still want to play bridge with you once they learned all the finer details."

Mrs Trentham rose quickly to her feet, clenched both her fists and advanced towards him menacingly. Daniel stood his ground.

"No hysterics, Grandmother. Don't forget I know everything about you." He felt acutely aware that he actually knew very little.

Mrs Trentham stopped, and even retreated a pace. "And if I agree to your demands?"

"I shall walk out of this room and you will never hear from me again as long as you live. You have my word on it."

She let out a long sigh, but it was some time before she replied.

"You win," she eventually said, sounding remarkably composed. "But I have a condition of my own if I am expected to comply with your demands."

Daniel was taken by surprise. He hadn't planned for any conditions coming from her side. "What is it?" he asked suspiciously.

He listened carefully to her request and, although puzzled by it, could see no cause for any alarm.

"I accept your terms," he said finally.

"In writing," she added quietly. "And now."

"Then I shall also require our little arrangement in writing," said Daniel, trying to score a point of his own.

"Agreed."

Mrs Trentham walked shakily towards the writing desk. She sat down, opened the centre drawer, and took out two sheets of purple headed paper. Painstakingly she wrote out separate agreements before passing them over for Daniel to consider. He read through the drafts slowly. She had covered all the points he had demanded and had left nothing out, including the one rather long-winded clause she had herself insisted upon. Daniel nodded his agreement and passed the two pieces of paper back to her.

She signed both copies, then handed Daniel her pen. He in turn added his signature below hers on both sheets of paper. She returned one of the agreements to Daniel before rising to pull the bell rope by the mantelpiece. The butler reappeared a moment later.

"Gibson, we need you to witness our signatures on two documents. Once you have done that the gentleman will be leaving," she announced. The butler penned his signature on both sheets of paper without question or comment.

A few moments later Daniel found himself out on the street with an uneasy feeling everything hadn't gone exactly as he had anticipated. Once he was seated in a taxi and on his way back to the Dorchester Hotel he re-read the sheet of paper they had both signed. He could not reasonably have asked for more but remained puzzled by the clause Mrs Trentham had insisted on inserting as it made no sense to him. He pushed any such disquiet to the back of his mind.

On arrival at the Dorchester Hotel, in the privacy of room 309, he quickly changed out of the uniform and back into his civilian clothes. He felt clean for the first time that day. He then placed the uniform and cap in his suitcase before going back down to reception, where he handed in the key, paid the bill in cash and checked out.

Another taxi returned him to Kensington where the hairdresser was disappointed to be told that his new customer now wished all signs of the bleach to be removed, the waves to be straightened out and the parting to be switched back.

Daniel's final stop before returning home was to a deserted building site in Pimlico. He stood behind a large crane and when he was certain no one could see him he dropped the uniform and cap into a rubbish tip and set light to the photograph.

He stood shivering as he watched his father disappear in a purple flame.

MRS TRENTHAM

1938-1948

CHAPTER 32

"My purpose in inviting you up to Yorkshire this weekend is to let you know exactly what I have planned for you in my will." My father was seated behind his desk while I sat in a leather chair facing him, the one my mother had always favoured. He had named me after her, Margaret Ethel, but there the resemblance ended, as he never stopped reminding me. I watched him as he carefully pressed some tobacco down into the well of his briar pipe, wondering what he could possibly be going to say. He took his time before looking up at me again and announcing, "I have made the decision to leave my entire estate to Daniel Trumper."

I was so stunned by this revelation that it was several seconds before I could think of an acceptable response.

"But, Father, now that Guy has died surely Nigel must be the legitimate heir?"

"Daniel would have been the legitimate heir if your son had done the honourable thing. Guy should have returned from India and married Miss Salmon the moment he realised she was having his child."

"But Trumper is Daniel's father," I protested. "Indeed, he has always admitted as much. The birth certificate –"

"He has never denied it, I grant you that. But don't take me for a fool, Ethel. The birth certificate only proves that, unlike my late grandson, Charlie Trumper has some sense of responsibility. In any case, those of us who have watched Guy in his formative years and have also followed Daniel's progress can be in little doubt about the relationship between the two men."

I wasn't certain I had heard my father correctly. "You've actually seen Daniel Trumper?"

"Oh, yes," he replied matter-of-factly, picking up a box of matches from his desk. "I made a point of visiting St Paul's on two separate occasions. Once when the boy was performing in a concert I was able to sit and watch him at close quarters for over two hours – he was rather good, actually. And then a year later on Founders' Day when he was awarded the Newton Mathematics Prize, I shadowed him while he accompanied his parents to afternoon tea in the headmaster's garden. So I can assure you that not only does he look like Guy, but he's also inherited some of his late father's mannerisms."

"But surely Nigel deserves to be treated as his equal?" I protested, racking my brains to think of some rational response that would make my father reconsider his position.

"Nigel is not his equal and never will be," replied my father, as he struck a match before beginning that endless sucking that always preceded his attempt to light a pipe. "Don't let's fool ourselves, Ethel. We've both known for some time that the lad isn't even worthy of a place on the board of Hardcastle's, let alone to be considered as my successor."

While my father puffed energetically at his pipe, I stared blindly at the painting of two horses in a paddock that hung on the wall behind him and tried to collect my thoughts.

"I'm sure you haven't forgotten, my dear, that Nigel even failed to pass out of Sandhurst, which I'm told takes some doing nowadays. I have also recently been informed that he's only holding down his present job with Kitcat and Aitken because you led the senior partner to believe that in time they will be administering the Hardcastle portfolio." He punctuated each statement with a puff from his pipe. "And I can assure you that will not be the case."

I found myself unable to look straight at him. Instead my eyes wandered from the Stubbs on the wall behind his desk to the row upon row of books he had spent a lifetime collecting. Dickens, every first edition; Henry James, a modern author he admired, and countless Blakes of every description from treasured handwritten letters to memorial editions. Then came the second blow.

"As there isn't a member of the family who can readily replace me as head of the firm, I have reluctantly come to the conclusion that with war daily becoming more likely I will have to reconsider the future of Hardcastle's." The pungent smell of tobacco hung in the air.

"You would never allow the business to fall into anyone else's hands?" I said in disbelief. "Your father would –"

"My father would have done what was best for all concerned, and no doubt expectant relations would have been fairly low down on his list of priorities." His pipe refused to stay alight so a second match was brought into play. He gave a few more sucks before a look of satisfaction appeared on his face and he began to speak again. "I've sat on the boards of Harrogate Haulage and the Yorkshire Bank for several years, and more recently John Brown Engineering where I think I've finally found my successor. Sir John's son may not be an inspired chairman of the company but he's capable and more important he's a Yorkshireman. Any road, I have come to the conclusion that a merger with that company will be best for all concerned."

I was still unable to look directly at my father as I tried to take in all that he was saying.

"They've made me a handsome offer for my

shares," he added, "which will in time yield an income for you and Amy that will more than take care of your needs once I've gone."

"But, Father, we both hope you will live for many more years."

"Don't bother yourself, Ethel, with trying to flatter an old man who knows death can't be far away. I may be ancient but I'm not yet senile."

"Father," I protested again but he simply returned to the sucking of his pipe, showing total lack of concern at my agitation. So I tried another ploy.

"Does that mean Nigel will receive nothing?"

"Nigel will receive what I consider right and proper in the circumstances."

"I'm not sure I fully understand you, Father."

"Then I shall explain. I've left him five thousand pounds which after my death he may dispose of in any manner he wishes." He paused as if considering whether he should add to this piece of information. "I have at least saved you one embarrassment," he offered at last. "Although, following your death, Daniel Trumper will inherit my entire estate, he won't learn of his good fortune until his thirtieth birthday, by which time you will be well over seventy and perhaps find it easier to live with my decision."

Twelve more years, I thought, as a tear fell from my eye and began to run down my cheek.

"You needn't bother with crying, Ethel, or hysterics, or even reasoned argument for that matter." He exhaled a long plume of smoke. "I have made up my mind, and nothing you can say or do is going to budge me."

His pipe was now puffing away like an express train. I removed a handkerchief from my handbag in the hope it would give me a little more time to think.

"And should it cross your mind to try and have the will revoked at some later date, on the grounds of my insanity" – I looked up aghast – "of which you are quite capable, I have had the document drawn up by Mr Baverstock and witnessed by a retired judge, a cabinet minister and, perhaps more relevant, a specialist from Sheffield whose chosen subject is mental disorders."

I was about to protest further when there was a muffled knock on the door and Amy entered the room.

"I do apologise for interrupting you, Papa, but should I have tea served in the drawing room or would you prefer to take it in here?"

My father smiled at his elder daughter. "The drawing room is just fine, my dear," he said in a far gentler tone than he ever adopted when addressing me. He rose unsteadily from behind his desk, emptied his pipe in the nearest ashtray and, without another word, followed my sister slowly out of the room.

I remained fairly uncommunicative during tea while I tried to think through the implications of all my father had just told me. Amy, on the other hand, prattled happily on about the effect the recent lack of rain was having on the petunias in the flower-bed directly under my father's room. "They don't catch the sun at any hour of the day," she confided to us in worried tones as her cat jumped up on to the sofa and settled in her lap. The old tortoise-shell whose name I could never remember had always got on my nerves but I never said as much because I knew Amy loved the creature second only to my father. She began to stroke the animal, obviously unaware of the unease caused by the conversation that had just taken place in the study.

I went to bed early that evening and spent a sleepless night trying to work out what course of action had been left open to me. I confess I hadn't expected anything substantial from the will for Amy or myself, as we were both women in our sixties and without a great need of any extra income. However, I had always assumed that I would inherit the house and the estate while the company would be left to Guy and, following his death, Nigel.

By the morning I had come to the reluctant conclusion that there was little I could do about my father's decision. If the will had been drawn up by Mr Baverstock, his long-serving solicitor and friend, F. E. Smith himself would not have been able to find a loophole. I began to realise that my only hope of securing Nigel's rightful inheritance would have to involve Daniel Trumper himself.

After all, my father would not live for ever.

We sat alone almost unsighted in the darkest corner of the room. He began clicking the knuckles of his right hand one by one.

"Where is it at this moment?" I asked, looking across at a man to whom I had paid thousands of pounds since we had first met almost twenty years ago. He still turned up for our weekly meetings at the St Agnes wearing the same brown tweed jacket and shiny yellow tie, even if he did seem to have acquired one or two more shirts lately. He put down his whisky, pulled out a brown paper package from under his chair and handed it over to me.

"How much did you have to pay to get it back?"

"Fifty pounds."

"I told you not to offer him more than twenty pounds without consulting me."

"I know, but there was a West End dealer nosing around the shop at the time. I just couldn't risk it, could I?"

I didn't believe for one moment that it had cost Harris fifty pounds. However, I did accept that he realised how important the picture was to my future plans.

"Would you like me to hand the painting over to the police?" he asked. "I could then drop a hint that perhaps –"

"Certainly not," I said without hesitation. "The police are far too discreet in these matters. Besides, what I have in mind for Mr Trumper will be a great deal more humiliating than a private interview in the privacy of Scotland Yard."

Mr Harris leaned back in the old leather chair and began clicking the knuckles of his left hand.

"What else do you have to report?"

"Daniel Trumper has taken up his place at Trinity College. He's to be found on New Court, staircase B, room seven."

"That was all in your last report."

Both of us stopped speaking while an elderly guest selected a magazine from a nearby table.

"Also, he's started seeing quite a lot of a girl called Marjorie Carpenter. She's a third-year mathematician from Girton College."

"Is that so? Well, if it begins to look at all serious let me know at once and you can start a file on her." I glanced around to be sure no one could overhear our conversation. The clicking began again and I looked back to find Harris staring fixedly at me.

"Is something worrying you?" I asked as I poured myself another cup of tea.

"Well, to be honest with you there is one thing, Mrs Trentham. I feel the time might have come for me to ask for another small rise in my hourly rate. After all, I'm expected to keep so many secrets" – he hesitated for a moment – "secrets that might . . ."

"That might what?"

"Prove to be invaluable to other equally interested parties."

"Are you threatening me, Mr Harris?"

"Certainly not, Mrs Trentham, it's just that –"

"I'll say this once and once only, Mr Harris. If you ever reveal anything to anyone that has passed between us it won't be an hourly rate that you'll be worrying about but the length of time you'll be spending in prison. Because I also have kept a file on you which I suspect some of your former colleagues might well be interested to learn about. Not least the pawning of a stolen picture and the disposal of an army greatcoat after a crime had been committed. Do I make myself clear?"

Harris didn't reply, just clicked his fingers back into place, one by one.

Some weeks after war was declared I learned that Daniel Trumper had avoided being called up. It transpired that he was now to be found serving behind a desk in Bletchley Park and was therefore unlikely to experience the wrath of the enemy unless a bomb were to land directly on top of him.

As it happened, the Germans did manage to drop a bomb, right in the middle of *my* flats, destroying them completely. My initial anger at this disaster evaporated when I saw the chaos it left behind in Chelsea Terrace. For several days I gained considerable satisfaction from just standing on the opposite side of the road admiring the Germans' handiwork.

A few weeks later it was the turn of the Musketeer and Trumper's greengrocery shop to feel the brunt of the Luftwaffe. The only perceptible outcome of this second bombing was that Charlie Trumper signed up for the Fusiliers the following week. However much I might have desired to see Daniel disposed of by a stray bullet, I required Charlie Trumper to remain very much alive: it was a more public execution I had in mind for him.

It didn't require Harris to brief me on Charlie Trumper's new appointment at the Ministry of Food because it was fully reported in every national paper. However, I made no attempt to take advantage of his prolonged absence as I reasoned there could be little purpose in acquiring further property in the terrace while war was still being waged, and in any case

Harris's monthly reports revealed that Trumper's was steadily losing money.

Then, when I was least prepared for it, my father died of a heart attack. I immediately dropped everything and hurried off to Yorkshire in order to help oversee the arrangements for the burial.

Two days later Amy and I led the mourners at the funeral, which was held in Wetherby parish church. As titular head of the family, Amy was placed on the left-hand end of the front pew with Gerald and Nigel on her right. The service was well attended by family, friends and business associates alike, including the solemn Mr Baverstock, clutching on to his inevitable Gladstone bag that I noticed he never let out of his sight. Amy, who sat in the row directly in front of me, became so distressed during the archdeacon's address that I don't believe she would have got through the rest of the day had I not been there to comfort her.

After the mourners had left I decided to stay on in Yorkshire for a few more days while Gerald and Nigel returned to London. Amy spent most of the time in her bedroom which gave me the chance to look around the house and check if there was anything of real value that could be rescued before I returned to Ashurst. After all, the property would – once the will had been administered – at worst end up being divided between us.

I came across my mother's jewellery, which had obviously never been touched since her death, and the Stubbs that still hung in my father's study. I removed the jewellery from my father's bedroom, and as for the Stubbs Amy agreed – over a light supper in her room – that for the time being I could hang the painting at Ashurst. The only other item left of any real value, I concluded, was my father's magnificent library. However, I already had long-term plans for the collection that did not involve the sale of a single book.

On the first of the month I travelled down to

London to attend the offices of Baverstock, Dickens and Cobb to be informed officially of the contents of my father's will.

Mr Baverstock seemed disappointed that Amy had felt unable to make the journey but accepted the fact that my sister had not yet recovered sufficiently from the shock of my father's death to contemplate such a trip. Several other relations, most of whom I saw only at christenings, weddings and funerals, sat around looking hopeful. I knew exactly what they could expect.

Mr Baverstock took over an hour performing what seemed to me a simple enough responsibility, though to be fair he managed with some considerable dexterity not to reveal the name of Daniel Trumper when it came to explaining what would eventually happen to the estate. My mind began to wander as minor relations were informed of the thousand pound windfalls they would inherit and was only brought sharply back to the droning voice of Mr Baverstock when he uttered my own name.

"Mrs Gerald Trentham and Miss Amy Hardcastle will both receive during their lifetime in equal part any income derived from the Trust." The solicitor stopped to turn a page before placing the palms of his hands on the desk. "And finally, the house, the estate in Yorkshire and all its contents plus the sum of twenty thousand pounds," he continued, "I bequeath to my elder daughter, Miss Amy Hardcastle."

CHAPTER 33

"Good morning, Mr Sneddles."

The old bibliophile was so surprised the lady knew his name that for a moment he just stood and stared at her.

Eventually he shuffled across to greet the lady, giving her a low bow. She was, after all, the first customer he had seen for over a week – that is if he did not count Doctor Halcombe, the retired headmaster who would happily browse around the shop for hours on end but who had not actually purchased a book since 1937.

"Good morning, madam," he said in turn. "Was there a particular volume that you were hoping to find?" He looked at the lady, who wore a long lace dress and a large wide-brimmed hat with a veil that made it impossible to see her face.

"No, Mr Sneddles," said Mrs Trentham. "I have not come to purchase a book, but to seek your services." She stared at the stooping old man in his mittens, cardigan and overcoat, which she assumed he was wearing because he could no longer afford to keep the shop heated. Although his back seemed to be permanently semicircular and his head stuck out like a tortoise from its overcoat shell, his eyes were clear and his mind appeared sharp and alert.

"My services, madam?" the old man repeated.

"Yes. I have inherited an extensive library that I require to be catalogued and valued. You come highly recommended."

"It's kind of you to say so, madam."

Mrs Trentham was relieved that Mr Sneddles did not enquire as to who had made the particular recommendation.

"And where is this library, might I be permitted to ask?"

"A few miles east of Harrogate. You will find that it is quite an extraordinary collection. My late father, Sir Raymond Hardcastle – you may have heard of him? – devoted a considerable part of his life to putting it together."

"Harrogate?" said Sneddles as if it was a few miles east of Bangkok.

"Of course I would cover all your expenses, however long the enterprise might take."

"But it would mean having to close the shop," he murmured as if talking to himself.

"I would naturally also compensate you for any loss of earnings."

Mr Sneddles removed a book from the counter and checked its spine. "I fear it's out of the question, madam, quite impossible, you see –"

"My father specialised in William Blake, you know. You will find that he managed to get hold of every first edition, some still in mint condition. He even secured a handwritten manuscript of . . ."

Amy Hardcastle had gone to bed even before her sister arrived back in Yorkshire that evening.

"She gets so tired nowadays," the housekeeper explained.

Mrs Trentham was left with little choice but to have a light supper on her own before retiring to her old room a few minutes after ten. As far as she could tell nothing had changed: the view over the Yorkshire dales, the black clouds, even the picture of York Minster that hung above the walnut-framed bed. She slept soundly enough and returned downstairs at eight the following morning. The cook explained to her that Miss Amy had not yet risen so she ate breakfast alone.

Once all the covered dishes had been cleared away Mrs Trentham sat in the drawing room reading the *Yorkshire Post* while she waited for her sister to make an appearance. When over an hour later the old cat wandered in, Mrs Trentham shooed the animal away with a vicious wave of the folded newspaper. The grandfather clock in the hall had already struck eleven when Amy finally entered the room. She walked slowly towards her sister with the aid of a stick.

"I'm so sorry, Ethel, that I wasn't here to greet you when you arrived last night," she began. "I fear my arthritis has been playing me up again."

Mrs Trentham didn't bother to reply, but watched her sister as she came hobbling towards her, unable to believe the deterioration in her condition in less than three months.

Although Amy had in the past appeared slight she was now frail. And even if she had always been quiet she was now almost inaudible. If she had been perhaps a little pale, she was now grey and the lines on her face were so deeply etched she looked far older than her sixty-nine years.

Amy lowered herself on to the chair next to her sister and for some seconds continued to breathe deeply, leaving her visitor in no doubt that the walk from the bedroom to the drawing room had been something of an ordeal.

"It's so kind of you to leave your family and come up to be with me in Yorkshire," Amy said as the tortoise-shell cat climbed up on to her lap. "I must confess that since dear Papa died I don't know where to turn."

"That's quite understandable, my dear." Mrs Trentham smiled thinly. "But I felt it was nothing more than my duty to be with you – as well as being a pleasure, of course. In any case, Father warned me this might happen once he had passed away. He gave me specific instructions, you know, as to exactly what should be done in the circumstances."

"Oh, I'm so glad to hear that." Amy's face lit up for the first time. "Please do tell me what Papa had in mind."

"Father was adamant that you should sell the house as

quickly as possible and either come and live with Gerald and myself at Ashurst –"

"Oh, I could never dream of putting you to so much trouble, Ethel."

"– or alternatively you could move into one of those nice little hotels on the coast that cater specially for retired couples and single people. He felt that way you could at least make new friends and indeed even have an extended lease of life. I would naturally prefer you to join us in Ashurst, but what with the bombs –"

"He never mentioned selling the house to me," murmured Amy anxiously. "In fact, he begged me –"

"I know, my dear, but he realised only too well what a strain his death would be on you and asked me to break the news gently. You will no doubt recall the long meeting we held in his study when I last came up to see him."

Amy nodded her acknowledgment but the look of bewilderment remained on her face.

"I remember every word he said," Mrs Trentham went on. "Naturally, I shall do my utmost to see his wishes are carried out."

"But I wouldn't know how or where to begin."

"There's no need for you to give it a second thought, my dear." She patted her sister's arm. "That's exactly why I'm here."

"But what will happen to the servants and my dear Garibaldi?" Amy asked anxiously as she continued stroking the cat. "Father would never forgive me if they weren't all properly taken care of."

"I couldn't agree more," Mrs Trentham said. "However, as always he thought of everything and gave me explicit instructions as to what should be done with all the staff."

"How thoughtful of dear Papa. However, I am not altogether certain . . ."

It took Mrs Trentham two more days of patient encouragement before she was finally able to convince her sister that her plans for the future would all work out for the best and, more important, it was what "dear Papa" wanted.

From that moment on Amy only came down in the afternoons to take a short walk around the garden and occasionally attend to the petunias. Whenever Mrs Trentham came across her sister she begged her not to overdo things.

Three days later Amy dispensed with her afternoon walk.

The following Monday Mrs Trentham gave the staff a week's notice, with the exception of the cook whom she told to stay on until Miss Amy had been settled. That same afternoon she sought out a local agent and placed the house and the sixty-acre estate on the market.

On the following Thursday Mrs Trentham made an appointment to see a Mr Althwaite, a solicitor in Harrogate. On one of her sister's infrequent visits downstairs she explained to Amy that it had not been necessary to bother Mr Baverstock: she felt certain any problem that arose concerning the estate could be more easily dealt with by a local man.

Three weeks later Mrs Trentham was able to move her sister and a few of her belongings into a small residential hotel overlooking the east coast a few miles north of Scarborough. She agreed with the proprietor that it was unfortunate that they could not allow pets but felt sure that her sister would fully understand. Mrs Trentham's final instruction was to send the monthly bills direct to Coutts in the Strand, where they would be settled immediately.

Before Mrs Trentham bade farewell to Amy she got her sister to sign three documents. "So that you will have nothing more to worry about, my dear," Mrs Trentham explained in a gentle tone.

Amy signed all three of the forms placed in front of her without bothering to read them. Mrs Trentham quickly folded up the legal papers prepared by the local solicitor and deposited them in her handbag.

"I'll see you soon," she promised Amy before kissing

her sister on the forehead. A few minutes later she began her journey back to Ashurst.

The bell above the door clanged noisily in the musty silence as Mrs Trentham stepped smartly into the shop. At first there was no sign of movement until at last Mr Sneddles appeared from his little room at the rear carrying three books under his arm.

"Good morning, Mrs Trentham," he said. "How kind of you to respond to my note so quickly. I felt I had to contact you as a problem has arisen."

"A problem?" Mrs Trentham drew back the veil that covered her face.

"Yes. As you are aware, I have almost completed my work in Yorkshire. I am sorry it has taken so long, madam, but I fear I have been over-indulgent with my time, such was my appreciation of –"

Mrs Trentham waved a hand in a manner that indicated she was not displeased.

"And I fear," he continued, "that despite enlisting the good services of Doctor Halcombe as my assistant and also remembering the time it takes to travel up and down to Yorkshire it may still take us several more weeks both to catalogue and value such a fine collection – always aware that your late father spent a lifetime putting the library together."

"It's of no consequence," Mrs Trentham assured him. "You see, I'm not in a hurry. Do take your time, Mr Sneddles, and just let me know when you have completed the task."

The antiquarian smiled at the thought of being allowed to continue his cataloguing uninterrupted.

He escorted Mrs Trentham back to the front of the shop and opened the door to let her out. No one who saw them together would have believed they had been born in the same year. She stared up and down Chelsea Terrace before quickly dropping the veil across her face.

Mr Sneddles closed the door behind her and rubbed

his mittens together, then shuffled back to his room to join Doctor Halcombe.

Lately he had been annoyed whenever a customer entered the shop.

"After thirty years, I have no intention of changing stock-brokers," Gerald Trentham said curtly as he poured himself a second cup of coffee.

"But can't you understand, my dear, just what a boost it would give Nigel to secure your account for his company?"

"And what a blow it would be for David Cartwright and Vickers da Costa to lose a client whom they have served so honourably for over a hundred years? No, Ethel, it's high time Nigel carried out his own dirty work. Damn it all, he's over forty."

"All the more reason to help," his wife suggested as she buttered a second piece of toast.

"No, Ethel. I repeat, no."

"But can't you see that one of Nigel's responsibilities is to bring new clients into the firm? It's particularly important at this moment, as I feel sure that now the war is over, they will soon be offering him a partnership."

Major Trentham didn't try to hide his incredulity at this piece of news. "If that is the case, he should be making more use of his own contacts – preferably the ones he made at school and at Sandhurst, not to mention the City. He shouldn't always expect to fall back on his father's friends."

"That's hardly fair, Gerald. If he can't rely on his own flesh and blood, why should he expect anyone else to come to his aid?"

"Come to his aid? That just about sums it up." Gerald's voice rose with every word. "Because that's exactly what you've been doing since the day he was born, which is perhaps the reason he is still unable to stand on his own two feet."

"Gerald," Mrs Trentham said, removing a handkerchief from her sleeve. "I never thought –"

"In any case," the major replied, trying to restore some calm, "it's not as if my portfolio is all that impressive. As you and Mr Attlee know only too well, all our capital is bound up in land and has been for generations."

"It's not the amount that matters," Mrs Trentham chided him. "It's the principle."

"Couldn't agree with you more," said Gerald as he folded his napkin, rose from the breakfast table and left the room before his wife could utter another word.

Mrs Trentham picked up her husband's morning paper and ran her finger down the names of those who had been awarded knighthoods in the Birthday Honours. Her shaking finger stopped at the Ts.

During his summer vacation, according to Max Harris, Daniel Trumper had taken the *Queen Mary* to America. However, the private detective was quite unable to answer Mrs Trentham's next question – why? All that Harris could be sure of was that Daniel's college still expected the young don back for the start of the new academic year.

During the weeks that Daniel was away in America Mrs Trentham spent a considerable amount of time closeted with her solicitors in Lincoln's Inn Fields while they prepared a building application for her.

She had already sought out three architects, all of whom had recently qualified. She instructed them to prepare outline drawings for a block of flats to be built in Chelsea. The winner, she assured them, would be offered the commission while the other two would receive one hundred pounds each in compensation. All three happily agreed to her terms.

Some twelve weeks later, each presented his portfolio but only one of them had come up with what Mrs Trentham was hoping for.

In the opinion of the senior partner of the law practice, the submission by the youngest of the three, Justin Talbot, would have made Battersea Power Station look like the Palace of Versailles. Mrs Trentham did not divulge to her solicitor that she had been influenced in her selection by the fact that Mr Talbot's uncle was a member of the Planning Committee of the London County Council.

Even if Talbot's uncle were to come to his nephew's aid, Mrs Trentham remained unconvinced that a majority of the committee would accept such an outrageous offering. It resembled a bunker that even Hitler might have rejected. However, her lawyers suggested that she should state in her application that the primary purpose of the new building was to create some low-cost housing in the centre of London to help students and single unemployed men who were in dire need of temporary accommodation. Second, any income derived from the flats would be placed in a charitable trust to help other families suffering from the same problem. Third, she should bring to the committee's attention the painstaking efforts that had been made to give a young, recently qualified architect his first break.

Mrs Trentham didn't know whether to be delighted or appalled when the LCC granted its approval. After long deliberation over several weeks, they insisted on only a few minor modifications to young Talbot's original plans. She gave her architect immediate instructions to clear the bombed-out site so that the building could begin without delay.

The application to the LCC by Sir Charles Trumper for a new store to be erected in Chelsea Terrace came in for considerable national publicity, most of it favourable. However, Mrs Trentham noted that in several articles written about the proposed new building, there was mention of a certain Mr Martin Simpson who described himself as the president of the Save the Small Shops Federation, a body that objected to the whole concept of Trumper's. Mr Simpson claimed it could only harm the little shopkeeper in the long run; their livelihoods were, after all, being put at risk. He went on to complain that what made it even more unfair was that none of the local shopkeepers had the means of taking on a man as powerful and wealthy as Sir Charles Trumper.

"Oh, yes, they have," Mrs Trentham said over breakfast that morning.

"Have what?"

"Nothing important," she reassured her husband, but later that day she supplied Harris with the financial wherewithal to allow Mr Simpson to lodge an official objection to the Trumper scheme. Mrs Trentham also agreed to cover any out-of-pocket costs Mr Simpson might incur while carrying out his endeavours.

She began to follow the results of Mr Simpson's efforts daily in the national press, even confiding to Harris that she would have been happy to pay the man a fee for the service he was rendering; but like so many activists the cause was all he seemed to care about.

Once the bulldozers had moved in on Mrs Trentham's site and work had come to a standstill on Trumper's, she turned her attention back to Daniel and the problem of his inheritance.

Her lawyers had confirmed that there was no way of reversing the provisions in the will unless Daniel Trumper were voluntarily to resign all his rights. They even presented her with a form of words that would be necessary for him to sign in such circumstances, leaving Mrs Trentham the daunting task of actually getting his signature affixed to the paper.

As Mrs Trentham was unable to imagine any situation in which she and Daniel would ever meet, she considered the whole exercise futile. However, she carefully locked the lawyer's draft in the bottom drawer of her desk in the drawing room along with all the other Trumper documents.

"How nice to see you again, madam," said Mr Sneddles. "I cannot apologise too profusely over the length of time I have taken to complete your commission. I shall naturally charge you no more than the sum on which we originally agreed."

The bookseller was unable to see the expression on Mrs Trentham's face as she had not yet removed her veil. She followed the old man past shelf after shelf of dust-covered books until they reached his little room at the back of the shop. There she was introduced to Doctor Halcombe who, like Sneddles, was wearing a heavy overcoat. She declined to take the offered chair when she noticed that it too was covered in a thin layer of dust.

The old man proudly pointed to eight boxes that lay on his desk. It took him nearly an hour to explain, with the occasional interjection from Doctor Halcombe, how they had catalogued her late father's entire library, first alphabetically under authors, then by categories and finally with a separate cross-section under titles. A rough valuation of each book had also been pencilled neatly in the bottom right-hand corner of every card.

Mrs Trentham was surprisingly patient with Mr Sneddles, occasionally asking questions in whose answer she had no interest, while allowing him to indulge in a long and complicated explanation as to how he had occupied his time during the past five years.

"You have done a quite remarkable job, Mr Sneddles," she said after he flicked over the last card, "Zola, Emile (1840–1902)". "I could not have asked for more."

"You are most kind, madam," said the old man, bowing low, "but then you have always shown such a genuine concern in these matters. Your father could have found no more suitable person to be responsible for his life's work."

"Fifty guineas was the agreed fee, if I remember correctly," said Mrs Trentham, removing a cheque from her handbag and passing it over to the owner of the bookshop.

"Thank you, madam," Mr Sneddles replied, taking the cheque and placing it absent-mindedly in an ash-tray. He refrained from adding, "I would happily have paid *you* double the sum for the privilege of carrying out such an exercise."

"And I see," she said, studying the accompanying papers closely, "that you have placed an overall value on the entire collection of a little under five thousand pounds."

"That is correct, madam. I should warn you, however,

that if anything I have erred on the conservative side. You see, some of these volumes are so rare it would be difficult to say what they might fetch on the open market."

"Does that mean you would be willing to offer such a sum for the library should I wish to dispose of it?" asked Mrs Trentham, looking directly at him.

"Nothing would give me greater pleasure, madam," replied the old man. "But alas, I fear that I quite simply do not have sufficient funds to do so."

"What would your attitude be were I to entrust you with the responsibility for their sale?" asked Mrs Trentham, her eye never leaving the old man.

"I can think of no greater privilege, madam, but it might take me many months – possibly even years to carry out such an enterprise."

"Then perhaps we should come to some arrangement, Mr Sneddles."

"Some arrangement? I'm not sure I fully understand you, madam."

"A partnership perhaps, Mr Sneddles?"

CHAPTER 34

Mrs Trentham approved of Nigel's choice of bride; but then it was she who had selected the young lady in the first place.

Veronica Berry possessed all the attributes her future mother-in-law considered necessary to become a Trentham. She came from a good family: her father was a vice-admiral who had not yet been placed on the reserve list and her mother was the daughter of a suffragan bishop. They were comfortably off without being wealthy and, more important, of their three children, all daughters, Veronica was the eldest.

The wedding was celebrated at Kimmeridge parish church in Dorset where Veronica had been christened by the vicar, confirmed by the suffragan bishop and was now to be married by the Bishop of Bath and Wells. The reception was grand enough without being lavish and "the children", as Mrs Trentham referred to them, would, she told everyone, be spending their honeymoon on the family estate in Aberdeen before returning to a mews house in Cadogan Place that she had selected for them. It was so convenient for Chester Square, she explained when asked, and also when not asked.

Every one of the thirty-two partners of Kitcat and Aitken, the stockbrokers for whom Nigel worked, was invited to the nuptial feast, but only five felt able to make the journey to Dorset.

During the reception, held on the lawn of the vice-admiral's home, Mrs Trentham made a point of speaking to all those partners present. To her consternation none was particularly forthcoming about Nigel's future.

Mrs Trentham had rather hoped that her son might have been made a partner soon after his fortieth birthday as she was well aware that several younger men had seen their names printed on the top left-hand side of the letterpaper despite having joined the firm some time after Nigel.

Just before the speeches were about to begin a shower sent the guests scurrying back into the marquee. Mrs Trentham felt the bridegroom's speech could have been received a little more warmly. However, she allowed that it was quite hard to applaud when you were holding a glass of champagne in one hand and an asparagus roll in the other. Indeed, Nigel's best man, Hugh Folland, hadn't done a great deal better.

After the speeches were over Mrs Trentham sought out Miles Renshaw, the senior partner of Kitcat and Aitken, and after taking him on one side revealed that in the near future she intended to invest a considerable sum of money in a company that was planning to go public. She would therefore be in need of his advice as to what she described as her long-term strategy.

This piece of information did not elicit any particular response from Renshaw who still remembered Mrs Trentham's assurance over the future management of the Hardcastle portfolio once her father had died. However, he suggested that perhaps she should drop in to their City office and go over the details of the transaction once the official tender document had been released.

Mrs Trentham thanked Mr Renshaw and continued to work her way round the assembled gathering as if it were she who was the hostess.

She didn't notice Veronica's scowl of disapproval on more than one occasion.

It was the last Friday in September 1947 that Gibson tapped quietly on the door of the living room, entered and announced, "Captain Daniel Trentham."

When Mrs Trentham first saw the young man dressed in the uniform of a captain in the Royal Fusiliers, her legs almost gave way. He marched in and came to a halt in the middle of the carpet. The meeting that had taken place in that room some twenty-five years before immediately sprang to her mind. Somehow she managed to get herself across the room before collapsing on to the sofa.

Gripping its arm to make sure she didn't pass out completely Mrs Trentham stared up at her grandson. She was horrified at his resemblance to Guy, and felt quite sick at the memories he evoked. Memories which for so many years she had managed to keep at the back of her mind.

Once she had composed herself Mrs Trentham's first reaction was to order Gibson to throw him out, but she decided to wait for a moment as she was anxious to discover what the young man could possibly want. As Daniel delivered his carefully rehearsed sentences she began to wonder if possibly the meeting might be turned to her advantage.

Her grandson started by telling her how he had been to Australia that summer, not America as Harris had led her to believe. He went on to show he knew of her ownership of the flats, her attempt to block the planning permission for the store and the wording on the grave in Ashurst and even details of her meetings at the St Agnes Hotel. He continued his rendering with an assurance that his parents were unaware he had come to visit her that afternoon.

Mrs Trentham concluded that he must have discovered the full circumstances of her son's death in Melbourne. Otherwise why would he have stressed that, if the information he possessed were to fall into the hands of the popular press, it could only result in – to put it mildly – embarrassment for all concerned?

Mrs Trentham allowed Daniel to continue his speech while at the same time thinking furiously. It was during his prognosis on the future development of Chelsea Terrace that she wondered just how much the young man standing before her actually did know. She decided there was only one way of finding out, and that would require her to take one big risk.

When Daniel had finally come out with his specific demand, Mrs Trentham simply replied, "I have a condition of my own."

"What condition?"

"That you relinquish any claim you might have to the Hardcastle estate."

Daniel looked uncertain for the first time. It was obviously not what he had expected. Mrs Trentham suddenly felt confident that he had no knowledge of the will: after all, her father had briefed Baverstock not to allow the young man to be privy to its contents until his thirtieth birthday; and Mr Baverstock was not a man to break his word.

"I can't believe you ever intended to leave me anything in the first place," was Daniel's first response.

She didn't reply and waited until Daniel at last nodded his agreement.

"And it must be in writing," she added.

"So must my part of the deal," he demanded brusquely.

Mrs Trentham felt certain that he was no longer relying on the safety of a prepared script and was now simply reacting to events as they took place.

She rose, walked slowly over to her desk and unlocked a drawer. Daniel remained in the middle of the room, swaying slightly from foot to foot.

Having located two sheets of paper and retrieved the lawyer's draft wording that she had left locked in the bottom drawer, Mrs Trentham wrote out two identical agreements which included Daniel's demand for her withdrawal both of her application to build the flats and her objections to his father's application for planning permission to build Trumper Towers. She also included in the agreements her lawyer's exact words for Daniel's waiver of his rights to his great-grandfather's estate.

She handed over the first draft for her grandson to study. At any moment she expected him to work out what he must be sacrificing by signing such a document.

Daniel finished reading the first copy of the agreement then checked to see that both drafts were identical in every detail. Though he said nothing, Mrs Trentham still felt he must surely fathom out why she needed the agreement so badly. In fact, had he demanded that she also sell the land in Chelsea Terrace to his father at a commercial rate she would happily have agreed, just to have Daniel's signature on the bottom of the agreement.

The moment Daniel had signed both documents Mrs Trentham rang the bell and called for the butler to witness the two signatures. Once this task had been completed she said curtly, "Show the gentleman out, Gibson." As the uniformed figure left the room she found herself wondering just how long it would be before the boy realised what a poor bargain he had struck.

When on the following day Mrs Trentham's solicitors studied the one-page document they were stunned by the simplicity of the transaction. However, she offered no explanation as to how she had managed to achieve such a coup. A slight bow of the head from the senior partner acknowledged that the agreement was watertight.

Every man has his price, and once Martin Simpson realised his source of income had dried up, a further fifty pounds in cash convinced him that he should withdraw his objection to Trumper Towers from proceeding as planned.

The following day Mrs Trentham turned her attention to other matters: the understanding of offer documents.

In Mrs Trentham's opinion Veronica became pregnant far too quickly.

Her daughter-in-law produced a son, Giles Raymond, only nine months and three weeks after she and Nigel had been married. At least the child had not been born prematurely. As it was, Mrs Trentham had already observed the servants counting the months on their fingers on more than one occasion.

It was after Veronica had returned from hospital with

the child that Mrs Trentham had the first difference of opinion with her daughter-in-law.

Veronica and Nigel had wheeled Giles round to Chester Square for the proud grandmother to admire. After Mrs Trentham had given the infant a cursory glance Gibson pushed the pram out and the tea trolley in.

"Of course you'll want the boy to be put down for Aysgarth and Harrow without delay," said Mrs Trentham, even before Nigel or Veronica had been given a chance to select a sandwich. "After all, one wants to be certain that his place is guaranteed."

"Actually, Nigel and I have already decided how our son will be educated," said Veronica, "and neither of those schools have entered our deliberations."

Mrs Trentham placed her cup back on its saucer and stared at Veronica as if she had announced the death of the King. "I'm sorry, I don't think I heard you correctly, Veronica."

"We are going to send Giles to a local primary school in Chelsea and then on to Bryanston."

"Bryanston? And where is that, may one ask?"

"In Dorset. It's my father's old school," Veronica added before removing a salmon sandwich from the plate in front of her.

Nigel looked anxiously across at his mother as he touched his blue and silver striped tie.

"That may well be the case," said Mrs Trentham. "However, I feel sure we still need to give a little more consideration as to how young Raymond – she stressed the name – should start off in life."

"No, that will be unnecessary," said Veronica. "Nigel and I have already given quite sufficient thought as to how Giles should be educated. In fact, we registered him for Bryanston last week. After all, one wants to be certain that his place is guaranteed."

Veronica leant forward and helped herself to another salmon sandwich.

* * *

Three chimes echoed from the little carriage clock that stood on the mantelpiece on the far side of the room.

Max Harris pushed himself up out of the armchair in the corner of the lounge the moment he saw Mrs Trentham enter the hotel lobby. He gave a half-bow as he waited for his client to be seated in the chair opposite him.

He ordered tea for her and another double whisky for himself. Mrs Trentham frowned her disapproval as the waiter scurried off to carry out the order. Her attention fixed on Max Harris the moment she heard the inevitable clicks.

"I assume you would not have requested this meeting, Mr Harris, unless you had something important to tell me."

"I think I can safely say that I am the bearer of glad tidings. You see, a lady by the name of Mrs Bennett has recently been arrested and charged with shoplifting. A fur coat and a leather belt from Harvey Nichols, to be exact."

"And of what possible interest could this lady be to me?" asked Mrs Trentham as she looked over his shoulder, annoyed to see that it had started raining and remembering that she had left the house without an umbrella.

"She turns out to have a rather interesting relationship with Sir Charles Trumper."

"Relationship?" said Mrs Trentham, looking even more puzzled.

"Yes," said Harris. "Mrs Bennett is none other than Sir Charles's youngest sister."

Mrs Trentham turned her gaze back on Max Harris. "But Trumper only has three sisters if I remember correctly," she said. "Sal, who is in Toronto and married to an insurance salesman; Grace, who has recently been appointed matron of Guy's hospital, and Kitty who left England some time ago to join her sister in Canada."

"And has now returned."

"Returned?"

"Yes, as Mrs Kitty Bennett."

"I don't begin to understand," said Mrs Trentham, becoming exasperated by the cat and mouse game Harris was so obviously enjoying.

"While she was in Canada," Harris continued, oblivious to his client's irritation, "she married a certain Mr Bennett, a longshoreman. Not unlike her old man, in fact. It lasted for almost a year before ending in a messy divorce in which several men were petitioned. She returned to England a few weeks ago, but only after her sister Sal had refused to take her back."

"How did you come by this information?"

"A friend of mine at Wandsworth nick pointed me in the right direction. Once he had read the charge sheet in the name of Bennett, *née* Trumper, he decided to double-check. It was 'Kitty' that gave the game away. I popped round immediately to be sure we had the right woman." Harris stopped to sip his whisky.

"Go on," said Mrs Trentham impatiently.

"For five pounds she sang like a canary," said Harris. "If I were in a position to offer her fifty I've a feeling she'd sound awfully like a nightingale."

When Trumper's announced they were preparing to go public Mrs Trentham was holidaying on her husband's estate in Aberdeenshire. Having read the short piece in the *Telegraph* she concluded that, although she now had control over the combined monthly incomes left to her sister as well as herself and a further windfall of twenty thousand pounds, she would still need all the capital she had acquired from the sale of the Yorkshire estate if she were going to be able to purchase a worthwhile holding in the new company. She made three trunk calls that morning.

Earlier in the year she had given instructions for her own portfolio to be transferred to Kitcat and Aitken, and after several months of continually badgering her husband she had finally bludgeoned him into following suit. Despite this further commitment on her son's behalf Nigel was still not offered a partnership. Mrs Trentham would have advised him to resign had she been confident his prospects elsewhere would have been any better.

Despite this setback she continued to invite the partners of Kitcat to dinner at Chester Square in regular rotation. Gerald left his wife in no doubt that he did not approve of such tactics, and remained unconvinced that they helped their son's cause. He had been, however, aware that his opinion in such matters had made little impression on her for some time. In any case, the major had now reached an age when he had become too weary to put up more than token resistance.

After Mrs Trentham had studied the finer details of the Trumper's proposals in her husband's copy of *The Times*, she instructed Nigel to apply for five per cent of the company's shares the moment the prospectus was launched.

However, it was a paragraph towards the end of an article in the *Daily Mail* written by Vincent Mulchrone headed "The Triumphant Trumpers" that reminded her that she was still in possession of a picture that needed to fetch its proper price.

Whenever Mr Baverstock requested a meeting with Mrs Trentham it always seemed to her to be more of a summons than an invitation. Perhaps it was because he had acted for her father for over thirty years.

She was only too aware that, as her father's executor, Mr Baverstock still wielded considerable influence, even if she had managed to clip his wings recently over the sale of the estate.

Having offered her the seat on the other side of the partner's desk Mr Baverstock returned to his own chair, replaced his half-moon spectacles on the end of his nose and opened the cover of one of his inevitable grey files.

He seemed to conduct all his correspondence, not to mention his meetings, in a manner that could only be described as distant. Mrs Trentham often wondered if he had treated her father in the same way.

"Mrs Trentham," he began, placing the palms of his

hands on the desk in front of him and pausing to stare down at the notes he had written the previous evening. "May I first thank you for taking the trouble to come and see me in my offices and add how sad I am that your sister felt she had to once again decline my invitation. However, she has made it clear to me in a short letter I received last week that she is happy for you to represent her on this and indeed on any future occasion."

"Dear Amy," said Mrs Trentham. "The poor creature took the death of my father rather badly, even though I have done everything in my power to soften the blow."

The solicitor's eyes returned to the file which contained a note from a Mr Althwaite of Bird, Collingwood and Althwaite in Harrogate, instructing them to see that in future Miss Amy's monthly cheque should be sent direct to Coutts in the Strand for an account number that differed by only one digit from that to which Mr Baverstock already sent the other half of the monthly revenue.

"Although your father left you and your sister the income derived from his Trust," the solicitor continued, "the bulk of his capital will, as you know, in time be passed on to Doctor Daniel Trumper."

Mrs Trentham nodded, her face impassive.

"As you are also aware," Mr Baverstock continued, "the Trust is currently holding stocks, shares and gilts that are being administered for us by the merchant bankers Hambros and Co. Whenever they consider it prudent to make a sizeable investment on behalf of the Trust, we feel it equally important to keep you informed of their intentions, despite the fact that Sir Raymond gave us a free hand in these matters."

"That's most considerate of you, Mr Baverstock."

The solicitor's eyes returned to the file where he studied another note. This time it was from an estate agent in Bradford. The estate, house and contents of the late Sir Raymond Hardcastle had without his knowledge been sold for forty-one thousand pounds. After deducting commissions and legal fees, the agent had sent the balance of the monies direct to the same account at Coutts in the Strand as received Miss Amy's monthly payment.

"Bearing this in mind," continued the family lawyer, "I felt it nothing less than my duty to inform you that our advisors are recommending a considerable investment in a new company that is about to come on to the market."

"And which company might that be?" enquired Mrs Trentham.

"Trumper's," said Baverstock, watching carefully for his client's reaction.

"And why Trumper's in particular?" she asked, the expression on her face revealing no particular surprise.

"Principally because Hambros consider it a sound and prudent investment. But, perhaps more important, in time the bulk of the company's stock will be owned by Daniel Trumper, whose father, as I feel sure you know, is currently chairman of the board."

"I was aware of that," said Mrs Trentham, without further comment. She could see that it worried Mr Baverstock that she took the news so calmly.

"Of course, if you and your sister were both to object strongly to such a large commitment being made by the Trust it is possible our advisors might reconsider their position."

"And how much are they thinking of investing?"

"Around two hundred thousand pounds," the solicitor informed her. "This would make it possible for the Trust to purchase approximately ten per cent of the company's shares."

"Is that not a considerable stake for us to be holding in one company?"

"It certainly is," said Mr Baverstock. "But still well within the Trust's budget."

"Then I am happy to accept Hambros' judgment," said Mrs Trentham. "And I feel sure I speak for my sister in this matter."

Once again Mr Baverstock looked down at the file

where he studied an affidavit signed by Miss Amy Hardcastle, virtually giving her sister *carte blanche* when it came to decisions relating to the estate of the late Sir Raymond Hardcastle, including the transfer of twenty thousand pounds from her personal account. Mr Baverstock only hoped that Miss Amy was happy at the Cliff Top Residential Hotel. He looked up at Sir Raymond's other daughter.

"Then all that is left for me to do," he concluded, "is to advise Hambros of your views in this matter and brief you more fully when Trumper's eventually allocate their shares."

The solicitor closed the file, rose from behind his desk and began to walk towards the door. Mrs Trentham followed in his wake, happy in the knowledge that both the Hardcastle Trust and her own advisors were now working in tandem to help her fulfil her long-term purpose without either side being aware of what she was up to. It pleased her even more to think that the day Trumper's went public she would have control of fifteen per cent of the company.

When they reached the door Mr Baverstock turned to shake Mrs Trentham by the hand.

"Good day, Mrs Trentham."

"Good day, Mr Baverstock. You have been most punctilious, as always."

She made her way back to the car where a chauffeur held open the back door for her. As she was driven away she turned to look out of the rear window. The lawyer was standing by the door of his offices, the worried expression remaining on his face.

"Where to, madam?" asked the chauffeur as they joined the afternoon traffic.

She checked her watch: the meeting with Baverstock had not taken as long as she had anticipated and she now found herself with some spare time before her next appointment. Nevertheless she still gave the instruction, "The St Agnes Hotel," as she placed a hand on the brown paper parcel that lay on the seat beside her.

She had told Harris to book a private room in the hotel

and slip Kitty Bennett up in the lift at a time when he felt confident that no one was watching them.

When she arrived at the St Agnes clutching the parcel under one arm, she was annoyed to find that Harris was not waiting for her in his usual place by the bar. She intensely disliked standing alone in the corridor and reluctantly went over to the hall porter to ask the number of the room Harris had booked.

"Fourteen," said a man in a shiny blue uniform with buttons that did not shine. "But you can't –"

Mrs Trentham was not in the habit of being told "You can't" by anyone. She turned and slowly climbed the stairs that led up to the bedrooms on the first floor. The hall porter quickly picked up the phone on the counter beside him.

It took Mrs Trentham a few minutes to locate Number 14 and Harris almost as long to respond to her sharp knock. When Mrs Trentham was eventually allowed to enter the room she was surprised to discover how small it was: only just large enough to accommodate one bed, one chair and a wash-basin. Her eyes settled on the woman who was sprawled across the bed. She was wearing a red silk blouse and a black leather skirt – far too short in Mrs Trentham's opinion, not to mention the fact that two of the top buttons of the blouse were undone.

As Kitty made no attempt to remove an old raincoat that had been thrown across the chair, Mrs Trentham was left with little choice but to remain standing.

She turned to Harris, who was checking his tie in the only mirror. He had obviously decided that any introduction was superfluous.

Mrs Trentham's only reaction was to get on with the business she had come to transact so that she could return to civilisation as quickly as possible. She didn't wait for Harris to start the proceedings.

"Have you explained to Mrs Bennett what is expected of her?"

"I most certainly have," said the detective, as he put

on his jacket. "And Kitty is more than ready to carry out her part of the bargain."

"Can she be trusted?" Mrs Trentham glanced doubtfully down at the woman on the bed.

" 'course I can, long as the money's right," were Kitty's first words. "All I want to know is, 'ow much do I get?"

"Whatever it sells for, plus fifty pounds," said Mrs Trentham.

"Then I expect twenty quid up front."

Mrs Trentham hesitated for a moment, then nodded her agreement.

"So what's the catch?"

"Only that your brother will try to talk you out of the whole idea," said Mrs Trentham. "He may even attempt to bribe you in exchange for . . ."

"Not an 'ope," said Kitty. " 'e can talk 'is 'ead off as far as I'm concerned but it won't make a blind bit of difference. You see, I 'ate Charlie almost as much as you do."

Mrs Trentham smiled for the first time. She then placed the brown paper parcel on the end of the bed.

Harris smirked. "I knew you two would find you had something in common."

BECKY

1947-1950

CHAPTER 35

Night after night I would lie awake worrying that Daniel must eventually work out that Charlie wasn't his father.

Whenever they stood next to each other, Daniel tall and slim, with fair wavy hair and deep blue eyes, Charlie at least three inches shorter, stocky, with dark wiry hair and brown eyes, I assumed Daniel must in time comment on the disparity. It didn't help that my complexion is also dark. The dissimilarities might have been comic had the implications not been so serious. Yet Daniel has never once mentioned the differences in physical make-up or character between himself and Charlie.

Charlie wanted to tell Daniel the truth about Guy right from the start, but I convinced him that we should wait until the boy was old enough to understand all the implications. But when Guy died of tuberculosis there no longer seemed any point in burdening Daniel with the past.

Later, after years of anguish and Charlie's continued remonstrations, I finally agreed to tell Daniel everything. I phoned him at Trinity the week before he was due to sail for America and asked if I could drive him down to Southampton; that way at least I knew we would be uninterrupted for several hours. I mentioned that there was something important I needed to discuss with him.

I set out for Cambridge a little earlier than was

necessary and arrived well in time to help Daniel with his packing. By eleven we were heading down the A10. For the first hour he chatted away happily enough about his work at Cambridge – too many students, not enough time for research – but the moment the conversation switched to the problems we were facing with the flats, I knew he had presented me with the ideal opportunity to tell him the truth about his parentage. Then quite suddenly he changed the subject and I lost my nerve. I swear I would have broached the topic right there and then, but the moment had passed.

Because of all the unhappiness we subsequently experienced with the death of my mother and with the life of Mrs Trentham while Daniel was away in America, I decided my best chance of ever being frank with my son had been squandered. I begged Charlie to allow the matter to drop once and for all. I have a fine husband. He told me I was wrong; that Daniel was mature enough to handle the truth but he accepted that it had to be my decision. He never once referred to the matter again.

When Daniel returned from America I travelled back down to Southampton to pick him up. I don't know what it was about him but he seemed to have changed. For a start he looked different – more at ease – and the moment he saw me he gave me a big hug, which quite took me by surprise. On the way back to London we discussed his visit to the States, which he had obviously enjoyed, and without going into great detail I brought him up to date on what was happening to our planning application for Chelsea Terrace. He didn't seem all that interested in my news, but to be fair Charlie never involved Daniel in the day-to-day working of Trumper's once we both realised he was destined for an academic career.

Daniel spent the next few weeks with us before returning to Cambridge, and even Charlie, not always the most observant of people, commented on how much he had changed. He was just as serious and quiet, even as secretive, but he was so much warmer towards us both that I began to wonder if he had met a girl while he had been away. I hoped so, but despite the odd hint clumsily dropped, Daniel made no mention of anyone in particular. I rather liked the idea of him marrying an American. He had rarely brought girls home in the past and always seemed so shy when we introduced him to the daughters of any of our friends. In fact he was never to be found if Clarissa Wiltshire put in an appearance – which was quite often nowadays, as during their vacations from Bristol University both the twins were to be found working behind the counter at Number 1.

It must have been about a month after Daniel returned from America that Charlie told me Mrs Trentham had withdrawn all her objections to our proposed scheme for joining the two tower blocks together. I leapt with joy. When he added that she was not going ahead with her own plans to rebuild the flats I refused to believe him and immediately assumed that there had to be some catch. Even Charlie admitted, "I've no idea what she's up to this time." Certainly neither of us accepted Daphne's theory that she might be mellowing in her old age.

Two weeks later the LCC confirmed that all objections to our scheme had been withdrawn and we could begin on our building programme. That was the signal Charlie had been waiting for to inform the outside world that we intended to go public.

Charlie called a board meeting so that all the necessary resolutions could be passed.

Mr Merrick, whom Charlie had never forgiven for causing him to sell the Van Gogh, advised us to appoint Robert Fleming to be our merchant bankers in the run-up to the flotation. The banker also added that he hoped the newly formed company would continue to use Child and Co as their clearing bank. Charlie would have liked to have told him to "get lost" but knew only too well that if he changed banks a few weeks before going public, eyebrows would be raised in the City. The board accepted both pieces of advice, and Tim Newman of Robert Fleming's was duly invited to join the board. Tim brought a breath of fresh air to the company, representing a new breed of bankers. However, although I, like Charlie, immediately took to Mr Newman, I never really got on the same wavelength as Paul Merrick.

As the day for issuing the tender documents drew nearer, Charlie spent more and more of his time with the merchant banker. Meanwhile Tom Arnold took overall control of the running of the shops, as well as overseeing the building programme – with the exception of Number 1, which still remained my domain.

I had decided several months before the final announcement that I wanted to mount a major sale at the auction house just before Charlie's declaration of going public, and I was confident that the Italian collection to which I had been devoting a great deal of my time would prove to be the ideal opportunity to place Number 1 Chelsea Terrace on the map.

It had taken my chief researcher Francis Lawson nearly two years to gather some fifty-nine canvases together, all painted between 1519 and 1768. Our biggest coup was a Canaletto – *The Basilica of St Mark's* – a painting that had been left to Daphne by an old aunt of hers from Cumberland. "It isn't," she characteristically told us, "as good as the two Percy already has in Lanarkshire. However, I still expect the painting to fetch a fair price, my darling. Failure will only result in offering any future custom to Sotheby's," she added with a smile.

We placed a reserve on the painting of thirty thousand pounds. I had suggested to Daphne that this was a sensible figure, remembering that the record for a

Canaletto was thirty-eight thousand guineas, bid at Christie's the previous year.

While I was in the final throes of preparation for the sale Charlie and Tim Newman spent most of their time visiting institutions, banks, finance companies and major investors, to brief them on why they should take a stake in the "biggest barrow in the world".

Tim was optimistic about the outcome and felt that when the stock applications came to be counted we would be heavily oversubscribed. Even so, he thought that he and Charlie should travel to New York and drum up some interest among American investors. Charlie timed his trip to the States so that he would be back in London a couple of days before my auction was to take place and a clear three weeks before our tender document was to be offered to the public.

It was a cold Monday morning in January, and I may not have been at my brightest but I could have sworn I recognised the customer who was in deep conversation with one of our new counter assistants. It worried me that I couldn't quite place the middle-aged lady who was wearing a coat that would have been fashionable in the thirties and looked as if she had fallen on hard times and might be having to sell off one of the family heirlooms.

Once she had left the building I walked over to the desk and asked Cathy, our most recent recruit, who she was.

"A Mrs Bennett," said the young girl behind the counter.

The name meant nothing to me so I asked what she had wanted.

Cathy handed me a small oil painting of the Virgin Mary and Child. "The lady asked if this could still be considered for the Italian sale. She knew nothing of its provenance and looking at her I have to say I wondered if it might have been stolen. I was about to have a word with Mr Lawson."

I stared at the little oil and immediately realised it had been Charlie's youngest sister who had brought the painting in.

"Leave this one to me."

"Certainly, Lady Trumper."

I took the lift to the top floor and walked straight past Jessica Allen and on into Charlie's office. I handed over the picture for him to study and quickly explained how it had come into our possession.

He pushed the paperwork on his desk to one side and stared at the painting for some time without saying a word.

"Well, one thing's for certain," Charlie eventually offered, "Kitty is never going to tell us how or where she got hold of it, otherwise she would have come to me direct."

"So what shall we do?"

"Put it in the sale as she instructed, because you can be sure that no one is going to bid more for the picture than I will."

"But if all she's after is some cash, why not make her a fair offer for the picture?"

"If all Kitty is after was some cash, she would be standing in this office now. No, she would like nothing better than to see me crawling to her for a change."

"But if she stole the painting?"

"From whom? And even if she did there's nothing to stop us stating the original provenance in our catalogue. After all, the police must still have all the details of the theft on their files."

"But what if Guy gave it to her?"

"Guy," Charlie reminded me, "is dead."

I was delighted by the amount of interest the press and public were beginning to take in the sale. Another good omen was that several of the leading art critics and collectors were spotted during the preview week studying the pictures on display in the main gallery.

Articles about Charlie and myself began to appear, first in the financial sections, then spreading over to the feature pages. I didn't care much for the sound of "The Triumphant Trumpers", as one paper dubbed us, but Tim Newman explained to us the importance of public relations when trying to raise large sums of money. As feature after feature appeared in newspapers and magazines, our new young director became daily more confident that the flotation was going to be a success.

Francis Lawson and his new assistant Cathy Ross worked on the auction catalogue for several weeks, painstakingly going over the history of each painting, its previous owners and the galleries and exhibitions in which each had been exhibited before they were offered to Trumper's for auction. To our surprise, what went down particularly well with the public was not the paintings themselves but our catalogue, the first with every plate in colour. It cost a fortune to produce, but as we had to order two reprints before the day of the sale and we sold every catalogue at five shillings a time, it wasn't long before we recovered our costs. I was able to inform the board at our monthly meeting that following two more reprints we had actually ended up making a small profit. "Perhaps you should close the art gallery and open a publishing house," was Charlie's helpful comment.

The new auction room at Number 1 held two hundred and twenty comfortably. We had never managed to fill every seat in the past, but now, as applications for tickets kept arriving by every post, we quickly had to sort out the genuine bidders from the hangers-on.

Despite cutting, pruning, being offhand and even downright rude to one or two persistent individuals, we still ended up with nearly three hundred people who expected to be found seats. Several journalists were among them, but our biggest coup came when the arts editor of the Third Programme phoned to enquire if they could cover the auction on radio.

Charlie arrived back from America two days before the sale and told me in the brief moments we had together that the trip had proved most satisfactory – whatever that meant. He added that Daphne would be accompanying him to the auction – "Got to keep the major clients happy." I didn't mention the fact that I had quite forgotten to allocate him a seat, but Simon Matthews, who had recently been appointed as my deputy, squeezed a couple of extra chairs on the end of the seventh row and prayed that no one from the fire department would be among the bidders.

We decided to hold the sale at three o'clock on a Tuesday afternoon, after Tim Newman advised us that timing was all-important if we were to ensure the maximum coverage in the national papers the following day.

Simon and I were up all night before the auction with the saleroom staff, removing the pictures from the walls and placing them in the correct order ready for sale. Next we checked the lighting of the easel which would display each painting and finally placed the chairs in the auction room as close together as possible. By pulling the stand from which Simon would conduct the auction back by a few feet we were even able to add another row. It may have left less room for the spotters – who always stand by the side of the auctioneer during a sale searching for the bidders – but it certainly solved fourteen other problems.

On the morning of the auction we carried out a dress rehearsal, the porters placing each picture on the easel as Simon called the lot number, then removing it once he had brought the hammer down and called for the next lot. When eventually the Canaletto was lifted up on to the easel, the painting displayed all the polished technique and minute observation which had been the hallmark of the master. I could only smile when a moment later the masterpiece was replaced by Charlie's little picture of the Virgin Mary and Child. Despite considerable research by Cathy Ross she had been quite unable to trace its antecedents, so we had merely re-framed the painting and attributed it in the catalogue as sixteenth-century school. I marked it up in my book at an estimated two hundred guineas, although I was fully aware that Charlie intended to buy back the little picture whatever the price. It still worried me how Kitty had got hold of the oil, but Charlie told me continually to "stop fussing". He had bigger problems on his mind than how his sister had come into possession of Tommy's gift.

On the afternoon of the auction some people were already in their seats by two fifteen. I spotted more than one major buyer or gallery-owner who had not previously encountered a packed house at Trumper's and consequently had to stand at the back.

By two forty-five there were only a few seats left, and latecomers were already crammed shoulder to shoulder down the side walls, with one or two even perched on their haunches in the centre aisle. At two fifty-five Daphne made a splendid entrance, wearing a finely tailored cashmere suit of midnight blue which I had seen featured in *Vogue* the previous month. Charlie, who I felt looked a little tired, followed only a pace behind. They took their seats on the end of the seventh row, for sentimental reasons he had explained. Daphne appeared very satisfied with herself while Charlie fidgeted impatiently.

At exactly three o'clock I took my place next to the auctioneer's stand while Simon climbed the steps to his little box, paused for a moment as he scrutinised the crowd to work out where the major buyers were seated, then banged his gavel several times.

"Good afternoon, ladies and gentlemen," he

announced. "Welcome to Trumper's, the fine art auctioneers." He managed somehow to emphasise "the" in a most agreeable fashion. As he called for lot number one a hush came over the room. I checked the painting in my catalogue – although I think I knew the details of all fifty-nine lots by heart. It was a depiction of St Francis of Assisi by Giovanni Battista Crespi, dated 1617. I had the little oil marked in our code as QIHH pounds, so when Simon brought down the hammer at two thousand two hundred, seven hundred pounds more than I had estimated, I felt we were off to a good start.

Of the fifty-nine works on sale the Canaletto had been left until lot number thirty-seven as I wanted an atmosphere of excitement to build before the painting reached the stand, while not leaving it so late that people started to drift away. The first hour had raised forty-seven thousand pounds and we still had not come to the Canaletto. When eventually the four-foot-wide canvas was placed in the glare of the spotlight, a gasp came from those in the audience who were seeing the masterpiece for the first time.

"A painting of St Mark's Basilica by Canaletto," said Simon, "dated 1741" – as if we had another half-dozen stored away in the basement. "Considerable interest has been shown in this item and I have an opening bid of ten thousand pounds." His eyes scanned the hushed room, as I and my spotters searched to see where the second bid might come from.

"Fifteen thousand," said Simon as he looked towards a representative from the Italian government who was seated in the fifth row.

"Twenty thousand pounds at the back of the room" – I knew it had to be the representative from the Mellon Collection. He always sat in the second to back row, a cigarette dangling from his lips to show us he was still bidding.

"Twenty-five thousand," said Simon, turning again towards the Italian government representative.

"Thirty thousand." The cigarette was still emitting smoke: Mellon remained in the chase.

"Thirty-five thousand." I spotted a new bidder, sitting in the fourth row to my right: Mr Randall, the manager of the Wildenstein Gallery in Bond Street.

"Forty thousand," said Simon as a fresh puff of smoke emanated from the back. We were past the estimate I had given Daphne, although no emotion showed on her face.

"Fifty thousand." This was far too big a hike at this stage in my opinion. Looking towards the box, I noticed that Simon's left hand was shaking.

"Fifty thousand," he repeated a little nervously, when a new bidder in the front row, whom I didn't recognise, started nodding furiously.

The cigarette puffed once again. "Fifty-five thousand."

"Sixty thousand." Simon had turned his attention back in the direction of the unknown bidder, who confirmed with a sharp nod that he remained in the hunt.

"Sixty-five thousand." The Mellon representative still kept puffing away, but when Simon turned his attention back to the bidder in the front row he received a sharp shake of the head.

"Sixty-five thousand then, the bid is at the back of the room. Sixty-five thousand, are there any more bidders?" Once again Simon looked towards the underbidder in the front row. "Then I'm offering the Canaletto at sixty-five thousand pounds, sixty-five thousand pounds for the second time, then it's sold for sixty-five thousand pounds." Simon brought the gavel down with a thud less than two minutes after the first bid had been offered, and I marked ZIHHH in my catalogue as a round of applause spontaneously burst from the audience – something I had never experienced before at Number 1.

Noisy chatter broke out all over the room as Simon turned round to me and said in a low voice, "Sorry about the mistake, Becky," and I realised that the jump from forty to fifty thousand had been nothing more than a bout of auctioneer's nerves.

I began to compose a possible headline in tomorrow's papers: "Record amount paid for Canaletto in auction at Trumper's". Charlie would be pleased.

"Can't see Charlie's little picture fetching quite that sum," Simon added with a smile, as the Virgin Mary and Child replaced the Canaletto on the stand and he turned to face his audience once again.

"Quiet please," he said. "The next item, lot number thirty-eight in your catalogue, is from the school of Bronzino." He scanned the room. "I have a bid of one hundred and fifty" – he paused for a second – "pounds for this lot. Can I ask for one hundred and seventy-five?" Daphne, who I assumed was Charlie's plant, raised her hand and I stifled a smile. "One hundred and seventy-five pounds. Do I see two hundred?" Simon looked around hopefully but received no response. "Then I'll offer it for the first time at one hundred and seventy-five pounds, for the second time, for the third time then . . ."

But before Simon could bring the gavel down a stocky man with a brownish moustache, greying hair, dressed in a tweed jacket, checked shirt and a yellow tie leaped up from the back of the room and shouted, "That painting is not 'from the school of', it's an original Bronzino, and it was stolen from the Church of St Augustine, near Reims, during the First World War."

Pandemonium broke out as people stared first at the man in the yellow tie, then at the little picture. Simon banged his gavel repeatedly but could not regain control as the journalists began to scribble furiously across their pads. I glanced across to see Charlie and Daphne, their heads bowed in frantic conversation.

Once the outcry had died down, attention began to focus on the man who had made the claim. He remained standing in his place.

"I believe you are mistaken, sir," said Simon firmly. "As I can assure you, this painting has been known to the gallery for some years."

"And I assure you, sir," replied the man, "the painting is an original, and although I do not accuse the previous owner of being a thief, I can nevertheless prove it was stolen." Several in the audience immediately glanced down at their catalogues to see the name of the most recent owner. "From the private collection of Sir Charles Trumper" was printed in bold letters along the top line.

The hubbub, if anything, was now even louder, but still the man remained standing. I leaned forwards and tugged Simon's trouser leg. He bent over and I whispered my decision in his ear. He banged his gavel several times and at last the audience began to quieten. I looked across at Charlie who was as white as a sheet, then at Daphne, who remained quite calm and was holding his hand. As I believed there had to be a simple explanation to the mystery, I felt curiously detached. When Simon had finally restored order he announced, "I am advised that this lot will be withdrawn until further notice."

"Lot number thirty-nine," he added quickly as the man in the brown tweed jacket rose and hurriedly departed from the room, pursued by a gaggle of journalists.

None of the remaining twenty-one items reached their reserve prices, and when Simon brought the gavel down for the final time that afternoon, although we had broken every house record for an Italian sale, I was only too aware what the story in the next day's papers was bound to be. I looked across at Charlie who was obviously trying his best to appear unruffled. Instinctively I turned towards the chair which had been occupied by the man in the brown tweed jacket. The room was beginning to empty as people drifted towards the doors and I noticed for the first time that directly behind the chair sat an elderly lady sitting bolt upright, leaning forward, her two hands resting on the head of a parasol. She was staring directly at me.

Once Mrs Trentham was sure she had caught my eye, she rose serenely from her place and glided slowly out of the gallery.

The following morning the press had a field day. Despite the fact that neither Charlie nor I had made any statement our picture was on every front page except *The Times* alongside the little oil of the Virgin Mary and Child. There was hardly a mention of the Canaletto in the first ten paragraphs of any report and certainly no accompanying photograph.

The man who made the accusation had apparently disappeared without trace and the whole episode might have died down if Monsignor Pierre Guichot, the Bishop of Reims, hadn't agreed to be interviewed by Freddie Barker, the saleroom correspondent of the *Daily Telegraph*, who had uncovered the fact that Guichot had been the priest at the church where the original picture had hung. The bishop confirmed to Barker that the painting had indeed mysteriously disappeared during the Great War and, more important, he had at the time reported the theft to the appropriate section of the League of Nations responsible for seeing that, under the Geneva Convention, stolen works of art were returned to their rightful owners once hostilities had ceased. The bishop went on to say that of course he would recognise the picture if he ever saw it again – the colours, the brushwork, the serenity of the Virgin's face; indeed the genius of Bronzino's composition would remain clearly in his memory until the day he died. Barker quoted him word for damning word.

The *Telegraph* correspondent rang my office the day the interview appeared and informed me that his paper intended to fly the distinguished cleric over at their expense so that he could study the painting at first hand and thus establish its provenance beyond doubt. Our legal advisors warned us that we would be unwise not to allow the bishop to view the painting; to deny him access would be tantamount to acknowledging we were trying to hide something. Charlie agreed without hesitation and simply added, "Let the man see the picture. I'm confident that Tommy left that church with nothing other than a German officer's helmet."

The next day, in the privacy of his office, Tim Newman warned us that if the Bishop of Reims identified the picture as the original Bronzino, then the launch of Trumper's as a public company would have to be held up for at least a year, while the auction house might never recover from such a scandal.

The following Thursday the Bishop of Reims flew into London, to be greeted by a bank of photographers whose flash-bulbs popped again and again before the monsignor was driven off to Westminster, where he was staying as a guest of the archbishop.

The bishop had agreed to visit the gallery at four the same afternoon, and anyone walking through Chelsea Terrace that Thursday might have been forgiven for thinking Frank Sinatra was about to make a personal appearance. A large gathering had formed on the kerbside as they waited keenly for the cleric's arrival.

I met the bishop at the entrance to the gallery and introduced him to Charlie, who bowed before kissing the episcopal ring. I think the bishop was somewhat surprised to discover that Charlie was a Roman Catholic. I smiled nervously at our visitor who appeared to have a perpetual beam on his face – a face that was red from wine, not sun, I suspected. He glided off down the passage in his long purple cassock as Cathy led him in the direction of my room, where the picture awaited him. Barker, the reporter from the *Telegraph*, introduced himself to Simon as if he were dealing with someone from the underworld. He made no attempt to be civil when Simon tried to strike up a conversation with him.

The bishop came through to my little office and accepted a proffered cup of coffee. I had already placed the picture on an easel, having at Charlie's insistence refitted the original old black frame on the painting. We all sat round the table in silence as the priest stared at the Virgin Mary.

"*Vous permettez?*" he asked, holding out his arms.

"Certainly," I replied, and handed over the little oil.

I watched his eyes carefully as he held the painting in front of him. He seemed to take just as much interest in Charlie, whom I had never seen so nervous, as he did in the picture itself. He also glanced at Barker, who in contrast had a look of hope in his eyes. After that the bishop returned his attention to the painting, smiled and seemed to become transfixed by the Virgin Mary.

"Well?" enquired the reporter.

"Beautiful. An inspiration for any non-believer."

Barker also smiled and wrote his words down.

"You know," the priest added, "this painting brings back many memories" – he hesitated for a moment and I thought my heart was going to stop before he pronounced – "but, *hélas*, I must inform you, Mr Barker, that it is not the original. A mere copy of the madonna I knew so well."

The reporter stopped writing. "Only a copy?"

"Yes, *je le regrette*. An excellent copy, *peut-être* painted by a young pupil of the great man, would be my guess, but none the less a copy."

Barker was unable to hide his disappointment as he placed his pad down on the table, looking as if he wished to make some protest.

The bishop rose and bowed in my direction. "It

is my regret that you have been troubled, Lady Trumper."

I too rose and accompanied him to the door, where he was faced once again with the assembled press. The journalists fell silent as they waited for the priest to utter some revelation and I felt for a moment that he might actually be enjoying the experience.

"Is it the real thing, Bishop?" shouted a reporter in the crowd.

He smiled benignly. "It is indeed a portrait of the Blessed Virgin, but this particular example is only a copy, and of no great significance." He did not add a word to this statement before climbing back into his car to be whisked away.

"What a relief," I said once the car was out of sight. I turned round to look for Charlie, but he was nowhere to be seen. I rushed back to my office and found him holding the picture in his hands. I closed the door behind me so that we could be alone.

"What a relief," I repeated. "Now life can return to normal."

"You realise, of course, that this *is* the Bronzino," Charlie said, looking straight at me.

"Don't be silly," I said. "The bishop –"

"But did you see the way he held her?" said Charlie. "You don't cling on to a counterfeit like that. And then I watched his eyes while he came to a decision."

"A decision?"

"Yes, as to whether or not to ruin our lives, in exchange for his beloved Virgin."

"So we've been in possession of a masterpiece without even knowing it?"

"It would seem so, but I'm still not sure who removed the painting from the chapel in the first place."

"Surely not Guy . . ."

"Why not, he's more likely to have appreciated its value than Tommy."

"But how did Guy discover where it ended up, let alone what it was really worth?"

"Company records, perhaps, or a chance conversation with Daphne might have put him in the right direction."

"But that still doesn't explain how he found out it was an original."

"I agree," said Charlie. "I suspect he didn't, and simply saw the picture as another way of discrediting me."

"Then how the blazes . . . ?"

"Whereas Mrs Trentham has had several years to stumble across . . ."

"Good God, but where does Kitty fit in?"

"She was a distraction, nothing more, used by Mrs Trentham simply to set us up."

"Will that woman go to any lengths to destroy us?"

"I suspect so. And one thing's for certain, she isn't going to be pleased when she discovers her 'best laid plans' have once again been scuppered."

I collapsed on the chair beside my husband. "What shall we do now?"

Charlie continued to cling to the little masterpiece as if he were afraid someone might try to seize it from him.

"There's only one thing we can do."

I drove us to the archbishop's house that night and parked the car outside the tradesmen's entrance. "How appropriate," Charlie remarked, before knocking quietly on an old oak door. A priest answered our call and without a word ushered us in before leading us through to see the archbishop, whom we found sharing a glass of wine with the Bishop of Reims.

"Sir Charles and Lady Trumper," the priest intoned.

"Welcome, my children," said the archbishop as he came forward to greet us. "This is an unexpected pleasure," he added, after Charlie kissed his ring. "But what brings you to my home?"

"We have a small gift for the bishop," I said as I handed over a little paper parcel to His Grace.

The bishop smiled the same smile as when he had declared the picture to be a copy. He opened the parcel slowly, like a child who knows he's being given a present when it isn't his birthday. He held the little masterpiece in his hands for some time before passing it to the archbishop for his consideration.

"Truly magnificent," said the archbishop who studied it carefully before handing it back to the bishop. "But where will you display it?"

"Above the cross in the chapel of St Augustine I consider would be appropriate," the bishop replied. "And possibly in time someone far more scholarly on such matters than myself will declare the picture to be an original." He looked up and smiled, a wicked smile for a bishop.

The archbishop turned towards me. "Would you and your husband care to join us for dinner?"

I thanked him for the kind offer and muttered some excuse about a previous engagement before we both bade them goodnight and quietly slipped out the way we had come.

As the door closed behind us I heard the archbishop say, "You win your bet, Pierre."

CHAPTER 36

"Twenty thousand pounds?" said Becky as she came to a halt outside Number 141. "You must be joking."

"That's the price the agent is demanding," said Tim Newman.

"But the shop can't be worth more than three thousand at most," said Charlie, staring at the only building on the block he still didn't own. "And in any case I signed an agreement with Mr Sneddles that when – "

"Not for the books, you didn't," said the banker.

"But we don't want the books," said Becky, noticing for the first time that a heavy chain and bolt barred them from entering the premises.

"Then you can't take possession of the shop, because until the last book is sold your agreement with Mr Sneddles cannot come into operation."

"What are the books really worth?" Becky asked.

"In his typical fashion, Mr Sneddles has pencilled a price in every one of them," said Tim Newman. "His colleague, Doctor Halcombe, tells me the total comes to around five thousand pounds with the exception – "

"So buy the lot," said Charlie, "because knowing Sneddles he probably undervalued them in the first place. Then Becky can auction the entire collection some time later in the year. That way the shortfall shouldn't be more than about a thousand."

"With the exception of a first edition of Blake's *Songs of Innocence*," added Newman. "Vellum bound, that are marked up in Sneddle's inventory at fifteen thousand pounds."

"Fifteen thousand pounds at a time when I'm expected to watch every penny. Who imagines that . . . ?"

"Someone who realises you can't go ahead with the building of a department store until you are in possession of this particular shop?" suggested Newman.

"But how could she – ?"

"Because the Blake in question was originally purchased from the Heywood Hill bookshop in Curzon Street for the princely sum of four pounds ten shillings and I suspect the inscription solves half the mystery."

"Mrs Ethel Trentham, I'll be bound," said Charlie.

"No, but not a bad guess. The exact words on the flyleaf, if I remember correctly, read: From your loving grandson, Guy. 9 July 1917."

Charlie and Becky stared at Tim Newman for some time until Charlie finally asked, "What do you mean – half the mystery?"

"I also suspect she needs the money," replied the banker.

"What for?" asked Becky incredulously.

"So she can purchase even more shares in Trumper's of Chelsea."

On 19 March 1948, two weeks after the bishop had returned to Reims, the official tender document for Trumper's was released to the press to coincide with full-page advertisements taken in *The Times* and the *Financial Times*. All Charlie and Becky could do now was sit and wait for the public's response. Within three days of the announcement the share issue was oversubscribed and within a week the merchant bankers had received double the applications necessary. When all the requests had been counted, Charlie and Tim Newman were left with only one problem: how to allocate the shares. They agreed that institutions who had applied for a large holding should be taken up first, as that would give the board easy access to the majority of shares should any problem arise in the future.

The only application that puzzled Tim Newman came from Hambros who offered no explanation as to why they should wish to purchase one hundred thousand shares which would give them control of ten per cent of the company. However, Tim recommended that the chairman should accept their application in full while at the same time offering them a place on the board. This Charlie agreed to do, but only after Hambros had confirmed that the bid had not come from Mrs Trentham or one of her proxies. Two other institutions applied for five per cent: Prudential Assurance which had serviced the company from its outset, and a United States source which Becky discovered was simply a front for one of the Field family trusts. Charlie readily accepted both these applications and the rest of the shares were then divided between another one thousand seven hundred ordinary investors, including one hundred shares, the minimum allowed, which were taken up by an old-age pensioner living in Chelsea. Mrs Symonds had dropped Charlie a line to remind him that she had been one of his original customers when he opened his first shop.

Having distributed the shares, Tim Newman felt the next matter Charlie should consider was further appointments to the board. Hambros put up a Mr Baverstock, a senior partner of the solicitors Baverstock, Dickens and Cobb, whom Charlie accepted without question. Becky suggested that Simon Matthews, who virtually ran the auction house whenever she was absent, should also be appointed. Again Charlie acquiesced, bringing the full complement on the board to nine.

It was Daphne who told Becky that 17 Eaton Square was coming on the market, and Charlie only needed to see the eight-bedroomed house once before he decided that was where he wanted to spend the rest of his life. It didn't seem to cross Charlie's mind that someone would have to supervise the move at the same time as Trumper's was being built. Becky might have complained if she too hadn't fallen in love with the house.

A couple of months later Becky held a house-warming party at Eaton Square. Over a hundred guests were invited to join the Trumpers for a dinner that had to be served in five different rooms.

Daphne arrived late and complained about being held up in a traffic jam on her way back from Sloane Square, while the colonel travelled down from Skye without a murmur. Daniel came over from Cambridge accompanied by Marjorie Carpenter and to Becky's surprise Simon Matthews arrived with Cathy Ross on his arm.

After dinner, Daphne made a short speech and presented Charlie with a scale model of Trumper's crafted in the form of a silver cigar case.

Becky judged the gift to be a success because after the last guest had left, her husband carried the case upstairs and placed it on his bedside table.

Charlie climbed into bed and took one last look at his new toy as Becky came out of the bathroom.

"Have you considered inviting Percy to be a director?" she said as she climbed into bed.

Charlie looked across at her sceptically.

"The shareholders might appreciate having a marquess on the company letterhead. It would give them a feeling of confidence."

"You're such a snob, Rebecca Salmon. Always were and always will be."

"You didn't say that when I suggested the colonel should be our first chairman twenty-five years ago."

"True enough," said Charlie, "but I didn't think he'd say yes. In any case, if I wanted another outsider I'd rather have Daphne on the board. That way we get the name as well as her particular brand of common sense."

"I should have thought of that."

When Becky approached Daphne with an invitation to join the board of Trumper's as a non-executive director the

Marchioness was overwhelmed and accepted without a second thought. To everyone's surprise, Daphne approached her new responsibilities with immense energy and enthusiasm. She never missed a board meeting, always read the papers thoroughly and whenever she considered Charlie hadn't fully covered an item under discussion or, worse, was trying to get away with something, she nagged at him until she got a full explanation as to what he was up to.

"Are you still hoping to build Trumper's at the price you recommended in your original offer document, Mr Chairman?" she asked time and time again during the next two years.

"I'm not so sure it was a good idea of yours to invite Daphne to become a director," Charlie grumbled to Becky following one particularly raucous meeting in which the marchioness had got the better of him.

"Don't blame me," Becky replied. "I would have happily settled for Percy, but then I'm a snob."

It took nearly two years for the architects to complete the twin towers of Trumper's, their adjoining walkway and the five floors of offices above Mrs Trentham's empty space. The task was not made any easier by Charlie's expecting business in the remaining shops to proceed as if nothing was going on around them. It was a source of wonder to all concerned that during the changeover period Trumper's lost only nineteen per cent of its annual revenue.

Charlie set about supervising everything, from the exact siting of the one hundred and eighteen departments to the colour of the twenty-seven acres of carpet, from the speed of the twelve lifts to the wattage of the one hundred thousand light bulbs, from the displays in the ninety-six windows to the uniforms of over seven hundred employees, each of whom displayed a little silver barrow on their lapel.

Once Charlie realised how much storage space he would need, not to mention facilities for an underground car park now so many customers had their own vehicles, the costs went considerably over budget. However, the contractors somehow managed to complete the building by 1 September 1949, mainly because Charlie appeared on the site at four thirty every morning and often didn't leave to go back home much before midnight.

On 18 October 1949 the Marchioness of Wiltshire, escorted by her husband, performed the official opening ceremony.

A thousand people raised their glasses once Daphne had declared the building open. The assembled guests then did their best to eat and drink their way through the company's first year's profits. But Charlie didn't seem to notice; he moved happily from floor to floor checking that everything was exactly as he expected it to be and made sure that the major suppliers were being properly looked after.

Friends, relations, shareholders, buyers, sellers, journalists, hangers-on, gatecrashers and even customers were celebrating on every floor. By one o'clock Becky was so tired that she decided to start looking for her husband in the hope that he might agree to go home. She found her son in the kitchen department examining a refrigerator that would have been too large for his room in Trinity. Daniel assured his mother that he had seen Charlie leaving the building about half an hour before.

"Leaving the building?" Becky said, in disbelief. "Surely your father wouldn't have gone home without me?" She took the lift to the ground floor and walked quickly towards the main entrance. The doorman saluted her as he held open one of the massive double doors that led out on to Chelsea Terrace.

"Have you seen Sir Charles, by any chance?" Becky asked him.

"Yes, m'lady." He nodded in the direction of the far side of the road.

Becky looked across to see Charlie seated on his bench, an old man perched by his side. They were chatting animatedly as they stared across at Trumper's. The old man pointed at something that had attracted his attention and

Charlie smiled. Becky quickly crossed the road but the colonel had sprung to attention long before she had reached his side.

"How lovely to see you, my dear," he said as he leaned forward to kiss Becky on the cheek. "I only wish Elizabeth had lived to see it."

"As I understand it, we're being held to ransom," said Charlie. "So perhaps it's time we took a vote on the issue."

Becky looked around the boardroom table, wondering which way the vote would fall. The full board had been working together for three months since Trumper's had opened its doors to the public, but this was the first major issue on which there had been any real disagreement.

Charlie sat at the head of the table, looking unusually irritable at the thought of not getting his own way. On his right was the company secretary, Jessica Allen. Jessica did not have a vote but was there to see that whenever there was one it would be faithfully recorded. Arthur Selwyn, who had worked with Charlie at the Ministry of Food during the war, had recently left the civil service to replace Tom Arnold on his retirement as managing director. Selwyn was proving to be an inspired choice, shrewd and thorough, while being the ideal foil to the chairman as he tended to avoid confrontation whenever possible.

Tim Newman, the company's young merchant banker, was sociable and friendly and almost always backed Charlie, though he was not averse to giving a contrary view if he felt the company finances might suffer. Paul Merrick, the finance director, was neither sociable nor friendly and continued to make it abundantly clear that his first loyalty would always be to Child's Bank and its investment. As for Daphne, she rarely voted the way anyone might expect her to, and certainly was no placeman for Charlie – or anyone else, for that matter. Mr Baverstock, a quiet, elderly solicitor who represented ten per cent of the company stock on behalf of Hambros, spoke rarely, but when he did everyone listened, including Daphne.

Ned Denning and Bob Makins, both of whom had now served Charlie for nearly thirty years, would rarely go against their chairman's wishes, while Simon Matthews often showed flashes of independence that only confirmed Becky's initial high opinion of him.

"The last thing we need at the moment is a strike," said Merrick. "Just at a time when it looks as if we've turned the corner."

"But the union's demands are simply outrageous," said Tim Newman. "A ten-shilling rise, a forty-four-hour week, before overtime becomes automatic – I repeat, they're outrageous."

"Most of the other major stores have already agreed to those terms," interjected Merrick, consulting an article from the *Financial Times* that lay in front of him.

"Chucked the towel in would be nearer the mark," came back Newman. "I must warn the board that this would add to our wages bill by some twenty thousand pounds for the current year – and that's even before we start to consider overtime. So there's only one group of people who will suffer in the long run, and that's our shareholders."

"Just how much does a counter assistant earn nowadays?" asked Mr Baverstock quietly.

"Two hundred and sixty pounds a year," said Arthur Selwyn without having to check. "With incremental rises so that if they have completed fifteen years' service with the company, the sum could be as high as four hundred and ten pounds a year."

"We've been over these figures on countless occasions," said Charlie sharply. "The time has come to decide – do we stand firm or just give in to the union's demands?"

"Perhaps we're all overreacting, Mr Chairman," said Daphne, who hadn't spoken until then. "It may not prove to be quite as black or white as you imagine."

"You have an alternative solution?" Charlie made no attempt to hide his incredulity.

"I might have, Mr Chairman. First, let's consider

what's at stake if we do give our staff the rise. An obvious drain on resources, not to mention what the Japanese would call 'face'. On the other hand, if we don't agree to their demands, it's possible that we might lose some of the better as well as the weaker brethren to one of our main rivals."

"So what are you suggesting, Lady Wiltshire?" asked Charlie, who always addressed Daphne by her title whenever he wished to show he didn't agree with her.

"Compromise, perhaps," replied Daphne, refusing to rise. "If Mr Selwyn considers that to be at all possible at this late stage. Would the trade unions, for example, be willing to contemplate an alternative proposal on wages and hours, drawn up in negotiation with our managing director?"

"I could always have a word with Don Short, the leader of USDAW, if the board so wishes," said Arthur Selwyn. "In the past I've always found him a decent, fair-minded man and he's certainly shown a consistent loyalty to Trumper's over the years."

"The managing director dealing direct with the trade union's representative?" barked Charlie. "Next you'll want to put him on the board."

"Then perhaps Mr Selwyn should make an informal approach," said Daphne. "I'm confident *he* can handle Mr Short with consummate skill."

"I agree with Lady Wiltshire," said Mr Baverstock.

"Then I propose that we allow Mr Selwyn to negotiate on our behalf," continued Daphne. "And let's hope he can find a way of avoiding an all-out strike without actually giving in to everything the unions are demanding."

"I'd certainly be willing to have a try," said Selwyn. "I could report back to the board at our next meeting."

Once again Becky admired the way Daphne and Arthur Selwyn between them had defused a time-bomb the chairman would have been only too happy to let explode on the boardroom table.

"Thank you, Arthur," Charlie said a little begrudgingly. "So be it. Any other business?"

"Yes," said Becky. "I would like to bring to the board's attention a sale of Georgian silver that will be taking place next month. Catalogues will be sent out during the coming week and I do hope any directors who are free on that particular day will try to attend."

"How did the last antiques sale work out?" asked Mr Baverstock.

Becky checked her file. "The auction raised twenty-four thousand seven hundred pounds, of which Trumper's kept seven and a half per cent of everything that came under the hammer. Only three items failed to reach their reserve prices, and they were called back in."

"I'm only curious about the success of the sale," said Mr Baverstock, "because my dear wife purchased a Charles II court cupboard."

"One of the finest items in the sale," said Becky.

"My wife certainly thought so because she bid far more for the piece than she had intended. I'd be obliged if you didn't send her a catalogue for the silver sale."

The other members of the board laughed.

"I've read somewhere," said Tim Newman, "that Sotheby's are considering raising their commission to ten per cent."

"I know," said Becky. "That's exactly why I can't contemplate the same move for at least another year. If I'm to go on stealing their best customers I must stay competitive in the short term."

Newman nodded his understanding.

"However," Becky continued, "by remaining at seven and a half per cent, my profits for 1950 won't be as high as I might have hoped. But until the leading sellers are willing to come to us, that's a problem I'll continue to face."

"What about the buyers?" queried Paul Merrick.

"They aren't the problem. If you have the product to sell, the buyers will always beat a path to your door. You see, it's the sellers that are the life-blood of an auction house, and they're every bit as important as the buyers."

"Funny old outfit you're running," said Charlie with a grin. "Any other business?"

As no one spoke, Charlie thanked all the members of the board for their attendance and rose from his place, a signal he always gave to indicate that the meeting was finally over.

Becky collected up her papers and started walking back to the gallery with Simon.

"Have you completed your estimates on the silver sale yet?" she asked as they jumped into the lift just before the doors closed. She touched the "G" and the lift began its slow journey to the ground floor.

"Yes. Finished them last night. One hundred and thirty-two items in all. I reckon they might raise somewhere in the region of seven thousand pounds."

"I saw the catalogue for the first time this morning," said Becky. "It looks to me as if Cathy has done another first-class job. I was only able to pick up one or two minor errors but I'd still like to check over the final proofs before they go back to the printer."

"Of course," said Simon. "I'll ask her to bring all the loose sheets up to your office this afternoon." They stepped out of the lift.

"That girl has turned out to be a real find," said Becky. "Heaven knows what she was doing working in a hotel before she came to us. I shall certainly miss her when she goes back to Australia."

"Rumour has it that she's thinking of staying."

"That's good news," said Becky. "I thought she was only hoping to spend a couple of years in London before she returned to Melbourne?"

"That's what she had originally planned. However, I may have been able to convince her that she should stay on a little longer."

Becky would have asked Simon to explain in greater detail but once they had set foot in the gallery she was quickly surrounded by staff anxious to gain her attention.

After Becky had dealt with several queries, she asked

one of the girls who worked on the counter if she could locate Cathy.

"She's not actually around at the moment, Lady Trumper," the assistant told her. "I saw her go out about an hour ago."

"Do you know where she went?"

"No idea, I'm sorry."

"Well, ask her to come to my office the moment she returns. Meanwhile, could you send up those catalogue proofs for the silver sale?"

Becky stopped several times on the way back to her room to discuss other gallery problems that had arisen in her absence, so that by the time she sat down at her desk, the proofs for the silver sale were already awaiting her. She began to turn the pages slowly, checking each entry against its photograph and then the detailed description. She was studying the photograph of the Georgian mustard pot that Charlie had overbid for at Christie's some years before when there was a knock on the door and a young woman popped her head in.

"You asked to see me?"

"Yes. Do come in, Cathy." Becky looked up at a tall, slim girl with a mass of curly fair hair and a face that hadn't quite lost all its freckles. She liked to think that her own figure had once been as good as Cathy's but the bathroom mirror unflatteringly reminded her that she was fast approaching her fiftieth birthday. "I only wanted to check over the final catalogue proofs for the silver sale before they went back to the printer."

"I'm sorry I wasn't around when you returned from the board meeting," Cathy said. "It's just that something's come up that worried me. I may be overreacting, but I felt you ought to know about it in any case."

Becky took off her glasses, placed them on the desk and looked up intently. "I'm listening."

"Do you remember that man who stood up during the Italian auction and caused all that trouble over the Bronzino?"

"Will I ever forget him?"

"Well, he was in the gallery again this morning."

"Can you be sure?"

"I'm fairly confident. Well-built, greying hair, a brownish moustache and sallow complexion. He even had the nerve to wear that awful tweed jacket and yellow tie again."

"What did he want this time?"

"I can't be certain of that, although I kept a close eye on him. He didn't speak to any member of the staff, but took a great deal of interest in some of the items that were coming up in the silver sale – in particular lot nineteen."

Becky replaced her glasses and turned the catalogue pages over quickly until she came to the item in question: "A Georgian silver tea-set made up of four pieces, teapot, sugar bowl, tea strainer and sugar tongs, hallmarked with an anchor." Becky looked down at the letters "AH" printed in the margin. "Estimated value seventy pounds. One of our better items."

"And he obviously agrees with you," Cathy replied, "because he spent a considerable time studying each individual piece, then made copious notes before he left. He even checked the teapot against a photograph he had brought with him."

"Our photograph?"

"No, he seemed to have one of his own."

"Did he now?" said Becky as she rechecked the catalogue photo.

"And the reason I wasn't around when you came back from the board meeting was because when he left the gallery I decided to follow him.

"Quick thinking," said Becky, smiling. "And where did our mystery man disappear to?"

"Ended up in Chester Square," said Cathy. "A large house halfway down on the right-hand side. He dropped a package through the letter-box but didn't go in."

"Number 19?"

"That's right," said Cathy, looking surprised. "Do you know the house?"

"Only from the outside," said Becky without explanation.

"Is there anything else I can do to help?"

"Yes, there is. To start with, can you remember anything about the customer who brought that particular lot in for sale?"

"Certainly can," replied Cathy, "because I was called to the front desk to deal with the lady." She paused for a moment before adding, "Can't remember her name but she was elderly and rather – genteel is the way I think you would describe her." Cathy hesitated then continued, "As I remember, she had taken a day trip down from Nottingham. She told me that she'd been left the tea-set by her mother. She didn't want to sell a family heirloom but 'needs must'. I remember that expression, because I'd never heard it before."

"And what was Mr Fellowes's opinion when you showed him the set?"

"As fine an example of the period as he'd seen come under the hammer – each piece is still in almost mint condition. Peter's convinced the lot will fetch a good price, as you can see from his estimate."

"Then we'd better call in the police straight away," said Becky. "We don't need our mystery man standing up again announcing that this particular item has been stolen too."

She picked up the telephone on her desk and asked to be put through to Scotland Yard. A few moments later an Inspector Deakins of the CID came on the line and, having listened to the details of what had taken place that morning, agreed to come round to the gallery during the afternoon.

The inspector arrived a little after three, accompanied by a sergeant. Becky took them both straight through to meet the head of the department. Peter Fellowes pointed to a minute scratch he had come across on a silver salver. Becky frowned. He stopped what he was doing and walked over to the centre table where the four-piece tea-set was already out on display.

"Beautiful," said the inspector as he bent over and checked the hallmark. "Birmingham around 1820 would be my guess."

Becky raised an eyebrow.

"It's my hobby," the inspector explained. "That's probably why I always end up getting these jobs." He removed a file from the briefcase he was carrying and checked through several photographs along with detailed written descriptions of recently missing pieces of silverware from the London area. An hour later he had to agree with Fellowes: none of them fitted the description of the Georgian tea-set.

"Well, we've had nothing else reported as stolen that matches up with this particular lot," he admitted. "And you've polished them so superbly," he said, turning to Cathy, "that there's no hope of our identifying any prints."

"Sorry," said Cathy, blushing slightly.

"No, miss, it's not your fault, you've done a fine job. I only wish my little pieces looked so good. Still, I'd better check with the Nottingham police in case they have something on their files. If they haven't, I'll issue a description to all forces throughout the United Kingdom, just in case. And I'll also ask them to check on Mrs . . . ?"

"Dawson," said Cathy.

"Yes, Mrs Dawson. That may take a little time, of course, but I'll come back to you the moment I hear anything."

"Meanwhile our sale takes place three weeks next Tuesday," Becky reminded the inspector.

"Right, I'll try and give you the all-clear by then," he promised.

"Should we leave that page in the catalogue, or would you prefer the pieces to be withdrawn?" asked Cathy.

"Oh, no, don't withdraw anything. Please leave the catalogue exactly as it is. You see, someone might recognise the set and then get in touch with us."

Someone has already recognised the set, thought Becky.

"While you're at it," continued the inspector, "I'd be obliged if you could give me a copy of the catalogue picture, as well as use of one of the negatives for a day or two."

When Charlie was told about the Georgian tea-set over dinner that night, his advice was simple: withdraw the pieces from the sale – and promote Cathy.

"Your first suggestion isn't quite that easy," said Becky. "The catalogue is due to be sent out to the general public later this week. What explanation could we possibly give to Mrs Dawson for removing her dear old mother's family heirloom?"

"That it wasn't her dear old mother's in the first place and you withdrew it because you've every reason to believe that it's stolen property."

"If we did that, we could find ourselves being sued for breach of contract," said Becky, "when we later discover that Mrs Dawson's totally innocent of any such charge. If she then took us to court we wouldn't have a leg to stand on."

"If this Dawson lady is as totally innocent as you think, then why is Mrs Trentham showing such an interest in her tea-set? Because I can't help feeling she already has one of her own."

Becky laughed. "She certainly has. I know, because I've even seen it, though I never did get the promised cup of tea."

Three days later Inspector Deakins telephoned Becky to let her know that the Nottingham police had no record of anything that had been stolen in their patch fitting the tea-set's description and they were also able to confirm that Mrs Dawson was not previously known to them. He had therefore sent the details out to every other constabulary in the land. "But," he added, "outside forces aren't always that co-operative with the Met when it comes to trading information."

As Becky put the phone down, she decided to give the green light and send the catalogues out, despite Charlie's apprehension. They were posted the same day along with invitations to the press and selected customers.

A couple of journalists applied for tickets to the sale. An unusually sensitive Becky checked them out, only to find that both worked for national newspapers, and had covered Trumper's sales several times in the past.

Simon Matthews considered that Becky was over-reacting, while Cathy tended to agree with Sir Charles that the wise course would be to withdraw the tea-set from the auction until they had been given the all-clear by Deakins.

"If we're to withdraw a lot every time that man takes an interest in one of our sales we may as well close our front doors and take up star-gazing," Simon told them.

The Monday before the sale was to take place Inspector Deakins telephoned to ask if he could see Becky urgently. He arrived at the gallery thirty minutes later, again accompanied by his sergeant. This time the only item he removed from his briefcase was a copy of the Aberdeen *Evening Express* dated 15 October 1949.

Deakins asked to be allowed to inspect the Georgian tea-set once more. Becky nodded her agreement and the policeman studied each piece carefully against a photograph that was on an inside page of the newspaper.

"That's them all right," he said, after double-checking. He showed Becky the photograph.

Cathy and Peter Fellowes also studied each item while looking carefully at the picture from the newspaper and had to agree with Deakins that the match was perfect.

"This little lot was stolen from the Aberdeen Museum of Silver some three months ago," the inspector informed them. "The bloody local police didn't even bother to let us know. No doubt they considered it was none of our business."

"So what happens now?" asked Becky.

"The Nottingham constabulary have already visited Mrs Dawson, where they found several other pieces of silver and jewellery hidden around the house. She's been taken to her local station in order to, as the press would have it, help the police with their enquiries." He placed the newspaper back in his briefcase. "After I've phoned them back to confirm my piece of news, I expect that she'll be charged later today. However, I'm afraid I shall have to take the tea-set away with me for processing at Scotland Yard."

"Of course," said Becky.

"My sergeant will write out a receipt for you, Lady Trumper, and I'd like to thank you for your co-operation." The inspector hesitated as he looked lovingly at the tea-set. "A month's salary," he said with a sigh, "and stolen for all the wrong reasons." He raised his hat and the two policemen left the gallery.

"So what do we do now?" said Cathy.

"Not much we can do," Becky sighed. "Carry on with the auction as if nothing had taken place and when the lot comes up, simply announce that the piece has been withdrawn."

"But then our man will leap up and say, 'Isn't this yet another example of advertising stolen goods and then having to withdraw them at the last moment?' We won't look so much like an auction house," said Simon, his voice rising with anger. "More like a pawnbroker. So why don't we just put three balls outside the front door, and a fence to give a clue as to the class of person we're hoping to attract?"

Becky didn't react.

"If you feel so strongly about it, Simon, why not try and turn the whole episode to our advantage?" suggested Cathy.

"What do you mean?" asked Becky as both she and Simon swung round to face the young Australian.

"We must get the press on our side for a change."

"I'm not sure I understand what you're getting at."

"Phone that journalist from the *Telegraph* – what was his name? Barker – and give him the inside story."

"What good would that do?" asked Becky.

"He'll have our version of what happened this time, and he'll be only too pleased to be the one journalist on the inside, especially after that fiasco with the Bronzino."

"Do you think he'd be at all interested in a silver set worth seventy pounds?"

"With a Scottish museum involved and a professional fence arrested in Nottingham? He'll be interested all right. Especially if we don't tell anyone else."

"Would you like to handle Mr Barker yourself, Cathy?" Becky asked.

"Just give me the chance."

The following morning, the *Daily Telegraph* had a small but prominent piece on page three reporting that Trumper's, the fine art auctioneers, had called in the police after they had become suspicious about the ownership of a Georgian tea-set that was later discovered to have been stolen from the Aberdeen Museum of Silver. The Nottingham police had since arrested a woman whom they later charged with handling stolen goods. The article went on to say that Inspector Deakins of Scotland Yard had told the *Telegraph*: "We only wish every auction house and gallery in London were as conscientious as Trumper's."

The sale that afternoon was well attended, and despite losing one of the centre-pieces of the auction Trumper's still managed to exceed several of the estimates. The man in the tweed coat and yellow tie didn't make an appearance.

When Charlie read the *Telegraph* in bed that night he remarked, "So you didn't take my advice?"

"Yes and no," said Becky. "I admit I didn't withdraw the tea-set immediately, but I did promote Cathy."

CHAPTER 37

On 9 November 1950 Trumper's held their second AGM. The directors met at ten o'clock in the boardroom so that Arthur Selwyn could take them slowly through the procedure he intended to follow once they faced the shareholders.

At eleven o'clock sharp he guided the chairman and his eight directors out of the boardroom and into the main hall as if they were school children being led in a crocodile on their way to morning assembly.

Charlie introduced each member of the board to the assembled gathering, who numbered around one hundred and twenty – a respectable turn-out for such an occasion, Tim Newman whispered in Becky's ear. Charlie went through the agenda without a prompt from his managing director and was only asked one awkward question. "Why have your costs gone so much over budget in the first full year of trading?"

Arthur Selwyn rose to explain that the expense of the building had exceeded their original estimate and launching had incurred certain one-off costs which would not arise again. He also pointed out that strictly on a trading basis Trumper's had managed to break even in the first quarter of their second year. He added that he remained confident about the year ahead, especially with the anticipated rise in the number of tourists attracted to London by the Festival of Britain. However, he warned shareholders it might be necessary for the company to raise more capital, if they hoped to increase their facilities.

When Charlie declared the AGM closed he remained seated because the board received a small ovation, which quite took the chairman by surprise.

Becky was about to return to Number 1 and continue with her work on an Impressionist sale she had planned for the spring when Mr Baverstock came over and touched her gently on the elbow.

"May I have a word with you in private, Lady Trumper?"

"Of course, Mr Baverstock." Becky looked around for a quiet spot where they could talk.

"I feel that perhaps my office in High Holborn would be more appropriate," he suggested. "You see, it's a rather delicate matter. Would tomorrow, three o'clock suit you?"

Daniel had phoned from Cambridge that morning and Becky couldn't remember when she had heard him sounding so chatty and full of news. She, on the other hand, was not chatty or full of news: she still hadn't been able to fathom why the senior partner of Baverstock, Dickens and Cobb should want to see her on "a rather delicate matter".

She couldn't believe that Mr Baverstock's wife wanted to return the Charles II court cupboard or required more details on the forthcoming Impressionist sale, but as in her case anxiety always ruled over optimism, Becky spent the next twenty-six hours fearing the worst.

She didn't burden Charlie with her troubles, because the little she did know of Mr Baverstock made her certain that if her husband were involved the lawyer would have asked to see them both. In any case, Charlie had quite enough problems of his own to deal with without being weighed down with hers.

Becky couldn't manage any lunch and arrived at the solicitor's office a few minutes before the appointed hour. She was ushered straight through to Mr Baverstock's rooms.

She was greeted with a warm smile by her fellow-director, as if she were some minor relation of his large family. He offered her the seat opposite his on the other side of a large mahogany desk.

Mr Baverstock, Becky decided, must have been about fifty-five, perhaps sixty, with a round, friendly face and the few strands of grey hair that were left were parted neatly down the centre. His dark jacket, waistcoat, grey striped trousers and black tie could have been worn by any solicitor who practised within five square miles of the building in which they now sat. Having returned to his own chair he began to study the pile of documents that lay in front of him before removing his half-moon spectacles.

"Lady Trumper," he began. "It's most kind of you to come and see me." In the two years they had known each other he had never once addressed her by her christian name.

"I shall," he continued, "come straight to the point. One of my clients was the late Sir Raymond Hardcastle." Becky wondered why he had never mentioned this fact before and was about to protest when Mr Baverstock quickly added, "but I hasten to say that Mrs Gerald Trentham is not and never has been a client of this firm."

Becky made no effort to disguise her relief.

"I must also let you know that I had the privilege of serving Sir Raymond for over thirty years and indeed considered myself not only to be his legal advisor but towards the end of his life a close friend. I tell you this as background information, Lady Trumper, for you may feel such facts are relevant when you've heard all that I have to say."

Becky nodded, still waiting for Mr Baverstock to get to the point.

"Some years before he died," continued the solicitor, "Sir Raymond drew up a will. In it he divided the income from his estate between his two daughters – an income, I might add, that has grown considerably since his death, thanks to some prudent investment on his behalf. The elder of his daughters was Miss Amy Hardcastle, and the younger, as I feel sure you know, Mrs Gerald Trentham. The income from the estate has been sufficient to give both these ladies a standard of living equal to, if not considerably higher, than the one to which they had grown accustomed to before his death. However – "

Will dear Mr Baverstock ever get to the point? Becky was beginning to wonder.

"– Sir Raymond decided, in his wisdom, that the share capital should remain intact, after he allowed the firm that his father had founded and he had built up so successfully to merge with one of his greatest rivals. You see, Lady Trumper, Sir Raymond felt there was no member of the family who could obviously fill his shoes as the next chairman of Hardcastle's. Neither of his two daughters, or his grandsons for that matter – of whom I shall have more to say in a moment – did he consider competent to run a public company."

The solicitor removed his glasses, cleaned them with a handkerchief which he took out of his top pocket and peered through the lenses critically before returning to the task at hand.

"Sir Raymond, you see, had no illusions about his immediate kith and kin. His elder daughter, Amy, was a gentle, shy lady who nursed her father valiantly through his final years. When Sir Raymond died she moved out of the family house into a small seaside hotel where she resided until her death last year.

"His younger daughter, Ethel Trentham," he continued, "let me put this as delicately as I can – Sir Raymond considered had perhaps lost touch with reality and certainly she no longer acknowledged any attachment to her past. Anyway, I know it particularly saddened the old man not to have produced a son of his own, so when Guy was born his hopes for the future became focused on the young grandson. From that day he lavished everything on him. Later he was to blame himself for the boy's eventual downfall. He did not make the same mistake when Nigel was born, a child for whom he had neither affection nor respect.

"However, this firm was instructed to keep Sir Raymond briefed at all times with any information that came into our hands concerning members of his immediate family. Thus when Captain Trentham resigned his commission in 1922, somewhat abruptly, we were asked to try to find out the real cause behind his leaving the colours. Sir Raymond certainly did not accept his daughter's story about an appointment as a partner with an Australian cattle broker, and indeed at one stage was sufficiently concerned that he even contemplated sending me to that continent to find out the real story. Then Guy died."

Becky sat in her chair wanting to wind Mr Baverstock up like a gramophone and set him going well above 78 rpm, but she had already come to the conclusion that nothing she said was going to accelerate him along the track he had set himself.

"The result of our investigations," continued Baverstock, "led us to believe – and at this point, Lady Trumper, I must apologise for any indelicacy, for I do not intend to offend – that Guy Trentham and not Charles Trumper was the father of your child."

Becky bowed her head and Mr Baverstock apologised once again before he continued.

"Sir Raymond, however, needed to be convinced that Daniel was his great-grandson, and to that end he made two separate visits to St Paul's after the boy had won a scholarship to that school."

Becky stared at the old lawyer.

"On the first occasion he watched the boy perform in a school concert – Brahms, if I remember correctly – and on a second saw Daniel receive the Newton Prize for Mathematics from the High Master on Founders' Day. I believe you were also present on that occasion. On both visits Sir Raymond went out of his way to be sure that the boy was unaware of his presence. After the second visit, Sir Raymond was totally convinced that Daniel was his great-grandchild. I'm afraid all the men in that family are stuck with that Hardcastle jaw, not to mention a tendency to sway from foot to foot when agitated. Sir Raymond accordingly altered his will the following day."

The solicitor picked up a document bound in a pink ribbon which lay on his desk. He untied the ribbon slowly. "I was instructed, madam, to read the relevant clauses of his will to you at a time I considered appropriate but not until the boy had celebrated his thirtieth birthday. Daniel was thirty a few weeks ago, if I am not mistaken."

Becky nodded.

Baverstock acknowledged the nod and slowly unfolded the stiff sheets of parchment.

"I have already explained to you the arrangements concerning the disposal of Sir Raymond's estate. However, since Miss Amy's death Mrs Trentham has had the full benefit of any interest earned from the Trust, now amounting to some forty thousand pounds a year. At no time to my knowledge did Sir Raymond make any provision for his elder grandson, Mr Guy Trentham, but since he is now deceased that has become irrelevant. Subsequently he made a small settlement on his other grandson, Mr Nigel Trentham." He paused. "And now I must quote Sir Raymond's exact words," he said, looking down at the will. He cleared his throat before continuing.

"After all other commitments have been honoured and bills paid, I leave the residue of my messuage and estate to Mr Daniel Trumper of Trinity College, Cambridge, the full benefit of which will come into his possession on the death of his grandmother, Mrs Gerald Trentham."

Now that the lawyer had at last come to the point Becky was stunned into silence. Mr Baverstock paused for a moment in case Becky wished to say something, but as she suspected that there was still more to be revealed she remained silent. The lawyer's eyes returned to the papers in front of him.

"I feel I should add at this point that I am aware – as

indeed Sir Raymond was – of the treatment you have suffered at the hands both of his grandson and his daughter, so I must also let you know that although this bequest to your son will be considerable, it does not include the farm at Ashurst in Berkshire or the house in Chester Square. Both properties, since the death of her husband, are now owned by Mrs Gerald Trentham. Nor does it include – and I suspect this is of more importance to you – the vacant land in the centre of Chelsea Terrace, which forms no part of Sir Raymond's estate. However, everything else he controlled will eventually be inherited by Daniel, although, as I explained, not until Mrs Trentham has herself passed away."

"Is she aware of all this?"

"Indeed, Mrs Trentham was made fully conversant with the provisions in her father's will some time before his death. She even took advice as to whether the new clauses inserted after Sir Raymond's visits to St Paul's could be contested."

"Did that result in any legal action?"

"No. On the contrary, she quite suddenly, and I must confess inexplicably, instructed her lawyers to withdraw any objections. But whatever the outcome, Sir Raymond stipulated most clearly that the capital could never be used or controlled by either of his daughters. That was to be the privilege of his next of kin."

Mr Baverstock paused and placed both palms down on the blotting paper in front of him.

"Now I will finally have to tell him," murmured Becky under her breath.

"I feel that may well be the case, Lady Trumper. Indeed, the purpose of this meeting was to brief you fully. Sir Raymond was never quite sure if you had informed Daniel who his father was."

"No, we never have."

Baverstock removed his glasses and placed them on the desk. "Please take your time, dear lady, and just let me know when I have your permission to contact your son and acquaint him with his good fortune."

"Thank you," said Becky quietly, sensing the inadequacy of her words.

"Finally," said Mr Baverstock, "I must also let you know that Sir Raymond became a great admirer of your husband and his work, indeed of your partnership together. So much so that he left a recommendation with this office that, were Trumper's ever to go public, which he anticipated they would, we were to invest a sizeable stake in the new company. He was convinced that such an enterprise could only flourish and therefore prove to be a first-class investment."

"So that's why Hambros invested ten per cent when we went public," said Becky. "We always wondered."

"Precisely," Mr Baverstock added with a smile, almost of satisfaction. "It was on my specific instructions that Hambros applied for the shares on behalf of the Trust, so that there could never be any reason for your husband to be apprehensive about such a large outside shareholder.

"The amount was in fact considerably less than the estate received from dividends during that year. However, more important, we were aware from the offer documents that it was Sir Charles's intention to retain fifty-one per cent of the company, and we therefore felt it might be some relief for him to know that he would have a further ten per cent under his indirect control should any unforeseen problem arise at some time in the future. I can only hope that you feel we have acted in your best interests, as it was always Sir Raymond's wish that you should be told the full facts at a time that I considered appropriate, the only stipulation as I have already explained was that such information was not to be revealed to your son before his thirtieth birthday."

"You couldn't have been more considerate, Mr Baverstock," said Becky. "I know Charlie will want to thank you personally."

"That is most kind of you, Lady Trumper. May I also add that this meeting has been a genuine delight for me. Like Sir Raymond, I have had considerable pleasure over the years in following the careers of all three of you, and I am delighted to be playing a small part in the company's future."

Having completed his task, Mr Baverstock rose from his side of the desk and accompanied Becky silently to the front door of the building. Becky began to wonder if the solicitor spoke only when he had a brief.

"I shall wait to hear from you, dear lady, as to when I may be permitted to contact your son."

CHAPTER 38

The weekend after Becky's visit to Mr Baverstock she and Charlie drove to Cambridge to see Daniel. Charlie had insisted that they could procrastinate no longer and had telephoned Daniel that evening to warn him that they were coming up to Trinity as there was something of importance they needed to tell him. On hearing this piece of news Daniel had replied, "Good, because I've also got something rather important to tell you."

On the journey to Cambridge, Becky and Charlie rehearsed what they would say and how they were going to say it; but still came to the conclusion that however carefully they tried to explain what had happened in the past, they could not anticipate how Daniel would react.

"I wonder if he'll ever forgive us?" said Becky. "You know, we should have told him years ago."

"But we didn't."

"And now we're only letting him know at a time when it could be to our financial benefit."

"And ultimately to his. After all, he'll eventually inherit ten per cent of the company, not to mention the entire Hardcastle estate. We'll just have to see how he takes the news and react accordingly." Charlie accelerated when he came to a stretch of dual carriageway. For some time neither of them spoke until Charlie suggested, "Let's go through the order once again. You'll start by telling him how you first met Guy –"

"Perhaps he already knows," said Becky.

"Then he surely would have asked –"

"Not necessarily. He's always been so secretive in the past, especially when dealing with us."

The rehearsal continued until they had reached the outskirts of the city.

Charlie drove slowly down the Backs past Queens' College, avoiding a bunch of undergraduates who had strayed on to the road, and finally right into Trinity Lane. He brought his car to a halt in New Court and he and Becky walked across to entrance C and on up the worn stone staircase until they reached the door with "Doctor Daniel Trumper" painted above it. It always amused Becky that she hadn't even discovered that her son had been awarded his PhD until someone addressed him as Doctor Trumper in her presence.

Charlie gripped his wife's hand. "Don't worry, Becky," he said. "Everything will be all right, you'll see." He gave her fingers a squeeze before knocking firmly on Daniel's door.

"Come on in," shouted a voice that could only have been Daniel's. The next moment he pulled open the heavy oak door to greet them. He gave his mother a huge hug before ushering them both through to his untidy little study where tea was already laid out on a table in the centre of the room.

Charlie and Becky sat down in two of the large and battered leather chairs the college had provided. They had probably been owned by the past six inhabitants of the room, and brought back memories for Becky of the chair that she had once removed from Charlie's home in Whitechapel Road and sold for a shilling.

Daniel poured them both a cup of tea and began to toast a crumpet over the open fire. Nobody spoke for some time and Becky wondered where her son had come across such a modern cashmere sweater.

"Good journey down?" Daniel asked eventually.

"Not bad," said Charlie.

"And how's the new car running in?"

"Fine."

"And Trumper's?"

"Could be worse."

"Quite a little conversationalist, aren't you, Dad? You ought to apply for the recently vacated chair of Professor of English."

"Sorry, Daniel," said his mother. "It's just that he's got rather a lot on his mind at the moment, not least the subject we have to discuss with you."

"Couldn't be better timing," said Daniel, turning the crumpet over.

"Why's that?" asked Charlie.

"Because, as I warned you, there's something rather important I have to discuss with you. So – who goes first?"

"Let's hear your news," said Becky quickly.

"No, I think it might be wise if we went first," Charlie intervened.

"Suits me." Daniel dropped a toasted crumpet on to his mother's plate. "Butter, jam and honey," he added, pointing to three small dishes that rested on the table in front of her.

"Thank you, darling," said Becky.

"Get on with it then, Dad. The tension's becoming too much for me to bear." He turned a second crumpet over.

"Well, my news concerns a matter we should have told you about many years ago and indeed would have done so only –"

"Crumpet, Dad?"

"Thank you," said Charlie, ignoring the steaming offering that Daniel dropped on to his plate "– circumstances and a chain of events somehow stopped us from getting round to it."

Daniel placed a third crumpet on the end of his long toasting fork. "Eat up, Mum," he said. "Otherwise yours will only get cold. In any case, there'll be another one on its way soon."

"I'm not all that hungry," admitted Becky.

"Well, as I was saying," said Charlie. "A problem has arisen concerning a large inheritance that you will eventually –"

There was a knock on the door. Becky looked desperately towards Charlie, hoping that the interruption was nothing more than a message that could be dealt with quickly. What they didn't need at that moment was an undergraduate with an interminable problem. Daniel rose from the fender and went over to the door.

"Come in, darling," they heard him say and Charlie stood up as Daniel's guest entered the room.

"How nice to see you, Cathy," Charlie said. "I had no idea you were going to be in Cambridge today."

"Isn't that typical of Daniel," said Cathy. "I wanted to warn you both, but he wouldn't hear of it." She smiled nervously at Becky.

Becky glanced across at the two of them seated next to each other – something worried her.

"Pour yourself some tea, darling," said Daniel. "You're just in time for the next crumpet and you couldn't have arrived at a more exciting moment. Dad was just about to let me into the secret of how much I might expect to be left in his will. Am I to inherit the Trumper empire or shall I have to be satisfied with his season ticket to the West Ham Football Club?"

"Oh, I'm so sorry," said Cathy, half rising from her seat.

"No, no," said Charlie, waving her back down. "Don't be silly, it wasn't that important. Our news can wait until later."

"They're very hot, so watch it," said Daniel, dropping a crumpet on to Cathy's plate. "Well, if my inheritance is of such monumental insignificance then I shall have to impart my own little piece of news first. Roll of drums, curtain up, opening line" – Daniel raised the toasting fork as if it were a baton – "Cathy and I are engaged to be married."

"I don't believe it," said Becky, immediately springing

up from her chair to hug Cathy in delight. "What wonderful news."

"How long has this been going on?" asked Charlie. "I must have been blind."

"Nearly two years," admitted Daniel. "And to be fair, Dad, even you couldn't expect to have a telescope capable of focusing on Cambridge every weekend. I'll let you into another little secret: Cathy wouldn't allow me to tell you until Mum had invited her to join the management committee."

"As someone who's always been a dealer, my boy," said Charlie beaming, "I can tell you you've got the better of this bargain." Daniel grinned. "In fact, I think Cathy's probably been short-changed. But when did all this happen?"

"We met at your house-warming party nearly eighteen months ago. You won't remember, Sir Charles, but we bumped into each other on the stairs," Cathy said, nervously fingering the little cross that hung around her neck.

"Of course I remember, and please call me Charlie. Everyone else does."

"So have you decided on a date?" asked Becky.

"We were planning to be married during the Easter vacation," said Daniel. "If that suits you?"

"Next week suits me," said Charlie. "I couldn't be happier. And where do you plan to hold the wedding?"

"The College chapel," said Daniel without hesitation. "You see, both Cathy's parents are dead so we thought down here in Cambridge might be best, in the circumstances."

"And where will you live?" asked Becky.

"Ah, that all depends," said Daniel mysteriously.

"On what?" asked Charlie.

"I've applied for a chair in mathematics at King's, London – and I'm reliably informed that their choice will be announced to the world in two weeks' time."

"Are you at all hopeful?" asked Becky.

"Well, let me put it this way," said Daniel. "The Principal has asked me to have dinner with him next Thursday at his lodgings, and as I've never set eyes on the gentleman in question before –" He broke off as the telephone interrupted his flow.

"Now, whoever can that be?" he asked rhetorically. "The monsters don't usually bother me on a Sunday." He picked up the receiver and listened for a moment.

"Yes, she is," he said after a few more seconds. "May I say who's calling? I'll let her know." He turned to face his mother. "Mr Baverstock for you, Mum."

Becky pushed herself out of her chair and took the telephone from Daniel as Charlie looked on apprehensively.

"Is that you, Lady Trumper?"

"Yes, it is."

"Baverstock here. I'll be brief. But first, have you informed Daniel about the details of Sir Raymond's will?"

"No. My husband was just about to do so."

"Then please don't mention the subject to him until I have had the chance to see you again."

"But – why not?" Becky realised it was now going to be necessary to conduct a one-sided conversation.

"It isn't something I feel comfortable about discussing over the telephone, Lady Trumper. When are you expecting to be back in town?"

"Later this evening."

"I think we should meet as soon as possible."

"Do you consider it's that important," said Becky, still mystified.

"I do. Would seven o'clock this evening suit you?"

"Yes, I feel sure we'll be back by then."

"In that case I'll come round to Eaton Square at seven. And please, whatever you do, don't mention anything about Sir Raymond's will to Daniel. I apologise about the mystery but I fear I have been left with little choice. Goodbye, dear lady."

"Goodbye," said Becky and put the receiver down.

"Problem?" asked Charlie, raising an eyebrow.

"I don't know." Becky looked her husband straight in the eye. "It's just that Mr Baverstock wants to see us about those papers he briefed me on last week." Charlie grimaced. "And he doesn't wish us to discuss the details with anyone else for the time being."

"Now that does sound mysterious," said Daniel, turning to Cathy. "Mr Baverstock, my darling, is on the board of the barrow, a man who would consider phoning his wife during office hours a breach of contract."

"That sounds like the right qualifications for a place on the board of a public company."

"You've met him once before, as a matter of fact," said Daniel. "He and his wife were also at Mum's house-warming party, but I fear he isn't exactly memorable."

"Who painted that picture?" said Charlie suddenly, staring at a watercolour of the Cam that hung above Daniel's desk.

Becky only hoped the change of subject hadn't been too obvious.

On the journey back to London Becky was torn between delight at the thought of having Cathy as a daughter-in-law and anxiety over what Mr Baverstock could possibly want to see them about.

When Charlie asked yet again for details, Becky tried to repeat the conversation she'd conducted with Baverstock word for word, but it left neither of them any the wiser.

"We'll know soon enough," said Charlie as they left the A10 to go through Whitechapel and on into the City. It always gave Charlie a thrill whenever he passed all the different barrows displaying their colourful wares and heard the cries of the merchants shouting their outrageous claims.

I don't offer you these for . . .

Suddenly Charlie brought the car to a halt, turned off the engine and stared out of the window.

"Why are you stopping?" asked Becky. "We haven't any time to spare."

Charlie pointed at the Whitechapel Boys' Club: it

looked even more run-down and dilapidated than usual.

"You've seen the club a thousand times before, Charlie. And you know we mustn't be late for Mr Baverstock."

He took out his diary and began unscrewing the top of his fountain pen.

"What *are* you up to?"

"When will you learn, Becky, to look more carefully?" Charlie was busy scribbling down the number of the estate agent on the "For Sale" sign.

"You surely don't want to open a second Trumper's in Whitechapel?"

"No, but I do want to find out why they're closing my old boys' club," said Charlie. He returned the pen to his inside pocket and pressed the button to start up the engine.

The Trumpers arrived back at 17 Eaton Square with just over half an hour to spare before Mr Baverstock was due to visit them; and Mr Baverstock, they both were painfully aware, was never late.

Becky immediately set about dusting the tables and plumping up the cushions in the drawing room.

"Everything looks fine to me," said Charlie. "Do stop fussing. In any case, that's what we employ a housekeeper for."

"But it's a Sunday night," Becky reminded him. She continued to check under objects she hadn't touched for months and finally put a match to the well-laid fire.

At exactly seven the front door bell rang and Charlie left to greet his guest.

"Good evening, Sir Charles," said Mr Baverstock, removing his hat.

Ah, yes, thought Charlie, there *is* someone I know who never calls me Charlie. He took Mr Baverstock's coat, scarf and hat and hung them on the hallstand.

"I am sorry to bother you on a Sunday evening," Mr Baverstock said as he followed his host into the drawing room carrying his Gladstone bag. "But I hope when you learn my news, you will feel I came to the right decision."

"I'm sure we will. We were naturally both intrigued by

your call. But first let me offer you a drink. Whisky?"

"No, thank you," said Mr Baverstock. "But a dry sherry would be most acceptable."

Becky poured Mr Baverstock a Tio Pepe and her husband a whisky before she joined the two men round the fire and waited for the lawyer to explain his uncharacteristic interruption.

"This isn't easy for me, Sir Charles."

Charlie nodded. "I understand. Just take your time."

"Can I first confirm with you that you did not reveal to your son any details of Sir Raymond's will?"

"We did not. We were saved that embarrassment first by the announcement of Daniel's engagement to be married and then by your fortuitous telephone call."

"Oh, that is good news," said Mr Baverstock. "To the charming Miss Ross, no doubt. Please do pass on my congratulations."

"You knew all along?" said Becky.

"Oh, yes," said Mr Baverstock. "It was obvious for everyone to see, wasn't it?"

"Everyone except us," said Charlie.

Mr Baverstock permitted himself a wry smile before he removed a file from his Gladstone bag.

"I'll waste no more words," continued Mr Baverstock. "Having talked to the other side's solicitors during the past few days, it has come to light that at some time in the past Daniel paid a visit to Mrs Trentham at her home in Chester Square."

Charlie and Becky were unable to hide their astonishment.

"Just as I thought," said Baverstock. "Like myself, you were both obviously quite unaware that such a meeting had taken place."

"But how could they have met when – ?" asked Charlie.

"That we may never get to the bottom of, Sir Charles. However, what I do know is that at that meeting Daniel came to an agreement with Mrs Trentham."

"And what was the nature of this agreement?" asked Charlie.

The old solicitor extracted yet another piece of paper from the file in front of him and re-read Mrs Trentham's handwritten words: "'In exchange for Mrs Trentham's withdrawing her opposition to any planning permission for the building to be known as Trumper Towers, and in addition for agreeing not to proceed with her own scheme for the rebuilding of a block of flats in Chelsea Terrace, Daniel Trumper will waive any rights he might be entitled to now or at any time in the future from the Hardcastle estate.' At that time, of course, Daniel had no idea that he was the main beneficiary of Sir Raymond's will."

"So that's why she gave in without putting up a fight?" said Charlie eventually.

"It would seem so."

"He did all that without even letting us know," said Becky as her husband began to read through the document.

"That would appear to be the case, Lady Trumper."

"And is it legally binding?" were Charlie's first words after he had finished reading the page of Mrs Trentham's handwriting.

"Yes, I'm afraid it is, Sir Charles."

"But if he didn't know the full extent of the inheritance – ?"

"This is a contract between two people. The courts would have to assume Daniel had relinquished his interest to any claim in the Hardcastle estate, once Mrs Trentham had kept her part of the bargain."

"But what about coercion?"

"Of a twenty-six-year-old man by a woman over seventy when he went to visit her? Hardly, Sir Charles."

"But how did they ever meet?"

"I have no idea," replied the lawyer. "It seems that she didn't confide the full circumstances of the meeting even to her own solicitors. However, I'm sure you now understand why I considered this wasn't the most appropriate time to raise the subject of Sir Raymond's will with Daniel."

"You made the right decision," said Charlie.

"And now the subject must be closed for ever," said Becky, barely louder than a whisper.

"But why?" asked Charlie, placing an arm around his wife's shoulder.

"Because I don't want Daniel to spend the rest of his life feeling he betrayed his great-grandfather when his only purpose in signing that agreement must have been to help us." The tears flowed down Becky's cheeks as she turned to face her husband.

"Perhaps I should have a word with Daniel, man to man."

"Charlie, you will never even consider raising the subject of Guy Trentham with my son again. I forbid it."

Charlie removed his arm from around his wife and looked at her like a child who has been unfairly scolded.

"I'm only glad it was you who has brought us this unhappy news," said Becky, turning back to the solicitor. "You've always been so considerate when it comes to our affairs."

"Thank you, Lady Trumper, but I fear I have yet more unpalatable news to impart."

Becky gripped Charlie's hand.

"I have to report that on this occasion Mrs Trentham has not satisfied herself with one blow at a time."

"What else can she do to us?" asked Charlie.

"It seems that she is now willing to part with her land in Chelsea Terrace."

"I don't believe it," said Becky.

"I do," said Charlie. "But at what price?"

"That is indeed the problem," said Mr Baverstock, who bent down to remove another file from his old leather bag.

Charlie and Becky exchanged a quick glance.

"Mrs Trentham will offer you the freehold on her site in Chelsea Terrace in exchange for ten per cent of Trumper's shares" – he paused – "and a place on the board for her son Nigel."

"Never," said Charlie flatly.

"If you should reject her offer," the solicitor continued, "she intends to sell the property on the open market and accept the highest bidder – whoever that might be."

"So be it," said Charlie. "We would undoubtedly end up buying the land ourselves."

"At a far higher price than the value of ten per cent of our shares, I suspect," said Becky.

"That's a price worth paying after what she's put us through."

"Mrs Trentham has also requested," continued Mr Baverstock, "that her offer should be presented to the board in detail at your next meeting and then voted on."

"But she doesn't have the authority to make such a demand," said Charlie.

"If you do not comply with this request," said Mr Baverstock, "it is her intention to circulate all the shareholders with the offer and then call an extraordinary general meeting at which she will personally present her case and bring the issue to a vote."

"Can she do that?" For the first time Charlie sounded worried.

"From everything I know about that lady, I suspect she wouldn't have thrown down such a gauntlet before taking legal advice."

"It's almost as if she can always anticipate our next move," said Becky with feeling.

Charlie's voice revealed the same anxiety. "She wouldn't need to bother about our next move if her son was on the board. He could just report back to her direct after every meeting."

"So what it comes to is that we may well *have* to give in to her demands," said Becky.

"I agree with your judgment, Lady Trumper," said Mr Baverstock. "However, I felt it was only proper that I should give you as much notice as possible of Mrs Trentham's demands as it will be my painful duty to acquaint the board with the details when we next meet."

There was only one "apologies for absence" when the board met the following Tuesday. Simon Matthews had to be in Geneva to conduct a rare gems sale and Charlie had assured him that his presence would not be vital. Once Mr Baverstock had finished explaining the consequences of Mrs Trentham's offer to the board, everyone around the table wanted to speak at once.

When Charlie had restored some semblance of order, he said, "I must make my position clear from the outset. I am one hundred per cent against this offer. I don't trust the lady in question and never have. What's more, I believe that in the long term her only purpose is to harm the company."

"But, surely, Mr Chairman," said Paul Merrick, "if she is considering selling her land in Chelsea Terrace to the highest bidder, she could always use the cash from that sale to purchase another ten per cent of the company's shares at any time that suited her. So what real choice are we left with?"

"Not having to live with her son," said Charlie. "Don't forget, part of this package means offering him a place on the board."

"But if he were in possession of ten per cent of the company," said Merrick, "and perhaps an even higher stake for all we know, it would be nothing less than our duty to accept him as a director."

"Not necessarily," said Charlie. "Especially if we believed his sole reason for joining the board was eventually to take over the company. The last thing we need is a hostile director."

"The last thing we need, is to pay more than is necessary for a hole in the ground."

For a moment no one spoke while the rest of the board considered these contrary statements.

"Let's assume for one moment," said Tim Newman, "the consequences of not accepting Mrs Trentham's terms but instead bidding for the empty plot ourselves on the open market. That might not prove to be the cheapest route, Sir

Charles, because I can assure you, that Sears, Boots, the House of Fraser and John Lewis – to name but four – would derive considerable pleasure from opening a new store right in the middle of Trumper's."

"Rejecting her offer may therefore turn out to be even more expensive in the long run, whatever your personal views are of the lady, Mr Chairman," said Merrick. "In any case, I have another piece of information that the board may feel is relevant to this discussion."

"What's that?" asked Charlie, warily.

"My fellow-directors may be interested to know," began Merrick rather pompously, "that Nigel Trentham has just been made redundant by Kitcat and Aitken, which is simply a euphemism for being sacked. It seems he's not proved up to the task in these leaner times. So I can't imagine his presence around this table is likely to provide us with a great deal of anxiety now or at any time in the future."

"But he could still keep his mother briefed on every move we make," said Charlie.

"Perhaps she needs to know how well the knickers are selling on the seventh floor?" suggested Merrick. "Not to mention the trouble we had with that burst water main in the gents' lavatory last month. No, Mr Chairman, it would be foolish, even irresponsible, not to accept such an offer."

"As a matter of interest, Mr Chairman, what would you do with the extra space, should Trumper's suddenly get hold of Mrs Trentham's land?" asked Daphne, throwing everyone off balance for a moment.

"Expand," said Charlie. "We're already bulging at the seams. That piece of land would mean at least fifty thousand square feet. If I could only get my hands on it it would be possible for me to open another twenty departments."

"And what would such a building programme cost?" Daphne continued.

"A lot of money," Paul Merrick interjected, "which we may not have at our disposal if we are made to pay well over the odds for that vacant site in the first place."

"May I remind you that we're having an exceptionally good year," said Charlie, banging the table.

"Agreed, Mr Chairman. But may I also remind you that when you last made a similar statement within five years you were facing bankruptcy."

"But that was caused by an expected war," insisted Charlie.

"And this isn't," said Merrick.

The two men stared at each other, unable to disguise their mutual loathing.

"No, our first duty must always be to the shareholders," continued Merrick, as he looked around the boardroom table. "If they were to find out that we had paid an excessive amount for that piece of land simply because of – and I put this as delicately as I can – a personal vendetta between the principals, we could be heavily censured at the next AGM and you, Mr Chairman, might even be called on to resign."

"I'm willing to take that risk," said Charlie, by now almost shouting.

"Well, I'm not," said Merrick calmly. "What's more, if we don't accept her offer we already know that Mrs Trentham will call an extraordinary general meeting in order to put her case to the shareholders, and I've little doubt where their interests will lie. I consider the time has come to take a vote on this matter, rather than carry on with any further pointless discussion."

"But wait a moment –" Charlie began.

"No. I will not wait, Mr Chairman, and I propose that we accept Mrs Trentham's generous offer of releasing her land, in exchange for ten per cent of the company's shares."

"And what do you propose we do about her son?" asked Charlie.

"He should be invited to join the board without delay," replied Merrick.

"But –" began Charlie.

"No buts, thank you, Mr Chairman," said Merrick. "The time has come to vote. Personal prejudices shouldn't be allowed to cloud our better judgment."

There was a moment's silence before Arthur Selwyn said, "As a formal proposal has been made will you be kind enough to record the votes, Miss Allen?" Jessica nodded and glanced round at the nine members of the board.

"Mr Merrick?"

"For."

"Mr Newman?"

"For."

"Mr Denning?"

"Against."

"Mr Makins?"

"Against."

"Mr Baverstock?"

The lawyer placed the palms of his hands on the table and seemed to hesitate, as if in some considerable dilemma over the decision.

"For," he said finally.

"Lady Trumper?"

"Against," Becky said without hesitation.

"Lady Wiltshire?"

"For," said Daphne quietly.

"Why?" said Becky, unable to believe her response.

Daphne turned to face her old friend. "Because I'd rather have the enemy inside the boardroom causing trouble, than outside in the corridor causing even more."

Becky couldn't believe her ears.

"I assume you're against, Sir Charles?"

Charlie nodded vigorously.

Mr Selwyn raised his eyes.

"Does that mean it's four votes each?" he enquired of Jessica.

"Yes, that's correct, Mr Selwyn," said Jessica after she had run her thumb down the list of names a second time.

Everyone stared across at the managing director. He

placed the pen he had been writing with on the blotting pad in front of him. "Then I can only do what I consider to be in the best long-term interests of the company. I cast my vote in favour of accepting Mrs Trentham's offer."

Everyone round the table except Charlie started to talk.

Mr Selwyn waited for some time before adding, "The motion has been carried, Mr Chairman, by five votes to four. I will therefore instruct our merchant bankers and solicitors to carry out the necessary financial and legal arrangements to ensure that this transaction takes place smoothly and in accordance with company regulations."

Charlie made no comment, just continued to stare in front of him.

"And if there is no other business, Mr Chairman, perhaps you should declare the meeting closed."

Charlie nodded but didn't move when the other directors rose to leave the boardroom. Only Becky remained in her place, halfway down the long table. Within moments they were alone.

"I should have got my hands on those flats thirty years ago, you know."

Becky made no comment.

"And we should never have gone public while that bloody woman was still alive."

Charlie rose and walked slowly over to the window, but his wife still didn't offer an opinion as he stared down at the empty bench on the far side of the road.

"And to think I told Simon that his presence wouldn't be vital."

Still Becky said nothing.

"Well, at least I now know what the bloody woman has in mind for her precious Nigel."

Becky raised an eyebrow as Charlie turned to face her.

"She plans that he will succeed me as the next chairman of Trumper's."

CATHY

1947-1950

CHAPTER 39

The one question I was never able to answer as a child was, "When did you last see your father?" Unlike the young cavalier, I simply didn't know the answer. In fact I had no idea who my father was, or my mother for that matter. Most people have no idea how many times a day, a month, a year one is asked such a question. And if your reply is always, "I simply don't know, because they both died before I can remember," you are greeted with looks of either surprise or suspicion – or, worse still, disbelief. In the end you learn how to throw up a smoke-screen or simply avoid the issue by changing the subject. There is no variation on the question of parentage for which I haven't developed an escape route.

The only vague memory I have of my parents is of a man who shouted a lot of the time and of a woman who was so timid she rarely spoke. I also have a feeling she was called Anna. Other than that, both of them remain a blur.

How I envied those children who could immediately tell me about their parents, brothers, sisters, even second cousins or distant aunts. All I knew about myself was that I had been brought up in St Hilda's Orphanage, Park Hill, Melbourne. Principal: Miss Rachel Benson.

Many of the children from the orphanage did have relations and some received letters, even the occasional visit. The only such person I can ever recall was an elderly, rather severe-looking woman, who wore a long black dress, black lace gloves up to her elbows and spoke with a strange accent. I have no idea what her relationship to me was, if any.

Miss Benson treated this particular lady with considerable respect and I remember even curtsied when she left; but I never learned her name and when I was old enough to ask who she was Miss Benson claimed she had no idea what I was talking about. Whenever I tried to question Miss Benson about my own upbringing, she would reply mysteriously, "It's best you don't know, child." I can think of no sentence in the English language more likely to ensure that I tried even harder to find out the truth about my background.

As the years went by I began to ask what I thought were subtler questions on the subject of my parents – of the vice-principal, my house matron, kitchen staff, even the janitor – but I always came up against the same blank wall. On my fourteenth birthday I requested an interview with Miss Benson in order to ask her the question direct. Although she had long ago dispensed with "It's best you don't know, child," she now replaced this sentiment with, "In truth, Cathy, I don't know myself." Although I didn't question her further, I didn't believe her, because some of the older members of the staff would from time to time give me strange looks, and on at least two occasions began to whisper behind my back once they thought I was out of earshot.

I had no photographs or mementoes of my parents, or even any proof of their past existence, except for a small piece of jewellery which I convinced myself was silver. I remember that it was the man who shouted a lot who had given me the little cross and since then it had always hung from a piece of string around my neck. One night when I was undressing in the dormitory Miss Benson spotted my prize and demanded to know where the pendant had come from; I told her Betsy Compton had swopped it with me for a dozen marbles, a fib that seemed to satisfy her at the time. But from that day onwards I kept my treasure well hidden from anyone's prying eyes.

I must have been one of those rare children who loved going to school from the first day its doors were opened to me. The classroom was a blessed escape from my prison and its warders. Every extra minute I spent at the local school was a minute I didn't have to be at St Hilda's, and I quickly discovered that the harder I worked the longer the hours I was allowed to remain behind. These became even more expandable when, at the age of eleven, I won a place at Melbourne Church of England Girls' Grammar School, where they had so many extra-curricular activities going on, from first thing in the morning until late every evening, that St Hilda's became little more than the place where I slept and had breakfast.

While at MGS I took up painting, which made it possible for me to spend several hours in the art room without too much supervision or interference; tennis, where by dint of sheer hard work and application I managed to gain a place in the school second six, which produced the bonus of being allowed to practise in the evening until it was dusk; and cricket, for which I had no talent, but as team scorer not only was I required never to leave my place until the last ball had been bowled but every other Saturday I was able to escape on a bus for a fixture against another school. I was one of the few children who enjoyed away matches in preference to home fixtures.

At sixteen I entered the sixth form and began to work even harder: it was explained to Miss Benson that I might possibly win a scholarship to the University of Melbourne – not an everyday occurrence for an inmate from St Hilda's.

Whenever I received any academic distinction or

reprimand – the latter became rarer once I had discovered school – I was made to report to Miss Benson in her study, where she would deliver a few words of encouragement or disapproval, before placing the slip of paper that marked these occurrences in a file which she would then return to a cabinet that stood behind her desk. I always watched her most carefully as she carried out this ritual. First she would remove a key from the top left-hand drawer of her desk, then she would go over to the cabinet, check my file under QRS, place the credit or misdemeanour inside my entry, lock the cabinet and then replace the key in her desk. It was a routine that never varied.

Another fixed point in Miss Benson's life was her annual holiday, when she would visit "her people" in Adelaide. This took place every September and I looked forward to it as others might a holiday.

Once war had been declared I feared she might not keep to her schedule, especially as we were told we would all have to make sacrifices.

Miss Benson appeared to make no sacrifices and despite travel restrictions and cutbacks departed for Adelaide on exactly the same day that summer as she always had. I waited until five days after the taxi had driven her off to the station before I felt it was safe to carry out my little escapade.

On the sixth night I lay awake until just after one in the morning, not moving a muscle until I was certain all sixteen girls in the dormitory were fast asleep. Then I rose, borrowed a pen torch from the drawer of the girl who slept next to me and headed off across the landing towards the staircase. Had I been spotted en route, I already had an excuse prepared about feeling sick, and as I had rarely entered the sanatorium at any time during my twelve years at St Hilda's, I felt confident I would be believed.

I crept cautiously down the staircase without having to use the torch: since Miss Benson had departed for Adelaide, I had practised the routine each morning with my eyes closed. Once I had reached the principal's study, I opened the door and slipped in, only then switching on the pen torch. I tiptoed over to Miss Benson's desk and cautiously pulled open the top left-hand drawer. What I hadn't been prepared for was to be faced with about twenty different keys, some in groups on rings while others were detached but unmarked. I tried to remember the size and shape of the one Miss Benson had used to unlock the filing cabinet, but I couldn't, and with only a pen torch to guide me several trips to the cabinet and back were necessary before I discovered the one that would turn one hundred and eighty degrees.

I pulled open the top drawer of the filing cabinet as slowly as I could but the runners still seemed to rumble like thunder. I stopped, and held my breath as I waited to hear if there were any movement coming from the house. I even looked under the door to be sure no light was suddenly switched on. Once I felt confident I hadn't disturbed anyone I leafed through the names in the QRS box file: Roberts, Rose, Ross . . . I pulled out my personal folder and carried the heavy bundle back to the principal's desk. I sat down in Miss Benson's chair and, with the help of the torch began to check each page carefully. As I was sixteen and had now been at St Hilda's for around twelve years, my file was necessarily thick. I was reminded of misdemeanours as long ago as wetting my bed as well as several credits for painting, including the rare double credit for one of my watercolours that still hung in the dining room. Yet however much I searched through that folder there was no trace of anything about me before the age of three. I began to wonder if this was a general rule that applied to everyone who had come to live at St Hilda's. I took a quick glance at the details of Jennie Rose's record. To my dismay, I found the names of both her father (Ted, deceased) and her mother

(Susan). An attached note explained that Mrs Rose had three other children to bring up and since the death of her husband from a heart attack had been quite unable to cope with a fourth child.

I locked the cabinet, returned the key to the top left-hand drawer of Miss Benson's desk, switched off the pen torch, left the study and walked quickly up the stairs to my dormitory. I put the pen torch back in its rightful place and slipped into bed. I began to wonder what I could possibly do next to try and find out who I was and where I'd come from.

It was as if my parents had never existed, and I had somehow started life aged three. As the only alternative was virgin birth and I didn't accept that even for the Blessed Mary, my desire to know the truth became irrepressible. I must eventually have fallen asleep, because all I remember after that is being woken by the school bell the following morning.

When I was awarded my place at the University of Melbourne I felt like a long-term prisoner who has finally been released. For the first time, I was given a room of my own and was no longer expected to wear a uniform – not that the range of clothes I could afford was going to set the Melbourne fashion houses alight. I remember working even longer hours at university than I had done at school, as I was apprehensive that if I didn't pass my first year general papers they would send me back to spend the rest of my days at St Hilda's.

In my second year I specialised in the history of art, and English while continuing with painting as a hobby, but I had no idea what career I wanted to pursue after leaving university. My tutor suggested I should consider teaching, but that sounded to me rather like an extension of St Hilda's, with me ending up as Miss Benson.

I didn't have many boyfriends before going to university, because the boys at St Hilda's were kept in a separate wing of the house and you were not allowed to talk to them before nine in the morning and after five o'clock at night. Until the age of fifteen I thought kissing made you pregnant so I was determined not to make that mistake, especially after my experience of growing up with no family of my own.

My first real boyfriend was Mel Nicholls, who was captain of the university football team. Having finally succeeded in getting me into bed he told me that I was the only girl in his life and, more important, the first. After I had admitted it was true for me too and lay back on the pillow Mel leant over and began to take an interest in the only thing I was still wearing.

"I've never seen anything quite like that before," he said, taking my little piece of jewellery between his fingers.

"Another first."

"Not quite." He laughed. "Because I've seen one very similar."

"What do you mean?"

"It's a medal," he explained. "My father won three or four of them himself but none of them's made of silver."

Looking back on it now, I consider that this particular piece of information was well worth losing my virginity for.

In the library of the University of Melbourne there is a large selection of books covering the First World War, biased not unnaturally towards Gallipoli. However, tucked away among the pages of heroic deeds performed by Australian infantrymen was a chapter on British gallantry awards, complete with several coloured plates.

I discovered that there were VCs, DSOs, DSCs, CBEs, OBEs – the variations seemed endless until finally on page four hundred and nine I found what I was searching for: the Military Cross, a ribbon of white watered silk and purple vertical stripes and a medal forged in silver with the Imperial crown on each of its four arms. It was awarded to officers below the rank of major "for conspicuous gallantry when under fire". I began to hypothesise that my father was a war hero who had died at an early age from terrible wounds. At least that would have explained his perpetual shouting as something that had been brought on by so much suffering.

My next piece of detective work came when I visited an antique shop in Melbourne. The man behind the counter simply studied the medal, then offered me five pounds for it. I didn't bother to explain why I wouldn't have parted with my prize had he offered me five hundred pounds, but at least he was able to inform me that the only real medal dealer in Australia was a Mr Frank Jennings, of Number 47 Mafeking Street, Sydney.

At that time I considered Sydney to be the other side of the globe, and I certainly couldn't afford to make such a long journey on my tiny grant. So I had to wait patiently until the summer term when I applied to be scorer for the university cricket team. They turned me down on account of my sex. Women couldn't really be expected to understand the game fully, it was explained to me by a youth who used to sit behind me in lectures so that he could copy my notes. This left me with no choice but to spend hours of practice on my ground strokes and almost as many on my overhead smash until I was selected for the ladies' second tennis team. Not a major achievement but there was only one match on the calendar that interested me: Sydney (A).

On the morning we arrived in Sydney, I went straight to Mafeking Street and was struck by how many young men who passed me on the street were in uniform. Mr Jennings himself studied the medal with considerably more interest than the dealer from Melbourne had shown.

"It's a miniature MC all right," he told me, peering at my little prize through a magnifying glass. "It would have been worn on a dress uniform for guest nights in the regimental mess. These three initials printed down the edge of one of the arms, barely discernible to the naked eye, ought to give us a clue as to who was awarded the decoration."

I stared through Mr Jennings' magnifying glass at something I had never been aware of until then, but I could now clearly see the initials "G.F.T.".

"Is there any way of finding out who G.F.T. is?" I asked hopefully.

"Oh, yes," said Mr Jennings, turning to a shelf behind him, from which he removed a leather-bound book and flicked through its pages until he came to Godfrey S. Thomas and George Victor Taylor, but could find no trace of anyone with the initials G.F.T.

"Sorry, but I can't help you on this one," he said. "Your particular medal can't have been awarded to an Australian, otherwise it would be catalogued right here." He tapped the leather cover. "You'll have to write to the War Office in London if you want any further information. They still keep on file the names of every member of the armed forces awarded any decoration for gallantry."

I thanked him for his help but not before he had offered me ten pounds for the medal. I smiled and returned to join the tennis team for my match against Sydney University. I lost 6-0, 6-1, being quite unable to concentrate on anything except G.F.T. I wasn't selected for the university tennis team again that season.

The next day I followed Mr Jennings's advice and wrote to the War Office in London. I didn't get a letter back from them for several months, which was hardly surprising as everyone knew they had other things on their mind in 1944. However, a buff envelope eventually came and when opened informed me that the holder of my medal could have been either Graham

Frank Turnbull of the Duke of Wellington's regiment or Guy Francis Trentham of the Royal Fusiliers.

So was my real name Turnbull or Trentham?

That same evening I wrote to the British High Commissioner's office in Canberra asking whom I should contact for information regarding the two regiments referred to in the letter. I received a reply a couple of weeks later. With the new leads I had acquired I despatched two more letters to England: one to Halifax, the other to London. I then sat back again and resigned myself to another long wait. When you have already spent eighteen years of your life trying to discover your true identity, another few months doesn't seem all that important. In any case, now that I had begun my final year at university I was up to my eyes in work.

The Duke of Wellington's were the first to reply, and they informed me that Lieutenant Graham Frank Turnbull had been killed at Passchendaele on 6 November 1917. As I was born in 1924 that let Lieutenant Turnbull off the hook. I prayed for Guy Francis Trentham.

It was several weeks later that I received a reply from the Royal Fusiliers to inform me that Captain Guy Francis Trentham had been awarded the MC on 18 July 1918, following the second battle of the Marne. Fuller details could be obtained from the Regimental Museum library at their headquarters in London, but this had to be done in person as they had no authority to release information about members of the regiment by post.

As I had no way of getting to England I immediately began a new line of investigation, only this time I drew a complete blank. I took a whole morning off in order to search for the name of Trentham in the birth records of the Melbourne city registry on Queen Street. I found there was not one Trentham listed. There were several Rosses but none came anywhere near my date of birth. I began to realise that someone had gone to considerable lengths to make sure I was unable to trace my roots. But why?

Suddenly my sole purpose in life switched to how I could get myself to England, despite the fact that I had no money and the war had only recently ended. I checked every graduate and undergraduate course that was on offer and all that my tutor considered it might be worth applying for was a scholarship to the Slade School of Art in London, which offered three places each year to students from Commonwealth countries. I began to put in hours that even I hadn't realised existed, and was rewarded by a place on the short list of six for a final interview to be held in Canberra.

Although I became extremely nervous on the train journey to the Australian capital, I felt the interview went well and indeed the examiners told me that my papers on the history of art were of particular merit, even if my practical work was not of the same high standard.

An envelope marked The Slade was dropped in my cubbyhole a month later. I ripped it open in anticipation and extracted a letter that began:

Dear Miss Ross,

We are sorry to inform you

The only worthwhile thing that came out of all the extra work I had put in was that I sailed through my finals and was awarded a First Class honours degree when the graduation results were announced. But I was still no nearer to getting myself to England.

In desperation I telephoned the British High Commission and was put through to the labour attaché. A lady came on the line and informed me that with my qualifications there would be several teaching posts on offer. She added that I would have to sign a three-year contract and be responsible for my own travel arrangements – nicely worded, I considered, as I still wasn't able to afford the trip to Sydney, let alone the United Kingdom. In any case, I felt I would only need to spend about a month in England to track down Guy Francis Trentham.

The only other jobs that were available, the lady explained the second time I called, were known as "slave traders". These consisted of positions in hotels, hospitals or old people's homes, where you were virtually unpaid for one year in return for your passage to England and back. As I still had no plans for any particular career and realised this was virtually the only chance I might ever have of getting myself to England and finding someone I was related to, I called into the labour attaché's department and signed on the dotted line. Most of my friends at university thought I had taken leave of my senses, but then they had no idea of my real purpose in wanting to visit Britain.

The boat we sailed to Southampton on couldn't have been much of an improvement on the one the first Australian immigrants took coming the other way some one hundred and fifty years before. They put three of us "slave traders" to a cabin no larger than my room on the university campus, and if the ship listed more than ten degrees Pam and Maureen ended up in my bunk. We had all signed on to work at the Melrose Hotel in Earl's Court, which we were assured was in central London. After a journey of some six weeks we were met at the dockside by a clapped-out army lorry which took us up to the capital and deposited us on the steps of the Melrose Hotel.

The housekeeper allocated our accommodation and I ganged up with Pam and Maureen, again. I was surprised to discover that we were expected to share a room of roughly the same size as the cabin in which we had suffered together on board ship. At least this time we didn't fall out of bed unexpectedly.

It was over two weeks before they gave me enough time off to visit Kensington Post Office and check through the London telephone directory. There wasn't a Trentham to be found.

"Could be ex-directory," the girl behind the counter explained. "Which means they won't take your call in any case."

"Or there just isn't a Trentham living in London," I said, and accepted that the Regimental Museum was now my only hope.

I thought I had worked hard at the University of Melbourne, but the hours they expected us to do at the Melrose would have brought a combat soldier to his knees. All the same, I was damned if I was going to admit as much, especially after Pam and Maureen gave up the struggle within a month, cabled their parents in Sydney for some money and returned to Australia on the first available boat. At least it meant I ended up with a room to myself until the next boatload arrived. To be honest I wish I could have packed up and gone home with them, but I hadn't anyone in Australia to whom I could cable back for more than about ten pounds.

The first full day I had off and wasn't totally exhausted, I took a train to Hounslow where the museum was situated now. When I left the station the ticket collector directed me to the Royal Fusiliers' Depot and Museum. After walking about a mile I eventually reached the building I was looking for. It seemed to be uninhabited except for a single receptionist. He was dressed in khaki uniform, with three stripes on both arms. He sat dozing behind a counter.

I walked noisily over and pretended not to wake him.

"Can I 'elp you, young lady?" he asked, rubbing his eyes.

"I hope so."

"Australian?"

"Is it that obvious?"

"I fought alongside your chaps in North Africa," he explained. "Damn great bunch of soldiers, I can tell you. So 'ow can I help you, miss?"

"I wrote to you from Melbourne," I said, producing a handwritten copy of the letter. "About the holder of this medal." I slipped the piece of string over my head and handed my prize to him. "His name was Guy Francis Trentham."

"Miniature MC," said the sergeant without hesitation as he held the medal in his hand. "Guy Francis Trentham, you say?"

"That's right."

"Good. So let's look 'im up in the great book: 1914–1918, yes?"

I nodded.

He went over to a massive bookshelf weighed down by heavy volumes and removed a large leather-bound book. He placed it on the counter with a thud, sending dust in every direction. On the cover were the words, printed in gold, "Royal Fusiliers, Decorations 1914–1918".

"Let's have a butcher's, then," he said as he started to flick through the pages. I waited impatiently. "There's our man," he announced triumphantly. "Guy Francis Trentham, Captain." He swung the book round so that I could study the entry more carefully. I was so excited it was several moments before I could take the words in.

Captain Trentham's citation went on for twenty-two lines and I asked if I might be allowed to copy out the details in full.

"Of course, miss," he said. "Be my guest." He

handed over a large sheet of ruled paper and a blunt army-issue pencil. I began to write:

> On the morning of 18th July, 1918, Captain Guy Trentham of the Second Battalion of the Royal Fusiliers led a company of men from the Allied trenches towards the enemy lines, killing several German soldiers before reaching their dug-outs, where he wiped out a complete army unit single-handed. Captain Trentham continued in pursuit of two other German soldiers and chased them into a nearby forest where he succeeded in killing them both.
>
> The same evening, despite being surrounded by the enemy, he rescued two men of his own company, Private T. Prescott and Corporal C. Trumper, who had strayed from the battlefield, and were hiding in a nearby church. After nightfall, he led them back across open terrain while the enemy continued to fire intermittently in their direction.
>
> Private Prescott was killed by a stray German tracer bullet before he managed to reach the safety of his own trenches. Corporal Trumper survived despite a continual barrage of firepower from the enemy.
>
> For this singular act of leadership and heroism in the face of the enemy, Captain Trentham was awarded the MC.

Having written out every word of the citation in my neatest hand, I closed the heavy cover and turned the book round to face the sergeant.

"Trentham," he said. "If I remember correctly, miss, 'e still 'as 'is picture up on the wall." The sergeant picked up some crutches, manoeuvred himself from behind the counter and limped slowly to the far corner of the museum. I hadn't realised until that moment that the poor man only had one leg. "Over 'ere, miss," he said. "Follow me."

My palms began to sweat and I felt a little sick at the thought of discovering what my father looked like. I wondered if I might resemble him in any way.

The sergeant hobbled straight past the VCs before we came to a row of MCs. They were all lined up, old sepia pictures, badly framed. His finger ran along them – Stevens, Thomas, Tubbs. "That's strange. I could have sworn 'is photo was there. Well, I'll be damned. Must 'ave got lost when we moved from the Tower."

"Could his picture be anywhere else?"

"Not to my knowledge, miss," he said. "I must 'ave imagined it all along, but I'd swear I'd seen 'is photo when the museum was at the Tower. Well, I'll be damned," he repeated.

I asked him if he could supply me with any more details of Captain Trentham and what might have happened to him since 1918. He hobbled back to the counter and looked up his name in the regimental handbook. "Commissioned 1916, promoted to second lieutenant 1916, captain 1917, India 1920–1922, resigned 'is commission August 1922. Since then nothing known of 'im, miss."

"So he could still be alive?"

"Certainly could, miss. 'e'd only be fifty, fifty-five, most."

I checked my watch, thanked him and ran quickly out of the building, suddenly aware of how much time I had spent at the museum and fearful that I might miss the train back to London and wouldn't be in time to clock on for my five o'clock shift.

After I had settled in a corner of a dingy third-class compartment I read over the citation again. It pleased me to think that my father had been a First World War hero; but I still couldn't fathom out why Miss Benson had been so unwilling to tell me anything about him. Why had he gone to Australia? Had he changed his name to Ross? I felt I would have to return to Melbourne if I was ever going to find out exactly what had happened to Guy Francis Trentham. Had I possessed the money to pay for my return fare, I would have gone back that night, but as I had to work out my contract at the hotel for another nine months before they would advance me enough cash to cover the one-way ticket home I settled down to complete my sentence.

London in 1947 was an exciting city for a twenty-three-year-old so despite the dreary work there were many compensations. Whenever I had any time off I would visit an art gallery, a museum or go to a cinema with one of the girls from the hotel. On a couple of occasions I even accompanied a group of friends to a dance at the Mecca ballroom just off the Strand. One particular night I remember a rather good-looking bloke from the RAF asked me for a dance and, just moments after we had started going round the hall, he tried to kiss me. When I pushed him away he became even more determined and only a firm kick on his ankle followed by a short dash across the dance floor made it possible for me to escape. A few minutes later I found myself out on the pavement and heading back to the hotel on my own.

As I strolled through Chelsea in the general direction of Earl's Court I stopped from time to time to admire the unattainable goods on display in every shop window. I particularly craved a long blue silk shawl draped over the shoulders of an elegant slim mannequin. I stopped window-shopping for a moment and glanced up at the name over the door: "Trumper's". There was something familiar about the name but I couldn't think what. I walked slowly back to the hotel but the only Trumper I could recall was the legendary Australian cricketer who had died before I was born. Then in the middle of the night it came back to me. Trumper, C. was the corporal mentioned in the citation written about my father. I jumped out of bed, opened the bottom drawer of my little desk and checked the words I had copied out during my visit to the Royal Fusiliers Museum.

The name was not one I'd come across since arriving in England, so I wondered if the shopkeeper might be related in some way to the corporal and therefore might help me find him. I decided to return to the museum in Hounslow on my next day off and see if my one-legged friend could be of any further assistance.

"Nice to see you again, miss," he said as I walked up to the counter. I was touched that he remembered me.

"More information you're after?"

"You're right," I told him. "Corporal Trumper, he's not the . . . ?"

"Charlie Trumper the 'onest trader. Certainly is, miss; but now 'e's Sir Charles and owns that large group of shops in Chelsea Terrace."

"I thought so."

"I was about to tell you all about 'im when you ran off last time, miss." He grinned. "Could 'ave saved you a train journey and about six months of your time."

The following evening, instead of going to see Greta Garbo at the Gate Cinema in Notting Hill, I sat on an old bench on the far side of Chelsea Terrace and just stared at a row of windows. Sir Charles seemed to own almost every shop on the street. I could only wonder why he had allowed such a large empty space to remain right in the middle of the block.

My next problem was how I could possibly get to see him. The only idea that occurred to me was that I might take my medal into Number 1 for a valuation – and then pray.

During the next week I was on the day shift at the hotel so I was unable to return to Number 1 Chelsea Terrace before the following Monday afternoon, when I presented the girl on the front counter with my MC and asked if the medal could be valued. She considered my tiny offering, then called for someone else to examine it more carefully. A tall, studious-looking man spent some time checking the piece before he offered an opinion. "A miniature MC," he declared, "sometimes known as a dress MC because it would be worn on a mess or dinner jacket for regimental nights, value approximately ten pounds." He hesitated for a moment. "But of course Spink's at 5 King Street SW1 would be able to give you a more accurate assessment should you require it."

"Thank you," I said, having learned nothing new and finding myself quite unable to think of any way I might phrase a question about Sir Charles Trumper's war record.

"Anything else I can help you with?" he asked as I remained rooted to the spot.

"How do you get a job here?" I bleated out, feeling rather stupid.

"Just write in, giving us all the details of your qualifications and past experience and we'll be back in touch with you within a few days."

"Thank you," I said and left without another word.

I sat down that evening and drafted a long handwritten letter, setting out my qualifications as an art historian. They appeared a bit slender to me when I looked at them on paper.

The next morning I rewrote the letter on the hotel's finest stationery before addressing the envelope to "Job Enquiries" – as I had no name as a contact other than Trumper's – Number 1 Chelsea Terrace, London SW3.

The following afternoon I hand-delivered the missive to a girl on the front desk of the auction house, never really expecting to receive a reply. In any case, I wasn't actually sure what I would do if they did offer me a job, as I planned on returning to Melbourne in a few weeks and I still couldn't imagine how working at Trumper's would ever lead to my meeting Sir Charles.

Ten days later I received a letter from the personnel officer, saying they would like to interview me. I spent four pounds fifteen shillings of my hard-earned wages on a new dress that I could ill afford and arrived over an hour early for the interview. I ended up having to walk round the block several times. During that hour I discovered that Sir Charles really did seem to sell everything any human being could desire, as long as you had enough money to pay for it.

At last the hour was up and I marched in and presented myself at the front counter. I was taken up some stairs to an office on the top floor. The lady who interviewed me said she couldn't understand what I was doing stuck in a hotel as a chambermaid with my qualifications, until I explained to her that hotel work was the only job available to those who couldn't afford to pay their passage over to England.

She smiled before warning me that if I wanted to work at Number 1 everyone started on the front desk. If they proved to be any good they were promoted fairly quickly.

"I started on the front desk at Sotheby's," my interviewer went on to explain. I wanted to ask her how long she'd lasted.

"I'd love to come and work at Trumper's," I told her, "but I'm afraid I still have two months of my contract to complete before I can leave the Melrose Hotel."

"Then we'll have to wait for you," she replied without hesitation. "You can start at the front desk on 1st September, Miss Ross. I will confirm all the arrangements in writing by the end of the week."

I was so excited by her offer that I quite forgot why I'd applied for the job in the first place: until my interviewer sent her promised letter and I was able to decipher her signature scribbled across the foot of the page.

CHAPTER 40

Cathy had worked on the front desk of Trumper's Auction House for just eleven days when Simon Matthews asked her to help him prepare the catalogue for the Italian sale. He was the first to spot how, as the auction house's premier line of defence, she handled the myriad enquiries that were thrown at her without constantly having to seek a second opinion. She worked just as hard for Trumper's as she had done at the Melrose Hotel, but with a difference: she now enjoyed what she was doing.

For the first time in her life Cathy felt she was part of a family, because Rebecca Trumper was invariably relaxed and friendly with her staff, treating them all as equals. Her salary was far more generous than the bare minimum she had received from her previous employer, and the room they gave her above the butcher's shop at Number 135 was palatial in comparison with her hideaway at the back of the hotel.

Trying to find out more about her father began to seem less important to Cathy as she set about proving she was worth her place at Number 1 Chelsea Terrace. Her primary task in preparing the catalogue for the Italian sale was to check the history of every one of the fifty-nine pictures that were to come under the hammer. To this end she travelled right across London from library to library and telephoned gallery after gallery in her quest to track down every attribution. In the end only one picture completely baffled her, that of the Virgin Mary and Child, which bore no signature and had no history attached except that it had originally come from the private collection of Sir Charles Trumper and was now owned by a Mrs Kitty Bennett.

Cathy asked Simon Matthews if he could give any lead on the picture and was told by her head of department that he felt it might have come from the school of Bronzino.

Simon, who was in charge of the auction, went on to suggest that she should check through the press cuttings books.

"Almost everything you need to know about the Trumpers is in there somewhere."

"And where will I find them?"

"On the fourth floor in that funny little room at the end of the passage."

When she eventually found the cubicle that housed the files she had to brush off a layer of dust and even remove the odd cobweb as she browsed through the annual offerings. She sat on the floor, her legs tucked beneath her, as she continued to turn the pages, becoming more and more engrossed in the rise of Charles Trumper from his days when he owned his first barrow in Whitechapel to the proposed plans for Trumper's of Chelsea. Although the press references were sketchy in those early years, it was a small article in the *Evening Standard* that stopped Cathy in her tracks. The page had yellowed with age and on the top right-hand corner, barely discernible, was printed the date: 8 September 1922.

A tall man in his late twenties, unshaven and dressed in an old army greatcoat, broke into the home of Mr and Mrs Charles Trumper of 11 Gilston Road, Chelsea yesterday morning. The intruder escaped with a small oil painting thought to be of little value. Mrs Trumper, seven months pregnant with her second child, was in the house at the time and collapsed

> from the shock. She was later rushed to Guy's hospital by her husband.
>
> On arrival an emergency operation was carried out by the senior surgeon Mr Armitage, but their little girl was still-born. Mrs Trumper is expected to remain at Guy's hospital under observation for several days.
>
> The police would like to interview anyone who may have been in the vicinity at the time.

Cathy's eyes moved on to a second piece, dated some three weeks later.

> Police have come into possession of an abandoned army greatcoat that may have been worn by the man who broke into 11 Gilston Road, Chelsea, the home of Mr and Mrs Charles Trumper, on the morning of 7 September. The ownership of the coat has been traced to a Captain Trentham, formerly of the Royal Fusiliers, who until recently was serving with his regiment in India.

Cathy read the two pieces over and over again. Could she really be the daughter of a man who had tried to rob Sir Charles and had been responsible for the death of his second child? And where did the painting fit in? Just how had Mrs Bennett come into possession of it? More important, why had Lady Trumper taken such an interest in a seemingly unimportant oil by an unknown artist? Unable to answer any of these questions, Cathy closed the cuttings book and pushed it back to the bottom of the pile. After she had washed her hands she wanted to return downstairs and ask Lady Trumper all her questions one by one, but knew that wasn't possible.

When the catalogue had been completed and on sale for over a week Lady Trumper asked to see Cathy in her office. Cathy only hoped that some frightful mistake hadn't been unearthed, or someone hadn't come across an attribution for the Virgin Mary and Child that she should have discovered in time to be credited in the catalogue.

As Cathy stepped into her office Becky said, "My congratulations."

"Thank you," said Cathy, not quite sure what she was being praised for.

"Your catalogue has been a sell-out and we're having to rush through a reprint."

"I'm only sorry that I couldn't discover any worthwhile attribution for your husband's painting," said Cathy, feeling relieved that was not the reason Rebecca had wanted to see her. She also hoped her boss might confide in her how Sir Charles had come into possession of the little oil in the first place, and perhaps even throw some light on the connection between the Trumpers and Captain Trentham.

"I'm not that surprised," Becky replied, without offering any further explanation.

You see, I came across an article in the files that mentioned a certain Captain Guy Trentham and I wondered . . . Cathy wanted to say, but she remained silent.

"Would you like to be one of the spotters when the sale takes place next week?" Becky asked.

On the day of the Italian sale, Cathy was accused by Simon of being "full of beans" although in fact she had been unable to eat a thing that morning.

Once the sale had started, painting after painting passed its estimate and Cathy was delighted when *The Basilica of St Mark's* reached a record for a Canaletto.

When Sir Charles's little oil replaced the masterpiece she suddenly felt queasy. It must have been the way the light caught the canvas, because there was now no doubt in her mind that it too was a masterpiece. Her immediate thought was that if only she possessed two hundred pounds she would have put in a bid for it herself.

The uproar that followed once the little picture had been removed from the easel made Cathy yet more anxious. She felt the accuser might well be right in his claim that the painting was an original by Bronzino. She had never seen a better example of his classic chubby babies with their sun-lit halos. Lady Trumper and Simon placed no blame on Cathy's shoulders as they continued to assure everyone who asked that the picture was a copy and had been known to the gallery for several years.

When the sale eventually came to an end, Cathy began to check through the dockets to be sure they were in the correct order so that there could be no doubt who had purchased each item. Simon was standing a few feet away and telling a gallery owner which pictures had failed to reach their reserve price and might therefore be sold privately. She froze when she heard Lady Trumper turn to Simon, the moment the dealer had left, and say, "It's that wretched Trentham woman up to her tricks again. Did you spot the old horror at the back of the room?" Simon nodded, but had made no further comment.

It must have been about a week after the Bishop of Reims had made his pronouncement that Simon invited Cathy to dinner at his flat in Pimlico. "A little celebration," he added, explaining he had asked all those who had been directly involved with the Italian sale.

Cathy arrived that night to find several of the staff from the Old Masters department already enjoying a glass of wine, and by the time they sat down to dinner only Rebecca Trumper was not present. Once again Cathy felt aware of the family atmosphere the Trumpers created even in their absence. The guests all enjoyed a sumptuous meal of avocado soup followed by wild duck which they learned Simon had spent the whole afternoon preparing. She and a young man called Julian, who worked in the rare books department, stayed on after the others had left to help clear up.

"Don't bother with the washing-up," said Simon. "My lady who 'does' can deal with it all in the morning."

"Typical male attitude," said Cathy as she continued to wash the dishes. "However, I admit that I remained behind with an ulterior motive."

"And what might that be?" he asked as he picked up a dishcloth and made a token attempt to help Julian with the drying.

"Who is Mrs Trentham?" Cathy asked abruptly. Simon swung round to face her, so she added awkwardly, "I heard Becky mention her name to you a few minutes after the sale was over and that man in the tweed jacket who made such a fuss had disappeared."

Simon didn't answer her question for some time, as if he were weighing up what he should say. Two dry dishes later he began.

"It goes back a long way, even before my time. And don't forget I was at Sotheby's with Becky for five years before she asked me to join her at Trumper's. To be honest, I'm not sure why she and Mrs Trentham loathe each other quite so much, but what I do know is that Mrs Trentham's son Guy and Sir Charles served in the same regiment during the First World War, and that Guy Trentham was somehow involved with that painting of the Virgin Mary and Child that had to be withdrawn from the sale. The only other piece of information that I've picked up over the years is that Guy Trentham disappeared off to Australia soon after . . . hey, that was one of my finest coffee cups."

"I'm so sorry," said Cathy. "How clumsy of me." She bent down and started picking up the little pieces of china that were scattered over the kitchen floor. "Where can I find another one?"

"In the china department of Trumper's," said Simon. "They're about two shillings each." Cathy laughed. "Just take my advice," he added. "Remember that the older staff have a golden rule about Mrs Trentham."

Cathy stopped gathering the pieces.

"They don't mention her name in front of Becky unless

she raises the subject. And never refer to the name of Trentham in the presence of Sir Charles. If you did, I think he'd sack you on the spot."

"I'm not likely to be given the chance," Cathy said. "I've never even met him. In fact, the nearest I've been to the man was watching him in the seventh row at the Italian sale."

"Well, at least we can do something about that," said Simon. "How would you like to accompany me to a house-warming party the Trumpers are giving next Thursday at their new home in Eaton Square?"

"Are you serious?"

"I certainly am," replied Simon. "Anyway, I don't think Sir Charles would altogether approve of my taking Julian."

"Mightn't they consider it somewhat presumptuous for such a junior member of staff to turn up on the arm of the head of the department?"

"Not Sir Charles. He doesn't know what the word 'presumptuous' means."

Cathy spent many hours during her lunch breaks poking around the dress shops in Chelsea before she selected what she considered was the appropriate outfit for the Trumpers' house-warming party. Her final choice was a sunflower yellow dress with a large sash around the waist which the assistant who served her described as suitable for a cocktail party. Cathy became fearful at the last minute that its length, or lack of length, might be a little too daring for such a grand occasion. However, when Simon came to pick her up at 135 his immediate comment was "You'll be a sensation, I promise you." His unreserved assurance made her feel more confident – at least until they arrived on the top step of the Trumpers' home in Eaton Square.

As Simon knocked on the door of his employers' residence, Cathy only hoped that it wasn't too obvious that she had never been invited to such a beautiful house before. However, she lost all her inhibitions the moment the butler invited them inside. Her eyes immediately settled on the feast that awaited her. While others drank from the seemingly endless bottles of champagne and helped themselves from the passing trays of canapés, she turned her attention elsewhere and even began to climb the staircase, savouring each of the rare delicacies one by one.

First came a Courbet, a still life of magnificent rich reds, oranges and greens; then a Picasso of two doves surrounded by pink blossom, their beaks almost touching; after a further step her eyes fell on a Pissarro of an old woman carrying a bundle of hay, dominated by different shades of green. But she gasped when she first saw the Sisley, a stretch of the Seine with every touch of pastel shading being made to count.

"That's *my* favourite," said a voice from behind her. Cathy turned to see a tall, tousle-haired young man give her a grin that must have made many people return his smile. His dinner jacket didn't quite fit, his bow tie needed adjusting and he lounged on the banisters as if without their support he might collapse completely.

"Quite beautiful," she admitted. "When I was younger I used to try and paint a little myself, and it was Sisley who finally convinced me I shouldn't bother."

"Why?"

Cathy sighed. "Sisley completed that picture when he was seventeen and still at school."

"Good heavens," the young man said. "An expert in our presence." Cathy smiled at her new companion. "Perhaps we should sneak a look at some more works on the upper corridor?"

"Do you think Sir Charles would mind?"

"Wouldn't have thought so," the young man replied. "After all, what's the point of being a collector if other people are never given the chance to admire what you've acquired?"

Buoyed up by his confidence Cathy mounted another step. "Magnificent," she said. "An early Sickert. They hardly ever come on the market."

"You obviously work in an art gallery."

"I work at Trumper's," Cathy said proudly. "Number 1 Chelsea Terrace. And you?"

"I sort of work for Trumper's myself," he admitted. Out of the corner of her eye, Cathy saw Sir Charles appearing from a room on the upstairs landing – her first close encounter with the chairman. Like Alice, she wanted to disappear through a keyhole, but her companion remained unperturbed, seemingly quite at home.

Her host smiled at Cathy as he came down the stairs. "Hello," he said once he'd reached them. "I'm Charlie Trumper and I've already heard all about you, young lady. I saw you at the Italian sale, of course, and Becky tells me that you're doing a superb job. By the way, congratulations on the catalogue."

"Thank you, sir," said Cathy, unsure what else she should say as the chairman continued on down the stairs, delivering a rat-a-tat-tat of sentences while ignoring her companion.

"I see you've already met my son," Sir Charles added as he looked back towards her. "Don't be taken in by his donnish façade; he's every bit as much of a rogue as his father. Show her the Bonnard, Daniel." With this Sir Charles disappeared into the drawing room.

"Ah yes, the Bonnard. Father's pride and joy," said Daniel. "I can think of no better way of luring a girl into the bedroom."

"You're Daniel Trumper?"

"No. Raffles, the well-known art thief," Daniel said as he took Cathy's hand and guided her up the stairs and on into his parents' room.

"Well – what about that?" he asked.

"Stunning," was all Cathy could think of saying as she stared up at the vast Bonnard nude – of his mistress Maria drying herself – that hung above the double bed.

"Father's immensely proud of that particular lady," Daniel explained. "As he never stops reminding us, he only paid three hundred guineas for her. Almost as good as the . . ." but Daniel didn't complete the sentence.

"He has excellent taste."

"The best untrained eye in the business, Mother always says. And as he's selected every picture that hangs in this house, who's to argue with her?"

"Your mother chose none of them?"

"Certainly not. My mother's by nature a seller, while my father's a buyer, a combination unequalled since Duveen and Berenson cornered the art market."

"Those two should have ended up in gaol," said Cathy.

"Whereas," said Daniel, "I suspect my father will end up in the same place as Duveen." Cathy laughed. "And now I think we ought to go back downstairs and grab some food before it all disappears."

Once they entered the dining room Cathy watched as Daniel walked over to a table on the far side of the room and switched round two of the place cards.

"Well, I'll be blowed, Miss Ross," Daniel said, pulling back a chair for her as other guests searched for their places. "After all that unnecessary banter, I find we're sitting next to each other."

Cathy smiled as she sat down beside him and watched a rather shy-looking girl circle the table desperately hunting for her place card. Soon Daniel was answering all her questions about Cambridge while he in turn wanted to know everything about Melbourne, a city he had never visited, he told her. Inevitably the question arose, "And what do your parents do?" Cathy replied without hesitation, "I don't know. I'm an orphan."

Daniel smiled. "Then we're made for each other."

"Why's that?"

"I'm the son of a fruit and veg man and a baker's daughter from Whitechapel. An orphan from Melbourne, you say? You'll certainly be a step up the social ladder for me, that's for sure."

Cathy laughed as Daniel recalled his parents' early careers, and as the evening went on she even began to feel this might be the first man she would be willing to talk to about her somewhat unexplained and unexplainable background.

When the last course had been cleared away and they sat lingering over their coffee, Cathy noticed that the shy girl was now standing immediately behind her chair. Daniel rose to introduce her to Marjorie Carpenter, a mathematics don from Girton. It became obvious that she was Daniel's guest for the evening and had been surprised if not a little disappointed to find that she had not been seated next to him at dinner.

The three of them chatted about life at Cambridge until the Marchioness of Wiltshire banged a spoon on the table to attract everyone's attention, then made a seemingly impromptu speech. When she finally called for a toast they all stood and raised their glasses to Trumper's. The marchioness then presented Sir Charles with a silver cigar case in the form of a scale model of Trumper's and from the expression on his face it obviously brought their host considerable delight. After a witty, and Cathy suspected not impromptu, speech, Sir Charles resumed his place.

"I ought to be going," Cathy said a few minutes later. "I have an early start in the morning. It was nice to have met you, Daniel," she added, sounding suddenly formal. They shook hands like strangers.

"Talk to you soon," he said as Cathy went over to thank her hosts for what she told them had been a memorable evening. She left on her own, but not before she had checked that Simon was deep in conversation with a fair-haired young man who had recently come to work in rugs and carpets.

She walked slowly back from Eaton Square to Chelsea Terrace, savouring every moment of the evening, and was upstairs in her little flat above Number 135 a few minutes after midnight, feeling not unlike Cinderella.

As she began to undress, Cathy mused over how much she had enjoyed the party, especially Daniel's company and the joy of seeing so many of her favourite artists. She wondered if . . . Her thoughts were interrupted by the sound of a phone ringing.

As the time was now well past midnight she picked up the receiver assuming the caller must have dialled a wrong number.

"Said I'd talk to you soon," said a voice.

"Go to bed, you chump."

"I'm already in bed. Talk to you again in the morning," he added. She heard a click.

Daniel telephoned a little after eight the following morning.

"I've only just got out of the bath," she told him.

"Then you must be looking like Maria. I'd better come over and select a towel for you."

"I already have a towel safely wrapped round me, thank you."

"Pity," said Daniel. "I'm rather good at drying up. But failing that," he added before she could reply, "would you join me at Trinity on Saturday? They're holding a college feast. We only have a couple a term, so if you turn the invitation down there's no hope of seeing me again for another three months."

"In which case I'll accept. But only because I haven't had a feast since I left school."

The following Friday, having taken Saturday off from work, Cathy travelled up to Cambridge by train to find Daniel standing on the platform waiting for her. Although Trinity High Table has been known to intimidate the most confident of guests, Cathy felt quite at ease as she sat among the dons. Nevertheless she couldn't help wondering how so many survived to old age if they ate and drank like this regularly.

"Man cannot live by bread alone," was Daniel's only explanation during the seven-course meal. She imagined that the orgy must have ended when they were invited back to the master's lodge only to find she was being offered even more savouries, accompanied by a port decanter that circled endlessly and never seemed to settle or empty. She eventually escaped, but not before the clock on Trinity tower had struck midnight. Daniel escorted her to a guest room on the far side of Great Court and suggested that they might attend matins at King's the following morning.

"I'm so glad you didn't recommend I make an appearance at breakfast," said Cathy as Daniel gave her a kiss on the cheek before saying goodnight.

The little guest room that Daniel had booked Cathy into was even smaller than her digs above 135, but she fell asleep the moment she placed her head on the pillow and was woken only by a peal of bells that she assumed must be coming from King's College Chapel.

Daniel and Cathy reached the chapel door only moments before the choristers began their crocodile procession down the nave. The singing seemed even more moving than on the gramophone record that Cathy possessed, with only the choristers' pictures on the sleeve to hint what the real experience might be like.

Once the blessing had been given Daniel suggested a walk along the Backs "to get rid of any left-over cobwebs". He took her hand, not releasing it again until they had returned to Trinity an hour later for a modest lunch.

During the afternoon he showed her round the Fitzwilliam Museum, where Cathy was mesmerised by Goya's *Devil Eating the Children*. "Bit like Trinity High Table," suggested Daniel before they walked over to the Queens', where they listened to a student string quartet give a recital of a Bach fugue. By the time they left, the lights along Silver Street had started flickering.

"No supper, please," begged Cathy in mock protest as they strolled back across the Mathematical Bridge.

Daniel chuckled and, after they had collected her case from Trinity, drove her slowly back to London in his little MG.

"Thank you for a wonderful weekend," said Cathy once Daniel had parked outside 135. "In fact, 'wonderful' is quite inadequate to describe the last two days."

Daniel kissed her gently on the cheek. "Let's do it again next weekend," he suggested.

"Not a hope," said Cathy. "That is, if you meant it when you claimed you liked thin women."

"All right, let's try the whole thing without the food and perhaps even have a game of tennis this time. It may be the only way I'll ever find out the standard of the Melbourne University 2nd VI."

Cathy laughed. "And would you also thank your mother for that superb party last Thursday? It's been a truly memorable week."

"I would, but you'll probably see her before I do."

"Aren't you staying overnight with your parents?"

"No. I must get back to Cambridge – got supervisions to give at nine tomorrow."

"But I could have taken the train."

"And I would have had two hours less of your company," he said as he waved goodbye.

CHAPTER 41

The first time they slept together, in his uncomfortable single bed in his comfortable little room, Cathy knew she wanted to spend the rest of her life with Daniel. She just wished he wasn't the son of Sir Charles Trumper.

She begged him not to tell his parents that they were seeing each other so regularly. She was determined to prove herself at Trumper's, she explained, and didn't want any favours because she was going out with the boss's son.

After the silver sale, her coup over the man in the yellow tie and later her tip-off to the journalist from the *Telegraph*, she began to feel more confident about letting the Trumpers know she had fallen in love with their only child.

On the Monday following the silver sale, Becky invited Cathy to join the management board of the auction house, which up until then had consisted of only Simon, Peter Fellowes – the head of research – and Becky herself.

Becky also asked Cathy to prepare the catalogue for the autumn Impressionist sale and take on several other responsibilities, including overall supervision of the front counter. "Next stop, a place on the main board," teased Simon.

She phoned Daniel to tell him the news later that morning.

"Does that mean we can at last stop fooling my parents?"

* * *

When Daniel's father telephoned him some weeks later to say he and his mother wanted to come down to Cambridge, as they needed to discuss something "rather important" with him, Daniel invited them both to have tea in his rooms on the following Sunday, warning them he too had something "rather important" to tell them.

Daniel and Cathy spoke to each other on the telephone every day that week and she began to wonder if it might not be wise at least to warn Daniel's parents that she would also be present when they came to tea. Daniel wouldn't hear of it, claiming that it was not often he had the chance of stealing a march on his father and he had no intention of letting the moment pass without the full satisfaction of seeing their surprised faces.

"And I'll let you into another secret," said Daniel. "I've applied for a post of Professor of Mathematics at King's College, London."

"That's some sacrifice you're making, Doctor Trumper," said Cathy, "because once you come to live in London I'm never going to be able to feed you the way they do at Trinity."

"Good news. That can only mean fewer visits to my tailor."

The tea that Daniel held in the rooms could not have been a happier occasion, Cathy felt, although at first Becky seemed on edge and, if anything, became even more anxious following an unexplained telephone call from someone called Mr Baverstock.

Sir Charles's delight at the news that she and Daniel planned to be married during the Easter vacation was so obviously genuine and Becky was positively overjoyed at the whole idea of having Cathy as a daughter-in-law. Charlie surprised Cathy when he suddenly changed the subject and enquired who had painted the watercolour that hung above Daniel's desk.

"Cathy," Daniel told him. "An artist in the family at last."

"You can paint as well, young lady?" Charlie asked in disbelief.

"She certainly can," said Daniel, looking towards the watercolour. "My engagement present," he explained. "What's more, it's the only original Cathy has painted since she came to England, so it's priceless."

"Will you paint one for me?" asked Charlie, after he had studied the little watercolour more carefully.

"I'd be delighted to," Cathy replied. "But where would you hang it? In the garage?"

After tea the four of them all walked along the Backs and Cathy was disappointed that Daniel's parents seemed quite anxious to return to London and felt unable to join them for evening chapel.

When they had returned from evensong they made love in Daniel's little bed and Cathy warned him that Easter might not be a moment too soon.

"What do you mean?" he asked.

"I think my period's already a week overdue."

Daniel was so overjoyed by the news he wanted to phone his parents immediately and share his excitement with them.

"Don't be silly," said Cathy. "Nothing's confirmed yet. I only hope that your mother and father won't be too appalled when they find out."

"Appalled? They're hardly in a position to be. They didn't even get married until the week after I was born."

"How do you know that?"

"Checked the date on my birth certificate in Somerset House against the date of their marriage certificate. Fairly simple really. It seems to begin with no one was willing to admit I belonged to anyone."

That one statement convinced Cathy that she must finally clear up any possibility of her being related to Mrs Trentham before they were married. Although Daniel had taken her mind off the problem of her parentage for over a year, she couldn't face the Trumpers thinking at some later date that she had set out to deceive them or worse, was somehow related to the woman they loathed above all others. Now that Cathy had unwittingly discovered where Mrs Trentham lived she resolved to write a letter to the lady just as soon as she was back in London.

She scribbled out a rough copy on Sunday evening and rose early the following morning to pen a final draft:

135 Chelsea Terrace
London SW3

November 27th, 1950

Dear Mrs. Trentham,

I write to you as a complete stranger in the hope that you might be able to help me to clear up a dilemma that I have been facing for several years.

I was born in Melbourne, Australia and have never known who my parents are as I was abandoned at an early age. I was in fact brought up in an orphanage called St. Hilda's. The only memento that I have of my father's existence is a miniature Military Cross which he gave me when I was a small child. The initials "G.F.T." are inscribed down one arm.

The curator of the Royal Fusiliers Museum at Hounslow has confirmed that the medal was awarded to a Captain Guy Francis Trentham on July 22nd 1918 following his brave action at the second battle of the Marne.

Are you by any chance related to Guy, and could he be my father? I would appreciate any information you may be able to give me on this matter and I apologise for intruding on your privacy.

I look forward to hearing from you.

Yours sincerely,

Cathy Ross

Cathy dropped the envelope in the post-box on the corner of Chelsea Terrace before going into work. After years of hoping to find someone to whom she was related, Cathy found it ironic that she now wanted that same person to deny her.

The announcement of Cathy's engagement to Daniel Trumper was on the court and social page of *The Times* the following morning. Everyone at Number 1 seemed delighted by the news. Simon toasted Cathy's health in champagne during the lunch break and told everyone, "It's a Trumper plot to be certain we don't lose her to Sotheby's or Christie's." Everyone clapped except Simon who whispered in her ear, "And you're exactly the right person to put us in the same league." Funny how some people think of possibilities for you, Cathy thought, even before you consider them for yourself.

On Thursday morning Cathy picked up off the front door mat a purple envelope with her name written in spidery handwriting. She nervously opened the letter to find it contained two sheets of thick paper of the same colour. The contents perplexed her, but at the same time brought her considerable relief.

19 Chester Square
London
SW1

November 29th, 1950

Dear Miss Ross,

Thank you for your letter of last Monday, but I fear I can be of little assistance to you with your enquiries. I had two sons, the younger of whom is Nigel, who has recently separated. His wife now resides in Dorset, with my only grandson, Giles Raymond, aged two.

My elder son was indeed Guy Francis Trentham, who was awarded the Military Cross at the second battle of the Marne, but he died of tuberculosis in 1922 after a long illness. He never married and left no dependants.

The miniature version of his MC went missing soon after Guy had paid a fleeting visit to distant relatives in Melbourne. I am happy to learn of its reappearance after all these years, and would be most grateful if you felt able to return the medal to me at your earliest convenience. I feel sure you would no longer wish to hold on to a family heirloom now that you are fully acquainted with its origins.

Yours sincerely

Ethel Trentham

Cathy was delighted to discover that Guy Trentham had died the year before she was born. That meant it was quite impossible for her to be related to the man who had caused her future parents-in-law so much distress. The MC must somehow have got into the hands of whoever her father was, she concluded; on balance she felt she ought, however reluctantly, to return the medal to Mrs Trentham without delay.

After the revelations of Mrs Trentham's letter, Cathy was doubtful that she would ever be able to find out who her parents were, as she had no immediate plans to return to Australia now that Daniel was so much part of her future. In any case, she had begun to feel that further pursuit of her father had become somewhat pointless.

As Cathy had already told Daniel on the day they met that she had no idea who her parents were, she travelled down to Cambridge that Saturday evening with a clear conscience. She was also relieved that her period had at last begun. As the train bumped over the points on its journey to the university city, Cathy could never remember feeling so happy. She fingered the little cross that hung around her neck now hanging from a gold chain Daniel had given her on her birthday. She was sad to be wearing the memento for the last time: she had already made the decision to send the medal back to Mrs Trentham following her weekend with Daniel.

The train drew into Cambridge station only a few minutes after its scheduled time of arrival.

Cathy picked up her small suitcase and strolled out on to the pavement, expecting to find Daniel parked and waiting for her in his MG: he had never once been late since the day they had met. She was disappointed to find no sign of him or his car, and even more surprised when twenty minutes later he still hadn't shown up. She walked back on to the station concourse and placed two pennies in the telephone box before dialling the number that went straight through to Daniel's room. The ringing tone went on and on, but she didn't need to press Button A because no one answered.

Puzzled by not being able to locate him, Cathy left the station once again and asked one of the drivers from the rank to take her to Trinity College.

When the taxi drove into New Court Cathy was even more bemused to discover Daniel's MG was parked in its usual space. She paid the fare and walked across the court to the now familiar staircase.

Cathy felt the least she could do was tease Daniel for failing to pick her up. Was this to be the sort of treatment she could expect once they were married? Was she now on the same level as any undergraduate who turned up without his weekly essay? She climbed the worn stone steps up to his room and knocked quietly on the door in case he still had a pupil with him. As there was no answer after a second knock, she pushed open the heavy wooden door, having decided that she would just have to wait around until he returned.

Her scream must have been heard by every resident on staircase C.

The first undergraduate to arrive on the scene found the prostrate body of a young woman lying face down in the middle of the floor. The student fell to his knees, dropped the books he had been carrying by her side and proceeded to be sick all over her. He took a deep breath, turned round as quickly as he could, and began to crawl back out of the study past an overturned chair. He was unable to look up again at the sight that had met him when he had first entered the room.

Doctor Trumper continued to swing gently from a beam in the centre of the room.

CHARLIE

1950-1964

CHAPTER 42

I couldn't sleep for three days. On the fourth morning, along with so many of Daniel's friends, colleagues and undergraduates, I attended his funeral service at Trinity Chapel. I somehow survived that ordeal and the rest of the week, thanks not least to Daphne's organising everything so calmly and efficiently. Cathy was unable to attend the service as they were still detaining her for observation at Addenbrooke's hospital.

I stood next to Becky as the choir sang "Fast Falls the Eventide". My mind drifted as I tried to reconstruct the events of the past three days and make some sort of sense of them. After Daphne had told me that Daniel had taken his own life – whoever selected her to break the news understood the meaning of the word compassion – I immediately drove up to Cambridge, having begged her not to tell Becky anything until I knew more of what had actually happened myself. By the time I arrived at Trinity Great Court some two hours later, Daniel's body had already been removed, and they had taken Cathy off to Addenbrooke's where she was not surprisingly still in a state of shock. The police inspector in charge of the case couldn't have been more considerate. Later, I visited the morgue and identified the body, thanking God that at least Becky hadn't experienced that ice-cold room as the last place she was alone with her son.

"*Lord, with me abide . . .*"

I told the police that I could think of no reason why Daniel should want to take his own life – that in fact he had just become engaged and I had never known him happier. The inspector then showed me the suicide note: a sheet of foolscap containing a single handwritten paragraph.

"They generally write one, you know," he said.

I didn't know.

I began to read Daniel's neat academic hand:

> Now that it's no longer possible for Cathy and me to marry, I have nothing left to live for. For God's sake take care of the child.
>
> Daniel

I must have repeated those twenty-eight words to myself over a hundred times and still I couldn't make any sense out of them. A week later the doctor confirmed in his report to the coroner that Cathy was not pregnant and had certainly not suffered a miscarriage. I returned to those words again and again. Was I missing some subtle inference, or was his final message something I could never hope to comprehend fully?

"*When other helpers fail . . .*"

A forensic expert later discovered some writing paper in the grate, but it had been burnt to a cinder and the black brittle remains yielded no clue. Then they showed me an envelope that the police believed the charred letter must have been sent in and asked if I could identify the writing. I studied the stiff, thin upright hand that had written the words "Doctor Daniel Trumper" in purple ink.

"No," I lied. The letter had been hand-delivered, the detective told me, some time earlier that afternoon by a man with a brown moustache and a tweed coat. This was all the undergraduate who caught sight of him could remember, except that he seemed to know his way around.

I asked myself what that evil old lady could possibly have written to Daniel that would have caused him to take his own life; I felt sure the discovery that Guy Trentham was his father would not have been sufficient for such a drastic course of action – especially as I knew that he and Mrs Trentham had already met and come to an agreement some three years before.

The police found one other letter on Daniel's desk. It was from the Provost of King's College, London, formally offering him a Chair in Mathematics.

"*And comforts flee . . .*"

After I had left the mortuary I drove on to Addenbrooke's hospital, where they allowed me to spend some time at Cathy's bedside. Although her eyes were open, they betrayed no recognition of me: for nearly an hour she simply stared blankly up at the ceiling while I stood there. When I realised there was nothing I could usefully do I left quietly. The senior psychiatrist, Doctor Stephen Atkins, came bustling out of his office and asked if I could spare him a moment.

The dapper, little man in a beautifully tailored suit and large bow tie explained that Cathy was suffering from psychogenic amnesia, sometimes known as hysterical amnesia, and that it could be some time before he was able to assess what her rate of recovery might be. I thanked him and added that I would keep in constant touch. I then drove slowly back to London.

"*Help of the helpless, O abide with me . . .*"

Daphne was waiting for me in my office and made no comment about the lateness of the hour, I tried to thank her for such endless kindness, but explained that I had to be the one who broke the news to Becky. God knows how I carried out that responsibility without mentioning the purple envelope with its tell-tale handwriting, but I did. Had I told Becky the full story I think she would have gone round to Chester Square that night and killed the woman there and then with her bare hands – I might even have assisted her.

They buried him amongst his own kind. The college chaplain, who must have carried out this particular duty so many times in the past, stopped to compose himself on three separation occasions.

"*In life, in death, O Lord, abide with me . . .*"

Becky and I visited Addenbrooke's together every day that week, but Doctor Atkins only confirmed that Cathy's condition remained unchanged; she had not yet spoken. Nevertheless, just the thought of her lying there alone needing our love gave us something else to worry about other than ourselves.

When we arrived back in London late on the Friday afternoon Arthur Selwyn was pacing up and down outside my office.

"Someone's broken into Cathy's flat, the lock's been forced," he said even before I had a chance to speak.

"But what could a thief possibly hope to find?"

"The police can't fathom that out either. Nothing seems to have been disturbed."

To the puzzle of what Mrs Trentham could have written to Daniel I added the mystery of what she could possibly want that belonged to Cathy. After checking over the little room myself I was none the wiser.

Becky and I continued to travel up and down to Cambridge every other day, and then midway through the third week Cathy finally spoke, haltingly to start with, then in bursts while grasping my hand. Then suddenly, without warning, she would go silent again. Sometimes she would rub her forefinger against her thumb just below her chin.

This puzzled even Doctor Atkins.

Doctor Atkins had since then, however, been able

to hold extensive conversations with Cathy on several occasions and had even started playing word games to probe her memory. It was his opinion that she had blotted out all recollection of anything connected with Daniel Trumper or with her early life in Australia. It was not uncommon in such cases, he assured us, and even gave the particular state of mind a fine Greek name.

"Should I try and get in touch with her tutor at the University of Melbourne? Or even talk to the staff of the Melrose Hotel – and see if they can throw any light on the problem?"

"No," he said, straightening his spotted bow tie. "Don't push her too hard and be prepared for that part of her mind to take some considerable time to recover."

I nodded my agreement.

"Back off" seemed to be Doctor Atkins' favourite expression. "And never forget your wife will be suffering the same trauma."

Seven weeks later they allowed us to take Cathy back to Eaton Square, where Becky had prepared a room for her. I had already transferred all Cathy's possessions from the little flat above the butcher's shop, still unsure if anything was missing following the break-in.

Becky had stored all Cathy's clothes neatly away in the wardrobe and drawers while trying to make the room look as lived in as possible. Some time before I had taken her watercolour of the Cam from above Daniel's desk and rehung it on the staircase between the Courbet and the Sisley. Yet when Cathy first walked up those stairs on the way to her new room, she passed her own painting without the slightest sign of recognition.

I enquired once again of Doctor Atkins if perhaps we should now write to the University of Melbourne and try to find out something about Cathy's past, but he still counselled against such a move, saying that she must be the one who came forward with any information, and then only when she felt able to do so, not as the result of any pressure from outside.

"But how long do you imagine it might be before her memory is fully restored?"

"Anything from fourteen days to fourteen years, from my experience."

I remember returning to Cathy's room that night, sitting on the end of her bed and holding her hand. I noticed with pleasure that a little colour had returned to her cheeks. She smiled and asked me for the first time how the "great barrow" was rumbling along.

"We've declared record profits," I told her. "But far more important, everyone wants to see you back at Number 1."

She thought about this for some time. Then quite simply she said, "I wish you were my father."

In February 1951 Nigel Trentham joined the board of Trumper's. He took his place next to Paul Merrick, to whom he gave a thin smile. I couldn't bring myself to look directly at him. He was a few years younger than me but I vainly considered no one round that table would have thought so.

The board meanwhile approved the expenditure of a further half a million pounds "to fill the gap", as Becky referred to the half-acre that had for ten years lain empty in the middle of Chelsea Terrace. "So at last Trumper's can all be housed under one roof," I declared. Trentham made no comment. My fellow-directors also agreed an allocation of one hundred thousand pounds to rebuild the Whitechapel Boys' Club which was to be renamed "The Dan Salmon Centre". I noticed Trentham whispered something in Merrick's ear.

In the event, inflation, strikes and escalating builders' costs caused the final bill for Trumper's to be nearer seven hundred and thirty thousand pounds than the estimated half-million. One outcome of this was to make it necessary for the company to offer a further rights issue in order to cover the extra expense. Another was that the building of the boys' club had to be postponed.

The rights issue was once again heavily oversubscribed, which was flattering for me personally, though I feared Mrs Trentham might be a major buyer of any new stock: I had no way of proving it. This dilution of my equity meant that I had to watch my personal holding in the company fall below forty per cent for the first time.

It was a long summer and as each day passed Cathy became a little stronger, Becky a little more communicative. Finally the doctor agreed that Cathy could return to Number 1. She came back to work the following Monday and Becky said it was almost as if she had never been away – except that no one ever mentioned the name of Daniel in her presence.

One evening, it must have been about a month later, I returned home from the office to find Cathy pacing up and down the hall. My immediate thoughts were that she must be agonising over the past. I couldn't have been more wrong.

"You've got your staffing policy all wrong," she said as I closed the door behind me.

"I beg your pardon, young lady?" I had not even been given enough time to shed my topcoat.

"It's all wrong," she repeated. "The Americans are saving thousands of dollars in their stores with time and motion studies while Trumper's are behaving as if they're still roaming around on the ark."

"Captive audience on the ark," I reminded her.

"Until it stopped raining," she replied. "Charlie, you must realise that the company could be saving at least eighty thousand a year on wages alone. I haven't been idle these last few weeks. In fact, I've put together a report to prove my point." She thrust a cardboard box into my arms and marched out of the room.

For over an hour after dinner I rummaged into the box and read through Cathy's preliminary findings. She had spotted an over-manning situation that we had all missed and characteristically explained in great detail how the situation could be dealt with without offending the unions.

Over breakfast the following morning Cathy continued to explain her findings to me as if I had never been to bed. "Are you still listening, Chairman?" she demanded. She always called me "Chairman" when she wanted to make a point. A ploy I felt sure she had picked up from Daphne.

"You're all talk," I told her, which caused even Becky to glance over the top of her paper.

"Do you want me to prove I'm right?" Cathy asked.

"Be my guest."

From that day on, whenever I carried out my morning rounds, I would invariably come across Cathy working on a different floor, questioning, watching or simply taking copious notes, often with a stop-watch in her other hand. I never asked her what she was up to and if she ever caught my eye all she would say was, "Good day, Chairman."

At weekends I could hear Cathy typing away in her room for hour after hour. Then, without warning, one morning at breakfast I discovered a thick file waiting for me in the place where I had hoped to find an egg, two rashers of bacon and the *Sunday Times*.

That afternoon I began reading through what Cathy had prepared for me. By the early evening I had come to the conclusion that the board must implement most of her recommendations without further delay.

I knew exactly what I wanted to do next but felt it needed Doctor Atkins' blessing. I phoned Addenbrooke's that evening and the ward sister kindly entrusted me with his home number. We spent over an hour on the phone. He had no fears for Cathy's future, he assured me, especially since she'd begun to remember little incidents from her past and was now even willing to talk about Daniel.

When I came down to breakfast the following morning I found Cathy sitting at the table waiting for me. She didn't say a word as I munched through my toast and marmalade pretending to be engrossed in the *Financial Times*.

"All right, I give in," she said.

"Better not," I warned her, without looking up from my paper. "Because you're item number seven on the agenda for next month's board meeting."

"But who's going to present my case?" asked Cathy, sounding anxious.

"Not me, that's for sure," I replied. "And I can't think of anyone else who'd be willing to do so."

For the next fortnight whenever I retired to bed I became aware when passing Cathy's room that the typing had stopped. I was so filled with curiosity that once I even peered through the half-open bedroom door. Cathy stood facing a mirror, by her side was a large white board resting on an easel covered in a mass of coloured pins and dotted arrows.

"Go away," she said, without even turning round. I realised there was nothing for it but to wait until the board was due to meet.

Doctor Atkins had warned me that the ordeal of having to present her case in public might turn out to be too much for the girl and I was to get her home if she began to show any signs of stress. "Be sure you don't push her too far," were his final words.

"I won't let that happen," I promised him.

That Thursday morning the board members were all seated in their places round the table by three minutes to ten. The meeting began on a quiet note, with apologies for absence, followed by the acceptance of the minutes of the last meeting. We somehow still managed to keep Cathy waiting for over an hour, because when we came to item number three on the agenda – a rubber-stamp decision to renew the company's insurance policy with the Prudential – Nigel Trentham used the opportunity simply as an excuse to irritate me – hoping, I suspected, that I would eventually lose my temper. I might have done, if he hadn't so obviously wanted me to.

"I think the time has come for a change, Mr Chairman," he said. "I suggest we transfer our business to Legal and General."

I stared down the left-hand side of the table to focus on the man whose very presence always brought back memories of Guy Trentham and what he might have looked like in late middle age. The younger brother wore a smart well-tailored double-breasted suit that successfully disguised his weight problem. However, there was nothing that could disguise the double chin or balding pate.

"I must point out to the board," I began, "that Trumper's have been with the Prudential for over thirty years. And what is more, they have never let the company down in the past. Just as important, Legal and General are highly unlikely to be able to offer more favourable terms."

"But they're in possession of two per cent of the company's stock," Trentham pointed out.

"The Pru still have five per cent," I reminded my fellow-directors, aware that once again Trentham hadn't done his homework. The argument might have been lobbed backwards and forwards for hours like a Drobny–Fraser tennis match had Daphne not intervened and called for a vote.

Although Trentham lost by seven to three, the altercation served to remind everyone round that table what his long-term purpose must be. For the past eighteen months Trentham had, with the help of his mother's money, been building up his shareholding in the company to a position I estimated to be around fourteen per cent. This would have been controllable had I not been painfully aware that the Hardcastle Trust also held a further seventeen per cent of our stock – stock which had originally been intended for Daniel but which would on the death of Mrs Trentham pass automatically to Sir Raymond's next of kin. Although Nigel Trentham lost the vote, he showed no sign of distress as he rearranged his papers, casting an aside to Paul Merrick who was seated on his left. He obviously felt confident that time was on his side.

"Item seven," I said and leaning over to Jessica asked if she would invite Miss Ross to join us. When Cathy entered the room every man around that table stood. Even Trentham half rose from his place.

Cathy placed two boards on the easel that had already been set up for her, one full of charts, the other covered in statistics. She turned to face us. I greeted her with a warm smile.

"Good morning, ladies and gentlemen," she said. She paused and checked her notes. "I should like to begin by . . ."

She may have started somewhat hesitantly, but she soon got into her stride as she explained, point by point, why the company's staffing policy was outdated and the steps we should take to rectify the situation as quickly as possible. These included early retirement for men of sixty and women of fifty-five; the leasing of shelf space, even whole floor sections, to recognised brand names, which would produce a guaranteed cash-flow without financial risk to Trumper's, as each lessee would be responsible for supplying their own staff; and a larger percentage discount on merchandise for any firms who were hoping to place orders with us for the first time. The presentation took Cathy about forty minutes, and when she concluded it was several moments before anyone round the table spoke.

If her initial presentation was good, her handling of the questions that followed was even better. She dealt with all the banking problems Tim Newman and Paul Merrick could throw at her, as well as the trade union anxieties Arthur Selwyn raised. As for Nigel Trentham, she handled him with a calm efficiency that I was only too painfully aware I could never equal. When Cathy left the boardroom an hour later all the men rose again except Trentham, who stared down at the report in front of him.

As I walked up the path that evening Cathy was on the doorstep waiting to greet me.

"Well?"

"Well?"

"Don't tease, Charlie," she scolded.

"You were appointed to be our new personnel director," I told her, grinning. For a moment even she was speechless.

"Now you've opened this can of worms, young lady," I added as I walked past her, "the board rather expects you to sort the problem out."

Cathy was so obviously thrilled by my news that I felt for the first time perhaps Daniel's tragic death might be behind us. I phoned Doctor Atkins that evening to tell him not only how Cathy had fared but that, as a result of her presentation, she had been elected to the board. However, what I didn't tell either of them was that I had been forced to agree to another of Trentham's nominations to the board in order to ensure that her appointment went through without a vote being called for.

From the day Cathy arrived at the boardroom table it was clear for all to see that she was a serious contender to succeed me as chairman and no longer simply a bright girl from Becky's fold. However, I was well aware that Cathy's advancement could only be achieved while Trentham remained unable to gain control of fifty-one per cent of Trumper's shares. I also realised that the only way he could hope to do that was by making a public bid for the company, which I accepted could well become possible once he got his hands on the money held by the Hardcastle Trust. For the first time in my life I wanted Mrs Trentham to live long enough to allow me to build the company to such a position of strength that even the Trust money would prove inadequate for Nigel Trentham to mount a successful takeover bid.

On 2 June 1953 Queen Elizabeth was crowned, four days after two men from different parts of the Commonwealth conquered Everest. Winston Churchill best summed it up when he said: "Those who have read the history of the first Elizabethan era must surely look forward with anticipation to participating in the second."

I took up the Prime Minister's challenge and Cathy threw all her energy into the personnel project the board had entrusted her with, and was able to show a saving of forty-nine thousand pounds in wages during 1953 and a further twenty-one thousand pounds in the first half of 1954. By the end of that fiscal year I felt she knew more about the running of Trumper's at staff level than anyone around that table, myself included.

During 1955 overseas sales began to fall sharply, and as Cathy no longer seemed to be extended and I was keen for her to gain experience of other departments I asked her to sort out the problems of our international department.

She took on her new position with the same enthusiasm with which she tackled everything, but during the next two years began to clash with Nigel Trentham over a number of issues, including a policy to return the difference to any customer who could prove he had paid less for a standard item when shopping at one of our rivals. Trentham argued that Trumper's customers were not interested in some imagined difference in price that could be compared with a lesser-known store, but only in quality and service, to which Cathy replied, "It isn't the customers' responsibility to be concerned with the balance-sheet, it's the board's on behalf of our shareholders."

On another occasion Trentham came near to accusing Cathy of being a communist when she suggested a "workers' share participation scheme" which she felt would create company loyalty that only the Japanese had fully understood – a country, she explained, where it was not uncommon for a company to retain ninety-eight per cent of its staff from womb to tomb. Even I was unsure about this particular idea, but Becky warned me in private that I was beginning to sound like a "fuddy duddy", which I assumed was some modern term not to be taken as a compliment.

When Legal and General failed to get our insurance business they sold their two per cent holding outright to Nigel Trentham. From that moment I became even more anxious that he might eventually get his hands on enough stock to take over the company. He also proposed another nomination to the board which, thanks to Paul Merrick seconding, was accepted.

"I should have secured that land thirty-five years ago for a mere four thousand pounds," I told Becky.

"As you have reminded us so often in the past, and what's worse," Becky reminded me, "is that Mrs Trentham is now more dangerous to us dead than alive."

Trumper's took the arrival of Elvis Presley, Teddy boys, stilettos and teenagers all in its stride. "The customers may have changed, but our standards must not be allowed to," I continually reminded the board.

In 1960 the company declared a seven hundred and fifty-seven thousand pound net profit, a fourteen per cent return on capital, and a year later went on to top this achievement by being granted a Royal Warrant from the monarch. I instructed that the House of Windsor's coat of arms should be hung above the main entrance to remind the public that the Queen shopped at the barrow on a regular basis.

I couldn't pretend that I had ever seen Her Majesty carrying one of our familiar blue bags with its silver motif of a barrow, or spotted her as she travelled up and down the escalators during peak hours, but we still received regular telephone calls from the Palace when they found themselves running short of supplies: which only proved yet again my old granpa's theory that an apple is an apple whoever bites it.

The highlight of 1961 for me was when Becky finally opened the Dan Salmon Centre in Whitechapel Road – another building that had run considerably over cost. However, I didn't regret one penny of the expenditure – despite Merrick's niggling criticism – as I watched the next generation of East End boys and girls swimming, boxing, weightlifting and playing squash, a game I just couldn't get the hang of.

Whenever I went to see West Ham play soccer on a Saturday afternoon, I would always drop in to the new club on my way home, and watch the African, West Indian and Asian children – the new East Enders – battle against each other just as determinedly as we had done against the Irish and Eastern European immigrants.

"The old order changeth, yielding place to new, And God fulfils himself in many ways, Lest one good custom should corrupt the world." Tennyson's words, chiselled in the stone on the archway above the centre, brought my mind back to Mrs Trentham, who was never far from my thoughts, especially while her three representatives sat around the boardroom table eager to carry out her bidding. Nigel, who now resided at Chester Square, seemed happy to wait for everything to fall into place before he marshalled his troops ready for the attack.

I continued to pray that Mrs Trentham would live to a grand old age as I still needed more time to prepare some blocking process to ensure that her son could never take over the company.

It was Daphne who first warned me that Mrs Trentham had taken to her bed and was receiving regular visits from the family GP. Nigel Trentham still managed to keep a smile on his face during those months of waiting.

Without warning, on 7 March 1962, Mrs Trentham, aged eighty-nine, died.

"Peacefully in her sleep," Daphne informed me.

CHAPTER 43

Daphne attended Mrs Trentham's funeral, "Just to be certain that the wretched woman really was buried," she explained to Charlie later, "though it wouldn't surprise me if she found some way of rising from the dead." She went on to warn Charlie that Nigel had been overheard, even before the body had been lowered into the ground, telling everyone that we should expect thunderbolts as soon as the board met again. He only had a few days to wait.

That first Tuesday of the following month Charlie checked around the boardroom table to see that every director was present. He could sense they were all waiting to see who would strike first. Nigel Trentham and his two colleagues wore black ties like some official badge of office, reminding the board of their newly acquired status. In contrast, for the first time in Charlie's memory, Mr Baverstock wore a garish pastel-coloured tie.

Charlie had already worked out that Trentham would wait until item number six – a proposal to expand the banking facilities on the ground floor – before he made any move. The original scheme had been one of Cathy's brainchilds, and soon after returning from one of her monthly trips to the States she had presented a detailed proposal to the board. Although the new department had experienced some teething problems by the end of its second year it was just about breaking even.

The first half-hour was peaceful enough as Charlie took

the board through items one to five. But when he called for, "Item number six. The expansion of . . ."

"Let's close the bank and cut our losses," were Trentham's opening words even before Charlie had been given the chance to offer an opinion.

"For what reason?" asked Cathy defiantly.

"Because we're not bankers," said Trentham. "We're shopkeepers – or barrow pushers, as our chairman so often likes to remind us. In any case, it would give us a saving on expenditure of nearly thirty thousand pounds a year."

"But the bank is just beginning to pay its way," said Cathy. "We should be thinking of expanding the facilities, not curtailing them. And with profits in mind, who knows how much money cashed on the premises is then spent on the premises?"

"Yes, but look at the amount of extra counter space the banking hall is taking up."

"In return we give our customers a valuable service."

"And lose money hand over fist by not using the space for more profitable lines of business," fired back Trentham.

"Like what, for example?" said Cathy. "Just tell me one other department that would provide a more useful service for our customers and at the same time show a better return on our investment. Do that and I'll be the first to agree we should close down the banking hall."

"We're not a service industry. It's our duty to show a decent return on capital for our shareholders," said Trentham. "I demand a vote on this," he added, not bothering to rebut Cathy's arguments any further.

Trentham lost the vote by six to three and Charlie assumed after such an outcome they would then pass on to item number seven – a proposed staff outing to the film of *West Side Story*, playing at the Odeon, Leicester Square. However, once Jessica Allen had recorded the names for the minutes, Nigel Trentham rose quickly to his feet and said, "I have an announcement to make, Mr Chairman."

"Wouldn't it be more appropriate under 'Any other business'?" asked Charlie innocently.

"I will no longer be here when you come to discuss any other business, Mr Chairman," said Trentham coldly. He proceeded to move a piece of paper from an inside pocket, unfolded it and began reading from what was obviously a prepared script.

"I feel it is my duty to inform the board," he stated, "that within a few weeks I will be the sole owner of thirty-three per cent of Trumper's shares. When we next meet, I shall be insisting that several changes be made to the structure of the company, not least in the composition of those presently seated around this table." He stopped to stare at Cathy before he added, "I intend to leave now, in order that you can discuss more fully the implications of my statement."

He pushed back his chair as Daphne said, "I'm not quite sure I fully understand what you're suggesting, Mr Trentham."

Trentham hesitated for a moment before he replied, "Then I shall have to explain my position more fully, Lady Wiltshire."

"How kind of you."

"At the next board meeting," he continued unabashed, "I shall allow my name to be proposed and seconded as chairman of Trumper's. Should I fail to be elected, I shall immediately resign from the board and issue a press statement of my intention to make a full takeover bid for the remaining shares of the company. You must all be aware by now that I will have the necessary facility to mount such a challenge. As I only require a further eighteen per cent of the stock to become the majority shareholder, I suggest it might be wise for those of you who are currently directors to face up to the inevitable and offer your resignations in order to avoid the embarrassment of being dismissed. I look forward to seeing one or two of you again at next month's board meeting." He and his two colleagues rose and followed him out of the room.

The silence that followed was broken only by another question from Daphne.

"What's the collective noun for a group of shits?"

Everybody laughed, except Baverstock, who said under his breath, "A heap."

"So, now we've been given our battle orders," said Charlie. "Let's hope we all have the stomach for a fight." Turning to Mr Baverstock he asked, "Can you advise the board on the present position concerning those shares currently held by the Hardcastle Trust?"

The old man raised his head slowly and looked up at Charlie. "No, Mr Chairman, I cannot. Indeed, I'm sorry to have to inform the board that I, too, must tender my resignation."

"But why?" asked Becky, aghast. "You've always supported us in the past through thick and thin."

"I must apologise, Lady Trumper, but I am not at liberty to disclose my reasons."

"Couldn't you possibly reconsider your position?" Charlie asked.

"No, sir," Baverstock replied firmly.

Charlie immediately closed the meeting, despite everyone trying to talk at once, and quickly followed Baverstock out of the boardroom.

"What made you resign?" Charlie asked. "After all these years?"

"Perhaps we could meet and discuss my reasons tomorrow, Sir Charles?"

"Of course. But just tell me why you felt it necessary to leave us at exactly the time when I most need you."

Mr Baverstock stopped in his tracks. "Sir Raymond anticipated this might happen," he said quietly. "And instructed me accordingly."

"I don't understand."

"That is why we should meet tomorrow, Sir Charles."

"Do you want me to bring Becky along?"

Mr Baverstock considered this suggestion for some time before saying, "I think not. If I am to break a confidence for the first time in forty years, I'd prefer to have no other witnesses present."

When Charlie arrived at the offices of Baverstock, Dickens and Cobb the following morning, the senior partner was standing at the door waiting to greet him. Although Charlie had never once been late for an appointment with Mr Baverstock in the fourteen years they had known each other, he was touched by the old-world courtesy the solicitor always extended to him.

"Good morning, Sir Charles," said Baverstock before guiding his guest along the corridor to his office. Charlie was surprised to be offered a seat near the unlit fire rather than his usual place on the other side of the partner's desk. There wasn't a clerk or secretary in attendance on this occasion to keep a record of the meeting and Charlie also noticed that the phone on Mr Baverstock's desk had been taken off the hook. He sat back, realising that this was not going to be a short meeting.

"Many years ago when I was a young man," began Baverstock, "and I sat my pupil's exams, I swore to keep a code of confidentiality when dealing with my clients' private affairs. I think I can safely say that I have honoured that undertaking throughout my professional life. However, one of my clients, as you well know, was Sir Raymond Hardcastle and he – " There was a knock on the door and a young girl entered, carrying a tray bearing two cups of hot coffee and a sugar bowl.

"Thank you, Miss Burrows," said Baverstock as one of the cups was placed in front of him. He did not continue with his exposition until the door was closed behind her. "Where was I, old fellow?" Baverstock asked, as he dropped a sugar lump into his cup.

"Your client, Sir Raymond."

"Oh, yes," said Baverstock. "Now, Sir Raymond left a will of which you may well feel you are cognisant. What you could not know, however, is that he attached a letter to that document. It has no legal standing, as it was addressed to me in a personal capacity."

Charlie's coffee lay untouched as he listened intently to what Baverstock had to say. "It is because that letter is not a legal document but a private communication between old friends that I have decided you should be a party to its contents."

Baverstock leaned forward and opened the file that lay on the table in front of him. He removed a single sheet of paper transcribed in a bold, firm hand. "I should like to point out, Sir Charles, before I read this letter to you that it was written at a time when Sir Raymond assumed that his estate would be inherited by Daniel and not by his next of kin."

Mr Baverstock pushed his spectacles up the bridge of his nose, cleared his throat and began to read:

Dear Baverstock,

Despite everything I have done to ensure that my final wishes are carried out to the letter, it may still be possible that Ethel will find some way of seeing that my great grandson, Daniel Trumper, does not inherit the residue of my estate. If such circumstances should come about please use your common sense and allow those most affected by the decisions in my will to be privy to its finer details.

Old friend, you know exactly to whom and what I am referring.

Yours as ever

Ray.

Baverstock placed the letter back on the table and said, "I fear he knew my little weaknesses every bit as much as his daughter's." Charlie smiled for he appreciated the ethical dilemma with which the old lawyer was so obviously grappling.

"Now, before I make reference to the will itself I must let you into another confidence."

Charlie nodded.

"You are painfully aware, Sir Charles, that Mr Nigel Trentham is now the next of kin. However, it should not pass unobserved that the will is so worded that Sir Raymond couldn't even bring himself actually to name him as the recipient. I suspect that he hoped that Daniel might produce progeny of his own who would have taken precedence over his grandson.

"The current position is that Mr Nigel Trentham will, as Sir Raymond's closest living descendant, be entitled to the shares in Trumper's and the residue of the Hardcastle estate – a considerable fortune, which I can confirm would provide him with adequate funds to mount a full takeover bid for your company. However, that was not my purpose in wanting to see you this morning. No, that was because there is one clause in the will you could not have previously been aware of. After taking into account Sir Raymond's letter, I believe it to be nothing less than my duty to inform you of its import."

Baverstock burrowed into his file and retrieved a sheaf of papers, sealed in wax and bound in pink ribbon.

"The first eleven clauses of Sir Raymond's testament took me some considerable time to compose. However, their substance is not relevant to the issue at hand. They relate to minor legacies left by my client to nephews, nieces and cousins who have already received the sums bequeathed.

"Clauses twelve to twenty-one go on to name charities, clubs and academic institutions with which Sir Raymond had long been associated and they too have received the benefit of his munificence. But it is clause twenty-two that I consider crucial." Baverstock cleared his throat once again before looking down at the will and turning over several pages.

" 'The residue of my estate shall pass to Mr Daniel Trumper of Trinity College, Cambridge, but should he fail to survive my daughter Ethel Trentham then that sum shall be equally divided between his offspring. Should he have no issue, then the estate shall pass to my closest living descendant.' Now to the relevant paragraph, Sir Charles. 'If these circumstances arise I instruct my executors to go to any lengths they feel necessary to find someone entitled to make a claim on my inheritance. In order that this option might be properly executed, I also deem that final payment of the residue of the estate shall not be made until a further two years after my daughter's death.' "

Charlie was about to ask a question when Mr Baverstock raised his hand.

"It has become clear to me," continued Baverstock, "that Sir Raymond's purpose in including clause twenty-two was simply to give you enough time to marshal your forces and fight any hostile takeover bid Mr Nigel Trentham might have in mind.

"Sir Raymond also left instructions that, at a suitable time following his daughter's death, an advertisement should be placed in *The Times*, the *Telegraph*, the *Guardian* and any other newspaper I considered appropriate when seeking to discover if there were any other persons who feel they might have some claim on the estate. If this should be the case, they can then do so by making direct contact with this firm. Thirteen such relations have already received the sum of one thousand pounds each, but it is just possible there could be other cousins or distant relatives of whom Sir Raymond was unaware who may still be entitled to make such a claim. This provision simply gave the old man an excuse for the two-year clause. As I understand it, Sir Raymond was quite happy to allocate another thousand pounds to some unknown relative if at the same time it afforded you some breathing space. By the way," said Baverstock, "I have decided to add the *Yorkshire Post* and the *Huddersfield Daily Examiner* to the list of newspapers named in the will because of the family connections in that county."

"What a shrewd old buzzard he must have been," said Charlie. "I only wish I'd known him."

"I think I can say with some confidence, Sir Charles, that you would have liked him."

"It was also extremely kind of you to put me in the picture, old fellow."

"Not at all. I feel sure," said Baverstock, "that had he been placed in my position it is no more and certainly no less than Sir Raymond would have done himself."

"If only I'd told Daniel the truth about his father . . ."

"If you save your energies for the quick," said Baverstock, "it is possible Sir Raymond's foresight may still not have been wasted."

On 7 March 1962, the day on which Mrs Trentham had died, Trumper's shares stood at one pound two shillings on the FT Index; only four weeks later they had risen by a further three shillings.

Tim Newman's first piece of advice to Charlie was to cling on to every share he still possessed and under no circumstances during the next couple of years to agree to any further rights issues. If between them Charlie and Becky were able to lay their hands on any spare cash, they should purchase shares as and when they came on the market.

The problem with following this particular piece of advice was that every time a substantial block of shares did come on to the market they were immediately taken up by an unknown broker who obviously had instructions to purchase stock whatever the price. Charlie's stockbroker managed to get his hands on a few shares but only from those unwilling to trade on the open market. Charlie was loath to pay over the odds, as he had never forgotten how close he had come to bankruptcy when he last extended his credit. By the end of the year Trumper's shares stood at one pound seventeen shillings. There were even fewer sellers left in the market place after the *Financial Times* had warned their readers of a possible takeover battle for the company and gone on to predict it would take place within the next eighteen months.

"That damned paper seems to be as well briefed as any member of the board," Daphne complained to Charlie at their next meeting, adding that she no longer bothered with the minutes of past meetings as she could always read an excellent summary of what had taken place on the front page of the *Financial Times*, which appeared to have been dictated to them verbatim. As she delivered these words her eyes never left Paul Merrick.

The paper's latest story was inaccurate in only one small detail, as the battle for Trumper's was no longer taking place in the boardroom. As soon as it became known that a two-year holding clause existed in Sir Raymond's will Nigel Trentham and his nominees had stopped attending the monthly meetings.

Trentham's absence particularly annoyed Cathy, as quarter after quarter the new in-house bank began to show increased profits. She found herself addressing her opinions to three empty chairs – though she too suspected Merrick was reporting back every detail to Chester Square. As if to compound matters, in 1963 Charlie informed the shareholders at the AGM that the company would be declaring another record profit for the year.

"You may have spent a lifetime building up Trumper's only to hand it over on a plate to the Trenthams," Tim Newman reflected.

"There's certainly no need for Mrs Trentham to be turning in her grave," admitted Charlie. "Ironic, after all she managed during her life that it's only by her death that she's been given the chance to deliver the *coup de grâce*."

When, early in 1964, the shares rose yet again – this time to over two pounds – Charlie was informed by Tim Newman that Nigel Trentham was still in the market place with instructions to buy.

"But where's he getting hold of all the extra cash that would be needed to bankroll such an operation – when he's still not yet got his hands on his grandfather's money?"

"I picked up a hint from a former colleague," replied Tim Newman, "that a leading merchant bank has granted him a large overdraft facility in anticipation of his gaining control of the Hardcastle Trust. Only wish you had a grandfather who'd left you a fortune," he added.

"I did," said Charlie.

Nigel Trentham chose Charlie's sixty-fourth birthday to announce to the world that he would be making a full bid for Trumper's shares at a price of two pounds four shillings, a mere seven weeks before he was entitled to lay claim to his inheritance. Charlie still felt confident that with the help of friends and institutions like the Prudential – as well as some shareholders who were waiting for the price to rise even higher – he could still lay his hands on almost forty per cent of the stock. Tim Newman estimated that Trentham must now have at least twenty per cent, but once he was able to add the Trust's seventeen per cent he might then be in possession of as much as forty-two to forty-three. Picking up the extra eight or nine per cent required to gain control should not prove too hard for him, Newman warned Charlie.

That night Daphne threw a birthday party in Charlie's honour at her home in Eaton Square which Cathy was unable to attend, as she was in New York on a buying trip. No one mentioned the name of Trentham until the port had been passed round for a second time, when a slightly maudlin Charlie recited the relevant clause in Sir Raymond's will, which he explained had been put there with the sole purpose of trying to save him.

"I give you Sir Raymond Hardcastle," said Charlie, raising his glass. "A good man to have in your team."

"Sir Raymond," the guests echoed, all raising their glasses, with the exception of Daphne.

"What's the problem, old gel?" asked Percy. "Port not up to scratch?"

"No, as usual it's you lot who aren't. You've all totally failed to work out what Sir Raymond expected of you."

"What *are* you on about, old gel?"

"I should have thought it was obvious for anyone to

see, especially you, Charlie," she said, turning from her husband to the guest of honour.

"I'm with Percy – I haven't a clue what you're on about."

By now everyone round the table had fallen silent, while they concentrated on what Daphne had to say.

"It's quite simple really," continued Daphne. "Sir Raymond obviously didn't consider it likely that Mrs Trentham would outlive Daniel."

"So?" said Charlie.

"And I also doubt if he thought for one moment that Daniel would have any children before he died."

"Possibly not," said Charlie.

"And we are all painfully aware that Nigel Trentham was a last resort – otherwise Sir Raymond would happily have named him in his will as the next beneficiary and not have been willing to pass his fortune on to an offspring of Guy Trentham, whom he had never even met. He also wouldn't have added the words: should he have no issue then the estate shall pass to my closest living descendant."

"Where's all this leading?" asked Becky.

"Back to the clause Charlie has just recited. 'Please go to any lengths you feel necessary to find someone entitled to make a claim on my inheritance.'" Daphne read from the jottings she had scribbled in biro on her damask tablecloth. "Are those the correct words, Mr Baverstock?" she asked.

"They are, Lady Wiltshire, but I still don't see –"

"Because you're as blind as Charlie," said Daphne. "Thank God one of us is still sober. Mr Baverstock, please remind us all of Sir Raymond's instructions for placing the advertisement."

Mr Baverstock touched his lips with his napkin, folded the linen square neatly and placed it in front of him. "An advertisement should be placed in *The Times*, the *Telegraph* and the *Guardian* and any other newspaper I consider relevant and appropriate."

"I consider relevant and appropriate," said Daphne,

slowly enunciating each word. "As broad a hint as you might hope from a sober man, I would have thought." Every eye was now fixed on Daphne and no one attempted to interrupt her. "Can't you see those are the crucial words?" she asked. "Because if Guy Trentham did have any other children, you certainly wouldn't find them by advertising in the London *Times*, the *Telegraph*, the *Guardian*, *Yorkshire Post* or for that matter the *Huddersfield Daily Examiner*."

Charlie dropped his slice of birthday cake back on to his plate and looked across at Mr Baverstock. "Good heavens, she's right, you know."

"She certainly may not be wrong," admitted Baverstock, shuffling uneasily in his chair. "And I apologise for my lack of imagination, because as Lady Wiltshire rightly points out, I've been a blind fool by not following my master's instructions when he advised me to use my common sense. He so obviously worked out that Guy might well have fathered other children and that such offspring were most unlikely to be found in England."

"Well done, Mr Baverstock," said Daphne. "I do believe I should have gone to university and read for the bar."

Mr Baverstock felt unable to correct her on this occasion.

"There may still be time," said Charlie. "After all, there's another seven weeks left before the inheritance has to be handed over, so let's get straight back to work. By the way, thank you," he added, bowing towards Daphne.

Charlie rose from his chair and headed towards the nearest phone. "The first thing I'm going to need is the sharpest lawyer in Australia." Charlie checked his watch. "And preferably one who doesn't mind getting up early in the morning."

Mr Baverstock cleared his throat.

During the next two weeks, large box advertisements appeared in every newspaper on the Australian continent with a circulation of over fifty thousand. Each reply was quickly followed up with an interview by a firm of solicitors in Sydney that Mr Baverstock had been happy to recommend. Every evening Charlie was telephoned by Trevor Roberts, the senior partner, who remained on the end of the line for several hours when Charlie would learn the latest news that had been gathered from their offices in Sydney, Melbourne, Perth, Brisbane and Adelaide. However, after three weeks of sorting out the cranks from the genuine enquirers Roberts came up with only three candidates who fulfilled all the necessary criteria. However, once they had been interviewed by a partner of the firm they also failed to prove any direct relationship with any member of the Trentham family.

Roberts had discovered that there were seventeen Trenthams on the national register, most of them from Tasmania, but none of those could show any direct lineage with Guy Trentham or his mother, although one old lady from Hobart who had emigrated from Ripon after the war was able to present a legitimate claim for a thousand pounds, as it turned out she was a third cousin of Sir Raymond.

Charlie thanked Mr Roberts for his continued diligence but told him not to let up, as he didn't care how many staff were allocated to the job night or day.

At the final board meeting to be called before Nigel Trentham officially came into his inheritance, Charlie briefed his colleagues on the latest news from Australia.

"Doesn't sound too hopeful to me," said Newman. "After all, if there is another Trentham around he or she must be well over thirty and surely would have made a claim by now."

"Agreed, but Australia's an awfully big place and they might even have left the country."

"Never give up, do you?" remarked Daphne.

"Be that as it may," said Arthur Selwyn, "I feel the time is long overdue for us to try and come to some agreement with Trentham, if there is to be a responsible takeover of the company. In the interests of Trumper's and its customers, I would like to see if it is at all possible for the principals involved to come to some amicable arrangement –"

"Amicable arrangement!" said Charlie. "The only arrangement Trentham would agree to is that he sits in this chair with a built-in majority on the board while I am left twiddling my thumbs in a retirement home."

"That may well be the case," said Selwyn. "But I must point out, Mr Chairman, that we still have a duty to our shareholders."

"He's right," said Daphne. "You'll have to try, Charlie, for the long-term good of the company you founded." She added quietly, "However much it hurts."

Becky nodded her agreement and Charlie turned to ask Jessica to make an appointment with Trentham at his earliest convenience. Jessica returned a few minutes later to let the board know that Nigel Trentham had no interest in seeing any of them before the March board, when he would be happy to accept their resignations in person.

"Seventh of March: two years to the day since the death of his mother," Charlie reminded the board.

"And Mr Roberts is holding for you on the other line," Jessica reported.

Charlie rose and strode out of the room. The moment he reached the phone he grabbed at it as a drowning sailor might a lifeline. "Roberts, what have you got for me?"

"Guy Trentham!"

"But he's already buried in a grave in Ashurst."

"But not before his body was removed from a gaol in Melbourne."

"A gaol? I thought he died of tuberculosis."

"I don't think you can die of tuberculosis while you're hanging from the end of a six-foot rope, Sir Charles."

"Hanged?"

"For the murder of his wife, Anna Helen," said the solicitor.

"But did they have any children?"

"There's no way of knowing the answer to that."

"Why the hell not?"

"It's against the law for the prison service to release the names of the next of kin to anyone."

"But why, for heaven's sake?"

"For their own protection."

"But this could only be to their benefit."

"They've heard that one before. Indeed, I have had it pointed out to me that in this particular case we've already advertised for claimants from one coast to the other. What's worse, if any of Trentham's offspring had changed their name, for understandable reasons, we've little chance of tracing him or her at all. But be assured I'm still working flat out on it, Sir Charles."

"Get me an interview with the chief of police."

"It won't make any difference, Sir Charles. He won't – " began Roberts, but Charlie had already hung up.

"You're mad," said Becky, as she helped her husband pack a suitcase an hour later.

"True," agreed Charlie. "But this may well be the last chance I have of keeping control of the company, and I'm not willing to do it on the end of a phone, let alone twelve thousand miles away. I have to be there myself, so at least I know it's me who's failed and not a third party."

"But what exactly are you hoping to find when you get there?"

Charlie looked across at his wife as he fastened his suitcase. "I suspect only Mrs Trentham knows the answer to that."

CHAPTER 44

When, thirty-four hours later on a warm, sunlit evening, Flight 012 touched down at Kingsford Smith airport in Sydney, Charlie felt what he most needed was a good night's sleep. After he had checked through customs he was met by a tall young man dressed in a light beige suit who stepped forward and introduced himself as Trevor Roberts, the lawyer who had been recommended by Baverstock. Roberts had thick, rusty-coloured hair and an even redder complexion. He was of a solid build and looked as if he might still spend his Saturday afternoons in a different type of court. He immediately took over Charlie's laden trolley and pushed it smartly towards the exit marked "Car park".

"No need to check this lot into a hotel," said Roberts as he held the door open for Charlie. "Just leave everything in the car."

"Is this good legal advice you're giving me?" asked Charlie, already out of breath trying to keep up with the young man.

"It certainly is, Sir Charles, because we've no time to waste." He brought the trolley to a halt at the kerbside and a chauffeur heaved the bags into the boot while Charlie and Mr Roberts climbed into the back. "The British Governor-General has invited you for drinks at six at his residence, but I also need you to be on the last flight to Melbourne tonight. As we only have six days left, we can't afford to waste any of them being in the wrong city."

Charlie knew he was going to like Mr Roberts from the moment the Australian passed over a thick file. Charlie began to listen attentively to the young lawyer as he went over the proposed schedule for the next three days. While the car travelled towards the outskirts of the city. Charlie continued to pay attention to everything he had to say, only occasionally asking for something to be repeated or gone over in greater detail as he tried to accustom himself to the difference in style between Mr Roberts and any solicitor he had dealt with in England. When he had asked Mr Baverstock to find him the sharpest young lawyer in Sydney, Charlie hadn't imagined that he would select someone in quite such a different mould from his old friend.

As the car sped along the highway towards the Governor-General's residence Roberts, with several files balanced on his knees, continued with his detailed briefing. "We're only attending this cocktail party with the Governor-General," he explained, "in case during the next few days we need some help in opening heavy doors. Then we're off to Melbourne because every time someone from my office comes up with anything that might be described as a lead it always seems to end up on the Chief Commissioner of Police's desk in that city. I've made an appointment for you to see the new chief in the morning, but as I warned you the commissioner's not proving to be at all co-operative with my people."

"Why's that?"

"He's recently been appointed to the job, and is now desperately trying to prove that everyone will be treated impartially – except 'Poms'."

"So what's his problem?"

"Like all second-generation Australians he hates the British, or at least he has to pretend he does." Roberts grinned. "In fact, I think there's only one group of people he dislikes more."

"Criminals?"

"No, lawyers," replied Roberts. "So now you'll realise why the odds are stacked against us."

"Have you managed to get anything out of him at all?"

"Not a lot. Most of what he has been willing to reveal was already on public record, namely that on 27 July 1926 Guy Trentham, in a fit of temper, killed his wife by stabbing her several times while she was taking a bath. He then held her under the water so as to be sure that she didn't survive – page sixteen in your file. We also know that on 23 April 1927 he was hanged for the crime, despite several appeals for clemency to the Governor-General. What we've been quite unable to discover is if he was survived by any children. The Melbourne *Age* was the one newspaper that carried a report of the trial, and they made no mention of a child. However, that's hardly surprising, as the judge would have ruled against any such reference in court unless it threw some light on the crime."

"But what about the wife's maiden name? Surely that's a better route to take."

"You're not going to like this, Sir Charles," said Roberts.

"Try me."

"Her name was Smith – Anna Helen Smith – that's why we concentrated what little time we had on Trentham."

"But you've still come up with no firm leads?"

"I'm afraid not," said Roberts. "If there was a child in Australia at the time bearing the name of Trentham we certainly haven't been able to trace them. My staff have interviewed every Trentham that's shown up on the national register, including one from Coorabulka that has a population of eleven and takes three days to reach by car and foot."

"Despite your valiant efforts, Roberts, my guess is there might still be some stones we need to look under."

"Possibly," said Roberts. "I even began to wonder if perhaps Trentham had changed his name when he first came to Australia, but the chief of police was able to confirm that the file he holds in Melbourne is under the name of Guy Francis Trentham."

"So if the name's unchanged then surely any child would be traceable?"

"Not necessarily. I dealt with a case quite recently in which I had a client whose husband was sent to gaol for manslaughter. She reverted to her maiden name, which she also gave to her only child and was able to show me a foolproof system for then having the original name expunged from the records. Also, remember that in this case we're dealing with a child who could have been born any time between 1923 and 1925 and the removal of just one piece of paper could well have been enough to eliminate any connection he or she might have with Guy Trentham. If that's the case, finding such a child in a country the size of Australia would be like searching for the proverbial needle in the haystack."

"But I've only got six days," said Charlie plaintively.

"Don't remind me," said Roberts, as the car drove through the gates of the Governor-General's residence at Government House, dropping its speed to a more sedate pace as they continued up the drive. "I've allocated one hour for this party, no more," the young lawyer warned. "All I want out of the Governor-General is a promise that he'll telephone the chief of police in Melbourne before our meeting tomorrow, to ask him to be as co-operative as possible. But when I say we must leave, Sir Charles, I mean we must leave."

"Understood," said Charlie, feeling like a private back on parade in Edinburgh.

"By the way," said Roberts, "the Governor-General is Sir Oliver Williams. Sixty-one, former Guards officer, comes from some place called Tunbridge Wells."

Two minutes later they were striding into the grand ballroom of Government House.

"So glad you could make it, Sir Charles," said a tall, elegantly dressed man who wore a double-breasted striped suit and a Guards tie.

"Thank you, Sir Oliver."

"And how was the journey over, old chap?"

"Five stops for refuelling and not one airport that knew how to brew a decent cup of tea."

"Then you'll need one of these," suggested Sir Oliver, handing Charlie a large whisky that he removed deftly from a passing tray. "And to think," continued the diplomat, "they're predicting that our grandchildren will be able to fly the entire journey from London to Sydney non-stop in less than a day. Still, yours was a lot less unpleasant an experience than the early settlers had to endure."

"A small compensation." Charlie couldn't think of a more appropriate reply as he considered what a contrast Mr Baverstock's nominee in Australia was to the Queen's representative.

"Now, do tell me what brings you to Sydney," continued the Governor-General. "Are we to anticipate that the second biggest barrow in the world is about to be pushed round to this side of the globe?"

"No, Sir Oliver. You'll be saved that. I'm here on a brief private visit, trying to sort out some family business."

"Well, if there's anything I can do to assist you," said his host, taking a gin from another passing tray, "just let me know."

"That's kind of you, Sir Oliver, because I do need your help over one small matter."

"And what might that be?" asked his host, at the same moment allowing his eyes to wander over Charlie's shoulder in the direction of some late arrivals.

"You could call the chief of police in Melbourne and ask him to be as co-operative as possible when I visit him tomorrow morning."

"Consider the call made, old fellow," said Sir Oliver as he leaned forward to shake the hand of an Arab sheikh. "And don't forget, Sir Charles, if there's anything I can do to help – and I mean anything – just let me know. Ah, *Monsieur l'Ambassadeur, comment allez-vous*?"

Charlie suddenly felt exhausted. He spent the rest of the hour just trying to remain on his feet while talking to diplomats, politicians and businessmen, all of whom seemed well acquainted with the biggest barrow in the world. Eventually a firm touch on his elbow from Roberts signalled that the proprieties had been observed and he must now leave for the airport.

On the flight to Melbourne Charlie was just about able to stay awake, even if his eyes weren't always open. In answer to a question from Roberts he confirmed that the Governor-General had agreed to telephone the chief of police the following morning. "But I'm not certain he appreciated how important it was."

"I see," said Roberts. "Then I'll be back in touch with his office first thing tomorrow. Sir Oliver's not renowned for remembering promises he makes at cocktail parties. 'If there's anything I can do to assist you, old chap, and I mean anything,' " – which even managed to elicit a sleepy grin from Charlie.

At Melbourne airport another car was waiting for them. Charlie was whisked away, and this time he did fall asleep and didn't wake again until they drew up outside the Windsor Hotel some twenty minutes later. The manager showed his guest to the Prince Edward suite and as soon as he had been left on his own Charlie quickly undressed, had a shower and climbed into bed. A few minutes later he fell into a heavy sleep. However, he still woke around four the next morning.

Propped uncomfortably up in bed supported by foam rubber pillows that wouldn't stay in one place, Charlie spent the next three hours going through Roberts's files. The man might not have looked or sounded like Baverstock but the same stamp of thoroughness was evident on every page. By the time Charlie let the last file drop to the floor he had to accept that Roberts's firm had covered every angle and followed up every lead; his only hope now rested with a cantankerous Melbourne policeman.

Charlie had a cold shower at seven and a hot breakfast just after eight. Although his only appointment that day was at ten o'clock he was pacing round his suite long before Roberts was due to pick him up at nine thirty, aware that if nothing came out of this meeting he might as well pack his bags and fly back to England that afternoon. At least that would give Becky the satisfaction of being proved right.

At nine twenty-nine Roberts knocked on his door; Charlie wondered how long the young lawyer had been standing outside in the corridor waiting. Roberts reported that he had already telephoned the Governor-General's office and that Sir Oliver had promised to call the chief of police within the hour.

"Good. Now tell me everything you know about the man."

"Mike Cooper is forty-seven, efficient, prickly and brash. Climbed up through the ranks but still finds it necessary to prove himself to everyone, especially when he's in the presence of a lawyer, perhaps because crime statistics for Melbourne have risen at an even faster rate than our Test averages against England."

"You said yesterday he was second generation. So where does he hail from?"

Roberts checked his file. "His father emigrated to Australia at the turn of the century from somewhere called Deptford."

"Deptford?" repeated Charlie with a grin. "That's almost home territory." He checked his watch. "Shall we be off? I think I'm more than ready to meet Mr Cooper."

When twenty minutes later Roberts held open the door of the police headquarters for his client, they were greeted with a large formal photograph of a man in his late forties that made Charlie feel every day of his sixty-four years.

After Roberts had supplied the officer on duty with their names they were kept waiting for only a few minutes before Charlie was ushered through to the chief's office.

The policeman's lips formed a reluctant smile when he shook hands with Charlie. "I am not sure there's a lot I can do to help you, Sir Charles," began Cooper, motioning him to take a seat. "Despite your Governor-General taking the trouble to call me." He ignored Roberts, who remained standing a few feet behind his client.

"I know that accent," said Charlie, not taking the offered chair.

"I beg your pardon?" replied Cooper, who also remained standing.

"Half a crown to a pound says your father hails from London."

"Yes, you're right."

"And the East End of that city would be my bet."

"Deptford," said the chief.

"I knew it the moment you opened your mouth," said Charlie now sinking back into a leather chair. "I come from Whitechapel myself. So where was he born?"

"Deptford Church Street," said the chief. "Just off–"

"Just a stone's throw away from my part of the world," said Charlie in a thick Cockney accent.

Roberts had not yet uttered a word, let alone given a professional opinion.

"Millwall supporter, I suppose," said Charlie.

"The Gunners," said Cooper, firmly.

"What a load of rubbish," said Charlie. "Arsenal are the only team I know who read the names of the crowd to the players."

The chief laughed. "I agree," he said. "I've almost given up hope for them this season. So who do you support?"

"I'm a West Ham man myself."

"And you were hoping I'd co-operate with you?"

Charlie laughed. "Well, we did let you beat us in the Cup."

"In 1930," said Cooper, laughing.

"We've got long memories down at Upton Park."

"Well, I never expected you to have an accent like that, Sir Charles."

"Call me Charlie, all my friends do. And another thing, Mike, do you want him out of the way?" Charlie cocked a thumb at Trevor Roberts who still hadn't been offered a seat.

"Might help," said the chief.

"Wait outside for me, Roberts," said Charlie, not even bothering to glance in the direction of his lawyer.

"Yes, Sir Charles." Roberts turned and started walking towards the door.

Once they were alone Charlie leaned across the desk and said, "Soddin' lawyers, they're all the same. Overpaid toffee-nosed Brussels sprouts, charge the earth and then expect you to do all the work."

Cooper laughed. "Especially when you're a grass-hopper," he confided.

Charlie laughed. "Haven't heard a copper described that way since I left Whitechapel." The older man leaned forward. "This is between you and me, Mike. Two East End boys together. Can you tell me anything about Guy Francis Trentham that *he* doesn't know?" Charlie pointed his thumb towards the door.

"I'm afraid there isn't a lot Roberts hasn't already dug up, to be fair to him, Sir Charles."

"Charlie."

"Charlie. Look, you already know that Trentham murdered his wife and you must be aware by now that he was later hanged for the crime."

"Yes, but what I need to know, Mike, is, were there any children?" Charlie held his breath as the policeman seemed to hesitate.

Cooper looked down at a charge sheet that lay on the desk in front of him. "It says here, wife (deceased), one daughter."

Charlie tried not to leap out of his chair. "Don't suppose that piece of paper tells you her name?"

"Margaret Ethel Trentham," said the chief.

Charlie knew he didn't have to re-check the name in the files that Roberts had left with him overnight. There hadn't been a Margaret Ethel Trentham mentioned in any of them. He could recall the names of the three Trenthams born in Australia between 1923 and 1925, and all of those were boys.

"Date of birth?" he hazarded.

"No clue, Charlie," said Cooper. "It wasn't the girl who was being charged." He pushed the piece of paper over the desk, so that his visitor could read everything he had already been told. "They didn't bother too much with those sort of details in the twenties."

"Anything else in that file you think might 'elp an East End boy not on his 'ome ground?" asked Charlie, only hoping he wasn't overdoing it.

Cooper studied the papers in the Trentham file for some time before he offered an opinion. "There are two entries on our records that might just be of some use to you. The first was pencilled in by my predecessor and there's an even earlier entry from the chief before him which I suppose just might be of interest."

"I'm all ears, Mike."

"Chief Parker was paid a visit on 24 April 1927 by a Mrs Ethel Trentham, the deceased's mother."

"Good God," said Charlie, unable to hide his surprise. "But why?"

"No reason given, nor any record of what was said at that meeting either. Sorry."

"And the second entry?"

"That concerns another visitor from England enquiring after Guy Trentham. This time on 23 August 1947" – the police chief looked down at the file again to check the name – "a Mr Daniel Trentham."

Charlie went cold as he gripped the arms of his chair.

"You all right?" asked Cooper, sounding genuinely concerned.

"Fine," said Charlie. "It's only the effects of jet-lag. Any reason given for Daniel Trentham's visit?"

"According to the attached note, he claimed to be the deceased's son," said the chief. Charlie tried not to show any emotion. The policeman sat back in his chair. "So now you know every bit as much about the case as I do."

"You've been very 'elpful, Mike," said Charlie as he pushed himself up to his feet before leaning across to shake hands. "And if you should ever find yourself back in Deptford, look me up. I'd be only too happy to take you to see a real football team."

Cooper smiled and continued to trade stories with Charlie as the two men made their way out of his office to the lift. Once they were on the ground floor the policeman accompanied him to the steps of police headquarters, where Charlie shook hands with the chief once again before joining Trevor Roberts in the car.

"Right, Roberts, it seems we've got ourselves some work to do."

"May I be permitted to ask one question before we begin, Sir Charles?"

"Be my guest."

"What happened to your accent?"

"I only save that for special people, Mr Roberts. The Queen, Winston Churchill and when I'm serving a customer on the barrow. Today I felt it necessary to add Melbourne's chief of police to my list."

"I can't begin to think what you said about me and my profession."

"I told him you were an overpaid, toffee-nosed boy scout who expected me to do all the work."

"And did he offer an opinion?"

"Thought I might have been a little too restrained."

"That's not hard to believe," said Roberts. "But were you able to prise any fresh information out of him?"

"I certainly was," said Charlie. "It seems Guy Trentham had a daughter."

"A daughter?" repeated Roberts, unable to hide his excitement. "But did Cooper let you know her name, or anything about her?"

"Margaret Ethel, but our only other clue is that Mrs Trentham, Guy's mother, paid a visit to Melbourne in 1927. Cooper didn't know why."

"Good heavens," said Roberts. "You've achieved more in twenty minutes than I achieved in twenty days."

"Ah, but I had the advantage of birth," said Charlie

with a grin. "Now where would an English lady have rested her genteel head in this city around that time?"

"Not my home town," admitted Roberts. "But my partner Neil Mitchell should be able to tell us. His family settled in Melbourne over a hundred years ago."

"So what are we waiting for?"

Neil Mitchell frowned when his colleague put the same question to him. "I haven't a clue," he admitted, "but my mother's sure to know." He picked up his phone and started dialling. "She's Scottish, so she'll try and charge us for the information." Charlie and Trevor Roberts stood in front of Mitchell's desk and waited, one patiently, one impatiently. After a few preliminaries expected of a son, he put his question and listened carefully to her reply.

"Thank you, Mother, invaluable as always," he said. "See you at the weekend," he added before putting down the phone.

"Well?" said Charlie.

"The Victoria Country Club apparently was the only place someone from Mrs Trentham's background would have dreamed of staying in the twenties," Mitchell said. "In those days Melbourne only had two decent hotels and the other one was strictly for visiting businessmen."

"Does the place still exist?" asked Roberts.

"Yes, but it's badly run-down nowadays. What I imagine Sir Charles would describe as 'seedy'."

"Then telephone ahead and let them know you want a table for lunch in the name of Sir Charles Trumper. And stress Sir Charles."

"Certainly, Sir Charles," said Roberts. "And which accent will we be using on this occasion?"

"Can't tell you that until I've weighed up the opposition," said Charlie as they made their way back to the car.

"Ironic when you think about it," said Roberts, as the car headed out on to the freeway.

"Ironic?"

"Yes," said Roberts. "If Mrs Trentham went to all this trouble to remove her granddaughter's very existence from the records, she must have required the services of a first-class lawyer to do so."

"So?"

"So there must be a file buried somewhere in this city that would tell us everything we need to know."

"Possibly, but one thing's for certain: we don't have enough time to discover whose filing cabinet it's hidden in."

When they arrived at the Victoria Country Club they found the manager standing in the hallway waiting to greet them. He led his distinguished guest through to a quiet table in the alcove. Charlie was only disappointed to find how young he was.

Charlie chose the most expensive items from the *à la carte* section of the menu, then selected a 1957 bottle of Chambertin. Within moments he was receiving attention from every waiter in the room.

"And what are you up to this time, Sir Charles?" asked Roberts, who had satisfied himself with the set menu.

"Patience, young man," Charlie said in mock disdain as he tried to cut into an overcooked, tough piece of lamb with a blunt knife. He eventually gave in, and ordered a vanilla ice-cream, confident they couldn't do much harm to that. When finally the coffee was served, the oldest waiter in the room came slowly over to offer them both a cigar.

"A Monte Cristo, please," said Charlie, removing a pound note from his wallet and placing it on the table in front of him. A large old humidor was opened for his inspection. "Worked here for a long time, have you?" Charlie added.

"Forty years last month," said the waiter, as another pound note landed on top of the first.

"Good memory?"

"I like to think so, sir," said the waiter, staring at the two banknotes.

"Remember someone called Mrs Trentham? English,

strait-laced, might have stayed for a couple of weeks or more round 1927," said Charlie, pushing the notes towards the old man.

"Remember her?" said the waiter. "I'll never forget her. I was a trainee in those days and she did nothing except grumble the whole time about the food and the service. Wouldn't drink anything but water, said she didn't trust Australian wines and refused to spend good money on the French ones – that's why I always ended up having to serve on her table. End of the month, she ups and offs without a word and didn't even leave me a tip. You bet I remember her."

"That sounds like Mrs Trentham all right," said Charlie. "But did you ever find out why she came to Australia in the first place?" He removed a third pound note from his wallet and placed it on top of the others.

"I've no idea, sir," said the waiter sadly. "She never talked to anyone from morning to night, and I'm not sure even Mr Sinclair-Smith would know the answer to that question."

"Mr Sinclair-Smith?"

The waiter motioned over his shoulder to the far corner of the room where an elderly gentleman sat alone, a napkin tucked into his collar. He was busy attacking a large piece of Stilton. "The present owner," the waiter explained. "His father was the only person Mrs Trentham ever spoke civilly to."

"Thank you," said Charlie. "You've been most helpful." The waiter pocketed the three banknotes. "Would you be kind enough to ask the manager if I could have a word with him?"

"Certainly, sir," said the old waiter, who closed the humidor and scurried away.

"The manager is far too young to remember –"

"Just keep your eyes open, Mr Roberts, and possibly you might just learn a trick or two they failed to teach you in the business contracts class at law school," said Charlie as he clipped the end of his cigar.

The manager arrived at their table. "You asked to see me, Sir Charles?"

"I wonder if Mr Sinclair-Smith would care to join me for a liqueur?" said Charlie, passing the young man one of his cards.

"I'll have a word with him immediately, sir," said the manager who at once turned and walked towards the other table.

"It's back to the lobby for you, Roberts," said Charlie, "as I suspect that my conduct over the next half-hour might just offend your professional ethics." He glanced across the room, where the old man was now studying his card.

Roberts sighed, rose from his chair and left.

A large smile appeared on Mr Sinclair-Smith's podgy lips. He pushed himself up out of his chair and waddled over to join his English visitor.

"Sinclair-Smith," he said in a high-pitched English accent before offering a limp hand.

"Good of you to join me, old chap," said Charlie. "I know a fellow countryman when I see one. Can I interest you in a brandy?" The waiter scurried away.

"How kind of you, Sir Charles. I can only hope that my humble establishment has provided you with a reasonable cuisine."

"Excellent," said Charlie. "But then you were recommended," he said as he exhaled a plume of cigar smoke.

"Recommended?" said Sinclair-Smith, trying not to sound too surprised. "May I ask by whom?"

"My ancient aunt, Mrs Ethel Trentham."

"Mrs Trentham? Good heavens, Mrs Trentham, we haven't seen the dear lady since my late father's time."

Charlie frowned as the old waiter returned with two large brandies.

"I do hope she's keeping well, Sir Charles."

"Never better," said Charlie. "And she wished to be remembered to you."

"How kind of her," replied Sinclair-Smith, swirling the brandy round in his balloon. "And what a remarkable memory, because I was only a young man at the time and had just started working in the hotel. She must now be . . ."

"Over ninety," said Charlie. "And do you know the family still has no idea why she ever came to Melbourne in the first place," he added.

"Nor me," said Sinclair-Smith as he sipped his brandy.

"You never spoke to her?"

"No, never," said Sinclair-Smith. "Although my father and your aunt had many long conversations, he never once confided in me what passed between them."

Charlie tried not to show his frustration at this piece of information. "Well, if you don't know what she was up to," he said, "I don't suppose there's anyone alive who does."

"Oh, I wouldn't be so sure of that," said Sinclair-Smith. "Slade would know – that is, if he hasn't gone completely ga-ga."

"Slade?"

"Yes, a Yorkshireman who worked at the club under my father, in the days when we still had a resident chauffeur. In fact, the whole time Mrs Trentham stayed at the club she always insisted on using Slade. Said no one else should drive her."

"Is he still around?" asked Charlie as he blew out another large cloud of smoke.

"Good heavens no," said Sinclair-Smith. "Retired years ago. Not even sure he's still alive."

"Do you get back to the old country much nowadays?" enquired Charlie, convinced that he had extracted every piece of relevant information that could be gained from this particular source.

"No, unfortunately what with . . ."

For the next twenty minutes, Charlie settled back and enjoyed his cigar as he listened to Sinclair-Smith on everything from the demise of the Empire to the parlous state of English cricket. Eventually Charlie called for the bill, at which the owner took his leave and slipped discreetly away.

The old waiter shuffled back the moment he saw another pound note appear on the tablecloth.

"Something you needed, sir?"

"Does the name Slade mean anything to you?"

"Old Walter Slade, the club's chauffeur?"

"That's the man."

"Retired years ago."

"I know that much, but is he still alive?"

"No idea," said the waiter. "Last I heard of him he lived somewhere out in the Ballarat area."

"Thank you," said Charlie, as he stubbed out his cigar in the ash-tray, removed another pound note and left to join Roberts in the lobby.

"Telephone your office immediately," he instructed his solicitor. "Ask them to track down a Walter Slade who may be living at somewhere called Ballarat."

Roberts hurried off in the direction of the telephone sign, while Charlie paced up and down the corridor praying the old man was still alive. His solicitor returned a few minutes later. "Am I allowed to know what you're up to this time, Sir Charles?" he asked as he passed over a piece of paper with Walter Slade's address printed out in capital letters.

"No good, that's for sure," said Charlie, as he took in the information. "Don't need you for this one, young man, but I will require the car. See you back at the office – and I can't be sure when." He gave a small wave as he pushed through the swing doors leaving a bemused Roberts standing on his own in the lobby.

Charlie handed over the slip of paper to the chauffeur who studied the address. "But it's nearly a hundred miles," said the man, looking over his shoulder.

"Then we haven't a moment to waste, have we?"

The driver switched on the engine and swung out of the country club forecourt. He drove past the Melbourne Cricket Ground where Charlie could see someone was 147 for 2. It annoyed him that on his first trip to Australia he didn't even have enough time to drop in and see the Test Match. The journey on the north highway lasted for another hour and a half, which gave Charlie easily enough time to consider what approach he would use on Mr Slade, assuming he wasn't, to quote Sinclair-Smith, "completely ga-ga". After they had sped past the sign for Ballarat, the driver pulled into a petrol station. Once the attendant had filled the tank he gave the driver some directions and it took another fifteen minutes before they came to a halt outside a small terraced house on a run-down estate.

Charlie jumped out of the car, marched up a short, weed-covered path and knocked on the front door. He waited for some time before an old lady wearing a pinafore and a pastel-coloured dress that nearly reached the ground answered his call.

"Mrs Slade?" asked Charlie.

"Yes," she replied, peering up at him suspiciously.

"Would it be possible to have a word with your husband?"

"Why?" asked the old lady. "You from the social services?"

"No, I'm from England," said Charlie. "And I've brought your husband a small bequest from my aunt Mrs Ethel Trentham, who has recently died."

"Oh, how kind of you," said Mrs Slade. "Do come in." She guided Charlie through to the kitchen, where he found an old man dressed in a cardigan, clean check shirt and baggy trousers dozing in a chair in front of the fireplace.

"There's a man come all the way from England, specially to see you, Walter."

"What's that?" said the man, raising his bony fingers to rub the sleep out of his eyes.

"A man come from England," repeated his wife. "With a present from that Mrs Trentham."

"I'm too old to drive her now." His tired eyes blinked at Charlie.

"No, Walter, you don't understand. He's a relative come all the way from England with a gift. You see, she died."

"Died?"

Both of them were now staring quizzically at Charlie

as he quickly took out his wallet and removed every note he possessed before handing the money over to Mrs Slade.

She began to count the notes slowly as Walter Slade continued to stare at Charlie, making him feel distinctly uneasy as he stood on their spotless stone floor.

"Eighty-five pounds, Walter," she told him, passing the money over to her husband.

"Why so much?" he asked. "And after so long?"

"You did her a great service," said Charlie, "and she simply wished to repay you."

The old man began to look more suspiciously at Charlie.

"She paid me at the time," he said.

"I realise that," said Charlie, "but –"

"And I've kept my mouth shut," he said.

"That's just another reason why she had cause to be grateful to you," said Charlie.

"Are you saying that you came all the way from England, just to give me eighty-five pounds?" said Mr Slade. "Doesn't make any sense to me, lad." He suddenly sounded a lot more awake.

"No, no," said Charlie, feeling that he was losing the initiative. "I've had a dozen other bequests to deliver before coming out here, but you weren't that easy to find."

"I'm not surprised. I've stopped driving these twenty years."

"You're from Yorkshire, aren't you?" said Charlie with a grin. "I'd know that accent anywhere."

"Aye, lad, and you're from London. Which means you're not to be trusted. So why did you really come to see me? Because it wasn't to give us eighty-five pounds, that's for sure."

"I can't find the little girl who was with Mrs Trentham when you drove her," said Charlie, risking everything. "You see, she's been left a large inheritance."

"Fancy that, Walter," said Mrs Slade.

Walter Slade's face registered nothing.

"And it's my duty somehow to locate her and then inform the lady of her good fortune."

Slade's face remained impassive as Charlie battled on. "And I thought you'd be the one person who might be able to help."

"No, I won't," Slade replied. "What's more you can have your money back," he added, throwing the notes at Charlie's feet. "And don't bother to show your face round these parts again, with your phoney trumped-up stories about fortunes. Show the gentleman the door, Elsie."

Mrs Slade bent down and carefully picked up the scattered notes before passing them up to Charlie. When she had handed over the last one, she silently led the stranger back towards the front door.

"I do apologise, Mrs Slade," said Charlie. "I had no intention of offending your husband."

"I know, sir," said Mrs Slade. "But then Walter has always been so proud. Heaven knows, we could have done with the money." Charlie smiled as he stuffed the bundle of notes into the old lady's pinafore and quickly put a finger up to his lips. "If you don't tell him, I won't," he said. He gave a slight bow before turning to walk back down the little path towards the car.

"I never saw no little girl," she said in a voice that barely carried. Charlie froze on the spot. "But Walter once took a snooty lady up to that orphanage on Park Hill in Melbourne. I know because I was walking out with the gardener at the time, and he told me."

Charlie turned to thank her, but she had already closed the door and disappeared back into the house.

Charlie climbed into the car, penniless and with just one name to cling on to, aware that the old man could undoubtedly have solved the entire mystery for him. Otherwise he would have said "No, I can't" and not "No, I won't" when he had asked for his help.

He cursed his stupidity several times on the long journey back to the city.

"Roberts, is there an orphanage in Melbourne?" were

Charlie's opening words as he strode into the lawyer's office.

"St Hilda's," said Neil Mitchell, before his partner could consider the question. "Yes, it's up on Park Hill somewhere. Why?"

"That's the one," said Charlie, checking his watch. "It's about seven o'clock in the morning London time and I'm shattered, so I'm off to my hotel to try and grab some sleep. In the meantime I need a few questions answered. To start with, I want to know everything that can possibly be found out about St Hilda's, starting with the names of every member of staff who worked there between 1923 and 1927, from the head concho down to the scullery maid. And if anyone's still around from that period find them because I want to see them – and within the next twenty-four hours."

Two of the staff in Mitchell's office had begun scribbling furiously as they tried to take down every word Sir Charles said.

"I also want to know the name of every child registered at that orphanage between 1923 and 1927. Remember, we're looking for a girl who couldn't have been more than four years old, and may have been called Margaret Ethel. And when you've found the answers to all those questions wake me – whatever time it is."

CHAPTER 45

Trevor Roberts arrived back at Charlie's hotel a few minutes before eight the following morning to find his client tucking into a large breakfast of eggs, tomato, mushrooms and bacon. Although Roberts looked unshaven and tired, he was the bearer of news.

"We've been in touch with the principal of St Hilda's, a Mrs Culver, and she couldn't have been more co-operative." Charlie smiled. "It turns out that nineteen children were registered with the orphanage between 1923 and 1927. Eight boys and eleven girls. Of the eleven girls we now know that nine of them didn't have a mother or father alive at the time. Of those nine we have managed to contact seven, five of whom have a relative still alive who could vouch for who their father was, one whose parents were killed in a car crash and the other who is an aboriginal. The last two, however, are proving more difficult to track down, so I thought you might like to visit St Hilda's and study the files yourself."

"What about the staff at the orphanage?"

"Only a cook survives from around that period, and she says there never was a child at St Hilda's called Trentham or any name like that, and she can't even remember a Margaret or an Ethel. So our last hope may prove to be a Miss Benson."

"Miss Benson?"

"Yes, she was the principal at the time and is now a resident at an exclusive old people's home called Maple Lodge on the other side of the city."

"Not bad, Mr Roberts," said Charlie. "But how did you manage to get Mrs Culver to be so co-operative at such short notice?"

"I resorted to methods that I suspect are more familiar to the Whitechapel school of law than Harvard, Sir Charles."

Charlie looked at him quizzically.

"It seems that St Hilda's are currently organising an appeal for a minibus –"

"A minibus?"

"So badly needed by the orphanage for trips –"

"and so you hinted that I –"

"might be possible to help with a wheel or two if –"

"they in return felt able to –"

"co-operate. Precisely."

"You're a quick learner, Roberts, I'll give you that."

"And as there's no more time to be wasted, we ought to leave for St Hilda's immediately so you can go over those files."

"But our best bet must surely be Miss Benson."

"I agree with you, Sir Charles. And I've planned for us to pay her a visit this afternoon, just as soon as you've finished at St Hilda's. By the way, when Miss Benson was principal, she was known as 'The Dragon' not only by the children but also by the staff, so there's no reason to expect she'll be any more co-operative than Walter Slade."

When Charlie arrived at the orphanage he was greeted at the front door by the principal. Mrs Culver wore a smart green dress that looked as if it might have been freshly pressed. She had obviously decided to treat her potential benefactor as if he were Nelson Rockefeller because all that was lacking was a red carpet as Charlie was ushered through to her study.

Two young lawyers who had been going assiduously through files all night and learning all there was to know about dormitory times, exeats, kitchen duties, credits and misdemeanours stood as Charlie and Trevor Roberts entered the room.

"Any further progress with those two names?" asked Roberts.

"Oh, yes, down to two. Isn't this exciting?" said Mrs Culver, as she bustled round the room moving anything that seemed to be out of place. "I was wondering – "

"We have no proof as yet," said a bleary-eyed young man, "but one of them seems to fit the bill perfectly. We can come up with no information on the girl before the age of two. What's more important, she was registered with St Hilda's at precisely the same time as Captain Trentham was awaiting execution."

"And the cook also remembers from the days when she was a scullery maid," said Mrs Culver, jumping in, "that the girl came in the middle of the night, accompanied by a well-dressed, severe-looking lady who had a lah-de-dah accent who then – "

"Enter Mrs Trentham," said Charlie. "Only the girl's name is obviously not Trentham."

The young assistant checked the notes that lay spread across the table in front of him. "No, sir," he said. "This particular girl was registered under the name of Miss Cathy Ross."

Charlie felt his legs give way as Roberts and Mrs Culver rushed forward to help him into the only comfortable chair in the room. Mrs Culver loosened his tie and undid his collar.

"Are you feeling all right, Sir Charles?" she asked. "I must say you don't look too . . ."

"Right in front of my eyes all the time," said Charlie. "Blind as a bat is how Daphne would rightly describe me."

"I'm not sure I understand," said Roberts.

"I'm not sure I do myself as yet." Charlie turned back to face the anxious messenger responsible for delivering the news.

"Did she leave St Hilda's to take up a place at Melbourne University?" he asked.

This time the assistant double-checked his notes. "Yes, sir. She signed on for the class of '42, leaving in '45."

"Where she studied history of art and English."

The assistant's eyes again scanned the papers in front of him. "That's correct, sir," he said, unable to hide his surprise.

"And did she play tennis, by any chance?"

"The occasional match for the university second six."

"But could she paint?" asked Charlie.

The assistant continued to leaf through the files.

"Oh, yes," said Mrs Culver, "and very good she was too, Sir Charles. We still have an example of her work hanging in the dining room, a woodland scene influenced by Sisley, I suspect. Indeed, I would go as far as to say – "

"May I be allowed to see the picture, Mrs Culver?"

"Of course, Sir Charles." The principal removed a key from the top right-hand drawer of her desk and said, "Please follow me."

Charlie rose unsteadily to his feet and accompanied Mrs Culver as she marched out of her study and down a long corridor towards the dining room, the door of which she proceeded to unlock. Trevor Roberts, striding behind Charlie, continued to look puzzled, but refrained from asking any questions.

As they entered the dining room Charlie stopped in his tracks and said, "I could spot a Ross at twenty paces."

"I beg your pardon, Sir Charles?"

"It's not important, Mrs Culver," Charlie said as he stood in front of the picture and stared at a woodland scene of dappled browns and greens.

"Beautiful, isn't it, Sir Charles? A real understanding of the use of colour. I would go as far as to say – "

"I wonder, Mrs Culver, if you would consider that picture to be a fair exchange for a minibus?"

"A very fair exchange," said Mrs Culver without hesitation. "In fact I feel sure . . ."

"And would it be too much to ask that you write on the back of the picture, 'painted by Miss Cathy Ross', along with the dates that she resided at St Hilda's?"

"Delighted, Sir Charles." Mrs Culver stepped forward

and lifted the picture off its hook, then turned the frame round for all to see. What Sir Charles had requested, although faded with age, was already written and clearly legible to the naked eye.

"I do apologise, Mrs Culver," said Charlie. "By now I should know better of you." He removed his wallet from an inside pocket, signed a blank cheque and passed it over to Mrs Culver.

"But how much – ?" began the astonished principal.

"Whatever it costs," was all Charlie replied, having finally found a way of rendering Mrs Culver speechless.

The three of them returned to the principal's study where a pot of tea was waiting. One of the assistants set about making two copies of everything in Cathy's file while Roberts rang ahead to the nursing home where Miss Benson resided to warn the matron to expect them within the hour. Once both tasks had been completed Charlie thanked Mrs Culver for her kindness and bade her farewell. Although she had remained silent for some time she somehow managed, "Thank you, Sir Charles. Thank you."

Charlie clung tightly on to the picture as he walked out of the orphanage and back down the path. Once he was in the car again he instructed the driver to guard the package with his life.

"Certainly sir. And where to now?"

"Maple Lodge Residential Home, on the north side," instructed Roberts, who had climbed into the other side. "I do hope you're going to explain to me what happened back there at St Hilda's. Because I am, as the good book would have it, 'sore amazed'."

"I'll tell you as much as I know myself," said Charlie. He began to explain how he had first met Cathy almost fifteen years before at a house-warming party in his home at Eaton Square. He continued with his story uninterrupted until he had arrived at the part when Miss Ross had been appointed a director of Trumper's and how since Daniel's suicide she had been unable to tell them much about her background because she still hadn't fully recovered her memory of those events that had taken place before she came to England. The lawyer's opening response to this information took Charlie by surprise.

"You can be sure it wasn't a coincidence that Miss Ross visited England in the first place, or for that matter that she applied for a job at Trumper's."

"What are you getting at?" said Charlie.

"She must have left Australia with the sole purpose of trying to find out about her father, believing him still to be alive, perhaps even living in England. That must have been her original motivation to visit London, where she undoubtedly discovered some connection between his and your family. And if you can find that link between her father, her going to England and Trumper's, you will then have your proof – proof that Cathy Ross is in fact Margaret Ethel Trentham."

"But I have no idea what that link could be," said Charlie. "And now that Cathy remembers so little of her early life in Australia, I may never be able to find out."

"Well, let's hope Miss Benson can point us in the right direction," said Roberts. "Although, as I warned you earlier, no one who knew her at St Hilda's has a good word to say for the woman."

"If Walter Slade's anything to go by, it won't be easy to get the time of day out of her. It's becoming obvious that Mrs Trentham cast a spell over everyone she came into contact with."

"I agree," said the lawyer. "That's why I didn't reveal to Mrs Campbell, the matron of Maple Lodge our reason for wanting to visit the home. I couldn't see any point in warning Miss Benson of our impending arrival. It would only give her enough time to have all her answers well prepared."

Charlie grunted his approval. "But have you come up with any ideas as to what approach we should take with her?" he asked, "because I certainly made a balls-up of my meeting with Walter Slade."

"No, I haven't. We'll just have to play it by ear and hope she'll prove to be co-operative. Though heaven knows which accent you will be required to call on this time, Sir Charles."

Moments later they were driven between two massive wrought iron gates and on down a long shaded drive which led up to a large turn-of-the-century mansion set in several acres of private grounds.

"This can't come cheap," said Charlie.

"Agreed," said Roberts. "And unfortunately they don't look as if they're in need of a minibus."

The car drew up outside a heavy oak door. Trevor Roberts jumped out and waited until Charlie had joined him before pressing the bell.

They did not have long to wait before a young nurse answered their call, then promptly escorted them down a highly polished tiled corridor to the matron's office.

Mrs Campbell was dressed in the familiar starched blue uniform, white collar and cuffs associated with her profession. She welcomed Charlie and Trevor Roberts in a deep Scottish burr, and had it not been for the uninterrupted sunshine coming through the windows, Charlie might have been forgiven for thinking that the matron of Maple Lodge Residential Home was unaware that she had ever left Scotland.

After the introductions had been completed Mrs Campbell asked how she could be of help.

"I was hoping you might allow us to have a word with one of your residents."

"Yes, of course, Sir Charles. May I enquire who it is you wish to see?" she asked.

"A Miss Benson," explained Charlie. "You see –"

"Oh, Sir Charles, haven't you heard?"

"Heard?" said Charlie.

"Yes. Miss Benson's been dead this past week. In fact, we buried her on Thursday."

For a second time that day Charlie's legs gave way and Trevor Roberts had quickly to take his client by the elbow and guided him to the nearest chair.

"Oh, I am sorry," said Matron. "I had no idea you were such a close friend." Charlie didn't say anything.

"And have you come all the way from London especially to see her?"

"Yes, he did," said Trevor Roberts. "Has Miss Benson had any other visitors from England recently?"

"No," said the matron without hesitation. "She received very few callers towards the end. One or two from Adelaide but never one from Britain," she added with an edge to her voice.

"And did she ever mention to you anyone called Cathy Ross or Margaret Trentham?"

Mrs Campbell thought deeply for a moment. "No," she said eventually. "At least, not to my recollection."

"Then I think perhaps we should leave, Sir Charles, as there's no point in taking up any more of Mrs Campbell's time."

"I agree," said Charlie quietly. "And thank you, Matron." Roberts helped him to his feet and Mrs Campbell accompanied them both back along the corridor towards the front door.

"Will you be returning to Britain shortly, Sir Charles?" she asked.

"Yes, probably tomorrow."

"Would it be a terrible inconvenience if I were to ask you to post a letter for me once you are back in London?"

"It would be my pleasure," said Charlie.

"I wouldn't have bothered you with this task in normal circumstances," said the matron, "but as it directly concerns Miss Benson . . ."

Both men stopped in their tracks and stared down at the prim Scottish lady. She also came to a halt and held her hands together in front of her.

"It's not simply that I wish to save the postage, you understand, Sir Charles, which is what most folk would accuse my clan of. In fact, the exact opposite is the case, for my only desire is to make a speedy refund to Miss Benson's benefactors."

"Miss Benson's benefactors?" said Charlie and Roberts in unison.

"Aye," the matron said, standing her full height of five feet and half an inch. "We are not in the habit at Maple Lodge of charging residents who have died, Mr Roberts. After all, as I'm sure you would agree, that would be dishonest."

"Of course it would be, Matron."

"And so, although we insist on three months' payment in advance, we also refund any sums left over when a resident has passed away. After any outstanding bills have been covered, you understand."

"I understand," said Charlie as he stared down at the lady, a look of hope in his eyes.

"So if you will be kind enough to wait just a wee moment, I'll be away and retrieve the letter from my office." She turned and headed back to her room a few yards further down the corridor.

"Start praying," said Charlie.

"I already have," said Roberts.

Mrs Campbell returned a few moments later holding an envelope which she handed over for Charlie's safekeeping. In a bold copperplate hand were written the words: The Manager, Coutts and Company, The Strand, London WC2.

"I do hope you won't find my request too much of an imposition, Sir Charles."

"It's a greater pleasure than you may ever realise, Mrs Campbell," Charlie assured her, as he bade the matron farewell.

Once they were back in the car, Roberts said, "It would be quite unethical of me to advise you as to whether you should or should not open that letter, Sir Charles. However –"

But Charlie had already ripped open the envelope and was pulling out its contents.

A cheque for ninety-two pounds was attached to a detailed, itemised bill for the years 1953 to 1964: in full and final settlement for the account of Miss Rachel Benson.

"God bless the Scots and their puritan upbringing," said Charlie, when he saw to whom the cheque had been made out.

CHAPTER 46

"If you were quick, Sir Charles, you could still catch the earlier flight," said Trevor Roberts as the car pulled into the hotel forecourt.

"Then I'll be quick," said Charlie, "as I'd like to be back in London as soon as possible."

"Right, I'll check you out, then phone the airport to see if they can change your reservation."

"Good. Although I've a couple of days to spare there are still some loose ends I'd like to tidy up at the London end."

Charlie had jumped out of the car even before the driver could reach the door to open it for him. He made a dash for his room and quickly threw all his possessions into a suitcase. He was back in the lobby twelve minutes later, had settled the bill and was making a dash towards the hotel entrance within fifteen. The driver was not only standing by the car waiting for him but the boot was already open.

Once the third door had been closed, the chauffeur immediately accelerated out of the hotel forecourt and swung the car into the fast lane, as he headed towards the freeway.

"Passport and ticket?" said Roberts.

Charlie smiled and removed them both from an inside pocket like a child having his prep list checked.

"Good, now let's hope we can still reach the airport in time."

"You've done wonders," said Charlie.

"Thank you, Sir Charles," said Roberts. "But you must understand that despite your gathering a considerable amount of evidence to substantiate your case most if it remains at best circumstantial. Although you and I may be convinced that Cathy Ross is in fact Margaret Ethel Trentham, with Miss Benson in her grave and Miss Ross unable to recall all the relevant details of her past there's no way of predicting whether a court would find in your favour."

"I hear what you're saying," said Charlie. "But at least I now have something to bargain with. A week ago I had nothing."

"True. And having watched you operate over the past few days I'm bound to say that I'd give you odds of better than fifty-fifty. But whatever you do, don't let that picture out of your sight: it's as convincing as any fingerprint. And see that at all times you keep Mrs Campbell's letter in a safe place until you've been able to make a copy. Also be sure that the original plus the accompanying cheque are then posted on to Coutts. We don't want you arrested for stealing ninety-two pounds. Now, is there anything else I can do for you this end?"

"Yes, you could try to get a written statement out of Walter Slade admitting that he took Mrs Trentham and a little girl called Margaret to St Hilda's, and that she left without her charge. You might also attempt to pin Slade down to a date."

"That might not prove easy after your encounter," suggested Roberts.

"Well, at least have a go. Then see if you can find out if Miss Benson was in receipt of any other payments from Mrs Trentham before 1953 and if so the amounts and dates. I suspect she's been receiving a banker's order every quarter for over thirty-five years, which would explain why she was able to end her days in such comparative luxury."

"Agreed, but once again it's entirely circumstantial and there's certainly no way that any bank would allow me to delve into Miss Benson's private account."

"I accept that," said Charlie. "But Mrs Culver should be able to let you know what Miss Benson was earning while she was principal and if she appeared to live beyond her salary. After all, you can always find out what St Hilda's needs other than a minibus."

Roberts began to make notes as Charlie rattled out a series of further suggestions.

"If you were able to wrap up Slade and prove there were any previous payments made to Miss Benson, I would then be in a far stronger position to ask Nigel Trentham to explain why his mother was willing to keep on doling out money to someone who was principal of an orphanage situated on the other side of the globe if it wasn't for his elder brother's offspring."

"I'll do what I can," promised Roberts. "If I come up with anything I'll contact you in London on your return."

"Thank you," said Charlie. "Now, is there anything I can do for you?"

"Yes, Sir Charles. Would you be good enough to pass on my kindest regards to Uncle Ernest?"

"Uncle Ernest?"

"Yes, Ernest Baverstock."

"Kindest regards be damned. I shall report him to the Law Society."

"I must advise you that there is no case to answer, Sir Charles, as nepotism is not yet a crime. Though to be honest it's my mother who's to blame. You see, she produced three sons, all lawyers, and the other two are now representing you in Perth and Brisbane."

The car drew up to the kerb alongside the Qantas terminal. The driver jumped out and removed the suitcases from the boot as Charlie ran off in the direction of the ticket counter, with Roberts a yard behind carrying Cathy's picture.

"Yes, you can still make the early flight to London," the girl at the check-in desk assured Charlie. "But please be quick as we'll be closing the gates in a few minutes' time." Charlie breathed a sigh of relief and turned to say goodbye to Trevor Roberts as the driver arrived with his suitcase and placed it on the weighing machine.

"Damn," said Charlie. "Can you lend me ten pounds?"

Roberts removed the notes from his wallet and Charlie quickly passed them on to the driver, who touched his cap and returned to the car.

"How do I ever begin to thank you?" he said as he shook Trevor Roberts by the hand.

"Thank Uncle Ernest, not me," said Roberts. "He talked me into dropping everything to take on this case."

Twenty minutes later Charlie was climbing up the steps of Qantas Flight 102 ready for the first stage of his journey back to London.

As the plane lifted off ten minutes after schedule Charlie settled back and tried, with the knowledge he had gained in the last three days, to begin fitting the pieces together. He accepted Roberts's theory that it was no coincidence that Cathy had come to work at Trumper's. She must have discovered some connection between them and the Trenthams, even if Charlie couldn't work out exactly what that connection was or her reason for not telling either of them in the first place. Telling them . . . ? What right did he have to comment? If only he had told Daniel, the boy might still be alive today. Because one thing was certain: Cathy could not have realised that Daniel was her half-brother, although he now feared that Mrs Trentham must have found out, then let her grandson know the awful truth.

"Evil woman," said Charlie to himself.

"I beg your pardon," said the middle-aged lady who was seated on his left.

"Oh, I'm sorry," said Charlie. "I wasn't referring to you." He returned to his reverie. Mrs Trentham must have somehow stumbled on that truth. But how? Did Cathy go to see her as well? Or was it simply the announcement of their engagement in *The Times* that alerted Mrs Trentham to an illegal liaison that Cathy and Daniel could not have been aware of themselves? Whatever the reason, Charlie realised that his chances of piecing together the complete story were now fairly remote, with Daniel and Mrs Trentham in their graves and Cathy still unable to recall much of what had happened to her before she arrived in England.

It was ironic, thought Charlie, that so much of what he had discovered in Australia had all the time been lodged in a file at Number 1 Chelsea Terrace, marked Cathy Ross, job application. But not the missing link. "Find that," Roberts had said, "and you will be able to show the connection between Cathy Ross and Guy Trentham." Charlie nodded in agreement.

Lately Cathy had been able to recollect some memories from her past, but still nothing significant when it came to recalling her early days in Australia. Doctor Atkins continued to advise Charlie not to press her, as he was delighted with her progress, especially over her willingness to talk quite openly about Daniel. But if he were to save Trumper's he surely had to press her now? He decided that one of the first calls he should make the moment the plane touched down on English soil would have to be to Doctor Atkins.

"This is your captain speaking," said a voice over the intercom. "I'm sorry to have to inform you that we have encountered a slight technical problem. Those of you seated on the right-hand side of the aircraft will be able to see that I have turned off one of the starboard engines. I can assure you that there is no need for any anxiety, as we still have three engines working at their full capacity and in any case this aircraft is capable of completing any leg of the journey on just one." Charlie was pleased to learn this piece of news. "However," continued the captain, "it is company policy, with your safety in mind, that when any such fault arises we should land at the nearest airport, in order that repairs can be carried out immediately." Charlie frowned. "As we have not yet reached the halfway point on our outward leg of the journey to Singapore, I am advised by air traffic control that we must return to Melbourne at once." A chorus of groans went up throughout the aircraft.

Charlie made some hasty calculations about how much time he had to spare before he needed to be back in London, then he remembered that the aircraft he had been originally booked on was still due out of Melbourne at eight twenty that night.

He flicked open his seat-belt, retrieved Cathy's picture from the rack above him and moved across to the nearest available first-class seat to the cabin door, his mind now fully concentrated on the problems of getting himself re-booked on the BOAC carrier bound for London.

Qantas Flight 102 touched down at Melbourne airport at seven minutes past seven. Charlie was the first off the aircraft, running as fast as he could, but having to lug Cathy's picture under one arm slowed him down and made it possible for several other passengers, who obviously had the same idea, to overtake him. However, once he'd reached the booking counter Charlie still managed to be eleventh in the queue. One by one the line shortened as those ahead of him were allocated seats. But by the time Charlie reached the front they could only offer him a standby. Despite pleading desperately with a BOAC official he could make no headway: there were several other passengers who felt it was every bit as important for them to be in London.

He walked slowly back to the Qantas desk to be informed that Flight 102 had been grounded for engine repairs and would not be taking off again until the following morning. At eight forty he watched the BOAC Comet that he had been originally booked on lift off the tarmac without him.

All the passengers were found beds for the night at one of the local airport hotels before having their tickets transferred to a ten twenty flight the following morning.

Charlie was up, dressed and back at the airport two hours before the plane was due to take off, and when the flight was finally called he was the first on board. If all went to schedule, he worked out, the plane would still touch down at Heathrow early on the Friday morning, giving him a clear day and a half to spare before Sir Raymond's two-year deadline was up.

He breathed his first sigh of relief when the Comet took off, his second as the flight passed the halfway mark to

Singapore, and his third when they had landed at Paya Lebar airport a few minutes ahead of time.

Charlie left the plane, but only to stretch his legs. He was strapped back into his seat and ready for take-off an hour later. The second stage from Singapore to Bangkok landed at Don Muang airport only thirty minutes behind schedule, but the plane then sat parked in a queue on the runway for a further hour. It was later explained that they were short-staffed at air traffic control. Despite the delay, Charlie was not unduly worried; but that didn't stop him from checking his half-hunter every few minutes. They took off an hour behind schedule.

When the aircraft landed at Palam airport in New Delhi, he began another hour of strolling around the duty free while the plane was being refuelled. He became bored by seeing the same watches, perfume and jewellery being sold to innocent transit passengers at prices he knew still had a fifty per cent mark-up on them. When the hour had passed and there had been no further announcements about re-boarding, Charlie walked over to the enquiry desk to discover what was causing the hold-up.

"There seems to be some problem with the relief crew on this section of the flight," he was told by the young woman behind the general enquiries sign. "They haven't completed their twenty-four hours' rest period, as stipulated by IATA regulations."

"So how long have they had?"

"Twenty hours," replied the girl, looking embarrassed.

"So that means we're stuck here for another four hours?"

"I'm afraid so."

"Where is the nearest phone?" Charlie asked, making no attempt to hide his irritation.

"In the far corner, sir," said the girl, pointing to her right.

Charlie joined yet another queue and when he reached the front managed to get through to the operator twice, connected to London once but to speak with Becky never.

By the time he eventually climbed back on to the aircraft, having achieved nothing, he was exhausted.

"This is Captain Parkhouse. We are sorry for the delay in this flight's taking off," said the pilot in a soothing voice. "I can only hope that the hold-up has not caused you too much inconvenience. Please fasten your seat-belts and prepare for take-off. Flight attendants place cabin doors to automatic."

The four jets rumbled into action and the plane inched forward before building up momentum as it sped along the tarmac. Then, quite suddenly, Charlie was thrown forward as the brakes were locked in place and the plane came to a screeching halt a few hundred yards from the end of the runway.

"This is your captain speaking. I am sorry to have to tell you that the hydraulic pumps that lift the undercarriage up and down at take-off and landing are indicating red on the control panel and I am not willing to risk a take-off at this time. We shall therefore have to taxi back to our stand and ask the local engineers to fix the problem as quickly as possible. Thank you for being so understanding."

It was the word "local" that worried Charlie.

Once they had disembarked from the plane, Charlie ran from airline counter to airline counter trying to find out if there were any flights bound for anywhere in Europe due out of New Delhi that night. He quickly discovered the only flight due out that night was destined for Sydney. He began to pray for the speed and efficiency of Indian engineers.

Charlie sat in a smoke-filled waiting lounge, leafing through magazine after magazine, sipping soft drink after soft drink, as he waited for any information he could garner on the fate of Flight 102. The first news he picked up was that the chief engineer had been sent for.

"Sent for?" said Charlie. "What does that mean?"

"We have sent a car for him," explained a smiling airport official in a clipped staccato accent.

"Sent a car?" said Charlie. "But why isn't he at the airport where he's needed?"

"It's his day off."

"And haven't you got any other engineers?"

"Not for a job this big," admitted the harassed official.

Charlie slapped his forehead with the palm of his hand. "And where does the chief engineer live?"

"Somewhere in New Delhi," came back the reply. "But don't you worry yourself, sir, we should have him back within the hour."

The trouble with this country, thought Charlie, is they tell you exactly what they think you want to hear.

For some reason the same official was unable to explain later why it had taken two hours to locate the chief engineer, a further hour to bring him back to the airport and yet another fifty minutes before he discovered the job would require a full team of three qualified engineers, who had themselves recently signed off for the evening.

A rickety old bus delivered all the passengers from Flight 107 to the Taj Mahal Hotel in the centre of the city where Charlie sat on his bed and spent most of the night once more attempting to make contact with Becky. When he eventually succeeded in reaching her he was cut off even before he had time to explain where he was. He didn't bother to try and sleep.

When the bus dropped them back at the airport the following morning the Indian airport official was there to greet them, his large smile still in place.

"The plane will take off on time," he promised.

On time, thought Charlie; in normal circumstances he would have laughed.

The plane did take off an hour later and when Charlie enquired of the purser at what hour they expected to land at Heathrow he was told at some time Saturday mid-afternoon: it was hard to be precise.

When the aircraft made a further unscheduled landing at Leonardo da Vinci on Saturday afternoon Charlie telephoned Becky from the airport. He didn't even give her time to speak. "I'm in Rome," he said, "and I'll need Stan to pick me up from Heathrow. As I can't be sure what time

I'll arrive, tell him to go out to the airport right now and sit tight. Got that?"

"Yes," said Becky.

"And I'll also need Baverstock back in his office, so if he's already disappeared off to the country for the weekend ask him to drop everything and return to London."

"You sound a little harassed, dear."

"Sorry," said Charlie. "It's not been the easiest of journeys."

With the picture under one arm and no interest as to what was wrong with the aircraft this time or where his suitcase might end up, he took the first European flight available that afternoon for London, and once it had taken off checked his watch every ten minutes. When the pilot crossed the English Channel at eight o'clock that evening, Charlie felt confident that four hours would still be ample time for him to register Cathy's claim – so long as Becky had tracked down Baverstock.

As the plane began to circle London in a familiar holding pattern Charlie looked out of the little oval window and stared down at the snake-like Thames.

It was another twenty minutes before the lights of the runway glared up in two straight lines at Charlie, followed by a puff of smoke as the wheels touched the ground and the plane taxied to its allotted gate. The doors of the aircraft were finally opened at eight twenty-nine.

Charlie grabbed the picture and ran all the way to passport control and on through customs.

He didn't stop until he saw a telephone box, but as he hadn't any coins to make a local call he told the operator his name and asked to transfer the charge. A moment later he was put through.

"Becky, I'm at Heathrow. Where's Baverstock?"

"On his way back from Tewkesbury. Expects to be in his office around nine thirty, latest ten."

"Good, then I'll come straight home. I should be with you in about forty minutes."

Charlie slammed down the phone, checked his watch

and realised that he hadn't left himself enough time to phone Doctor Atkins. He ran out on to the pavement, suddenly aware of the chill breeze. Stan was waiting by the car for him. Over the years the former sergeant-major had become accustomed to Charlie's impatience and drove him smoothly through the outskirts of London, ignoring the speed limit until they reached Chiswick, after which only a motor-bike could have been stopped for speeding. Despite the teeming rain he had his boss back at Eaton Square by nine sixteen.

Charlie was about halfway through telling a silent Becky all he had discovered in Australia when Baverstock phoned to say he was back at his office in High Holborn. Charlie thanked him, passed on his nephew's best wishes and then apologised for ruining his weekend.

"You won't have ruined it if your news is positive," said Baverstock.

"Guy Trentham had another child," said Charlie.

"I didn't imagine that you'd dragged me back from Tewkesbury to tell me the latest Test score from Melbourne," said Baverstock. "Male or female?"

"Female."

"Legitimate or illegitimate?"

"Legitimate."

"Then she can register her claim with the estate at any time before midnight."

"She has to register her claim with you in person?"

"That is what the will stipulates," said Baverstock. "However, if she's still in Australia she can register with Trevor Roberts, as I've given him – "

"No, she's in England and I'll have her in your office by midnight."

"Good. By the way, what's her name?" asked Baverstock. "Just so that I can prepare the paperwork."

"Cathy Ross," said Charlie. "But ask your nephew to explain everything as I haven't a moment to spare," he added, replacing the receiver before Baverstock could react. He ran out into the hall searching for Becky.

"Where's Cathy?" he shouted, as Becky appeared at the top of the stairs.

"She went to a concert at the Festival Hall. Mozart, I think she said, with some new beau from the City."

"Right, let's go," said Charlie.

"Go?"

"Yes, go," said Charlie at the top of his voice. He had already reached the door and climbed into the back seat of the car before he realised there was no driver.

He jumped out and was on his way back to the house as Becky came rushing out in the opposite direction.

"Where's Stan?"

"Probably having some supper in the kitchen."

"Right," said Charlie, passing over his own keys. "You drive, I'll talk."

"But where are we off to?"

"The Festival Hall."

"Funny," Becky said, "after all these years and I had no idea you cared for Mozart." As she took her seat behind the wheel Charlie ran round to join her in the front. She pulled out and moved deftly through the evening traffic as Charlie continued to explain the full implications of his discoveries in Australia and how imperative it was that they find Cathy before midnight. Becky listened intently but did not attempt to interrupt her husband's flow.

By the time Charlie asked her if she had any questions they were crossing Westminster Bridge, but Becky still remained silent.

Charlie waited for a few moments before he demanded, "Have you nothing to say?"

"Yes," said Becky. "Don't let's make the same mistake with Cathy as we did with Daniel."

"Namely?"

"Fail to tell her the whole truth."

"I'll have to speak to Doctor Atkins before I can even consider taking that risk," said Charlie. "But our more immediate problem is to make sure she registers in time."

"Not to mention the even more immediate problem of

where you expect me to leave the car," said Becky as they swung left into Belvedere Road and on towards the entrance of the Royal Festival Hall with its double yellow lines and "No Parking" signs.

"Right outside the front door," said Charlie, which Becky obeyed without question.

As soon as the car had come to a halt Charlie jumped out, ran across the pavement and pushed through the glass doors.

"What time does the concert end?" he asked the first uniformed official he spotted.

"Ten thirty-five, sir, but you can't leave your car there."

"And where's the manager's office?"

"Fifth floor, turn right, second door on the left as you get out of the lift. But . . ."

"Thank you," shouted Charlie, already running past him towards the lift. Becky had just about caught up with her husband by the time the light above the lift indicated G.

"Your car, sir –" said the doorman, but the lift doors were already closing on the gesticulating official.

When the lift doors slid apart at the fifth floor Charlie jumped out, looked right and saw a door to his left marked "Manager". He knocked once before charging in, to find two men dressed in dinner jackets enjoying a cigarette and listening to the concert over an intercom. They turned to see who had interrupted them.

"Good evening, Sir Charles," said the taller of the two as he rose, stubbed out his cigarette, and stepped forward. "Jackson. I'm the theatre manager. Can I help you in any way?"

"I only hope so, Mr Jackson," said Charlie. "I have to get a young lady out of your concert hall as quickly as possible. It's an emergency."

"Do you know her seat number?"

"No idea." Charlie looked towards his wife who only shook her head.

"Then follow me," said the manager, who strode straight out of the door and back towards the lift. When the doors reopened the first official Charlie had come across was now standing in front of them.

"Any problems, Ron?"

"Only that this gentleman's left his car bang outside the front door, sir."

"Then keep an eye on it, will you, Ron?" The manager pressed the third-floor button and, turning to Becky, asked, "What was the young lady wearing?"

"A burgundy dress with a white cape," said Becky urgently.

"Well done, madam," said the manager. He stepped out of the lift and led them quickly through to a side entrance adjoining the Ceremonial Box. Once inside Mr Jackson removed a small picture of the Queen opening the building in 1957 and flicked back a disguised shutter so that he could observe the audience through a one-way mirror. "A security precaution in case there's ever any trouble," he explained. The manager then unhooked two pairs of opera glasses from their little stands under the balcony and handed one each to Charlie and Becky.

"If you can locate where the lady is seated, one of my staff will discreetly pull her out." He turned to listen to the strains of the final movement for a few seconds before adding, "You've got about ten minutes before the concert ends, twelve at the most. There are no encores planned for tonight."

"You take the stalls, Becky, and I'll cover the dress circle." Charlie began to focus the little opera glasses on the audience seated below them.

They both covered the one thousand nine hundred seats, first quickly then slowly up and down each row. Neither could spot Cathy in the stalls or dress circle.

"Try the boxes on the other side, Sir Charles," suggested the manager.

Two pairs of glasses swung over to the far side of the theatre. There was still no sign of Cathy, so Charlie and

Becky turned their attention back to the main auditorium, once again scanning quickly over the seats.

The conductor brought his baton down for the final time at ten thirty-two and the applause followed in waves as Charlie and Becky searched the standing throng until the lights eventually went up and the audience began to make their way out of the theatre.

"You keep on looking, Becky. I'll go out front and see if I can spot them as they're leaving." He dashed out of the Ceremonial Box and down the stairs followed by Jackson, nearly knocking over a man who was leaving the box below them. Charlie turned to apologise.

"Hello, Charlie, I didn't know you liked Mozart," a voice said.

"I never used to but suddenly he's top of the pops," said Charlie, unable to mask his delight.

"Of course," said the manager. "The one place you couldn't see was the box below ours."

"May I introduce –"

"We haven't time for that," said Charlie. "Just follow me." He grabbed Cathy by the arm. "Mr Jackson, would you be kind enough to ask Becky, my wife, to explain to this gentleman why I need Cathy. You can have her back after midnight," said Charlie, smiling at the bemused young man. "And thank you, Mr Jackson."

He checked his watch: ten forty. "We still have enough time."

"Enough time for what, Charlie?" said Cathy as she found herself being pulled across the foyer and out on to Belvedere Road. The uniformed man was now standing to attention by the car.

"Thank you, Ron," said Charlie as he tried to open the front door. "Damn, Becky's locked it," he said. He turned to watch a cab as it came off the waiting rank. He hailed it.

"I say, old fellow," said a man standing in the front of the taxi queue, "I think you'll find that's my cab."

"She's just about to give birth," said Charlie as he

opened the door and pushed the wafer-thin Cathy into the back of the taxi.

"Oh, jolly good luck," said the man, taking a pace backwards.

"Where to, guvn'r?" asked the cabbie.

"One hundred and ten High Holborn and don't hang about," said Charlie.

"I think we're more likely to find a solicitor than a gynaecologist at that particular address," suggested Cathy. "And I do hope you've a worthwhile explanation as to why I'm missing dinner with the one man who's asked me out on a date in weeks."

"Not right now," Charlie confessed. "All I need you to do for the moment is sign a document before midnight, then I promise the explanations will follow."

The taxi pulled up outside the solicitor's office a few minutes after eleven. Charlie stepped out of the cab to find Baverstock was standing by the door waiting to greet them.

"That'll be eight and six, guvn'r."

"Oh, God," said Charlie, "I haven't got any money."

"That's the way he treats all his girls," said Cathy, as she passed the cabbie a ten-shilling note.

They both followed Baverstock through to his office where a set of documents was already laid out on his desk. "Since you called I have had a long conversation with my nephew in Australia," said Baverstock, facing Charlie. "So I think I'm well acquainted with everything that took place while you were over there."

"Which is more than I am," said Cathy, sounding bewildered.

"All in good time," said Charlie. "Explanations later." He turned back to Baverstock. "So what happens now?"

"Miss Ross must sign here, here and here," the solicitor said without further explanation, indicating a space between two pencilled crosses at the bottom of three separate sheets of paper. "As you are in no way related to the beneficiary or a beneficiary yourself, Sir Charles, you may care to act as the witness to Miss Ross's signature."

Charlie nodded, placed a pair of opera glasses beside the contract and took a pen from his inside pocket.

"You've always taught me in the past, Charlie, to read documents carefully before putting my signature to them."

"Forget everything I've taught you in the past, my girl, and just sign where Mr Baverstock is pointing."

Cathy signed all three documents without another word.

"Thank you, Miss Ross," said Mr Baverstock. "And now if you could both bear with me for one moment, I must inform Mr Birkenshaw of what has taken place."

"Birkenshaw?" said Charlie.

"Mr Trentham's solicitor. I must obviously let him know immediately that his client is not the only person who has registered a claim to the Hardcastle estate."

Cathy, looking even more bewildered, turned to Charlie.

"Later," said Charlie. "I promise."

Baverstock dialled the seven digits of a Chelsea number.

No one spoke as they waited for the telephone to be answered. Eventually Mr Baverstock heard a sleepy voice say, "Kensington 7192."

"Good evening, Birkenshaw, Baverstock here. Sorry to have to bother you at this time of night. Indeed, I wouldn't have done so if I hadn't considered the circumstances fully warranted such an intrusion on your privacy. But may I first ask what time you make it?"

"Have I heard you correctly?" said Birkenshaw, his voice now sounding more alert. "You've telephoned me in the middle of the night to ask what the time is?"

"Precisely," said Baverstock. "You see, I need to confirm that it is still before the witching hour. So do be a good fellow and tell me what time you make it."

"I make it eleven seventeen, but I fail to understand – "

"I make it eleven sixteen," said Baverstock, "but on the matter of time I am happy to bow to your superior judgment. The purpose of this call, by the way," he continued, "is to let you know that a second person – who appears to be a more direct descendant of Sir Raymond than your client – has laid claim to the Hardcastle estate."

"What's her name?"

"I suspect you already know that," replied the old lawyer before he replaced the telephone. "Damn," he said, looking across at Charlie, "I should have recorded the conversation."

"Why?"

"Because Birkenshaw is never going to admit that he said 'her'."

CHAPTER 47

"Are you saying that Guy Trentham was my father?" asked Cathy. "But how . . . ?

After waking up Doctor Atkins, a man more used to being disturbed during the night, Charlie felt able to explain to Cathy what he had discovered during his visit to Australia, and how everything had been borne out by the information she had supplied to Becky when she first applied for a job at Trumper's. Baverstock listened intently, nodding from time to time, while regularly checking the copious notes he had made following a long conversation with his nephew in Sydney.

Cathy listened to everything Charlie had to report and although she now had some recollections of her life in Australia, she was still fairly vague about her days at the university of Melbourne, and could remember almost nothing of St Hilda's, while the name Miss Benson just didn't register at all.

"I've tried so hard to recall more details of what happened before I came to England, but nothing much comes back despite the fact that I can remember almost everything that took place after I landed at Southampton. Doctor Atkins isn't that optimistic, is he?"

"There are no rules is all he keeps reminding me."

Around four the following morning Charlie phoned for a taxi to take them back to Eaton Square, having agreed with Baverstock that he should set up a face-to-face meeting with the other side as soon as it could be arranged. When they returned home Cathy was so exhausted that she went straight to bed but as Charlie's time-clock didn't allow him to sleep he closeted himself in the study and continued his mental search for the missing link, only too aware of the legal battle that lay ahead of him even if he succeeded.

The following day he and Cathy travelled up to Cambridge together and spent a fraught afternoon in Doctor Atkins' little office at Addenbrooke's. For his part the consultant seemed far more interested in the file on Cathy that had been supplied by Mrs Culver than the fact she might in some way be related to Mrs Trentham and therefore eligible to inherit the Hardcastle Trust.

He took her slowly through each item in the file – art classes, credits, misdemeanours, tennis matches, Melbourne Church of England Girls' Grammar School, University of Melbourne – but he always met with the same response: deep thought, but only vague recollections. He tried word associations – Melbourne, Miss Benson, cricket, ship, hotel – to which he received the replies, Australia, Hedges, scorer, Southampton, long hours.

"Scorer" was the only word that interested Doctor Atkins but pressed further Cathy's only memories of Australia remained a sketchy description of Melbourne Grammar School, some clear recollections of the university and a boy called Mel Nicholls, followed by a long trip on a ship to London. She could even tell them the names of Pam and Maureen who had travelled over with her, but not where they came from.

Cathy went into great detail when the subject turned to the Melrose Hotel and Charlie was able to confirm the accuracy of Cathy's recollections of her early life at Trumper's.

The description of her first meeting with Daniel, down to his changing the place cards at the Trumpers' housewarming party, brought tears to Charlie's eyes. But on the subject of her parentage and the names of Margaret Ethel Trentham and Miss Rachel Benson she still had nothing to offer.

By six o'clock Cathy was drained. Doctor Atkins took Charlie on one side and warned him that in his opinion it was most unlikely that she would remember much more of what took place in her life before she arrived in London. Perhaps minor incidents might come back to her from time to time, but nothing of any real significance.

"I'm sorry, I wasn't much help to you, was I?" said Cathy as Charlie drove her back to London.

He took her hand. "We're not beaten yet," he promised her, although he was beginning to feel that Trevor Roberts's odds of fifty-fifty of proving that Cathy was the rightful claimant to the Hardcastle Trust were looking distinctly optimistic.

Becky was there to welcome them home and the three of them had a quiet supper together. Charlie made no reference to what had taken place at Cambridge earlier in the day until after Cathy had retired to her room. When Becky heard how Cathy had responded to Doctor Atkins' examination she insisted that from now on the girl was to be left in peace.

"I lost Daniel because of that woman," she told her husband. "I'm not willing to lose Cathy as well. If you're going to continue your fight for Trumper's you must do it without involving her."

Charlie nodded his agreement though he wanted to shout out: How am I expected to save everything I've built up from being taken away from me by yet another Trentham without being allowed to push Cathy to the brink?

Just before he switched out the bedroom light the phone rang. It was Trevor Roberts calling from Sydney, but his news did not advance their cause. Walter Slade had refused to release any new information on Ethel Trentham and wouldn't even sign a document confirming he had driven her. Charlie once again cursed himself for the crass way he had handled the interview with the old Yorkshireman.

"And the bank?" he asked, not sounding too hopeful.

"The Commercial Bank of Australia say they wouldn't allow access to the details of Miss Benson's private account unless we could prove a crime had been committed. What Mrs Trentham did to Cathy might well be described as evil, but I fear it wasn't strictly criminal."

"It hasn't been a good day for either of us," admitted Charlie.

"Never forget that the other side doesn't know that."

"True, but how much *do* they know?"

"My uncle's told me about Birkenshaw's slip of the tongue with 'her', so my bet is they know almost as much as we do. When you confront them, better assume they do, while at the same time never stop looking for that missing link."

After Charlie had put down the phone, he lay awake for some time and didn't move again until he could hear Becky breathing deeply. Then he slid out of bed, donned his dressing-gown and crept down to his study. He opened a notebook and began to write out every fact he had gathered during the last few days in the hope that it might just trigger off some memory. The following morning Cathy found him slumped, head on his desk, sound asleep.

"I don't deserve you, Charlie," she whispered, kissing him on the forehead. He stirred and raised his eyes.

"We're winning," he said sleepily and even managed a smile, but he realised from the expression on her face that she didn't believe him.

Becky joined them for breakfast an hour later and talked of everything except the face-to-face meeting that had been arranged to take place in Mr Baverstock's rooms that afternoon.

As Charlie stood up to leave the table, Cathy said, quite unexpectedly, "I'd like to be present at the showdown."

"Do you think that's wise?" asked Becky, glancing anxiously towards her husband.

"Perhaps not," said Cathy. "But I'm still certain I want to be there, not just learn about the outcome later, second-hand."

"Good girl," said Charlie. "The meeting will be at three in Baverstock's office, when we will get the chance to present our case. Trentham's lawyer will be joining us at four. I'll pick you up at two thirty, but if you want to change your mind before then, it won't worry me in the slightest."

Becky turned to see how Cathy had reacted to this suggestion and was disappointed.

When Charlie marched in to his office at exactly eight thirty, Daphne and Arthur Selwyn were already waiting for him as instructed.

"Coffee for three and please, no interruptions," Charlie told Jessica, placing his night's work on the desk in front of him.

"So where do we start?" asked Daphne, and for the next hour and a half they rehearsed questions, statements and tactics that could be used when dealing with Trentham and Birkenshaw, trying to second-guess every situation that might arise.

By the time a light lunch was sent in just before twelve they all felt drained; no one spoke for some time.

"It's important for you to remember that you're dealing with a different Trentham this time," said Arthur Selwyn eventually, as he dropped a sugar lump into his coffee.

"They're all as bad as each other as far as I'm concerned," said Charlie.

"Perhaps Nigel's every bit as resolute as his brother, but I don't believe for one moment that he has his mother's cunning – or Guy's ability to think on his feet."

"Just what are you getting at, Arthur?" asked Daphne.

"When you all meet this afternoon Charlie must keep Trentham talking as much as possible, because I've noticed over the years during board meetings that he often says one sentence too many and simply ends up defeating his own case. I'll never forget the time he was against the staff having their own canteen because of the loss of revenue it was bound to incur, until Cathy pointed out that the food came out of the same kitchen as the restaurant and we actually ended up making a small profit on what would otherwise have been thrown away."

Charlie considered this statement as he took another bite out of his sandwich.

"Wonder what his advisors are telling him are my weak points."

"Your temper," said Daphne. "You've always lived on a short fuse. So don't give them the chance to light it."

At one o'clock Daphne and Arthur Selwyn left Charlie in peace. After the door had closed behind them Charlie removed his jacket, went over to the sofa, lay down and for the next hour slept soundly. At two o'clock Jessica woke him. He smiled up at her, feeling fully refreshed: another legacy from the war.

He returned to his desk and read through his notes once again before leaving his office to walk three doors down the corridor and pick up Cathy. He quite expected her to have changed her mind but she already had her coat on and was sitting waiting for him. They drove over to Baverstock's office arriving a full hour before Trentham and Birkenshaw were due to put in an appearance.

The old lawyer listened carefully to Charlie as he presented his case, occasionally nodding or making further notes, though from the expression on his face Charlie had no way of knowing what he really felt.

When Charlie had come to the end of his monologue Baverstock put his fountain pen down on the desk and leaned back in his chair. For some time he didn't speak.

"I am impressed by the logic of your argument, Sir Charles," he said eventually, as he leant forward and placed the palms of his hands on the desk in front of him. "And indeed with the evidence you have gathered. However, I'm bound to say that without the corroboration of your main witness and also with no written affidavits from either

Walter Slade or Miss Benson, Mr Birkenshaw will be quick to point out that your claim is based almost entirely on circumstantial evidence.

"None the less," he continued, "we shall have to see what the other side has to offer. I find it hard to believe following my conversation with Birkenshaw on Saturday night that your findings will come as a complete revelation to his client."

The clock on his mantelpiece struck a discreet four chimes; Baverstock checked his pocket watch. There was no sign of the other side and soon the old solicitor started drumming his fingers on the desk. Charlie began to wonder if this was simply tactics on behalf of his adversary.

Nigel Trentham and his lawyer finally appeared at twelve minutes past four; neither of them seemed to feel it was necessary to apologise for their lateness.

Charlie stood up when Mr Baverstock introduced him to Victor Birkenshaw, a tall, thin man, not yet fifty, prematurely balding with what little hair he had left combed over the top of his head in thin grey strands. The only characteristic he seemed to have in common with Baverstock was that their clothes appeared to have come from the same tailor. Birkenshaw sat down in one of the two vacant seats opposite the old lawyer without acknowledging that Cathy was even in the room. He removed a pen from his top pocket, took out a pad from his briefcase and rested it on his knee.

"My client, Mr Nigel Trentham, has come to lay claim to his inheritance as the rightful heir to the Hardcastle Trust," he began, "as clearly stated in Sir Raymond's last will and testament."

"Your client," said Baverstock, picking up Birkenshaw's rather formal approach, "may I remind you, is not named in Sir Raymond's will, and a dispute has now arisen as to who is the rightful next of kin. Please don't forget that Sir Raymond insisted that I call this meeting, should the need arise, in order to adjudicate on his behalf."

"My client," came back Birkenshaw, "is the second son of the late Gerald and Margaret Ethel Trentham and the grandson of Sir Raymond Hardcastle. Therefore, following the death of Guy Trentham, his elder brother, he must surely be the legitimate heir."

"Under the terms of the will, I am bound to accept your client's claim," agreed Baverstock. "Unless it can be shown that Guy Trentham is survived by a child or children. We already know that Guy was the father of Daniel Trumper – "

"That has never been proven to my client's satisfaction," said Birkenshaw, busily writing down Baverstock's words.

"It was proven sufficiently to Sir Raymond's satisfaction for him to name Daniel in his will in preference to your client. And following the meeting between Mrs Trentham and her grandson we have every reason to believe that she also was in no doubt as to who Daniel's father was. Otherwise why did she bother to come to an extensive agreement with him?"

"This is all conjecture," said Birkenshaw. "Only one fact is certain: the gentleman in question is no longer with us, and as far as anyone knows produced no children of his own." He still did not look in Cathy's direction while she sat listening silently as the ball was tossed backwards and forwards between the two professionals.

"We were happy to accept that without question," said Charlie, intervening for the first time. "But what we didn't know until recently was that Guy Trentham had a second child called Margaret Ethel."

"What proof do you have for such an outrageous claim?" said Birkenshaw, sitting bolt upright.

"The proof is in the bank statement that I sent round to your home on Sunday morning."

"A statement, I might say," said Birkenshaw, "that should not have been opened by anyone other than my client." He glanced towards Nigel Trentham who was busy lighting a cigarette.

"I agree," said Charlie, his voice rising. "But I thought I'd take a leaf out of Mrs Trentham's book for a change."

Baverstock winced, fearing his friend might be on the verge of losing his temper.

"Whoever the girl was," continued Charlie, "she somehow managed to get her name on to police files as Guy Trentham's only surviving child and to paint a picture that remained on the dining room wall of a Melbourne orphanage for over twenty years. A painting, I might add, that could not be reproduced by anyone other than the person who originally created it. Better than a fingerprint, wouldn't you say? Or is that also conjecture?"

"The only thing the painting proves," retorted Birkenshaw, "is that Miss Ross resided at an orphanage in Melbourne at some time between 1924 and 1945. However, I'm given to understand that she is quite unable to recall any details of her life at that orphanage, or indeed anything about its principal. Is that not the case, Miss Ross?" He turned to face Cathy directly for the first time.

She nodded her reluctant agreement, but still didn't speak.

"Some witness," said Birkenshaw, not attempting to disguise the sarcasm. "She can't even support the story you are putting forward on her behalf. Her name is Cathy Ross, that much we do know, despite your so-called evidence there's nothing to link her with Sir Raymond Hardcastle."

"There are several people who can support her 'story', as you call it," said Charlie, jumping back in. Baverstock raised an eyebrow as no evidence had been placed before him to corroborate such a statement, even if he did want to believe what Sir Charles was saying.

"Knowing that she was brought up in an orphanage in Melbourne doesn't add up to corroboration," said Birkenshaw, pushing back a strand of hair that had fallen across his forehead. "I repeat, even if we were to accept all your wild claims about some imagined meeting between Mrs Trentham and Miss Benson, that still doesn't prove Miss Ross is of the same blood as Guy Trentham."

"Perhaps you'd like to check her blood group for yourself?" said Charlie. This time Mr Baverstock raised both eyebrows: the subject of blood groups had never been referred to by either party before.

"A blood group, I might add, Sir Charles, that is shared by half the world's population." Birkenshaw tugged the lapels of his jacket.

"Oh, so you've already checked it?" said Charlie with a look of triumph. "So there must be some doubt in your mind."

"There's no doubt in my mind as to who is the rightful heir to the Hardcastle estate," Birkenshaw said, before turning to face Baverstock. "How long are we expected to drag out this farce?" His question was followed by an exasperated sigh.

"As long as it takes for someone to convince me who is the rightful heir to Sir Raymond's estate," said Baverstock, his voice remaining cold and authoritative.

"What more do you want?" Birkenshaw asked. "My client has nothing to hide, whereas Miss Ross seems to have nothing to offer."

"Then perhaps you could explain, Birkenshaw, to my satisfaction," said Baverstock, "why Mrs Ethel Trentham made regular payments over several years to a Miss Benson, the principal of St Hilda's Orphanage in Melbourne, where I think we all now accept Miss Ross lived between 1927 and 1942?"

"I didn't have the privilege of representing Mrs Trentham, or indeed Miss Benson, so I'm in no position to offer an opinion. Nor, sir, for that matter, are you."

"Perhaps your client is aware of the reason for those payments and *would* care to offer an opinion," interjected Charlie. They both turned to Nigel Trentham who calmly stubbed out the remains of his cigarette but still made no attempt to speak.

"There's no reason why my client should be expected to answer any such hypothetical question," Birkenshaw suggested.

"But if your client is so unwilling to speak for himself," said Baverstock, "it makes it all the more difficult for me to accept that he has nothing to hide."

"That, sir, is unworthy of you," said Birkenshaw. "You of all people are well aware that when a client is represented by a lawyer it is understood he may not necessarily wish to speak. In fact, it was not even obligatory for Mr Trentham to attend this meeting."

"This isn't a court of law," said Baverstock sharply. "In any case, I suspect Mr Trentham's grandfather would not have approved of such tactics."

"Are you denying my client his legal rights?"

"Certainly not. However, if because of his unwillingness to offer any opinion I feel unable to come to a decision myself I may have to recommend to both parties that this matter be settled in a court of law, as stated clearly in clause twenty-seven of Sir Raymond's will."

Yet another clause that he didn't know about, Charlie reflected ruefully.

"But such a case might take years just to reach the courts," Birkenshaw pointed out. "Furthermore, it could end up in vast expenses to both sides. I cannot believe that would have been Sir Raymond's purpose."

"That may be so," said Baverstock. "But at least it would ensure that your client was given the opportunity to explain those quarterly payments to a jury – that is, if he knew anything about them."

For the first time Birkenshaw seemed to hesitate but Trentham still didn't speak. He just sat there, drawing on a second cigarette.

"A jury might also consider Miss Ross to be nothing more than an opportunist," suggested Birkenshaw, changing tack. "An opportunist who, having stumbled upon rather a good tale, managed to get herself over to England where she then made the facts fit in neatly with her own circumstances."

"Very neatly indeed," said Charlie. "Didn't she do well at the age of three to get herself registered at an orphanage in Melbourne? At exactly the same time as Guy Trentham was locked up in the local jail – "

"Coincidence," said Birkenshaw.

"– having been left there by Mrs Trentham, who then makes out a quarterly payment to the principal of that orphanage which mysteriously ceases the moment Miss Benson dies. That must have been some secret she was keeping."

"Once again circumstantial and, what's more, inadmissible," said Birkenshaw.

Nigel Trentham leaned forward and was about to make a comment when his lawyer placed his right hand firmly on his arm. "We shall not fall for those sort of bully-boy tactics, Sir Charles, that I suspect are more commonplace in the Whitechapel Road than in Lincoln's Inn."

Charlie leapt out of his chair, his fist clenched, and took a pace towards Birkenshaw.

"Calm yourself, Sir Charles," said Baverstock sharply.

Charlie reluctantly came to a halt a couple of feet in front of Birkenshaw, who did not flinch. After a moment's hesitation he recalled Daphne's advice and returned to his chair: Trentham's lawyer continued to stare defiantly at him.

"As I was saying," said Birkenshaw, "my client has nothing to hide. And he will certainly not find it necessary to resort to physical violence to prove his case."

Charlie unclenched his fist but did not lower his voice: "I do hope your client will resort to answering leading counsel when he enquires as to why his mother continued to pay large sums of money to someone from the other side of the world whom she, so you claim, never met. And why a Mr Walter Slade, a chauffeur with the Victoria Country Club, took Mrs Trentham to St Hilda's on 20 April 1927 accompanied by a little girl of Cathy's age called Margaret, but left without her. And I'll bet if we ask a judge to delve into Miss Benson's bank account, we'll find that those payments go back to within a day of when Miss Ross was registered at St Hilda's. After all, we already know that the banker's order was cancelled the week Miss Benson died."

Once again Baverstock appeared horrified by Charlie's reckless nerve, and raised a hand in the hope that he might stop any further outbursts.

Birkenshaw in contrast couldn't resist a wry smile. "Sir Charles, in default of your being represented by a lawyer, I really should remind you of one or two home truths. For a start, let me make one point abundantly clear: my client has assured me that he had never heard of Miss Benson until yesterday. In any case, no English judge has the jurisdiction to delve into an Australian bank account unless he has reason to believe a crime has been committed in both countries. What is more, Sir Charles, two of your key witnesses are sadly in their graves while the third, Mr Walter Slade, will not be making any trips to London. What is more, you won't be able to subpoena him.

"So now let us turn to your claim, Sir Charles, that a jury would be surprised if my client did not appear in the witness box to answer on behalf of his mother. I suspect they would be even more staggered to learn that the principal witness in this case, the claimant, was also unwilling to take the stand to answer on her own behalf because she has little or no recollection of what actually took place at the time in question. I do not believe that you could find a counsel in the land who would be willing to put Miss Ross through such an ordeal if the only words she is likely to utter in reply to every question put to her in the witness box were, 'Sorry, I can't remember.' Or is it possible that she simply has nothing credible to say? Let me assure you, Sir Charles, we would be only too happy to go to court, because you would be laughed out of it."

Charlie could tell from the look on Baverstock's face that he was beaten. He glanced sadly across at Cathy whose expression had not changed for the past hour.

Baverstock slowly removed his spectacles and made great play of cleaning them with a handkerchief he had taken out of his top pocket. Eventually he spoke: "I confess, Sir Charles, that I cannot see any good reason to take up the courts' time with this case. In fact, I believe it would be irresponsible of me to do so, unless of course Miss Ross is able to produce some fresh evidence of her identity that has so far not been considered or at least can corroborate all the statements you have made on her behalf." He turned to Cathy. "Miss Ross, is there anything you would like to say at this juncture?"

All four men turned their attention to Cathy who, sitting quietly, was rubbing a thumb against the inside of her forefinger, just below her chin. "I apologise, Miss Ross," said Baverstock. "I didn't realise that you had been trying to gain my attention."

"No, no, it is I who should apologise, Mr Baverstock," said Cathy. "I always do that when I'm nervous. It reminds me of the piece of jewellery that my father gave me when I was a child."

"The piece of jewellery your father gave you?" said Mr Baverstock quietly, not sure that he had heard her correctly.

"Yes," said Cathy. She undid the top button of her blouse and took out the miniature medal that hung from the end of a gold chain.

"Your father gave you that?" said Charlie.

"Oh, yes," said Cathy. "It's the only tangible memory I have of him."

"May I see the necklace, please?" asked Baverstock.

"Certainly," said Cathy, slipping the gold chain over her head and passing the medal to Charlie. He examined the miniature for some time before handing it on to Mr Baverstock.

"Although I'm no expert on medals I think it's a miniature MC," said Charlie.

"Wasn't Guy Trentham awarded the MC?" asked Baverstock.

"Yes, he was," said Birkenshaw, "and he also went to Harrow, but simply wearing their old school tie doesn't prove my client was his brother. In fact, it doesn't prove anything and certainly couldn't be produced as evidence in a court of law. After all, there must be hundreds of MCs still around. Indeed, Miss Ross could have picked up such a medal in any junk shop in London once she'd planned to make the facts surrounding Guy Trentham fit in with her background. You can't really expect us to fall for that old trick, Sir Charles."

"I can assure you, Mr Birkenshaw, that this particular medal was given to me by my father," said Cathy, looking directly at the lawyer. "He may not have been entitled to wear it, but I will never forget him placing it around my neck."

"That can't possibly be my brother's MC," said Nigel Trentham, speaking for the first time. "What's more, I can prove it."

"You can prove what?" asked Baverstock.

"Are you certain – ?" began Birkenshaw, but this time it was Trentham who placed a hand firmly on his lawyer's arm.

"I will prove to your satisfaction, Mr Baverstock," continued Trentham, "that the medal you now have in front of you could not have been the MC won by my brother."

"And just how do you propose to do that?" asked Baverstock.

"Because Guy's medal was unique. After he had been awarded his MC my mother sent the original to Spink's and at her request they printed Guy's initials down the edge of one of the arms. Those initials can only be seen under a magnifying glass. I know, because the medal he was presented with on the Marne still stands on the mantelpiece of my home in Chester Square. If a miniature had ever existed my mother would have had his initials stamped on it in exactly the same way."

No one spoke as Baverstock opened a drawer in his desk and took out an ivory-handled magnifying glass that he normally used to decipher illegible handwriting. He held up the medal to the light and studied the edges of the little silver arms one by one.

"You're quite right," admitted Baverstock, as he looked back up at Trentham. "Your case is proven." He passed both the medal and the magnifying glass over to Mr

Birkenshaw who in turn studied the MC for some time before returning the medal to Cathy with a slight bow of the head. He turned to his client and asked, "Were your brother's initials G.F.T.?"

"Yes, that's right. Guy Francis Trentham."

"Then I can only wish that you had kept your mouth shut."

BECKY

1964-1971

CHAPTER 48

When Charlie burst into the drawing room that evening it was the first time that I really believed Guy Trentham was finally dead.

I sat in silence while my husband strode around the room recalling with relish every last detail of the confrontation that had taken place in Mr Baverstock's office earlier that afternoon.

I have loved four men in my life with emotions ranging from adoration to devotion, but only Charlie encompassed the entire spectrum. Yet, even in his moment of triumph, I knew it would be left to me to take away from him the thing he most loved.

Within a fortnight of that fateful meeting, Nigel Trentham had agreed to part with his shares at the market price. Now that interest rates had risen to eight per cent it was hardly surprising that he had little stomach for a protracted and bitter wrangle over any claim he might or might not have to the Hardcastle estate.

Mr Baverstock, on behalf of the Trust, purchased all his stock at a cost of a little over seven million pounds. The old solicitor then advised Charlie that he should call a special board meeting as it was his duty to inform Companies House of what had taken place. He also warned Charlie that he must, within fourteen days, circulate all other shareholders with the details of the transaction.

It had been a long time since I'd looked forward to a board meeting with such anticipation.

Although I was among the first to take my place at the boardroom table that morning, every other director was present long before the meeting was scheduled to begin.

"Apologies for absence?" requested the chairman on the dot of ten.

"Nigel Trentham, Roger Gibbs and Hugh Folland," Jessica intoned in her best matter-of-fact voice.

"Thank you. Minutes of the last meeting," said Charlie. "Is it your wish that I should sign those minutes as a true record?"

I glanced round the faces at the boardroom table. Daphne, dressed in a perky yellow outfit, was doodling away all over her minutes. Tim Newman was looking as suave as ever and simply nodded, while Simon took a sip from the glass of water in front of him and when he caught my eye raised it in a mock toast. Ned Denning whispered something inaudible in Bob Makins's ear while Cathy placed a tick by item number two. Only Paul Merrick looked as if he wasn't enjoying the occasion. I turned my attention back to Charlie.

As no one appeared to be showing any dissent, Jessica folded back the last page of the minutes to allow Charlie to scrawl his signature below the bottom line. I noticed Charlie smile when he re-read the final instruction the board had given him on the last occasion we had met: "Chairman to try and come to some amicable agreement with Mr Nigel Trentham concerning the orderly takeover of Trumper's."

"Matters arising from the minutes?" Charlie asked. Still no one else spoke, so once again Charlie's eyes returned to the agenda. "Item number four, the future of –" he began, but then every one of us tried to speak at once.

When some semblance of order had been regained, Charlie suggested that it might be wise if the chief executive were to bring us up to date on the latest position. I joined the "Hear, hears" and nods that greeted this suggestion.

"Thank you, Mr Chairman," said Arthur Selwyn, removing some papers from a briefcase by the side of his chair. The rest of the board waited patiently. "Members of the board will be aware that," he began, sounding like the senior civil servant he had once been, "following the announcement by Mr Nigel Trentham that it was no longer his intention to mount a takeover bid for Trumper's, the company's shares subsequently fell from their peak of two pounds four shillings to their present price of one pound nineteen shillings."

"We're all capable of following the vagaries of the stock market," said Daphne, butting in. "What I would like to know is: what has happened to Trentham's personal shareholding?"

I didn't join in with the chorus of approval that followed as I already knew every last detail of the agreement.

"Mr Trentham's stock," said Mr Selwyn, continuing as if he had not been interrupted, "was, following an agreement reached between his lawyers and Miss Ross's, acquired a fortnight ago by Mr Baverstock on behalf of the Hardcastle Trust at a cost of two pounds one shilling per share."

"And will the rest of the board ever be privy to what brought about this cosy little arrangement?" asked Daphne.

"It has recently come to light," answered Selwyn, "that Mr Trentham has, during the past year, been building up a considerable holding in the company on borrowed money, causing him to accumulate a large overdraft – an overdraft, I am given to understand, he can no longer sustain. With that in mind he has sold his personal holding in the company – some twenty-eight per cent – direct to the Hardcastle Trust at the going market rate."

"Has he now?" said Daphne.

"Yes," said Charlie. "And it may also interest the board to know that during the past week I have received three letters of resignation, from Mr Trentham, Mr Folland and Mr Gibbs, which I took the liberty of accepting on your behalf."

"That was indeed a liberty," said Daphne sharply.

"You feel we shouldn't have accepted their resignations?"

"I certainly do, Mr Chairman."

"May one ask your reasons, Lady Wiltshire?"

"They're purely selfish, Mr Chairman." I thought I detected a chuckle in her voice, as Daphne waited to be sure she had the full attention of the board. "You see, I'd been looking forward to proposing that all three of them should be sacked."

Few members of the board were able to keep a straight face at this suggestion.

"Not to be recorded in the minutes," said Charlie, turning towards Jessica. "Thank you, Mr Selwyn, for an admirable summary of the present situation. Now, as I cannot believe there is anything to be gained by continuing to rake over those particular coals, let us move on to item number five, the banking hall."

Charlie sat back contentedly while Cathy reported to us that the new facility was making a respectable monthly return and she could see no reason why the figures should not continue to improve for the foreseeable future. "In fact," she said, "I believe the time has come for Trumper's to offer its regular customers their own credit card as . . ."

I stared at the miniature MC that hung from a gold chain around Cathy's neck, the missing link that Mr Roberts always insisted had to exist. Cathy was still unable to recall a great deal of what had taken place in her life before she had come to work in London, but I agreed with Doctor Atkins' assessment that we should no longer waste our time with the past but let her concentrate on the future.

None of us doubted that when the time came to select a new chairman we wouldn't have far to look. The only problem I had to face now was how to convince the present chairman that perhaps the time had come for him to make way for someone younger.

"Do you have any strong feelings about upper limits, Mr Chairman?" asked Cathy.

"No, no, it all makes good sense to me," said Charlie, sounding unusually vague.

"I'm not so sure that I'm able to agree with you on this occasion, Mr Chairman," said Daphne.

"And why's that, Lady Wiltshire?" asked Charlie, smiling benignly.

"Partly because you haven't been listening to a single word that's been said for about the last ten minutes," Daphne declared, "so how can you possibly know what you're agreeing to?"

"Guilty," said Charlie. "I confess my mind was on the other side of the world. However," he continued, "I did read Cathy's report on the subject and I suggest that the upper limits will have to vary from customer to customer, according to their credit rating, and we may well need to employ some new staff in future who have been trained in the City, rather than on the high street. Even so, I shall still require a detailed timetable if we're to consider seriously the introduction of such a scheme, which should be ready for presentation at the next board meeting. Is that possible, Miss Ross?" Charlie asked firmly, no doubt hoping that yet another example of his well-known "thinking on his feet" had released him from the jaws of Daphne.

"I will have everything ready for the board to consider at least a week before our next meeting."

"Thank you," said Charlie. "Item number six. Accounts."

I listened intently as Selwyn presented the latest figures, department by department. Once again I became aware of Cathy questioning and probing whenever she felt we were not being given a full enough explanation for any loss or innovation. She sounded like a better informed, more professional version of Daphne.

"What are we now projecting will be the profit forecast for the year 1965?" she asked.

"Approximately nine hundred and twenty thousand pounds," replied Selwyn, running his finger down a column of figures.

That was the moment when I realised what had to be achieved before I could convince Charlie he should announce his retirement.

"Thank you, Mr Selwyn. Shall we move on to item number seven?" said Charlie. "The appointment of Miss Cathy Ross as deputy chairman of the board." Removing his glasses, Charlie added, "I don't feel it will be necessary for me to make a long speech on why –"

"Agreed," said Daphne. "It therefore gives me considerable pleasure to propose Miss Ross as deputy chairman of Trumper's."

"I should like to second that proposal," volunteered Arthur Selwyn. I could only smile at the sight of Charlie with his mouth wide open, but he still managed to ask, "Those in favour?" I raised my hand along with all but one director.

Cathy rose and gave a short acceptance speech in which she thanked the board for their confidence in her and assured them of her total commitment to the future of the company.

"Any other business?" asked Charlie, as he began stacking up his papers.

"Yes," replied Daphne. "Having had the pleasure

of proposing Miss Ross as deputy chairman I feel the time has come for me to hand in my resignation."

"But why?" asked Charlie, looking shocked.

"Because I shall be sixty-five next month, Mr Chairman, and I consider that to be a proper age to make way for younger blood."

"Then I can only say –" began Charlie and this time none of us tried to stop him making a long and heartfelt speech. When he had finished we all banged the table with the palm of a hand.

Once order had been regained, Daphne said simply, "Thank you. I could not have expected such dividends from a sixty-pound investment."

Within weeks of Daphne leaving the company, whenever a sensitive issue came under discussion with the board Charlie would admit to me after the meeting was over that he missed the marchioness's particular brand of maddening common sense.

"And I wonder if you'll miss me and my nagging tongue quite as much when I hand in my resignation?" I asked.

"What are you talking about, Becky?"

"Only that I'll be sixty-five in a couple of years and intend to follow Daphne's example."

"But –"

"No buts, Charlie," I told him. "Number 1 now runs itself – more than competently since I stole young Richard Cartwright from Christie's. In any case, Richard ought to be offered my place on the main board. After all, he's taking most of the responsibility without gaining any of the credit."

"Well, I'll tell you one thing," Charlie retorted defiantly, "I don't intend to resign, not even when I'm seventy."

During 1965, we opened three new departments: "Teenagers", which specialised in clothes and records with its own coffee shop attached; a travel agency, to cope with the growing demand for holidays abroad; and a gift department, "for the man who has everything". Cathy also recommended to the board that after nearly twenty years perhaps the whole barrow needed a face-lift. Charlie told me that he wasn't quite sure about such a radical upheaval, reminding me of the Fordian theory that one should never invest in anything that eats or needs to be repainted. But as Arthur Selwyn and the other directors seemed in no doubt that a refurbishment programme was long overdue he only put up token resistance.

I kept to my promise – or threat as Charlie saw it – and resigned three months after my sixty-fifth birthday, leaving Charlie as the only director who still survived from the original board.

For the first time in my recollection, Charlie admitted that he was beginning to feel his age. Whenever he called for the minutes of the last meeting, he admitted, he would look around the boardroom table and realise how little he had in common with most of his fellow directors. The "bright new sparks", as Daphne referred to them, financiers, takeover specialists, and public relations men, all of whom seemed somehow detached from the one element that had always mattered to Charlie – the customer.

They talked of deficit financing, loan option schemes and the necessity to have their own computer, often without bothering to seek Charlie's opinion.

"What can I do about it?" Charlie asked me after a board meeting at which he admitted he had hardly opened his mouth.

He scowled when he had heard my recommendation.

The following month Arthur Selwyn announced at the company's AGM that the pre-tax profits for 1966 would be £1,078,600. Charlie stared down at me as I nodded firmly from the front row. He waited for "Any other business" before he rose to tell the assembled company that he felt the time had come for him to resign. Someone else must push the barrow into the seventies, he suggested.

Everyone in the room looked shocked. They spoke of the end of an era, "no possible replacement", and said that it would never be the same again; but not one of them suggested Charlie should reconsider his position.

Twenty minutes later he declared the meeting closed.

CHAPTER 49

It was Jessica Allen who told the new chairman that a Mr Corcran had phoned from the Lefevre Gallery to say that he accepted her offer of one hundred and ten thousand pounds.

Cathy smiled. "Now all we have to do is agree on a date and send out the invitations. Can you get Becky on the line for me, Jessica."

The first action Cathy had proposed to the board after being elected unanimously as the third chairman of Trumper's was to appoint Charlie as Life President and hold a dinner in his honour at the Grosvenor House Hotel. The occasion was attended by all Trumper's staff, their husbands, wives and many of the friends Charlie and Becky had made over nearly seven decades. Charlie took his place at the top table that night, one of the one thousand, seven hundred and seventy people who filled the great ballroom.

There followed a five-course meal that even Percy was unable to fault. After Charlie had been supplied with a brandy and had lit up a large Trumper's cigar, he leaned over and whispered to Becky, "I wish your father could have seen this spread." He added, "Of course, he wouldn't have come – unless he'd supplied everything from the meringues glacés to the bread rolls."

"I wish Daniel could have shared the evening with us as well," Becky replied quietly. A few moments later Cathy stood and delivered a speech that could have left no one in any doubt that they had elected the right person to follow Charlie. She ended by inviting the assembled company to toast the health of the founder and first Life President. After the applause had died away, she bent down and removed something from beneath her chair. "Charlie," she said, "this is a small memento from us all to thank you for the sacrifice you once made in order to keep Trumper's afloat." Cathy turned and handed over an oil painting to Charlie, who beamed in anticipation until he saw what the subject was. His mouth opened and his cigar fell on the table as he stared in disbelief. It was some time before he could let go of *The Potato Eaters* and rise to respond to the calls of "Speech, speech!"

Charlie began by reminding his audience once again how everything had begun with his grandfather's barrow in Whitechapel, a barrow that now stood proudly in the food hall of Trumper's. He paid tribute to the colonel, long since dead, to the pioneers of the company, Mr Crowther and Mr Hadlow, as well as to two of the original staff, Bob Makins and Ned Denning, both of whom had retired only weeks before he himself had. He ended with Daphne, Marchioness of Wiltshire, who had loaned them their first sixty pounds to make it all possible.

"I wish I was fourteen years old again," he said wistfully. "Me, my barrow and my regulars in the Whitechapel Road. Those were the 'appiest days of my life. Because at 'eart, you see, I'm a simple fruit and vegetable man." Everybody laughed, except Becky, who gazed up at her husband and recalled an eight-year-old boy in short trousers, cap in hand, standing outside her father's shop, hoping to get a free bun.

"I'm proud to 'ave built the biggest barrow in the world and tonight to be among those who 'ave 'elped me push it from the East End all the way into Chelsea Terrace. I'll miss you all – and I can only 'ope you'll allow me back into Trumper's from time to time."

As Charlie sat down, his staff rose to cheer him. He leaned over, took Becky by the hand and said, "Forgive me, but I forgot to tell 'em it was you what founded it in the first place."

Becky, who had never been to a football match in her life, had to spend hours listening to her husband on the subject of the World Cup, and how no fewer than three West Ham players had been selected for the England squad.

For the first four weeks after Charlie had retired as chairman he seemed quite content to allow Stan to drive him from Sheffield to Manchester, and from Liverpool to Leeds, so they could watch the early rounds together.

When England won a place in the semi-final, Charlie used every contact he could think of to obtain two stand tickets, and his efforts were rewarded when the home side won a place in the final.

However, despite those contacts, a willingness to pay over the odds, and even writing to Alf Ramsey, the England team manager, Charlie still failed to get even a standing ticket for the final. He told Becky that he had come to the reluctant conclusion that he and Stan would have to watch the match on television.

On the morning of the game, Charlie came down to breakfast to find two stand tickets wedged in the toast rack. He was unable to eat his eggs and bacon for sheer excitement. "You're a genius, Mrs Trumper," he said several times, interspersed with: "However did you manage it?"

"Contacts," was all Becky would say, resolved not to let Charlie know that the new computer had revealed that Mrs Ramsey held an account at Trumper's, and Cathy had suggested she should join that select group of customers who received a ten per cent discount.

The four–two victory over West Germany, with three goals scored by Geoff Hurst of West Ham, not only brought Charlie to the edge of delirium but even made Becky briefly wonder if her husband had now put Trumper's behind him and would allow Cathy a free hand as chairman.

Yet within a week of returning home from Wembley Stadium Charlie seemed perfectly content just to potter around the house, but it was during the second week that Becky realised something had to be done if she wasn't to be driven mad – as well as lose most of her domestic staff at

Eaton Square. On the Monday of the third week, she dropped into Trumper's to see the manager of the travel department and during the fourth week tickets were delivered from the offices of Cunard to Lady Trumper – for a trip to New York on the *Queen Mary* – followed by an extensive tour of the United States.

"I do hope she can run the barrow without me," said Charlie, as they were driven down to Southampton.

"I expect she'll just about scrape by," said Becky, who had planned that they should be away for at least three months, to be sure that Cathy had a free hand to get on with the refurbishment programme, which they both suspected Charlie would have done everything in his power to hold up.

Becky became even more convinced this would have been the case the moment Charlie had walked into Bloomingdale's and started grumbling about the lack of proper space allocated to view the goods. She moved him on to Macy's where he complained of the non-existent service, and when they arrived in Chicago he told Henry Field that he no longer cared for the window displays that had at one time been the hallmark of the great store. "Far too garish, even for America," he assured the owner. Becky would have mentioned the words "tact and subtlety" had Henry Field not agreed with his old friend's every pronouncement while placing the blame firmly on a new manager who believed in "flower power" whatever that was.

Dallas, San Francisco and Los Angeles were no better, and when three months later Becky and Charlie climbed back on board the great liner in New York, the name of Trumper's was once again on Charlie's lips. Becky began to dread what might happen when they set foot back on English soil.

She only hoped that five days of calm seas and a warm Atlantic breeze might help them relax and allow Charlie to forget Trumper's for a few moments. But he spent most of the voyage back explaining his new ideas for revolutionising the company, ideas he felt should be put into operation the moment they reached London. It was then that Becky decided she had to make a stand on Cathy's behalf.

"But you're not even a member of the board any longer," Becky reminded him, as she lay on the deck sunbathing.

"I'm the Life President," he insisted, after he had finished telling her his latest idea for tagging garments to combat shoplifting.

"But that's a purely honorary position."

"Poppycock. I intend to make my views felt whenever –"

"Charlie, that's not fair on Cathy. She's no longer the junior director of a family venture but chairman of a vast public company. The time has surely come for you to stay away from Trumper's and allow Cathy to push the barrow along on her own."

"So what am I expected to do?"

"I don't know, Charlie, and I don't care. But whatever you do it's no longer going to take place anywhere near Chelsea Terrace. Do I make myself clear?"

Charlie would have replied if a deck officer hadn't come to a halt beside them.

"Sorry to interrupt you, sir."

"You're not interrupting anything," said Charlie. "So what do you want me to do? Arrange a mutiny or organise the deck tennis draw?"

"Both those are the purser's responsibility, Sir Charles," said the young man. "But the captain wonders if you would be kind enough to join him on the bridge. He's received a cablegram from London which he feels you would want to know about immediately."

"I hope it's not bad news," said Becky, as she sat up quickly and placed the novel she had been trying to read on the deck beside her. "I told them not to contact us unless it was an emergency."

"Rubbish," said Charlie. "You're such an old pessimist. With you a bottle is always half empty." He stood up and stretched himself before accompanying the young officer along the after-deck towards the bridge, explaining how he would organise a mutiny. Becky followed a yard behind, offering no further comment.

As the officer escorted them on to the bridge the captain turned to greet them.

"A cablegram has just come over the wires from London, Sir Charles, which I thought you would want to see immediately." He handed the message over.

"Damn, I've left my glasses back on the deck," Charlie mumbled. "Becky, you'd better read it to me." He passed the slip of paper to his wife.

Becky opened the cablegram, her fingers trembling slightly and read the message to herself first as Charlie studied his wife's face for a clue as to its contents.

"Come on then, what is it? Half full or half empty?"

"It's a request from Buckingham Palace," she replied.

"What did I tell you," said Charlie, "you can't leave them to do anything for themselves. First day of the month, bath soap, she prefers lavender; toothpaste, he likes Euthymol, and loo paper . . . I did warn Cathy –"

"No, I don't think it's the loo paper Her Majesty is fussing about on this occasion," said Becky.

"So what's the problem?" asked Charlie.

"They want to know what title you'll take."

"Title?" said Charlie.

"Yes," said Becky, turning to face her husband. "Lord Trumper of where?"

Becky was surprised and Cathy somewhat relieved to discover how quickly Lord Trumper of Whitechapel appeared to become absorbed in the daily workings of the upper house. Becky's fears of his continually interfering with the day-to-day business of the company evaporated the moment Charlie had donned the red ermine. For his wife, the routine brought back memories of those days during the Second World War when Charlie had worked under Lord Woolton in the Ministry of Food and she could never be sure what time of night he'd arrive home.

Six months after being told by Becky he was not to go anywhere near Trumper's, Charlie announced that he had been invited to become a member of the Agricultural Committee, where he felt he could once again use his expertise to the benefit of his fellow-members. He even returned to his old routine of rising at four thirty each morning so that he could catch up with those parliamentary papers that always needed to be read before important meetings.

Whenever Charlie returned home for dinner in the evening he was always full of news about some clause he had proposed in committee that day, or how an old duffer had taken up the House's time during the afternoon with countless amendments to the hare coursing bill.

When in 1970 Britain applied to join the Common Market Charlie told his wife that he had been approached by the Chief Whip to chair a sub-committee on food distribution in Europe and felt it was his duty to accept. From that day on, whenever Becky came down for breakfast she would discover countless order papers or copies of the Lords' daily *Hansard* strewn untidily all the way from Charlie's study to the kitchen, where the inevitable note had been left to explain that he had to attend yet another early sub-committee meeting or briefing from some continental supporter of Britain's entry into Europe who happened to be in London. Until then Becky had no idea how hard members of the upper house were expected to work.

Becky continued to keep in touch with Trumper's by regular Monday morning visits. She would always go in at a time when business was fairly quiet, and to her surprise had become Charlie's main source of information as to what was happening at the store.

She always enjoyed spending a couple of hours strolling through the different departments. She couldn't help noticing how quickly fashions changed, and how Cathy always managed to keep a step ahead of her rivals, while never giving regular customers cause to grumble about unnecessary change.

Becky's final call was inevitably at the auction house to

see whose paintings were due to come under the hammer. It had been some time since she had handed over her responsibility to Richard Cartwright, the former chief auctioneer, but he always made himself available to show her round the latest preview of pictures to be auctioned. "Minor Impressionists on this occasion," he assured her.

"Now at major prices," Becky replied as she studied works by Pissarro, Bonnard and Vuillard. "But we'll still have to make sure Charlie doesn't find out about this lot."

"He already has," Richard warned her. "Dropped in last Thursday on his way to the Lords, put a reserve on three lots and even found time to complain about our estimates. Claimed he had bought a large Renoir oil from you called *L'homme à la Pêche* only a few years ago for the price I was now expecting him to pay for a small pastel by Pissarro that was nothing more than a study for a major work."

"I suspect he might be right about that," said Becky as she flicked through the catalogue to check the different estimates. "And heaven help your balance sheet if he finds out that you failed to reach the reserve price on any picture he's interested in. When I ran this department he was always known as 'our loss leader'."

As they were chatting an assistant walked over to join them, nodded politely to Lady Trumper and handed Richard a note. He studied the message before turning to Becky. "The chairman wonders if you would be kind enough to drop in and see her before you leave. Something she needs to discuss with you fairly urgently."

Richard accompanied her to the lift on the ground floor, where Becky thanked him once again for indulging an old lady.

As the lift travelled grudgingly upwards – something else that Cathy wanted to change as part of the refurbishment plan – Becky pondered on why the chairman could possibly want to see her and only hoped that she wasn't going to have to cancel dinner with them that night, as their guests were to be David and Barbara Field.

Although Cathy had moved out of Eaton Square some

eighteen months before into a spacious flat in Chelsea Cloisters they still managed dinner together at least once a month, and Cathy was always invited back to the house whenever the Fields or the Bloomingdales were in town. Becky knew that David Field, who still sat on the board of the great Chicago store, would be disappointed if Cathy was unable to keep her appointment that night, especially as the American couple were due to return home the following day.

Jessica ushered Becky straight through to the chairman's office, where she found Cathy on the phone, her brow unusually furrowed. While she waited for the chairman to finish her call, Becky stared out of the bay window at the empty wooden bench on the far side of the road and thought of Charlie, who had happily swapped it for the red leather benches of the House of Lords.

Once Cathy had replaced the receiver, she immediately asked, "How's Charlie?"

"You tell me," said Becky. "I see him for the occasional dinner during the week and he has even been known to attend breakfast on a Sunday. But that's about it. Has he been seen in Trumper's lately?"

"Not that often. To be honest, I still feel guilty about banning him from the store."

"No need to feel any guilt," Becky told her. "I've never seen the man happier."

"I'm relieved to hear it," said Cathy. "But right now I need Charlie's advice on a more urgent matter."

"And what's that?"

"Cigars," said Cathy. "I had David Field on the phone earlier to say that his father would like a dozen boxes of his usual brand and not to bother to send them round to the Connaught because he'll be only too happy to pick them up when he comes to dinner tonight."

"So what's the problem?"

"Neither David Field nor the tobacco department have the slightest idea what his father's usual brand is. It seems Charlie always dealt with the order personally."

"You could check the old invoices."

"First thing I did," said Cathy. "But there's no record of any transaction ever taking place. Which surprised me, because if I remember correctly old Mr Field regularly had a dozen boxes sent over to the Connaught whenever he came to London." Cathy's brow furrowed again. "That was something I always considered curious. After all, when you think about it, he must have had a large tobacco department in his own store."

"I'm sure he did," said Becky, "but it wouldn't have stocked any brands from Havana."

"Havana? I'm not with you."

"Some time in the fifties US Customs banned the import of all Cuban cigars into America and David's father, who had been smoking a particular brand of Havanas long before anyone had heard of Fidel Castro, saw no reason why he shouldn't be allowed to continue to indulge himself with what he considered was no more than his 'Goddamn right'."

"So how did Charlie get round the problem?"

"Charlie used to go down to the tobacco department, pick up a dozen boxes of the old man's favourite brand, return to his office, remove the bands around each cigar, then replace them with an innocuous Dutch label before putting them back in an unidentifiable Trumper's box. He always made sure that there was a ready supply on hand for Mr Field in case he ever ran out. Charlie felt it was the least we could do to repay all the hospitality the Fields had lavished on us over the years."

Cathy nodded her understanding. "But I still need to know which brand of Cuban cigar is nothing more than Mr Field's 'Goddamn right'."

"I've no idea," admitted Becky. "As you say, Charlie never allowed anyone else to handle the order."

"Then someone's going to have to ask Charlie, either to come in and complete the order himself or at least tell us which brand Mr Field is addicted to. So where can I expect to find the Life President at eleven thirty on a Monday morning?"

"Hidden away in some committee room at the House of Lords would be my bet."

"No, he's not," said Cathy. "I've already phoned the Lords and they assured me he hadn't been seen this morning – and what's more they weren't expecting him again this week."

"But that's not possible," said Becky. "He virtually lives in the place."

"That's what I thought," said Cathy. "Which is why I called down to Number 1 to ask for your help."

"I'll sort this out in a trice," said Becky. "If Jessica can put me through to the Lords, I know exactly the right person to speak to."

Jessica returned to her office, looked up the number and, as soon as she had been connected, put the call through to the chairman's desk, where Becky picked up the receiver.

"House of Lords?" said Becky. "Message board please . . . Is Mr Anson there? No, well, I'd still like to leave an urgent message for Lord Trumper . . . of Whitechapel . . . Yes, I think he's in an agricultural sub-committee this morning . . . Are you sure? . . . That can't be possible . . . You do know my husband? . . . Well, that's a relief . . . Does he . . . ? How interesting . . . No, thank you . . . No, I won't leave a message and please don't trouble Mr Anson. Goodbye."

Becky replaced the phone and looked up to find Cathy and Jessica staring at her like two children at bedtime waiting to hear the end of a story.

"Charlie hasn't been seen in the Lords this morning. There isn't an agricultural sub-committee. He's not even a member of the full committee, and what's more they haven't set eyes on him for the past three months."

"But I don't understand," said Cathy. "How have you been getting through to him in the past?"

"With a special number supplied by Charlie that I keep by the hall phone in Eaton Square. It connects me to a

Lords messenger called Mr Anson, who always seems to know exactly where Charlie can be found at any time of the day or night."

"And does this Mr Anson exist?" asked Cathy.

"Oh, yes," said Becky. "But it seems he works on another floor of the Lords and on this occasion I was put through to general enquiries."

"So what happens whenever you do get through to Mr Anson?"

"Charlie usually rings back within the hour."

"So there's nothing to stop you phoning Mr Anson now?"

"I'd rather not for the moment," said Becky. "I think I'd prefer to find out what Charlie's been up to for the past two years. Because one thing's for certain, Mr Anson isn't going to tell me."

"But Mr Anson can't be the only person who knows," said Cathy. "After all, Charlie doesn't live in a vacuum." They both swung round to face Jessica.

"Don't look at me," said Jessica. "He hasn't had any contact with this office since the day you banned him from Chelsea Terrace. If Stan didn't come in to the canteen for lunch from time to time I wouldn't even know Charlie was still alive."

"Of course," said Becky, snapping her fingers. "Stan's the one person who must know what's going on. He still picks up Charlie first thing in the morning and brings him home last thing at night. Charlie couldn't get away with anything unless his driver was fully in his confidence."

"Right, Jessica," said Cathy as she checked her diary. "Start by cancelling my lunch with the managing director of Moss Bros, then tell my secretary I'll take no calls and no interruptions until we find out exactly what our Life President has been up to. When you've done that, go down and see if Stan's in the canteen and if he is phone me back immediately."

Jessica almost ran out of the room as Cathy turned her attention back to Becky.

"Do you think he might have a mistress?" said Becky quietly.

"Night and day for nearly two years at the age of seventy? If he has, we ought to enter him as the Bull of the Year at the Royal Agricultural Show."

"Then what can he be up to?"

"My bet is that he's taking his master's degree at London University," said Cathy. "It's always riled Charlie whenever you tease him about never properly completing his education."

"But I'd have come across the relevant books and papers all over the house."

"You already have, but they were only the books and papers he intended you to see. Don't let's forget how cunning he was when he took his BA. He fooled you for eight years."

"Perhaps he's taken a job with one of our rivals."

"Not his style," said Cathy. "He's far too loyal for that. In any case, we'd know which store it was within days, the staff and management alike would be only too happy to keep reminding us. No, it has to be simpler than that." The private phone rang on Cathy's desk. She grabbed the receiver and listened carefully before saying, "Thank you, Jessica. We're on our way."

"Let's go," she said, replacing the phone and jumping up from behind her desk. "Stan's just finishing his lunch." She headed towards the door. Becky quickly followed and without another word they took the lift to the ground floor where Joe, the senior doorman, was surprised to see the chairman and Lady Trumper hail a taxi when both their drivers were patiently waiting for them on meters.

A few minutes later Stan appeared through the same door and climbed behind the wheel of Charlie's Rolls before proceeding at a gentle pace towards Hyde Park Corner, oblivious of the taxi that was following him. The Rolls continued down Piccadilly and on through Trafalgar Square before taking a left in the direction of the Strand.

"He's going to King's College," said Cathy. "I knew I was right – it has to be his master's degree."

"But Stan's not stopping," said Becky, as the Rolls passed the college entrance and weaved its way into Fleet Street.

"I can't believe he's bought a newspaper," said Cathy.

"Or taken a job in the City," Becky added as the Rolls drove on down towards the Mansion House.

"I've got it," said Becky triumphantly, as the Rolls left the City behind them and nosed its way into the East End. "He's been working on some project at his boys' club in Whitechapel."

Stan continued east until he finally brought the car to a halt outside the Dan Salmon Centre.

"But it doesn't make any sense," said Cathy. "If that's all he wanted to do with his spare time why didn't he tell you the truth in the first place? Why go through such an elaborate charade?"

"I can't work that one out either," said Becky. "In fact, I confess I'm even more baffled."

"Well, let's at least go in and find out what he's up to."

"No," said Becky, placing a hand on Cathy's arm. "I need to sit and think for a few moments before I decide what to do next. If Charlie is planning something he doesn't want us to know about, I'd hate to be the one who spoils his bit of fun, especially when it was me who banned him from going into Trumper's in the first place."

"All right," said Cathy. "So why don't we just go back to my office and say nothing of our little discovery? After all, we can always phone Mr Anson at the Lords, who as we know will make sure Charlie returns your call within the hour. That will give me easily enough time to sort out David Field and the problem of his cigars."

Becky nodded her agreement and instructed the bemused cabbie to return to Chelsea Terrace. As the taxi swung round in a circle to begin its journey back towards the West End, Becky glanced out of the rear window at the

Centre named after her father. "Stop," she said without warning. The cabbie threw on the brakes and brought the taxi to a sudden halt.

"What's the matter?" asked Cathy.

Becky pointed out of the back window, her eyes now fixed on a figure who was walking down the steps of the Dan Salmon Centre dressed in a grubby old suit and flat cap.

"I don't believe it," said Cathy.

Becky quickly paid off the cab driver while Cathy jumped out and began to follow Stan as he headed off down the Whitechapel Road.

"Where can he be going?" asked Cathy, as they kept Stan well within their sights. The shabbily dressed chauffeur continued to march along the pavement, leaving any old soldier who saw him in no doubt of his former profession while causing the two ladies who were pursuing him to have occasionally to break into a run.

"It ought to be Cohen's the tailors," said Becky. "Because heaven knows the man looks as if he could do with a new suit."

But Stan came to a halt some yards before the tailor's shop. Then, for the first time, they both saw another man, also dressed in an old suit and flat cap, standing beside a brand-new barrow on which were printed the words: "Charlie Salmon, the honest trader. Founded 1969".

"I don't offer you these at two pounds, ladies," declared a voice as loud as that of any of the youngsters on the pitches nearby, "not one pound, not even fifty pence. No, I'm going to give 'em away for twenty pence."

Cathy and Becky watched in amazement as Stan Russell touched his cap to Charlie, then began to fill a woman's basket, so that his master could deal with the next customer.

"So what'll it be today, Mrs Bates? I've got some lovely bananas just flown in from the West Indies. Ought to be selling 'em at ninety pence the bunch, but to you, my old duck, fifty pence, but be sure you don't tell the neighbours."

"What about those 'tatoes, Charlie?" said a heavily made-up, middle-aged woman who pointed suspiciously at a box on the front of the barrow.

"As I stand 'ere, Mrs Bates, new in from Jersey today and I'll tell you what I'll do. I'll sell 'em at the same price as my so-called rivals are still peddling their old ones for. Could I be fairer, I ask?"

"I'll take four pounds, Mr Salmon."

"Thank you, Mrs Bates. Serve the lady, Stan, while I deal with the next customer." Charlie stepped across to the other side of the barrow.

"And 'ow nice to see you this fine afternoon, Mrs Singh. Two pounds of figs, nuts and raisins, if my memory serves me right. And how is Doctor Singh keeping?"

"Very busy, Mr Salmon, very busy."

"Then we must see that 'e's well fed, mustn't we?" said Charlie. "Because if this weather takes a turn for the worse, I may need to come and seek 'is advice about my sinus trouble. And 'ow's little Suzika?"

"She's just passed three A-levels, Mr Salmon, and will be going to London University in September to read engineering."

"Can't see the point of it myself," said Charlie as he selected some figs. "Engineerin', you say. What will they think of next? Knew a girl once from these parts who took 'erself off to university and a fat lot of good it did 'er. Spent the rest of 'er life living off 'er 'usband, didn't she? My old granpa always used to say –"

Becky burst out laughing. "So what do we do now?" she asked.

"Go back to Eaton Square, then you can look up Mr Anson's number at the Lords and give him a call. That way at least we can be sure that Charlie will contact you within the hour."

Cathy nodded her agreement but both of them remained transfixed as they watched the oldest dealer in the market ply his trade.

"I don't offer you these at two pounds," he declared,

holding up a cabbage in both hands. "I don't offer 'em for one pound, not even fifty pence."

"No, I'll give 'em away for twenty pence," whispered Becky under her breath.

"No, I'll give 'em away for twenty pence," shouted Charlie at the top of his voice.

"You do realise," said Becky as they crept back out of the market, "that Charlie's grandfather carried on to the ripe old age of eighty-three and died only a few feet from where His Lordship is standing now."

"He's come a long way since then," said Cathy, as she raised her hand to hail a taxi.

"Oh, I don't know," Becky replied. "Only about a couple of miles – as the crow flies."